The Jennifer Grey Mysteries

The Jennifer Grey Mysteries

Six Complete Books

by

Jerry B. Jenkins

MOODY PRESS
CHICAGO

Library of Congress Cataloging in Publication Data

Jenkins, Jerry B.
   The Jennifer Grey mysteries.

      Contents: Heartbeat—Three days in winter—
Too late to tell—[etc.]
      1. Detective and mystery stories, American.
I. Title.
PS3560.E485A6   1986   813'.54   86-21679
ISBN 0-8024-4345-1

                    1 2 3 4 5 6 7 Printing/AF/Year 91 90 89 88 87 86

Printed in the United States of America.

CONTENTS

HEARTBEAT

ONE

At 12:53 A.M., Tuesday, December 6, Jennifer Grey awoke to the sound of the telephone beside her bed. "I know you don't want me to call you unless it's important, but I think this is hot." It was the voice of Robert Block, her young assistant at the *Chicago Day.*

"That's all right, Bobby," she said, "What've you got?"

"Another big internal bust. Lots of top names from the Sixteenth Precinct, but somebody went down tonight."

"Someone was shot?"

"Yup, don't know who yet. Rumor is someone from Internal Affairs."

"Killed?"

"Think so, but nobody's talking."

"Where are you?"

"The office. Leo told me you'd want to handle this yourself and to just stay by the phone."

"He's right."

"I could handle it for you, Jennifer, if you wanted me to, I mean."

Jennifer smiled at his earnest naiveté. "I'll call you from the Sixteenth, Bobby. But thanks anyway."

Jennifer spent less than two minutes washing her face and applying light makeup. She pulled her long, light-brown hair into a ponytail and threw on what she always thought of as her emergency outfit—a white, button-down blouse under a burnt-orange V-neck sweater, a brown plaid, pleated skirt, and zippered boots.

She grabbed her calf-length camel hair coat and slung over her shoulder a large bag containing the usual essentials plus her reporter's spiral note pad.

She paused near the phone in the living room, wondering if this was the one time she could justify taking advantage of her relationship with Jim. She had enjoyed a lovely dinner with him just hours before at a quiet spot not frequented by newspaper people or policemen.

She knew it was risky, if not wrong, for a police reporter to be seeing a policeman. But she rationalized that if she didn't use him as a source of information and left writing about him to the feature writers—his current assignment took him into elementary and junior high schools as Officer Friendly—no one had to know.

Besides, she wasn't sure how she felt about him. It was clear how he felt about her. But a widow of fewer than three years who still thought of her late husband every day was not jumping into any new relationship.

There was no need to bother Jim in the middle of the night. Chiding herself for having even thought of waking him, she sat on the edge of the sofa and dialed the Sixteenth Precinct station instead.

"Yeah, somethin' went down, honey," Desk Officer Flannigan told Jennifer. "But if I tell ya over the phone, that means I won't get to see yer pretty face down here tonight, right?"

"Please, Herb," she said, "you can't joke about someone getting killed, can you?"

Silence.

"Herb?"

"Who bought it, Jenny? I didn't know anybody bought it. I heard a guy took a coupla slugs in the gut, but I didn't know he died."

"Who was it, Herb?"

"Somebody from IAD, but you know I can't tell you anything. You sure he died? I didn't hear he died."

"My source wasn't sure either, Herb. I just thought you might know."

"You don't know any more'n I do. What're you doin' talking about somebody dyin' when you don't know?"

"I'm sorry, all right? Can I talk to Campbell? Is he on tonight?"

"He's on, but he's talkin' to nobody, 'specially the press. And I'm not supposed to either. You understand?

"If I come down there, can I see him?"

"I doubt it, but then I'd get to see you, so don't let me talk you out of it."

Jennifer might have appreciated the tacky compliment under other circumstances. But she had been poking around the grimy precinct station houses for almost a year since graduating from obituaries and school board meetings, and she had no inkling of more Internal Affairs Division activity right under her nose. A major operation had taken place with her on the beat every day, yet she knew nothing about it.

Worse yet, someone from Internal Affairs was probably fighting for his life. A new widow might be in the making, and she felt that pain again.

She phoned downtown headquarters, but she got no new leads. *Jim will understand,* she decided. But the phone at his apartment just rang and rang.

Shortly after midnight, a task force for the Internal Affairs Division of the Chicago Police Department had scheduled the operation that would rock the department to its core.

Yet another contingent of Chicago's finest had been caught wallowing in its own mire. Not yet a year and a half since the biggest internal scandal in its history had seen dozens of police officers sentenced to prison for trafficking in dope, another black eye on the police department's reputation was swelling.

No one—least of all the guilty officers—knew of the investigation. Most officials and citizens and even the press assumed that the last housecleaning had scoured the department of the worst offenders and probably scared the small-timers into staying straight.

But a tiny, close-knit unit from IAD had been keeping an eye on suspicious activity in the Sixteenth Precinct for nearly thirty months—in fact, since long before the more publicized crackdown had even been initiated.

This band of four were players in one of the most dangerous games in the world. Not even their families could know of their activities. They had been given routine assignments, many requiring uniforms, while in actuality they were undercover agents, spying and ratting on their own colleagues.

There can be no more despised good guy than the one who must make his living deceiving his friends, being a snitch, a stool pigeon. It took a special kind of person to even be considered for such an assignment, and only those a cut above the rest lasted a year.

When you were suspected of reporting to Internal Affairs, you were shunned even by your friends, even by good cops who had nothing to hide. You were quietly ridiculed for being a goody-two-shoes, an idealist, a superpatriot, a God-squadder. And soon enough, of course, you had to be reassigned. A known employee of Internal Affairs was worthless.

Thus, the noisy crackdown that resulted in arrests and convictions and sentences for so many Chicago cops made the smallest IAD unit fear for the success of their own surveillance of the Sixteenth Precinct.

Would their activities be revealed in the course of the trial? Would the success of the bigger mission scare off their prey before they could lower the net? No one from the special unit had been involved in the major crackdown, but would all the publicity somehow tip their hands?

Would Jennifer Grey, the woman they begrudgingly admired for always being in the right place at the right time, somehow sniff out this terribly delicate operation? Could she or the *Day* be persuaded that their First Amendment rights should be voluntarily limited for the sake of human lives?

For months after the publicity of the previous noisy crackdown, IAD laid low, finally realizing that their mission had not been aborted. Their targets had become more cautious, but the lure of profit had finally brought them scurrying back into the cesspool.

And the men from IAD, the ones who had avoided suspicion and had been able to rise above the feeling that they were betraying their comrades, if dope-dealing policemen could be considered comrades, were waiting.

They waited for the perfect time. They waited for the perfect opportunity. They waited until they had something solid on each of the three men and one woman they had been tailing.

The midnight roundup was to be a simple maneuver. At a meeting earlier in the day, the four IAD officers had mapped careful strategy, plotting the whereabouts of their marks. Lieutenant Frank Akeley would be easy. He'd leave his favorite watering hole on Wells Street at exactly midnight, and IAD Chief John Lucas and two specially assigned patrolmen—who would not know what they were going to be involved in until about half an hour in advance—would make the arrest, booking Akeley downtown in an attempt to avoid publicity as long as possible.

The two others would be trickier. Sergeant Bill Much was a family man and would be asleep at home, if everything went as expected. No one looked forward to the prospect of an arrest in the dead of night, especially when a man's family would suddenly realize what was going on.

They'd think it was a mistake, of course, but Sergeant Much would know. And he could be armed. And there could be trouble. IAD Special Investigator Ray Bequette had the assignment, and he also would take two uniformed police officers with him.

For Officer James Purcell, IAD had decided on a ruse. He was a bachelor, living alone in an apartment on Oak Street near Rush. IAD investigator Donald Reston, a rangy, athletic, youthful man in his late thirties, would call Purcell from the lobby and tell him he had information on one of his cases. Reston would say he was sorry to bother him, but could they come up, and all the rest. When Purcell activated the buzzer and let them in downstairs, they could only hope he would still be unaware of what they were up to.

At least the bust that would end Reston's stint in IAD (anything publicized ruined future effectiveness) would be one the public would love. They turn on their heroes the first chance they get, and Purcell was a bona fide turncoat against the public trust.

Any bad cop was, of course, but this one would go down the throat of John Q. Public like nectar. A bad cop with a good reputation who gets his comeuppance. For Reston, it was too good to be true.

Officer Trudy Janus would be on duty on the street. Her partner would be directed to phone the station for a personal message. When he stopped to place the call, IAD's Eric O'Neill, a uniformed officer, and a police matron would arrest Janus.

It was set. Warrants had been issued. And not more than eight people in the world knew what would be going down. Fewer than that knew when and who and how. The mayor and the police commissioner knew the basics. IAD Chief Lucas, the three others in the operation, and a secretary knew everything.

Lucas was convinced that his men had not breathed a word to anyone, not anyone. Not a friend, not a relative, not a lover. If ever there was a business in which you couldn't trust *anyone,* this was it. Not that a man like Ray Bequette couldn't trust his wife of twenty years, but who might she tell? What might slip? Who knew what information might get to the wrong ears?

That was one reason that short terms with IAD were the norm. A man couldn't carry the burden of guilt and suspicion long without being able to tell even his own loved ones.

The operation was to be simultaneous, with the four suspects being brought downtown by 12:30 A.M. Sergeant Bill Much would be last, as his arrest would take place on the city's far West Side. Many more officers and civilians were involved, of course, but one thing was sure: these four were the ringleaders, the principal drug buyers and suppliers. And when they fell, they'd bring a massive network down with them.

At 11:00 P.M. IAD Chief John Lucas had sat in his personal car on the other side of the street and a half block to the south of the tiny parking lot of The Illusion bar near the corner of Wells and Ontario. Unmarked squad cars would never work for Internal Affairs; they were just as recognizable by cops as were the standard blue and white patrols.

Lucas, a tall, thin, graying man in his late fifties, was as respected as a man in his position could be. His was a thankless job. Neither he nor the people above him ever really liked what he ferreted out. Yet no one, not even those who had been burned by his professional approach and his incredible reputation for confidentiality in a huge police department, questioned his motives.

He was always impeccably dressed and soft-spoken. He shunned publicity. He personally handled the arrests of police officers above the rank of sergeant, and as difficult as it must have been for him, he was somehow usually able to pull them off with the least humiliation for the suspect.

That, he told his superiors more than once, would come in greater measure than he could ever personally mete out, when the man had to face his own family and the press and the public in court. "It is not my job to destroy a man before his subordinates. By the time I get to him, he has already accomplished that on his own. My role is to clean house quickly and deliver the man to his fate."

His prey had entered the bar, as usual, a few minutes after ten-thirty. While Lucas's men began to close their stakeout nets around Sergeant Bill Much's West Side bungalow and Officer James Purcell's Near North apartment and Trudy Janus's squad car, Lucas himself unhurriedly left his car and strode to a phone booth on the corner, another half block north.

He could still keep an eye on the bar's side exit—the one Lieutenant Frank Akeley would use to get to his car. Lucas and his men had talked about having a squad car merely pull Akeley over with a story of a burned out taillight or some other minor infraction. Then, when his guard was down, he would be arrested and read his rights.

But Lucas had decided against it. Too dangerous, he believed. Akeley was usually able to pilot himself to his apartment, despite the fact of driving while under the influence. But Lucas didn't know specifically what kind of a drunk Frank Akeley made. He was armed. Would he cry or pass out, or would he reach for his piece? It was too great a risk for the patrolman or two who would have no idea what it was all about until it was over.

Lucas dialed. "Sixteenth Precinct, Flannigan."

"Good evening, Officer Flannigan," Lucas began carefully. "Chief Lucas calling for the sergeant on duty."

"Yeah, who's 'is again?"

"Chief Lucas calling."

"An' you want Sergeant Campbell?"

"If he's the sergeant on duty, yes sir."

"Is this Lucas from IAD?"

"Yes, sir."

"What's goin' down? Somethin' big?"

"Flannigan," Lucas grew cold. "I need to speak with your watch commander. Will you put him on please?"

Lucas directed Campbell to assign two patrolmen to meet him at the phone booth as soon as possible. "Oh, please, Chief, you're not gonna bust somebody right here on my shift, are ya?" Campbell pleaded.

"As a matter of fact, no, Sergeant, and you know I can't discuss it further. May I expect a couple of officers?"

"Yes, sir."

Lucas turned his collar up against the cold wind and buried his hands deep in the pockets of his long trench coat. When a squad car pulled to the curb, he slipped into the backseat and briefed the officers.

They began by radioing in that they would be unavailable for more than an hour. Lucas told them precisely what he was doing and—not so precisely—why. "You will station yourself in front of the bar, out of the light," he told the one, "and you will be in front of the next building to the north. When I leave my car and cross the street, I will approach Lieutenant Akeley and call him by name, as if in a greeting.

"If he merely looks up in surprise, just fall in behind me in the parking lot to back me up. I'll identify myself officially, show him my badge, and ask him to surrender his weapon. If he resists, I'll ask you to assist me. Don't draw your guns unless I ask you to or unless it becomes obviously necessary."

The officers, one young and the other old, were stony. Neither liked his assignment, but Lucas didn't detect any treason in their silence. He didn't much like his own assignment for that matter. Nonetheless, this wasn't the time for convincing the patrolmen of the lieutenant's guilt. They wouldn't attempt to tip anyone off by radio, because they knew he would be monitoring the frequency in his own car.

"Take your positions at eleven fifty-five, unless you see me leave my car earlier."

Lucas headed back to his own car and maintained his vigil, shaking his head slightly at the thought of the watch commander worrying that one of his own men might be used by IAD. *What will he think when he finds out it's his boss, the lieutenant who likes to work the three to eleven shift, but always leaves for The Illusion at ten-thirty?*

On the West Side, Ray Bequette had rolled to a stop about a block from Bill Much's home. The only light visible in the house was a flickering television from an upstairs window. Bequette had briefed his assigned officers on the way from downtown. One moved quietly between houses to cover the back door; the other carefully hid in the shrubbery at the front of the small house.

"I'll ring the bell, and we'll just have to see what he does," the stocky forty-five-year-old veteran whispered. He had aspired to a position with IAD since its inception when he was a young cop. When he secretly supplied information leading to the arrest of not only three men on his shift, but also his own partner, in a shakedown scheme, IAD was able to keep his name out of it and put him on other cases while providing another assignment as the perfect front. He was ostensibly in charge of records and vehicles at the smallest precinct in the city. There was no way to keep his name out of this one. When he personally arrested a sergeant, the word would spread quickly and his undercover days in IAD would end.

At the Oak Street apartment of Officer James Purcell, Donald Reston had worried that Purcell would smell a rat. So when Purcell sounded not the least bit perturbed at being awakened by a phone call from the lobby and quickly agreed to let Reston and two others come up to see him, Reston sent one cop to one end of the hall and the other one to the other end and approached Purcell's door carefully.

Eric O'Neill had arranged for an emergency personal call to be placed to the precinct station for the partner of Officer Trudy Janus. When the dispatcher related the message, "Ten-twenty-one the station, personal," Janus's partner stopped at the next call box. As he neared the phone, the uniformed officer approached to tell him what was happening, while O'Neill and the matron closed in on the unsuspecting woman in the squad car.

TWO

Officer Trudy Janus's partner had been puzzled when he was interrupted before reaching for the call-box phone. "There's no call," Eric O'Neill's backup told him. "IAD just needed you out of the car for a minute." He wheeled around to see O'Neill flash his badge through the passenger side window of the squad while the matron positioned herself near the taillight on the other side.

Janus angrily yanked at the door handle, but O'Neill pressed against the door, both palms facing her. "You can step out," he said, "but I want to see those hands."

"What're you, bustin' me?" she asked.

"You got it. Lemme see those hands."

"I'm not goin' for the gun," she said, disgusted and swearing. "Hey, you can't collar me without a woman here anyway!" O'Neill pointed to the matron. When Janus craned her neck to look, O'Neill opened the door and asked her to unsnap her holster.

"Was my partner in on this setup?" she demanded.

"No."

"What's this all about?"

"You wanna just come downtown with me and find out, Trudy, or you want me to read you your rights right here while a crowd gathers?"

She stepped from the car and slammed the door.

"Should I have her search you, or you wanna give me your other piece?"

Janus pulled a tiny .22 from her left ankle.

"Is that everything?"

She nodded, glaring.

James Purcell had opened his apartment door to find Donald Reston out of his direct line of sight in the hall with his snub-nosed .38 in his hand. "Whoa! I'm unarmed, Don," Purcell said, barefoot in pajama bottoms and a T-shirt. "Search me."

"I'm on a job from IAD," Reston told him, almost apologetically, and holstered his pistol. He signaled his backups, and they entered the apartment.

"What's it all about, Don?" Purcell asked.

"It's about dope," Reston said. "Isn't it usually about dope?"

"Not always," Purcell said.

Reston squinted at him, wondering what he meant. "You wanna just come with us, or do you need me to officially arrest you here?"

"Nah. I'll come." Purcell didn't even appear offended.

When Ray Bequette had rung the front doorbell at the Bill Much residence, a huge figure appeared at the window upstairs. Ray waved, and Much opened the window. "Who'sat? Bequette? What're you doin' here, Ray?"

"I'm here for IAD, Bill. I'm sorry."

Much was bending over with both hands on the windowsill, his massive body still. He stared down at Bequette, a man he'd never worked with, but who had been a classmate at recruit school more than twenty years before.

Much's shoulders heaved and he began to sob. "Do I gotta come with you right now?" he whined.

"Yeah," Bequette whispered.

"Oh, no." Still Much didn't move except to draw a hand to his mouth and muffle his whimpering. "Oh, no, no." And he swore.

"C'mon down, Bill," Bequette said. "Just come on downtown with us, huh?"

"You're not alone?" the big man said.

"I got somebody at the back and somebody here with me," Ray said, and his front yard man extricated himself self-consciously from the bushes.

"Oh, you didn't have to do that, Ray. You know me. I ain't gonna hurt nobody. I'll come with ya. Just give me a minute."

"Bill?"

"Yeah."

"You come without your piece, hear?"

"'Course, Ray. I don't wanna hurt nobody." Lights began to come on in other rooms.

When Sergeant Bill Much, who would never wear a badge again, emerged from his house, he wore bedroom slippers, no socks, work pants with an elastic waistband, a sweatshirt, and a short, unbuttoned jacket. He carried a paper bag with a change of clothes. And no gun.

"Am I gonna be gone long?" he asked Bequette.

"Probably so."

"My wife can bring my other stuff in the morning," he said absently. He sat in the front seat next to Bequette, carefully placed the bag next to him, pressed his fingers to his forehead, and cried quietly all the way downtown.

When Bequette drove through the underground garage to the elevator that would take Much to the interrogation room, he saw Reston's and O'Neill's cars. John Lucas had not arrived yet, so Bequette, as special investigator, had to officially arrest and charge Much, Purcell, and Janus and see that they were properly booked.

Janus sat in a straight-backed wooden chair, coolly answering O'Neill's questions. She looked up in disgust at Bill Much's red, puffy eyes. Jim Purcell leaned against a counter, chatting amiably with a booking clerk.

He jerked quickly to attention with a stricken look when the rumor reached the booking room that "Lucas is down! They've taken him to Henrotin Hospital!" Much grimaced. Janus suppressed a smile.

John Lucas's backup officers had moved into position at 11:55 P.M. as instructed, and Lieutenant Frank Akeley left the bar six minutes later. He may have been tipsy, but it didn't show in his walk. He was in plainclothes, moving briskly between vehicles to his own car.

Lucas's path intersected Akeley's line of vision, but the lieutenant apparently decided not to turn and look, despite the fact that he had to have seen Lucas peripherally. "Frank!" Lucas called, yet still the man didn't slow or turn.

By continuing, Lucas would have blocked Akeley, but he hesitated, then stepped forward again, falling in behind Akeley. "Frank!" he tried again, knowing full well that even an inebriated man would have heard him.

Akeley stopped, but he didn't turn around. Lucas signaled for his backups and put his hand on Akeley's shoulder. "What *do* you want, Lucas?" Akeley shouted, his back still to him.

"You know what I want, Frank. Don't make it difficult for both of us." He was glad Akeley's hands were in his overcoat pockets and that the coat was buttoned. He couldn't go for his shoulder holster without unbuttoning his coat.

But as Akeley turned around, the hand hidden by his body pulled a .22 from his coat pocket, and he fired three times as he faced Lucas. The IAD chief lurched forward, his face ashen, and he grabbed Akeley's lapels, dragging him to the ground before releasing his grip. Lucas was unconscious, bleeding from two holes in his abdomen and one hole in his chest.

"Police! Freeze!" the uniformed officers screamed as they dropped to crouching positions, each with both hands on service revolvers pointed at Akeley's head.

"Self-defense, self-defense! Lucas tried to kill me!" He still had the weapon in his hand.

"Drop it, or you're dead!"

"I'm your superior!" Akeley said, trying to pull himself up from under Lucas's weight.

"The man never made a move on you, Lieutenant!" the officer said, pulling back the hammer of the .38 with his thumb. Akeley let the .22 slip from his fingers and slumped again to the pavement as the other cop kicked it away.

"You probably killed the man," the first said. "We gotta call an ambulance."

Jennifer Grey tried to watch her speed as she hurried to the Sixteenth Precinct station house. She remembered the warning of Leo Stanton, her city editor, that he would bail her out of jail for whatever it took for her to get a story—except a traffic ticket.

His idea of police reporting and hers were light years apart. But he was the one with thirty-five years in the business who had been on the police beat "when cops were cops and newspapers were newspapers."

With Leo Stanton in the slot, the *Chicago Day* would always have an old-fashioned, high quality, complete city news section, "even if," he was fond of saying, "the rest of the rag goes to psycho-babble, pinko columnists, and how to develop a meaningful relationship with your dog."

She enjoyed working for Leo, even if she couldn't stand the unlit cigar lodged in the corner of his mouth. Occasionally he'd slide it free with two fingers and a thumb and she'd have to endure looking at the soggy end, but he was a bit more articulate when his plug was pulled.

He'd had the crazy thing in the first night when she turned in a story he didn't like. She was new on the police beat and had written what he called "a feminine piece."

"But I'm a woman," she had tried. "I'm going to sound more like a woman than a man. I can't change that can I?" He glared at her. "Should I?"

"You should sound like a newspaper reporter, not a man *or* a woman. People don't want to read *you*. They want to read your story. Write it like a reporter, not like a pretty little lady."

He shoved her story back across the desk, and she couldn't resist yanking it from his grip. She knew she shouldn't have, but she was fuming, talking to herself. She headed back to her typewriter, but he called her back.

"This time," he said, "remember that you're in the city room now, not the society page or wherever in the world we inherited you from. Write it on the tube and patch it over to mine. I'll edit it on the screen."

It had taken her until midnight to learn the rudiments of the video display terminal so she could rewrite the story. Robert Block, a journalism intern from Northwestern University who was to be her assistant, walked her through it and even showed her how to transmit her story to Leo when she was ready.

Twice she had lost everything but her notes, but finally the piece was finished. She sent it electronically to Leo's machine. When it came up on the screen, he hollered across the city room, "This better be good; I'm two hours into overtime now, and everybody knows *I* don't get paid overtime."

She was still mad. *Everybody's seen your salary posted with all the other Guild rates too,* she thought, *and if we made that kind of money, we wouldn't care about overtime.* And as she sat waiting for his reaction, she realized how good it was to feel some real emotion again after so long.

After Scott had been killed in an auto accident just before their first anniversary, Jennifer had retreated to her parent's home in Rockford. She wanted to do nothing, to say nothing, to think nothing. When the shock wore off and the pain invaded, she slept twelve to sixteen hours at a stretch and didn't want to eat.

Her parents had been supportive, but her father brought her back to reality with his gentle speculation that her sleep was just a substitute for what she really wanted. She wanted to die, he said. She wanted to join Scott. She knew in an instant that he was right. And that she couldn't. And that the same God she had trusted as a child and had worshiped and prayed to all her life would bring her through this.

She knew it in her head, but that didn't make her feel any better. Though her father's counsel forced her back into a semblance of normal routine, the numbness, the absence of any emotion, hung with her like a colorless cloud even after she had moved away from home again. She found her own apartment and finished the last few hours of her journalism degree. Then she landed a job on the new *Day,* mostly because they wanted an entire staff that had not worked on a Chicago paper before.

She wrote obituaries and then covered board meetings, and her no-nonsense reporting style caught Leo's eye. Whenever he got on her case about anything, she reminded herself that *he* had sought *her* out, not the other way around. He was the one who thought she had the makings of an excellent police reporter. He was the one who said she could go places and that there was no better starting place than the toughest beat in the city.

"You'll be up against the best the *Tribune* and the *Times* have to offer," he said. "And they won't give you a thing."

On that first night, her anger at her new boss made her realize that she was emerging again. After a couple of years in emotional limbo, the temper that had so tried her mother, the temper she had even hidden from her young husband, the temper she had tentatively and unsuccessfully tried to turn on God when He snatched her love away came bubbling up to make her feel alive again.

Everyone knew what it was like to work for Leo. And everyone wanted to. You'd never learn so much so fast or be pushed to such limits or set such standards for yourself working for anyone else. But that didn't lessen her ire any when he read her rewrite and yelled at her again.

She stood at the rim of his horseshoe desk and heard him say one word she didn't understand. Was it *good? Bad? Better? Worse?*

"I'm sorry?" she said.

He repeated it, only this time it sounded like a foul expletive. It wasn't that she hadn't ever heard the word before; she just wasn't sure she'd heard it this time.

"I didn't hear you," she said.

He pulled his cigar from his lips, as if to aid his articulation, then thought better of it and waved her back to her desk. When she arrived, her screen was blinking. She called up the message and blinked herself. There on the screen, from her new boss, was the four-letter word she thought she'd heard.

She didn't want Leo to see her redden, more from anger than embarrassment. She tapped out a return message. "Does that mean you like my story, or you don't?"

"I don't," came the reply.

"Can you tell me why, or is vulgarity all I get?"

"There's no more time to mess with it. I'll rewrite it."

"Then you take the byline in the morning paper."

"The city editor take a byline on the front page? It's your stuff, your work. Anyway, I'm in charge of who gets bylines."

"It feels ridiculous writing you messages from twenty-five feet away. Just know that I'm going to succeed in this job and make you like me; appreciate me, anyway."

"*It* doesn't feel ridiculous. *You* do. So do I. And my liking you is of little consequence to the job we're paid to do. Appreciate you? I already do. Now go home, and in the morning, enjoy the story under your name. It'll be good."

And it had been good. Leo was a pro. The best. Earthy, but a mentor, nonetheless. They had not communicated, except face to face, since that first night. In fact, he had apologized for his language.

"I didn't know you were religious," he explained.

"I wouldn't call myself religious," she had said. "We can talk about it sometime."

"No, we can't. And I'm glad you don't call yourself religious, because religion doesn't go far on the police beat. You'll see."

A pro, a good mentor and all, but not always right. Jennifer had seen how the police beat and her faith jibed or didn't jibe all right, and she had to wonder how she would have survived without it.

She prayed now as she parked on the street across from the Sixteenth Precinct. She prayed for the injured cop, whoever he was. For his wife. For his family. For the people who would be hurt by this latest internal crackdown, whatever it was all about. For the people who had been hurt by unscrupulous cops in the first place, because there were always civilian victims when policemen went bad.

As she trotted across the street and up the steps to face the greasy Flannigan, she prayed for her Jim. He hadn't been pressed into late duty for months. She knew he wasn't scheduled for tonight.

But if the internal affairs arrests were significant or widespread, maybe a lot of the guys in the Sixteenth would be on the street.

THREE

James Purcell had been one of the first men Jennifer had met in her new role with the *Day.* He'd been a detective in the Vice Control Division who had requested a transfer due to his personal scruples.

Much had been made of it in the papers because scruples hadn't been a problem in the Chicago Police Department for as long as anyone could remember. "I don't want to come off like a Sunday school type," the *Sun-Times* had quoted him. "But there are things a VCD detective has to do that make it hard for me to sleep at night. I want to see vice controlled in Chicago, but it takes a different kind of a man to do this job."

The public had taken him to its heart. What he really wanted, he said, was an assignment in the Homicide Division. There was a "Jim Purcell" day and even a fan club. But it all blew over shortly after the police commissioner announced that it was not up to an individual officer to choose his assignment. The commissioner said he and his command officers would decide whether a man could beg off an assignment, and that even if they decided that such requests might be tolerated, there would be no selecting of the new assignment.

The implications were clear. An officer might request a transfer, but it would not have to be honored, and there was no guarantee he wouldn't be sentenced to some Siberia within the department, like the night desk clerk's job in the Sixteenth Precinct. Which is what Purcell received.

When Jennifer was making the rounds that first week, she found herself coming back again and again to the shy, younger-than-his-years-looking bachelor at the Sixteenth. She hadn't even entertained a thought of interest in him or any man, but she was scrambling in her job and she needed help. Other desk officer types on her beat leered at her. The brass tolerated her but hardly talked to her. Some tested her. Some made passes at her. Many treated her as a child.

She wanted to do a good job. She wasn't there to do public relations work for the police department, but she wasn't out to get anybody either. All she wanted was information. Solid, truthful, no games, complete information she could use to write a story the public had the right to hear.

Jim Purcell seemed to understand that when no one else did. And though he had said he didn't want to be considered a Sunday school type, he *was* a Sunday school type, and the kids he taught on Sunday mornings demanded an explanation after that quote appeared.

He was like an oasis. She could count on a smile from him even when she stopped at the station house in the middle of the night. She knew that at the end of the counter in front of his desk, she'd find a little wire basket full of copies of all the reports of arrests in the precinct since she'd dropped in last.

Her predecessor had told her about the wire baskets that were unpublicized sources of information to the press and the public. No one used them but the police reporters, and they were not to take the sheets or make photocopies. The desk officers in many station houses thought it cute to "misplace" all but the stray dog or cat-up-a-tree reports or, worse, drop in bogus reports.

Jim had rescued her from that humiliation as well. She showed up one night, took her usual copious notes based on the reports in the basket, heard once again that the watch commander didn't have time to talk to her about any of them, and proceeded to tell Jim of a report she had read in the last station house.

Jim's eyes grew wide with mock wonder as she recounted the story of a young mother who had reportedly been startled by an intruder. "But she just took the matters into her own hands. She shushed him with a finger to her lips as she rocked the baby, giving the intruder a look that said he'd better not wake the baby, whatever he did. Then she continued singing lullabies to the baby while the man sat on the floor. Within a few minutes, he was sound asleep, and she called the police. They got there just as he was waking up and—Jim! I've been had, haven't I?"

"Just one question," Jim said. "Did the watch commander talk with you about the report?"

"Yes."

"Has he ever talked to you about a case before?"

"No."

"Yeah. I'd say you've been had."

Jennifer turned it into points with her boss though, and she even turned the joke around on the men who started it. She wrote the story as if it were fact, until she got to the bottom line where she quoted herself, "And any reporter who'd buy this has to also believe in the Easter Bunny."

Leo got a good laugh out of it and told her he was glad she saw through it. She wanted to tell him that her new friend at the Sixteenth was really responsible for saving her from it. But Leo had warned her enough about not fraternizing that she thought better of it.

Then she got a buddy from the composition room to doll the story up in type as it might appear in the paper, had it laminated, and presented it to the desk officer. It quoted both him and his boss, and the look on his face when he thought it would be in the next day's paper was worth the embarrassment she had suffered in believing it in the first place.

When Jim Purcell was reassigned, after just a couple of months, to the role of Officer Friendly, it might have meant the end of their contact had it not been for Jennifer's independence. She remembered being disappointed the night he told her that he would no longer be on the desk after the end of the month, but still she felt no stirrings. He was just a nice guy, a rare Christian among a rough bunch of men. They knew little about each other, and neither was really supposed to fraternize with the other—though this was only traditional on both sides, not written policy.

Then the night she had car trouble right in front of the station house, she was tempted to run back in and ask his help. But that would have been unprofessional. It might have even looked forward.

But she didn't have time to wait for a tow truck, and who knew what gas station would send one this time of night anyway? Should she call Bobby and have him come and get her? Who needed the heat that would bring from Leo? Leo didn't care if you were a man or a woman, he always said, "You've got your job to do and your deadlines to meet and you do it, that's all."

So she had called a cab, but she didn't use the pay phone in the precinct. She used a phone down the block where she waited for the cab until just after 11:00 P.M. But the car that finally pulled to the curb was not a cab. A man, alone, rolled down the passenger side window. She started back toward the station.

"Hey! It's me, Jim! You need a ride?"

She felt foolish. "No, thanks, Jim. I've got a cab coming. I just called for one."

"You *called* a cab? You can hail one faster. The called ones never come. C'mon, where you going? I can run you over to the paper."

She hesitated, then got in.

"What's wrong with your car?"

"I wish I knew. Won't turn over."

"I'll drop you at the paper, from a block away if you're worried someone will see." She smiled. "And then I'll come back here and take a look. Can't be anything serious. Has it been acting up?"

"Not at all."

"Probably nothing big then."

"Oh, Jim, no. I can't let you do that. I'll get a garage to look at it tomorrow. If you can just run me to my office, someone can take me home, and I'll work it out, no problem."

"Forget it. By the time you're off work, I'll be back to pick you up and take you to your car. Fair enough?"

"I really can't let you do that. It's sweet of you, but no."

"C'mon! My one chance to be a white knight? Don't ruin it for me. Don't forget, I'm gonna be Officer Friendly."

She laughed and removed her car keys from her key ring for him. He chided her. "That's right. Hang onto those apartment keys, just like Officer Friendly would advise. Too easy to copy."

When she got off work that night, she hoped Bobby—a sweet kid, but a climber and sometimes a big mouth—didn't notice that Jim was waiting out in front. Jim took her back to her car and explained the minor problem that had interrupted the ignition. She thanked him profusely. He asked if he could see her again since he wouldn't be seeing her on business much any more.

"I shouldn't," she said.

"If I was still going to see you every night on duty, I might not have asked you this soon."

"I'd better not."

"You'd better."

"I don't know."

"I won't beg."

"I wouldn't want you to."

"Please, oh please!"

And they both laughed. "You can call me," she said finally. "But no promises."

"Ah, so it depends on where I'm going to take you. How do you feel about professional wrestling?"

"Are you kidding?"

"Of course."

"Whew!"

"I was thinking more in terms of a concert at Ravinia."

"Now that I'd love," she said.

"Saturday?"

"Saturday."

There had been many Saturdays since then. And Sundays at his church. And hers. And Friday nights. And last night. He was perfect for what ailed her. He wasn't pushy. He wasn't demanding. He let her talk about Scott. He let her cry.

It almost embarrassed him that he grew to love his Officer Friendly role. "It's not something I want to do the rest of my life," he said, "because I'd still like to land in Homicide eventually, but I *do* like working with kids."

"I wouldn't think investigating homicides would be something you'd want to do the rest of your life either," she said.

"It wouldn't always be pleasant. But it would always be a challenge, and a worthy one. If we believe God is the author of life, we should want to oppose those who take lives." But she wondered what it would be like to be married to a man who dealt with bodies and blood and murderers all day.

Then she scolded herself for even thinking that way. What Jim Purcell did with his life was his business, and besides, they weren't past the hand-holding stage. No commitments had been made, no love expressed.

Did she love him? She could. She was capable. She might someday. But now? Did she? She wasn't sure. She figured she'd know when she did. She knew one thing: she loved to watch him with kids. With his Sunday school kids, his friends from church. Even with her nieces and nephews.

And though people in both churches and both families had started making assumptions, she and Jim had not even said they wouldn't see other people yet. No one from their respective places of work knew anything about their relationship. They liked each other. A lot. And she thought he probably loved her. He had expressed it in many ways. She missed him when she didn't see him. She was happier when she was with him.

Sounds like love, she thought. *Feels like love.* But she had been through it before. And the loss, even the potential of the loss of one she could hold so dear, scared her, slowed her, made her careful.

Now, as she entered the Sixteenth Precinct on what she sensed was as important a day in police news since she'd been on the beat, she was thinking of Jim and the quiet dinner they had enjoyed. Simultaneously, she reached into her bag for her note pad.

"Good evening, Herb," she said to Flannigan. "What've you got? Who can I see?"

"Nothin' and nobody. How's that?"

She started to smile, but he wasn't kidding. "What's the matter, Herb? Is everything under wraps? You must know by now who was hit. Anybody I know?"

"I can't tell you anything. It's a guy from IAD, and he's brass. He's at Henrotin, and if you tell anybody I tol' you, it's the last thing you'll ever get from me."

"I appreciate it, Herb. You know I do. Now what was the bust?"

"I'm afraid it was right here in the Sixteeth," he said. "And I'm serious, I can't say a word. I wouldn't tell you who if you paid me."

"Campbell in?"

"He's in, but the official answer is no, if you know what I mean."

"No way he'll see me?"

"No way."

Jennifer pursed her lips and headed for the pay phone near the stairs. "Hi, it's Grey," she said. "Let me talk to Leo."

While she waited for Leo, she was tempted to try Jim at home again and, short of that, asking Flannigan if Jim had been called in for emergency duty.

"Yeah, Jenn!"

"Leo, I'm at the Sixteenth and getting nothing. I'm going over to Henrotin where they've got this Chief of Internal Affairs."

"Lucas?"

"Is that his name?"

"'Course that's his name. You don't have your department directory with you?"

"No."

"John Lucas. Very big name. Very impressive. Big news if he's been hit. You know this for sure? I'll start a bio."

"I can't be sure yet if it's Lucas, but it sounds like he's in pretty bad shape, whoever he is. You think I'll get anybody in Public Information this time of night?"

"I doubt it, but it's worth a try. I can only hold page one until three A.M., and I mean three. You call me at quarter to with whatever you've got, and I gotta tell ya, it better be more than you've got now. You know how many were busted?"

"No."

"Better get to Henrotin. We'll get the arrested officers from the TV or the wires. Concentrate on the shot cop, and Bobby'll track down the rest."

I'll bet he will, Jennifer thought, feeling as if she had failed already. She didn't want help. She didn't want to be reminded what she'd forgotten. She didn't want to have to concentrate on just one aspect of the story, regardless of the time pressure. She was mad.

Pushing open the glass door to the lobby she called to Flannigan. "Give me the number for Public Information, fast!"

He didn't have time to think about it. He peeled open the dog-eared department directory and yelled out the number. When the switchboard downtown answered, Jennifer identified herself and asked for the Public Information Director. "No, it's not an emergency," she said with more sarcasm than she should have.

She was told he was unavailable. "Are you telling me he's not in the office? Because I don't think his wife will be too thrilled to take a call right now, especially if he isn't home."

"He's here, but unavailable."

"Tell him it's the *Chicago Day,* and don't tell me he isn't out talking to the broadcast people right now. Tell him I just need him for a second."

Jennifer looked at her watch and panicked. If she was just getting information that Bobby could get elsewhere and she missed the one part of the story Leo told her to stay on, she'd be in big trouble. She tapped her foot impatiently and began preparing herself to run to her car as soon as she talked to the Public Information Director.

"This is Nelson, sir. What is it?"

"First of all, I'm not a sir, but don't apologize. I'm Jennifer Grey with the *Day* and—"

"Yes, I've seen your stuff—"

"Good, I need to know what Sixteenth Precinct officers were arrested this morning."

"I'm sorry, Grey, but those announcements don't come from this office. They are always handled by Internal Affairs, and I'm afraid they're incapacitated at this moment."

"Because John Lucas is in intensive care at Henrotin?"

"Who told you that?"

"You did. I was just guessing. Thanks, Nelson."

"You're welcome."

"Just one more thing. Where are the arrested officers being booked?"

"Down here."

"Can I come?"

"Suit yourself. But we won't even be giving out the names."

You might not be, Jennifer thought, *but somebody down there is always eager to tell what they know.*

FOUR

Jennifer sped to Henrotin Hospital on the Near North Side and debated parking in the emergency lane. Instead, she parked as close as she could to the door and popped her press card on the dash. *That's one way to beg for a ticket,* she thought.

She was among the press latecomers in the emergency room, asking all the questions everyone else had already tried. And getting the same answer. No comment. She walked the halls and asked doctors, nurses, aides, and custodians if they knew anything at all about the condition of the man in intensive care.

They had been briefed well. That or they'd been through this before, Henrotin being a popular site for the most common emergencies in the world of crime that surrounded it. Jennifer spotted a pay phone and dialed the emergency room. She could hear the nurse on duty live in one ear and by phone in the other. She turned toward the wall so the effect wouldn't be reversed.

"This is Jennifer Grey calling from the Near North Side," she said. "I must know immediately if you called the morgue and whether you will be transferring Mr. Lucas's body there?"

"I didn't call the morgue," she said. "I don't believe Mr. Lucas has expired, ma'am."

"Is that correct? I understood that he may have already died."

"One moment please."

A male voice came on. "This is Dr. Burris. May I help you?"

"I need to know the condition of Mr. Lucas as soon as you can put me in touch with someone in authority."

"Well, we'll be releasing this to the press at about three-thirty A.M. anyway if there has been no change: His condition is grave. He is suffering from wounds to the abdomen and the cardiovascular system. He has not been conscious since the time of the shooting. We have been able to remove only one bullet at this time, and further surgery must be postponed until his condition stabilizes, probably not for several hours. All vital signs are weak."

"What kind of chance would you give him, Doctor?"

"One in ten."

"Thank you."

Jennifer phoned the news in to Leo and headed downtown. There'd be no one falling for an innocent phone call down at headquarters, however straightforward. She had never been able to justify lying, which Leo felt was fair. She always told the party her name and what she wanted to know, emphasizing the urgency of it and appealing to their rank. If they asked her more specifically why she wanted to know, she told them, but they seldom asked.

Jennifer arrived at 2:30 A.M. Again she was a latecomer. Her colleagues pressed around Public Information Director Nelson, who was asking how many were on a hot deadline. "I am," Jennifer called, remembering the days when it was all she could do to muster the courage to ask a simple question at a press conference.

"I oughta head for the phone right now," one of her competitors quipped. The *Day* stayin' open after sundown is front page stuff!"

Everyone guffawed, but Jennifer ignored them and talked directly to Nelson again. "I'm looking at fifteen minutes," she said. "I'll take whatever you've got."

"All I have is four names."

"We've all got the names," she said, taking a chance, assuming Leo and Bobby had been able to get that much. She lost the gamble. Everyone turned and stared, then shouted at Nelson, demanding to know why she had information that they didn't.

He held up both hands. "She's bluffing," he said. "No one has the names because I just got them myself. Now, Grey, the names are all I have except a few details. If you've already got what I'm about to give, you might as well head back to the *Day.*" She stared him down.

"Now, then, ladies and gentlemen, a few ground rules. I have very brief, very sketchy reports for you. I will read them verbatim the way I have been instructed. I will not be able to comment further on them. I have nothing more on the arrests themselves, and I cannot release the names of the arresting officers.

"I can tell you that at around midnight, the Internal Affairs Division of the Chicago Police Department made four arrests of police personnel, charging them with trafficking in controlled substances. These four arrested officers are being held without bail in this facility. The police commissioner is releasing the following statement: 'These arrests come after lengthy preparation by the Internal Affairs Division. However, we will consider the arrested officers innocent until proven guilty. Any so found will not only be dismissed from the police force but will be prosecuted to the full extent of the law.'

"That statement was prepared in advance. With the wounding of IAD Chief John Lucas, the commissioner has added this: 'Our prayers are with the wounded officer and his family.'

"Lucas's is the only name I can give you from the list of arresting officers. He was critically wounded during the arrest of Lieutenant Frank Akeley of the Sixteenth Precinct. The arrest was made in the parking lot of The Illusion bar on Wells Street. I know none of the details except that Chief Lucas was hit three times by small caliber ammunition and is in intensive care at Henrotin Hospital at this time. No one else was injured."

"Did this Akeley shoot him?"

"I am not at liberty to comment on that."

"How many officers were at the scene?"

"I do not know."

"Is he expected to live?"

"I'm sorry, gentlemen—and ladies. As I told you, this is all I have. Now there is more on the other arrests, if you'd care to hear it."

"Yeah, but you got stats on Akeley?"

"Yes. White, male, age fifty-nine, five feet eleven inches, one hundred eighty-five pounds. The highest ranking officer arrested this evening. An employee of the City of Chicago for thirty-two years."

"Family?"

"That's all I have."

"Stats on Lucas?"

"Yes. White, male, age fifty-six, six feet two inches, one hundred ninety pounds. Thirty-year employee."

"Family?"

"Wife, four grown daughters."

"The other arrested officers included Sergeant William Much, also Sixteenth Precinct. Arrested at his home on the West Side. He's married, two teenage sons and a younger daughter. White, male, age forty-three, six feet four inches, two hundred sixty-five pounds. Employed by Chicago PD for nineteen years."

"Who arrested him?" Laughter.

"I don't have that information."

"Is the arresting officer still alive?" More laughter. Nelson ignored it.

"That name sounds familiar. Has he ever been up on charges before?"

"No, but we've released stories about him from our office twice in the last year. One—which none of you used—was a feature on the fact that he's our singing policeman. The other—which you all used—was that he was our biggest policeman and that he had been ordered to lose weight before the end of this year."

"How's he doing? He gonna make it?"

Nelson was not amused. He looked as if he wanted to say he didn't have that information, but of course he had the file on the old feature story. He ignored the question anyway.

"Arrested on duty, and again, I am not at liberty to give you the name of the arresting officer, was Patrol Officer Trudy Janus, white, female, age twenty-seven, five feet five inches, one hundred forty pounds. Single. Employed here three years."

"First female in that precinct?"

"Yes."

"First female officer ever arrested?"

"I believe so. Better not quote me on that."

"Any of these resist arrest?"

"No comment."

"Did more than one resist arrest?"

"No."

"There's one more?"

"James Purcell, a specially assigned Patrol Officer, white, male, age twenty-nine, six feet one inch, one hundred seventy pounds, six-year employee. Arrested at his Near North Side apartment."

Jennifer squinted and stared unblinking at Nelson. Her throat had tightened at the first mention of Jim's name, and her desperate hope that it was another James Purcell was dashed immediately with the cold recitation of his statistics. The numbness that had plagued her after the death of her husband swept over her once more.

There has to be a mistake, she thought as she stiffly backed away from the scene. She was terrified for Jim and what he must be going through. She didn't want to face the news. It was too stark, too impersonal, too awful. It took her back three years to the phone call that asked her if she were Mrs. Scott Alan Grey. She knew by the way she had been asked that something terrible had happened.

The caller had identified himself as a state trooper and asked cordially if she would be home for the next half hour or so and could he please drop by for a moment. She had known so certainly then that she called her father and told him to come to Arlington Heights, that Scott had been killed, and that she needed her parents.

She never once doubted the truth of her conviction, and, of course, she was right. She made it easy on the young trooper. "How did it happen?" she asked, refusing his suggestion that she sit down.

"Multiple car accident, icy roads. No one's fault."

"Anyone else hurt?"

"Yes, ma'am. No other fatalities, however."

"Could you stay with me for a half hour or so until my parents arrive?"

"Of course. Would you like me to call them for you? It wouldn't be any trouble."

"They're on their way."

Jennifer's first thought as she backed through the door now was to stop at the pay phone and call her father. But she couldn't. There were too many reasons she couldn't. She wanted to shut this out, to wake up from it, to be done with it.

Her deadline was closing in, and she was a newspaper woman. She was not a woman in love. She was not a person with a second chance at life. She was Leo Stanton's ace police reporter. Maybe she had wobbly legs, and maybe she was on the verge of hysterics. But a grown woman doesn't wake up her father in the middle of the night when she has a job to do.

So she phoned Leo. While the rest of the pack were running for other phones and howling about Officer Friendly being a dope dealer and "Wasn't this the guy who wanted out of vice control because he wasn't old enough? No, he found out there wasn't as much money in it!" Jennifer told Leo that he'd better get another hour from the pressmen.

"I told you, Jenn, three means three. We go to press in a few minutes. What's the matter with you anyway? You sound strange."

"I'm sitting on the biggest story of my career, Leo. Trust me. I'll come straight in and give you a lead story for page one in the first draft. If you don't hold the press for this piece, we'll be blown out by all the other news media."

"You know what you're asking, Jennifer?"

"Leo, I asked myself what you would do in this situation, and that's what I'm doing."

Stanton laughed a rueful laugh. "I can't argue with that. I'll get you a four o'clock pressrun; you get in here and give me the story."

Jennifer knew she couldn't drive, so she grabbed a cab and paid him in advance so she could jump out when he slid up to the night entrance at the *Day.* She hid her face in her hands and tried to control her sobs, but she couldn't.

The public has a right to hear this story whether these people are guilty or innocent, she told herself over and over. *He just has to be innocent! He couldn't! He wouldn't! I know him too well! Who am I kidding? I don't know him at all. I've been taken. He used me. But the story can't be vindictive. It has to be straight. It has to be the piece I would write if I'd never heard of the man. God, don't let this be true! Please make it all be a mistake!*

She hurried into the city room, shedding her coat and her bag and reading her notes as she walked. Bobby approached and handed her a story. "Leo let me take a shot at the Lucas piece. What do you think?"

She sensed Bobby's gloating and tried to scan the piece through her tears.

> John Lucas, 56, is fighting for his life at Henrotin Hospital this morning after suffering multiple gunshot wounds during a midnight arrest on the Near North Side.
>
> The long-time veteran with a reputation for incorruptiblity was personally handling the arrest of Chicago Police Lieutenant Frank Akeley, 59, who allegedly opened fire in the parking lot of . . ."

"Yeah, yeah, I think that'll be OK," Jennifer managed, wondering which story Leo would lead with. Not that she cared. In a selfish, protective way, she could wish that he would bury her story. She would beg him to leave her name off it, maybe even threaten to quit if he didn't comply.

Leo gave her a puzzled look, and she slowed as she passed his desk, wondering if she didn't owe him some sort of an explanation. He started to pull his cigar from his lips, then remembered the time and just left it. He clicked his fingers and pointed to her video display terminal, and she kept walking.

It was warm in the city room, or was it just Jennifer? She pulled her sweater over her head and sat, still steaming, in her blouse. She set up her note pad next to the machine while trying to remove her boots with her free hand. No luck.

She bent down and put her head under the desk to get a better vantage point from which to attack the zippers. While in that ridiculous position, it hit her what she was about to do.

She was going to write a story for the fastest growing newspaper in Chicago that would end a man's career forever, guilty or innocent. *But the story won't, can't, say he's guilty,* she reasoned.

And the facts will be broadcast on radio and television and printed in all the other papers anyway. There's no way I can protect him. And why should I? Because I know he can't be guilty, that's why. Don't I? And either way, it's a story. A valid story. Either way, it's news that he was arrested. And there's irony in his present assignment.

She had to do it. Leo stared at her taking so long to take off her boots. She'd been running since Bobby had called her just before 1:00 A.M. She needed a shower. She needed a shampoo. She needed a change of clothes. She needed a bed.

What she wanted was her parents. *Why do I have to be such a baby?* Her dad had told her that it took more of a woman to admit she needed someone than to need someone and pretend she didn't.

That was sage advice, as usual, from Dad. But this time it didn't fit. Because this time what she wanted and what she needed were two different things. She would have said to herself, and did, that she wanted her parents. She wanted to go home to Rockford, home to her old bedroom, home to long days of sleeping her cares away.

But what she needed? What she really needed? If she'd had her choice of all the options in the world, would she really go home? No. She would go to Jim. She would tell him she believed him, whatever his story was.

And she knew when she even let that thought enter her head that it was ludicrous. It was the thought of a crazy woman. It was the kind of thing a woman in love would say. *I love him,* she told herself. *I finally know that I love him, and I have every reason to believe he's a criminal.*

Surer of her love than of his innocence, she straightened up, gave one hard glance back at Leo—who had been about to tell her to make good on her page one story or hit the bricks—and turned to her machine.

Her tears began afresh, and as they rolled down her face, she punched in the toughest story she would ever write. Knowing it would go out over the *Day* syndicate as well, she datelined it Chicago and began:

> James Purcell, 29, the Sunday school teaching Chicago policeman who begged off from his unsavory assignment to the Vice Control Division early this year and has been serving as Officer Friendly in areas schools, was one of four 16th Precinct police officers arrested early this morning and charged with buying and selling illegal drugs.
>
> In the quadruple arrests that took place at four separate locations simultaneously, Internal Affairs Division Chief John Lucas was critically wounded. (See separate story.) The other three arrests, including Purcell, veteran Sergeant William Much, 43, and Patrol Officer Trudy Janus, 27, were without incident. . . .

FIVE

It was all Jennifer could do to finish the article, she wanted so badly to see Jim.

But at the lockup she was faced with a brick wall. "No, Jennifer, absolutely not, no way. Sorry."

"What're you talking about, Bradley?" she pleaded with the lanky, dark deskman. "You've taken me in to see your *own* prisoners before!"

"Maybe that's why I got stuck on desk duty, Jenn. I've got orders. Nobody sees these four except their lawyers. That's it, so don't beg."

"Can you give him a message for me?"

Bradley appeared to consider it. "Not without clearance from my boss, Jennifer."

"How long would that take?"

"I dunno. He works the day shift, and I ain't gonna call him at home. I could leave it for him."

"Forget it," she said, trying to keep from screaming. "Is there really no way I can get in there for a few minutes, if I promise to keep your name out of it?"

"C'mon, Jennifer, I told you not to beg. I'm in charge of the keys until tomorrow, so there's no way anyone can keep my name out of anything if you get in there. I'm sorry, OK?"

Jennifer couldn't speak, not even to thank him for listening to her. She trudged to her car, fighting tears and suddenly feeling the fatigue that the last few hectic hours had made her ignore. She banged both hands against the steering wheel, fighting the sobs that were just beneath the surface.

She made a conscious decision not to cry. She wanted to be with Jim, but she couldn't be, and that was that. Sleep was what she needed.

The morning papers and the radio talk shows made the most of the arrests, speculating on how many police officers would wind up indicted when all the results were in.

They had great fun, of course, with the singing policeman—the biggest man on the force—being brought down by the scandal. But their ire was reserved for Jim Purcell, the one they said had played the "all-American boy" image to the hilt.

While hearts bled for John Lucas, and hourly hospital reports sounded worse and worse, Jennifer sat in her apartment unable to turn away from the radio call-in programs. People who knew nothing except what they'd read in the paper, and—she knew many of them had read only her article—ranted and raved about the fact that "this man, or at least this person who calls himself a man, spends his days telling kids that the police department is on their side and spends his nights selling heroin to the same children!"

Leo had reluctantly complied with her ultimatum, and she wondered if she would have had the fortitude to follow through with her threat to resign if he had crossed her. After hearing the diatribes all morning, she knew she would have. Still, even without the byline, Jim Purcell would know who wrote those stories.

And why was she still worried about that? If it had all been a mistake and he was cleared, he'd have to understand, wouldn't he? Wouldn't any sane adult know that the story was news? That it would have appeared everywhere else anyway? And that she and the *Day* would have looked suspicious for not covering it?

But the more she thought about it, the more she knew that it was something else that was bothering her. It was the possibility that it was all true. That she had been duped by a con man second to none. If she was wrong about Jim, she could never trust another human being as long as she lived.

The man was special. He reminded her of her own father. The kindness, the understanding, the gentleness, the insight. Could a person be that confused, that deceived, that totally swept away by someone?

It was inconceivable! She wracked her brain for clues to a side of him she never knew. He was idealistic. He was sometimes unrealistic. Yet he was responsible. He was one of those who volunteered for unpopular duty, working weekends and holidays when the family men wanted to trade days off.

Were there times when he was unavailable, and she didn't know why or he didn't explain? She could think of none. There seemed to be a lot of meetings, staff meetings. And not always at the precinct house. Could that have been when he was doing his dirty work? She had no reason to believe that.

No reason except for the sketchy reports coming out of Internal Affairs that this surveillance had been under way for longer than Jim had been in the precinct. She decided she could live with the bad news more easily than with no news. If she could find out for sure that he was the scoundrel the stories implied, she would deal with the pain, the remorse, the grief of it, the same way she had dealt with the loss of Scott.

There were similarities; of course there were. Especially after the realization at her keyboard in the wee hours that she was indeed in love with Jim. Memories of their praying together stabbed through her. *Could he be a phony? Is it possible? Could a man drag God into a sham? I suppose a real pro could.*

But Jim was sincere in his distaste for the work he'd been assigned in the Vice Control Division. Having to play up to prostitutes and pay off informants. Deciding which crime was more important and letting the small-time criminal go, and maybe even helping him or her out, in exchange for the bigger prey.

He said he'd been raised straight and had never really been in serious trouble, certainly not involving the seamier side of life. He was not only repulsed by the after-dark world of Chicago, but he also found himself fascinated and even tempted by parts of it. He found himself thinking thoughts he'd never entertained before, seeing pictures in his mind he wondered if he could ever erase.

He wasn't a prude, he'd said. It wasn't that he didn't know what went on behind closed doors. But he'd always appreciated the counsel of an older Christian policeman who had said that a Christian officer "must be fully acquainted with sin but not partake of it."

This vice control business was for someone else, according to Jim. And when Jennifer heard his view of it, she had to agree. There were bad, horrible, awful sides to other parts of police work too—like trying to solve grisly murders. But while they, too, left memory pictures that needed cleansing, they didn't begin to work on a young man's imagination or make him remember the alluring sights of the underworld. And only a blind man could deny that they were there.

No man would admit to his family that he wanted all that went with the action in the sleazy strip joints and hangouts. There was filth and disease and burned-out men and women. But could the same man say that there weren't sights that appealed to his lower nature, possibilities that excited his fantasies?

Jim, Jennifer felt, had decided he didn't need that kind of input. He was admitting to the world that it took either a stronger man for the work or one who didn't care about the purity of his thought life.

Jim had told Jennifer more than he had told any other reporter—because he was telling her off-the-record as a friend, even though he never stipulated such. He had told her that his reason was his faith in Christ, his eagerness to do and to be and to become all that God wanted him to.

Somehow she couldn't make those lofty ideals fit the worst con man in the business. But maybe they were what made him the best.

She rose from the couch, where fits of exhausted sleep left her more tired than refreshed, and shuffled to the phone. She called Leo at home. "Well, I guess we've got another paper to put out for tomorrow morning," she said.

"Yeah, I suppose we do, Jenn. You all right?"

"I think so."

"We're going to have to talk about it, you know that, don't you?"

"Talk about what?"

"C'mon, Jenn. You're talking to Leo. And Leo knows. You ought to know that by now. But better than that, just like your mom, Leo cares. Thing is, you can snow Mom. You can't snow Leo."

"I know. I'm sorry."

"Don't be sorry. Just talk to me. What's happening with you, Jennifer? Why are you taking this story so hard? You get too close to these people or something? Know them too well? I warned you about taking sides, about seeing yourself as one of the cops instead of a reporter, standing between them and the readers."

"Yeah, well, maybe that was it, Leo. It does hurt to see people hurt."

"But *they* hurt people, Jennifer. It was *their* fault. You've got to see that, to separate yourself from them, to see the public's side. If you're going to be a bleeding-heart cheerleader for the cops, you're no good to us in your job."

"Maybe you're right. Maybe I'm no good in the job."

"We both know that's garbage. You called me. You said we've got another paper to put out. That tells me you're ready for an assignment today. I was going to give you a day off, but if you're ready—"

"You were? You were going to give me a break? I don't know what to think about that, Leo. What am I supposed to think about that?"

"Since when are you asking me what you're supposed to think? That'll be the day."

"No, I just mean, are you feeling sorry for me? Wondering if I can handle the job? What?"

"You worked hard last night, and it was getting to you. It showed. You can't deny that."

"It showed in my piece?"

"No, your story was as nice as you've done since you've been with me. But you do a great job, you cry at your desk, you don't want your name on the story. I'm no psychiatrist, Jenn, but I've got to think my star reporter needs a day to herself."

"That's thoughtful, Leo. But no, I think I'll do better working than sitting around here all day thinking."

"You're sure?"

"Yeah."

"You want an assignment?"

"Sure."

"You know it's going to be right in the middle of this Internal Affairs bust."

"Sure."

"Well, there *have* been a few developments I'd like you to check out. First, the names of the arresting officers have leaked out. Bobby's got 'em at the office. You can try to contact them. Second, Lucas has taken a turn for the worse. The doctors are saying it's only a matter of time. Third, no one but their lawyers is allowed in to see the four busted cops, but get this: only three of them even have lawyers. Akeley, who's been formally charged now with resisting arrest, assault with a deadly weapon, and attempted murder, has procured this Williams, you remember the guy?"

"The Williams who represented the City of Chicago in federal court? Big stuff."

"Yeah, that's the guy. But I have a feeling that with the testimony of two of his own precinct cops against him, Akeley's going to need more than Williams. Anyway, it appears this Bill Much, the—"

"Sergeant."

"Yeah, Much is broke and is using a public defender. That's worth a few laughs when you think about it. A defender of the public violates the public trust, then hires a public defender to defend himself against the public. It's too good. But not funny. I'm sorry. I forgot how you're reacting to this."

"It's all right."

"OK, Janus has a guess-what lawyer?"

"A woman."

"You got it."

"A known feminist defender."

"Right again."

"You're telling me the fourth defendant doesn't have counsel yet?"

"That's the story, Jenn. He isn't going to have counsel. What's his name?"

"Purcell."

"Right. This James Purcell, the Holy Joe, has waived his right to a lawyer."

"Temporarily, surely."

"Maybe. But what's his game? That's what I want you to find out. What would you think of visiting his church? Talking to his pastor, some of his friends? They'll say they're shocked and all that, never would have thought it. Maybe they'll stick up for him. But go deeper. Find out what the parents of the kids he teaches in Sunday school think about letting their kids stay in his class if he gets out on bond. Or if the church will let him keep his class. What do the people think? I don't suppose you could get to one of the kids, but that would be interesting too. My guess is the kids will not believe it yet."

"Do you believe it, Leo?"

"I missed that."

"Do you believe Purcell is guilty?"

Leo swore. "They're all guilty, Jenn. Once in a great while there'll be smoke with no fire. But when you're talking official corruption, your cops and your politicians and your government employees, uh-uh. In the *Day,* just like in every other rag that wants to be fair and ethical, our pieces will be full of alleged this and allegedly that and all the rest. But let me tell you something: the alleged Akeley who allegedly shot the alleged chief of the alleged IAD is going to be in a heap of alleged trouble if his victim allegedly dies. Yeah, Jenn, they're all as guilty as sin, and when you've been on this beat long—in fact, probably after this coverage right here—you'll never doubt it again."

Jennifer was silent, trying to keep from crying.

"C'mon, Jennifer. Be realistic. I don't want to be such a cynic any more than anyone else, but you've got to snap out of this Pollyanna business. I like a reporter who can be optimistic and look on the bright side of things. But there is no bright side to a cop scandal. Talking to a guy's Sunday school class might seem a little crass. But did you ever see a story of a mass murderer that doesn't carry quotes from the people he grew up with, people who taught him?"

"I guess not."

"Of course you didn't. Now what do you want to take today? You get first choice of course. Bobby and I'll take the rest, along with a couple stringers we're borrowing from the newsroom."

"I'll tell you what I want to do, if you don't mind, Leo. I'd like to take you up on your offer of a day off. I could really use the time."

This time Leo was silent.

"Is that OK?"

"Sure, Jenn. How much time you need?"

"Just a day. I'll see you tomorrow afternoon."

"You going to get some rest, kid?"

"I don't know. I might go see my parents in Rockford."

"I'll be thinking about you. Give me a call if you need me, huh?"

"Thanks, Leo. Thanks a lot."

Six

Though she was hounded by it all the way up the Northwest Tollway, Jennifer couldn't decide what significance there was to Jim's decision not to procure a lawyer. Was it lack of money? Could she help? Should she? Would she have to quit her job first? What if she was wrong about him and quit her job to help him, all in vain? They'd both be ruined.

She wouldn't have thought twice about sacrificing her career for him if he was innocent. But how could she be sure? What was she saying? That she loved him enough to sacrifice for him, yet she didn't know if he was innocent?

She saw the familiar postbox with her parents' names—George and Lillian Knight—and pulled into the drive, realizing immediately that she had made a mistake. She had forgotten that her mother had invited her older brother, Drew, his nagging wife, Francene, and their three toddlers for a week.

Drew she loved. Francene she tolerated, trying to forgive her nasal twang (a gift from birth) and her constant badgering of her husband and the kids by blaming it on the burden of trying to manage such a household.

Tolerating Francene was a full-time job even without the kids crying, wetting, fighting, and running through every conversation in the house. When Jennifer's mother and dad saw her in the driveway, they ran out.

Her mother had that look of joy that accompanies the thought of having most of her family together. "Hi, honey," she called, embracing Jennifer. "Now if only Tracy could be here!"

George Knight, however, had the concerned look that went with having read the *Morning Star* and knowing something about his daughter that he had not yet told his wife. And Jennifer could tell.

"How are you, Jenny?" He asked, taking her hands in his and looking deep into her eyes. He was the only person who called her Jenny anymore, and it always transported her back to treehouses and sandboxes and long walks in the woods. He called her Jenny right through high school when they had their one-on-one talks that would go till after midnight.

He'd never said she was his favorite, but she knew. And he loved her, he always said, even when she was ornery. That always got to her. She'd be mean or terrorize her mother with that temper of hers, and he would sit her down and give her the Dutch-uncle routine. She'd sulk and pout and refuse to admit she'd been wrong. She'd try the silent treatment, defying him with her eyes, and he'd say in a way that endeared him to her forever: "You can't make me not like you, Jenny Knight. And you can't stay mad at your old dad because I love you even when you're ornery."

And if she'd been so mean that she couldn't force a smile, she'd break down and cry, and he'd hold her. He never forced an apology out of her. But after she had seen herself in contrast to this sensitive, gentle man, she wanted more than anything to be like him, to get things right again, to forgive and forget and be forgiven.

Now he was staring into her eyes and asking her how she was, and she knew he knew what was going on. Somehow she sensed that he had not told the others. Mom wasn't a newspaper reader, unless Jennifer had written the story. Drew was way above front-page news, always with his nose in some science magazine. And Francene hadn't sat still long enough to read a paragraph since her firstborn, her four-year-old wonder, had come along.

"Oh, Drew!" came the dreaded whine. "Look who's here! Hi, Jennifer. How are you?"

Jennifer saw her father's face soften into an understanding smile. She rolled her eyes. "Hi, Fran! Good to see you."

"How long can you stay?" Mrs. Knight wanted to know.

"Not long," Jennifer said, having wished she could stay overnight, but realizing now that it would do her psyche and her problem no good to try to survive a houseful of relatives.

"Well, come in and sit down," her mother said. "Have a bite."

Drew pecked her on the cheek as she came through the door, and he rounded up all the kids to say hi to Aunt Jennifer. They came, kicking and screaming, performing their duties and heading off to see what more havoc could be wreaked.

When her mother was at the stove, Jennifer's father leaned close. "Where's your head?" he whispered.

"Right here," she said, pointing to her heart. He nodded with an I-thought-so look. "I forgot they were going to be here," she said, and he nodded again. "What I really need, Dad, is a long talk with you."

"I think we can work that out," he said. "What do you think, Mom?"

"What's that, Dear?"

"You think Jenny and I could sneak away for an hour or so before dinner?"

"Sure. Be back by five-thirty though."

The frozen path that led to the woods behind the house seemed so much smaller than it had the last time they had walked there. Fatigue had set in, and Jennifer needed to rest. They sat on dry stumps in the middle of a tiny alcove, and she wondered aloud what her mother would think when she read about Jim.

"Let me worry about that," her father said. "I'm more concerned with what *you're* thinking right now."

So she told him. The whole story. How she heard. What she felt. What she did. What she said to Leo. That she knew she loved Jim, and mostly, that she was surer of her love than of his innocence.

She had finished, and, as was her father's custom, he didn't respond immediately. He just sat. Thinking. Waiting. Giving her a chance to restate anything she had not said the way she wanted to. Letting her own words echo in her ears to see how they sounded out in the open rather than in the echoing valleys of her mind.

She wasn't tempted to ask him what he thought. She knew he'd tell her. When he had sifted it through, he would ask her a few questions she hadn't thought to ask herself. He would give her insight she could have had on her own. He would lead her to her own decisions, never trying to force one on her.

It hadn't always been that way. He wasn't perfect. He had tried so hard to hold on to her when she was an adolescent that he had, a time or two, tried to push his will onto her. It never worked, and they both learned from it. But he was so eminently forgivable, if for no other reason than that line about loving her even when she was ornery.

"What will it do to your love for him if you find that he's guilty?" he said at last.

Jennifer couldn't answer. As she had silently predicted, it was something she hadn't considered. His guilt she had considered. How would it affect her feelings for him? She had assumed, she thought, that her love for him was dependent upon his character.

"I think I love the man I thought he was," she said. "Does that make sense?"

"Do you think it does?"

"I know it sounds conditional, but that was all I knew of him. You can only love what you know, can't you?"

"Can you?"

"I learned things about Scott after we were married, and I loved him in spite of some of those."

"And vice-versa?"

"Of course. But, Dad, those were little things. Irritations, idiosyncrasies. Not character things. Not dishonest things."

He looked at her without speaking.

"I'm saying my love is conditional, aren't I?"

He smiled.

"Can't my love be conditional? Is there something wrong with falling out of love if you've been betrayed, if someone is not only not what you thought they were, but the exact opposite?"

"Are you asking me or telling me?"

"I'm asking you, Dad, but I know how you counsel. You'll tell me it's not what *you* think that matters, but what *I* think. But I'm so confused right now that I need some feedback from you. What kind of crazy lady doesn't know she loves someone until he's in trouble? I mean, I know now that I was in love with him before without realizing it. But why does it hit me with such force when it appears he's everything I hate in a person?"

"You're not loving him because he's in jail, Jenny. You're loving him for the same reason you loved him those last few times you brought him up here."

"You knew?"

"Of course, we could tell. You can't hide something like that. Other people always know before the stricken one knows. But now maybe you know for sure because he needs you. If he was hurt or missing or victimized in some other way, it would have hit you the same way. It's not so paradoxical as it seems."

"But what will it do to my love for him if I find out he's guilty?"

"That question sounds familiar."

"He could be, you know, Dad."

"He could be guilty?"

"Of course. The odds are that he is. They've been watching that precinct for so long. They don't make arrests like that without something solid. Oh, I've been through all this."

"That's all right. You'll go through it a lot more before you come to any conclusions, Honey. You'd better just keep kicking it around in your head until it settles into place."

"If I had to answer you now—"

"Which you don't."

"I know, and I appreciate that. But if I had to answer you now, I'd say that finding out he was guilty would spoil my love for him. My love is built on trust and faith. If he had fallen, made a mistake, taken a wrong turn, that would be one thing. I think I could love him through that. But if he's been involved in this since before we met and has been living a lie before me all this time—then, no, that would be the end."

"You couldn't forgive him?"

"Ah, touché. I don't know."

Her father fell silent again.

"I know that's what God would do, Dad. But I'm not God."

"No, none of us are God. But we're supposed to be imitators of Him."

"You are."

"I'm not, Jenny. But it *is* my goal."

"Mine too. But I'm not there. I can't judge Jim. I can't know his heart, his motives, his sincerity. I'm afraid if I knew he was guilty, that he had been thumbing his nose at my pure love—and I don't apologize for calling it that—then I would find it very difficult to accept an apology. Unless it was somehow very convincing."

"What does that make you think of, Jenny?"

"I know."

"Do you ever wonder if God believes you're sincere after you've, what did you call it, thumbed your nose at His pure love?"

"Yes. And there were times when I knew I *wasn't* sincere, and I knew He knew it, and it made me feel so guilty that I got sincere real quick."

George Knight smiled broadly and wrapped an arm around his daughter's waist as they walked back. "You've got a lot of thinking to do, girl." She nodded. "I do have one little bit of advice for you, though."

She stopped, surprised. "This is a switch."

"I won't say anything if you don't want me to," he said, "but I believe you really are confused and at the end of yourself. I don't mind telling you, I haven't seen you this troubled since—"

"Since Scott."

"Yes."

"I want your advice, Dad. Whatever it is, I want it."

"I can't tell you whether Jim is guilty or innocent. No one can. That will have to be proven. But all I want to tell you—and you can throw it out or take it or whatever you want—is that I think you'll handle this thing better if you give Jim the benefit of the doubt until you know for sure."

"I might look like a fool in the end."

"Maybe. But if he's a phony, he's already made a fool of you. And you'll have a lot of company. I like the man. Your mother likes him. The people in his church love him. You love him. If he's betrayed us all, then you can know it and go on from there.

"But what if he hasn't, Jenny? You can only gain by giving him the benefit of the doubt. Believe with all your heart that he's innocent. That there's an explanation. That it'll all work out in the end. If you're wrong, you were just prolonging how wrong you'd been from the start. But if you're right, you'll be glad you stuck by him."

They walked on in silence for several minutes. "My boss says the opposite, you know," she said finally.

"Doesn't surprise me. But he's talking to you as a newspaper woman. What was his line? Where there's smoke and all that? That's true enough. We both know the odds are against you. You said it yourself. You do your reporting job the best way you know how. But as God's person, as my daughter, as Jim's love, you believe in him until you're proven wrong. It's a much better angle from which to work, don't you think?"

"Don't I think? No, why should I think when I've got a dad like you to do my thinking for me?" And she hugged him.

When they got to the backyard, Lillian Knight was at the door. "Jenn! Your boss called. Wants you to call him right away. Say's he sorry to bother you, but it's urgent."

SEVEN

In person, Leo Stanton ranted and raved and used his expressions and gestures to make his points. On the phone, when he was really angry, he was terse, cold, impersonal.

"Jennifer," he said, "I think you'd better get back here as quickly as possible."

"What is it, Leo?"

"We can discuss it when you get here. When may I expect you?"

"You want me to leave right now?"

"I think that would be wise."

"Give me about an hour and a half then."

"Thank you," he said, hanging up without another word.

Jennifer tried to treat her fast departure as a minor crisis at the office, but in the car the mystery nearly drove her mad. Who did Leo think he was, demanding that she come back from her parents' without telling her what was going on? Had Lucas died? Did they simply need her at the office? Was that it? Couldn't he have just said that?

Maybe it was more. Maybe Leo had found out about her and Jim. She hoped not. That would ruin the plan that had been taking shape in her mind from the moment—just minutes before—when her father encouraged her to give Jim the benefit of the doubt.

She hadn't had time to sort it all out, but she agreed that taking the positive approach would save her—or at least postpone—a lot of grief. She'd be good for nothing in any effort to help clear Jim if she continually tormented herself with doubt.

She wanted to inform Leo of her chats with Jim—not of their relationship exactly, but of the discussions they'd had about his philosophy of life. She'd write these, she thought, in feature form, just providing curious readers with background on one of the arrested officers.

She didn't know what Leo would think. Worse, she didn't know what Jim would think. He didn't want a lawyer for some reason; maybe he didn't want her defending him either. Of course, he had told her all those things as a friend. But he hadn't ever *said* they were off-the-record, and he knew he was talking to a reporter, didn't he?

She knew she wasn't making sense, but this was something that could only help Jim. Readers who didn't believe him would have a field day—that's how she would sell it to Leo. A story about a guy who still maintains his innocence in the face of serious charges. Leo should love that.

All the while, of course, she would be hoping and praying that Jim's boyish honesty would come through and that someone would be convinced. Maybe the readers would get behind him again, the way they had when he took his stand against some of the things required of him as a Vice Control Division undercover cop.

But when Jennifer slowed to a stop and rolled down her window to toss money into the tollbooth basket, the frigid air brought her back to her senses, and she knew that Leo would see right through it. She was being naive. No one would buy it. If she was going to clear Jim, she'd have to do it with hard evidence.

But where would she get that? She didn't have access to the kind of information that would clear a man of a serious crime. Anyway, she hadn't even seen the evidence against him. What was she going to do if she found he'd been meeting with hoodlums or passing dope to kids in school yards?

She scolded herself again for thinking negatively. It wasn't going to be easy, following her father's advice. She usually assumed the worst in an effort to protect herself. She didn't want to get her hopes up anymore—not since Scott's life had been stolen from her.

That's the way she saw it. Someone had stolen Scott. She knew it was the enemy, the author of death, the one who comes to steal and to kill and to destroy. That supreme scoundrel had nearly ruined her life. She knew her God would be ultimately victorious and that He was still in absolute control. But she had learned a painful, bitter lesson from that loss. For as long as she was on this earth, she could take nothing for granted. She could look to a bright future, a time of consummation, an eternal home of peace. But she fought expecting too much from this present world.

That's why it took her so long to realize her true feelings about Jim. She was not only building her defenses against another disappointment. She was running full speed away from her feelings. She had enjoyed Jim. She had looked forward to seeing him. She had delighted in the quiet, peaceful, unpressured moments with him.

But she had not allowed herself to even consider that she might be falling in love with him. She wasn't blind. She knew what he was thinking, though he was cautious, sensitive, biding his time.

He wasn't pushy, wasn't rushing anything. She was amazed, when she thought about it, how childlike and innocent their relationship had been for so long—especially in this day and age (as her mother always said).

Perhaps he could have expected more from her. More encouragement. More affection. More response. It was clear theirs was not a brother-sister relationship; yet it could have appeared that way.

They told life stories, told secrets, told what they liked about each other. They walked hand-in-hand for hours, yet she worked hard—maybe too hard—at giving clues that said she was not open to an embrace or a ki s.

He'd been so understanding, though they never discussed it. It was one of the things she so appreciated about him. Could he sense that it was her loss that made her want to move so slowly, not just in the physical aspect, but in the whole area of commitment?

It wasn't that he made advances and then didn't act upset when she didn't respond. No, he could read her better than that. She didn't think she had been obnoxious about it; she had simply not encouraged it. And somehow, he understood.

With Scott, the relationship was probably typical, she thought. They liked each other. Then they missed each other. They wanted to be together. They talked about it, kidded about it, flirted, and joked about their marriage long before they had known each other well enough to be discussing it seriously. As they grew in their love, their jokes about being man and wife evolved into serious discussions of their plans.

Jennifer didn't know what she would have done if that same progression had begun with Jim. It would have put her off, certainly. She would have seen the similarities, known where it was leading, and she would have tried to jump off the carousel.

Not that she didn't care for Jim or had any reservations about him at all. But she was going to be careful this time. She was going to be sure; she was going to be realistic; she was going to be even a little fatalistic, though she had been counseled not to be.

Both her father and her pastor had told her that she wouldn't really protect herself by locking herself in a cocoon and insuring herself against another devastating disappointment. Both felt she would do better to concentrate on the tremendous odds—morbid though it might be to consider them—against someone suffering two such painful blows in one lifetime.

"Then you're saying that since it's so unlikely that I'd be twice widowed," she asked her pastor, "that I should just put it out of my mind and not worry about it?"

"I'm aware how unrealistic that has to sound to someone whose wound is so fresh," he had said. And she nodded. "And also coming from someone who has never suffered that kind of pain." And she nodded again, not intending to be cruel. "But Jennifer, you can survive this thing when you are able to pull yourself up and out of it with the help of your friends and your family and your God."

It had sounded so pompous and pietistic; and yet, as she mulled it over during the many hard months to follow, she saw the wisdom of it. She also knew the absence of anything else to say to the bereaved. The less said the better, she decided. She had learned, at least, how to best comfort grieving loved ones. You stand there, you hold their hand, you put your arm around them, you sit with them, you cry with them, you do something for them without offering or being asked, and you keep your mouth shut. Because when you say that you don't know what to say, you're proving just that. And when you think that there's nothing you can say that will change anything or assuage the grief, you are right on the money, and your quiet actions speak so much louder than your empty words that Jennifer almost missed her exit. *What's wrong with me?* she wondered. *Am I so worried about Leo that I'm burying myself in these gloomy thoughts?* She turned on an all-news radio station to hear if there was anything that would prepare her for Leo. After a few minutes, the city's most popular topic was in the news again.

"Two of the four police officers arrested just after midnight this morning have already been released on bond. Originally, no bond was set for the four, but attorneys for both Sergeant William Much and Patrol Officer Trudy Janus won emergency bond concessions late this morning, citing precedence in the previous police shakeup during which all charged officers had been released to the custody of their attorneys, pending hearings.

"No bond has been set in the case of Sixteenth Precinct Lieutenant Frank Akeley, who has been charged with the near fatal shooting of

Internal Affairs Division Chief John Lucas during Akeley's arrest. Akeley's attorney, the noted municipal barrister, Carl Williams, has sought no concessions for his client at this point.

"The fourth arrested officer, specially assigned Patrol Officer James Purcell, has still not secured representation and has reportedly refused the offer of a public defender. So though bond is apparently available for those officers who did not resist arrest, Purcell remains in the headquarters lockup at this hour.

"There has been speculation that Frank Akeley's high-powered attorney might enter a self-defense plea and that counsel for Sergeant Bill Much may have already made overtures toward plea bargaining by offering his client as a state's witness.

"The attorney for Ms. Janus, however, has released a statement that her client will be entering an emphatic not guilty plea.

"In a related humorous note, if anything about this case can be considered funny, Jake Rogers, columnist for the *Chicago Day* writing in a special midday edition, has noted the irony of Singing Policeman Bill Much offering to continue to sing about his and his colleagues roles in this latest scandal. . . ."

Jennifer had always enjoyed Jake's columns. Until today. Her personal involvement in this case made it impossible for her to see any humor in it. She wondered if she would have anyway. There was something terribly sad about whatever it was that caused people to leave their ideals and bring shame on themselves and their families and their co-workers.

She wondered what bond had been set. If it was less than $50,000, perhaps she could scrape together the 10 percent of that necessary to get Jim out.

Jennifer parked behind the *Day* building on Michigan Avenue, wishing she'd stopped by her apartment to pick up her notes. She didn't know if Leo wanted her to work or what. But by his tone on the phone, it could have been anything from a change of his mind to a new break in the story or even a true calling on the carpet. She hadn't faced his anger since that first week under his supervision, but his tongue lashings were legendary.

She planned to stop at the washroom mirror for one last peek, but she saw Bobby Block heading down the back hallway toward her.

"Hi, Jenn! Didn't know you were going to be in today."

"Neither did I. What's happening, Bobby?"

"In the big one? Not much. Lucas has stabilized, but the docs are still doubtful about his recovery. Still on machines and everything. The arresting officers' names are out. Everybody's got 'em. Can't imagine how long they thought they were gonna keep those quiet with all the uniformed guys they pulled in for assistance."

"Yeah, Leo told me when he called."

"Guess their days with Internal Affairs are just about over. You know, once all the other cops know—"

"Yes, I know."

"Guess your time with the *Day* is just about over too, huh?"

Jennifer eyed him warily. "What are you talking about, Bobby?"

"Leo didn't tell you a couple of them were in here today?"

"Who?"

"The arresting officers. The ones who busted that singing sergeant and the young 'all-American boy' type. They were with Leo and the big boss more'n an hour, showing them pictures and reports and stuff, as far as I could tell. Leo didn't tell me anything, but I'm guessing they were telling Leo and Cooper about you and that cop."

Jennifer was stunned, but chose to ignore Bobby's attack for the moment. "*Max Cooper* was in on it?" she said.

"Who'd you think I meant by big boss? Nobody around here bosses the publisher, do they?" He looked smug. After months of playing the dutiful subordinate, Bobby had sensed his opening and turned on her.

Jennifer looked at her watch. It had been an hour and forty-five minutes since she'd talked to Leo. "Gotta run, Bobby. But thanks a lot for the loyalty and for telling Leo about me."

He smiled condescendingly. "I didn't have to, Jennifer. But I would have."

She shot through the swinging doors to the newsroom and moved straight through to the city room. No one looked up from their desks, for which she was glad. She didn't want to appear rude, but she *was* late.

She unbuttoned her coat as she neared her desk and draped it on her chair on the way by, noticing several memos and a stack of mail. It hadn't seemed that long since she'd been in. Leo was at his desk in his window-enclosed office, pretending to edit copy, but she knew him too well for that.

He had seen her the minute she hit the city room, and his pencil hadn't moved since. She tried to take a few deep breaths and be ready for anything, but her anxiety caught up with her and left her huffing and puffing.

Forgetting to knock, she breezed into Leo's office with an apology for being late. "Ran into Bobby in the hall and shouldn't have stopped to talk."

Without standing when she entered—as was his custom—Leo motioned to a chair and took off his reading glasses. He looked at her with raised brows, his chin still lowered as if he could have just as easily stayed with his work. She fell silent, deciding on the safest course, but her chest heaved as she tried to catch her breath without gasping.

Leo leaned forward and slowly pulled his day-old unlit cigar from his cheek and laid it gently in his personal ashtray, one which hadn't ever seen an ash. He picked up the tray and placed it behind him on an overhanging bookshelf, out of consideration for her, Jennifer hoped.

He turned around again to face her and leaned back in his chair, putting his feet on the desk and his hands behind his head. With his slightly frumpy Ivy League look, sleeves rolled up and tie loosened, she couldn't help thinking what an archetypical newspaper editor he was. And how right now he was milking his authority over her for all it was worth.

She wanted to say, "Let's get on with it, Leo. What's on your mind?" But she wouldn't dare do that with Leo Stanton. And just when she thought she'd burst if he *didn't* get on with it, he spoke.

"You were running late, but you stopped in the hall to chat with Bobby."

"Yes, I shouldn't have. I'm sorry."

It's all right. At least, it's understandable. I mean, he works for you. Admires you. Looks up to you. Aspires to be like you."

"Oh, I wouldn't say—"

"I'm not trying to flatter you, Jennifer. I'm trying to make a bigger point, because there's something about your stopping to talk with Bobby that *isn't* understandable. You know what that is?"

She shook her head.

"The fact that you would tell me that was why you were late. I'm your boss. You should try to impress me. You *do* try to impress me. And that's OK. I do the same thing with my boss. Only I do it in a different way.

"If I was late to a meeting with my boss, I'd tell him it was the traffic, or car trouble, or anything other than the truth if the truth were so lame that it made me look bad. Don't you think it made you look bad that you were late to what you have to know is a very important meeting with your boss because you lost track of the time?"

"Well, yes, that's why I told you I was sorry, and I really am. It was inexcusable, and I hope you'll forgive me."

"If it's inexcusable, how can I forgive you?"

"Leo, I don't understand. I'm sorry. You're right. I was wrong. It won't happen again. If you want the whole truth, frankly I was gently pumping Bobby to see what would make you call me back to work from a day off."

"*You* don't understand? *I* don't understand. You're not just so honest that you tell me the real reason you were late; you tell me *more*. I've always appreciated your honesty, Jenn. It's one of the many things I like about you."

"Thank you, Leo, but it's not like you to beat around the bush. It's apparent you're leading up to something."

"If you don't mind my saying so, Jennifer, it's your whole honesty kick that leaves me so disappointed in you today."

He paused as if expecting a reaction from her. She had decided to say nothing more until he got to his point. Leo's lips tightened and he slid his feet off the desk to the floor and sat forward again.

"Jennifer, Jennifer. Why didn't you tell me about you and James Purcell?"

EIGHT

"There was nothing to tell, Leo."

Her boss shook his head sadly and looked away from her, making her feel low. "A police reporter fraternizing with a police officer and there was nothing to tell? Tell me we've never discussed the danger of this, Jennifer."

"Of course we have, but the man was one of my first contacts. He was desk officer at the Sixteenth when I started. And when he was reassigned to duty that would never be something I would cover, I didn't see the harm in seeing him."

"Do you now?"

"I guess, but—"

"You guess? Can you tell me that wasn't the reason you were crying over that article last night?"

"It was, but it didn't show in the piece, did it?"

"You shouldn't have written the article. You were biased."

"But it didn't show."

"You think the man is innocent."

"And you think he's guilty, Leo. Doesn't that make you biased?"

"I have every reason to believe he's guilty. Everyone believes he guilty. Everyone but you."

"I hadn't planned to start seeing him, Leo. And I've never used him for information."

"But it had to color your view of the police, didn't it?"

"No, it didn't. It really didn't. I have no doubt that Akeley shot Lucas, and not out of self-defense. Much has all but admitted he was guilty by offering himself up as a state's witness. And Janus has been a pistol ever since she joined the force. Her involvement in this wouldn't surprise me."

"Me either, Jenn. I agree with you all the way down the line except in one specific case: your boyfriend. Your relationship *had* to affect your view of him. They're all guilty and he's not? How do you reconcile that? Because you know him? What if you knew the others and developed a little sympathy for them? What if you'd heard Bill Much singing "The Big Brown Bear" to a bunch of elementary school kids and knew he had a sixth-grade daughter with braces and that he coached his boys through Little League? Then would you say, 'Well, Akeley shot a man and Trudy Janus is a pistol, but my boyfriend and good ol' Bill Much, they're innocent'?"

"You don't understand," Jennifer said quietly.

"I didn't hear you."

"You don't understand how well I know Jim."

"I don't? I don't think I *want* to understand how well you know him! I'm trying to figure out this little game of deceit about your relationship with him and how that all fits in with your church and Sunday school thing; now don't get real honest with me and tell me you're having an affair with the man."

"I'm not. Of course I'm not. We haven't even kissed."

Leo almost had to suppress a smile. "I don't want to hear all of it, Jennifer. If you church types carry on serious romantic relationships without even kissing, that's just too interesting. I'm telling you you deceived me by saying nothing about it. You should have told me the first night he picked you up from the office."

"You would have taken me off the police beat," she said slowly.

"Possibly."

"That would have been unnecessary."

"You see what's happened and you can say that? The man is the laughingstock of this town because of his fresh-scrubbed image and now being up on charges, and you tell me it isn't significant that my police reporter is a very close personal friend?"

"How do you know how close or how personal or how much of a friend? He helped me with my car one night, and we've dated a few times."

Leo stood. "Can't you see it's too late to try to snow me about this?"

"I've never tried to snow you!"

"No, but you don't tell me everything either, do you?"

"I didn't tell you about Jim because I was afraid you would misunderstand something that did not and is not and will not affect my work."

"You're right that I would have misunderstood. You're wrong that it isn't or won't affect your work."

"It didn't."

"Granted."

"It isn't."

"If you'd seen yourself hunched over your VDT and bawling your eyes out last night, you wouldn't say that."

"But Leo! The story didn't show it!"

"Granted."

"It won't affect me in the future; I can promise that. I can be objective."

"Wrong. You don't want to write a piece about the 'real' Jim Purcell? You're not tempted to try to unload a piece on me about some of the things he's said over the past several months that prove that he just couldn't be the man everyone thinks he is?"

Jennifer was stunned. It was as if Leo had read her mind. But she *had* finally decided against that strategy. "No," she said weakly.

"How many times have you dated Purcell?"

"I don't know. Quite a bit."

"How much is 'quite a bit'?"

"I don't know, Leo. What are you driving at?"

"You want to know how many times you've seen him since that night your car broke down in front of the Sixteenth Precinct?"

"Did I say that's where it broke down?"

"Am I wrong? Where did it break down?"

"You're right."

"Do you want me to tell you where you went that night and the next Saturday? And the weekend after that? And Monday evening before the arrest? You want me to tell you where you had dinner and how long you stayed there and whether he opened the door for you? You want to see pictures of yourself in the parking lot with him?"

Jennifer couldn't speak.

"I don't enjoy this, Jennifer. But I think you're going to regret not telling me that you've been seeing a man on your beat." And he sat back down, rolled his chair back to his credenza, pulled open a file drawer, and produced a manila envelope full of black and white photographs.

He spread them on the desk before him. Jim and Jennifer at Ravinia. Jim and Jennifer at the beach. At dinner. At a concert. At a ball game. In the parking lot of her apartment building. At her church. At his church. Everywhere but at her home.

"You want pictures of you in a car with him on the Northwest Tollway?"

She shook her head. Her face was hot. "So you had me followed. You found out about Jim, and you put a tail on me. That's low. But what do you see in your pictures? Anything out of line? Anything more than holding hands?"

Leo stood again and sat on the edge of his desk, staring down at Jennifer and slowly shaking his head. "Jenn, you can't really think I'd do that. That's not me. I would have confronted you. I haven't the time or the money to put a tail on you. For what reason would I do that? To build some sort of a case against you? If I had known, I would have taken you off the beat, that's all. You wouldn't have been able to talk me into leaving you on. You wouldn't have been able to convince me that it could work, because it never does. It's Murphy's Law, kid. Look what happened. You wouldn't have predicted this in a million years."

"So where'd you get the pictures, Leo?"

Leo pulled two business cards from his pocket and read them. "From Special Investigator Raymond Bequette and Detective Donald Reston, IAD."

"I'll bite," she said. "What's it all about?"

"They'd like to talk to you."

"About *what?*"

"About your relationship with a man who has been under surveillance and under suspicion for dealing dope for more than a year, since before he left Vice Control Division."

"They think he sold me dope? Or that I supplied it? Did they get any pictures of that?"

"If you'd done that, they'd had pictures, you can be sure of that."

"Their pictures tell the whole story of our relationship. They know where we went and how long we stayed there and how many times we went out. That's more than I know. What could I tell them?"

"They don't know, but you spent as much time with him as anyone during the time he was trafficking in drugs. They think you might be able to shed a little light on the subject for them."

"What do you think, Leo? I've told you why I didn't think our relationship was anything you needed to be aware of, and I admit I was breaking the rules, rationalizing, whatever you want to call it. I love my job, and I love working for you, and I wanted that *and* my relationship with Jim. I can see how it's gotten me into bigger trouble, and I'm sorry it cost you your confidence in me. But do you think that I could be aware that Jim was doing what they think he was doing and still keep seeing him? Could I have become aware of his activity and then not told you of my mistake?"

"I can't imagine."

"Thanks for that, anyway."

"You're welcome, but I also can't understand you're being so close to the man for this long and not catching on."

"Catching on to what? Have you considered the possibility that I know the man better than people who shoot pictures with a telephoto lens from a hundred yards away? I'm telling you that Jim Purcell is the farthest thing from a dope dealer I've ever met. He never talked about it. He never used it. He never possessed it. He never ran in those circles. It just isn't true, Leo."

Leo reached back into the same drawer and produced another envelope full of photographs. He scooped up the ones of Jim and Jennifer and replaced them with a couple dozen shots of James Purcell with other people.

Jennifer put a trembling hand up to her mouth, and, as much as she wanted to pull away and run from the room, she couldn't take her eyes off the pictures. Even in dark glasses, Jim was recognizable. Even in shots taken by infrared camera in the dead of night, it was most definitely him.

There were pictures of him in broad daylight, some in uniform, some in clothes she didn't recognize, some with his hair styled differently. But it was him. He was talking with Frank Akeley at a street corner, taking something from Trudy Janus in the parking lot of a shopping center on Western Avenue, in conference with Bill Much somewhere in Uptown, looking around to be sure no one was watching.

There he was with known hoodlums from outside the police department too. The mob-related figure from south of the Loop whom Jennifer had written a story about when he was sentenced in the spring. The gang leader from the West Side ghetto who was up on charges six times before being sent to Stateville Penitentiary in Joliet a few months earlier. The police officer who was fired after being convicted of stealing truckloads of auto tires in a suburban heist.

"You recognize some of these creeps?"

She nodded, shuddering.

"Your boyfriend got too close to the fire one too many times, and IAD got him. You want to see more?"

She didn't, but part of her needed to. She wasn't about to let this thing drop until she had talked to Jim. Love may not have been what she felt for the sad looking creature in the photos, but she did pity him. He surely wouldn't have a friend in the world once all the dirt came out.

So this was what was going to happen to her love if she found he was guilty. It wasn't so much anger and resentment. It was pity. And wonder. And curiosity. When had it started? What caused it? What made him so good at concealing it from even the woman he appeared to love?

Why would he risk his cover by spending time with a police reporter? Did knowing that she had been fooled give him the false sense of security that allowed him to be the subject of so much surveillance without his catching on? Did it ultimately lead to his arrest? Should she take some morbid comfort in that? That she may have been partially responsible for his finally being stopped by providing him a sense of well-being that he shouldn't have had?

She had a feeling the bitterness would return—the bitterness she had felt when she first suspected him. But for now she was stunned. "Let me see the other photos," she said.

"The other material isn't photos. It's documents, affidavits."

She scanned a few. Depositions taken from policemen at lower levels. Civilian dope dealers, some in prison, some still on the street, telling of their contacts within the police department. Some of it dated back many years. Much of it related to the big scandal a year and a half before.

But the parts that related to Jim Purcell went back to just before he had left VCD. That's where it had started. Had he been sincere about his reasons for getting out? She had thought of sexual temptation, maybe financial temptation. She'd never thought of drugs, let alone dealing.

But maybe that was it. He left VCD to clean up his act, to get an assignment—he had hoped in Homicide—where drugs were irrelevant. But he got into the wrong precinct. He got in where the big stuff was going on, and he couldn't stay out.

Why was she pitying him? If he had lived a lie for all those months and—as she had told her father—thumbed his nose at her love, he didn't deserve anything from her.

"What does this all mean for me, Leo?"

"I've been thinking a lot about that, Jenn. I can see you were hoodwinked by this guy, and that makes me feel bad. I never really figured that you knew all this, or I'd have let you go without even talking with you. But that wouldn't have been fair. Now that I've talked to you, I have to lay it out straight.

"I'm suspending you indefinitely for insubordination for not telling me of a relationship that was potentially dangerous for the *Day*. You have no idea what it was like for me today, begging the boys from IAD not to release your name to any other media. They agreed not to, but they couldn't guarantee for how long. They want to talk to you, as I said, but there's no telling what might happen after that.

"So you're off the beat and off the job until this whole police thing is over. That could be a year. And the only way I can let you back is if your guy is acquitted or if your name *never* gets into it. Now we both know Purcell is as good as up the river. And I've got to tell you that I'd have to wait two years of not seeing your name associated with this thing anywhere before I'd be comfortable in putting you back on the beat."

It was as if he had punched her in the stomach. He hadn't said she was actually fired, but he might as well have. What was she supposed to do for two years? Hibernate? Go to a competitor? With his sense of justice, Leo would tell anyone who called for a reference that they should be careful of her for a while.

Now what? Run home again? He had said IAD wanted to talk to her. He had also said that if he had let her go without even talking to her, it wouldn't have been fair. Was she being fair to Jim? Didn't she owe it to him, if not to herself, to talk to him before she abandoned him?

Her father had said to believe in Jim until he was proven guilty. Neither of them knew how quickly that might happen. But had he meant "proven" guilty, or "found" guilty by a court? Was she grasping at straws? Perhaps. But she decided she would do everything in her power to follow her father's advice, at least until she talked to Jim. IAD first, then Jim.

"I understand, Leo," she said lifelessly. "Are you going to be able to keep this out of the *Day,* I mean with Bobby knowing?"

"Bobby knows?"

She nodded.

"You told Bobby, but you didn't tell me?"

"*I* didn't tell him, Leo. I thought *he* told *you!*"

"He never told me anything, the little—" He caught himself. "Ah, anyway, I'll deal with him. I'm sorry, Jenny. I'm going to miss you. I loved you liked a sister. A daughter anyway."

His calling her Jenny grated on her, and she almost asked him not to ever call her that again. But then she realized that she likely wouldn't have to worry about it.

NINE

Jennifer appeared upset enough as she cleaned out her desk that no one had the courage to ask what was going on. It was apparent she was leaving, and not just for a few days. They'd have to find out from Leo.

One of her messages was from Donald Reston of the IAD. It said she could locate him the next afternoon at the Numbers Racket Club on Dearborn. Jennifer was grateful that she didn't have to talk to him right away.

She went home and tried to sort things out. Jennifer knew she was tired, but she just couldn't sleep. Most of the night she sat by the window, staring into the dark—talking to herself and thinking and praying.

She realized how bone weary she was the next day when she stepped from her car on Dearborn. Money for this meter would not be reimbursed by the *Day*. It was a good thing Scott had left her some money. More than half of it had been spent on the funeral and the cost of settling his modest estate, but there was enough left to live on for a while if necessary. But probably not enough to last long if she used any of it to bail Jim Purcell out of jail.

I must be tired, she thought. *Still thinking about getting him out after seeing those pictures Leo has. What's the matter with me?* She decided she was so enamored of her own father that she had been somehow catapulted into a benefit-of-the-doubt-giving posture that couldn't be shaken, even by condemning pictures and affidavits.

There was something about the whole ordeal that still didn't sit well with her, but she couldn't put her finger on it. It wasn't that she thought she was above being conned. Nor that Jim would have been incapable of it. But she thought she had glimpsed the core of the man. And what she had seen in Jim was not what she'd seen in the photographs. Oh, those were pictures of him, all right. But if she had to choose between the two personas, she'd choose the one she knew, not just because that was the way she wanted it or because that would make it all pleasant, but because she really felt—down deep—that she knew the real Jim Purcell. And she loved him.

Did she, could she, love him if the Jim in the pictures was the real character? No, she decided. She couldn't. She wouldn't be reacting this way if she knew for sure that he was guilty. But she didn't know if she was reacting this way because she wasn't convinced of his guilt, or if she wasn't convinced of his guilt because of the way she was reacting. That would sound crazy to a person like Don Reston. It even sounded crazy to Jennifer.

She asked for Reston at the counter and was directed to racquetball court number three. She watched from the cutout in the wall upstairs and tried to guess which player was Reston. Not knowing the game, it was hard for Jennifer to tell who was winning or what was going on. But the most agile, the most in-shape player was a tall, almost gangly, dark-haired man in red shorts and a blue cutoff sweatshirt. He was playing barefoot, which she didn't understand either.

Decked out in a jogger's ensemble was an older man, probably mid-forties, who was paunchy, sweated a lot, and was always stopping to catch his breath. He was an all right player, she guessed. But the taller man dominated. He started each play, when he was in control of the ball, by bouncing it very lightly on the floor so that it rose only a few inches, and then he didn't hit it until it was on its way down again.

The taller man stepped and twisted his whole body and drove his racket into the ball with such force that it slammed off the front wall and came hurtling at the ankles of his opponent, usually causing him to dance just to get his racket on it.

Jennifer folded her coat neatly over her arm and leaned against the ledge. She watched and thought for several minutes, guessing the taller man was Reston. Suddenly the other man lost his balance while stepping into a low shot close to the front wall. As she watched him tumble to the floor, she nearly missed seeing the ball careen off the wall and head straight at her. As she dropped out of sight, she saw the tall man whirl to follow the flight of the ball.

"A little help, please," he called.

She ran after the ball and retrieved it just before it would have bounced down the carpeted stairway. Embarrassed, she tossed it through the opening again without showing her face. But when she didn't hear the game begin again, she cautiously peered down.

Both men were looking at her. They smiled and looked at each other. "It's her," the older one said.

"Jennifer Grey?" asked the younger.

She nodded.

"Can you give me a minute to polish off this turkey, and we'll be right with you?"

She'd been right. It was Reston. When they'd finished, he hollered back up at her. "We'll grab a shower, then we can talk right here, if that's all right with you."

They looked both tired and refreshed later in casual clothes as they sat across from her in overstuffed chairs in the upstairs lounge. She found herself strangely nervous, though she'd interviewed cops hundreds of times.

"I'm Don Reston; call me Don. This is Ray Bequette; call him Gramps." The men laughed. Jennifer tried to.

"Let's get right to the point, Miss Grey."

"Mrs."

"Oh, I'm sorry. I guess we just figured—"

"You figured that since I'm dating, I couldn't be a widow."

"I'm sorry, ma'am; I was unaware of that. Your boss told you by now, no doubt, that the Internal Affairs Division has been observing you and Officer Purcell for many months. Were you totally unaware of his involvement in the drug scene?"

"I still am."

"I beg your pardon?"

"I still am totally unaware of his involvement in the drug scene."

"I was under the impression that Mr. Stanton was to show you some of the results of our surveillance."

"I saw your photographs and your affidavits."

"Then you can't really say you are completely in the dark about our suspicions of Purcell."

"Fair enough. I know what you think about him, and I know what people have said about him. But I never had an inkling about this, and I'm not ready to accept it."

"What more will it take to convince you?"

"I need to talk to him, of course."

"We can arrange that."

"You can?"

"Certainly."

"What's in it for you?"

"We need a little information. We thought you might be willing to help us get it."

"You mean trying to get something out of him that I would then pass along to you? You've got to be kidding. I couldn't do that."

"You're above that?"

"I'm not an undercover cop. Maybe if I were I'd throw my scruples to the wind."

"Your boss told us he thought you were in the dark about Purcell until now too."

"He was right. Can you tell me something? How much of your information did you get from my assistant at the *Day?*"

The two looked at each other. "I didn't even know you had an assistant until I heard from your boss. Stanton called this morning and told me that he had reprimanded your assistant because he knew about you and Purcell and never said a word to Stanton about it. Stanton figured he was trying to set you up so he could have your job."

Jennifer sat back and stared at the wall.

"Do you mind if we get back to your boyfriend?"

"You mean back to the dirty work you just asked me to do?"

"Purcell betrayed you."

"Possibly."

"You wouldn't like to return the favor?"

Jennifer removed her coat from her lap and draped it on a nearby chair. She looked first at Reston, then at Bequette. "Maybe if I really thought he was guilty, I could justify this."

"How are you going to find out?"

"I'm going to ask him. To the best of my knowledge, he has never lied to me. He's answered everything I've ever asked him. I know him well, I think. If he's doing a number on me, I'll know when I ask him straight out."

"And if you determine that he is what we think he is?"

"I'll be disappointed, of course."

"Of course. But will you tell us what he says?"

"I'll think about it."

"We can only arrange a meeting for you if you agree to give us information afterward."

"And what if I become convinced during our conversation that he is innocent?"

Reston and Bequette looked at each other. Reston shrugged. Bequette took over in a fatherly manner. "Mrs. Grey, I hate to tell you, but apparently you'e not getting our drift. The man is guilty. There is no doubt about that. We have enough evidence to put him away for years. We don't want information from you that will incriminate him. We simply want all we can get from him in the event that he doesn't turn state's witness. Frankly, this move of his not to seek counsel was a crafty thing to do, and it makes us nervous. Whatever he was trying to accomplish with it, it worked. We don't know what he's up to, but apparently he's stalling for some reason."

"It could be he's worried about some of his key contacts, worried that they'll try to harm him now that he's been burned. That's a good reason to stay in jail. Maybe someone else is clearing out of town while he's stalling us. This is our last case with IAD, and we'd like to clean the thing up right, wouldn't you?"

"I have no problem with what you're trying to do. It's just that I would have to be totally convinced that Jim's guilty before I could ever cooperate with you in trying to implicate other people by getting information out of him."

Bequette turned to Reston and talked quietly, though not trying to keep Jennifer from hearing. "Don, I frankly don't think the man will try to maintain his innocence any longer. He hasn't announced how he'll plead, but he's got to know what we've got on him. If she goes in there under the assumption that he's guilty and that the sham is over, my guess is he'd give it up and would try to determine if Mrs. Grey here would stick by him or throw him over. If he does that—and we might be able to help that happen by getting him special permission to talk with her longer in a more casual setting than the interview cells—then she'll know, and, if I'm reading her right, she'll help us out all she can."

Reston looked to Jennifer. She tilted her head and pursed her lips as if to say, "I suppose." What she did say was, "Well, if Jim *tells* me he's guilty, I can't argue with that, can I?"

"I don't see how he can say otherwise," Bequette said. "I've been concentrating on Bill Much for several months, but of course I've helped Don tail Purcell at times too. We've all worked together on this case, each specializing on one of the four and helping out with the others."

"Jim was your mark?" Jennifer asked Reston.

"Yes, ma'am. I'd been seeing a lot of you two together lately."

"Yeah, well, I'm not too thrilled about that. But tell me, what did you see Jim do?"

"With you?"

"No, I know that. What your camera saw was all there was to see."

"That's what we thought. You never spent time with him at his place or yours, did you?"

"I've never even been *in* his place."

Reston shook his head in wonder. "So anyway, you were asking?"

"What you saw Jim do while you were tailing him all this time. I didn't see your name in the affidavits, did I?"

"No, my deposition and testimony will come nearer the time of the trials. It takes us weeks to prepare our presentations, and of course, each of us will talk about what we saw all four suspects doing."

"And what I give you—if I do—from my talk with Jim—will go into your testimony?"

"Absolutely."

"Then I'd better be sure he's guilty. And that he willfully betrayed me. And that I'm up to this kind of revenge."

"I don't think you should call it revenge," Reston said. "It's the civic duty of any law-abiding citizen."

"That's a little idealistic after what I've been through with Jim the past several months," she said.

"I've been through a few things with him too," Reston said.

"Are you going to give me some examples?"

"What do you want to hear?"

Jennifer was growing impatient. "Anything. Something solid. Something incriminating. Something that will convince me the way you're convinced."

Reston stood and walked to the iron railing that overlooked the first floor. Joggers were padding past. He put both hands on the rail and hung his head low to his chest. He turned and came back, sitting right next to Jennifer, which startled her. His dark eyes looked weary.

"Let me tell you something," he said. "I don't much like the job I've had to do the last couple of years. I don't like spying on cops, even bad ones. I don't get any big kick out of building a case against someone and knowing it's going to ruin him forever. I know these guys deserve it, and I know that ruining them for life is the price we pay to get them off the street—and getting them off the street is something I have no qualms about because we deal with the results of dope addiction in nearly every case we handle, week in and week out.

"And when that surveillance work is over, like it is now, the toughest part of the process begins. We take our notes and our photos and our tape recordings, and we start a written case against someone, a case that is so airtight that we never have to worry that our work has been in vain.

"I could sit here and tell you stories about James Purcell that would take me all night. Places I've seen him, people I've seen him with, marked money I've seen him take, dope I've checked in that he's sold to undercover narcs. You want just one incident? I wouldn't know where to start.

"There's something we don't do, Mrs. Grey. We don't arrest them and then see them on the street again. When IAD has busted a guy, he stays busted. Because we wouldn't even go to the trouble of the dangerous arrest of an armed man unless we had him so dead to rights that we didn't have to worry that he was going to get away with something.

"My boss, one of the best in the business, is probably never going to wake up again, never see his wife and his daughters again, never be a great example to young cops again because your boyfriend's boss tried to kill him. A cop shot a cop, and don't let anybody ever tell you that Frank Akeley didn't know who he was firing on Tuesday morning."

Reston had grown emotional, and Bequette looked concerned. Jennifer's last vestiges of hope were fleeting. He sounded so sure. He ought to be sure. He *was* sure.

"I put the responsibility for the shooting of John Lucas right in the laps of every one of the big four in the Sixteenth Precinct. Every one of 'em ought to get the chair if he dies, because they all had a hand in it. They were the reason he was on the street that night, doing a job that a lesser boss wouldn't have done.

"So you see why I don't want to talk about the specifics in the James Purcell case? You see why these guys, all of them, make me sick when I think about them? You'll get your specifics. They'll all come out in the trial, and they'll be in every paper in town."

Jennifer was sorry she had asked. She couldn't speak, but she tried to tell him with her expression that she at least understood what he was trying to say.

Bequette broke the tension. "You still want to see Purcell?"

She nodded.

"All right. We'll set it up. You'll get a call. Probably from Purcell himself; he hasn't used his call yet. And you'll be able to talk to him in the anteroom downtown. You'll be searched and will be allowed to take nothing in or out with you. But we'll give you all the time you need."

"When?"

"Tomorrow morning at nine."

TEN

The next morning Jennifer dressed as if she were going on the most important date of her life. She was, of course. But the mirror told the story of the night before. She had been in bed twelve hours, yet she did more praying than sleeping, more thinking than dreaming.

She tried covering the dark circles under her eyes with makeup, but that backfired. She decided she looked like a raccoon and hoped that Jim would think her clothes were so nice he wouldn't notice her face.

Why am I thinking about trivia anyway? she chided herself. *How I look will be the last thing on his mind, and on mine if I can keep my thoughts straight.*

She had settled it, she decided in her car. If Jim was guilty—and she would know either by his not trying to hide it anymore or by seeing through him if he did—she felt no responsibility for his actions or for protecting him. She would lose whatever it was she felt for him, and she would feel no compulsion to keep from IAD anything he might say incriminating anyone else.

It was when she reached police headquarters downtown that she realized she had never received a confirming call—not from Jim, not from IAD, not from anyone. Should she wait until she saw Bequette or Reston? Or should she just go in and see if she was expected? There were plenty of unmarked squad cars, but how would she know if any of them belonged to men from IAD?

"I would like to see a prisoner," she told the sergeant at the desk.

"Name?"

"Officer James Purcell."

"No! *Your* name!"

"Jennifer Grey."

"Press is not allowed to see prisoners, especially that one."

"I'm not here as press, Sergeant. I have been cleared to talk with Officer Purcell."

"You got papers?"

"No, I assumed you would have received something."

"I got nothing."

"Well, could you please check? It was cleared through IAD and—"

"IAD don't cut any ice around here, lady. I run the jail."

"But wouldn't you have clearance papers for certain visitors?"

"Lemme look," he said, disgusted. He rummaged around on his desk and came up with a yellow carbon copy of something. "Well, whadya know?" She edged closer.

"You're to see Purcell at nine o'clock in the anteroom. It's all set."

"Thank you."

"Except—"

"Except?"

"Except it ain't nine o'clock yet, is it? I got to make sure I got personnel that'll allow you to be in the anteroom."

"I was told there would be no one else in there but us."

"Yeah, so I gotta have men outside the windows and outside the door, don't I?"

"How long will that take? It's ten to nine."

"I don't know. I'll let you know when the room and the prisoner are ready for you, Miss Grey."

"Mrs."

"Whatever."

Jennifer sat on a wood bench for nearly forty minutes, doing everything in her power to avoid asking what was taking so long. Every time she would come to the end of her patience and start to move toward the sergeant again, he would hold up a hand and mouth silently, "I will let you know."

Crazy ideas floated through her head. Jim was a drug addict. A schizophrenic. He would cry and beg her to forgive him. He would deny it, but she would see through him. He had been moved to another facility. He had finally hired a lawyer and was out on bond. He had tried to escape. He had been caught. He had escaped.

"Miss Grey!'

Mrs., Jennifer thought as she jumped up and ran over to the sergeant, but she said nothing.

"The prisoner has declined the conference," the man said.

"What?"

"He don't wanna see anybody."

"Does he know who's here to see him?"

"Yes, ma'am, if you want it like that, he don't wanna see you."

Jennifer spun in a circle, confused. What was she supposed to make of this? Didn't he realize that until he got a lawyer, she was probably the only friend he had? She had held out hope—she still did—and she shouldn't have after all she'd heard. Something was still unresolved. Something he didn't know but should have. He needed to know that she loved him. That was really why she was here. Guilty or not, a future for them or not, whether she loved him when she knew the whole truth or not, he needed to know that she loved the man she knew. She had to tell him.

She hadn't been gone from her job long enough to lose her ingenuity. "Can you get a message to him?"

"I could if I wanted to. I tol' ya—I run the jail. But I don't wanna. Bye-bye."

"Maybe this message is as much for you as it is for him then. How would you like me to make a scene, right here in the lobby? How would you like it to appear in every paper in town that the former police reporter for the *Chicago Day* couldn't get in to see a prisoner and that she caused such a ruckus she had to be thrown out?"

"That I don't need. I'm in enough trouble as it is with all the baloney that goes on *inside* the bars. That'd be great; a fruitcake *outside* the bars goes nuts."

"That's what you're going to have to answer for."

"Awright, what's the message?"

"Just that. I'll make a scene that'll embarrass him and you if he won't see me."

"He'll see ya. Wait in the anteroom."

Jennifer couldn't believe herself. *I've gone from a halfway intelligent police reporter to a conniving, unemployed, boisterous, lovesick woman in two days!*

She sat at the end of a long gray table, wondering what she should do when he entered. Embrace him? Smile at him? Tear into him verbally? The door opened, and a matron came in. Jennifer was searched, and her handbag and coat and jewelry were taken. She sat back down but hadn't even had time to collect herself when Jim walked in. Her heart raced. She stood, but he sat at the other end of the table. She felt foolish standing there and sat back down.

He looked like his old self except that he was wearing city-issue blue denims. He still had that shy look, that gentle air. She didn't know what she had expected. A monster? A shouter? A hard-looking criminal?

"How are you?" she said, her voice quavering.

He ignored the question. "I'm sorry I said I didn't want to see you, Jennifer. But it's just that the timing isn't right. I didn't want you to see me in here like this. I know you've been around these places, but you don't like seeing me in this get-up, do you?"

"That's not the reason you didn't want to see me," she tried weakly, fighting tears. "If I didn't see you here, where was I ever going to see you?"

"You could have seen me later. Soon."

"Where?"

"Jennifer, the truth is there's something going on here that you know nothing about. I never told you anything about it because I simply couldn't. You don't understand it, and you won't be able to understand it until I'm able to tell you all about it."

"I'm afraid I *do* know about it, Jim. I know more than I want to know. I can't believe you could have kept it from me all this time. I feel so stupid, so used. Betrayed."

"But you understand why I couldn't talk about it, don't you?"

"No! Did you think I wouldn't understand?"

"Would you have?"

She bit her lip and stood, walking to the window where she saw three uniformed guards kibbitzing. "I don't understand how you could do this to me."

"Jenn, there was no other way. If I had told you, it would have spoiled everything. I couldn't take the chance."

"You don't think everything's spoiled now?"

"All we have right now is a timing problem, Jennifer."

"You think time will heal *this* wound?"

"Jennifer, I'm gratified to hear that you miss me, and I miss you too, but this is temporary, and—"

"It goes much deeper than missing you, Jim. I love you. I need you. And now I'm so disappointed in you that I don't know what to think."

Jim stared at her, his eyes narrowing. She pressed her lips together to keep from crying. "There, you see?" she said, scolding him. "I love you in spite of this, and I had decided not to!"

He stood and moved toward her, but she turned her back to him. "Jennifer. You're disappointed in me? You love me in spite of this? In spite of what?"

"What have we just been talking about Jim? I know all about it! I've seen the pictures! I've read the reports! I've talked with the people from IAD! What are you going to do, deny it all now? What have you been saying about my not understanding what you couldn't tell me, if you're claiming now that you don't see what's come between us?"

He turned and rested both palms on the table, leaning over from the waist. Then he stood up and drew his palms to his face and slid them slowly down his cheeks. He let out a short sigh of surprise and whispered, "You believe I've really been busted!"

Jennifer was speechless. Her mouth fell open, and she just turned to stare at him. He looked at her without turning his head and grinned. "Jennifer! You don't really think—no, you—oh, Jenn, I'm sorry. You couldn't have thought—"

"Jim, what are you saying?"

"You said you talked to the guys at IAD? Who'd you talk to?"

"Don Reston and Ray somebody."

"Bequette?"

"Yes."

"And they didn't tell you?"

"They told me everything, Jim, and you're in a lot of trouble."

"They're not telling you the truth because you're a reporter," he guessed, but his smile had frozen. He'd lost his edge, his confidence. Jennifer read the worst into it.

"I'm not a reporter anymore, Jim. I lost my job because of you. And it would be worth it if I knew it had all been a big mistake."

"You lost your job? Well, it was no mistake, Jenn. But I'm not supposed to tell you about it yet, that's all. Someone will be bailing me out soon—in fact they should have already—and then the whole story will come out."

Jennifer sat down. "Jim, if you're trying to tell me that you were in on this from IAD's side, I've got to tell you, I don't believe it. I don't know who's trying to con who, but they showed me some stuff that makes you look pretty bad."

Jim's confusion and fear showed. "Why would they show you that stuff? Did they know you'd lost your job?"

"They wanted me to pump you for information on other people who might be incriminated in the case. They showed the stuff to my boss too, and to the publisher."

"What for, Jenn? What's it all about?"

"They thought I would know all about your dope-dealing because I'd spent so much time with you the past several months. Jim, what is going on?"

"I'm not sure. I'll feel like a fool if I'm supposed to be going along with this and then I tell you everything at the drop of a hat. Maybe it's a test. Maybe I shouldn't have told you anything, but just played along, pretended I'd been caught. But I can't do that to you, Jenn. I never thought you'd really think I'd been busted. But since you did, I probably should have let you go on thinking it until this thing blew over."

"If you think this thing is going to blow over, you'd better talk to Don Reston. He was nearly in tears today, telling me that he holds you and Much and Janus every bit as responsible for Lucas's death as Akeley."

"Lucas died?" Jim said, almost shouting.

"No, I didn't mean that; he was saying *if* Lucas died."

"Reston's a good actor. Could he have been bluffing you?"

"For what reason? Anyway, I don't think so. He'd have had to be a better con man than you are."

"Jenn, I want to tell you the whole story, but I have to make sure I'm not messing up the operation. We've been on this one for too long."

"You lost me a long time ago."

"You never told me you loved me before."

"Jim, how can you change the subject like that?"

"I love you too, you know."

"Don't do this to me, Jim. I can't make it compute."

"I couldn't tell you I loved you before because I knew we were being watched and photographed, and I didn't want you to be embarrassed by anything we did."

"You *knew* we were being photographed? And you knew by whom?"

"Of course."

"I've got to tell you something, Jim. If you think you have friends in IAD, you don't. Either those men I talked to today think you're as guilty as you look, or I am the worst judge of character who ever walked the earth."

"You're serious."

"You bet I am."

"All right, Jennifer. I'm going to tell you what's been going on, but you can't tell anyone. If you love me, you'll protect my confidence."

"Jim, don't put that on me, please! I've got all this evidence on one side showing that you've been living a lie in front of me for months, and I've got you on the other, telling me not to tell the people who sent me here that you told me anything. I came here under the condition that I would tell them what you said. You think you're breaking confidences; how do you like that one?"

"I don't know what to think, Jenn, but you're going to have to hear me out on this. I may be the worst undercover cop Chicago's ever had, but I don't know what else to do with a woman who says she loves me."

Jennifer hid her face in her hands. She wanted whatever she was about to hear to be true. She raised her head and looked Jim full in the face as if to say, "I'm listening. Pour it on."

Eleven

"When I first requested a transfer from Vice Control Division, I got in hot water from my captain."

"Why did you want to transfer?"

"I already told you that, Jenn. I may have kept a lot from you, but I never lied to you, OK?"

"OK, so you quit VCD because you had a hard time reconciling it with your faith."

"Exactly. And I took a lot of heat for that inside the department, especially from my boss and his boss. They sent memos around, even up to the commissioner, trying to head off this precedent of people deciding they didn't like their assignments and all that."

"Yes, and it was in all the papers."

"Right, but that was by design."

"Meaning?"

"It was staged, planned, set up. You know, Jenn, that you never got anything the police department didn't want you to have, and you never missed something they wanted you to cover. You may not have run with what they gave you, but they tried anyway."

"I don't follow."

"They're news manipulators. And they're good at it. I know from having spent enough time with you that you would not agree with tactics like that, but I think in some instances they have their place. It's debatable. That's why I thought Bequette and Reston were setting you up. But if they went to your boss and higher and showed them all the stuff, well I may have a serious problem—one that depends a lot on the health of John Lucas."

"You think they could indict all of you in connection with his death?"

"No, you're still not getting it, are you?"

"No, but I'm trying. Keep going."

"Anyway, the word inside the department was that I was some kind of a goody-goody, and there was a lot of speculation about whether they'd make a scapegoat of me so other guys wouldn't try the same thing with their assignments. Of course, most of them *want* Vice Control duty. They get a charge out of it.

"Well, right about that time, I got contacted by John Lucas. He said he liked my attitude and that he had gotten permission to consider me for IAD. He wanted to do some checking and interview me for several days. We met at various places and talked for hours. The one thing he told me never to forget was that a good internal affairs man has to keep secrets even from himself."

"What did he mean by that?"

"It was an exaggeration to make a point. Most people can't keep a secret for half a day. Internal Affairs tests their guys all the time, starting rumors and seeing where they lead, how long it takes the story to get distorted and come back, and all that. Confidentiality was a major prerequisite. But it wasn't as important as an unimpeachable record.

"Lucas had checked me out and decided I was the type of person he wanted in IAD. He set it up with the commissioner for me to appear to suffer for my request of a change of assignment, and people within and without the department bought it. The people in the Sixteenth thought they were really getting me and doing the commissioner a favor by giving me the dog assignments, the night desk and then the Officer Friendly thing. It couldn't have been more perfect for what I was really assigned to do.

"Lucas gave me a couple of drug-related assignments in VCD before I was transferred. He gave me the dope and the money, and he had his men check me out. He was pleased when they reported back that I was somebody they could nail and that they should keep an eye on me.

"My point is this, Jennifer. For the past year or so, I have ultimately reported to John Lucas. We hardly ever saw each other because he had not even told his own men. And he trained them to stay on my tail. That made it nearly impossible for me to ever meet with him."

"When was he going to tell his men?"

"He wasn't sure. He said he thought he might not tell them until the night of the big four arrests. You know, when Reston busted me that night, I only played along for the sake of the uniformed men with him. But I wondered if he had been told yet because he played it so straight. No winks, no jokes, no anything."

"Well, Jim, someone else had to know. Even if Lucas decided not to tell anyone until after you were in jail, his secretary had to know, didn't she? And who checked you out for him in the first place?"

"That was just it. He did most of the checking himself, and then he assigned the ones who had checked me out first to tail me a while. After the first few drug sales in VCD, they were all convinced I was bad. Lucas told me he was getting a real kick out of having his own inside guy that no one else knew about. He didn't think it was too dangerous because it was only temporary, and his real reason was to give him a fail-safe look at his own team. They did well."

"They did too well, Jim. But the commissioner knows, right?"

"The commissioner *should* know. Lucas reports directly and confidentially to him. Has to. That's the only way Internal Affairs can work."

Jennifer leaned back in her chair and studied James Purcell's eyes. "An undercover undercover undercover man. If I didn't want to believe it so badly, I probably wouldn't."

He smiled. "Lucas called me that once, not in those words. Said I was his triple threat. When the undercover guys investigating the undercover guys are not worthy, he's got one more ace up his sleeve."

"Jim, do you think Bequette and Reston were putting me on today and that they really know?"

"If I thought that, I'd have played along with *them.* Sorry to have to tell you that, but it has been my job for more than a year. Their talking to you and your boss and everybody and costing you your job, that's what scares me. Reston becoming emotional is nothing new. He's sincere, but he can playact that bit as well as anyone I've ever seen."

"What do we do about them?"

"I don't worry about them unless something happens to Lucas."

"Something could have already happened to Lucas, Jim. He's that bad."

Purcell stood and paced. "You want to help?"

"Why do you think I'm here?"

"To help the people who think I'm guilty, isn't that what you said?"

"I was confused. Of course I want to help. I believe you, Jim."

He stepped behind where she sat and put his hands on her shoulders. "That's the second-nicest thing you've said to me today," he said. "Anyway, I think you'd better get to Lucas's secretary and Eric O'Neill, he's the one who busted—"

"Janus. I know. I covered this story, remember?"

"Hey, if you clear me, will you get your job back?"

"I guess. Somehow that seems insignificant right now. Anyway, I'll go and see anyone you say. Who else?"

"Well, you *could* talk to the commissioner, but let's save him as a last resort. If you don't get anywhere with the guys from IAD, send Reston and Bequette to see me. I'll see what I can do. Maybe there's something I can tell them about Lucas, some inside joke, some special name he has for them, something that will convince them that I work for the man too."

Jennifer smiled for the first time since she had chatted with her father. "It's nice to have a job to do," she said. "I'm sorry I doubted you, Jim, but it was all so—"

"I know. Listen, you were looking at dirt dug up by the Chicago PD IAD, and they're the best in the business. If I saw all they had on me, I might doubt me too. Listen, Jenn, if you don't mind, find out what you can as soon as you can, because if these guys are serious and Lucas doesn't pull through, I might as well be guilty, because I won't have a chance."

"I'll do everything I can; you know I will. I'll be praying for you."

"You know who *I'll* be praying for?"

"Who?"

"Lucas."

Jennifer stood and found herself face to face with Jim Purcell, the man she realized she would have loved in spite of herself, in spite of himself, and in the middle of the most confusing time of her life. They held each other for several minutes, her face buried in his shoulder. And she cried.

Perhaps she had not done as well as her father might have hoped in her attempt to give Jim the benefit of the doubt. But now there was no longer any doubt, and she could think of no greater joy.

She drove to her apartment and bounded up the steps, wanting to laugh and cry and sing and scream all at the same time. She was reminded of her seventh birthday when her father gave her her first bicycle. He had sent her to the garage on an errand, and she had seen that beautiful bike with a big blue bow and a card with her name on it, and she ran back in tears to thank him before she even touched it. What a gift that had been. And what a gift this had been.

When she lost Scott, there was no bringing him back. She prayed that it had all been a bad dream, but it wasn't, and she knew it would always hurt. But now she had Jim. She would not let this love be snatched away, not if she had anything to say about it. And the beauty was, she had everything to say about it.

She called Don Reston and asked him to meet her as soon as possible. They met at a coffee shop on LaSalle Drive. She happily, earnestly spilled the story. "So if you were trying to get to me through him for some reason, it didn't work because it scared him. You can be straight with me now if you know that he's working with IAD too."

Reston stated at her sullenly. "I'm sorry, Mrs. Grey, but I think you're a victim of a vivid imagination."

"I'm not imagining anything. I talked to him, just like you said, and—"

"I'm talking about *his* imagination," Reston said. "It's just not true. Lucas would have told us, and believe me, he didn't."

"Would anyone else in IAD know?"

"I'll call Bequette, but I'm afraid you're in for a big disappointment. I'm not happy that you blew our assignment either, because if you had just told him you knew he was guilty—"

"I *did!* But he told me everything."

Reston shook his head sadly. "This is no game, ma'am. I'd have no reason to continue any ruse if what you were saying was true. But it's not. Let me call Ray."

He slid out of the booth, and she called after him, "See if you can get ahold of Mr. O'Neill for me too. Someone had to know about this."

He nodded and was on the phone for several minutes. Jennifer looked at her watch, wondering if she could squeeze in a meeting with John Lucas's secretary before she left for lunch. She was nervous. Her foot tapped, fingers on both hands drummed the table, her eyes darted all around the room. She was on a mission she had planned to enjoy, but she didn't need any more negative reactions.

Reston returned. He looked glum. "Listen," Jennifer said, "why don't you and Bequette visit Jim and talk to him yourselves?"

"We'd never get permission for something like that. It could spoil everything we're preparing for the trial. I'd really like Purcell's story to be true, for your sake. But I saw what I saw. I suppose it's possible that James Purcell was doing that stuff as part of a bigger setup. But I'm afraid unless John Lucas himself says so, I'd never be able to even admit the longshot possibility of it to anybody but you."

"What did Mr. Bequette say?"

"His reaction was the same as mine. I tried to hit him with it before betraying my own feelings on it, just to be fair to you. He says he heard rumors years ago that Lucas liked to do this sort of thing once in a great while, but never for this long or with stakes this high. You can forget about meeting with O'Neill too. He was with Bequette. You don't want to know what *he* thought of your idea."

"Yes I do."

"He called it a million-to-one shot."

Jennifer accepted the odds and headed to John Lucas's office where she waited until noon to see Gladys Balderson, the chief's secretary. She was a fussy, precise little woman—friendly, yet formal.

"No, Mrs. Grey," she said sweetly. "I never heard Mr. Lucas mention the name Purcell. But then much of his affairs were private, even from me. He has a file that I do not have a key to, but that is always off limits and has, in fact, in light of the shooting, been impounded."

"How would I gain access to it? It must have Jim's name in it somewhere, even if only his initials in a meeting schedule or something. Surely Mr. Lucas couldn't have kept all his clandestine meetings in his head."

"Surely you don't know Mr. Lucas. I would have thought you might have run into him in your work."

"I've never talked with the man."

"I'm sorry, you asked about access to his private file. I believe only a municipal judge or the commissioner of police could grant that, and I would find it highly unlikely in light of your occupation."

Jennifer didn't bother setting her straight about her current employment situation. She was running out of options. "I know it's a long shot," she said, "but I wouldn't forgive myself if I didn't at least try the commissioner. Could I impose on what must be your close relationship with his secretary, your both being at the executive secretarial level and all, and see if you can get me in to see him just for a moment this afternoon?"

"What would you want him to do, honey, open the file for you? I'm sure he wouldn't. Probably couldn't."

"Perhaps he could look for me. I wouldn't have to see anything. I'd just like to see if there's anything at all in that file that would indicate that Mr. Lucas was working with Jim."

"Well, it's a possibility," Miss Balderson said. "I'll call Joan and see." While dialing, she said, "Did you hear that Mr. Lucas rallied this morning?"

"No! Really? Tell me!"

"He apparently gained consciousness early this morning, and the doctors asked the family to join him. One moment."

While Lucas's secretary was talking with the commissioner's secretary, Jennifer prayed that God would spare the man's life. Even as she prayed it, she knew it was selfish. She couldn't care as much for a man she had never spoken with as she did about Jim, whom she loved.

"Tell me your man's full name again, dear," Miss Balderson said, holding a hand over the mouthpiece.

"Officer James Purcell."

When Gladys hung up she said, "You're in luck. The commissioner's secretary took all the information and will check it out herself. She is recording the contents of the entire file verbatim, and if she sees his initials or his name or anything remotely connected with him, if the commissioner approves, she will let you know this afternoon when you arrive for your appointment. Three o'clock. She even remembered that he is Officer Friendly, and she will look up his badge number to see if Mr. Lucas referred to him by that."

"Oh, that's too kind," Jennifer said.

"I don't mind telling you I'm jealous."

"I'm sorry?"

"The man's secret file ought to be handled by his own secretary, wouldn't you think?"

TWELVE

Police Commissioner Joseph Masek appeared ill at ease with Jennifer. He began the conversation with a scowl. "You're with the *Day,* aren't you?"

Jennifer spent several minutes explaining why she was no longer with the *Day.* "I see," he said slowly, pressing his fingertips together and staring at her as he leaned back in his chair.

"I can understand your concern," he said. "Yes, I *do* remember the request from Chief Lucas to investigate the young man who wanted out of Vice Control Division. I believe he thought Purcell would be the kind of guy who might make it in IAD. Frankly, my fear at the time, and I expressed it forcefully to John, was that I thought Purcell might look *too* much like an IAD candidate. He had that fresh-scrubbed look, you know—well, of course you know, don't you? Regardless, John felt he would like to check the man out and then bring him in very gradually, test him a little, that sort of thing. I approved that, but then, of course, I removed myself from the situation."

"You removed yourself?"

"Yes. I'm very big on letting the individual chiefs run their respective areas. Of course, in this case, John was requesting permission to maneuver between departments, so he came to me. Now, as a rule, all of John's activity is interdepartmental, and he doesn't need permission when he is investigating any untoward conduct, even within this office."

"Your office?"

"Absolutely. It's the only way an IAD can work properly. He has my full backing and cooperation, and unless he's looking for personnel from another branch, he doesn't get any input from me."

Jennifer took a deep breath. "Well, sir, I just want to assure you that the only reason I'm here is because I'm convinced a huge misunderstanding has occurred, and I didn't know where else to turn."

Commissioner Masek appeared somber. "Mrs. Grey, Officer Purcell is a close personal friend of yours, am I right?"

"Yes."

"I have to tell you that what you have described, John Lucas using a man undercover *within* IAD, is so highly improbable and unusual—though a very, very interesting idea—that I would have to doubt even its remotest possibility."

"Of course it's unusual," Jennifer pleaded, "but that was the only way it could work. Once it comes out, it probably would never work again."

"The point is, I really don't think John would work that way, and he and I go back many, many years. He's been a friend since the early nineteen fifties."

"I didn't know that. You must be very worried."

"I am indeed. My wife and I have been with Sylvia, John's wife, and two or three of the daughters off and on at the hospital ever since Tuesday morning. It doesn't look good."

"But I understood he had rallied this morning."

"Well, he gained consciousness for the first time since the shooting, but by the time I arrived there, he was sleeping again. Whether he had lapsed into a coma again, I don't know. But the doctor confided that not a great deal of optimism was justified. John's vital signs are still very weak, very bad."

"May I ask another—"

"I don't hesitate to say," the commissioner continued, staring past Jennifer, "that I am sick in my heart that one police officer would fire on another. It goes much deeper than just the shooting, though, Mrs. Grey. If a younger officer had done it, it might even be easier to take. Then I could say that they don't make cops like they did in my day. But Lucas and I are close to the same age, and Frank Akeley is even older. How does this happen? How does a man with a fine record get mixed up in things like this?"

Jennifer felt sudden compassion for Masek. He was lost in his grief and his fear for the life of his friend. She knew she'd feel the same for Lucas if she spent any time with him. But Lucas was almost an enemy at this point. She constantly pleaded with God to spare his life, knowing all the while that her motive was not as pure as it could be.

She wanted to feel for the man and his wife and his family, but she was thinking of Jim. She admitted silently that she was thinking of herself. Rescuing Jim from this nightmare meant new life for her too.

Commissioner Masek had asked a question to which there was no answer. But he had also interrupted Jennifer's, and she wanted to get back to it.

"Could I ask you a hypothetical question, Commissioner?"

He nodded, still staring past her.

"If John Lucas were to try something innovative as Jim, as Officer Purcell, has suggested, would you have known about it?"

"Not necessarily, no."

"Would it have been likely that you would know?"

"No, I suppose not."

"Then the fact that it sounds so unique to you doesn't really rule out the possibility of it."

He squinted at her. "Are you asking me or telling me?"

"Asking, and I'm sorry if it sounded otherwise."

"That's all right," he said slowly. "Let me tell you something, may I?"

"Please."

"I, uh, have been quite aware of you for some time."

"You have?"

He ignored her. "I am always very interested when a major newspaper puts a new reporter on the police beat. I frankly wasn't sure what I thought of a woman handling the job. That's not to betray any feeling I may or may not have about women in other professions, particularly my own. But I read all three Chicago papers everyday. I care about what they say about law enforcement in this city. And I think you're a good police reporter."

"Thank you."

"That's why I was disappointed when your name came up in this case."

Jennifer held her breath and slowly let it out as he continued.

"Truthfully, I was most disappointed when the top secret documents from John Lucas arrived at my home on Sunday, indicating the names of four officers who would be arrested in the Tuesday morning operation. My heart is always broken when I receive that kind of news.

"It comes in the form of a dossier containing all the essentials on the officer, his record, his years of service, everything. And it culminates in a careful listing—not detailed like it will be for the trial—but a listing of the offenses which have necessitated the arrests.

"Yes, ma'am, I recognized that Officer Purcell was a man John had once considered for work with IAD. But you'd be amazed at how many men who are considered for that kind of work either don't want to do it or aren't qualified. We won't touch a man with *anything* on his record. If he had a tardiness problem when he was a rookie, it's a red flag."

He paused for a long minute. Jennifer didn't know what to make of it. "Are you saying that something in Jim's file disqualified him for IAD?"

"You see, Mrs. Grey, I wouldn't know that. I gave permission for him to be considered, and more than a year later I read a file that contains a very damaging, very horrifying list of offenses against society, against the department, against the law."

"But it was a setup! He was working for Lucas!"

Commissioner Masek leaned forward and rested his chin on his fist, his elbow on the massive desk. He looked into her eyes with a blank expression. She could read nothing. He spoke slowly, carefully. "You have a reason to want to believe that. The only reason I want to believe it is because it saddens me to think that even one patrol officer is involved in the kinds of things in which these four were involved. If for some reason that number could be reduced to three, it would soften the blow for me by just that much. But, Mrs. Grey, the idea of it is preposterous. I'm sorry to have to tell you that. I believe you are sincere; but I'm afraid your young friend is lying to you."

Jennifer started to protest, but he raised a hand to silence her. "Let me put it this way," he tried again. "Let's say I wanted to give you the benefit of the doubt. What could I do? I have no knowledge past what I told you. Yes, I find it ironic that a man who had a tremendous record, a man who was once considered for IAD, was eventually arrested by them. But that *is* the truth as I know it. And unless someone in IAD tells me otherwise, I have to rely on the arrest documentation. And that looks extremely bad for Officer Purcell."

Jennifer didn't want to cry. She wouldn't. How could this have happened? Was it possible Lucas thought his idea was so novel that he wanted *no one* else to know? Apparently, he had not considered this eventuality. But then no one had.

"Can you tell me anything from Chief Lucas's private file?"

"Yes, but I must first ask you to sign a statement that stipulates that you have been granted access to classified information and that if you ever disseminate it in any fashion, you can be prosecuted."

His secretary dug out the form and brought it in. Jennifer signed quickly as Commissioner Masek scanned the typed list of the contents of Lucas's file. "I'll read you only the pertinent items; I prefer not to show anything to you. The only thing I see here that could have any bearing on Officer Purcell is a list of appointments over the last year with individuals to whom he gives code names: Apollo, Cruiseship, Delta, Eagle."

Jennifer pressed her fingers to her temples and stared at the floor. "None of them mean anything to me," she said sadly.

"They don't have to mean anything, and probably don't. When we use code names, we use them in categories, that's all. Sometimes it's birds—Robin, Dove, Sparrow, and all the rest. Sometimes it characters from a classic. John was apparently using names from the space program."

"What if one of the names meant something to Jim?"

"Then we'd have only his word for it, wouldn't we?"

She nodded.

"Anyway," he said, "if I know John, he never would have told any of his contacts his code names for them."

Jennifer stood and reached for Masek's hand. "Thank you for seeing me on such short notice," she said. "Do I have any other recourse? Any at all?"

Masek covered her hand with both of his. "Nothing I can think of," he said. "Unless John Lucas says your man was working for him, Purcell's in a lot of trouble."

Jennifer stepped out of Masek's office just as his secretary was hanging up the phone. *God,* Jennifer prayed silently, *forgive my motive, forgive my selfishness, forgive anything I've done wrong in this whole mess. Just don't let Lucas die.*

His secretary pushed her intercom button. "Mr. Masek?"

"Yes, Joan."

"The hospital just called. Mrs. Lucas is asking for you."

"*Mrs.* Lucas?"

"Yes, sir. She would like you to come right away, if possible."

"What do I have this afternoon?"

"Sir, it was the doctor, and he said you should hurry."

"Thanks, Joan. Cancel everything. Call the car."

Masek flew out of his office, putting his coat on as he went. Jennifer had to run to keep up with him, a lump rising in her throat. *God, please!*

"Commissioner, may I go with you?"

As he waited for the elevator, he appeared annoyed that she would even ask. He shrugged as if he really didn't know, couldn't decide, and wished she weren't there.

They rode the elevator down together. He still hadn't said no, so she stayed with him. "I won't get in the way." He moved faster now, out the front door to his waiting car. "I want to be there," she said.

Suddenly he stopped and turned on her. "Why?" he demanded angrily. "Whatever for?"

"I don't know!" she said, almost shouting.

He climbed into the backseat and shut the door, leaving her standing there holding her coat, shivering and fighting tears. She was paralyzed, wondering if she should run around the building to her car and race to the hospital on her own. But she'd never get close to Lucas's room if she wasn't with the commissioner.

She clenched her fists and hung her head, then heard the commissioner's car stop at the corner and back up. It screeched to a stop in front of her, and the back door flew open. She didn't hesitate.

When Masek and Jennifer stepped off the elevator in the intensive care unit, they saw the Lucas family standing in a waiting area at the end of the hall, embracing each other and crying.

An emergency team with a crash cart was slowly leaving one of the rooms, and the commissioner and Jennifer knew. Lucas had died.

"No," Masek moaned as he walked slowly toward the family. Jennifer's arms hung straight at her sides, and she forced herself to keep moving on her rubbery legs. Her breath came in short gasps.

Sylvia Lucas noticed Masek and fell into his arms, sobbing loudly and holding him tight. "Oh, Joe, Joe," she said. "Thank you for coming!"

"I'm so sorry, Syl," he said, his long arms wrapped around her.

"He was awake, Joe. He was awake when they called you. He talked."

"He talked?"

"Yeah, Joe. Didn't make any sense, but he tried to talk to me."

Jennifer stepped closer, her heart racing.

"That's nice, Syl," Masek said. "He was tryin' to say good-bye to you; you know that."

"I don't know, Joe," she said, trying to gain control of herself. "He just said something crazy. It didn't make any sense to me. He said, 'Thank the Eagle for me. Thank Purcell.' What do you make of that?"

Masek turned in time to see Jennifer slump into a chair. She buried her face in her hands and sobbed. She and Masek had realized the bad news about John Lucas at the same instant. Now they both knew the good news about Jim. It was over.

THREE DAYS IN WINTER

ONE

Heather Lauren. Jennifer thought it was a beautiful name, a name you might find in the social register of a North Shore debutante. Not the name of a murder victim on a police blotter in the West Side Precinct station.

"But that's where I found it," she told her boss, *Chicago Day* City Editor Leo Stanton. "The cops don't like it."

"I don't like it either," the veteran editor said, the ever-present unlit cigar jammed in his teeth. "Four years old? Where'd they find her?"

"Tied in the cellar."

"Abused?"

"Beaten, burned. Malnourished."

Leo swore. "Burned?"

Jennifer nodded, her eyes tearing.

Leo shook his head. "I've seen most everything in this business," he said. "In fact, I've seen this kinda thing before. But I never get used to it." He stood and walked around to the front of his desk, leaning back against it and crossing his arms as he stared down at Jennifer. "What're you going to do with it?"

She pressed her lips tight. "I don't know," she said, just above a whisper. "Play it straight, I guess. Quote the cops. Try to recreate how she was found. Talk to the coroner, the neighbors, check with Social Services."

Leo Stanton rolled up his sleeves and tugged at the waistband of his pullover sweater vest. He closed his eyes and let his head fall back, then reached up and slowly took off his half glasses, gently placing them on the desk beside him. "What would you do with this story if you could do whatever you wanted?" he asked.

Jennifer dropped her head and stared into her lap for several seconds. "I saw the pictures, Leo," she said.

"Hm?"

"The photographs of Heather Lauren. Martin Grom, the Homicide Detective Sergeant on the West Side, showed them to me. I almost wish he hadn't."

"I know Grom. A good guy, right? Big man. A redhead."

"That's him."

"Gruesome photos, huh? Nothing we can use, I s'pose."

"We could use one, but not the other. She was a doll, Leo. Apparently the only good picture her mother had of her was taken at some local Park District function. The kids brought the pictures home to see if the parents wanted to buy them. Some did. Some kept them without buying them. That's what Mrs. Lauren did."

"And we can get that picture?"

"Sure."

"Get it."

"Even that picture makes me sick, Leo. It's so precious it makes me think of the horrible one I saw in Grom's office. Do I have to describe it?"

"To me? No. I don't get any more kick out of something like that than you do. In your piece, yes. The reader has to know what happened, Jennifer. You know that."

She nodded, still staring down. The old man put a hand on her shoulder. "Jennifer, you never answered my question, so I'm gonna answer it for you. I want you to whip out the straight story fast. We'll go with it on page one with the good photo. Then I want you to do a sidebar; anything you want."

"Oh, Leo, no. You won't print what I'd have to write."

"You're gonna tell me what I'd print?" he said, smiling. "Try me."

"It's not funny, Leo. It's just that I'm so angered by this thing that I don't know if I can even do the straight story without intruding on it."

"You know I can't print opinion in the straight piece, Jennifer. And I can't have you spouting off about your religion. But a little emotion, especially on a story like this, well, there's no harm in that. That's why I'm telling you to do two. Let *me* decide if I can print the sidebar or not. Regardless, the page one story has to be done within the hour, and you'd better send someone to the West Side to get that photograph. I don't s'pose we can scoop the *Trib* or the *Times* on the photo."

"No, but at least we won't be the only one without it, and that's saying something."

"That's saying something, all right," Stanton said, returning to his chair. "The *Trib* has Bob Greene and Dear Abby. The *Times* has Mike Royko and Gary Deeb. We're glad when we're not the only one *without* a hot photo. The only thing we've got is the best police reporter in town."

Jennifer would have enjoyed the compliment another day. Now she trudged to the video screen at her desk, sliding her leather shoulder bag to the floor and draping her calf-length camel hair coat over the back of the chair.

It was always hot in the newsroom. She unzipped her boots and sat in stocking feet, digging from her bag the spiral notebook containing her notes. She propped it up next to the screen, then called the West Side Precinct station house.

"Chicago Police."

"Homicide, please."

"Jis' a minute."

"Homicide, Henry."

"Sergeant Grom, please."

"He's busy. Can he call you back?"

"No, please tell him it's Jennifer Grey from the *Day*."

"Grey from the *Day* for Grom on the phone? I love it! Hang on."

"This is Grom. Hi, Jenn."

"Hi, Martin. Listen, I know you're in the middle of this thing, but can I send someone to get the picture?"

"Yeah. You wanted the Park District shot, right?"

"Of course. You're not releasing the one from the cellar, are you?"

"You want it?"

"No, but—"

"Your competitors want it."

"You're kidding!"

"Nope. The both want it."

"They going to run it?"

"You mean do they want to? I can't imagine. I'd never let it out. Would you want that photo in the paper if it was your kid?"

Jennifer thought she heard an edge in Martin Grom's voice she hadn't heard before. "You're in a mood, aren't you?" she tried.

"Ah," he said, pausing. "I got a young daughter myself. If I had it *my* way, I'd kill Wyatt Oliver right now."

Jennifer grabbed for her notebook so fast she knocked it to the floor. "You're saying you believe Cornelia Lauren's common-law husband murdered the child?"

"Oh, Jenn, you can't quote me on that, please! Can't I just spout off to you without getting my neck in a noose? I'd be assigned to the mayor's office for bug control if that came out in the paper."

"That didn't sound off-the-record to me, Martin. You know you have to tell me it's off-the-record *before* you say it, not after."

"Well, you gotta pretend I told you in time on this one, Jennifer. Don't pull any technicality on me and quote me just because I felt free to tell you what I was thinking. Promise me."

"You don't have to worry, Martin. Hang on a second so I can tell Bobby to go get the picture."

She signaled her assistant, Robert Block, who sat with his feet up on his desk reading *Newsweek*.

"West Side Precinct," she said. "An envelope is in my name at the desk. Get it to composition ASAP."

"Why didn't you get it when you were there?" he whined.

"They had to make copies for each of us—oh, Bobby, just hit the road, will you? Do I have to tell Leo that you're being—"

"No, but I have no doubt that you would, with half a reason."

"You waste any time getting that photo, and I'll have more than half a reason." She turned back to the phone. "Sorry, Martin. So, tell me, is Mrs. Lauren sticking with her story, or did she lead you to believe that this, uh, Oliver, uh, Wyatt Oliver guy killed Heather?"

"You're not gonna print what I said, right?"

"I promised, Martin."

"Awright. No, both she and Oliver are sticking with their story."

"And what you don't like about it is that if the daughter had really been missing for two days, they would have reported it to somebody?"

"Right."

"Ok, Martin, off-the-record. If Wyatt Oliver killed the kid, why would his common-law wife cover for him?"

"'Cause she's scared to death of him. Wouldn't you be?"

"Jennifer thought for a moment. "I guess. I'd rather not say how I feel about him right now, because I'm afraid you're right."

"We just want to book him soon, because there's another kid in the family—you know, the seven-year-old boy."

"Elliott?"

"Right."

"Is that his real name?"

"Yeah, Elliott Lauren."

"Another beautiful name for a poor, sad child."

"Yeah, I gotta go, Jenn. I'll call you if I get anything more."

"No you won't."

"You're right, I prob'ly won't. But I do owe ya one. You don't print what I said about Wyatt Oliver, and I may just call you if I get anything new."

"Thanks, Martin."

Jennifer turned to her keyboard and began tapping out the front page story:

> The burned, beaten, and emaciated body of a four-year-old girl was found tied to a post in the cellar of a West Side apartment building Wednesday afternoon after police responded to a call from the girl's mother, Mrs. Cornelia Lauren of 4326 W. Stivers. The Cook County coroner's office is still trying to determine the cause of death.
>
> Mrs. Lauren, 31, who lives in the building with her common-law husband, Wyatt Oliver, 36, and her son, Elliott, 7, told police her daughter Heather had not come home from a Park District preschool program Monday afternoon. She said she discovered the body at approximately 3:30 P.M. Wednesday.
>
> West Side Homicide Detective Sergeant Martin Grom said police had no record of a missing person's report having been filed in the case. Neighbors were apparently unaware that the girl had been missing. But Oliver, an unemployed truck driver, says he wouldn't have asked his neighbors for help anyway. Oliver and Lauren are one of few white couples in the neighborhood, and police have intervened in disputes in their building before.
>
> When asked to explain the apparent malnourishment, Mrs. Lauren said her daughter had always been a light eater and very thin. She said that whoever had abducted the child must have inflicted the bruises and burns, because "the only time Heather ever hurt herself was when she fell down the stairs and burned herself on a hot plate."
>
> Sergeant Grom refused to comment on any leads or suspects in the case, though he admitted that police would be questioning the couple.

Jennifer finished the article with a more detailed description of the child's injuries, along with other minor details and a menu of related articles the reader could expect over the next few days, including interviews with neighbors and acquaintances, the police, and the coroner. She transmitted the story to Leo's screen and waited.

In a few minutes her phone rang. "Remarkably detached," he said. "C'mon in."

"You can sense where my head is from the piece, though, can't you?" she asked, standing in his doorway.

"'Course. So will the reader. But everyone will have the same suspicions. The kid is missing two days before the mother finds her? No one has been looking, let alone even knows the kid has been gone? The woman is a lousy liar, Jenn. She admits the kid fell down the stairs at age three—which is unlikely—and that she got burned on a hot plate. Are we talking about a burned finger? You write here that the girl had burns and burn scars on 15 percent of her body. Maybe a kidnapper gave her the fresh burns and bruises, but burn scars? That many don't come from a hot plate unless she wrestled with the thing."

"I know. And I'm so livid I don't even want to take a shot at the sidebar."

"You don't understand, Jennifer," Leo said. "It's not a suggestion. I want that piece. If you go overboard, I'll edit you a little. Let's do it. Let's prove we know what the readers are thinking and identify with them once. People are sick and tired of people who hurt children. Let's show 'em we have the same feelings. What could you say that I wouldn't print, besides the fact that you think Jesus is the answer for everything?"

Jennifer looked pained.

"I'm sorry," Leo said. "That was a little cold."

"Not to mention a little simplistic."

"OK, guilty. But other than a sermonette, I want to see what's rattling around in your brain under all that brown hair. How 'bout it?"

Two

Jennifer padded back to her desk, still not sure what to do with the sidebar and wished she could talk to Jim before their late dinner in Geneva. But she was determined to stick with the agreement she had struck with Leo and the publisher: "You can date a police officer as long as you don't see him or talk to him when either of you are working, and provided you neither use him to gain information, nor personally handle a story in which he might be mentioned."

It was better than being reassigned to the society page, but there were days when she wondered if it was worth it. How could she not discuss this terrible story with him, just because he happened to be a policeman? She couldn't avoid it, it was as simple as that. She loved him; she needed him as a sounding board. She wouldn't be pumping him for information, and he wouldn't offer any—not even to tip her off as to who to talk to.

Her screen's red light came on. She called up the message. "Leo the Lion sez: Don't daydream too long. You've got about 40 minutes to give me the equivalent of 2 takes."

"Thanks, Mane Man," she tapped back, not feeling as light as her message. She hit the key to clear the screen and put away her notebook while the computer was doing its thing. She would do this piece off the top of her head.

She breathed a silent prayer and tried to keep her tears in check as she began:

> I saw a photograph today that made me an instant militant in the campaign for capital punishment.
>
> I don't know who beat or burned or starved or neglected four-year-old Heather Lauren to death in her own West Side basement this week, and something tells me I don't want to know.
>
> You can see the *before* picture on page one. That's her next to the grizzly headline and my just-the-facts story. If the picture were in color, you could see that she was a blue-eyed blonde with a pageboy haircut, a shy smile, and perfect little teeth.
>
> But the beauty of the child and the horrible manner of her death is not what moves me to temporarily leave my niche as a police reporter to tell you that I feel the same way you do about this story.
>
> I do, but then I hope you suspected that. Maybe you didn't. Maybe you think I've grown calloused over the last two years, writing about crime, about good cops and bad cops, white-collar criminals and blue-collar criminals.
>
> Maybe you think that to me it's all just more grist for the newspa-

per stories, something that allows me to fill my space, justify my existence, put food on my table. Maybe you think I can forget it and go home, only to return and hit it again the next day.

Well, I can't. I'm as depressed by bad news as you are. It affects me as much. And when I've seen the police department's photo of a lifeless little body—a photo so offensive that we wouldn't dare publish it in a family newspaper—perhaps it affects me even more than it does you.

When I leave the office after writing this article, I'll go home, I'll see my friends, I'll have dinner, I'll watch the news, I'll go to bed. And when I get up, I'll come back to work and investigate the story for days until someone is suspected, sought, found, charged, convicted, and sentenced.

And then we will all forget about Heather Lauren for awhile. Or will we? Will I? I'll see that picture again and again in my mind. I'll hear the story in court more times than I want to. And I'll be reminded constantly of the vulnerability of the child. Any child.

People who prey upon defenseless victims—the aged, the infirm, the young—should be punished. Of course, anyone who preys upon anyone else is wrong. But in the cases of the defenseless, the crimes are all the more heinous. For they are always perpetrated for the most selfish reasons.

Murderers murder the aged for their money. They murder the infirm for their money. They murder children for their silence, or to eliminate the haunting, hungry eyes that bring guilt. Maybe they're inconvenient.

I know this isn't the right era for tough laws, for punishment at the expense of rehabilitation, for inhumane treatment of society's misfits, for not understanding the difficult environments that produce someone capable of the crime that will be on our minds for weeks.

But if you saw the picture I saw today and compared it to the one on the front page of this newspaper, you'be be unable to swallow the lump in your throat. You'd be unable to hold back the tears. You'd be frightened of your feelings. And you'd want justice.

I can't help it. I want to see the guilty party pay for this crime. And when the bleeding heart letters come pouring in to call *me* inhumane, I'll call to memory that photograph just one more time and know I'll never change my mind.

Jennifer transmitted the story to Leo but didn't wait for his reaction. She pulled on her boots and coat and hurried down the back corridor toward the parking lot, passing Bobby on the way. She sniffed and managed, "Get it?"

"Yes, your highness," he said. "I can handle all dese tough jobs Massa Grey, ma'am. Anything else you wants of Bobby today?"

She ignored him and kept moving. He had tried so hard—and almost succeeded—to get her fired for seeing Jim while handling the police beat. Bobby would graduate from Northwestern and be her boss within a few years, she guessed, unless someone was made fully aware of his attitude.

He was good at hiding it, and he *did* have unusual talent. But he was a scoundrel who needed exposing, and if she couldn't change him or at least get him to see that he needed changing, she'd have to pull him out from under his slimy rock to protect others.

This was one of those days when Bobby Block didn't seem worth the effort.

A light snow had covered Jennifer's little car, and she hated to think what she was doing to her coat, leaning against the salty, slushy sides of the car to scrape the windows. She wanted to look nice for Jim tonight. He would have been at prayer meeting. Someday she would have an assignment that would free her to go with him. But for now, Wednesday evenings, after she got off work, were their late dinner nights.

She always looked forward to them, no matter how tired she was. And regardless what might come up at work or how late she had to stay, Officer James Purcell would never hear of canceling. He'd wait, he always said. And he always did. Once until eleven-thirty.

It wouldn't be that late tonight, but never had Jennifer been more tired or had more on her mind. She arrived at her apartment with just enough time to park, grab her mail, ride the elevator to her floor, freshen up, change clothes, and answer the doorbell. It was too early for Jim.

"You got a delivery, Miss Grey," old Mrs. Alexander yodeled. "You weren't here, and I knew you weren't here, so I told him you weren't here but that I knew you and that I would take if for you and that I would even pay him, and so I did. A dollar I gave him. For this."

Beaming, she held out a small, narrow box. Jennifer dug a dollar from her purse, deciding not to open the box until Mrs. Alexander was gone. She appreciated the kindness, but the contents of the box were none of her neighbor's business.

"Thank you very much," Jennifer said, smiling. "You're so kind."

"And so is Jim," the old woman said with a twinkle as she backed down the hall. "One red rose, and so lovely!"

It was all Jennifer could do to keep from slamming the door.

Well, the nosy old bat was right, anyway, she said to herself, sitting on the edge of the sofa opening the box. *It is lovely.*

The card read, *I'm looking forward to tonight. Pick you up at 9.*

She nearly panicked. Was there something special about this Wednesday night? Was there something she had forgotten? Was it an anniversary of sorts? She couldn't remember. Jim was thoughtful; she'd received deliveries before. But what did his card mean? Maybe nothing, but what if she'd forgotten something she should have remembered?

She put the rose in a tiny vase and scurried to finish her face and hair. *I hope he hasn't got anything up his sleeve,* she thought, surprised by how nervous and excited she always felt about seeing him again, even after a day like today.

She knew the real thing when it came along. She'd been through it before. After other experiences of puppy love and infatuation through high school and college, she fallen in love with Scott Grey. And it had been only recently that she had forgiven him for dying on an icy road early in their marriage.

That was why for so long she had hidden even from herself her true feelings for Jim. It couldn't be, she decided, that the first man she chose to see after finally emerging from her grief, would be a man she could love.

And so she didn't. She simply wouldn't allow herself to fall for him. Jim was patient. He knew. He understood. He waited. Bided his time. Proved himself. And when she had least expected it, her love for him burst from its hiding place.

She loved him unabashedly. And he loved her. They were unusually blessed with a relationship that lucky people approach only once in their lifetimes. He had been disappointed in love before. She had been happily married, then widowed. And now God had given them each other.

She looked at her watch. Eight fifty-five. Jim would arrive in five minutes, as usual. And she would be ready. As usual. She latched her watchband and folded her coat over her arm and sat again on the edge of the couch.

She could just as easily sleep as go out, and she realized she would not go out tonight for anyone in the world but Jim. Not even Leo. Dad? She'd probably try to beg off, but Dad could talk her into it. And if Jim was the only person besides her dad who she would go out with after an exhausting day, then that was as high a compliment as she could pay him.

She'd have done anything—and often had—for Scott too. It was good to be able to think about him rationally now. Finally. For how long had his absence been the first thing on her mind every day?

She hadn't been able to keep him from her mind, and when the memories intruded, they suffocated her with grief—longing, hoping, wishing his accident had never happened. No pleasant memory of him had ever wafted through her mind without ending in that remarkably stark and sterile conversation with the young state trooper who brought her the news that had changed her life.

Had she grown out of it, like a child who quits sucking his thumb? Had Jim taken Scott's place? No. Time, as much as she had always hated the platitude, truly had been a healer of the wound. Jim had been part of the healing process, of course, because he had not seemed threatened by her memories of Scott.

In fact, he wanted to hear about Scott. Jim felt flattered that she loved him after having been married to such an outstanding young man.

She leaped to her feet at the sound of the doorbell. There stood Jim, all tall and trim and bronze and blonde in his Ivy League earth tones, cardigan, herringbone jacket, and open trench coat.

"Hi, Sweetheart," he said, smiling and reaching for her.

She embraced him. "Hi, Scott," she said, wincing immediately and knowing he was doing the same. "Jim, I'm so sorry. I've never done that before, have I?"

He chuckled. "Been thinking again?"

"Yes, but mostly about you."

"Sounds like it," he said, still smiling.

"Really I was. I love you, Jim."

"I love you too. Get anything from me today?"

"Yes, and I loved it. It worried me though."

"Worried you?"

"Yes, have I forgotten something? Is there something special about this day or this dinner? If there is, I'm sorry, but it's passed me by."

"Does it have to be a special occasion for me to remind you that I look forward to dinner with you?" he said, reaching behind her and pulling the door shut, then walking her to the elevator.

"No, it's great, but if I forgot something, you remind me."

"What would you forget?"

"The first time we held hands or kissed or something."

"You mean we've already held hands and kissed?" he said, mocking, as the elevator door shut.

She planted a passionate one on him. "Now we have," she said, laughing.

He wrapped his arm tightly around her as they stepped into a frigid wind. "You look tired," he said.

"More than usual on Wednesday night?"

"Yeah. 'Fraid so. Tough day?"

"Always."

"But more so than usual?"

"How'd you know?"

"I know everything."

"You know about the little girl on the West Side, of course."

"Of course."

"You mind if we don't talk about it?"

"Whatever you want, Jenn." He opened the car door for her. "I would have thought you might want to bounce it off me, though," he said, shutting it.

"I thought so too," she said when he slid behind the wheel. "In fact, I've been looking forward to talking to you about it all afternoon. Now I want to talk about anything but."

He gave her an understanding glance and pulled away into the night toward the western suburbs.

THREE

Jim insisted on taking Jennifer home early when she nearly dozed off at dinner. He hadn't pressed her about her reactions to the Heather Lauren murder, but she did reveal why she felt she couldn't talk about it.

"I emptied myself in a sidebar, a personal column type thing, Jim. I think the Lord really gave me clarity of mind, because it came out just the way I wanted it to. I really don't know if I could have expressed it better, and I sure won't try to do it from memory. You'll see it in the morning *Day*. Let me know what you think."

"I can hardly wait. I know what I'll think. I'll think it's great, like all your stuff."

"You don't understand, Jim. This is so forthright that it may get me into trouble with the readership. In fact, for all I know, Leo might not even print it. I all but demand capital punishment for the perpetrator."

"You won't get any argument from my side of the street."

"Yeah, but everybody knows you cops are right-wing red-necks. We journalists are supposed to be liberal left-wingers, remember?"

Jennifer didn't protest the early end to the evening. It was the type of attention she appreciated so much in Jim. After praying and reading some Scripture, she mentally plotted her afternoon tasks for the next day. She'd start with the Park District preschool teacher, then contact the social worker assigned to the family. If that didn't give her enough for the next morning's paper, a last minute check with Sergeant Grom would.

But the next day came earlier than Jennifer expected. Leo called shortly after 9:00 A.M.

"No, it's all right, Leo, I was just getting up—in an hour or two."

"Sorry, but the big boss wants to see us in about an hour. Can you make it?"

"I dunno. How important is this guy to my career? Tell 'im I'm still in bed."

"You're cute."

"See you in forty-five, Leo. What's he want, anyway? You know?"

"Yeah, but I can't tell ya."

"Wonderful. Should I think raise or welfare?"

"Think anything you want; just get over here."

"You print the sidebar, Leo?"

"Didn't change a word."

"That mean you like it?"

"What do you think, Einstein?"

"Your kind of compliment. Thanks."

Max Cooper's office was on the top floor of the *Day* building on Michigan Avenue. Even Leo appeared nervous.

"This is Jennifer Grey," Leo said.

"Of course, sure," the tall, thin, intense, distinguished publisher said. He had a reputation for looking good but being a little rough around the edges in personality. "I shook hands with you at the Christmas party, didn't I?"

"No, I wasn't there. But I've seen you around, of course."

"Of course, and I know your stuff. Sit down, sit down."

Cooper joined Leo and Jennifer at a small wood table and grinned at them. *If my career has just bit the dust, he's pretty happy about it,* Jennifer decided.

"Let me get straight to the point, Miss Grey. I was serious about knowing your stuff. I read you every day, and I mean that. If you don't believe it, just quiz me."

"I believe you."

"Good, 'cause who knows how I'd do on a fool quiz! Ha!"

Leo laughed. Jennifer smiled. Cooper continued.

"I, ah, was a police reporter myself when I started out. 'Course, my old man owned the whole chain, so I sorta had my pick, if you know what I mean." Jennifer nodded. "But anyway, I've always kept a close eye on the police beat."

"Don't I know it?" Leo said.

"Yeah! You hear from me about that now and then, don't you, Lion? I call him Lion all the time, don't I, Lion?" Leo nodded. "Well, Leo here was a police reporter way back when too. Seems all the really good guys start there."

Jennifer smiled at Max Cooper, enjoying whatever it was he was trying to say.

"Now me, before I went administrative, I went from the police beat to the sports page, then sports columnist and sports editor. I don't s'pose you've got any aspirations that way, do you, Miss Grey?"

"No, not really."

"Well, 'course not. Not that a woman couldn't do a good job in sports. Wouldn't be against that at all if a qualified one wanted to or whatever, right? But you don't want that."

"No, sir."

"Well, I said I was going to get straight to the point, didn't I? I've been following your stuff for some time, and I've seen a spark there. I've seen attention to detail. I've seen a sensitivity there. I've seen the color, the depth, the care—the types of things that most people wouldn't think an old hack like me would notice if they stared him in the face."

"Thank you, sir."

"Well, thank *you*. I mean, let's put the credit where the credit's due. Anyway, I've been pushing on the Lion here to get you into a little more feature stuff, not tryin' to tell him his job or anything, but just to see what your potential is. 'Course Leo agrees with me anyway; fact is, he saw you were special long before I did and told me so. You've got an ally there, Miss Grey."

Jennifer smiled at Leo and refrained from telling Cooper that she was actually a *Mrs.,* as she usually did.

"Well, anyway, I didn't know what Leo had done this morning when I saw your sidebar on the little girl's murder. I mean, I wanted him to broaden your horizons a little, and you may have sensed he's been doing that, but letting you go and get so personal and opinionated and, uh, uh, earthy there—why, I just didn't know what to expect."

"How did you feel about it, Mr. Cooper?" Jennifer asked.

"Me? Well, there wasn't anything wrong with your position as far as I'm concerned. I mean, I s'pose it's the type of thing I would have had no problem with on the editorial page or in some signed column or something. You were speaking my mind there, Miss Grey, and everybody's I assume, except for some misguided do-gooders who think more of the criminal than of the victim."

"So, you don't feel it should have been placed next to the end of the story on page three?"

"I'm not saying that. I'm saying that I didn't know what to think when I saw it. I was moved by it, I must tell you that. I cried reading it, and I don't cry reading anything! The last time a newspaper piece moved me to tears was when Bob Greene did that thing in the *Trib* last year directed to the Tylenol killer. But I also must tell you that as soon as I got myself under control again, I was wearing my publisher's hat, and I started to worry. And I wanted to know why Leo had had you do it. I wasn't going to blame you. I was going to have the Lion's hide here if the phones started ringin' off the wall from the ACLU or who knows who else."

Jennifer was puzzled. What exactly was the man trying to say?

"I know what you're thinking, Miss Grey. I know you're thinking that it's awful small of me to decide who gets called on the carpet and who doesn't, based on what the readers think of what goes in the paper. And you're right. But it's the name of the game. If they like it, I'm happy. If enough of 'em don't like it, then we've got trouble, whether I agree with the article or not. Which, as I already told you, I do.

"You see, we're still the third paper in a town with three papers, and I gotta tell ya, we're not ignoring the *Defender,* which a lot of people don't think qualifies as one of the biggies. It's comin' on, and we may be a town with four major papers again one day.

"But we thought Chicago could use another daily, even when the *Today* and the *Daily News* couldn't compete. Everybody knows we've succeeded, and we've hurt the competition—at least we've taken some of their readers and advertisers. Personally, I think competition can only help a paper, unless it runs it out of business. And we have no intention of doing that.

"So, as tough and honest and real as I want our paper to be, we still have to be a little conservative in our policies so we don't lose big batches of readers at a time. One or two over a mistake or disagreement once in a while, OK. But not hundreds of readers at a crack. Can't afford it."

"And is that what's happening this morning, Mr. Cooper?"

The big boss squinted at her and then at Leo Stanton. He rose and smiled. "No, ma'am. Apparently you haven't been listening to the radio, watching the news, noticing the newspaper stands. Our pressrun ran out, Miss Grey. It *ran out!* Do you know the last time a daily paper in this town had to go back to press with the same edition, Miss Grey? Neither do I. You struck a nerve, lady. You hit big. You're the talk of the town. People want today's issue of the *Day.* And you know what that means? That means they're going to want tomorrow's, and the next day's, and the next—as long as there's a personal column by you in there."

Suddenly the man fell silent and sat again. Jennifer took it as her cue to rise. Both Cooper and Stanton were content to let her be the next to speak. They looked at each other and smiled. But she was troubled.

"Can I ask a question?" she said.

"Absolutely," Cooper said.

"What would I be hearing right now if the reaction had been the opposite?"

"Good question, young lady. And I want to be honest with you. You see, you and I think a lot alike; I could tell that from your previous work, but especially in your column this morning. I like you; I like what you say. But if the public reaction had been negative, you wouldn't be standing here right now. Stanton would have been in trouble, and you would have been put out to pasture somewhere until this thing blew over."

"If you don't mind my saying so, that sounds like a pretty shaky way to start a relationship as a columnist. Right or wrong, the public decides, correct?"

"It's a business, Miss Grey."

"*Mrs.* Grey."

"Excuse me."

"That's all right. So if I become a daily columnist and the public suddenly decides it doesn't like me, I'm through?"

"I know how that sounds, Miss, ah, Mrs. Grey."

"But that's the case."

"Yes, that's the case."

"I'll have to think about it."

"Columnists don't get Guild rates, Mrs. Grey. We pay them like executives. For you, that would mean nearly a 50 percent increase in pay."

"Because of one emotional column?"

"Of course not. I told you, I've been reading you."

"But the public reaction tipped the scales."

"That's right," Cooper said, suddenly sobering. "Listen, sit down and let me tell you something, Mrs. Grey. If Leo hadn't told me a little about you, you can understand how I could be a little offended by your reaction here."

"Yes, sir, I know, but it's just that—"

"I know. I know you're not motivated by money or power or prestige."

"I'm not above being flattered by all that, but—"

"I know you're a religious person and that—"

"I prefer not to refer to my faith as religion."

"Whatever, I know you're a churchgoing person and honest and all that."

"And that would have to come through in any column I would write. Not in *every* column, but if you want my personality on paper, that would have to be a factor."

Cooper furrowed his brow. "It wasn't overt in the column this morning."

"No, but I did pray about writing that."

"Well, listen. If the public goes for it, you can write sermons for all I care. I'm not a man without principles myself, but I need a columnist the people want to read, and right now they want to read you, so you're it. It's yours if you want it. I'll have Leo put you on the bottom of page one, just like Keegan in the *Trib*. You can write what you want, but I assume you'd stay on this Heather Lauren case until it's resolved."

"You may find that that's what got everyone so excited today. Not *me*, but the case itself."

"Well, you may be right. I don't think so, but who knows? If you're right, the public will let us know, and you'll be back on the police beat."

"Just like that?"

"Just like that. And let me ask you something. Where do you think Greene or Deeb or even Royko would be if the public suddenly decided they weren't worth the price of the paper every day?"

Jennifer blinked. "But they don't write what the public wants to hear just to keep their jobs."

"And we wouldn't want you to do that either. Just be yourself. As long as they love you, we'll have a tough time keeping you from jumping to one of the other papers."

"Can I think about it?"

"For how long?"

"Twenty-four hours?"

"On one condition. You do at least one more piece like today's for tomorrow morning's paper."

"I'm not sure I've got anything more to say like that."

"It doesn't have to be just like it. Do your usual digging on the story today, write a straight piece, and then do a reflective sidebar. Where is your head since you wrote the last one and turned up more evidence? That type of thing is what the readers want to know."

"I'll try," Jennifer said.

Leo clapped. "That's what she said last night, Max. Just before she wrote the winner."

FOUR

Jennifer's mind was jumbled as she swung off Bilford Boulevard onto the long and depressing Stivers Avenue. Just to drink in the atmosphere, she started four blocks from Lake Michigan and drove through more than eight miles of stoplights, crowded intersections, and elevated train underpasses from West Stivers.

She would have to have a talk with Leo. She had to smile at old man Cooper calling him Lion. Not Leo the Lion. Not The Lion. Just Lion. For how long had Leo been setting her up for this column possibility?

Already she'd heard on the radio that she wasn't exactly the hit of the *entire* town as Max Cooper had hoped. Indeed, the ACLU had released a statement demanding a retraction or an apology or a modification from her.

And there were rumors that another columnist, on her own paper, would be taking issue with her in the next edition. She wondered how Cooper would react to that. And what if Cooper was right, that *she* had hit the nerve, and thus her counterpart would be taking an unpopular stand? Would that mean a soon end of his stint as a columnist?

The ACLU thing had initiated a mini-barrage of callers telling a radio talk show host that they agreed she'd been wrong. If she hadn't been bolstered by the reactions of so many others, including her boss and his boss, she might have panicked, wondered if she had done the right thing, looked for a way out.

But she didn't even have to ask to see again the photo Martin Grom had showed her in the West Side Precinct station house the day before. She could remember. Would she ever be able to forget?

Jennifer had a 1:00 P.M. appointment with Angela Liachi, Heather Lauren's preschool supervisor. But with a little time to spare, she made a quick decision. She was going to drop in on Heather's mother and, she hoped, Wyatt Oliver.

She was ten minutes finding a parking place on the street, and then she wasn't confident her locked car was any more secure than if she had left the keys in it.

As she headed toward 4326, she heard the whistles and catcalls of groups of men she'd seen huddled around burning trash cans, bouncing on their toes, hands jammed in their pockets except when lighting cigarettes.

Such groups dotted all of Stivers Avenue from just west of the Loop all the way through the high-rise projects and into the low-rise duplexes. Now she was into the rows of three-story, full-basement apartments that teemed with occupants, usually more than one family per apartment, at least two apartments per floor.

Jennifer fingered a can of chemical spray in her right coat pocket. Her purse strap was wrapped around her left arm. In her left hand she clutched her key ring, which contained a police whistle and a tiny razor blade that could be exposed with one snap of the wrist.

She could blind one, slice one, and scare a few with the whistle, but she didn't want to have to. She never had before, and now she simply wished she'd dressed less bourgeois. What was it Jim had advised, besides all the artillery? "Walk as if you know where you're going, as if you're expected any second, and as if you just might be a cop."

More important, she thought, *is to actually know, and to actually be expected, and to actually be a cop.* Except for knowing where she was going, she had two strikes. If she didn't get an answer at the Oliver-Lauren residence, it was a good walk back to the car with at least one group of bored, unemployed men between it and her.

When she stole a glance back at them, however, it was apparent they had already given up on her. Now she noticed groups of preschool age children—some school age-—frolicking near chain link fences in a world of gray and brown.

Jennifer looked at her watch. Almost twelve-thirty. Not much time. But then she probably wouldn't need much.

She sensed the eyes of many neighbors as she approached the front door of the dingy three-floor apartment building. The sign at the front read, "Use Side Enterence." She didn't like the looks of the dark space between buildings that led to the side door.

What was left of a crumbling sidewalk echoed under her boots as she moved around the building. The wind picked up momentum in the small passageway, hidden from the sun. She gritted her teeth at the bone-chilling gusts and wondered about the makeshift screens on the windows and doors.

There were no storm windows, nor—she assumed—any insulation. The screen door at the side was loose on its hinges, and giant tears top and bottom made it worthless for the summer, let alone the winter.

Jennifer sensed no movement from inside the building, though she knew someone had to be home in at least one of the apartments. She was about to revert back to Plan A and drive the few blocks to locate Angela Liachi when she was startled by the rattle-crashing bursting open of the side door.

A tiny, sandy-haired boy, the size of a four- or five-year-old ran past her. "Are you Elliott?" she called after him.

He nodded once as he ran, not looking back. He accelerated and turned a corner out of her sight. "Is your mother home?" she called again, but suddenly the entire neighborhood was silent. Even the wind seemed to have stopped. It was as if no one could believe she had come there in her hotshot ensemble with her camel coat and her leather boots and her cover-girl makeup and her shining hair and then had the audacity to ask for someone.

Her eyes darted out from the darkness into the harsh sunlight that lit but didn't warm the street. The men were turning back to their oil drum fire. The kids stared at her from across the street. She waited until they lost interest and turned back to their games. Then she knocked on the warped wood of the screen door.

She felt conspicuous. Watched. Unwanted.

She pulled at the squeaky door and reached in to knock more loudly on the inner door, which wasn't in much better shape. The first firm tap of her knuckles pushed the door all the way open. Stunned, she stepped back and waited. Nothing.

Looking around one more time, Jennifer stepped inside and carefully shut the door behind her, feeling foolish. To her left, the stairs led to the cellar. To the right was an open archway into the kitchen of one of the first floor flats. Straight ahead, the stairs led up. Heather Lauren's family lived on the second floor.

It seemed to her to take ages to make up her mind. She decided that Sergeant Martin Grom would soon convince a judge that he had enough on Wyatt Oliver and Cornelia Lauren to hold them and maybe even charge them with child abuse, manslaughter, murder, or whatever he wanted. She would then be unable to interview them.

She poked her head into the kitchen on the first floor. "Anyone home?" she called quietly.

No response, even though she smelled food cooking.

She headed upstairs, holding her breath, listening for any sound of life. She knocked at a door, but footsteps on the third floor, resounding through the ceiling, scared her off. She hurried back down to the first floor and waited by the side door again.

There was no sound of steps on the stairs, so she crept down to the cellar. The musty dampness, combined with the stench of a makeshift bathroom where drunks apparently detoured before staggering into their apartments at night, nauseated her.

She located an area surrounding a simple metal pole that had been roped off by the police. There was no sign of a struggle or of blood, but a blunted chalk tracing around the base of the pole marked where Cornelia Lauren told police she had found the tied, slumped body of her daughter.

Jennifer felt the bile rise in her throat and the anger shorten her breath. Why wouldn't someone have heard the girl's cries? Where were the first-floor families when this happened? Where were they now?

She pressed her lips tight and hunched her shoulders against the chill, walking as close to the police rope as she could and peering into the shadows to try to imagine the scene. The memory of the horrible photo flooded her mind and she realized for the first time that it had been taken before the little body had been cut free.

Dear God, she prayed silently, fighting tears, *here's one I'll never understand. If it had to happen for some reason, at least help us find who did it.*

The sound of footsteps on the stairs above her froze Jennifer to her spot. Through the back of the stairs she could see bare feet and what appeared to be old, charcoal-colored suit pants. There was no exit except those stairs and nowhere to hide either.

Was he coming down to see if someone was there? Or because he knew someone was there? Or for a reason totally unrelated? The time for ducking behind something was past. She stood her ground and squinted at the small, muscley figure that had stopped at the bottom of the steps.

He glared at her without a word. He was not armed. His fingers were entwined in those Salvation Army barrel suit pants, holding them up for want of a belt. He wore a ribbed, sleeveless undershirt.

The light from the basement window shone on the back of his head, leaving his face dark, so Jennifer moved to her right to get a better look. His hair was long, greasy, and unkempt. He was unshaven. His eyes looked black. His muscles were taut.

Jennifer imagined she could smell him from ten feet away. She decided not to speak first. He spread his feet apart, as if ready to defend his position.

He looked Italian; he spoke truck driver with what Jennifer guessed was a CB-trained phony Southern accent. "The las' female found in this cellar was dead," he said.

"I don't intend to be found here," she said, surprising herself.

"Don't be too sure."

She switched to the offensive, trying to sound friendlier. "I, uh, was looking for the Lauren family. Mr. Oliver. Mrs. Lauren. Their son."

"Down here you was lookin' for 'em?"

"Upstairs too. I didn't see anyone."

"You knock?"

"Yes, sir."

"I don't answer the door, an' my wife is in mournin'."

"Are you also?"

"Ma'am?"

"Are you also in mourning, Mr. Oliver?"

"You want trouble, lady?" He swore. "Who are you anyway?"

"Jennifer Grey. I write for the *Chicago Day* newspaper. Are you familiar with it?"

"I can't afford no newspaper. We ain't even paid off the TV yet."

"Did you beat your wife's daughter, Mr. Oliver?"

His eyes narrowed. "I think you better get your little self outta my house."

"Is this your building?"

"I live here."

"You own this basement?"

"Don't make me throw you out, writer lady."

"Unless you have a weapon, you'll not be throwing me anywhere," Jennifer said, her heart smashing against her ribs. "Or are you going to tie me to a post and burn me and punch me?"

His hand shook. "Are *you* armed, lady?"

"Yes, sir."

He eyed her warily, then spoke softly. "I'm bettin' you're lying'," and he moved quickly toward her.

Jennifer yanked both hands from her pockets simultaneously, flicking open the razor blade in her left hand, chemical spray poised in her right. Wyatt Oliver instinctively raised his hands in surrender, but he grabbed at his waistband again as his pants started to fall. And Jennifer dashed past him, up the stairs, out the door, down the block, and, trembling as she fumbled with her keys, slid into her car. She didn't dare even look back as she sped toward the Park District center.

She pulled into the parking area a few minutes ahead of schedule and dropped her head to the steering wheel, closing her eyes and trying to calm herself. *If that was my answered prayer, Lord,* she prayed wryly, *it could have waited.*

As she caught her breath, someone knocked on the window. Without thinking or looking up, she jammed the key back into the ignition and turned it on, throwing the car into reverse.

But as she whirled around to guide the car out of the lot, she saw a short, dark-haired woman leap clear of the car, arms outstretched, terrified. Jennifer hit the brake and rolled down her window with an embarrassed smile. "Angela?"

"Miss Grey?" Angela said. "What's got you spooked?"

"Not what. Who."

"OK. Who?"

"Wyatt Oliver."

"Why doesn't that surprise me?" Angela asked.

"Doesn't it?" Jennifer said. "Tell me about it."

"On one condition. You've got to get out from behind the wheel."

FIVE

Angela Liachi was cute in a plump sort of way. Short. Dark. Intense. Fast-talking. New Yorkish. Her eyes shown as she smiled at Jennifer's jumpiness.

"Thought I was Wyatt Oliver, didja?"

Jennifer nodded.

"Let's take a walk. I don't wanna be anywhere near yer car, if you know what I mean."

They walked three blocks north to the parking lot of a boarded up former fast-food restaurant where they slowed and moseyed around the building, turning their collars up against the wind. They ignored occasional honks and waves of passersby who thought they might be hookers.

"I saw your article today," Angela said, stopping and facing the sun, squinting and enjoying the little heat she could drink from it.

Jennifer put a foot up on a cracked concrete carstop and studied the ground. "Yeah? Kinda extreme, huh?"

"Are you kiddin'? If there was anything wrong with it, it was only that it was prob'ly too easy."

Jennifer shot her a double take. "Too easy? You ever try writing?"

"Nah, I don't mean the writing part of it. I mean taking the position. Too easy. Who could disagree?"

"The ACLU."

Angela smiled a rueful smile and made an obscene gesture. "Bleeding heart liberals."

"People say social workers like you are bleeding heart liberal idealists," Jennifer said.

"Oh, they do, huh? Well, I don't consider myself a social worker, a bleeding heart, or a liberal."

"An idealist."

"Dyed in the wool."

The women smiled at each other.

"I have many questions for you about Heather Lauren—"

"And Wyatt Oliver, right?"

"Of course, if you know anything—"

"If I *know* anything! *I* could write you an article on Wyatt Oliver."

"I was going to say that I had a lot of questions for you about the case, and I appreciate your agreeing to see me, but first I wanted to talk about you."

That made Angela nervous. She started moving again, and Jennifer had to shift her weight quickly and get going to keep up. Angela swore. "It's cold," she added.

"It's nothing personal," Jennifer said. "I'm just curious."

"And you're not gonna print anything in the paper about me, are you?"

"No. Well, I might quote you on the Heather Lauren case, that's all."

"You can't quote everything I say about that. You wouldn't want to."

"We'll get to it. First, just tell me—"

"I know what you're going to ask."

"How do you know what I'm going to ask?" Jennifer was smiling, but becoming exasperated.

"Because I get it all the time. I gotta tell ya, I'm not good copy. Every few months, some well-dressed—nothing personal—reporter from some magazine or newspaper or radio or TV station comes into my little ghetto here and asks me what motivates me. That's the big word. *Motivation.* Tell me the truth, is that what you were going to ask?"

"Yes."

"Still want an answer?"

"I must have missed all those interviews you've done. I've never heard or read your answer."

"That's because they never use it. I don't give 'em enough."

"And if you did, you wouldn't let them print it or broadcast it, am I right?"

"That's not it, Miss, uh, Grey—"

"Call me Jennifer, please."

"Okay, Jennifer please," she said, smiling. "The point is that I don't have any grand story to tell. Why would a skilled, privileged, educated, established, unlimited-future-type like me come to the seediest part of Chicago and—they always put this in quotes—*give her life* to the blacks, Hispanics, and poor whites?"

"It's a good question, Angela. If all those reporters from all those different media ask it, it must be because they believe the public wants to know."

"But Jennifer, it would be a good question only if there was a good answer. I'd love to be able to spin a yarn for you, tell you that despite my privileged upbringing, a chance encounter with a not-so-fortunate person taught me the meaning of selfless love. I can't. Didn't happen. I'm not a socialist. I'm not religious; I wasn't called here. I just heard about the opportunity, thought it fit me, and it seemed like the right thing to do at the time."

"How long have you been here?"

"Eight years."

"Eight years! That's got to be some kind of a record, doesn't it?"

"For one program in one neighborhood, it is. By almost double."

"You're proud of that, I can tell."

"Granted."

"Why?"

"I don't know. I came here to do a job, and I'm doin' it. Does there have to be more than that? You see how unpublishable that is?"

"I'd publish it."

"And break your promise?"

"No, I mean I would if you'd let me."

"I won't."

"I figured that. Does anything make you angry?"

"I'm pretty even, Jennifer. I've seen it all here. I've been disappointed at slow progress. I miss kids when I feel I've gotten somewhere with them and then the parents move them away in the middle of the night to stay a step ahead of their creditors."

"Is this job dangerous?"

"Yeah, but I don't want to talk about that either. I live in the neighborhood. I'm known. I use lots of locks on the door. I don't own a car. I don't go out alone at night. If I was jumped or my place invaded, I'd give whoever it was anything they wanted. I survive. I've got friends."

"Do you arm yourself?"

"No, but I'll bet *you* do."

"I do," Jennifer admitted.

"Right again."

"Are you bitter, cynical?"

"Some. Hard not to be here. Aren't you, after spending a little time here?"

"Yes. You know, Angela, I asked you what I wanted to ask you, but I feel like I haven't found out anything. You're not the typical visionary, but something must make you tick, keep you here, motivate you—sorry."

"It's all right. I knew you'd get back to it. I love the kids. I don't know why. I honestly don't know why I love the kids. There was nothing in my background that pointed me this way. I was an only child. I studied literature at Alfred University. I had no degree in this kind of work, no training. I just applied. Not much competition, I can tell you that. We done with me?"

"I guess, but you fascinate me."

"That embarrasses me."

"I wouldn't have guessed that anything embarrasses you."

"I cover well. You've already gotten more out of me than anyone else ever did, and you promised not to use it. So let's quit wasting your time and talk about Heather Lauren."

"I don't consider it a waste of my time, but I don't want to waste yours."

"Talking about me wastes my time, but I'm not angry. I'm flattered. But I've also done enough of it."

It hadn't been said unkindly, but Jennifer got the message. "Why did you agree to talk with me about Heather?"

"Because Wyatt Oliver murdered her, and I'd like to see him fry for it."

"You *know* he did it?"

"I'd lay odds."

"Why?"

"The man is no good. I'm supposed to be used to his kind of people, but not everybody who has the misfortune to live around here is Wyatt Oliver's kind of person. His wife, for instance. She's limited."

"Limited?" Jennifer asked, taking Angela by the arm and leading her around a corner of the boarded up building to get out of the direct wind.

"Psychologically. She makes me mad, but I can sympathize with her."

"I'm sorry, I'm not following you."

"The woman is scared to death of Oliver. She needs him, she thinks, but she brings in more money than he does, which isn't much. He terrorizes her and the children, and she won't lift a finger. The cops have been over a time or two. But when the woman won't press charges, they lose interest in responding to the neighbors' calls when they've finally had enough of the screaming. You wonder where the other tenants were when that precious child was murdered in the basement?"

Jennifer nodded, but Angela's voice had broken and her chin quivered, and she couldn't speak. Jennifer tried to give her time to recover. "Yes, that's exactly what I thought when I was in the basement and saw where it had happened. It's an old rickety building, and the sound would carry. No one heard anything?"

"Have you asked them?" Angela managed. "That's part of your job, isn't it?"

"I will be asking, if I dare go back there."

Angela crossed her arms and raised her chin, closing her eyes, then opening them and lowering her gaze to Jennifer's. "I want to tell you that I'm used to the kinds of things that go on around here. I know the frustration, the sense of emptiness, the futility. I know why women stay with men they shouldn't and why teenagers do dope and pull robberies and why men come home drunk every night and can't keep jobs. I know why families scream at each other and fight and throw things."

She was becoming emotional again, but this time Jennifer just let her regain her composure in her own time. Angela turned sideways to Jennifer and leaned a shoulder against the building.

"I understand why the cops have to cruise the area and why they have to keep people from killing each other. But there's something I don't understand. I don't understand a woman, the real parent to her children, letting anyone lay a hand on them. Isolated instances, okay. Fits of rage, forgivable once in a great while. And I know a drunken bum, many times stronger than a woman, can intimidate her to the point where she feels powerless to help herself. But if he beat the kids one night, wouldn't you be hitting the bricks the next day, first chance you got?"

Jennifer nodded; she was moved. Angela fell silent, and Jennifer didn't know where to go from there. She had a feeling Angela wasn't finished, and she knew she'd have to ask again if Angela had any hard evidence against Wyatt Oliver.

In an uncharacteristic loss of concentration, Jennifer suddenly found herself wishing she didn't have to wait until Friday night to see Jim. She missed him. She wanted to talk with him about the column possibility. But they had limited themselves to Wednesdays and weekends.

She scolded herself for even thinking about that now. Angela was staring into the distance. *Interesting woman,* Jennifer decided. *She gets emotional, but she doesn't lose control. She doesn't break down.*

"Elliott came to the preschool program first," Angela said suddenly. "They had moved in from the South somewhere, and he was supposed to be in kindergarten. I didn't ask any questions. He was a good kid, quiet, but often short of energy and hungry.

"We give the kids milk, and once a week we get day-old pastries from one of the local bakeries. All the kids love 'em, of course, but Elliott inhaled 'em. I mean, he'd eat five or six. Every time I turned around, he'd sneak another. At first I was afraid he'd get sick, but then I feared it was all he was getting to eat."

"Not a very good diet," Jennifer said.

"Better than nothing. So I started smuggling him fruit. Terribly small, thin child, but when he got some food in him, he loved to run."

"He ran past me this morning."

"Yeah? The old man is feeding him good since Heather's been gone. Keeping him quiet is my guess."

"What makes you so sure about Oliver?"

"I've visited that place more than once. It's a hole, but I'm used to that. What I didn't like was that Wyatt Oliver didn't care that I was there; he treated his woman and her children the same as always. They waited on him hand and foot. They brought him beer and snacks, and he sat in front of a little color TV that must have cost him a month's unemployment money."

"He says he's still paying for it."

"I'll bet he *is*. Probably stole it. Anyway, I suggested that Heather was old enough to come to the program and also that it would be a good idea to be sure they had a good lunch on preschool days because we had so much activity. Mrs. Lauren appeared to understand, but Oliver was incensed. 'You just make 'em behave there, and we'll make 'em behave here.'

"I didn't know what that had to do with a good lunch, so I told him I'd never had a bit of trouble with Elliott and that I assumed I wouldn't with Heather either. He told me to just let him know if I did and I'd never have any more trouble."

"Scary."

"I should say. Scared me. I wanted to adopt both kids right then and there. Both so cute. Heather started coming to the Monday-Wednesday-Friday group after that. I couldn't get her to say a word to anyone, not even 'Hi'. But she always came. Would sometimes laugh at the stories, always participated in games. But my first clue of what was happening in that home was when we had an outing at the Y."

"A swimming party?"

"Right. A lot of the kids didn't even have suits, so they were provided by the Y. It was a bring-your-lunch and spend the day type of a thing. The Lauren kids didn't bring suits and wouldn't accept suits, either. That was the first time I heard Heather talk.

"I sat them down and told them how much fun they'd be missing, and I asked Elliott to tell me why they didn't want to swim. He looked past me as if he hadn't heard. I asked him again. He ignored me.

"I asked him again, and Heather piped up. 'We got ouchies,' she said, and Elliott leaped to his feet and screamed at her, 'Don't tell! Don't tell! Don't tell! Don't tell!'"

SIX

By the time Jennifer left Angela Liachi a couple of hours later, she had heard the full story of Angela's encounters with Wyatt Oliver.

After that day at the Y, when Angela had been forced to let Elliott and Heather just sit and watch the others, because—she assumed—they had sores on their bodies where people couldn't see them, she called the Department of Social Services.

"I talked to the woman there I deal with a lot. Nathalie Benedict. She set up a bogus physical exam for my group one Friday, sort of swooped in, pulled each kid behind a screen, and had a doctor check their pulses, look down their throats, and put a stethoscope to their bare chests.

"The idea was that the doctor would be so quick and intimidating that he could just whip through the exam and at the end tug their shirts up for a quick listen. By then, Elliott wasn't coming anymore. He'd started kindergarten.

"Little Heather, who hadn't spoken to me before or after the incident at the Y, kept looking at me fearfully as she stood in line, waiting for her turn with the doctor. Her huge, sad eyes begged me to rescue her, but I alternately ignored her or smiled at her to boost her courage.

"The woman from Social Services knew which one they were really after, and she played it just right. She just ushered Heather in and spoke softly and encouragingly to her, and when the time came to lift her little shirt, Heather flinched, but let the doctor do it.

"Heather came out teary and scowled at me, as if I should have protected her from that indecency, but I didn't know if they'd found anything or what."

"Did she make you feel guilty?"

"Hardly. The whole scheme was for her benefit. She couldn't know that, but I did it for her, and I wasn't about to feel bad about it. I was sorry she had to be embarrassed, but better embarrassed than killed in her own home."

"Did they find anything?"

Angela had started walking back toward the center. "I knew when it was all over and they were putting their equipment away. The kids, for the most part, had loved it. No shots. Quick and painless. They'd been tickled. They asked questions. The doctor stayed and answered a few, but it was obvious to me that both the doctor and Nathalie were upset; it showed all over their faces. They were grim. Boiling. They waited in the parking lot until the class was over and the kids started home."

"What had they found?"

Angela stopped and faced Jennifer. "Sores. Burns. Burn scars." She bit her lip and looked down. "I was angry, so mad I was going to run after Heather and keep her from going home. Nathalie had to calm me down. She said I could cause more trouble by doing that right then. She said there was no way to immediately pull a child from her home and that if we tried, the parents would get her back and punish her worse for telling on them.

"I didn't care. I wanted to grab the kid and hide her somewhere. You had to have seen this girl, Jennifer, to know what I mean. So quiet, so sweet, so giving and loving and lovable. Short cropped blonde hair, skinny little arms and legs. Never wore dresses or skirts. Always jeans. Probably owned one pair."

Jennifer put her hand on Angela's shoulder. "You through talking for today?"

Angela shook her head. "I want to finish this. I pushed Social Services to file a report and press charges, and I know they did, but it took so long that I took matters into my own hands."

"Meaning?"

"I visited Heather's home again. When Elliott saw me, he headed for the hills."

"Elliott?"

"Yup. He knew that whatever had started that day at the Y was coming to a head, and he didn't want to get punished for letting the cat out of the bag."

"What did you do, Angela—just confront Oliver?"

"No, I wasn't dumb enough to do that. Might as well have though; I didn't fool him. I said I wanted to talk about Heather's progress. He ignored me and just sat there watching his TV. Cornelia sat with me, looking fearful, as if she wanted me to finish and get going.

"I talked about general things, motor skills, Heather's shyness, that type of stuff. Then I said that it was apparent she'd been hurt somehow and that it hampered her during playtime. I just threw it out there without comment, hoping that her mother would at least try to explain it, even with a lie."

"She didn't?"

"She shot a terrified glance at Oliver and fell silent. I mean silent. She hardly moved. I said, 'Well, is she recovering from whatever happened, or would you like me to arrange for treatment? It'll be free.' With that, Oliver wrenched around in his chair and swore at me.

"He said, 'We can take care of our own here, and we don't need any charity. Just let the kid be. She's all right. Just quit babying her.'"

"He was admitting she'd been hurt," Jennifer said.

"I thought so, and it made me mad. Maybe he could see through my offer and caught the veiled threat that if something didn't stop in that household, I was going to city authorities. I knew I was about to say something I'd regret, so I forced myself to put it in the form of a question rather than an accusation.

"I said, 'What happened to her anyway, Mr. Oliver? She looks as if she's had some sort of an accident that burned her.' He stood quickly and kicked the TV switch off, sending the stand rocking and almost tipping the whole set over. I was frozen in my chair.

"He swore again and said, 'How do you know what kinda sores she's got on her body? I never seen any sores on her.' Now I was livid. I said, 'Why don't you ask her mother or call her in here and see for yourself?' It was the first time I sensed any vulnerability in the man. He said, 'She fell down the stairs about a month ago and she burned herself on the hot plate about a week later.'"

"Did you believe him?"

"Would you have? Being burned on a hot plate is a mighty unusual injury, other than on a finger. Anyway, the Social Services doctor put in his report that many of the burns appeared to have been caused by cigarettes. I stood and moved toward the door. I thanked him for his time and left him with a not-so-veiled threat.

"I said, 'I'd hate to have to report to Social Services that this is an unsafe home for a little girl.'"

"He let you get away with saying that?"

"Not entirely. He said, 'You're gonna find out that this ain't a safe place for you.' And he started toward me. His wife cried out, and as I ran down the stairs I heard him laughing. By the time I reached the door on the first floor, he was screaming at her."

"I'm surprised he let Heather come to preschool after that," Jennifer said, "now that the cat was out of the bag. These guys usually protect themselves."

"She didn't come again for more than a month. I panicked. I asked her friends if she was still around, and they assured me she was. I walked through the neighborhood several times, and occasionally I'd see her, but when she saw me, she'd run away. Finally I talked to Elliott."

"Really? You hadn't talked to him for quite a while by then."

"Right, but I ran into him at the park and asked him how he liked school. We probably talked more for those few minutes than we had all the time he'd been in preschool. It was so sweet. I asked him if there was anyone at school who sneaked him doughnuts and rolls, and he smiled so shyly and with such obvious gratefulness at the memory that it made my whole career here worthwhile."

Angela invited Jennifer into the building and into her tiny, cluttered office where she poured two cups of black coffee. "I have to admit," Jennifer said, "even after all you've told me, I don't feel like I know those two kids."

"That's just it," Angela said. "I never felt that way either. When kids don't express themselves, you tend to assume characteristics based on how they look, how cute they are, how shy they are. I'm sure I've got both Elliott and Heather idealized in my mind. To me, they were both precious children. Victimized. They had that look like you had, that look Oliver gives people."

"That look?"

"Like they've just seen the devil himself."

"He left you with that look twice, didn't he, Angela?"

"Three times."

"Three?"

"I saw him once more. This is the good part. I threatened him."

"Whoa, back up a little!"

"Well, Heather started coming to preschool again; and she appeared healthy. There were no signs of any injuries. She was running and playing and talking with the other kids. Things were fine for probably six months."

"That long?"

"I'm not saying she wasn't still being abused. I'm sure she was. But the man was being careful. I mean, he'd always been careful enough to keep from hurting her where it would show. But I noticed no tentativeness, no physical tenderness, and she finally even started talking to me."

"Really?"

"Nothing big. Just greetings and questions. Very shyly, very quietly. I tried desperately to build a relationship with her so she would tell me the next time she got hurt. That was a pipe dream, but I tried."

"And did she?"

"Tell me, you mean? No. I found out about the next incident through Nathalie at Social Services. They got a call from the emergency room at St. Anthony's. The mother had brought Heather in during the middle of the night with an unbelievable injury."

Angela stopped talking. Jennifer waited. Angela straightened papers on her desk and stacked some books on the shelf. When she finally spoke again, her voice was thick. "Jennifer," she said, "if you want a crusade, a campaign, an issue, it's the red tape in this city! We're choking on it!"

Jennifer didn't understand, but she wasn't about to interrupt Angela now that her anger was boiling over. She had apparently been so crushed by the death of Heather Lauren that she had been unable to fully express it. If it was coming out this way, that was fine. It would be good for her.

"It's not Social Services' fault. They have no more power than the Park District does. All they can do is file reports and make recommendations. I think they should have recommended Heather and Elliott's removal from that home after the first physical exam, but they advised observation instead.

"But when they got the report from St. Anthony's, they moved quickly. As far as I know, the paperwork is still floating through city hall somewhere."

"Can you tell me about the injury?"

"The girl was nearly dead, Jennifer! They had to perform artificial resuscitation on her twice in the emergency room!"

"What had happened to her?"

"She was in shock. She could have died from the shock. Shock is probably what really killed her a few days ago."

"The autopsy will show that. But why was she in shock that first time?"

"Lots of bruises and burns, but a horrible injury to her seat." Again Angela was too upset to talk, but Jennifer wanted to hear it all.

"To her seat?"

"Oh, Jennifer," Angela whispered, "Nathalie showed me a picture that I can't erase from my mind." And she cried.

"I saw one of those recently too."

"You saw that picture?"

"I saw the one taken by the police in the cellar where she was found."

"I don't want to see that one. The emergency room photo was all I ever care to see."

"Can you tell me about it?"

Angela walked to the window and stared out across the parking lot. The sun was now hidden, and the day had turned gray. "The skin was burned black, and the only thing recognizable was the brand name of the hot plate, which had been seared into her in reverse. Someone had sat her on that hot plate!"

"What was the mother's story?"

"She just wanted them to hurry, because she said her husband, whom she listed as Wyatt Lauren, had forbidden her to bring the girl in, but he was sleeping and she needed to get treatment and hurry back. The hospital wanted to admit Heather, but her mother refused. That's when they called the police."

"The police were involved in this before? I didn't even know that."

"You didn't know that the West Side homicide sergeant wanted the kids out of there but couldn't get the clearance?"

"No, but I'll be asking him about that today. What did Mrs. Lauren tell the police?"

"Her story was that Heather had sleepwalked, fallen down the stairs, landed on the hot plate, and passed out from the pain or from hitting her head or something. They asked why her husband had not wanted her brought in for treatment, and she said he didn't have money or insurance and thought they could take care of her themselves."

"And the police believed her?"

"No. In fact, Wyatt Oliver was held overnight for questioning."

"I wonder why none of the media are aware of that," Jennifer said. "You're sure of this?"

"That's what Social Services told me when I screamed at them about getting the kids out of that house. They said they'd done everything they could think of. *I* could think of something else."

"Such as."

"If you can't separate the children from the parents, you have to separate the parents from the children."

"How do you do that?"

"When Wyatt Oliver was released and I realized the full import of what was going on—"

"Meaning?"

"Meaning that the man had apparently almost killed the girl and was now back in the same home situation. I stewed for a day, then walked through the neighborhood. Heather was outside, watching the other kids play. Elliott was very attentive to her, checking with her every few minutes.

"She was pale, cold, stiff. When she walked, she hardly bent her knees. It was pitiful. I stormed to her apartment building and charged up the stairs. I surprised the life out of Wyatt Oliver.

"I banged on the door so loudly that they didn't want to answer. I said, 'I know you're in there, you lazy bum. Answer the door!' His wife opened the door, and he stood behind her with a small stick in his hand.

"'You gonna use that on me?' I asked him, 'or do you only beat up little girls?' His wife hid her face in her hands and started to move away, and he acted like he was going to come at me. I wish he had. I'd have killed him."

"Do you really think you would have?"

"I know I would have. He's a strong guy, but I was so pumped up I could have torn him in two with my bare hands. He saw it in my eyes, Jennifer, because he was scared to come closer. I said, 'Come here, you slime,' and he tried to slam the door on me. I put my foot in it and took a good bruise to the ankle, but not before I promised to make him pay with his life."

"You really did?"

"You bet. I said, 'If one more thing happens to those kids, Oliver, I'll kill you.'"

SEVEN

"I'm glad, for your sake, that you didn't fulfill your promise, Angela."

"There's still time."

"Don't say that."

"I read your column, Jennifer. Don't tell me you and a lot of other people wouldn't love to do it for me."

"I wouldn't."

"Then your column was a lie?"

"I didn't say in my column that *I* wanted to mete justice out to the murderer."

"Oh, I see. You want him to die for the crime, but you wouldn't want *your* pretty hands soiled in the process."

"Angela, you're upset. You know what I mean, and I know what you mean. And I have to believe that you don't seriously intend to do harm to a person you can't even be sure is guilty."

"I'm sure. Are you saying you're not?"

"How could I know?"

"You know. Don't you know? You had an encounter with the murderer today, didn't you?"

"How could I know he was the murderer, Angela?"

"Will you get off this Pollyanna kick? You look into your heart of hearts and tell me you've got one shred of doubt whether that scoundrel murdered his own daughter."

Jennifer couldn't speak.

"One shred," Angela challenged again.

Jennifer stared at her.

"All right," Angela said, "so get off your high horse."

"But Angela, you're a mature adult. You know you can't throw your life and career away by actually killing a man."

"I know what you're saying, Jennifer, but I'm so tired of the bureaucracy, the stalling, the jive. Who needs this? Society lets this man get away with everything short of murder, and now it appears he's going to get away with *that!*"

"He won't get away with it."

"Not if I have anything to do with it, he won't."

"What would you do, Angela, if he really did slip through somehow? If through further investigation, they couldn't find enough evidence to convict him?"

Angela Liachi sat heavily across from Jennifer and looked deep into her eyes. "If it happened today?" she said. "If I learned it today and I saw him today and I had the opportunity, I fear I would kill the man. And I mean that."

"Do you want me to protect you from yourself?" Jennifer offered.

"What do you mean?"

"You want to take a few days off and cool down, come and stay with me for awhile? You sound serious."

"I *am* serious. You think I'd like that, don't you? You think I'd welcome the chance to get out of this rat hole, start thinking like a rational human being, and enjoy the comforts of your Uptown place."

"It isn't that."

"It isn't? Then what is it? You want me for column material? You promised not to write about my motivation for working here, but you didn't promise you wouldn't write about my motivation for murder. Am I gonna read about this in the paper tomorrow morning?"

"Of course not."

Apparently Angela believed her, because she finally broke down and sobbed. "I appreciate you," she admitted through her tears. "And I'm sorry I said that. I've known you only a little while, but I can tell you wouldn't use me."

"And the little I've known *you*," Jennifer said, "tells me you really don't want to end your career by committing a murder."

Angela's shoulders heaved. She shook her head. "I don't really," she said. "I'm like you; I want someone else to do it. It scares me though. I really think I'd do it if I saw the man today."

Jennifer stood and poured more coffee. Angela appeared surprised that Jennifer would feel free to do that. She thanked her and asked, "Want something on-the-record that even the cops don't know yet?"

Jennifer was almost too shocked to respond. "Are you serious?"

"Sure. Get out your pad. You remember Mrs. Lauren told the cops that Heather didn't come home from preschool? And that she didn't report her missing or tell anyone else outside the family until she found her in the basement two days later? Well, Heather hadn't been to preschool for weeks, and she definitely wasn't there Monday."

"I don't get it."

"Neither do I."

"The police didn't come asking?"

"No, and they should have, shouldn't they?"

"Of course."

"I'd been asking around about Heather. The kids said she was still in the neighborhood but that she couldn't come to preschool. I thought maybe she was being abused again, and I walked through the neighborhood a few times, but I always missed her. Either that or she avoided me."

"Likely?"

"Under threat of her father, if you can call him that? Sure."

"So you really hadn't seen her for a long time?"

"Not since right after she'd been treated for the hot plate burns."

"Why didn't you come forward when you saw the misinformation in the paper?"

"I just did," Angela said.

"And I can quote you on this?"

"That's what I said."

"Thanks for everything, Angela. And do me a favor, will you? Don't do anything rash, regardless of what happens with Wyatt Oliver."

Angela forced a smile, but said nothing.

Not a half hour later, Jennifer was waiting to see Nathalie Benedict at the West Side Social Services Center. The receptionist kept relaying questions from the inner office. "You won't need much time? You'll accept no-comment reactions when Mrs. Benedict feels they're necessary? She can be off-the-record when she requests it?"

Jennifer agreed to everything. Finally, she was ushered in. Nathalie Benedict was a tall, pleasant, healthy-looking, almost handsome woman—classy but past her prime. In her mid-fifties, she still carried the evidence of an early season tan, aided by heavy make-up, coiffed hair, lots of jewelry, and expensive clothes. Her nails were long and painted lavender to go with her layered outfit.

"You're covering the Lauren case?" she asked.

"Yes, ma'am, thank you for seeing me. I wonder if you can tell me about the time you had Heather Lauren examined by a Social Services doctor."

Mrs. Benedict grew cold and stared at her. "When I what?"

"When you took a doctor into the West Side Park District preschool at the request of the teacher and staged a bogus class physical so the doctor could get a look at what Heather Lauren had told the teacher were 'ouchies.'"

Mrs. Benedict lit a cigarette and squinted as she took a deep drag and, instead of blowing the smoke away, merely opened her mouth and let it curl up in a thick column. "I have no comment about that," she said evenly.

"Are you saying it didn't happen?"

"I'm saying I prefer not to comment about it."

"Did you yourself see the injuries on Heather Lauren's body?"

"No," she said, and quickly realizing the implication of that, added, "comment."

"No? Or no comment?"

"No comment."

"Can you tell me about the injury to Heather Lauren that your office was made aware of several weeks ago when she was taken to St. Anthony's emergency room in the middle of the night with third-degree burns to the buttocks?"

"We were made aware of that, yes."

"And did you make a recommendation based on that?"

"Our recommendations to the police and other agencies are matters of public record."

"Then you won't mind telling me what that was?"

"Our recommendations? I don't remember. You may feel free to look it up at city hall."

"Did you not recommend that both Heather Lauren and her older brother, Elliott, be removed from their home?"

"I don't recall."

"Does it not sound logical?"

"Without studying the documents, I couldn't comment—"

"Are you saying there's a possibility that you *didn't* recommend that a child be removed from a home where such injuries had been inflicted?"

Mrs. Benedict had not appreciated being interrupted, and while it was not Jennifer's usual style, she sensed there wasn't a lot of time on this case. Wyatt Oliver either had to be indicted or exonerated, and she was beginning to share Angela Liachi's frustration over the red tape.

"I will talk with you off-the-record," Mrs. Benedict said suddenly, surprising Jennifer. "Do I have your word?"

"Yes, ma'am." But Nathalie didn't start talking until Jennifer returned her notebook to her purse.

"I know you have been talking to Miss Liachi, because you couldn't have known of the physicals otherwise. And I want you to know I share her anger and misery over this death. But I also want to make clear that I need my job, I want my job, and I have never made a practice of bad-mouthing my agency or the police or the courts."

"I understand. Is there something you would tell me off-the-record about them, however?"

"I must have your word."

"Absolutely confidential."

"My prediction is that this Oliver will never come to trial. They so seldom do. It was obvious from the way Cornelia Lauren acted that night in the emergency room that he had abused the child and also that the whole family was terrified of him. She would not budge from the crazy sleepwalking story, and she has never pressed charges against the man for any reason.

"Strange as it may seem, as many times as our agency has been in that home and been aware of the abuse, and as many times as Angela Liachi has taken it upon herself to do our work—and I don't blame her for a little zeal—the man has never been charged with one crime similar to what was committed this week."

"Nothing? No public disturbance, family quarrel, anything?"

"The only thing on his record, and the police will bear this out, is some public drunkenness. We have recommendations in, yes. I would like to see the kids, well, the boy now, removed from that environment. But someone had better get something on that quote/unquote father, or Elliott will grow up right where he is. If Oliver doesn't kill him, too."

"You know these people, don't you? I mean, you know their names as if you're familiar with the case."

Mrs. Benedict nodded. "All I can give you on-the-record is that we are aware of the case, we hope the guilty party will be found, and that our previous recommendations regarding the disposition of the family are on public record."

"That's it?"

"That's it. I wish I could be of more help."

"Off-the-record again, then. What are the answers for cases like this? What can anyone do to speed things along, to get action, to protect children from such an environment?"

"Besides killing the abusive parent you mean? I wish I knew."

"I wish you hadn't said that."

"You *have* been talking with my friend, Angela, haven't you?"

"Uh-huh."

"Don't worry about her. She blows off a lot of steam, and she's usually right on the money. But she's not going to do anything more to Wyatt Oliver than yell and scream at him like she did once."

"She's not serious about wanting to kill him?"

"Oh, she's serious enough. I just don't think she would or could if she wanted to. Anyway," she concluded with a weary sigh, "if she really wants to, she'd better take a number and get in line."

EIGHT

Jennifer had a few hard questions for Sergeant Martin Grom at the West Side Precinct station. But he wasn't there when she arrived. That surprised her. He knew she was coming.

As she waited in the lobby and idly read the plaques and citations and Police Youth League trophies, she smiled at the memory of her first encounter with the man the officers call The Lug.

Grom was a big redhead, about six feet three inches and broad in a soft sort of way that wasn't flabby, but was miles from being in shape. He walked with his elbows away from his body, swinging his arms like a robot. People tended to stay out of his way.

He was gruff and blunt, but he waxed fatherly in the presence of the opposite sex. Jennifer's Jim had always gotten a kick out of Martin, and he seemed to have a decent reputation in the department. He often brought his kids in on his days off. Couldn't stay away, but had to babysit. He had a bunch of 'em, but all were boys except his five-year-old.

"Your daughter's name again?" Jennifer asked when The Lug finally arrived and waved her into his cubicle.

"Jackie," he said, not beaming as usual. "We call her Red."

"Everyone in your family have a nickname?"

"No, she's the only one."

Jennifer smiled, assuming no one called Grom The Lug to his face. "I don't think I've ever seen you in uniform before, Martin. You still in homicide?"

"Oh, yeah. I wear it now and then. Special occasions and so forth."

"This is a special occasion?"

"Nah." But he didn't appear eager to elaborate.

"Martin, can I ask you some questions?"

"I figured that's why you were here, Hon," he said. "Fire away, but let's make it fast."

That wasn't like him either. She studied him for a moment, but he wouldn't return her gaze. "Why didn't you tell me Heather Lauren had been burned before?"

"What're you talking about?"

"I'm talking about St. Anthony's, the middle of the night, third-degree burns with a hot plate, holding Oliver for questioning."

"Ah, that *was* Oliver, wasn't it?"

"Oh, I get it. You didn't remember till just now."

"That's right."

"That's ridiculous. A man of your ability, your concentration, your attention to detail?"

"So what? What do you want from me, Jenn? OK, we tried to book the guy the first time around—"

"But that *wasn't* the first time around, Martin. Social Services wanted you to look into the family when they discovered injuries on the girl's body in a physical exam."

"Oh, yeah? You're onto everything, huh? Well, did whoever tell you that also tell you what kinda heat Social Services got for that little sham or how the fur would have flown if we'd used that little bit of information on this Oliver creep?"

"What are you saying?"

"You tell me, Brenda Starr, you know so much."

"Martin, don't be mean with me."

"I'm sorry, Jenn, but this girl has been dead probably since Monday, discovered only yesterday, and already I'm getting pressure to arrest somebody."

"Pressure from whom?"

"What'dya mean from whom? From downtown, from the papers, from everybody. From you."

"Did I say anything like that?"

"Come on, Jennifer! You sit here all but askin' me why I don't have Wyatt Oliver in the slam. You think I don't get your drift?"

"I wasn't driving at that, Martin."

"Then what *were* you driving at?"

"I just want to know why there has been so much activity on the man, admittedly with no convictions, but without the press knowing anything about it?"

"We don't have to tell you anything you don't ask."

"But you have in the past, and I've appreciated it."

"I haven't given you much."

"That's the most accurate thing you've said so far." He looked pained, but she plunged ahead. "Tell me what kind of trouble Social Services would have been in if you'd used the evidence they turned up in the class physicals."

Grom stood and rested an elbow on a bookshelf next to his desk. He sighed. "Awright, you can't give physicals without parental consent. All we needed to do was use that information and it would have come out that they'd pulled a bogus deal. Other parents with kids in that class would've demanded to know if their children had been examined in that scheme, and then the whole city would have come down on our heads. The evidence would have been inadmissible."

"So you had to forget it, even when she turned up terribly burned at St. Anthony's several months later?"

"We put a lot of heat on the man, Jennifer. Hank Henry and I handled the interrogation, and I'd like to think we had the guy on the ropes. But the woman wouldn't point the finger at him. The little girl wasn't talking. The neighbors heard only screaming and crying and an argument about taking her to the hospital. Oliver didn't give Cornelia Lauren permission to take Heather to the hospital, so she had to wait until she could get him dead drunk, and she almost waited too long."

"That's not enough to focus on him?"

"It's nothing! The woman was there! Without her testimony, for all we know the kid *could* have fallen down the stairs onto the hot plate!"

"Martin! What would the hot plate be doing at the bottom of the stairs? And how could have she have landed on it in a perfect sitting position and stay there until she'd suffered third-degree burns and branded herself? And why would the hot plate be turned on in the middle of the night?"

"OK, Jennifer, the man is guilty, all right? I know it. You know it. Social Services knows it. Cornelia Lauren knows it. Heaven knows Heather knows it. And you can bet Elliott knows it too."

"Then why can't anything be done? I don't understand it."

"It's the system, Jenn."

"The system! Martin, this sounds like a B movie! Everyone's powerless to fight the system?"

"I tried! I offered to take those kids into my own home! You've got to have a smoking pistol, or the next best thing, in court. I go in there with circumstances and shouting in the night, and I'll come out with an acquittal. That's worse than no indictment in the first place. I'm trying to get the District Attorney to indict now, but we can't use Wyatt Oliver's history."

"Why not?"

"Because according to the law, if he wasn't convicted, it never happened."

"Let me change subjects here for a minute, Martin. How do you know Heather Lauren didn't return from preschool Monday?"

"You got our official statement. It came right off Mrs. Lauren's written statement."

"May I see that?"

"The written statement?"

"Yes."

"You promise not to quote directly from it?"

"Of course."

Sergeant Grom dug it out from a pile in the middle of his desk, leafed through it, and produced a photocopy of a thick, handwritten sheaf. Jennifer scanned it quickly until she came to the following:

> I send Heather of to scool at 12.30. She dont com home at 2.30 lik everday. I wate and wate and send Elliott to lok.

"Did you check this out?" Jennifer asked.

"I assume someone corroborated it."

"Who?"

"I don't know. We have a lot of people on this, Jenn."

"Has anyone talked to her preschool classmates?"

"What do three- and four-year-olds know that can help us?"

"That she wasn't at school that day."

Grom stared at her, unblinking. "She never made it to school?"

"Did you talk with the preschool teacher?"

"I assume someone did."

"You're assuming too much, Martin. I talked with her, and no one from the police department has asked her anything."

"And she's saying the kid didn't make it to preschool that day?"

"She's saying Heather hadn't been coming for weeks. She didn't expect her that day."

"What's this woman's name?"

"Angela Liachi."

"I'll check it out. Liachi, you say?"

"Liachi."

"We've got something on her."

"Meaning what?"

"We got a complaint about her."

"From whom?"

"Are you ready for this? From Wyatt Oliver."

"You're serious?"

"Yeah. Just a minute. Hank!"

"Yeah!"

"Bring me that complaint Wyatt Oliver filed on the Liachi woman, will ya?"

Jennifer could hear grumbling from over the partitions as a pudgy, grimy detective brought in a manila folder. "In uniform today, huh Sarge?" he said.

Grom grunted and thanked him. He shuffled back out.

"Here it is," Grom said, sitting again and picking his way through the carbon paper. "Threatened my life," he read, "said she would kill me if she saw another bruise on one of my kids. I don't have to take that from anyone, blah, blah, blah."

"So what'd you do with it?"

"Sent somebody over to tell her that a threat on someone's life was illegal and that she could be charged with assault, not to mention battery, manslaughter, and/or murder if she ever followed through with her threats."

"She deny making them?"

"No. Told us if we wouldn't do our job relating to Wyatt Oliver, she would. We don't make a big deal of this type of a thing. We try to get the parties to talk and resolve their differences. In this case, it was apparent that that would not be the best approach, so we just let it drop."

"Is that why you never asked her to corroborate the mother's story? You were afraid she would do something drastic?"

Martin studied her. "You have a lot of insight," he said.

"And you guys are pretty naive. You think she wouldn't find out about the murder unless you told her?"

He was taken aback. "Are you turning on me, Jenn?"

"I'm not turning on you, Martin. But I'm saying you've got more than enough to lock up Wyatt Oliver."

"You gonna say that in the paper?"

"I don't know. Probably."

"That's gonna make us look bad, Jennifer."

"You *do* look bad, Martin."

"I've got to ask you not to do it."

"I can make no promises."

"It'll be the end of our friendship, Jennifer. It'll be the end of any information you get outta me."

"Do you think I care about any of that, Sergeant? I want to be objective. I want to play this straight. I don't want to be a crusader, and it's not my place to tell you what to do or how to do it. But I have to tell you, you've got a woman and a child living with a murderer who should have been locked up months ago. I don't know how you can sleep at night, Martin. I should think you'd have Heather Lauren's blood on your hands."

He stood quickly and glared down at her, and she knew she'd been too harsh. *Who do you think you are?* she asked herself. *One day with a column assignment and you start accusing cops of killing kids!* She raised both hands to him. "I went too far, Martin. I'm sorry—"

But he wasn't listening. His intercom had buzzed, and he pushed the lever to answer. "What is it?" he bellowed.

"A death, possible homicide, forty-three twenty-six West Stivers."

Jennifer gasped and stood as Grom came charging around the desk, pulling his dress blue coat off the hook. She found herself in his way, but only temporarily. He clubbed her just below the neck with the back of his hand on his way out and knocked her back into her chair without even looking at her.

Her elbow had banged the arm of the chair and throbbed. She caught her breath and jumped up to follow Grom, but as she neared the front door, he was already climbing into an idling squad car. She sprinted the half block to her car and gave chase, but she lost him and had to rely on her memory to get to the Oliver-Lauren residence.

She screeched to a stop a block away and found the 4300 block cordoned off by squad cars, paddy wagons, an ambulance, and several unmarked squad cars.

People were streaming from the surrounding buildings to as close to the scene as they could get. Jennifer joined them, wondering who Oliver had killed this time. As she neared the roped off area, she saw Elliott Lauren in the backseat of a squad car with a woman she assumed was Cornelia Lauren.

She detoured and asked the woman to roll down the window. "Are you Cornelia Lauren?" she asked the ashen face.

The woman nodded, but the officer at the wheel lurched around and shouted, "Hey! Get away! Roll up that window!"

"I'm with the press," Jennifer said.

"Get away!"

At least *they* were safe. She moved to the edge of the rope and started to crawl under. "You can't come in here, lady," a cop told her.

"I'm Press," she said.

"I don't care if you're the Queen of England," he said. "Nobody but police are allowed in here right now."

"What happened, Officer?"

"Somebody got snuffed, that's all I know."

"Did Wyatt Oliver do it?"

"I didn't hear any names. Clear the way!"

Evidence technicians were jogging up the walk, with cameras and black boxes at their sides. Jennifer knew that as soon as they had marked the spot where the body had been found, they'd release it, and the medics would carry it out.

"You really don't know if the perp has been apprehended or who was murdered?"

The cop shook his head and ignored her.

In a few minutes, plainclothes detectives escorted a middle-aged black man from the apartment building. He was not handcuffed, so apparently he would simply be questioned. He stared at Jennifer as they approached, and as they passed, he shouted:

"That's her! That's her! That's the chick I saw in the house the last time I saw Oliver alive!"

NINE

A detective with the black man told the uniformed policeman, " Don't let her out of your sight," and kept moving.

"Hey, Officer, uh—"

"Officer Huber, ma'am, please stay right here with me."

"Officer Huber, you don't have to worry about me. I'm Jennifer Grey with the *Chicago Day.* I was here earlier, yes, but on assignment. I saw Oliver, but—"

"So, who's Oliver? The dead man?"

"I assume, yes, but—"

"I know nothing about the case, lady. I just can't let you outta my sight."

"Well, listen, when people come out of that house, I may be moving up and down the line here asking them questions. Can I do that?"

He looked worried.

"I'll keep waving at you to let you know I'm still here," she said. "Fair enough?"

"I don't know."

"Here, take my wallet, better yet, take my car keys. I can't get far without these."

"Lady, I don't want any of your stuff. You just stay right here, 'cause I'm gonna hafta answer for you."

Martin Grom emerged from the building, leading another couple of cops and the paramedics, who wheeled a litter containing a covered body. The crowd edged forward. Jennifer felt strange, being the only media person on the scene. They'd be here soon enough, she decided.

"Who's the dead man, Sergeant?" she called.

"You know who he is, Jennifer," Grom growled.

"See, Officer Huber, I know the sergeant."

He just stared at her.

"Martin," she called, grabbing his arm and slowing him, "will you tell this guy I can be trusted?"

Grom was disgusted. "What's the trouble?" he asked.

"The black guy they're questioning says he saw her here before the murder," Huber explained. "Cap'n Halliday told me to keep an eye on her."

"I was here for a few minutes before going to see Angela Liachi, Martin," Jennifer said. "She can prove I wasn't here when Oliver was killed."

"Don't kid yourself, Jenn," Martin said. "Angela Liachi is our prime suspect."

Jennifer was speechless. *Of course,* she realized, *a person who had made a definite threat and was even named in a complaint would have to be the first suspect.* There had been a prerequisite to her threat—harm to one of the Lauren kids—and that had been fulfilled. Could Angela have been worked up to such a frenzy by their chat that she had actually followed through with her plans? Jennifer couldn't believe it.

"Then can I go?" she called after Grom.

"Just stay accessible, you hear?" he yelled back.

She nodded.

"It's all right, Huber!" Grom added. "We know where to find her."

Several other uniformed and plainclothes cops emerged from the building. "How'd he die?" Jennifer asked.

"No comment."

"Angela Liachi the only suspect?"

The men looked at each other and at her. "We have no suspects as yet."

"How'd he die?" she asked again, hoping someone in the back of the group had not heard the "no comment" from the front.

"Fork," someone said.

"Fork?"

"Fork to the back."

"Common kitchen utensil?"

"You got it."

"From his own house?"

"Can't tell yet."

"Fingerprints?"

"Don't know yet."

"Where was he found?"

"On the landing between the first and second floors."

"Happen there?"

"Probably outside his door on two."

"Thank you. May I go in?"

"Not till the evidence techs come out."

"His wife and child see the murder?"

"No comment."

"She a suspect?"

"No suspects yet."

Jennifer, as was her custom at such scenes, returned to her car and waited for the crowd to disperse. There wasn't much to see once the body had been removed, and people generally drifted away, just as the broadcast media rolled up to take long shots of the building.

After about twenty minutes, TV camera crews began setting up out front in the growing darkness, their lights illuminating street reporters in the front yard reading somber messages from cue cards, telling of the bizarre slaying of a man whose daughter had been found in this very building the day before, and whom many had considered a suspect in that death.

Jennifer walked around the block and came through the back alley to the side door. The cops supposed to be watching that door were ogling the TV reporters in the front yard. She took in the scene and casually walked through the open door and up the steps, careful to touch nothing.

Evidence technicians were crouched everywhere, dusting for prints and tracks, taking blood samples from the stairs. They basically ignored her except to direct her around the areas where they worked.

She began to realize the idiocy of walking through the scene of a crime in which she herself was a suspect, but she was more overcome with the sense of evil in this place. She'd been at murder scenes before. But never this soon after the event.

She believed Satan was the author of death, the robber of life, and when a murder motivated by anger or hatred was perpetrated with such horrible violence, it carried the stench of evil. A feeling of fear and dread was almost physical in the place.

She prayed silently as she mounted the stairs. *Lord, protect me, cleanse me, be with me.*

The door to the Oliver-Lauren apartment was open, and the lights were off. "Have you been in there yet?" she asked the technicians.

"No, ma'am. Not yet."

She hurried back down the steps and out the door, drawing a surprised look from Officer Huber, who was now stationed at the side of the building. "Good evening, Officer," she said. He nodded.

Jennifer couldn't make it all compute. Why would the apartment door be open and the lights off? If Cornelia Lauren had been the perpetrator, wouldn't she have done it while he slept? Had she been there when it happened? If so, she would have either seen or had a good idea who had murdered Wyatt Oliver.

Had Elliott been home? Was he capable of such an act? She doubted it. Surely he could have had a motive if he had been treated as his sister had. But he was so small, and Oliver was so strong. Maybe, if he had surprised the man— But with a fork? Unlikely. The fork pointed to Cornelia. But what was that Jennifer had seen in the backseat of the squad car? A bag of groceries? Had she been out and discovered him when she returned? Who would know?

Jennifer went back out into the alley and to the other side of the building next door. She rapped on the door and jumped back as a black face appeared immediately at the window. *Of course,* she realized, *everyone's been watching everything.*

"Excuse me," she said, "but could I ask you a few questions?"

"Depends on who you are," said a male voice.

"I'm Jennifer Grey of the *Chicago Day.*"

"If I talk to you, I might be in the paper?"

"You might be, unless you don't want to be."

"I do. Come on in."

Jennifer hesitated, knowing immediately that her hesitation would probably offend the man. She walked in slowly and up a short flight of stairs to a tiny kitchen. The man, who looked to be in his early twenties, was long and lanky and wore a new white T-shirt and blue jeans with no belt. He was barefoot.

"Chair?" he said, pointing to a vinyl covered, aluminum framed one.

"Thank you."

"Coffee?"

"Thank you."

He scowled as if he'd wished she'd said no, and moved toward the stove.

"Oh, if it's any trouble—" she said.

"No trouble," he said, unconvincingly.

"You don't mind talking to me and being quoted in the paper?"

"Are you kidding?" he said. "Might be the highlight of my life."

She smiled. "Name?"

"Lionel Whalum," and he spelled it for her.

"Age?"

"Twenty-five."

"Occupation?"

"None."

"You live here alone?"

"Nobody lives in this neighborhood alone," he said, sitting across from her and waiting for the coffee to perk.

"Family?"

"I live here with my mother and her brother. We're the only people on this block without kids."

"Can you tell me what you saw today?"

"Everything."

"Meaning?"

"I saw you earlier today."

"You did? You did see everything then, didn't you?"

"Yes, ma'am."

"What else did you see?"

"You mean around the time Oliver bought it?"

"Uh huh."

"Kids were playing all over the place. Elliott was with them."

"How far from his apartment?"

"Down the block."

"Where was Mrs. Lauren?"

"His old lady? She was out with somebody from Social Services."

"How do you know that?"

"I saw the car. Someone from the agency comes every now and then and takes her shopping, showing her how to get more food for less money and food stamps, that kinda stuff. They do the same for us."

"And then they brought her back when?"

"They didn't bring her back. She walked home."

"Is that normal?"

"Yeah. Store's not that far away. They come for you because they know you probably wouldn't show otherwise. But they don't have to take you home too."

"Does this happen on some kind of a schedule?"

"Yeah, but nobody knows what it is 'cept Social Services. They just call and say they're coming to take you to the store, and it's usually within a few days after you get your check and your food stamps."

"Uh huh. Did you see who it was from Social Services?"

"No, I just saw Cornelia get in the car."

"Did Elliott go along?"

"No, he went back into the house for awhile. Then he came back out to play."

"What else did you see today, Lionel?"

"I saw another reporter. At least, I think he was a reporter."

"What did he look like?"

"Big, tall. Young. Dark hair. Big glasses. Wore boots. Walked around the front of that building and took a lot of notes. I don't know if he actually went in or not, 'cause from where I am I can only see the front and the sidewalk and the back alley, I can't actually see the side door."

"Was this guy wearing a denim suit?"

"Right. You know him?"

"I think so." She sure did. It sounded like Bobby Block. *What would he have been doing there? Maybe murdering Wyatt Oliver and trying to make it look like I did it? Good grief, Jennifer, you're paranoid. The kid is a scroundrel, but he wouldn't go that far to get your job!*

"What did you see me do today?"

"I knew you went inside because I saw you go around the side and heard you holler at Elliott. And then you didn't turn up in the back alley or come back out the front until you came running. I figured you must've met up with Oliver in there. I was hoping you'd killed him, but I saw him in the backyard about a half hour later."

"You'll swear to that?"

"Sure."

"And he was healthy?"

"Yeah!"

"And the other reporter came when?"

"While Mrs. Lauren was gone."

"You see anybody else?"

"I saw the preschool teacher."

"Angela Liachi?"

"Uh huh." He poured the coffee.

"When was this?"

"I saw her two or three times. Mid-afternoon, before Mrs. Lauren left. Then while she was gone."

"Did she go into the building?"

"I don't think so. I saw her in front and in back, but never at the side."

"What was she doing?"

"Just talking with the kids and watching them and roaming. Just like always."

"How do you know her, Mr. Whalum?"

"We know everybody who comes through here. It's safer that way."

"I suppose it is."

"For everybody 'cept Wyatt Oliver anyway. We don't do much to protect that man."

"Apparently not."

"Can you blame us?"

"Do you think he killed Heather?"

"Everybody knows that. He's been beatin' on those kids since they moved in here."

"Who found him today?"

"She did."

"She?"

"His old lady, Cornelia. She came back from the store with a bag of groceries, waved 'hi' to Elliott, and the next thing I know she's out front of the building screaming to call the police, call the police."

"Did you call?"

"Me? No. I got enough trouble with the police. I don't need that. Anyway, there's enough people in her building to call. They never go anywhere."

"There didn't seem to be anyone there when I was there."

"They don't come to the door unless they know you. And they wouldn't have called the police for him."

"I thought you said they would."

"They would for her. Not for him. If it was him yelling to call the police, they'd have just shut the doors. They like her. She's good people."

"So then what happened?"

"Elliott came running to his mama, and she liked to tackle him to keep him outta that building. She set the grocery bag down and grabbed him in both arms and held on for all she was worth until the cops got here. That's when I knew Oliver musta bought it and was lyin' in there somewhere. 'Course, news travels fast, so soon enough I got the story."

"What *is* the story?"

"People in my building think someone in his building got him with his own silverware. This gonna be in the paper?"

TEN

"I've just been sitting here reading, wondering when I would hear from you," Jim said when Jennifer called.

"I assume you've heard what's going on," she said.

"Yeah. You need an ear?"

"I sure do, Love. But it might be kinda late. I've got two pieces to write tonight, and I have to talk my way out of being a suspect in this thing myself."

"*That* I hadn't heard!"

"I saw Wyatt Oliver before he was murdered, and I was seen. But I'm not worried about that. I'll tell you all about it later. Can I call you and meet you somewhere?"

"Sure."

"How late?"

"You name it. I'm off tomorrow, remember?"

"Oh, that's right! Thanks, Sweetheart. I'll call you as soon as I can."

Jennifer had broken a boot heel in the alley behind the Oliver apartment building, so while she was in the phone booth, she decided to let Leo know she would be stopping by her apartment on the way in.

"You know the cops are looking for you?" he asked.

"Yeah. Who called?"

"The redhead from the West Side. Is it serious?"

"Leo, for now I'm a suspect."

"Tell me you're kidding."

"I'm not. But I've also got a witness who saw me at the Oliver place and who also saw a healthy Wyatt Oliver after I left. And I was with Angela Liachi and then Nathalie Benedict and then Sergeant Grom the rest of the afternoon."

"The cops are placing the time of death at late in the afternoon, Jennifer. Were you en route somewhere around that time?"

"Sure, I could have been going to or from any one of those appointments. I was with Grom when the report came in."

"Did you go back to Oliver's late in the afternoon?"

"Not until after he was dead. That's where I'm calling from now."

"Give me the details on your eyewitness, and I'll try to get you cleared through Grom. That'll give you time to run home on your way in if you want to, and I should at least be able to get you enough time to do your two pieces before they send you to Sing Sing."

"Not funny, Leo."

"Sorry. But don't dawdle."

Jennifer knew the doorman at her building would keep an eye on her car, so she parked in front instead of in the underground garage and limped in the front door, gobbling a fast-food burger on the way.

"Your sister is waiting for you, ma'am," the doorman said.

"My sister?"

"Yes, ma'am."

"Thank you," she said, looking warily into the lobby. From an overstuffed chair in the corner, peeking over the top of a magazine, were the fearful eyes of Angela Liachi. "Angela!" Jennifer said, a little too loudly.

"Hi, Sis!" Angela said, making a show of embracing her. Then she whispered, "I've got to talk to you!"

Jennifer took her upstairs while she changed into low-heeled shoes and freshened up. "So, what are you doing here?" she asked, pointing Angela to the couch.

"I decided to take you up on your offer to get me out of that rat hole so I could cool off for a few days."

"Angela!" Jennifer said, emerging from the bathroom. "You know the police are looking for you?"

"I know. I did a very foolish thing, Jennifer." Her voice grew husky and her eyes filled.

"Oh, please—" Jennifer said, dreading what she was about to hear.

"I shouldn't have even walked over there."

"Angela, if you're about to make a confession, I—"

"It was a dumb thing to do," Angela continued in a monotone, ignoring Jennifer and staring past her. "I was in a mood after I talked to you. I thought about you sitting there with Nathalie Benedict and then going to see that homicide guy, and I knew you'd find out that they couldn't use the evidence they found by giving those phony physicals—"

"Angela, please, if, if, I don't even want to know right now if—"

"—and I knew that nothing would be done, because nothing ever gets done about people like Wyatt Oliver." She began to cry.

Jennifer stood over her with her hands on Angela's shoulders. "What are you going to do, Angela?"

"I want to stay here for awhile. May I?"

"I have to get into the office to write my stories. Is one of them supposed to say that I'm harboring the murderer of Wyatt Oliver?"

"I didn't say that, Jennifer! I *wanted* to kill him, but I couldn't bring myself to go inside! I hate myself because I didn't do it, but I'm sure glad it got done."

Jennifer flinched. She had suppressed the same reaction to the murder, knowing all the while that is was a horrible thought. To be glad that a man has been plunged into eternity, and knowing that he certainly met a godless end—

"So you didn't do it."

"No. Nathalie told me after my first episode with him, when I threatened him, that I would never really be able to do it."

"You discussed it with her?"

"Sure. She said she thought she could do it if she felt as strongly about Oliver as I did, but she didn't think I could."

"Dangerous talk."

"I know. But, Jennifer, you haven't worked with the low-lifes in this city the way we have. You haven't faced the system. You haven't seen innocent people suffer and guilty people go free because of delays, continuances, payoffs, deals, bargains, neglect, and incompetence."

"Do you think Nathalie Benedict could have murdered Wyatt Oliver?"

Angela buried her face in her hands. "I don't know," she said. "I really don't."

Jennifer looked at her watch. "I need a commitment from you, Angela."

"Hm?"

"I need you to look me in the eye and tell me you didn't see Wyatt Oliver today."

"I didn't."

"I want to believe you."

"You can."

"Based on what you're telling me, I'm going to take the risk of harboring you for a few hours."

"Harboring me?"

"You're wanted by the police, Angela, and I know it. That means I'm protecting you from them. But let me tell you this: If they ask, I'll have to tell them the truth."

"Could you call me and let me know if they're coming?"

"No, I couldn't do that. I shouldn't even do this, but if I give you to them, they'll detain me as well, and I've got work to do first."

"What do you want me to do?"

"Just stay here. Don't answer the door, and don't answer the phone unless it rings seventeen times. If it does, that's me."

"Thanks, Jennifer."

"Don't be too quick to thank me. We both may regret this soon enough. I've got to call Leo. That reminds me. Don't use the phone."

"I won't."

Jennifer dialed. "Leo, I'm leaving right now."

"I'm surprised to hear from you, Jennifer. Grom says they're staking out the parking garage in your building right now."

"Luckily, I parked in front, but I'd better hurry or they'll tow me away. They may be waiting down there for me now, or on their way up."

"I don't like it, Jenn, and neither does Cooper."

"Cooper knows about this?"

"He's got contacts everywhere. What are you going to do?"

"I'll do whatever you say, Leo."

"You sure you can clear yourself in this deal?"

"Of course."

"Grom says the eyewitness you quote is a known pimp."

"Terrific, Leo. If I'm going to try to get there without them seeing me, I've got to go right now. If you want me to just turn myself in, I will."

"Come on in. Let's see if you can get the stories done before we have to give you up."

Jennifer ran to the door, pointed back at Angela and said, "Remember what I told you. Just stay put. I may not be back until morning."

"What?" Angela said, but Jennifer was gone, sprinting past the elevators—she was sure the police were on their way up—and down the far stairway. She ran down nine flights of stairs, fearing at every turn that she would see cops who were supposed to be in the basement garage.

When she reached street level, she peered around the exit door a half block south to the front windows where the doorman was pointing two uniformed policemen to the elevators. Apparently they had not seen her car yet or were convinced that she was upstairs. She ran to her car and drove to the office.

Cooper and Stanton and Bobby Block were waiting for her when she got off the elevator at the far end of the city room. "Follow me," Leo said, and they headed for a small office that formerly housed the news wires and now was used for paper storage. A video display terminal had been plugged in.

"We're going to stall them for as long as we can," Cooper said, "but as soon as your stories are written, we're going to turn you over to them."

"You're going to stand by me, aren't you?"

"Of course we are," the big boss said. "If you say you're innocent, you're innocent. But we can't hide someone who's wanted by the police, and we won't. At least, not for long."

"I have a question for Bobby," Jennifer said.

Bobby squinted at her. Leo and Cooper looked at him.

"Any reason you can't do the straight story?" she asked.

He shrugged.

"What's she talking about, Block?" Leo said.

"How should I know? Ask her."

"Watch your mouth, Kid. You're talking to your boss's boss in front of his boss," Max Cooper said, showing a remarkable familiarity with the hierarchy.

"Well, I don't know what she's talkin' about!" Bobby whined.

"Why were you at the scene of the murder today, Bobby?" she asked.

"Who says I was?"

"I do."

"Are you saying you weren't?" Leo said.

"Well, no— "

"Then why were you? You weren't assigned!"

"Well, somebody has to handle the police beat while Susie Columnist here is posturing for the publisher!"

Everyone fell silent, but Max Cooper was hot. His forehead and ears reddened. Finally, he said, "Leo, I don't want to see this person anymore. Get rid of 'im."

Leo and Bobby headed down the hall, leaving old man Cooper with Jennifer for a moment. "Write me a good column, huh?" he said. "Leave out anything about you bein' a suspect; we'll deal with that. The straight piece oughta write itself. Put your energy into the column, 'cause it's your column that's gonna make this paper over the next few years."

He winked at her and left, and while she was flattered by his confidence, she hadn't decided to accept his long-term column offer, and she could have as easily burst into tears and begged for twelve solid hours' sleep as try to write.

Besides not knowing what to think about the fact that her salvation from being a suspect was in the hands of a known pimp, she wanted to see Jim and talk to him about all the dangling clues in the case.

Neither did she know yet whether Angela Liachi had been straight with her. For all Jennifer knew, Angela *had* murdered Wyatt Oliver. Jennifer's conscience was already nagging her for protecting Angela from the police, guilty or not. The same was true of her own flight from Sergeant Grom.

For a minute she toyed with insisting that Cooper and Leo turn her in, but at the same time she was nudging the elements of her column around in her head. As they fell into place, she began writing:

> I'm facing difficult emotions as I compose these words. The man most people assume murdered four-year-old Heather Lauren has himself been murdered, not a full day after I championed capital punishment for whoever had done it.
>
> And so now what am I supposed to think? How am I supposed to react? How are you reacting? Cornelia Lauren may now feel free to tell what really happened in that home, fearing no reprisal from her common-law husband.
>
> It won't surprise anyone to learn that Wyatt Oliver tortured the girl, let her go too long without eating, intimidated her mother to the point that she couldn't even protect her own daughter, went too far with his methods, and wound up killing Heather.
>
> We'll find that he carried her to the basement of the apartment building in the middle of the night, probably Monday, and tied the lifeless body to a post—for there are no signs of struggle or blood in that basement now—and attempted to make it look as if she had been abducted.
>
> We'll find that she died from shock, but that any of several injuries inflicted on that vulnerable, defenseless little frame could have done her in. And then we'll be glad that the perpetrator got his.
>
> Or will we? When we know for sure it was Wyatt Oliver, will we still be glad he's dead? You see my dilemma? If he murdered Heather Lauren, I'm glad justice was done. But the justice was not carried out in a just way.
>
> There was no trial. So, unless Cornelia Lauren, one of two people in the world with firsthand knowledge of the first slaying, committed this murder, the perpetrator was making assumptions. And evidence will surface to clear Mrs. Lauren.
>
> I spent time today with several people who are so frustrated with the "system" in this city, the bureaucracy that favors the guilty and harms the innocent, that any one of them could have had a motive to murder Wyatt Oliver. By the time I finished talking with them, I shared their feelings.
>
> I saw Wyatt Oliver alive today. I left him with no shadow of a doubt that he had killed his own daughter. It's a strange feeling to

see a man a few hours before he meets a violent death. And I wrestle with the emotion that tells me that as one who believes in the sovereignty of God, one who believes that vengeance is His, one who believes that God is the author of life and that Satan is the author of death, I should not have any positive feeling whatsoever related to the death of a child abuser.

I'll keep praying about it; and I don't say that flippantly.

ELEVEN

Jennifer was in the middle of rapping out the straight update article on the entire case when Leo knocked at the door.

"They're here," he said. "We've admitted you're here, and we've promised that you'll go with them if we can just let you finish your story. If you need it for the piece, Mrs. Lauren has been cleared, and she has named Oliver as Heather's murderer."

Jennifer was surprised half an hour later when she entered the city room and was arrested by Martin Grom himself. As he was quietly reading her her rights, Max Cooper caught her eye from behind the sergeant and pointed to Gerald Mayfield, the newspaper's counsel.

Jennifer was flabbergasted that they would have thought to call him and ask him to represent her. "I have counsel," she said. "Thank you."

Grom was surprised too. Mayfield introduced himself. "This isn't so magnanimous as it seems, Mrs. Grey." Mayfield said. "I happened to be in the Loop tonight anyway."

"Still, I'm grateful."

"Don't mention it. Sergeant, may my client and I have a few minutes?"

"Well, I gotta tell you, Counselor, my partner is waiting in the car, and the people here have been harboring this woman for quite some time—"

"Martin, you told me earlier that it was OK and that you knew were to find me," Jennifer said.

"Yeah, but when we looked at your place, all we found was Angela Liachi. We'll have to bust you for harboring her, at least."

"Well," Mayfield said, "which is it? Are you arresting her on suspicion of murder or for harboring a suspect?"

"We haven't decided yet."

"Then while you're thinking about it, surely you wouldn't mind if my client and I spent a few minutes in private."

Grom shrugged, grimacing.

Jennifer and the dapper Mayfield wended their way through clusters of desks and tables to the far end of the huge city room, finally sitting across from each other on a desk top. "I'm so sorry about this," Jennifer said. "It's all my fault, and I know I shouldn't have gone to the Oliver place today, and—"

"Just hold on a minute, Mrs. Grey. The worst thing you've done so far is to let this Liachi woman stay in your place. If she's guilty, that'll compound matters."

"She isn't."

"You can't know that."

"I'm pretty sure."

"Well, I should hope so."

"There's something strange going on here, Mr. Mayfield. Sergeant Grom said his partner was waiting in the car. Does it make sense that the numbers one and two men from West Side Homicide would be here looking for me? It seems anyone could come and round me up."

"True enough. So what are you saying?"

"I'm worried about Martin."

"Martin?"

"Grom, the sergeant. He's been very distraught since we spoke today. This case is really getting to him."

"That uniformed sergeant is the Homicide Chief on the West Side?"

"Yes."

"And his assistant would be whom?"

"Hank Henry."

"And Grom works for whom?"

"Captain Halliday, I believe, Chief of Investigative Operations."

"You have the number for the West Side Precinct?"

Jennifer recited it to him.

"Good evening. Gerald Mayfield of Bransfield, Mayfield, and Beckman calling for Captain Halliday, please . . . John? Gerry Mayfield here. How you doing? . . . Good! Me, too. Listen, do you have a minute? . . . Yeah, I know. I'm involved in it too now. I'm representing the *Day* and their reporter Jennifer Grey . . . Yes, she's been arrested actually. John, can you tell me who's heading up this investigation for you? . . . Oh, *you* are. Well, what about your Homicide Chief over there, Sergeant, uh . . . right, Grom. What's he doing? . . . Excuse me just a minute, John.

"Jennifer, Halliday tells me he's given Grom the rest of the night off. Says he's taken control of the operation himself."

She raised her eyebrows.

"John, the man is here right now. He's handling the arrest of Mrs. Grey himself. Is that what you want, or can I bring her over to you myself? . . . Sure, hang on."

"Mayfield hurried over to Martin Grom and told him he was wanted on the phone. After a few minutes of intense conversation with his boss, Grom stormed out of the city room. Mayfield took the phone again.

"What's his problem, John? . . . Ah, I see. Five-year-old, huh? Good man though, right? . . . Sure. We'll be over. Thanks, John."

Jennifer was puzzled.

"Let's go," Mayfield said. "We can talk in the car. I want you to tell me all about your day."

"Happy to," Jennifer said, following him out, "but what's happening with Grom?"

"Well, seems he's a father himself. Bunch of boys and a five-year-old daughter."

"I know."

"That's why he's taking this case so personally. He's been working on it around the clock. It's been affecting him."

"In what way?"

"Halliday says Grom wore his uniform today because he thought it was the day of the monthly meeting of the Fraternal Order of Police. But that's tomorrow."

"An easy mistake."

"Not for Grom. He's secretary of the Chicago chapter."

"What pushed Halliday into sending Grom home?" Jennifer asked as they approached Mayfield's car.

Mayfield stood at the open door as she got in. "When Grom and Henry brought the Liachi woman in, she told Halliday she'd never been questioned about Heather Lauren, even though Mrs. Lauren said she never came home from preschool."

"And?"

"Halliday was upset. To him, that was a major omission by a homicide sergeant, and he thought it was time Grom got some rest. They're all getting a lot of heat from downtown, and somebody is holding Halliday himself responsible for getting the thing cleared up."

"Am I going to be spending the night in the lockup, Mr. Mayfield? If I am, I need to call my boyfriend."

"I think you'll be able to see your boyfriend tonight, Jennifer. I'll try to have you out of there on your own recognizance—or mine—as soon as possible. John Halliday and I are old buddies."

Jennifer tried to give Gerald Mayfield every detail of her day, recreating much of it from her notes. He was not happy about her having entered the crime scene before the evidence technicians were finished.

"You know they have fantastic equipment," he said. "They'll find some trace of you there."

"Well, as I said, I had been there earlier in the day, too. And the evidence men *saw* me there, so there won't be any hiding that."

"I don't want to hide it. But if you hadn't been there at all, and there was therefore no trace that you had been there, they'd be hard pressed to try to say you had anything to do with Oliver's murder. You were there before *and* after, so who's to say you weren't there during?"

"You are."

Mayfield laughed. "True enough. But you've made my job a bit more difficult than it needed to have been."

"I'm sorry."

"Nonsense. I enjoy the challenge. You are innocent, aren't you?"

"Pardon me?"

"You are innocent, are you not? You didn't murder Wyatt Oliver, did you?"

"What do you think?"

"I think I'd better coach you on how to answer a direct question. I am not kidding when I ask you that, and neither will John Halliday be kidding. And you can be sure he will ask you. People will be asking you that, and every time you are asked, you would serve yourself well by looking the interrogator in the eye and telling him the truth."

"Even if I'm guilty?"

"Even more so. You'll notice that I didn't tell you what to say; I just said to tell the truth."

"I didn't murder Wyatt Oliver, Mr. Mayfield."

"Thank you. That was encouraging. Do you know who did?"

"No, sir."

"Very good. Do you have an idea who did?"

"I have fears."

"Care to speculate?"

"I don't know. There are so many people who wanted to. Myself included."

"It would be good if no one else in an official capacity heard you say that."

"But it's the truth."

"Fine, but if you are innocent and want others to believe you, you'll keep quiet about your own motive, means, and opportunity. You see, the fact that you were at the scene before and after means that you had the opportunity. Everybody in town had a motive, it seems. The means? Well, someone who was in that apartment got to the table or silverware drawer in time to use a fork on Oliver, probably to make it look as if his wife did it."

"I worry about Nathalie Benedict and Angela."

"So do I. Using a fork could be construed as a feminine means of attack."

"But I'm talking about the timing," Jennifer said. "It had to be someone who had access to the schedule of when Social Services was taking Mrs. Lauren shopping."

"A good point," Mayfield said. "I'm surprised too that Oliver would let his wife out of the house, since she was the one person who knew that he had murdered Heather."

"He probably had her convinced that she was as much at fault and that if he got in trouble for it, she would too."

"Yeah, but mother-love usually transcends things like that," he said, "especially after the daughter is gone."

"Who knows?" Jennifer said. "Maybe she *was* getting ready to spill the beans."

"Have you ruled out the son?"

"Elliott? Too small."

"Means, motive, opportunity," Mayfield reminded her.

"I don't think so."

"Neither do I, but don't overlook anyone. Including your eyewitness."

"*My* eyewitness? The pimp? How much help is he going to be?"

"His record and his occupation have little to do with his credibility."

"They should, Mr. Mayfield. That's another problem with the system."

"For now, don't knock it. He may be the only one who can clear you."

Twelve

As Gerald Mayfield and Jennifer entered the West Side Precinct station house, Jennifer caught sight of Jim waiting in the lobby. She ran to him.

"I heard about it on the radio," he said.

"Heard about what?"

"Bobby got fired."

"Yes, and—?"

"And he's gone to the news media saying that you're the prime suspect, that you went crazy with all the publicity today's column brought you, and you acted out your fantasy of capital punishment on the murderer of the child."

Jennifer was speechless. Jim held her.

"I suppose this bearer of good news is Jim," Mayfield muttered.

"Yes, I'm sorry," Jennifer said, making the introductions.

"Nice to meet you, Mr. Purcell. So what else did Bobby say?"

"He said another suspect was found in Jennifer's apartment and that there is speculation about conspiracy. Sounds crazy."

"It *is* crazy," Mayfield said. "We'd better go in, Jennifer. You'll probably have to wait, Purcell."

Before ushering Mayfield and Jennifer into Captain Halliday's office at the back of the building, the desk sergeant told Mayfield he had a message to call Leo Stanton at the *Day.* The conversation was brief, but after Mayfield hung up, he said, "We'll be initiating litigation against your former assistant, of course."

"Of course," Jennifer said.

Captain Halliday in many ways reminded Jennifer of an older Sergeant Grom. He didn't have the same mannerisms, and was in fact almost grandfatherly, but he was a large, rangy man. His white hair was thinning, and his full face was rosy, eyes sparkly.

He didn't rise when they entered but rather sat back and sized them up over the tops of his half glasses while pointing to chairs. Mayfield detoured to shake Halliday's hand first.

"Good to see you again, Gerry. And Jennifer, we've met. And I've worked with your intended a time or two."

"Oh really? Well, he's not really my intended, but—"

"Whatever, let's talk about why my crack homicide boys think you might have murdered this child killer, not that I wouldn't have wanted to do it myself."

"You know, John, that's what everybody's been saying all day," Mayfield jumped in. "People who read Mrs. Grey's column this morning, and even people who didn't. It seems she can't run into anyone who doesn't share that sentiment."

"Is that so? Well, I guess nobody loves somebody who could do something like that, do they? But nonetheless, we can't go around taking the law into our own hands, now can we?"

"Of course not," Mayfield said, "but—"

"Gerry, I'm gonna have to ask you to let Mrs. Grey here speak for herself."

"Well, John, I appreciate that, but I am her counsel, and I prefer to represent her."

"I don't mind, Mr. Mayfield," Jennifer said.

"Yeah," Halliday said, "and any way, this isn't anything official. I just want to have an off-the-record chat. I won't hold anything you say against you in a court o'law, as we have to say these days, an' you don't quote me in the paper, fair enough?"

"Sure!"

"Uh, can we stipulate something here, John?" Mayfield said. "I need to feel very comfortable here, as you're trying to make us feel, I think—"

Halliday winked at Jennifer, "These lawyers are never comfortable unless they're stipulatin' something, are they? All right, Gerry, just what is it you want stipulated?"

"I want to clarify that this is not an official interrogation and that nothing my client says here can or will be used against her in court."

Halliday swore and then excused himself to Jennifer. "Isn't that what I just said, Gerry? We go back a long way. You know me. I said I wanted to clear this up. I don't want any trouble with the media, and I don't want to detain this young lady any more than we have to. I said I wouldn't use anything against her, but I'll sure listen to everything that might clear her without further trouble. It's late, Gerry, and I'm sure we all want to go home. Don't you?"

"Yes, but—"

"Well, then just take me at my word like you've always known you could. All right, I know it's out of the ordinary for a cap'n to talk to a suspect off-the-record after she's been read her rights; do I hafta admit that Grom was way out of line to be bustin' somebody after I tol' him to go home? OK, let's get on with this, and I'm stipulatin' whatever it is you said, which I had already said. Let's work on getting this over with so I don't have to deal with a false arrest charge and you don't have to worry about court."

"I'll stipulate *this*," Mayfield said. "If we leave here tonight with no charges pending, there'll be no false arrest claim. And I haven't even cleared that with my client."

"OK with me," Jennifer said.

"Good," Halliday said. "Can we finally begin?"

They both nodded, smiling.

"I must tell you," the old man began, "that even though my little homicide crew is distraught and overworked and has made its share of errors here lately, they don't lightly arrest someone on suspicion of murder. As I understand it, you have been placed at the scene of the crime."

Jennifer nodded and started to speak. But Halliday continued.

"I'm also aware that one of the neighbors says he saw Oliver after you were there, and that he was healthy."

"Yes, when I came running out of there the first time, it could have looked like I had done something wrong."

"Well, it did. Do you have any idea how many people saw a well-dressed woman run from that building and speed away in her car? The next thing they know, it's several hours later and Oliver is dead. If this, uh, Whalum, Lionel Whalum, hadn't seen Oliver about mid-afternoon, you'd be in big trouble."

"I'm glad you talked to him, because I was relieved when he told me—"

"Yes, I'm aware that you also talked to him. That was not a wise thing to do."

"Why?"

"If you were aware of the man's profession, you wouldn't have wanted to be alone with him."

"I'm aware now."

"You saw his Cadillac with the multi-colored headlamps and the fur-lined rear window?"

"No. Was it there?"

"It usually is."

Hank Henry brought in some documents for the captain. "Did you get him home all right?" Halliday asked.

"Yes, sir," Henry whispered. "I'm sorry, sir, but I hadn't been apprised of the fact that he had been ordered off duty until he told me at the *Day* offices."

"That's all right. I know how intent he is on solving this one." He glanced at his watch. "You got here fast. He still lives on the Near North Side, doesn't he?"

"Yes, sir, but he just had me drop him off at the Chevy dealer up here on Lester. He'd dropped his van off there this morning."

"Surely they're not open this late, are they Hank?"

"No, sir. But he had extra keys, and they always let him settle up later."

"It's after midnight, Hank. You goin' home?"

"Yes, sir, but I'd kinda like to see this thing wrapped up too, and I thought maybe if you had time, I could run a few of my thoughts by you."

"If you want to hang around, Hank, I'll be here. But if you head home, I'll understand."

"I'll be here."

"Dedicated man," Halliday said. "You deal with him much, Jennifer?"

She shook her head. Halliday leafed through the papers Hank Henry had delivered. He read, half aloud and half to himself, so Mayfield and Jennifer caught only bits and pieces:

> Blood on stairs not an hour old when technicians arrived. Door casing to Oliver apartment had been shattered, apparently by a kick just under the doorknob. Lab tests show partial rubber print of sole and heel indicate possible oversized men's shoe, approximately thirteen, extra wide, possible quad E. Brand Apache Workmate.

"Good shoe. My dad wore 'em in the factory. Used to use 'em on the street when he walked the beats in the fifties. Not really regulation, but they were comfortable. Never wore out."

Door had knocked out jamb and swung all the way to wall, where knob drove hole into wall. Signs of struggle in the kitchen, silverware drawer open, blood on kitchen table, living room rug, wall near door, second floor landing, copious amounts on stairs and banister, body found on landing between first and second floor.

Coroner is estimating that the pound strength required to drive common kitchen fork through the latissimus dorsi muscle and to break a rib and puncture the heart would indicate that the perpetrator was either unusually strong or extremely agitated.

Halliday looked up. "Well, that kinda goes without saying, doesn't it? Somebody kicks Oliver's door in, beats him to the silverware drawer, starts poking him in the back in the kitchen, and chases him down a flight of stairs. I'd say whoever it was was agitated, wouldn't you?"

He didn't wait for an answer.

Coroner has determined eleven distinct puncture wounds, two to the deltoid muscle, seven to the latissimus, and two to the fleshy area in the lower right back. Assuming the victim was running away, the perpetrator was either significantly taller or inflicted all the wounds from a higher step on the stairs—unlikely because of the blood trail. Three of the puncture wounds affected the heart, and it's likely that the fatal blow was not the final wound, whatever that means.

"I suppose it means the murderer could have left after fewer stabs," Mayfield said. Jennifer felt sick.

"You don't look tall enough or strong enough or agitated enough to have done this, Mrs. Grey," Captain Halliday said. "Did you murder the man?"

She looked him straight in the eye. "No, sir, I did not."

"May we go," Mayfield asked.

"Not just yet. Let me see what else we've got here. Ah, interviews with neighbors in the building.

No love lost. Heard the door breaking, assumed it was Oliver himself. He's done it enough times. Heard the scuffling, thought he might be punishing the boy again. Heard feet running on the stairs and the tumbling to the landing. Heard male screaming, probably Oliver. Heard heavy footsteps running out. Saw no one.

"Yeah, I'll bet," Halliday said, then he continued.

Called cops? No. They never come for disturbances with Oliver anymore. Frankly, wishing he would get it one of these days. Figured maybe the wife did it, but when she screamed for cops, it was several minutes later.

Halliday peeked over his glasses again and looked at Jennifer, then at Mayfield. "The man's lucky his wife showed up. The neighbors probably would've just walked over him for a few weeks. This frankly makes me wonder if someone in the building didn't do it. Maybe a bunch of them did it, just like the *Murder on the Orient Express.*"
Halliday turned back to the report.

> What did neighbors notice unusual that day? Woman nosing around at about noon, running away within the half hour.

"That's you, huh?"

> Preschool teacher wandering through as usual, at least twice during the mid-afternoon.

"We've got her locked up in the back. Lot more points to her than you, frankly, but she doesn't look any too tall or strong either."

> Tall young man in western wear looking around, early afternoon.

"That one's worth checking out."
Jennifer caught Mayfield's eye, but said nothing.

> Mrs. Lauren went shopping in Social Services vehicle. Not unusual, except driver appeared to be the director herself, Mrs. Benedict.

"Don't know what to make of that. No one says she was in the building at all."

> Neighbors in the building and next door noticed police traffic at Whalum residence, approximately 4:00 P.M.

"Wonder what this is?"

> Kids in neighborhood corroborate this, and one also says he saw gray panel truck type vehicle pull into back alley. But no one else saw this, nor did youth see it pull away. Also unemployed men talking at corner saw unmarked squad car at Whalum residence for approximately twenty minutes.

Halliday looked agitated. "Hank! You still here?"
There was no response. Halliday grabbed his phone and dialed the desk. "Yeah, is Hank Henry out there? Tell 'im I wanna see 'im!"
Henry came chugging back and was surprised to see that Jennifer and Mayfield were still there.
"Sir?"
"These your notes?"

"Yes, sir."

"Well, what'sis all about, police activity at Whalum's around four o'clock? You tellin' me there were cops there that close to the time of the murder and we didn't hear or see anything?"

"At the time I wrote that, sir, I was unaware of the time similarity. Apparently I could have been in the neighborhood not long before the attack."

"You?"

"Yes sir, it was me."

"What were you doing at Whalum's, Hank?"

"Just putting a little heat on him, sir. Sergeant Grom, who used to deal with him a lot when he was in the Vice Control Division, got a call from VCD recently complaining that Whalum was apparently plying his trade unchecked on North Avenue and West Division. They were running the girls off, but they couldn't get to Whalum."

"So what was your assignment, Hank?"

"Grom asked if I would just pay him a call, mostly for looks. Let people see the un-marked squad in front of his place, embarrass him a little, that type of thing. I just talked with him for a while, told him the heat was on and that no one up here accepted any bribes or anything like that."

"Sounds pretty small time when we're on a much more important case, Hank."

"Yes, sir."

"But that's not your problem. I'll take it up with Grom."

"Frankly, sir, I didn't mind doing it. Sergeant Grom has had a lot on his mind, and with his daughter and all, he doesn't cater too much to, um, pimps, sir. He didn't want to handle it himself, and yet he didn't want to let down his friends in VCD."

"I understand." Halliday smiled. "Sometimes it is kinda fun just to intimidate one of these bad guys, you know what I mean? Well, uh, Hank, what else did you get from the neighbors inside Oliver's building?"

"Not much. The one black guy, the one who saw Mrs. Grey here, he was very helpful. He's the one who called when Mrs. Lauren started screaming."

"When does he say he saw Mrs. Grey?"

"Between twelve and one, just like everyone else."

"Any other witnesses say they saw Oliver alive after that?"

"Yes, sir. At least three, including Whalum. And some kids. The kids all know him. Scared of him. Hate him."

"Ha!" Halliday said. "Wonder if the kids did it?"

The captain stood and stretched, and Jennifer realized how tall the man was. He looked suddenly older and more tired than when they first came in. "You've got enough witnesses that say they saw Oliver alive after you went runnin' away, young lady. That's good enough for me. Now I gotta ask you not to use anything you heard in here tonight in the paper. OK?"

"That won't be easy," she said. "It was most interesting."

"But we have a deal, don't we? Your lawyer even stipulated it, remember?"

THIRTEEN

Jennifer had dark circles under her eyes and was dragging on her way out to the lobby, but she was alert enough to ask Gerald Mayfield for one more favor.

"Sure, what is it?"

"Could you get them to release Angela? From what he just read, she doesn't have any more strength or whatever than I do."

"I'll try, but it'll be tougher with her. She could have been agitated enough, and she is on record as having threatened the man."

"Can we at least bail her out?"

"I'll check."

It took another forty-five minutes, and Mayfield had to post a personal bond—"based solely on your word, Jennifer; I don't know this woman"—but Angela was released. Jim offered to take her home and Jennifer back to her car at the *Day* office. Mayfield was grateful. "I can't thank you enough, Mr. Mayfield," Jennifer said.

"It was fun," he said, heading for his car.

"Did I get you in a lot of trouble, Jennifer?" Angela asked in the car.

"Some. Not much. Most of it was my own doing. They're going to waive the harboring charge. How are you doing?"

"Well, that wasn't my favorite way to spend a late evening. I was almost asleep. I wouldn't have bet a penny I'd be bailed out tonight. Good experience, though. Just taught me more about the crazy system."

"We keep coming back to that, don't we?" Jennifer said.

"Yeah," Angela said, but she was preoccupied, staring out the window.

Jennifer let her be for a few minutes, then asked what she was thinking.

"I'm a little scared, that's all."

"You wanna stay with me tonight?"

"No, thanks, not that kind of scared. Scared of me."

Jennifer wanted to pump her, but she was too tired, and she figured Angela was too, so she probably wouldn't elicit much. She was wrong.

"My reaction to this whole thing bothers me a lot," Angela began suddenly. "I've gone through moments when I wondered if I actually *had* murdered Wyatt Oliver. I rehearsed it so many times. Not with a fork, of course, but whatever was handy."

She fell silent again, and Jennifer wondered aloud if there was anyone within blocks of where Wyatt Oliver lived who didn't have a motive to kill him.

"Probably not," Angela decided.

"And the one with the best motive of all didn't do it," Jim offered.

"Cornelia Lauren?" Angela said. "Don't be too sure. She's pretty shrewd in her limited way. She could have been planning this for a long time."

"But this soon after her daughter's murder?"

"What better time?"

Jim waited on the street until Angela was safely inside her building. "I'd love to hear every last detail," he said as he pulled away, "and I'm sure you're dying to tell me, Hon, but you'd better save it."

Jennifer lay her head on his shoulder, turned sideways in the seat, and slipped both her hands under his arm. "Jus' wake me when we get to the office," she slurred. "I gotta talk to Leo for a minute."

"He'll still be there?"

She nodded. "He's putting the first section to bed."

In the *Day* parking lot a half hour later, Jim gently pulled his arm from her grasp and wrapped it around her shoulders. "Sweetheart," he said quietly.

"Um hum," she said, eyes still closed.

"We're here."

She opened her eyes without moving. "So we are," she said. "I'm comfortable. How 'bout you?"

He chuckled. "Why don't you just let me drop you at your place, Jenn? You can talk to Leo tomorrow."

"No," she said, sitting up. "It can't wait. What time is it?"

"Almost two o'clock."

"Ouch. What time does the sun come up tomorrow morning?"

"You mean *this* morning? I don't know—about seven."

"I'll check."

And with that she dashed into the building and up to see Leo. "Hey, hey!" Leo said. "How's my little fugitive?"

"Bushed. I gotta talk to you."

"Coffee?"

"Why not? It's too late to keep me up."

He sent someone for two cups. "So, talk to me."

"You remember the agreement I made with you and Mr. Cooper about Jim and me and police reporting?"

"Yeah, you haven't violated that, have you?"

"No."

"Good."

"But I *would* like to know what you would do about the police beat if I left."

"If you left!"

"I mean, if I left the police beat, not the paper. With Bobby gone—"

"He's gone all right. I shoulda dumped him when he tried to get you in trouble the first time."

"Tried?"

"So, anyway, what would I do with the police beat if you left? Frankly, I'd have my pick of the news staff."

"You would?"

"Yeah. I told Cooper I thought you'd take the column—"

"You did?"

"Uh huh, and he suggested Bobby, but that was before this evening. After that, he said he would clear anyone I wanted, if they wanted to come."

"Got anybody in mind?"

"A few, yeah."

"Yeah? Are you to the point where you'll be disappointed if I stay?"

"I'll still be in charge of you, Jennifer, so I don't care what you do."

"You do too!"

"You're right. I want you to take this column. Your piece tonight was—"

"How badly do you want me to take it?"

"As badly as Cooper does."

"Is that badly enough that you two slave drivers will rescind our little agreement about Jim and me?"

"You set me up, you turkey!"

She laughed.

"I don't know," he said.

"Come on, it's not the police beat. There'd be no conflict of interest."

"But your stories would often overlap with police stories."

"Like now."

"Right. What would you do then?"

"I'd use him."

"You'd use Jim?"

"You bet I would."

"And if we back off about you and Jim, you'll take the column?"

"I don't know yet. I haven't prayed about it or talked to Jim about it yet."

"Will you?"

"I won't even consider it unless that agreement is eliminated."

"If I told you it was eliminated right now, when would I get your answer about the column?"

"Soon. Do you have the power to rescind it?"

"Are you kidding? You ever see Cooper cross the Lion?" They both laughed. "Forget the agreement," he added.

"You mean it?"

He nodded.

"Thanks, Leo!"

"The competition will be good."

"What do you mean?"

"C'mere, Jennifer. Let me give you a sneak preview of Jake Rogers's column, which will always appear opposite yours."

Jennifer read Jake's column off the film that would make up the front page of the morning's paper. He played critic, evaluating her work as a police beat writer ("gushy, gee-whiz reporting"), her two personal columns ("amateurish, sensational, emotional, religious"), and even the placement of the column ("call it professional jealousy if you will, but it took me six years of paying my dues before my column was placed on the front page").

"I'm shocked."

"Don't be. It's vintage Jake. And it's probably more entertainment than substance. I can't imagine he really feels that way, but he knows it'll sell papers."

"I have to tell you, I would never even acknowledge in print that kind of criticism."

"Of course you wouldn't, Jenn. If he keeps this up, we'll find out what the grassroots reader really wants."

"I don't want to take the column to prove something to Jake. I hardly know the man, and I usually enjoy his stuff, especially the humor. This doesn't humor me. But it does convince me that we're long overdue for an old-fashioned, conservative viewpoint."

"You know we are, Jennifer. Let me know soon, will you?"

"Leo, there's a method to my madness here, and I don't want to get thrown off the track by Jake Rogers' venom. Even if I don't take the column, I want you to rescind the agreement I made about Jim and me immediately, for the sake of tomorrow's column."

"You been working with him on something?"

"Of course not. I've lived up to my end of the bargain. But I'm about to ask him to help me with something. It may be crazy, but if it works, it could be a dynamite column. How 'bout it?"

"All right. But for tomorrow you're still writing two pieces, right? The straight one and the column."

"Right."

"And my pledge to you is that if you'll give me just forty-eight hours notice when you're going to take the column assignment, you'll be off the police beat immediately."

"Thanks, Leo."

Jim was dozing in the idling car and jumped when Jennifer opened the passenger side door. "I'm sorry, Jim." He smiled and drove toward her apartment building. "You have plans tomorrow?" she asked.

"Just sleeping in."

"Can I spoil 'em?"

"You're the one thing I'd even give up sleeping in for. How's that for a sentence, Mrs. Hemingway?"

"It got the point across. I have a plan for tomorrow morning, before sunrise."

He groaned.

"C'mon," she said. "You'll still get four hours or so of sleep. And it'll be fun. You still have your evidence kit from cadet training school?"

"'Course. Cost me more'n a hundred bucks."

"Got all the stuff?"

"Think so."

"You're gonna need it."

"You gonna get me in trouble?"

"No, unless there's something wrong with going over a crime scene after the evidence techs have already been there."

He thought a minute, parking in front of her building. "I guess not. What else can you tell me?"

"Dress warm. And be praying with me about my leaving the police beat and becoming a full-time columnist."

"I will. I'll miss you."

"Are you kidding? You'll see more of me than ever."

"Apparently so. Are we going to be too tired for dinner tomorrow night?"

"Highly unlikely," she said. And she kissed him good night.

FOURTEEN

It was cold in her apartment when Jennifer arose not four hours later. She liked to sleep with the window open slightly, even in the dead of winter. It made for good sleeping, but she paid dearly for it every morning on cold floors.

As she padded around the apartment in her bulky robe and slippers, she fought to keep her eyes open. Her breathing was deep and even, as if she were still in bed. But as she splashed cold water on her face and cranked up the coffeepot, her mind was racing.

She was convinced she would never get her eyes fully open and would probably look bedraggled to Jim, but she was still high with excitement. She'd had things rattling around in her brain ever since the conversation the night before with Captain John Halliday. She quickly ran down in her mind the list of things she had to accomplish to get out the front door by six; then she put herself on automatic pilot so they would get done even while she was thinking and praying.

One of the things she looked forward to in her future with Jim was the opportunity to spend time reading Scripture and praying with him everyday. She'd been doing it by herself for so long that she found she enjoyed it immensely when they shared it. Both were early risers by nature, so it would become a scheduled part of their morning routine.

She chastised herself for planning for married life with Jim when he hadn't even popped the question yet. But it was a foregone conclusion. They'd done a lot of talking about their future life together, but nothing close to a proposal had been made. That suited her. It had taken her a long time to get used to the idea of marrying again. In fact, for a long time it had kept her from even admitting to herself her deep feelings for Jim. But now she couldn't imagine a future without him.

Prayer was on her mind this morning too. She found herself thinking of the many people she'd been so intensely involved with the day before. Was it possible she had known Angela Liachi only one day? And Nathalie Benedict? She'd worked with Martin Grom before, but she'd never seen him near the edge like yesterday. Even Lionel Whalum came to mind, a man so removed from her life-style that she didn't know where to begin to pray for him.

How should she pray for such people? Not one of them, as far as she knew, was a churchgoer, though some had indicated a certain God-consciousness. She guessed that that was where she should start, praying that God would somehow impress Himself upon them, get them thinking, make them receptive.

And then she prayed for opportunities to talk with them. She didn't know if she'd ever even see Lionel Whalum again, but she would undoubtedly see Martin Grom. And she could make it a point to see Mrs. Benedict and Angela. She knew she had something they needed, and she knew God could give her the words that could draw them to Himself.

Angela seemed especially sensitive, just by her nature and personality and by what she had been going through for the past several months. But someone else was tugging at the recesses of Jennifer's mind, and when she stopped for a minute and forced it to the surface, she knew immediately. Bobby Block.

There was no doubt he had gotten what he deserved. And it was probably the best thing that had ever happened to him. Not only had he been crushed by being fired, but when his ridiculous claims and conclusions about Jennifer were proved false, which would likely happen this very day, he would look like a fool.

She prayed that God would give her the resources to not retaliate. To show Bobby either by her silence or by the right word, should their paths cross, that she bore no grudges, that she wished him no further humiliation.

She knew if she could somehow glue together the loose ends in her mind this morning and if everything came together to support her wild hunches, she would not only play a major role in solving this latest development in the Heather Lauren-Wyatt Oliver murders, but she could also clear away all suspicion about herself.

She hoped that whatever happened would provide opportunities for her to interact with the principals of the case on a less emotional and rushed basis. *And I hope Jim is praying about this column decision,* she thought, *because I don't even have the time to think about it.*

Except that down deep she wanted to graduate to that job more than anything she had wanted in a long time. *I'll have to remind Jim to pray for my humility,* she decided. *Getting this thing out of perspective or thinking it's something I deserve can be dangerous.*

She snapped on her watch. Only a few minutes to spare. One last look in the mirror on her way to the front closet showed her furry boots, corduroy Levis, a couple of layers of blouses and sweaters, topped by a cardigan buttoned all the way to the neck. She added a wool stocking cap and a down filled ski jacket and pulled on her mittens on the elevator—after pushing the buttons.

She nodded and smiled to the doorman, who sat at his station looking as if he were ready for bed. He looked surprised to see her again so soon, but he didn't ask any questions. The morning was even colder than Jennifer expected, shocking her fully awake as she swung out the door, notepads tucked under her arm.

"How can you look so good so early in the morning after such a short night?" Jim said as she slid into the car. "I'm dead."

"Ah, we're both dead," she said, "but you don't look so bad yourself." Except for the colors, they were dressed nearly alike.

"Where we goin', Nancy Drew?" he asked.

"Head toward West Stivers," she said. "I'll be reading to you as we go."

"It won't take long, this time of the morning," he said. "Read fast."

She did. She sped through both notepads, reading everything she'd written, commenting on most of it, and adding tidbits here and there from memory. Then she recounted the entire conversation she and Gerry Mayfield had had with Captain Halliday the night before, including all the exchanges between Halliday and Hank Henry.

"How can you remember all that, Jennifer?"

"I work on it. It's fun. I've always been able to do it. The only thing I regret about last night is that I agreed not to use any of the Halliday stuff in the paper. Would make great copy, don't you think?"

"Yeah. Now what do you want me to think about it? Much of it was new to me; some of it wasn't. I heard a few interesting things, but for the sake of time—that is if there's something you want to do before the sun comes up—you'd better coach me a little."

"Well, what is it you've always told me about investigative work? Haven't you said it's the little things that slip past the first time, the seemingly insignificant things, the apparently unrelated things that wind up making the difference?"

"Yeah. It's always amazing how the things you hear somehow fit together. Later they make sense and you wonder how you almost missed them, but most people do anyway. Did you hear something that you think no one else picked up on? That's the type of thing that'll break this case."

"I tried to recite the stuff to you straight, Jim, without any inflection to give away what I think is significant. Did you pick up on anything?"

"Not really, but then I'm not really awake yet."

So she went back and selectively read and recited various elements to see if he agreed they fit together. By his movement and tone of voice, she could tell he was warming to her speculations.

"First," she said, "settle in your mind who might have had access to the schedule on which Social Services takes people shopping. The murderer had to know that."

"Right, OK."

"Then consider this: Angela Liachi may have been a viable suspect early on because of her threat, which had been on record. And she had been seen in the neighborhood, as I had. But neither of us were really solid suspects after the evidence technicians finished their work and after West Side homicide detectives had talked to the neighbors."

"True enough. So?"

"Well, after the autopsy, when the angle of the puncture wounds and the strength needed to inflict wounds to that back muscle and rib cage was determined, we were both in the clear."

"Right, and after the evidence technicians determined the shoe size of the foot that kicked open Oliver's door, I gotta think Halliday and Grom and Henry are looking for a big man."

"Yeah, but they may be looking too far."

"I don't follow you, Jenn."

"Don't you think Angela and I were scapegoats for awhile?"

"You maybe; she was a solid suspect for long enough. And scapegoats for whom. You think they have a more solid suspect they're hiding?"

"Or protecting?"

"Hiding, I could see. Then they can reveal him at a press conference and take a lot of credit. Why would they protect a solid suspect?"

"Tell me this, Jim: why would Grom have arrested me at the office when his partner, Hank Henry, had already interviewed neighbors, three of whom said they had seen Oliver alive after they had seen me run from his building?"

"You said Henry was in the car when Grom was in your office, so he had to have told Grom."

"Sure he told him. Grom ignored it for some reason."

"Maybe he thought you knew too much, or he wanted to punish you for harboring Angela, whom he thought was the real murderer."

Jim approached the Oliver apartment building on West Stivers. "Pull around the side, Jim, but not in the alley. When I was in the alley last night, after being inside the building, I noticed only one place wide enough for a panel truck to fit. The driver could have pulled in and backed out, but he or she could not have driven all the way through the alley."

"Jenn, that gray, panel truck type vehicle business came from one kid. No one else saw it come or go."

"And what did you just tell me about little, insignificant pieces of evidence?"

"But does your whole case rest on whether that type of vehicle was in the alley?"

"Sort of."

"So that's why you wanted the evidence kit? For tire tracks?"

"Uh huh."

"No guarantees in this weather. The ground could have been so hard that no tracks were left; of course, a vehicle that big might leave tracks anyway. But if the ground has thawed and refrozen since it was here—if it was here—we'll get nothing."

Jim pulled the heavy case from the trunk, and he and Jennifer dropped to all fours with a flashlight and crawled into the alley from the north. Almost immediately Jim held up a hand to stop her. "Wide tracks," he whispered. "You were right. There's no proof it's the same vehicle, but there couldn't be too many trucks that go back here. A garbage truck couldn't even fit in here. Hey, I can see the evidence technicians have been here."

"Yeah," Jennifer said, "but they don't know where to start looking for tires to match the tracks."

"And you do?"

"Of course, Jim. You think I'd get up this early otherwise?"

In minutes, Jim had mixed a special plastic epoxy and poured ten-inch squares on three different patches of good tracks. He also poured some in a shoe heel track. "I got a C in fingerprinting," he said. "But I was real good on tire tracks in frozen ground!"

He waited five minutes, then carefully peeled up the reverse images, which had the consistency of rubber. He also measured the distance between the tracks. As they headed back to the car, he said, "Anything else?"

"Nope. Not unless you want to look for the tracks of a woman who broke a boot heel back here, a little farther south in the alley."

"It wouldn't be hard to find. Now where do we go?"

"First, Jim, tell me how difficult it would be for anyone in either Oliver's or Whalum's building to see a vehicle parked where you made the track impressions."

He crept past a wood wall behind a ramshackle garage. "You're right," he said. "I doubt you could see it from there even if you were watching for it."

"But no one was watching for it."

"How do you know that?"

"Because everyone except one kid was distracted by police activity in front of the Whalum residence. Hank Henry was there twenty minutes, giving Lionel a little heat, remember?"

"Yeah. What are you saying?"

"You'll see. Take me about three blocks north of the West Side Precinct station, and I'll keep track of how long it takes us. Just drive the speed limit."

FIFTEEN

Less than ten minutes later, Jim pulled up to the curb across from the Chevy dealer on North Lester Avenue. The sun was rising, and employees of the service department were pulling into the lot.

When the big garage door opened, Jim drove in. "You're a little early," a young mechanic said. "What can we do for you?"

"I need to talk to whoever worked on Sergeant Grom's van yesterday."

"Is that the cop's, the big silver and gray job with the one-way windows?"

"That's the one."

"Melvin!"

"Yeah!"

"Guy's got a question here about the cop's van!"

Melvin, who was already greasy with the day hardly begun, jogged over. "Who's askin'?"

"I am," Jim said.

"You a friend of Grom's?"

"Yes."

"Was there a problem? All we did was an oil change and lube job."

"No problem. He's gonna settle up today, huh?"

"I guess."

"Can I see the ticket? I'll be seeing him this morning, and I can tell him how much."

"Sure. I'll give you his copy. He's good for it."

The invoice showed that Grom had delivered the van a few minutes before eight o'clock in the morning, the previous day.

"He musta picked it up last night after closing, 'cause it was still here when I left."

"When was the work done?"

"Oh, let's see. I finished his by noon."

"You sure?"

"Yeah. Finished a Trans Am first, then Sarge's work comes next, every time."

"I'm sure he appreciates it."

"I hope so."

Captain John Halliday did not appreciate being awakened by Jennifer Grey after such a short night. But when he heard what she and Jim had uncovered, he agreed to meet them at the West Side station.

He arrived less than a half hour later—unshaven, wearing work clothes under a red and black woolen hunting jacket, and having just dragged a comb through his white hair. "This is terrible," he kept saying, "but let's not jump to any conclusions."

When presented with all of Jennifer's reasoning, he propped both elbows up on his desk and held his head in his hands. He buzzed the desk. "What have you got for Grom yesterday between three-thirty and four-thirty?"

"Just a minute, Cap. Ah, yeah, away from the office on foot. Coffee break."

"Get Hank Henry on the line for me, will ya? Thanks."

Jim and Jennifer sat silently, occasionally catching one another's eye, as Halliday slumped in his chair. The intercom crackled. "Hank Henry on line two, Cap."

Halliday grabbed the phone. "Hank, I need you in here right away. Something's breakin' on the Oliver murder. . . . I'll tell ya when you get here."

Jennifer started to speak as they waited for Henry to arrive, but Jim put a finger to his lips. Halliday wandered up and down the halls, reading messages he himself had posted on the walls, some of them years before, but which he probably hadn't noticed since.

When Hank Henry arrived, they all piled into Halliday's unmarked squad car for the drive to the Near North Side. Henry alternately nodded in recognition of the conclusions that were being drawn and shook his head at the realization that his boss was in terrible trouble.

At the modest home of Sergeant Martin Grom, the four stood on the porch and rang the bell. They could hear kids running through the living room and up and down the stairs. The TV was blaring.

The five-year-old girl answered the door. "Hi, Jackie," Jennifer said, eliciting a smile.

"Hi, Red," Halliday said. "Your daddy home?"

She ran to get him as her mother came to the door with a worried look. "Good morning, John," she said. "Is something wrong? Marty's still in bed."

"Just want to talk with him for a few minutes, Roberta. Can you get him?"

She turned to head up the stairs, but Martin was already coming down in a robe and slippers. He looked as if he hadn't slept. "Throw a coat on, Martin," Halliday suggested. "Wanna talk to you out here a minute."

Grom reached for a heavy parka from a hook by the door and pulled it on as he came out. "Let's take a little walk," Halliday suggested.

"I don't wanna walk around the neighborhood in my nightclothes, Captain."

"We aren't going far, Martin."

Mrs. Grom shut the door slowly as the unusual fivesome walked awkwardly down the front walk to the sidewalk, west a few dozen feet and back up the driveway toward the garage. Hank Henry looked as if he wished he could be anywhere else.

"Why did you arrest Mrs. Grey last night when you knew Henry had interviewed several neighbors who saw Oliver alive after she left him?"

Grom looked first at Hank, then at Halliday. "I had my reasons."

"I want to hear one."

"She was harboring another suspect."

"The other suspect wasn't much better, Martin. Why did you send Hank to see Whalum yesterday?"

"We often hassle these known baddies, Cap'n. You know that."

"Not in the middle of a murder investigation we don't. You sure you didn't send him as a decoy, something for the neighbors to watch while you did some business in the neighborhood yourself?"

Grom stood with his shoulders hunched and his hands deep in his pockets, the icy wind whipping at his pajama legs and bare ankles. His breath began to come in short gusts from his nose, his lips were pressed tight. He said nothing.

"You changed your clothes somewhere on the way to and from Oliver's place yesterday, did you, Martin?" Halliday pressed.

Grom couldn't hold his boss's gaze and looked at the ground. He began to tremble. Halliday continued.

"Our guys were supposed to be out this morning looking for a big guy, big feet, probably a blue-collar worker, maybe an old truck driving associate of Oliver's, somebody that mighta pulled a gray panel truck type of a vehicle into the alley behind his place."

Grom took his hands from his pockets and covered his face. "But the tracks from that alley aren't gonna fit some panel truck somewhere, are they Martin? We can call off our guys, the ones who would have been reporting to you today, can't we?"

Grom began to weep.

"You wanna open the garage door for us, Martin, and let us measure the wheelbase and compare the track molds and maybe look around in there for a big pair of bloody shoes, maybe some gloves, maybe some work clothes?"

Grom shook his head.

"We don't have to do that, Martin? You gonna save us the trouble? You wanna admit that you wore your uniform yesterday so people on Stivers wouldn't recognize you as the same guy who'd come through the backyard in the middle of the afternoon? And that you borrowed your own van from the Chevy lot during your coffee break so it would look like it had been at the garage all day?"

Grom nodded, sobbing, as his wife emerged from the back door to embrace him. He nearly collapsed in her arms. "If only that Lauren woman had told me the truth on Wednesday!" he wailed. "If only she'd said then that he had murdered the girl, this wouldn't have been necessary!"

"You'll have to get dressed and come with us, Martin," Halliday said sadly.

"He was going to get off scot-free!" Grom moaned. "I couldn't let that happen!"

Epilogue

Today I write a column I'd rather not write. In fact it's a column I will never want to remember, but shall never be able to forget.

Today I saw a man's life and career disintegrate, a man who had given himself in service for his community and his family for years. Two days ago he told me, "If I had it my way, I'd kill Wyatt Oliver right now," and then begged me not to quote him. I didn't, but it no longer matters.

Yesterday he had it his own way, and today he confessed to the slaying of a child killer. A father himself, Chicago Police West Side Homicide Detective Sergeant Martin Grom will face the penalty for taking the law into his own hands, for giving up on the system, for plotting and carrying out his own form of justice. . . .

TOO LATE TO TELL

ONE

As much as Jennifer Grey disliked Bobby Block, his mysterious note intrigued her.

He had always been a young man of complex problems, one she had never been able to figure. Clearly, he had always envied her, and after only a brief period of conniving, he showed his true colors and tried openly to destroy her. But Jennifer had survived.

Bobby had been a hulking, earnest, dark-haired graduate student from Northwestern University's Medill School of Journalism when they had met. He was already in place as a special intern assistant to the police reporter when Jennifer was handpicked by *Chicago Day* City Editor Leo Stanton to take over the police beat.

"You can dump Block, or you can teach him," Stanton said in his usual blunt fifty-seven-year-old Ivy League way. "Your choice."

"He could probably teach *me*," Jennifer had said, not kidding. "I'll keep him for now, at least until I learn the ropes."

Stanton had shrugged. "He's an OK kid, a little cocky. Lots of potential. We'll find a spot for him either way. I just don't want you to feel saddled. You've got the budget for part-time help, but you can hire your own if you wish."

Jennifer hadn't wished. At least not at first. There had been many times since then that she would have given anything to have taken Leo up on his offer.

Bobby had been fine the first few days—telling Jennifer where everything was, introducing her to the key contacts in all the precincts. But she sensed something behind his surfacy self-deprecating comments. It wasn't long before she realized that he was working against her.

Bobby Block may have doubted his own worth or ability, but his insecurities surfaced in quiet insubordination. At first, he had simply seemed eager to be in on everything and get his share of good by-lined stories.

But soon Bobby was thwarting Jennifer at every turn, withholding crucial information, leaking her best tips to the competition, and putting her in a bad light before Leo. Bobby wasn't openly hostile until he had gotten her into serious trouble; only then did it hit her that he had been the source of her problems.

In the middle of her coverage of an Internal Affairs Division (IAD) dragnet, Bobby chose to reveal Jennifer's relationship with Police Officer James Purcell, one of the charged officers. Until Purcell was cleared, Jennifer had lost her job—which, of course, had been Bobby's intention.

Months later, when Jennifer graduated to a front-page column, Bobby was so incensed that he took to snooping around her stories, trying to scoop her. That cost him *his* job, and within hours he was snapped up by the *Tribune*, from which he had waged a smear campaign against Jennifer. He even tried to implicate her in a murder that she and Jim Purcell eventually solved.

That cooled Bobby's jets for a while, and except for an occasional veiled barb at Jennifer, Bobby had settled into his role as police reporter at the *Tribune*. He had graduated with honors, alienated classmates and profs, annoyed his superiors and co-workers, and raised the hackles of the police officers he needed as sources. Yet still he flourished.

His secret was good writing laced with sarcasm and satire. The readers loved it. But Bobby had a growing list of professional enemies who soon realized that little he had ever said about Jennifer Grey had been true.

Jennifer, however, had been left with a nagging conscience over her failure to ever get next to Bobby—to find out what it was that made him so obnoxious, so committed to making waves, so unhappy unless he was fighting. She felt she and Jim had something to offer Bobby. But she realized she had been naive to think he would listen.

Twice she had called for appointments with him, hoping to bury the hatchet, to just chat, to grab a bite at Berghoffs. Neither time did Bobby even return her call. She had settled on what she would say, how she would begin. It wouldn't be that difficult, because she had grown to appreciate certain aspects of his writing.

She knew he was a better pure writer than she was, with less warmth and feeling and people-orientation perhaps, but with a certain concise purity nonetheless. And he had become a careful researcher. That surprised her. More than a few times she had recognized in his stories much careful homework and documentation of facts.

That was something she had tried to teach him over and over, yet he had been content to wing it, to guess, to assume. Maybe now that he was on his own at one of the top papers in the country, he felt forced to do it right. Or maybe someone was doing it for him.

Regardless, his writing had improved. She wanted to tell him that. But for a long time, Bobby pretended she didn't exist. She decided a cold war was better than his all-out efforts to ruin her had been in the past. Jennifer wished he would at least respond somehow, even if to say no to her invitation to lunch.

And then on Wednesday, his note had come. It read simply:

> Boy, Jennifer, do I ever need to talk to you!
> Yes, let's do lunch this week. So much to make you understand.
> B.B.

Jennifer called him right away and left a message for him to phone her. The next day she stood watching the Associated Press wire machine, looking for a Sunday column idea. Often the reporters resented the privileged columnists leaving their offices and getting in the way, so she was careful to stand aside any time anyone approached the machine.

"Hey, Jenn!" rewrite man Dick Harlan called from his desk, phone to his ear. "You know Block from the *Trib*?"

Several others looked up, annoyed, so Jennifer just nodded and approached Dick, assuming Bobby had finally returned her call.

"Found him dead," Harlan said.

Jennifer froze while others gathered around Harlan. "Just a minute," he said, listening. He hung up. Jennifer couldn't make her legs carry her farther, but she could hear Dick from where she stood.

"Didn't show up for work this morning, but nobody from the *Trib* checked until about noon. They couldn't get an answer, and the landlord said his car was still in the parking garage, so someone went over. His girlfriend had just shown up with the same idea when they got there. She had a key."

"How'd he die?" someone asked.

"Nobody knows yet. He do dope, Jenn?"

She shook her head, still rooted to her spot.

"We'll know soon," Harlan said. "In time for the fourth edition."

Jennifer walked stiff-legged back to her office. She phoned Jim. "I just heard about it," he said. "I don't know any more'n you do. You going over there?"

"Is there anything to see?"

"I s'pose. They just found him. Probably haven't even removed the body yet."

"I guess I will. Jim, this is doing a strange thing to me. I don't know why."

"It's always tough when you've known someone, Jennifer."

"I guess. See you later?"

"We hadn't planned anything tonight. You need to see me?"

"Maybe."

"Should I stay available?"

"Would you?"

"For you? I'll be here."

Jennifer fought tears in the car, wondering if it was because of some strange grief over Bobby Block and the frustration of likely never finding out what he wanted to tell her or the gratitude she felt for being loved by someone like Jim. Who knew what Jim might have had planned for tonight? The baseball season had just started; the Sox would be on television. He often had friends in to watch the game.

At Bobby Block's apartment a few blocks away, Jennifer slipped past police lines without a hitch. It had been many months since she'd had to show her press credentials to get in to a crime scene. She nodded to several acquaintances, none of whom spoke.

She had seen Bobby's girl, still a student at Northwestern, only once before. Jennifer almost didn't recognize her in her grubbies, but Adrienne Eden could have been Bobby's sister. Like him, she was taller and heftier than average.

In jeans and a baggy flannel shirt, her long, curly, black hair a mess, Adrienne sat at the end of the hall, pressing wads of tissue paper to her eyes as reporters crowded around her. Jennifer decided not to intrude just then. But when she turned to check out the apartment, Adrienne cursed her in a sob.

"Wonder if you were here earlier today!" she added. "Little Miss Righteousness!"

Jennifer flushed and ducked into the apartment, wondering if Adrienne could have known about Bobby's note and also realizing that if the other reporters had not known whom Adrienne was addressing, Adrienne would tell them. And now Jennifer found herself not ten feet from the bloated, discolored body of Robert A. Block, twenty-five, deceased. He was bare-chested and barefoot, wearing pajama bottoms. Police evidence technicians shot their final photographs, and the Cook County coroner made a few more notes before signaling paramedics to cover the body and lift it onto a litter.

The medical examiner was taken aback when Jennifer asked what he thought, because she was the only reporter in the room and didn't even have her notebook out. Dr. Jacob Steinmetz recognized her, though.

"Hard to say yet, Miss Grey. Didn't appear to be strangulation, and I found no preliminary signs of poisoning, though he apparently died while eating."

Jennifer peered past him into the kitchenette where a cold breakfast remained on the table.

"Could have been a heart attack. He carried a lot of weight for a young man."

"He couldn't have been murdered?"

"I couldn't say. Don't think so. No sign of foul play. If it was a poisoning, it was pretty sophisticated. Nothing common anyway. I thought he had choked on food, but I was wrong. You can see from the upended chair in there that he apparently bolted from the table into here and collapsed. Nasty head wound from hitting the floor, but I don't think that killed him. I'm guessing he was dead before he hit the floor. We'll see. If this had happened a few years ago, I'd fear cyanide—but I doubt it here."

Other reporters were crowding around. "I'll have a statement in a few hours," Dr. Steinmetz said. "Nothing now, thank you."

Several grumbled about his having talked to a columnist, but none followed him when he left. "Why does his girl friend hate you?" someone asked.

"I don't know," Jennifer said, wishing she could give them a "No comment" but knowing how they would despise it. "I hardly know the woman."

"She says you had it in for Block."

It wasn't a question, so Jennifer didn't respond.

"That true?" someone asked.

"Of course not."

"Had you two dated?"

"Don't be silly," Jennifer said. "Bobby had worked for me. You know that. I have nothing more to say."

"He was pretty tough on you in the paper. You fire him?"

"No."

"Who did?"

"My boss. I'm through talking."

"Why was he fired?"

"Ask my boss." Jennifer pushed her way through to the elevator. The questions continued until she was in her car, and she sensed the frustration of people who were subjected to that regularly. Her one consolation was that none of the three papers in Chicago was a scandal sheet. The reporters asked tough questions to elicit answers, but none would print the screaming headlines of the yellow journalist.

Was Bobby going to apologize for having caused Jennifer so much trouble? Was he going to explain himself, maybe make excuses? Did he know his life was in danger? Jennifer knew she would never know unless she searched for the answers herself.

Back at her office, she phoned the precinct station house to find that a Cap Duffy had been assigned to the case. She didn't recognize the name. "That a nickname?" she asked.

"I dunno," the desk sergeant said. "Prob'ly."

"Rank?"

"Just a detective."

"Homicide?"

"Yeah."

"Who decided this was a homicide?"

"Who's askin', lady? Young, healthy guy croaks at breakfast with no food in his throat. That sounds suspicious to me, homicide or not. We got to check out the suspicious deaths, right? So who would *you* put on a suspicious death, someone in vice control?"

Jennifer buzzed Dick Harlan.

"Rewrite."

"Yeah, Dick, Jennifer. Who've you got on the Block death? I didn't see anybody over there."

"I don't know if anybody's on it yet, Jenn. What were you doing there?"

"I have no restrictions."

"I know, but you wouldn't write about *that* death, would you?"

"I might. Why not?"

"Well, I mean, I don't know. Just seems sorta tacky, that's all. Forget it, what do I know? You want me to let you know when I find out who Leo assigns?"

"Nah, thanks. I'll ask him."

"It'll be a tough one to assign, won't it, Jenn?"

"How's that?"

"Just for fairness, we should find someone who didn't go to Medill, shouldn't we?"

"I guess," Jennifer said.

"That won't be easy around here."

"*I* didn't go to Medill."

"Yeah, but you're a star. And talk about fairness. No way you'll get assigned to this one. If you cover Bobby Block's death, you'll be doing it in your column, not in the news."

Two

"So, what did Leo say?" Jim asked at dinner, reaching for Jennifer's hand across the table.

"He agreed with Harlan."

"How about you? Don't you agree with Harlan?"

"Of course. But Leo says old man Cooper doesn't want me to deal with it even in my column, and there weren't supposed to be any limitations on my column."

Jim smiled and straightened as the waiter arrived, and Jennifer watched as he ordered. She had always envied Jim's ability to chat casually with perfect strangers. Usually his rosy complexion and pale blue eyes, offset by almost white blond hair, distracted listeners long enough for him to put them at ease.

When they were alone again, she interrupted her own story to thank Jim again for changing his plans for her.

He brushed it off. "I'd rather be with you than a bunch of divorced cops or married ones who should be home with their wives, anyway. And it's not like you haven't done the same for me."

"But you enjoy relaxing and watching a ball game."

"More than being with you? Someday I'll prove you wrong about that."

Jennifer didn't want to pursue *that* statement. If they were married, she'd watch the games with him, and they'd kill both birds with the same stone. But the mention of marriage was not going to come from her lips first. Maybe he didn't want to marry a widow anyway.

From the look in his eyes she would have guessed that indeed he did, and she couldn't help looking forward to his endearing good-bye. She never liked the thought of being apart from him, yet he was so loving, so gentle with her, embracing her as if she were a fragile china doll.

He lit old fires in her, yet he didn't push her, didn't exhibit the urgency that would have scared her off. She found him exciting; she loved him. And she couldn't shake the crazy feeling that, though the good-bye would mean she would be apart from him again, she longed for the thrill, the beauty, the purity of it.

After their salads came and they had prayed, she asked, "Do you think Max Cooper has a right to renege on his commitment to my freedom with the column?"

"Absolutely," Jim said, without hesitation.

It had been a rhetorical question, begging an answer that would allow Jennifer's soliloquy to masquerade as dialogue. Jim's response, of course, brought her up short.

"You *do*?"

"Of course. You believe in freedom of the press, don't you?"

"Ah, yes. But, uh, that was going to be *my* argument, Sweetheart. How does freedom of the press justify Cooper's position and not mine?"

"Freedom of the press belongs to the one who owns the press, not to the ones who are employed by him."

She sat silent. "But he promised," she said finally.

"That's *his* problem. He'll have to live with that. But certainly it's his prerogative to change his mind. And he *does* have a point in this case, Jenn."

"I was afraid you were going to get around to that," she said smiling. "I hate logic."

They ate in silence, occasionally gazing deep into each other's eyes. Jennifer wondered at herself and how she could unabashedly stare at Jim without even attempting to hide her pleasure in him. The April 21 evening was unseasonably warm, so after dinner they walked to the Oak Street Beach and sat on concrete benches.

"I shouldn't have reacted so impulsively to your question," Jim said, his arm around her waist. "You wanted an ear; I gave you a mouth."

"But you were right, Jim. It's just that I *want* to write about Bobby Block."

"Why?"

"I haven't thought that through. As soon as I was over the initial shock, I knew I had to get to know him as soon as possible. The sooner he's in the ground, the less chance that I'll know anything about him."

Jim squinted out at a blinking light a mile off the shore. "Are you sure there's anything there to know?" he asked. "Could it be that Block was just one of those selfish types who crash through life, destroying everything and everybody in their way?"

"Maybe."

"But it's not his death you want to write about?"

"Not really. There was a core of something there, something deeper than what everyone saw. It's what made him a decent police reporter after all, in spite of everything."

"Decency from indecency, huh? But you can't write about him, Jenn."

"Why not?"

"The guy in the city room—"

"Harlan?"

"Yeah, he's right. It would be tacky. If you're not investigating the death, you can only write about what you know. You haven't talked with the man for months. The only contact you had with him was unpleasant. He was a scoundrel. He was out to get you. He hurt you, slowed your career, never gave you a chance to fight back or even know what his beef was. Is that what you want to print about a dead man?"

Jennifer stood and faced Lake Shore Drive, watching the cars and buses and hearing the tires and horns. After two years of working in the city, those sounds had become a mere backdrop that no longer abused the senses.

Why did she want to pursue Bobby Block to his grave? Should she feel guilty for not having told him of her faith? She couldn't remember one opportunity. It seemed all she had done in his presence was defend herself or be careful not to implicate herself.

That wasn't it. In fact, Bobby knew where she stood and taunted her for it. It appeared to make him hostile, or threaten him somehow. She had tried not to intentionally turn him off. But he had been turned off anyway.

Jim stood behind her and massaged her shoulders. He said nothing. That was one of the reasons she loved him so. He knew when to counsel, when to talk, when to ask, when to be quiet.

"I know there's nothing I can write about him yet," she admitted. Jim rested his chin on her shoulder from behind so he could hear her over the din of the traffic. She turned and kissed him, and they walked back to his car.

Instead of letting him open the door for her, however, she leaned back against it and gently drew him to herself. "How about two good-byes tonight?" she asked.

He raised his eyebrows. "Hmm?"

"One now—and one at the door," she said.

"Twist my arm," he said, kissing her.

"I've got a couple of drawers worth of research on some interesting columns," she said in the car. "I'm going to try to bang out three tomorrow before two o'clock. That'll give me a few days to snoop around."

"Where are you going to snoop?"

"Northwestern."

"Yeah?" he said, as if making a list and waiting for the next location.

"And Bobby's apartment building."

"Yeah, OK, that'll be picked over pretty good by the time you get there."

"His family."

"Good. And?"

"And?"

"You're leaving out two perfectly logical places."

"I told you—"

"I know, you hate logic. But you're still logical, so where else will you dig?"

"The *Trib*."

"I love it."

"Why?"

"I knew you'd say the *Trib*, but think about it. Think how you'd respond if reporters from the *Sun-Times* waltzed over to research in *your* shop. How would they be received?"

"It wouldn't be a problem, Jim. It really wouldn't. In fact, I think we'd respect them and show them deference. It would be a good chance to show professionalism."

"Except that you aren't just a reporter, Jenn. And you're not just *any* columnist. You're Block's former boss. You're one of the reasons he was fired. You and he go back a long, shabby way."

"Meaning?"

"You had a motive to murder the man, Jenn."

"Come on, Jim."

"I know, but am I wrong?"

Jennifer stared straight ahead, as if studying the road as Jim pulled into the parking garage beneath her building. "I don't suppose they'd welcome me with open arms. So what's the other logical place I left out?"

"It's so obvious I'll spare you the embarrassment of telling you."

"You mean the Police Department?"

"Of course," Jim said.

"Well, sure, that's why I didn't mention it." They laughed.

On the elevator she asked Jim about the detective with the funny name.

"Yeah, I like Duffy a lot. We were uniformed beat cops together. I rode with him a few times. All he's ever wanted to be in his life was a detective."

"And he's a good one?"

"Oh, yes. One of the best."

"But he's not a sergeant or anything like that?"

"Doesn't want to be. Wants to be on the street—hustling, working."

"Will I like him?"

"Oh, sure. Question is, will he like you?"

Jennifer leaned back against her door and took Jim's hands in hers. "How could anybody not like me?" she asked, smiling.

He chuckled. "Cap has never been comfortable around women."

"Is he married?"

"Yes, and to the perfect match. He treats her like a queen, and apparently she doesn't grouse about his crazy hours and his idiosyncrasies."

"Which are?"

"Just like any career detective. He's *always* on a case. Any time of the day or night, talking about it, making calls, running here and there."

"A woman would really have to trust a man like that."

"Oh, and she does. When you meet him, you'll know he's trustworthy. It's written all over him."

"Children?"

"Nope."

"Interesting."

"That he is."

"Would he be working tonight?"

"Probably. Until he knows how Block died. Why?"

"Then I'm still working."

"Jenn, you're tired. You're not really going out again tonight, are you?"

"No, but I can call him, can't I?"

"Incurable," Jim said, shaking his head. And he kissed her good night a second time. Maybe next time, she decided, she'd try for three good-byes.

"Chicago Police."

"Detective Duffy, please."

"Who may I say is calling?"

"Jennifer Grey, *Chicago Day.*"

"Oh, hi, Miss Grey. Cap's on the street. Want me to have him call you?"

She gave him her private number at the *Day*. Then she called the night wire editor and asked if he would program the phone in Jennifer's office to ring at her apartment number, which Jennifer never publicized to outsiders.

She was nearly asleep an hour later when her phone rang.

"Jennifer Grey?"

"Who's calling, please?" she said.

"Duffy."

"Oh, yes! Mr. Duffy, how are you?"

"I'm, uh, fine, ma'am. How are you?"

"Fine, fine. Can we get together?"

"I don't think so. What can I do for you?"

"I'm calling regarding Robert Block. Have you determined the cause of death?"

"Well, that's not for me to determine, ma'am. That's up to the—"

"I know, Mr. Duffy. Has the medical examiner determined the cause of death?"

"Momentarily."

"Pardon me?"

"I'm calling from his office. We're expecting his statement any minute."

"Would you mind very much calling me with it?"

"Well, I don't know. If it's what I think it's going to be, I may be pretty busy."

"Keeping track of suspects?"

"Ma'am?"

"You know what I mean, Detective Duffy. The only thing you think it could be that would keep you busy would be murder. Why are you thinking it might be murder?"

"Well, not specifically murder."

"What else would concern you?"

"Well, manslaughter, justifiable homicide, stuff like that."

"But you're saying that you think it's probably a suspicious death, so—"

"Well, any death is suspicious until it's explained."

"I know, I know," Jennifer said, exasperated. Maybe Duffy was more charming in person. "Can you tell me why you it might be a death of other than natural causes?"

"You mean besides the fact that the man was only twenty-five years old?"

"Yes."

"No."

"No?"

"No."

"Why not?"

"Because I'm afraid you would be one of the suspects, ma'am, and frankly, you're the only one who's tried to reach *me* tonight."

Jennifer smiled, but kept from laughing. "I imagine I am," she said.

"Can you tell me the approximate time of death?"

"Not until I get your alibis, ma'am."

"Uh-huh. And I don't suppose you want those by phone."

"Not unless you want to give them to me."

"No," she said, not wanting to miss the privilege of meeting this man. "When and if the M.E. decides the cause of death, you know where to find me. But let me get a good night's sleep first, OK?"

"You won't be going anywhere?"

"Of course not."

"I may regret it, but I'm going to believe you, because you're such a visible person."

"Thank you."

"And because you're a friend of Jim Purcell."

"That's the real reason you trust me, isn't it?"

"Yes, ma'am," Duffy said, almost apologetically.

"He's the best credential I've got, even with my picture on the front page of the paper everyday."

"Yes, ma'am."

"Tell me something. Block died this morning while eating breakfast, right?"

"I'd rather interview you before we get into that, ma'am."

"I was there, Mr. Duffy. I saw him in his pajamas."

"Alive?"

"Of course not."

"But we might have found your prints in the apartment?"

"I'm not that careless after all these years. No, if you found unidentified prints in the apartment, unless they were on the arm of the medical examiner's coat, they aren't mine. You'll call me in the morning?"

"Yes, ma'am."

THREE

The next morning on her way to work, Jennifer heard a radio report from Coroner Steinmetz. He had determined the cause of Bobby's death as a slow, timed poison that could have entered the bloodstream as early as eighteen to twenty-four hours before he died.

In her office, Jennifer felt strangely distracted as she hunched over a two-drawer file and studied research on the three columns she hoped to finish by mid-afternoon.

This was the second time in her brief career with the *Day* that she'd been a possible suspect in a murder case—someone who had been in close enough proximity to the victim that she could not be ruled out without at least a hasty investigation.

Jennifer sensed someone in the doorway of her office and looked up into the wryly smiling face of City Editor Leo Stanton. He had his usual early morning look. Brown wing-tipped shoes, cuffed and pleated and perfectly seamed dark brown wool slacks, powder blue button-down shirt—already unbuttoned at the neck—with a slightly loosened blue and brown club tie of just the right width, and an unbuttoned, beige sweater vest.

Leo was classic, natty-but-casual East Coast establishment, and only the ever-present unlit cigar spoiled the effect. He had removed it from his lips so he could grin at Jennifer, but the sight of a well-dressed middle-aged man of success with a soggy cigar in his hand almost made Jennifer gag.

No one who liked the boss ever criticized him for his pacifier, and she liked him. She returned his smile.

"So how's my perennial murder suspect this morning?"

"I'm all right, Leo. How'd you know?"

"You must have your phone turned off or something. A detective has been calling and getting no answer, and he's afraid you've skipped town on him."

"Oh, no," she said, quickly reprogramming her phone.

"Not to worry, Ma Barker. I told him you were here."

"Is he coming?"

"No. Wants you to come there."

"Where's there?"

"Chicago Avenue Precinct Station." Jennifer started to assemble her things. "You've got time," Leo added. "You're supposed to be there at eleven. Anyway, don't I get to hear this story first?"

She pointed to a magazine-stacked chair. Leo lifted the stack and sat, holding the magazines in his lap. "What do you want to hear, Leo? You know I don't kill people."

He put his left hand atop the magazines for balance and returned the stogie to his mouth, jamming it between his teeth and the inside of his cheek so only half of it still showed. It left him remarkably articulate.

"You can't tell me you wouldn't have been tempted a time or two to waste Bobby Block."

"Leo, you know me better than that. I get mad at people, sure, and Bobby drove me crazy. But no, I never once thought of injuring the kid, let alone killing him." She had decided not to tell Leo about the note. At least not yet.

Leo grinned at her.

"You don't believe me?" she said.

"'Course I do. I was just thinking that *I* often thought of injuring him."

Jennifer fell silent, remembering the storied battles between the undisputed expert veteran of the staff and the know-it-all upstart from Medill who liked to preface his remarks with, "If I was running the city room—"

"Maybe *you* should be a suspect," Jennifer said finally.

Leo smiled again, then appeared deep in thought, the smile fading. "It's really sad, isn't it?" he said. "I can't say I've missed Block since we let him go, but it's weird to think that he's dead."

"Dead is one thing," Jennifer said. "Poisoned is something else."

"And he had done quite a job for the *Tribune*, hadn't he?" Leo said, as if he hadn't heard her.

"You wish you'd kept him and let *me* go?"

That brought Leo back. He turned to stare at her. "You kidding?"

They each looked down and said nothing. Leo stood and replaced the magazines. A short laugh sneaked from his throat. "Think of where we'd be now," he said. He moved to the door but stopped and turned on his way out. "If you want to talk when you get back, I'll be here."

"Thanks, Leo. I'm going to want to finish a couple of more columns today to give me a little breather."

He squinted at her. "You never needed a breather in your life. What are you up to?"

"I just want time to do my own snooping on this thing."

"Why?"

Jennifer stood and sat atop her cluttered desk. "I don't know, Leo. Block intrigues me somehow. I could never get next to him. You know how you usually know, or think you know, what someone's problem is?"

Leo nodded.

"With Bobby, I never knew. I thought I did. I guessed ambition, jealousy, that type of thing."

"Me too," Leo said. "I still think so."

"I don't. There was something more there." She wondered if she would have thought so, had she not received the note.

Leo looked at his watch. "You've got an hour before you have to see the detective," he said. "You got another minute for me?"

He shut the door. This time he put the magazines on the floor and leaned forward as he sat, elbows on his knees, eyes intense. "I've got to admit something to you, Jennifer.

It doesn't surprise me that you want to get into this case and probably write about it, am I right?"

She nodded.

"You also know how that would look?"

"I've been told by many people."

"Not by me," he said.

"No, but you're about to tell me I can't do it."

"Not necessarily. But you're going to have to take a different approach."

"Different from what, Leo? I haven't said anything about how I might do it."

"You forget that I know you, Jenn. If I had to guess, you'd either write about having worked with him and you'd hint about a troubling aspect of his personality, one you admit you have not figured out—"

Jennifer started to speak, but Leo continued, "or you'd write about how shocking and unsettling it is to know someone who has been robbed of life at a prime age. Those are old saws, Jenn, tearjerkers. And it doesn't take a top-notch columnist to do them. They're too easy."

"Well, you don't have to believe me, Leo, but that's not the approach I was going to take."

She told him of her plan to poke around the *Trib,* Block's apartment building, Northwestern, and the Police Department.

Leo shook his head. "Your strength is also your curse, Jenn. You've become too visible to be effective as an investigative reporter. Forget it."

Jennifer wasn't entirely convinced, but she'd heard it so many times she was beginning to waver. "You said you weren't going to tell me I couldn't do it. What's the new approach, the one you think *would* work?"

"You like to write continuing pieces as opposed to one-shot deals like you're trying to bat out today, right?"

She nodded.

"Cover the investigation. You always hear from cops that you learn more about someone's life from studying his death than you'd learn from him when he was alive."

Jennifer thought for a moment. "But that's been overdone too, hasn't it? The highly descriptive pieces about dingy station houses and scruffy cops who work around the clock?"

"So do it fresh," Leo said. "Give it the perspective of a woman who knew the victim. And avoid the clichés. You don't know if this detective is interesting or not."

"Jim thinks he is, but the guy wouldn't win any personality contests, at least based on our phone conversation last night."

"He's got an interesting name," Leo said. "You've got to give him that. Duffy. But why would they put a captain on this investigation?"

"He's not a captain."

"I thought he told me he was Captain Duffy from Homicide."

"No. *Cap* Duffy. He's not even a sergeant."

"I'm intrigued already. You?"

"I thought Cooper said I couldn't write about Block."

"I've already talked to him about this. You want to do it or not?"

"Of course I do. And thanks, Leo."

"You kickin' me out?"

"Hm?"

"That was a conversation-ending *thanks*, Jenn."

"Since when does the employee kick out the employer, Leo?"

"When the employee becomes as important to the paper as the City Editor, that's when."

"I appreciate that, Leo, but I'm not taking this visible celebrity thing seriously. I know who I am, and you know you're the brains behind my column, so don't think I'll ever get uppity about it. You taught me everything I know and gave me the confidence to do what I'm doing."

Leo stood, smiling a tight-lipped smile. "And don't you forget it," he said. "Seriously, Jennifer, that was nice. Do you really believe that?"

Jennifer grinned mischievously. "No, but it seemed like the right thing to say at the time."

"Ooh, you're bad," Leo said, pointing at her.

She stood and opened the door.

"Now you *are* kicking me out," he said.

"You got that right."

As he passed her she added seriously, "You know what's really good about this? I despise writing timeless columns that could run anytime, even if getting ahead does free me up a little."

"I know what you mean. Your column needs that daily freshness. And if people get hooked on one of your angles, they'll stay with you for a week or even two on the same topic. This should be worth at least that."

At 10:50 A.M. Jennifer announced herself at the desk of the Chicago Avenue Precinct station. She was directed to sit on an oily wood bench across from an identical one, on which was heavily settled an elderly woman, dressed as if for winter.

The woman wore dark, thick horn-rimmed glasses under a heavy scarf tied around her head. She wore a thick overcoat and stumpy rubber boots, flanked on either side by twine-handled shopping bags, both worn thin, but one ironically bearing the name of an exclusive shop in Water Tower Place. Jennifer wondered if the woman had been arrested for shoplifting or was just waiting for someone.

Jennifer tried to smile at the old woman, who stared straight ahead, as if seeing nothing, sleeping with her eyes open. Presently another woman, not as heavy but similarly dressed, trudged from the tile corridor and stood by her.

Without acknowledging her companion's presence, Rubber Boots slowly stood, grasped her bags, and wandered out to the front door with her friend. Jennifer's eyes followed them out, and when she turned back around, a seedy looking man had taken the woman's place on the opposite bench.

Jennifer had planned to kill her waiting time by making up stories about the women and the dastardly thing they might have done to result in their being hauled in by the police. But this man would be even more interesting to use as fiction fodder.

He was reading the racing form on the sports page, and Jennifer wondered if he had ever won a dime. He was thin and small, perhaps wiry, and he appeared down on his luck.

When she was sure he was deep into the fine print, she checked him out carefully. He wore thick-soled, soft fabric shoes; short, dark green, double-knit, polyester slacks that reached the tops of his ankles and revealed thin, light green socks with yellow triangles and elastic tops that had been through a hot dryer one time too many. A dingy dark green and off-white sports coat peeked out from under the bottom of a corduroy car coat, one of those with oblong buttons that poke through any remaining unbroken leatherette loops. It had zippered pockets, one of which still looked zippable.

His face was thin and pointed, and he had a cleft both in his chin and between his nostrils. His lips were a little too generous for his small mouth, and he had large, sad, gray eyes that were slightly bloodshot and peered out at the paper over puffy bags.

He appeared about ten days overdue for a haircut, with curly wisps showing from behind his neck. His sideburns were not only a tad too long, but also curling up in the middle. Jennifer wondered why his hair wasn't greasy, for it didn't seem to fit in with the rest of his appearance. His hands also were clean, and he was clean shaven.

Beside him on the bench was a hat that appeared to match his tie. It was pale green with yellow and brown plaid.

She looked at her watch and decided that if Detective Duffy was on time, she would have about a minute to guess Green and Brown's story. She was daydreaming a tale about his having lost his wallet at the racetrack and having come in to see if anyone had turned it in, when she realized he was looking at her from over the top of his newspaper.

Jennifer quickly looked away and ran her fingers between the back of her neck and her hair. When she stole a glance back at him, he was still looking at her, and she hoped she hadn't offended him by staring at him for so long.

She started to look away again, but she noticed him reach to the inside breast pocket of his sports coat and produce a pair of half glasses. He put them on and began digging through the paper.

She wondered why he needed his glasses to pore through the paper when he hadn't worn them to study the racing charts. He turned to the front page, and she noticed he was reading the *Day*. He folded it up so that her column and her mug shot stared out at him.

Did he recognize her? He looked at the column photo and then at her over the tops of his spectacles. Jennifer couldn't fight a blush as she nodded to acknowledge his gaze. He carefully placed the paper beneath his hat on the bench, ceremoniously took off his glasses, and replaced them in his pocket.

He clapped a palm on each of his knees and leaned forward, peering intently into Jennifer's eyes. "Jennifer Grey?" he asked in an almost sweet, mellow voice that didn't seem to fit.

She nodded again with an apologetic smile.

He reached to shake her hand and she slowly, cautiously complied.

"I'm Cap Duffy," he said, rising.

FOUR

Jennifer couldn't suppress an amazed expression, which made Duffy smile. "I'm sorry, but I often do this," he said. "I have trouble meeting people, so I just sit with them and get used to them first."

"Bizarre," she managed, and followed him back to his cubbyhole.

He cleared a place for her to sit, then stepped over her to the rickety chair wedged in behind his desk, which was jammed against one wall. The room was not built for two. "Be glad my partner's off today," Duffy said, then laughed. "Just kidding. I work alone."

"That's unusual, isn't it?"

"Nah. Some of us don't look like cops unless there's two of us. I can pass for anything, right?" Jennifer almost nodded. "But if I'm hangin' around with a guy in a trench coat and gum-soled shoes with a bulge at his hip, then all of a sudden we both might as well be wearin' uniforms, you follow me?"

Duffy wrenched off his car coat without standing and let it drape over the back of his chair. Jennifer did the same. As the detective dug in a file drawer for the case folder, she spoke.

"Forgive my reporter's curiosity. I know why I'm here and that you have a lot of questions to ask me, but could I ask you one first?"

"Sure."

"I'm intrigued by your name."

"Duffy? It's French."

Jennifer laughed.

Duffy straightened up and stared at her, a hint of a smile at his lips. "You got somethin' against the French?" he said.

"No, I was curious about your first name."

"You don't know my first name."

"It's Cap, isn't it?"

"You ever hear anybody go by the name of *Cap?*"

"Well, no, that's why I asked. That *is* your name, isn't it?"

"If you've never heard of anybody going by that name, then it's not my name, is it?"

"OK," she said, "I'll bite. What's your *real* first name?"

"Would a guy who goes by Cap to hide his real name wanna *tell* his real name?" Duffy was smiling broadly now. "Ah, I never was any good at games. My name is Harold."

"There's nothing wrong with the name Harold."

"I hate it."

"I don't."

"Then *you* can use it."

"I thought you were supposed to be shy around women."

"Who told you that? I'm not saying I'm not, but who told you? Oh, I know. That big mouth boyfriend of yours."

"So, where'd the name Cap come from?"

"I always wear one, that's all."

Jennifer sat smiling at Cap Duffy. She wanted to ask him if the rest of his ensemble was a put-on as well, but she didn't dare. He *could* use the clothes as sort of a Columbo facade, hiding the brilliant mind and all that. Then again, he could just be a cop with no sense of fashion.

Duffy suddenly grew serious, acting as if he wished they'd saved the informal banter until she'd been cleared. "I have several questions to ask you, if you don't mind."

"Not at all," she said.

"Do you wish to have a lawyer present?"

"Should I?"

"It's entirely up to you."

"Am I under arrest?"

"No, ma'am. If you were under arrest, I would read you your rights."

"I know. Why did you ask about a lawyer?"

"Just a suggestion."

"*Might* I be placed under arrest?"

"That's always a possibility. If your answers don't satisfy me or I can't corroborate them, I may be forced to arrest you, yes."

"Do you think it's possible that I murdered Bobby Block?"

"I've learned to never label anything an *im*possibility, let me put it that way."

"Well, fine then," she said, her heart pounding as she wondered if something in Duffy's investigation had already revealed that she and Block had been trying to get together for some time and that he had, in fact, written to her the day before he died. "Just ask your questions."

"I didn't mean to offend you, Miss Grey."

"*Mrs.* Grey."

"Excuse me, Mrs. Grey. You're married?"

"Widowed."

"I'm sorry."

"So am I."

"Mrs. Grey, I wasn't trying to offend you. I always suggest a lawyer as a courtesy. If I didn't think it was possible you had anything to do with Block's death, I wouldn't have asked you to come here. I'd love to be able to clear you, if for no other reason than to streamline my work. I don't need suspects all over town."

Jennifer was ashamed for having reacted so sharply, but she said nothing.

"Now, if I may begin. How long did you know the deceased?"

"I saw him around, knew who he was, ever since my first week on the staff of the *Day,* about two years ago. Then when I was assigned to the police beat about a year ago, I became his supervisor."

"How would you characterize your relationship?"

"Stormy."

Jennifer told him the whole story of Bobby's antagonism, his backstabbing, his deviousness. Duffy made detailed notes in a delicate script as she spoke.

"I know I haven't done myself any good by telling you this," she said, still holding her breath over the note.

"Honesty never hurts."

"Except that if I didn't believe I was supposed to love my enemies and pray for those who despitefully use me, what I just told you might have given me a motive for murder."

Duffy smiled, and it was apparent to Jennifer that, for a moment, his mind was miles away. "Yes," he said absently. "I suppose it might have." His eyes stared past her, and he appeared deep in thought. "Love your enemies, huh?" He smiled again. "That's the Bible, isn't it?"

She nodded, not wanting to bring him back from this strange reverie. "That was a memory verse we had to learn in Vacation Bible school," he said. "Thirty years ago." He grunted as if remembering the good old days.

Jennifer wanted to press, to find out if he was a Christian, but she decided this wasn't the time.

"You believe that, Mrs. Grey?"

"Yes."

"That's good. That's no defense, but that's good. I believe you."

"You believe I'm innocent?"

"Well, no, it's a little early for that. I just believe that you believe that you're supposed to love your enemies and pray for them. Whether you practiced that with Robert Block, I'm not sure yet. Can you tell me your general whereabouts beginning Tuesday at the end of your workday?"

"Sure. I worked a little late finishing up my column for Wednesday. Then I had to hurry home because I entertained my parents from Rockford and Jim, and I was expecting them at seven."

"You say that as if they didn't show up at seven."

"Well, they didn't. I did some fast grocery shopping, and by the time I got home just before six-thirty they were all already there and waiting in the hall. I was going to throw on some steaks and toss a salad, but my father insisted on taking us to dinner at Carson's."

"And then?"

"Back to my place for dessert."

"And they left when?"

"About eleven."

"And you didn't leave your apartment until the next morning when you left for work?"

"Correct."

"Do you remember Wednesday?"

"Of course; what do you mean?"

"The details. Where you went during the workday, that type of thing."

"I spent the morning on the phone with the mayor's press secretary, explaining why I had never written a column on the mayor and warning that if I *did* write one, it might be critical."

"This is off the subject, Mrs. Grey, but I'm curious. Why might it be critical?"

"No reason. I have nothing against the mayor. That's why I've never written a column about the mayor. But if I wrote one now, it would have to be about a press secretary who seeks favorable publicity."

"That *is* kinda base, isn't it?"

Jennifer nodded. "I went to lunch with Max Cooper and Leo Stanton at Hunan's."

"And they are?"

"Cooper is the publisher of the *Day,* and Stanton is my boss, the City Editor."

"No, I know. I mean, who are the Hunans?"

"That's a Chinese restaurant. The House of Hunan, Michigan Avenue."

"Good?"

"Great."

"OK, after that."

"Ah, let's see. Oh, yes. I went to Cabrini-Green where I talked with a Miss Hawkins about an opinion piece she had had printed in *Time* magazine. Made a good Friday column. You've seen it."

"Excuse me?"

"You may not have read it, but that's what you were looking at when you were pretending to be someone else out there."

"I wasn't pretending. I—"

"Whatever. You might want to read it."

"I probably will. How long were you with this Hawkins woman?"

"About three hours, until four o'clock."

"All that time for that short column?"

"You *did* read it!"

"Of course. It takes that long to get column material?"

"Sometimes more, sometimes less. There has to be more than you see in the paper everyday."

"I guess."

"Then I went back to the office for a few minutes, then home to get ready for prayer meeting."

"Prayer meeting?"

"Yes, Jim and I go together whenever he's off on Wednesday nights." She felt guilty now, because it was while she was back in the office for those few minutes that she had received the note from Bobby. She wondered how long she could go on telling Cap Duffy about loving her enemies and going to prayer meetings when she was withholding evidence in a murder case.

"And where is this?"

"At his church in Waukegan."

"Uh-huh. Prayer meeting. And then?"

"Out for a snack with another couple, the Barbers, and then home."

"He stay with you?"

"Excuse me?"

"Purcell stay with you?"

"Never."

"Never?"

"No, sir. We'll have plenty of time together someday. Please don't tell him I said that."

Duffy grinned. "And you were in all night until work the next morning?"

Jennifer nodded. "And then I was in the newsroom after lunch when I heard about Bobby."

"And you weren't gone from the office Thursday morning before that?"

"No."

"Went straight to work?"

"Yes."

"Out for lunch?"

"No, someone went for sandwiches."

"When was the last time you saw Bobby Block alive?"

"I saw him in January at a Chicago Press Club luncheon."

"Talk to him?"

"Tried to."

"Said hi and got no response?"

"Not even that much. I waved to him from across the room. He didn't acknowledge me. I moved toward him, and he moved away."

"That the last time?"

"I think so. No, I saw him at a Police Department press conference about a month later. Just from a distance. No contact." She pressed her lips together. News of the note was ready to burst from her, but she decided to hold it as long as she could. She didn't know why. It wasn't to protect herself. She knew better than that. It was just that this part of it was hers. It was the reason *she* wanted to investigate Bobby's death for herself.

Duffy sat staring at her. "I have a lot of people to talk to before I clear you," he said. He began reading from his list. "Your parents, Jim, the mayor's press secretary, Cooper and/or Stanton, Miss Hawkins, the Barbers, the doorman at your apartment, and the receptionist in your office."

"You have to talk to my parents?"

"Just routine. I do it in such a way that they don't worry."

"I don't suppose I can tail you around on this case for a week's worth of columns until I've been cleared myself."

"You got that right. Anyway, who said you could do that?"

"My boss."

"Don't *I* have any say in it?"

"Of course."

"I couldn't let you do that."

"Not even for a friend of Jim's?"

"What would my sergeant say?"

"What will *my* boss say? When Bob Greene runs out of column material over at the *Trib*, he writes about what it's like to shave with a razor for the first time at age thirty-five. Don't push me to that kind of fluff. If you're a good cop, it can only be good publicity, right? That's what the cops need right now, just like the mayor."

"Yeah, and I don't even have a press secretary begging for it. Listen, I'll think about it. But meanwhile, you stay outta my hair and stay accessible. I'm hoping for your sake that your story checks out."

"How long will that take?"

"Not long. I've got a lot of other suspects. This guy had very few friends, you know."

"He had a girlfriend."

"How well I know. She's a suspect too."

"Adrienne?"

"Excuse me?"

"Adrienne Eden is a suspect?"

"That's not the name I have down here." He rifled through his notebook. "I'm eager to talk to a Josie Sisk."

"You've got names I haven't got, and I've got names you haven't got. We could be good for each other, Mr. Duffy."

"Call me Cap."

FIVE

Back at her office, Jennifer worked on the first of her undated columns, just in case Duffy decided that—even if cleared—he didn't want her dogging his every move during the investigation. He seemed so strange, she couldn't even predict what he would decide when Leo and Max Cooper visited and asked.

"What really frosts my cake," the old publisher said in mock exasperation, "is that every time I turn around, you're a suspect in a murder case!"

"This is only the second time," Jennifer said weakly, sending Cooper into a laughing jag.

"Lemme know when you've been cleared," he said. "Anything we can do for you?"

"I'd like more information about the medical aspects of the death, but I don't want to step on anyone's toes in the newsroom."

Cooper nodded quickly to Leo who called in a secretary outside Jennifer's glassed-in office. "Yes, sir?"

"Stephanie, I want you to get me photocopies of everything we've got on the Block murder so far, and I mean *everything*. Reporters' notes, articles, sidebars, printed statements, wire copy, stuff from the City News Bureau, everything. Just tell 'em it's for me, and I want it ASAP. OK?"

"Certainly."

"Thanks, Leo," Jennifer said. "And thank you, Mr. Cooper."

"Don't mention it," Leo said. "Just be sure to give credit for anything you use. A hot quote or note from a reporter shows up in your column with no attribution, and we'll both be skinned."

"And rightly so," Cooper added.

"I've got one more big problem," Jennifer said. "I can't concentrate on anything but the murder. If I don't get this general column done and Duffy doesn't let me write about his investigation, I'll have no column for the Sunday edition."

"You want me to pull a few strings at Police Headquarters?" old man Cooper asked. "I hate to do it, but I would."

"No, I hate that type of thing too. The mayor's office tried to do it this morning, asking for a favorable column."

Cooper swore. "You oughta call the scoundrel back and tell 'im you'll think about it if he can get you permission to cover the murder investigation!"

"I'd rather do it without any obligations."

"You wouldn't *have* any! All you're tellin' 'im is that you'll think about it! You wouldn't actually do it!"

Jennifer smiled sympathetically, bringing the old timer back to his senses. "Listen to me," he said hoarsely, "goin' on like a senile, old fool. Well, I'll tell ya, Grey, I want a column from you in Sunday's rag as usual. I'd like it to be the first in your series on this murder investigation, but if it can't be, it can't be. If not, you'll have to come up with something else, and if it's not this afternoon, just make the deadline. Got it?"

"Yes, sir."

That was all Jennifer needed to take her mind off any alternative column and dig into the material which was soon delivered by Stephanie. She'd hear from Duffy in time to pull off a last minute column, if necessary. Meanwhile, she had homework to do in case his answer was good news.

After about forty-five minutes of poring over the material, Jennifer tried to get the coroner on the phone. It wasn't easy. He had gone home.

Even at his home number, she had to go through a receptionist and an aide, both of whom were reluctant to believe that she had learned the phone number from the good doctor himself. But she finally got through.

"I'm in the steam room," she heard him shout over a hissing noise. "So I was wrong about the poison, what else is new? You gonna fry me on the front page for it?"

"No," she laughed. "I've missed a few guesses in my day too. Just tell me about it, and I'll never breathe a word to anyone that you first thought it wasn't a poisoning."

"Well, Jennifer, the best I can determine, Block was done in by what my toxicological friends call a cumulative poison."

"Which means?"

"Which means that it was basically an irritant which probably entered the body as a liquid."

"But not through the mouth?"

"I was getting to that, but how did you know?"

"Just guessing that an irritant would injure the mouth, and you would have seen evidence of that when you did the preliminary examination of the body yesterday."

"Very good, Jennifer."

"But what do you mean *cumulative*, Jake? He had to get several doses or something?"

"No. The first dosage could have been enough, but it may have been in such a diluted solution that it would have been absorbed gradually. I suppose it's possible that he received increased dosages and that they finally took their toll, but this appears to me like a whizbang type of reaction to a time bomb sort of poison."

"For which you as yet have no name?"

"That's right. I saw no evidence of alcohol, barbiturates, or anything like that."

"How would a poison like that get into his system?"

"Well, of course, that's not for me to say. I did a quick study of the body to look for hypodermic holes. Just below his right hip there's about a one-inch square area that seems to at one time have been punctured repeatedly. Now he could have sat on something, or it could have been a series of injections, maybe all at once, maybe in his sleep."

"What are you saying?"

"I'm saying I don't know, and I don't want to speculate. I would not term this a suicide by any stretch of the imagination. The man could have been given an injection while he slept, but he would have had to have been a very sound sleeper to sleep through even one such injection, unless a surface anesthetic was applied. I found no evidence of that either."

"Jake, how will you find out just what the substance was and the effect it had?"

Dr. Steinmetz laughed ruefully. "I'm afraid we're already aware of the effect, girl."

"You know what I mean, Jake. What did it actually do to him to kill him?"

"Well, the big job now is left to the serologists. They have to separate the poison from the normal body fluids and purify it so they can fully identify it. Tomorrow a couple of pathology experts and I will be studying the injury the poison inflicted on the tissues of the major vital organs. This poison acted almost as a narcotic when it finally took effect, affecting the organs and resulting in respiratory and circulatory failure. The way he bolted from his chair and likely died before he hit the floor made me expect to find traces of botulin toxin in his mouth."

"That would have killed him that quickly?"

"Oh, yes. The most potent form of bacterial toxin causes acute food poisoning that can kill you if you get it past your lips."

"Could that be caused by bad food?"

"Unlikely. The cases of botulin toxin deaths I've studied have been deliberate poisonings. Every one."

"But there was no trace of that here?"

"No. But the effect was the same. This, based on what I know right now, was a cumulative poison that exploded upon his system when it was ready. And, as I said at the press conference this morning, it could have entered his bloodstream as long as eighteen to twenty-four hours before death."

"Thanks so much for taking time for me, Jake."

"Anytime, Jenn. Remember our bargain. I gave you a lot more than anyone else in town knows by now."

"Only because I tracked you down and caught you after you'd done more examining."

"True, true. But you're still gonna uphold your end, aren't you?"

"Sure. I'm writing the headline right now, Jake. How's this sound: 'Coroner Blows Another Diagnosis'?"

"Cute, Jennifer. Good-bye."

"You like that?"

"Good-bye, Jennifer."

"It'll be in Sunday's paper."

"Good-bye, Jennifer."

"Good-bye, Jake. Thanks again."

She hung up smiling, glad for some comic relief in such a grisly assignment.

Stephanie appeared at the door, and Jennifer waved her in. "There's a Duffy guy in the lobby asking to see you. Should I let him come up? The receptionist says he looks like one of those kooks who likes to get written up in the paper."

I wish, Jennifer thought. "Yeah, send him up," she said.

Her lower back tingled as she waited and wondered if she was as excited about being cleared as she was about whether Duffy knew about her note from Bobby. Or whether he would allow her to tag along, regardless.

She hadn't noticed before how smoothly Cap Duffy moved. He switched his hat from one hand to the other as he came through the door, sat without making a sound, crossed his legs, and settled back expectantly.

Jennifer stacked her papers neatly and entwined her fingers atop the desk, leaning forward to give full attention. It seemed to be what Duffy had been waiting for. "I have good news and bad news," he said seriously.

"The good news is I've been cleared," she guessed. "My references were not only able to corroborate my whereabouts, but they also sang my praises so that you wondered why I didn't go into full-time church work."

"Right, Joan of Arc."

"I sometimes wonder that myself."

"The bad news, however—"

"I know," she said. "The bad news is that you don't think you want me along on the investigation."

"Wrong."

"Really? I can?"

"No, you can't. But it's not that I don't *think* I want you along; I *know* I don't want you along."

Jennifer looked hurt.

"I didn't mean to be cold about that," he said. "It's just that I know how persistent you newspaper types are, and I needed to be able to shut the door on that little foray into loophole land you just tried to make."

"Pardon me?"

"When you said I didn't *think* I wanted you to go. That made it sound tentative, as if you still had some say in it, which you don't."

"You're not trying to sound mean?"

"No, ma'am, I'm truly not."

"That's good. I'd hate to be on the other end when you're working at it."

"I'm sorry."

"So am I. Why does this conversation sound familiar?"

"'Cause we had it this morning."

"Aren't you going to miss this, Mr. Duffy?"

"Call me—"

"I'm sorry, Cap. Aren't you going to miss this?"

"Miss what?"

"Our ease of conversation. You've got to admit you don't get much stimulating con-versation in a day's work."

"I get more than I want. All I do all day is talk to people."

"But you're not with them long enough to develop a relationship, to be able to volley back and forth with them. C'mon, I know I've quit conniving and gone to begging, but you know you'd enjoy it. I want to know how you work, where you look, what you're after. Most of all, why."

Duffy looked at her with his head cocked, apparently unimpressed. "You really want to get into the *why?*" he asked, incredulously.

"Sure, what did you think?"

"I figured lots of whats and hows and whos and wheres, if I remember Intro to Journalism one-oh-one."

"You know *why* is part of all that, Cap."

"Yeah, but not the *real* why."

"I would want to get into that. It would be a major part of what I'd want to say. Why does a man give himself to the kind of work you do? What motivates him? What keeps him sane? What keeps him straight? What keeps him from becoming a cynic?"

Duffy sat thinking, but Jennifer had not the slightest inkling that she was selling him.

"Well, that's encouraging," he said, "but no. You'd want no restrictions, no rules, no letting me see what you write before you print it."

"That's right," she said, almost wishing she didn't have to say it if it was going to determine whether she got to work with him. But she'd never forgive herself if she gave away her integrity and credibility.

"No, I'm afraid you'd put off my best leads, scare them, keep them from talking."

"I'd stay in the car when you talk to people at the *Trib*, if that's what you mean."

"But how about with Adrienne Eden?"

"You didn't even know about Adrienne before I put you onto her," Jennifer said.

"I would've gotten to her. He was two-timing her, after all."

"Really? See, I didn't know that."

"But she's got no love for you."

"OK, I'll stay in the background for that one too. But you'd have to tell me what she says."

"No, you're not going."

"Cap, you'll wish you'd let me."

"I will, huh? Gimme a reason."

"I've given you a bunch."

"Give me one reason that I'll wish I'd let you."

"Because I know lots of stuff and lots of people."

"Like what?"

She told him what she knew about the toxicologists and serologists and pathologists. She spoke quickly and clearly about what she thought they might find and what it would mean. Duffy's wheels were turning. She was giving him so much more than he had learned from the coroner earlier in the day.

He stood and thrust his hands deep into his coat pockets. She knew the time had come. She showed him the note. He read silently, but he took so long she knew he was going over it several times.

"I'm not too thrilled about this," he said without looking up.

"I know, and I'm sorry. And I swear it's the only thing I've held out on you."

He scowled at the note. "You'll be quiet when I'm interviewing people?"

She nodded enthusiastically.

"You won't ask me any questions in front of anyone?"

She shook her head.

"You won't interview my people. You'll stay out of the way when I say to. You'll let me be off-the-record when I say so. You won't call me at home. You'll give me every bit of information you dig up that I haven't come to yet."

She nodded like a little kid who realized her wish had been granted if she'd just agree to all the rules.

"Jim said you'd agree to everything if I held out long enough," he said.

"Ooh, you're kidding," she said. "He told you that?"

"Don't blame him. He talked me into it. I was dead set against it, but stringing you out for all the guarantees was a great idea."

"I'll wring his neck," she said.

"If he takes any heat for this, it's over," Duffy said.

"You two really have me over a barrel, don't you?"

"I'd say so."

"What would you say if I told you I put Jim up to talking you into it?" she said.

"I'd say you were fibbing."

"And you'd be right."

Six

Cap Duffy was breaking in a brand new unmarked squad car, and he didn't like it. "It looks more like a police car than a patrol car does! Two whip antennas, a spotlight, blackwalled tires, a municipal license number. Why don't we just put a badge decal on the door and a gumball machine on top?"

"I need to tell you something," Jennifer said.

"I know."

"You *know*?"

"Sure I know. You're gonna tell me that the *why* of my detective work isn't as big a reason as the note you got from Block for why you wanted to write about this investigation. That's all right."

"How did you know *that*?"

"A detective has to be a bit of a psychologist, Mrs. Grey."

"Jennifer."

"Thanks, Jennifer. I mean, let's face it. No matter what you had against this guy, you've got to be curious about his death, especially after that note."

"Even about his life, Cap."

"Well, sure, because you never got close, right?"

"Uh-huh. And it doesn't bother you that what makes you tick is not the primary reason behind this?"

"You never said it was. It's not like you lied to me or anything."

"But I never told you that note was the overriding reason."

"You didn't have to, Jennifer. I knew."

"I *will* write about you and why and how you do what you do, of course."

"It won't make much difference to me either way."

"Seriously? Most cops have at least a little ego, don't they?"

"Most have quite a bit of ego. I have an ego too, but it's not satisfied by seeing my name in the paper."

"What satisfies your ego?"

"Knowing I'm doing something that few other people could do, especially shy people."

"You really consider yourself shy?"

"Who would know better than me? I know I die inside when I have to confront people, but I play games, I playact, I overcome the barrier because I force myself. I know I have to, and so I do it, and I get great satisfaction from it."

"And each time it gets easier?"

"It *never* gets easier. Sometimes it's more difficult. And then I use every part of my being."

"Meaning."

"Sometimes it's my body. I'm in the best shape of any thirty-nine-year-old you know. I can run six miles in thirty minutes, do forty pull-ups, and one hundred push-ups in two minutes. I can lift one and a half times my body weight. Detective work is not all head knowledge and jive talk. When I get into a tight spot, I have more options than most. That's where my ego boost comes from."

"And it wouldn't give you a rush if people knew about that?"

"It embarrasses me a little to even tell you. Nobody else but my wife knows what I go through to stay in shape. Some of the guys are aware of my condition because we play racquetball, but most of the time I hide under the clothes."

"Tell me about the clothes."

"Clothes are irrelevant to me. I don't know or care what most people are wearing."

"But you dress, how should I say it—?"

"Tacky?"

"You said it, not me."

"I know," he said "Yeah. I do. And I'd like to be able to tell you it's for some strategic reason, but I dress the same way socially and formally. I'll tell you this, though. It works as strategy, because I'm seldom taken for a cop. Cops run the gamut from frumpy, old-fashioned 'Dragnet' TV show type outfits—trench coats, wide-brimmed hats, black shoes, and white socks—to the modern 'Barney Miller' style, like off the cover of *Gentlemen's Quarterly.*"

"You can't kid me, Cap. You *do* know fashion."

"OK, but I still think it's basically irrelevant, except for the cover it allows me before I have to identify myself. I often get more information when I'm just hanging around someone, before they know who I am, than I do when I'm peppering them with questions."

"Who are we going to pepper with questions this balmy Friday afternoon?"

"Don't start with the *we* business, Jennifer. I'm warning you."

He was only half-kidding.

"Sorry," she said. "Who are *you* going to question?"

"I'm going back to the *Tribune.*"

"Which means *I* have to sit in the car."

"But not for long. I've got a suspect in there who won't quit."

"Seriously? You think it's someone Bobby worked with?"

"Slow down, Brenda Starr," he said, pulling into a parking garage not far from *Tribune* Tower. "Choosing an early suspect is just one of my things. It helps me focus. I hone in, concentrate my energies, believe with everything I have that I've found the murderer, and I don't let up until I'm forced to."

"Guilty until proven innocent, huh?"

"That's right, except—of course—I never put someone in that category without a good reason."

"Was *I* in that category?"

"Not for a second."

"Who's your mark at the *Trib*?"

"Name's Young. Christopher Young."

"Chris *Young*? He used to be at the *Day*! He's a buddy of Bobby's, one of his very few. Are you sure you've got something on him?"

Duffy flashed her an impatient look. "No, I just don't like tall, skinny guys—so I thought I'd give him some grief."

"I'm sorry," Jennifer said, but not quickly enough. Duffy was out of the car, slamming the door and striding toward the garage elevator.

Chris Young? He'd gotten his start at the *Day*. In fact, hadn't he graduated a few years before Bobby and put in a good word for him with Leo? Chris was with the *Day* for three or four years and developed into a top-notch reporter and writer before landing a plum rewrite job at the *Trib* for excellent money.

Jennifer even vaguely remembered that it may have been Young who put the *Tribune* brass onto Bobby after Bobby had been fired from the *Day*. Chris and Bobby had been inseparable, and she had heard of no rift. But then she never heard much of anything from the *Tribune*.

What could have gone wrong in their relationship?

Duffy was back more quickly than Jennifer expected. "Stood me up," he said, fuming. "That only adds fuel to the fire."

"It doesn't necessarily mean anything," Jennifer said.

"It means he's avoiding me, and when I've got him in my sights, for valid reasons or not, it doesn't look good for him."

"Tell me why his scent is in your nose."

Duffy turned and grinned at her. "If it ain't Ernestine Hemingway! You gonna use that line in your column about ol' Cap Duffy, the bloodhound?"

Jennifer was embarrassed. "You know what I mean. And where are we going now?"

"Northwestern."

Inwardly, Jennifer felt proud of herself that Duffy was sniffing around the same places she would have. As he headed north, she asked again about Chris Young.

"Ah, it's nothing big, really. Just something I sensed when we first talked. He couldn't hide his bitterness over certain injustices in Block's life."

"Such as?"

"Such as the fact that Block was two-timing his girlfriend."

"You mean he was dating both this Josie girl you mentioned *and* Adrienne Eden?" Jennifer asked.

"Right. Josie Sisk is a Chicagoan. Eden is still on campus at Northwestern."

"But his buddy wouldn't kill him for that."

"Not as a rule. Unless Young was interested in one of the young ladies."

"Excuse me, Cap, but I don't know how to say this. The word around the *Day* was that Chris Young was more likely interested in the young men than the young ladies."

"Yeah, I heard the gay theory about Young too. So maybe he was interested in Block and was incensed that he was losing him to not just one woman, but two."

"Sounds pretty thin, Cap."

"Maybe, but there's more. I got the impression that Young wanted to take a lot of credit for Block's career."

"And he probably should. I seem to remember Chris got Bobby both his job at the *Day* and at the *Trib*."

"Well, I got that impression too, so I probed a little deeper. I told Young that I saw Block as one of the young stars at the *Trib*, in fact in all of Chicago journalism."

"Did that make him proud?"

"Hardly," Duffy said. "It opened a floodgate. Young burst forth with a lot of spiteful talk about the fact that the public should someday know the truth behind the newspaper writers in this city."

"What did he mean—that the behind-the-scenes guys, the rewrite men, are really the writers?"

"I assume."

"He's right, of course, Cap. *Our* rewrite men are chosen for their attitudes. That may be why Chris had to go to the *Trib* to get that kind of a position. He was too well-known at the *Day* as a hothead and a climber."

"Not the best type for a rewrite man?"

"No way. They sit there with earphones clamped to their heads for eight hours, trying to make readable copy out of poor reporting and horrible on-the-scene writing. A guy has to have the heart of a servant and love his work—not to mention his reporters—to be a good rewrite man. You can't buy or make them—they're born."

"In my book, Chris Young ain't one of 'em," Duffy decided.

Jennifer nodded. "He's got the ability. But not the psyche."

Duffy parked in a small lot on the far south side of Northwestern's campus, and they walked through the heart of the beautiful place, heading north. "Who are we looking for—excuse me, who are *you* looking for here?"

The detective dug out his leather notebook and leafed past several pages. "Ed McDevitt," he said carefully. "A sophomore. On the campus newspaper staff. A protégé of the great Bobby Block. He's a jock. Almost made the basketball team. Big in intramurals here. Tall, broad, rangy, good-lookin' kid with sandy blond hair. Real heartthrob type. Studying law. My favorite interview."

"Law students?"

"Yeah. They'll tell ya what you're doin' right and wrong, all that. I can usually tell right away if they've got something to hide."

"You have an appointment with this, uh—"

"McDevitt," Duffy said, sneaking a peek at his notes. "No, but he gets out of class in about fifteen minutes, and he should stroll right by here."

They sat on a wood bench behind a hedge and relaxed while Duffy kept an eye out for the big law student. "We talked about your technique, Cap," Jennifer said, "but we still haven't gotten into the why."

"Why do I do it? Why am I a cop? That type of thing?"

"Uh-huh."

"Like most honest cops, I'm on a justice trip, I guess. Growing up I noticed that the biggest and the strongest and the best-looking and the smartest people always got the breaks, and not only that, they got away with everything. Well, I can't be put in any of those classifications, but I can be sure that justice is done."

"But is justice always done?"

"No, 'course not. You mean because of the court system?"

Jennifer nodded.

"I hear you. We catch 'em red-handed, round 'em up, drag 'em to court. But we can't throw 'em in the slam. That's up to the judge, the jury, the court, the state, and the system. And it's too big and overcrowded. That's why you see guilty people go free. And that's why you see cops tempted to carry out justice on the spot and answer questions later. Because they see something bad going down—they themselves, the cops, you understand—are the witnesses. They testify in court, they've got the dude dead to rights, and to save time and money the judge lets the sucker cop a plea, and we've got murderers, rapists, armed robbers, you name it, on the streets with suspended or commuted sentences."

Jennifer looked up from her own notes. "But that's not enough to put you out of the profession?"

"Nah. If we all got discouraged with it, the whole thing would be up for grabs. A few guys get convicted, and we slow the rest down at least, make them hire lawyers and show up for court and post bond and all the rest. We make life tough for 'em anyway. There's some justice in that."

"But not enough, I hear you saying."

"You listen well, lady."

They fell silent and gazed across the campus. Suddenly, Duffy stood and peered through the hedge. He pulled a couple of pictures from his pocket. "I know that's McDevitt," he said, "but who's the girl?"

"Don't ask me," Jennifer said, craning her neck to see. A dreamy giant in a heavy woolen sweater loped down the sidewalk with a cute, little coed on his arm. At least, she looked like a coed.

"Look at this picture," Duffy said, shoving under her nose the likeness of a young woman with long, blond tresses and a short, compact body. "Imagine her with a pageboy haircut and tell me that isn't the girl he's with."

Jennifer compared the picture and the girl on the giant's arm. The couple neared the hedge. "That's her," Jennifer agreed.

"What in the world is he doing with Josie Sisk?" Duffy asked.

SEVEN

Duffy motioned to Jennifer to sit back down on the bench. He joined her, deftly pulling a newspaper from his side pocket, so he would appear to have been sitting there reading for some time when the couple walked by.

The move made both Jennifer and Duffy blend into the background. McDevitt and Sisk were about thirty feet past them when Jennifer whispered, "What now?"

"We follow them," Duffy said, rising. Jennifer wondered how Duffy thought he could look inconspicuous on *this* campus.

A hundred yards away McDevitt and Sisk stopped and leaned against the hood of a late model canary Porsche. Duffy sat under a tree and Jennifer wondered what she was supposed to do. She wasn't about to sit on the ground in her dress.

"Just mosey around," Duffy suggested. "If that's Josie's car, she'll be gone soon, and I'll intercept the big guy when he comes back this way."

Jennifer was frustrated but wandered off. In a few minutes Josie Sisk pulled away, and McDevitt started back up the walkway past Duffy. Jennifer headed that way too.

As the lanky student passed the detective, Duffy looked up from his newspaper. "Hey," he called, "aren't you Ed McDevitt?"

McDevitt whirled and glared at him, puzzled, but kept walking.

"The basketball player?" Duffy said. "Played high school ball in, ah, don't tell me, uh—"

"Michigan," McDevitt said, circling back. "Do I know you?"

Duffy looked around to be sure he wasn't creating a scene that would embarrass the big guy, then pulled out his badge and identified himself. "I want to talk to you about Bobby Block for a few minutes. Right here all right?"

"Who's the lady?" McDevitt asked, staring at Jennifer.

"She's with me," Duffy said.

"Uh-*huh*," McDevitt said, winking at her. She glared at him, and he smiled. She didn't. "Let's at least sit down," he suggested, and they found another bench. McDevitt sat in the middle. "What do you wanna know?" he asked.

"I just need preliminary information, some help," Duffy said.

"That's good," McDevitt said, "because you're out of your jurisdiction, aren't you? And if you made me sit here and talk to you without arresting me or informing me of my rights, I might have you for violating my security against unreasonable search and seizure."

"Oh, give the kid an A on that pop quiz," Duffy said with a grin. "If it ain't Perry Mason!"

McDevitt looked annoyed.

"Hey, just kiddin'," Duffy said. "Seriously, that was an impressive little rundown there for just a sophomore in prelaw."

"So, what else do you know about me?"

"I don't care about you, Ed. May I call you Ed? I care about your old buddy, Robert Block."

"All of a sudden everyone cares about Bobby. I don't remember that many people caring about him when he was alive."

"Only you?"

"A lot of the time only me. And Adrienne. I owed him."

"For what?"

"He took time for me. He talked me out of my major by telling me the odds against graduating high enough in law to get a decent job anywhere, and he said that while the journalism field has been flooded ever since Watergate and all that newspaper glamour, I had a chance if I stuck with it."

"Stuck with *him*, you mean?"

"Well, sort of, yeah. He taught me a lot of stuff, made me less naive. Pushed me to be tough, assertive, a digger."

"More cynical, Ed?"

"I guess. Especially now."

"Why now?"

"Like I said, everyone is finally interested in a good newspaperman, now that he's gone."

"How do you figure he died, Ed?"

"How should I know? He had plenty of enemies. Cops didn't like him. Criminals didn't like him. Co-workers didn't like him. What can I tell you? There must be a suspect list a mile long."

"Make that an A plus on the quiz, kid."

Ed McDevitt looked at his watch. "So what do you want from me?" he asked.

Duffy looked him square in the eye. "You really wanna know?"

McDevitt nodded carefully, as if fearing what he was getting into.

"I wanna know what you're doing holding hands and playing kissy-face with one of Block's girlfriends the day after he's found poisoned to death."

McDevitt uncrossed his long legs and stretched them out, crossing them again at the ankles, and folding his arms across his chest. "That make me a suspect?"

"Maybe."

"Then arrest me and charge me. You can't do anything more or less until I'm indicted before a grand jury."

"Oh, give me a break, Ed. You don't want me to do that any more than I do. It'd be a waste of time. I've got solid alibis on you even without your help. Just answer the question and save me a lot of grief."

McDevitt locked into Duffy's gaze. "All right," he said, speaking quickly. "You've done your home work, so I'll give you a few freebies and save you some time. First of all, Josie is *my* woman and has never been Bobby's. Bobby was engaged to Adrienne, though I don't think they ever got around to making it official with a ring. Bobby would have been a little too cheap for that."

"You telling me Adrienne doesn't think Bobby was seeing Josie on the side?"

"Of course she thinks that, and she was right."

"I'm not following you."

"Bobby saw Josie, OK? It was all right with me. I owed Bobby. Whatever was mine was his."

Jennifer couldn't contain herself. "You've got to be kidding!" she said. McDevitt flinched and Duffy stared her down. "Sorry," she said, putting a finger to her own lips.

"I'm an open-minded guy," McDevitt added. "It didn't really bother me."

"Baloney," Duffy said.

"It *didn't*!"

"Baloney."

"It wasn't a big issue."

"Baloney."

McDevitt appeared as if he knew Duffy had hit a weak spot. "You won't get me to admit it was a problem for me."

"Why?" Duffy pressed. "Because you were so enamored of Block that he was like a cult leader to you? Did he have you under mind control or something? I mean, what sane, healthy American in the twentieth century lets another man share his woman? Sounds a little kinky, man."

McDevitt glared at him.

"You couldn't have liked it, Ed. You may have given in, but you couldn't have liked it."

McDevitt said nothing.

"I'm saying it gave you a motive for murder," Duffy added.

"But you just said you had alibis for me."

"I do, so where am I, Ed? What've I got? Give an old gumshoe a break."

"You're driving at something, Duffy," McDevitt said.

"You're right. You wanna guess?"

"Not particularly."

"You wanna guess, ma'am?" Duffy asked Jennifer, avoiding her name.

"Sure," she said, eliciting another double take from McDevitt. "Ed has himself almost convinced that he didn't mind sharing his woman with Block, and he didn't want to trouble the waters for fear of losing Josie. Down deep, it troubles him greatly that she saw anything at all in a physical specimen as unimpressive as Block and that she would give any other man the time of day, let alone give him anything else. What you have, Ed, is a love-hate relationship with both Bobby *and* Josie."

Duffy fought a grin. McDevitt looked miserable. "Now you've got Josie all to yourself," Duffy said, "but you wonder how long that will last. You're hurt and disappointed, and you feel guilty because the feeling that Josie didn't care for you exclusively is stronger than the grief you feel over the loss of your friend."

McDevitt stared at the ground.

"Do you think you know who killed Bobby?" Jennifer asked.

Ed shook his head.

"Would you have liked to?"

He nodded, grimacing.

"Were you glad to hear about it?"

His shoulders heaved, but he didn't respond. Duffy put a hand gently on his arm—surprising Jennifer—and McDevitt broke down.

"The problem," Duffy said in the car, "is that the man has solid alibis; he couldn't have done it. But he sure had a motive."

"But so did Adrienne," Jennifer said.

"For sure. And if I can somehow eliminate Christopher Young from the list, she becomes prime."

"I hope you can eliminate him."

"Why? You got something in you that wants to see Adrienne Eden sentenced to death? I thought you hardly knew the woman."

"That's not it at all, Cap. Good grief, I don't want to see anyone die, though I share your interest in justice, especially in a murder case."

"You're one of those liberal left-wing news types that doesn't believe in capital punishment though, right?"

"If you've read my column for any length of time, you'd know how wrong you are about that."

"So why are you so eager to see Christopher Young cleared?"

"Because I don't know what I'd do with it in my column if a member of a competing paper's staff was a murderer."

Shocking Jennifer, Cap Duffy suddenly braked and pulled off to the shoulder of the expressway. He shifted into park and let the engine idle. With both hands gripping the wheel he turned to face her.

"I've finally found the chink," he said.

"The chink?"

"The chink in your armor. I knew you were too good to be true."

"What are you saying, Cap? Or should I ask, what did *I* say?"

"You just showed your true colors, that's all. Are you saying that your management wouldn't let you cover it in your paper if a competitor was guilty and that they would expect the same courtesy?"

"No, I'm saying *I* personally would have a problem with it. I wouldn't want to cover it, to deal with it, to write about it."

Duffy shook his head slowly and pulled back out into traffic.

"You're disappointed in me," Jennifer said. "I can see it all over your face."

"I guess I'm just a little surprised, that's all. I was kinda hoping—"

"Hoping what?"

"That you were different, like you seemed."

"That hurts. I'd like to think I'm different from most people in many ways."

"But not when it comes to fairness and objectivity."

He waited for a response, but she couldn't speak.

"What would you want me to do," he said, "if I found out the murderer was a cop? Sweep it under the rug? I've read your columns about *that*, haven't I? I applauded your stand on that, tough as it was. You called for consistency and firmness, quick and decisive justice. Cops were beneficiaries of the public trust, you said."

"You *do* read my column," she said wondering how he could remember her exact words.

"I read the ones that apply to me. You wanna know if I'm disappointed—yeah, I'm disappointed. I've got a columnist riding around with me, wanting to write about me and what I do. But what you'll write is gonna hinge on just who the murderer is and what walk of life he hails from, not whether or how we catch him—or her."

"I never said that, Cap."

"Well, you sure did!"

"I didn't mean that."

"Just what did you mean when you said you wouldn't be able to handle writing about a murderer who was from your profession, a competitor from another local paper?"

"Well, I didn't mean I actually wouldn't do it."

"But that's what you said."

"It is, isn't it? I'm sorry, because I know better."

"I hope so."

"I do."

"I wonder," Cap said.

"Don't say that. You couldn't hurt me more."

He looked at her with a puzzled look. "You're serious?"

She nodded, almost in tears.

"I really hoped your integrity meant that much to you," he said.

"Tomorrow I'll talk to Adrienne Eden and Christopher Young," Duffy said, parking behind the *Day* building.

"In other words, I won't be in on either of those."

"Probably not," Duffy said. "But you'll be close by, and I'll fill you in."

As Jennifer was opening her door and thanking him for putting up with her for the afternoon, a message crackled over the radio that he should telephone the station. "Ten-four" he said.

Few of the daytime staff were still in the office, so Jennifer let Duffy use Stephanie's phone, then checked her own desk for messages and tidied up her office.

Duffy appeared in the doorway, ashen faced. "You tired?" he asked.

It was a strange question, she decided. "Why?"

"We've got a big night ahead of us, if you're up to it."

Jennifer was baffled. "Well, what's happening, Cap? I'm supposed to meet Jim in about an hour, but if—"

"I'm on my way back to Evanston," he said. "Adrienne Eden was found by her roommate."

"She was found?"

"Dead."

EIGHT

As they sped north again, Jennifer told Cap Duffy that she was surprised to see him so affected by someone's death. "I would think you'd get used to murder after a while."

"There are days," he admitted, "when the bodies and crime scenes seem like nothing more than grist for the puzzle mill. On those days, it's just a job. Interesting, but just a task. But it always hits me hard when the victim is someone I've already talked to or someone who's a key to the investigation, as in this case."

Jennifer asked if Adrienne Eden had been a key in the investigation for any other reason than the fact that she knew Bobby was seeing Josie on the side.

"That, and the fact that she had a key to his apartment. A murderer needs motive, means, and opportunity. She had the first and the last. I'm not sure how poison injected into the system would be characteristic of her. She was a communications major, not a biologist."

The radio came alive again, informing Duffy that two eyewitnesses had placed the female in photograph number 08653 in the Block apartment building as late as midnight Wednesday night. Duffy reached into his breast pocket and tossed his whole packet of photographs to Jennifer.

She thumbed through them, pausing at the grisly autopsy photos of Bobby Block. There was McDevitt, Eden, Young, Sisk, and even herself. "The numbers are on the back," Duffy said. "See if Eden is the number he just read off."

"What was the number?"

"Zero-eight-six-five-three."

"How do you remember that?"

"The zero is easy. I pretended it was ten and the rest went down, two evens and two odds, in order."

"Incredible. Nope. That's not Eden's number."

"Is it yours? It better not be—or you and a lot of your friends lied to me."

Jennifer nearly panicked as she flipped her photo over. "Nope, not me either," she said.

"Sisk," he said. She turned over Josie's photo.

"Right," she said quietly.

"Do you realize," he said, "that the woman has had a drastic haircut since Thursday night?"

"And two people place her at the scene of the crime that night?"

"Yup."

"Can I ask you something a little off the subject? Have you been involved in enough autopsies to know how much weight a body should lose during one?"

"Yeah. A body can lose a lot of fluid, but if you're asking about those pictures of Block, they were taken before the autopsy, so he wouldn't have lost much weight there. Why?"

"I must not have been keeping up with him at all. His face seems a lot thinner than the way I remember him."

"Well, he was still a big boy there. I'd guess two hundred twenty-five pounds."

"But when he was at the *Day* he weighed more than two hundred fifty. When I saw him just a couple of months ago, he was as big as ever, so he would have had to have lost all that weight pretty quickly."

"Interesting," Duffy said, "because you know what we found, or I should say, what we didn't find?"

"Hm?"

"Evidence that he had eaten any of that breakfast on his table Thursday morning. It was as if he had fixed it for someone else and was waiting for them."

"Any evidence of Josie Sisk in the place?" Jennifer asked.

"Some unidentified fingerprints that we can perhaps trace to her. She shouldn't be hard to find."

"Have you matched the prints against Adrienne?"

"No, but that won't be too difficult now either, will it?"

Jennifer just stared at Duffy. "If she was murdered by the same *modus operandi,* she's no longer a suspect, is she?"

"As a rule, that's true," Duffy said.

"Who are you leaning toward now, Cap?" Jennifer asked, reorganizing the photos and returning them to him so she could take notes.

"Let's just say I'll be very interested to know if Christopher Young or Josie Sisk were seen in the vicinity of Adrienne's room during the last twenty-four hours."

"How will you find out?"

"There are no shortcuts to that," the detective said. "You just keep knocking on doors, asking questions, showing pictures, and hoping someone will have a good combination of memory and honesty. The honest ones usually can't remember, and the ones who remember will say they don't."

When Duffy and Jennifer arrived at the Northwestern security command post, campus guards and Evanston detectives were talking with Adrienne Eden's roommate, Lisa Johnson, a tiny girl with curly, dark brown hair and huge, square-lensed glasses. "I only roomed with her since January, and I learned to hate her with a passion, but this is horrible! She was lying face down at the door when I came back from dinner at five o'clock. She was a terrible person, but I wouldn't have killed her!"

Jennifer followed Duffy to the apartment, where the scene reminded her of Thursday afternoon at Bobby Block's. Jake Steinmetz would not cover this one himself, it being so far north, but Duffy quickly located a coroner's assistant.

"You wouldn't wanna help me with a little pre-autopsy, would you?" he asked.

The doctor glared at him. "You can't touch that body."

"I know," Duffy said, showing his badge. "I just need to know if there are any puncture wounds just below the right hip. It'll aid in the investigation, and I really can't wait until tomorrow."

The doctor pursed his lips and stared, then reached into his bag for a penlight. He draped a sheet over the fully clothed body and moved everyone else from the immediate area. Within minutes, he returned. "Bingo," he said. "About an inch square, maybe ten tiny puncture holes, none of them terribly recent."

"How recent?"

"The freshest could have been twenty-four hours ago."

Jennifer pulled Duffy aside. "What's going on?" she said. "Adrienne seems to have dropped a lot of weight fast too. When I saw her at Bobby's place, she was wearing a baggy top and I didn't notice, but she's lost maybe twenty pounds. What do you make of it?"

"They were both on diets? I don't know, Jennifer. What do *you* make of it?"

She shrugged. "I'd like to ask the roommate about it."

"I'd better," he said.

When they arrived back at the security office, Lisa Johnson was begging for somewhere else to stay. "I don't even want to go in there to get my things with a murderer on the loose. You've got to help me move! How am I supposed to concentrate on my studies?"

Duffy received permission to question her briefly. He asked about her roommate's weight loss.

"Yeah, it's just been over the last several weeks. I don't know. We never have meals together anyway, but she hasn't eaten a thing between meals like she used to. She never talked about it. She just quit snacking. Still did a lot of grass, though. I figured maybe she got on to some harder stuff and lost her appetite, but I never saw anything around the place."

"How about you?" Duffy said.

"How about me?"

"You do any dope?"

"Just a little grass, a long time ago."

"Nothing harder?"

"Cocaine. Once. Nearly scared me to death."

"Never dropped acid?"

"Never. What do you want from me?"

"Nothing. Thank you."

"I can go?"

"That's up to these gentlemen."

Jennifer and Duffy spent the rest of the evening, until quite late, questioning everyone within a quarter mile radius of the Eden-Johnson room.

Duffy was right. Most people were hostile, not wanting to talk when they found out what had happened. Others were just curious and asked more questions than they answered. Everyone knew Ed McDevitt, but no one had seen him around that area recently.

Everyone knew the Porsche that apparently belonged to his girlfriend, but no one had seen that around lately either.

The first break came just after Jennifer had called Jim to change their plans for the evening. He volunteered to come and help in the canvassing, but Duffy felt it unnecessary.

A senior girl, living alone on the top floor of Adrienne's building, had seen Christopher Young in the library earlier in the day. "It was about four o'clock, and he was talking with a tall, good-looking guy in a sweater, the guy who usually drives around in a yellow Porsche."

Had she seen either of them later? "No."

Had she seen the car that day? "Yes, right here at this building when I returned from the library. That's what struck me as strange, because I had seen the driver someplace else."

"Who was driving the car when you saw it?" Duffy wanted to know.

"I didn't see anyone in the car, but I passed a girl on the stairs, and the next time I looked out, the car was gone."

"Is this the girl?" Duffy asked, showing the photo of Josie Sisk.

"That's her," the senior said. "But that's not her hair. Either that's a wig, or she's had it cut since that picture was taken."

Duffy got the girl to agree to swear to what she had said, in court if necessary. Two others on the same floor corroborated much of her story. Duffy was elated.

"You think Josie could be your murderer?" Jennifer asked.

"I think we've got enough to warrant picking her up and fingerprinting her, don't you?"

Jennifer nodded.

"And if her prints match those found in Block's apartment?"

"Then I'd say the girl is in serious trouble."

The Chicago and Evanston police put out all points bulletins for Josie Sisk. When Duffy and Jennifer reached the city again, a message was waiting for Duffy to call Dr. Steinmetz.

"He's going to tell me that they found a similar patch of injection marks on the second body," he predicted.

He was wrong.

"I know you know all of that, Cap," Jake said. "I'm surprised you didn't ask for a full autopsy right there in the room. There's nothing too surprising to report, but there are two new developments, one of which I can tell you by phone, and the other I'd like to share with you in person."

"I wish you could tell me both by phone, Jake," Duffy said. "I'm about ready to drop."

"Sorry. I'll give you the first half now and the second whenever you say, but not by phone."

"OK, shoot."

"I don't know what this means. You can put it into the hopper and see what comes of it. But we found traces of an appetite suppressant in the tissues of both bodies."

"That significant?"

"You tell me. Could mean that both were on diets, but this suppressant is not available over-the-counter. It's like a hyper pre-sate and is usually administered only by injection, by a physician."

"Would that account for the needle marks?"

"Likely."

"Could the suppressant be lethal?"

"Only in mega-doses, and it would not cause the types of deaths we saw here. Both of these young adults died on what appears to be a timed release basis. If it hadn't happened twice, and if I weren't always hanging around you suspicious homicide types, I'd probably guess that someone blew the injection, gave the patient something other than what he was supposed to. But two? And people who knew each other? And no similar deaths reported? Too coincidental."

"You wanna trade jobs?" Duffy gibed.

"Over my dead bodies," the coroner said.

"Listen, Jake, do I really hafta wait until we can get together on your other tidbit?"

"Afraid so, Cap. I'm sorry. I'm not even sure it's any more significant than what I just gave you, but it just seems important to me to keep it for other than a phone conversation. Indulge me."

"Fair enough, if you'll indulge me."

"Anything."

"I want to bring Jennifer Grey along when you tell me."

"You can bring her around anytime. But seriously, Cap, you'd better get her to agree in advance that she won't print this information unless you or I give her the go-ahead, and even that will hinge on the wishes of the next of kin."

"The next of kin?"

"You heard me."

"You're gonna make me come out to see you tonight, aren't you?"

"No, I wouldn't do that. Really, Cap, it'll wait till morning, and we can meet in my office."

"You're going to be in on a Saturday morning?"

"You're working tomorrow, aren't you, Cap?"

"Well, yeah, but—"

"Well, I'm just as eager to see this thing solved as you are."

Jennifer slept fitfully, in spite of her exhaustion, and she wondered how a mind like Duffy's ever rested. She bet if she called him he'd be up pacing, making notes. But she didn't dare.

Jennifer's mind wandered, raced, slowed, slept, awoke, and thought some more. Did she have to decide between Chris Young, whom she hadn't seen for ages, and Josie Sisk, whom she'd never spoken to? Why would either of them murder both Bobby *and* Adrienne? It didn't make sense. And what was Chris doing talking with Ed after Ed had talked with Cap? Chris had stood up Cap.

At 3:00 A.M. the phone rang, and Jennifer didn't recognize it at first. *Why is that alarm so loud? Is it really six forty-five already?* When she realized it was the phone, it scared her. She didn't like surprise phone calls.

Could something have happened to Jim? "Hello?"

"Jennifer?"

"Jim?"

"No."

"Who's calling please?"

"Don't you recognize my voice? It's an old friend."

"Who's calling please? It's three o'clock in the morning."

"I know, and I'm sorry to bother you, Jennifer. But I have some information that might help you and your detective friend. Can I meet with you without him there?"

"Chris?"

"Yes. Can I?"

"Where?"

"Lincoln Park, tomorrow morning."

"Make it noon and you've got a deal."

"Noon then. But come alone."

NINE

For the sake of her sanity, Jennifer called Jim and met him for breakfast. She told him everything. Well, almost everything. Everything except the scheduled meeting with Christopher Young.

"What could the coroner possibly have up his sleeve?" she wondered aloud.

"Embalming fluid?" Jim tried.

Jennifer gagged. "You're as morbid as he is. You should have heard what he said to Duffy last night."

"You already told me."

Jennifer rested her head in her hands. "I'm sorry. I'm just exhausted. But think of Duffy."

"I'd rather think of you, but, yeah, I know the homicide guys put in some long hours. You can't schedule when the breaks will fall into your lap."

"I get the impression that Duffy makes more breaks than he waits for, though," she said.

"Impressive, huh? Didn't I tell you?"

"You didn't tell me half of what I've discovered in Cap Duffy. Really quite a character."

"I like him," Jim said.

"I'm not sure whether I like him yet," Jennifer said. "But he *is* interesting. I've already got a couple of columns rattling around in my head, and we've hardly started the investigation."

"Sounds like it's almost over, Jenn. If you can tie Young with Sisk somehow, you've got conspiracy, collusion, whatever you want. And if you can't tie 'em together, one is probably guilty."

"I don't know, Jim. It almost sounds too easy."

"Then make it hard, Jenn. It'll make for a better column."

"Eat your breakfast."

Cap Duffy was stony when Jennifer met him in the downstairs lobby of the building that housed the medical examiner's office. "You wanna talk about it," Jennifer said, "or are you just not a morning person?"

"I'm enough of a morning person," he said. "It's just that very few of the prints we pulled in Block's apartment match with the Eden girl, but plenty of 'em match Sisk."

"That should make you happy. Where'd you find Sisk?"

"That's just it. We didn't. She's blown. McDevitt isn't talking, and I tend to believe he really doesn't know where she is."

"Why is he so believable all of a sudden?"

"Because he gave us several leads on where we might find her. All dead ends so far, but I think he's really trying."

"If she's got his car, she'll be easy to track."

"She doesn't," Duffy said.

"How'd you get the prints if you don't have her?"

"We got a warrant and pulled a set from her apartment, which, by the way, is not too far from Block's. Then we got an old set from the state police. She was kind of a rowdy in high school and got busted a couple times when she was eighteen. Just old enough to make 'em keep her prints on file."

As they sat in Dr. Steinmetz's swank waiting room, Duffy continued. "We also got Sisk's prints from Adrienne's place."

"Doesn't that just about wrap it up, Cap?"

"You'd think so, but it's all circumstantial. Pretty impressive circumstances, I would say, with eyewitnesses placing her at the scenes of the deaths. Notice I didn't say she was placed at the scenes of the *crimes.*"

"What's your point?"

"Just that I'm not sure the places where we found Block and Eden dead were the places where the crimes were perpetrated. There's little evidence that Josie was at either place when the victims actually died."

"I can see why you're frustrated."

"That's not all of it. I'm also upset with this crazy Young character. I've got a much better suspect, yet Young chooses to run now. I tried to reach him at his office this morning, and he's on some three-day leave of absence. No one is saying where he went. If he's innocent, what's he running from?"

"Maybe he's involved in the thing with Sisk," Jennifer said.

Duffy apparently didn't want to waste time thinking about it. "Yeah, well, who knows?" he said. "He'd do himself a big favor by sticking around long enough to get cleared."

"If he's innocent, you mean."

Duffy cocked his head and pointed at Jennifer, as if conceding the point. Then they were called into Dr. Steinmetz's office, a beautiful, book-lined, mahogany sanctuary.

"It ain't much, but it's comfortable," Jake deadpanned.

"Yeah," Duffy added, "and paid for."

"That it's not," Steinmetz admitted. "Sit down, please."

They sat at a small antique table near a leather divan. The coroner had the Block file on the table, secured by two large rubber bands he never removed, though he frequently tugged at them and let them slap the manila folder.

"Did you inform Miss Grey that this is off-the-record until we say it isn't?"

Duffy nodded, and they both looked to Jennifer. "If you say it's off-the-record gentlemen, it's off-the-record. I *do* hope you'll cut off the restraint as soon as possible though, whatever the information is."

Steinmetz scowled and stared at his hands, then rose and slowly paced the room, stopping at the ten-foot window casing where he pulled back a heavy, dark drapery and peered out into brilliant sunlight. When he let go of the drape, the room returned to a yellow dullness, illuminated by just two table lamps.

"Well, Cap," Jake said, turning to face him with his hands in his pockets pushing his charcoal three-piece suit coat back, "as I said, I'm not sure of the significance of this, but here goes.

"Remember I told you that a couple of pathologists and I were doing some further work on the Block body the other night?"

Duffy nodded.

"We found something we didn't expect. We found something we couldn't have seen before because we weren't looking for it, and even if we had been, we were looking in the wrong place. The boy had colon cancer, Cap, and I would have given him fewer than six months to live."

Silence hung in the room for several minutes. Finally, Jennifer asked, "How long would he have had it?"

"Could have been a couple of years. It would have had the symptoms of colonitis at first and would have been terribly painful and depressing. The cancer then can be held in check for some time. But once it kicks up again after a brief remission, it's only a matter of time.

"My colleagues agree he was in the last stages of life. It was an ugly mess that would have killed him, even if it hadn't spread too far, which—we discovered—it had."

"Shouldn't you have been able to see that right away?" Cap asked.

"Another medical examiner might have. Then again, there was no reason to examine the colon the first time through. We found what we felt had killed him, and we saved the more careful work for later."

"Are you saying the cancer killed him?" Jennifer said.

"No, no, not at all. Don't misunderstand that. He still had several months, and he had to have known about it. But it was an as yet undetermined poison that shut down his cardiovascular and respiratory systems."

Duffy sat thinking, jotting a few notes in his neat script. No one spoke until he said, just above a whisper, "You wonder if we're looking at a suicide here, don't you, Jake?"

The doctor gave a wan smile. "That's not my department, Cap."

"Sure it is. You're supposed to speculate about the cause of death."

"I can tell you *what* did it, Cap. But when I list 'person or persons unknown,' I mean it. The person could have been Robert Block, but I don't know. I just don't know."

"Suicide crossed your mind?" Jennifer asked.

"I'll admit that."

"How about a double suicide?" Cap suggested, startling Jennifer.

"I thought of that too," Steinmetz said sadly. "He knew, she knew. His death was the trigger. She followed suit. It's possible."

"Yeah, it's possible," Duffy said. "But there are too many other people involved, and too few of them are in the clear yet. I'm still in the chase."

"And well you should be," Jake said. "I just thought you should know."

"I appreciate it, Doc. You know that."

Jennifer fought tears. "I appreciate it too, Jake."

"But you won't print it."

"No, of course not. Someday, maybe. To me it's vindication for Bobby in a way."

"You mean if it was a suicide."

"No, even if it wasn't. It explains him, his temperament, his attitude. It doesn't justify anything. Many people become courageous heroes in their final days, but at least it explains a few things. People, many people, should know that."

"But not now."

"Whenever you say," Jennifer said.

Neither Duffy nor Jennifer spoke as they rode the elevator to the first floor and trudged to the car. In fact, they had ridden around the city for twenty minutes before Jennifer finally asked where they were going. Cap admitted that he hadn't the foggiest idea.

"You got a column to write or anything?"

"Sure, but I don't want to miss anything."

"You won't," he said. "I'm just going back over all my notes and try to piece together the last full day of both victims' lives. I really can't do much now until I find Young or the APB turns up Josie Sisk. And when was the last time you heard of an all points bulletin working as fast as you'd like?"

"Could I watch you recreate the last days by going through your notes?" Jennifer asked.

"I'd really rather you not. It's kind of a silent process, and having to talk my way through it would ruin my concentration. If you don't mind."

"I don't mind," she said, feeling guilty about not telling him about Chris Young. "I should be back at the office by eleven-thirty anyway to make a noon appointment."

"You want me to call you if we turn up Sisk?"

"Sure."

"You can break your appointment if necessary?"

"Well, no, if you find her around noon, I'll just have to catch up with you later."

"You've got an hour," Duffy said. "You wanna get some coffee?"

For some reason, that sounded great to Jennifer. It would take her mind off Bobby's disease and her secret meeting at noon.

In a vinyl and linoleum designed coffee shop at the corner of Clark and Chicago, Jennifer asked Cap if she could ask him something totally unrelated to the case—sort of personal—and would he promise not to be offended or afraid to tell her to mind her own business.

"I'm already dying of curiosity," he said. "Fire away."

"Well, it's just that when we first met, you mentioned that you had been to vacation Bible school as a child."

"Yeah."

"I'm curious about that."

"Oh, it's just a thing that churches have and they invite all the kids from the neighborhood, whether they go to that church or not. I didn't go to the church. In fact, we didn't go to any church except some ethnic orthodox thing on Easter and Christmas. I don't even remember the name of that, but it was huge and scary."

"You talked about vacation Bible school as if you still remembered a lot of it. Did you go every year?"

"No, I only went once. It was a week or so long, and we had fun." For a moment Cap stared out the window at the traffic on Clark Street, but his eyes were unfocused. His speech slowed. He was a child of nine, running up the street to VBS.

"We made stuff," he said. "And there was this guy, Uncle Chuck he called himself. I never saw him before or since, though he came by the house a few times. My father wouldn't let him see me. He said the church had me for a week and almost ruined me for life, and that was all he was going to stand for."

"How did it almost ruin your life?"

"Oh, it didn't really. My dad was just scared. Afraid of the unknown. See, one day I came home saved, and it just about did him in."

"Saved?" Jennifer said, knowing exactly what Cap was talking about but wondering if *he* did.

"Yeah, saved. I was singing all the songs about having met Jesus at the crossroads and choosing to follow Him. I *had* chosen to follow Him too, and I mean I meant it. It was real. Isn't that funny?"

"I don't think it's funny at all, Cap."

"Well, ya know, I didn't either. I was devout for a kid who wasn't allowed to go back to where all the fun and the treats and the kids and the games and the stories were. I kept some of the papers and booklets and stuff and read them until they wore out. I still remember the verses, like the one that came back to me the other day. And I remember the Bible stories too."

"But you never went back to church?"

"Not until I was in the army. I tried a few churches that didn't appeal to me. And when we got married, my wife and I went to the same kind of church that she grew up in. But we just kind of faded away from it. You know, it's a funny thing—"

"What, Cap?"

"I'm glad you asked about that because I don't think I've ever in my whole life told anyone except my mom and dad about being saved. Not even my wife."

"That's sad."

"Yeah, it kinda is, because it was such a shaping experience for me."

"In what way?"

"I don't know. It made me a different person, it really did. For a long time I prayed to Jesus every day, asking Him what I should do or not do."

"And did He tell you?"

"Well, my conscience sure worked overtime. You know, I grew up in a pretty rough ethnic neighborhood. But after that, I never once got into serious trouble. I never stole anything again, I quit beating up kids, I never skipped school—that was unheard of— and I never smoked or drank. Well, I tried it a couple of times and didn't like it—so I never did it, not even in the service. And, you know, I never was unfaithful to my wife, even before we were married—you know what I mean."

Jennifer nodded. "And you credit that to this experience you had as a child?"

"Oh, I'm sure of it. I wasn't raised by any example of virtue, though my mother was a pretty decent woman. But you know, to this day I don't even lie. I've never cheated on my income tax. I don't take advantage of other people's mistakes that go in my favor."

"All because you were saved?"

"Well, why else?"

"You still pray?"

"No, not really."

"You still believe there's a God who loves you and a Jesus who saved you from your sins?"

"Sort of, yeah, I do. I know that sounds crazy, but there's no logical reason for the basically honest type of person I am. The odds all pointed in the other direction, but something happened to me in vacation Bible school when Uncle Chuck prayed with me."

"Can we talk more about this sometime, Cap?"

"Sure, if you want to. But I don't want any of this in the paper, Jennifer. You understand? None of it. All of this was off-the-record."

TEN

Jennifer cruised around Lincoln Park until she spotted Chris Young. He was leaning against the front door of his light blue, four-door, Ford Fairmont near a viaduct. His arms were folded across his chest, and his feet were crossed at the ankles. He wore sunglasses and stood so still he could have been asleep.

Jennifer pulled up next to him and rolled down her window, but she said nothing. Because of his dark shades, she couldn't tell if he saw her yet. She was tempted to honk the horn, but she didn't. She just sat there with the engine running.

Finally he grinned a tight-lipped smile and uncrossed his arms and legs. He put both hands atop her car and leaned from the waist to put his face next to hers. "Wanna go for a ride?" he asked.

"Not in your car," she said, amazing herself at her calmness.

"You don't trust me?"

"Should I?"

"What, that detective buddy of yours been filling your pretty little head with stories about the homicidal homosexual?"

"No, but I don't understand why you're avoiding him if you're innocent."

"I just don't need the hassle, Jennifer. Anyway, I wanted to give *you* my information, not him."

"What information?"

"My car or yours?" he asked.

"Not yours."

"You still don't trust me, and I'm doing you this favor?"

She didn't respond.

"All right then, I'll ride with you." He loped around to the other side of his car and pulled a brown paper-wrapped package from the glove compartment, secured with masking tape. Jennifer tried not to let her imagination run wild and decided she wouldn't ask about the package.

He slid into the passenger's seat and smiled at her. She was not about to be pleasant. "Will you take off those ridiculous glasses?" she asked. "It's overcast, for pete's sake!"

He looked disgusted with her but took them off and jammed them into his shirt pocket, pouting. "So where am I supposed to go?" she said.

"Anywhere. Just go up on the Drive, and you can pull off into one of the beach parking areas."

"You'll forgive me if I keep us in plain sight of the Drive."

He shook his head. "You really *are* paranoid, aren't you?"

"Shouldn't I be? Two people have been murdered in apparently bizarre ways, and you and I knew both of them. How do I know you're not going to drag me off somewhere and stick me with a needle and leave me gasping for breath?"

"How do *I* know *you* won't do the same to me? You had more of a motive for killing Bobby than I did."

"*You* afraid of *me*?" she said to the towering Young. "That'll be the day." She pulled off Lake Shore Drive into a parking area. "Now, let's get on with this."

"You in a hurry?"

Jennifer wanted to say yes, because no one knew where she was. But she decided that was just the kind of information Chris shouldn't have.

"I *will* be expected back soon," she said, knowing that at least her boss would wonder where she was.

"Let's take a quick walk, then."

"I'm not taking any quick walk, Chris! Honestly, do you have to be such a grandstander? Tell me whatever you're going to tell me or give me whatever you're going to give me and let me get out of here, OK?"

"OK!" he said, swearing. He shook his head again and turned away from her to stare out the window. "I've got something for you, but I've gotta be like Deep Throat in the Watergate thing."

"You've got to what?" she said, incredulously.

"I've got to remain anonymous. You can't write in your column where you got this stuff. I mean, it'll be obvious you got it from an insider, and you may want to say it was someone from the *Tribune* so people won't think it was from Josie."

"I'll at least be telling Duffy and Jim Purcell," she said.

"No! You can't! Then it's no deal!"

"What's the matter, Chris? You think I'm going to let Cap Duffy waste his time looking for you when there's no need? I'm already going to get royally chewed out for not telling him I was coming to see you."

Young stared at her. "You *really* didn't tell him? I can hardly believe that."

Jennifer could have kicked herself. What she didn't need was to make herself more vulnerable to this character. "No, I didn't. But I'm going to, and you can't stop me."

"Then maybe I won't give you what I was going to give you."

"Suit yourself, Chris," she said. "I'm tired of this game."

"I thought you were a curious reporter-columnist," he tried.

"I am. I'm curious to know if I'm going to survive this crazy meeting."

It was obvious he got great delight in imagining that she was really afraid of him. He could barely contain a smile. "You're really worried, aren't you?"

"Yes, I am. But let me tell you something, Chris. Unless you're armed, you're going to regret it if you try anything with me."

"Oh, excuse me, lady! I'm really scared now! What are you going to do—hit me with your purse?"

"I'm not saying I could defend myself for long, Chris, and you may wind up killing me, but I guarantee you'll regret it."

Young opened his door and staggered from the car, laughing hysterically and banging on the hood. "You're too good!" he shouted gleefully. "You're too funny!"

He had left his package on the seat between them, and when he turned his back to howl into the wind, Jennifer swept it to the floor and beneath her seat. She jumped from the car and smiled at him. "I guess I have been a little silly," she said. "I really don't think you're the murderer, Chris, and I know you wouldn't try to hurt me."

He was still laughing. "Really, Jennifer, what were you going to do to me? When you were really worried about me, I mean?"

She didn't appreciate being laughed at. She reached into her purse and pulled out her key ring, letting a tiny sheath of metal protrude between the ring and middle fingers of her right hand. "I would have used this," she said snapping her wrist and causing the metal to pivot away on its hinge and exposing a two-inch, razor-sharp blade.

Young flinched and stepped back, suddenly sober. "You would have seriously used that on me?" he said.

"If necessary. Of course."

"Well, I don't have, nor did I ever have, any plans to harm you, Jennifer. You should know that."

"Don't make my caution *my* problem, Chris. You're the murder suspect who's eluding the police, not me. I don't think it's so weird for me to be prepared to protect myself."

"So, you trust me enough now to take a little walk?"

"I don't trust you much, but I guess we can walk. Not far though. Not out of sight of the Drive."

As they walked through a small row of trees, he said,"I just want to give you something that belonged to Bobby. But first you have to promise that you won't tell anyone that you got it from me or that you even saw me."

Jennifer just kept walking, her head down, yet always aware of her proximity to Lake Shore Drive, the car, and Chris. When they were about 150 feet from the car, she stopped and looked up at him. "I already told you, I have to tell at least two people that I saw you. I—"

He interrupted with a string of profanities that sent her stomping back toward the car.

He hurried along beside her, berating her, begging her, trying to reason with her. "I can't give you his stuff unless you promise, Jennifer. I haven't even read it, haven't even *opened* it, so I don't know or care what's in there. I just had a hunch it might help in the investigation, that's all!"

"What do you care about the investigation?" she asked. "You won't even talk to Duffy."

"All right, that's it!" Young said. "Forget it! You're gonna tell him you saw me, but I'll be long gone when he comes looking for me, and I'll burn what I was going to give you!"

"Do whatever you have to do, Chris," Jennifer said.

He hurried ahead of her to the car and opened the passenger door. She prayed he wouldn't look under the seat. He backed out of the car and wailed. "Jennifer! We left the car unlocked! Now where's my package? Someone's stolen it! Jennifer!"

She tried to look concerned and hurried to him. "Where was it?" she asked.

"Right there on the seat!" he said, nearly in tears. "Jennifer, you tricked me! Someone's here! Someone's been watching us! You took the walk so someone could steal my package from the car!"

"How would they know you were going to leave anything in the car, Chris? Don't be ridiculous; there's no one here."

He lunged at her and grabbed her by both lapels, pulling her face up to his. His eyes were wild, and he grimaced as he spoke. "I've got to find that package," he hissed. "Even thinking of giving it to you was a betrayal of my dead friend. It was private! And if you tell *anyone* you saw me, you'll never get it." He began to cry. "Oh, Jennifer, I have to get it back! And you have to promise you won't tell anyone, so I can give it to you."

"Forget it," she said.

His hands slid up to her collar and his palms went to her neck, thumbs in front. She drove her right hand between his arms in an uppercut and stopped with the tip of her small blade resting lightly under his chin. He slowly released his grip on her neck and raised both hands, palms open, fear in his eyes.

She kept the blade under his chin with her right hand and gently guided him back, her left hand slipping a small chemical spray cannister from her pocket. She gave him a miniscule blast of mist in the face and pulled the blade away as he tripped backward over a carstop and sprawled in the gravel at the edge of the lot.

She turned and ran to her car, calling over her shoulder. "You can walk back to Lincoln Park!"

As she pulled away he scrambled to his feet and chased the car. He got close enough to bang both fists on the trunk before he fell face first to the pavement. He made a sickening sight in her rearview mirror, a tall, skinny, miserable excuse for an adult, lying face down, sobbing, and slamming his fists on the pavement.

Jennifer was shaking as she parked behind the *Day* building and reached beneath the seat. For several minutes, she worked at the masking tape on the package until she ruefully realized that the weapon she had so deftly used on Chris Young would also work on his package. It sliced open easily.

Inside she found twelve thin, neatly and alternately stacked reporter's spiral notebooks, the type that fit easily into a suit coat side pocket. Each was marked "Private and Confidential" and bore a sticker that said, "If found, please call Robert Block at the *Chicago Tribune* immediately. Reward."

Each was also dated, and a quick leaf through the first notebook, the one that began January 1, showed that Block had learned how to best use the reporter's most valuable tool. Each entry was dated and timed. The interview notes and miscellaneous information had been scribbled almost illegibly, but having worked with him, Jennifer was able to decipher it. Since such information had been ruled admissible in court—in the Watergate hearings—young reporters like Block had learned to protect themselves with meticulous records and direct quotes and research information.

It was a gold mine, Jennifer knew. From the trunk she grabbed the briefcase she seldom used, carefully placed the rewrapped package inside, and locked the latches. When she got to her office, the Saturday secretary, Gail, was waiting with a message for Jennifer to call Duffy at the Chicago Avenue station.

"You wanna talk by phone, or shall I come over there?" Jennifer asked when she reached him. "I've got some exciting stuff for you."

"Likewise," he said. "We've found both Sisk and Young."

"Are you serious?" she asked.

"'Course. Sisk wasn't far away and wound up turning herself in. Young was found wandering down Lake Shore Drive, crying and claiming he'd been the victim of a hit and run driver near the beach. What've you got for me?"

Jennifer was laughing so hard she couldn't speak. As she hung up she called out, "Gail! Please call Duffy back and ask him to call me when he's released Young. I'll go see him then."

ELEVEN

"Young is a first-class weirdo," Duffy told Jennifer just after three o'clock. "His eyes were bloodshot, and he couldn't quit crying. I still say he had a motive, but his alibis have all checked out since I last talked to him. We had to let him go. I have this nagging suspicion that he knows more than he's letting on, and he keeps saying cryptic things about what you should know."

"What *I* should know?"

"Right."

"Well, I'll fill you in on that after you bring me up to date on Sisk."

"I'll be interviewing her in the interrogation room in a few minutes. You can't be in there, but you can hear and see through a two-way mirror, if you'd like. You can't use anything either of us says in the paper unless you clear it with me, though. Now what have you turned up that's one, so important, and two, so hilarious that you hung up on me?"

But they were interrupted by a message that Miss Sisk was waiting in the interrogation room. Duffy positioned Jennifer where she could see and hear best, then told her to be ready for anything.

"What do you mean by that?"

"I'm gonna push her pretty hard. For one thing, she could be guilty."

"For sure, or is she just the one you're concentrating all your efforts on right now?"

He smiled at her. "Both."

He pulled back a curtain that allowed Jennifer to see clearly into the interrogation room where a matron sat in the corner and Josie Sisk sat on one side of a wood table, smoking idly, but tapping one foot on the floor.

Duffy appeared distracted as he entered the room and didn't look Josie in the eye at first. "Hi, Miss Sisk," he said quickly.

"Ms.," she corrected.

"Hi, *Miss* Sisk," he repeated with emphasis, surprising both Jennifer and the matron and causing Josie to widen her eyes, narrow her mouth, look up and around the room, and nod knowingly, as if she had just fully realized what she had gotten herself into.

"My name is Duffy—"

"I know who you are."

"—and this is Matron Gladys Sprague."

"I know who she is too."

"Well, good. Since you know who everyone is, I want to tell you that we appreciate your turning yourself in and saving us a lot of time, trouble, and expense trying to track you down."

"Don't mention it."

"You have the right to remain silent, Miss Sisk, and I suggest you exercise it." It was the first time Duffy had looked her in the eye. "Anything you say can and will be used against you in a court of law."

"I know my rights. I been busted before. Anyways, how come you're collarin' me when I came in on my own?"

"You have the right to have a lawyer present with you while you are being questioned. If you can't afford one, a lawyer will be appointed for you. Do you understand these rights as I have explained them to you?"

"Yeah, yeah."

"Do you waive the right to a lawyer?"

"I can afford judges—what do I need a lawyer for?"

"Then you're waiving the right to have an attorney present?"

"Yeah!"

"And you're obviously waiving your right to silence."

"Yeah."

"Do you understand that you are being placed under arrest for the murders of Robert Block and Adrienne Eden?"

"Both of 'em?"

"That's correct. Did you murder only one of them?"

"No! I didn't murder nobody! I just didn't know I was gettin' busted for both of 'em."

"Which murder did you think you were under suspicion for?"

"Adrienne."

"Why?"

"Because I was there at her place that day."

"You weren't at Block's before he was killed?"

"Plenty of times. I was s'posed to have breakfast with him that morning. Or at least breakfast at his place. He wasn't eatin'."

"Why not?"

"Who knows? He quit eatin' a couple months ago."

"Why didn't you show up?"

"For breakfast?"

"Uh-huh."

"He called and tol' me Adrienne was coming over."

"What time was this?"

"About seven-thirty I guess, quarter to eight."

"When were you supposed to have been there?"

"About eight-thirty."

"Why couldn't you be there if Adrienne was there?"

"What are you, crazy or somethin'? Adrienne didn't know about Bobby and me."

"Can I ask you a personal question, Miss Sisk?"

"You already have. Lots of 'em."

"I want to ask one more, and I don't mean to offend you."

"You're trying to get me on two murders I didn't do, and you don't want to offend me?"

"Miss Sisk, how did you get next to two reasonably intelligent men when you sound so stupid?"

She glared at him. "What're you sayin'?"

"I'm saying I don't understand how a newspaperman—a graduate of Medill School of Journalism—and another journalism student at the same respected university could see anything in a mush-mouth, uneducated type like you. Nothing personal."

It was all Jennifer could do to keep from bursting into laughter, though she was shocked at Duffy's approach, as was the matron whose eyes seemed to be popping out of her head.

"You don't know where I been educated, pal. I graduated from Senn High School and then I went away to college."

"You went *away* to college?" Duffy said, pulling his note pad from his pocket and quickly leafing to the right page. "You call flunking out of the nursing program after four weeks at Harper Community College in Palatine because of reading deficiency *going away* to college?"

"I had to live with a girlfriend in the suburbs for a while."

"You apparently aren't going to answer my question."

"About Ed and Bobby? Sure, I'll answer it. They never hit me as bein' so bright. What's so special about writin' for a newspaper or bein' an almost jock in college? Why do they like me? I'm a fun girl—what can I tell ya?"

"You lied to me about Adrienne not knowing about you."

"Well, she knew about me. She knew me, you know? But she didn't know I was seein' Bobby."

"Were you aware that she had a key to his apartment?"

"I never thought about it much, but I don't guess it surprises me. They were engaged."

"You didn't worry about being caught in there with him?"

"There's a chain lock. Nobody's gettin' in there while we're in there unless we let 'em."

"Where were you going to go if Adrienne showed up?"

"I don't know. I never thought about it. Never happened." She chuckled. "Luckily."

"How did Bobby Block die?" Duffy asked.

"TV news says somebody poisoned him. Only I don't know what they put it in, 'cause like I say, he wasn't eatin', far as I could tell. Maybe they put it in his water."

"What were you doing in his apartment the night before?"

"What are you talkin' about?"

"You were there. Several witnesses saw you come and go."

"I'm not sayin' I wasn't there. I'm just wonderin' if you really don't know."

"In other words, it was just a social call."

"Right, exactly. Social. I mean, let's face it, Bobby and I were not an item. We didn't go out, you know what I mean? Adrienne got around, had a lot of friends. Anyway, I'm going with Ed, and just because he doesn't mind me seein' Bobby now and then, when I go out, I go out with Ed."

"Uh-huh, and you really think Adrienne didn't know about you and Bobby?"

"I don't think so."

"What were you doing at Adrienne's the day she died?"

"I was going to threaten her."

Now even Duffy was shocked. "You were?"

"Yes, I was."

"Why?"

"Because I heard she was flirting with Ed."

"Adrienne was flirting with Ed?"

"That's right."

"And that's not good?"

She swore. "You're right."

"You can see Bobby on the side, even though he's engaged to Adrienne, but if Adrienne makes a move on your man, you're going to threaten her?"

"That's right."

"How does that compute?"

"How what?"

"How does that figure? Make that make sense for me—that it's OK for you to fool around with her guy, but it's not all right for her to make eyes at yours."

"I never said what I was doing was OK. But Ed didn't mind, and Adrienne didn't know, so I kept doin' it. If Ed didn't like it, he coulda tol' me. And if Adrienne found out, she shoulda put up a fuss, just like I was going to. If a woman don't fight for her man, she don't deserve to keep him."

"Uh-huh. So what were you going to do to Adrienne?"

"Just scare her a little. Hurt her if necessary."

"You're serious?"

"You heard me. I had a weapon. I'd have used it. I'd have killed her if she'd given me a reason."

"You amaze me, Josie."

"Yeah, why's that?"

"You're under arrest for murder, and I assume you want to talk your way out of it."

"Yeah."

"You're not doing a very good job."

"Well, I'm just tellin' the truth. I knew you had me at both places before Bobby and Adrienne were found, so I figured honesty was the best policy."

"That doesn't fit you."

"Honesty doesn't?"

"No."

"You heard me lie yet today?"

"You stretched it a little on going away to college."

"I did? I didn't mean to. Palatine may not seem far to you, buddy, but leavin' the city is a trip for me."

"So you went to Adrienne's to scare her and maybe even hurt her. What was your weapon?"

"A .22."

"Pistol?"

"Yeah."

"Ever use it before?"

"Nope."

"Would you have used it?"

"You bet."

"What would have made you use it?"

"If she gave me any grief."

"And did she?"

"Are you kidding? She answered my knock and dropped dead right there. I just shut the door and hit the bricks, man."

"How did you know she was dead?"

"I felt for a pulse at her neck. Nothing. Dead—and I mean right away. Didn't that medical guy say Bobby was dead before he hit the floor too?" Duffy nodded. "Must have been the same way here. I thought about Bobby and knew the same person prob'ly pulled both jobs. I didn't want any of it. But on the way out I saw a lot of people coming in, and I had to try to look like I hadn't just seen somebody drop dead right in front of me. Did a pretty good job hiding it too."

"Hiding it."

"The fact that I had just seen that. I think I looked pretty normal."

"Yeah, for someone driving a canary Porsche."

"Yeah, only it's yellow."

"Uh-huh."

Duffy stood and stretched. Josie lit another cigarette. "Something's still sticking in my craw," he said finally. She looked up. "It didn't bother you that this woman was still grieving the loss of her fiancé?"

"Oh, sure, that's what made me feel so bad later. Ed finally told me I shoulda gone to him before running over to her place, because whoever told me that she was seeing Ed didn't know the whole story. I asked him what *was* the whole story, and he said she was just cryin' on his shoulder. I believe him now."

"Who told you about Adrienne seeing Ed?"

"A guy at the *Tribune*. Chris."

"Really? Does Ed know that?"

"No, and he ain't gonna know either. He likes Chris."

"Does Chris like him?"

"I know what you're driving at, but it's not true."

"You know for sure?"

"I sure do. It's something Chris likes people to think about him, but it's definitely not true. Thing is, I knew Chris long before I met Ed or Bobby."

"Wonderful."

"So what happens to me now? Can I go?"

"I'm afraid not."

"You don't believe me? You think I murdered these two people?"

"Actually I don't, but you were at both scenes. You had a motive in at least one case. I don't know if you studied enough nursing at Harper to figure out how to poison someone. But if I didn't detain you until we could clear you, I'd be delinquent in my duty."

"I was a juvenile delinquent once."

"You'd better get a lawyer, Josie."

"OK."

TWELVE

Cap Duffy roared when he heard the Chris Young parking lot story. Then he asked Jennifer what she thought of his interview with Josie Sisk.

"You were pretty tough with her, Cap. But I'll tell you this—I think she's innocent. I don't think she's got the brains to pull off a sophisticated poisoning."

"Unless she's dumb like a fox and a great actress. She was consistent anyway, wasn't she? I mean, we're talking about a girl with no light at the top of the stairs."

"Any more on the poison?"

"Yeah, I got a call from Jake just after I got back to the office this morning. First he gave me an evaluation of some of the medicines and stuff we found in Block's apartment. Mostly vitamins and minerals, but lots of 'em, which Block would have had to have taken if he was really on a starvation-type diet. And protein powder, just like the kind you can get from these home-based mail-order businesses.

"Jake said he sent some tissue sample to the Center for Disease Control in Atlanta. Their preliminary finding is that Block, at least, died of dioxin poisoning. They found one hundred parts per billion dioxin in his body fluid. One part per billion is considered hazardous to human health and has been known to cause cancer, liver damage, and birth defects.

"Jake says it's one of the most toxic substances known, and that with as dense a concentration as was found in Block's tissue, the man didn't have a chance."

"Could it have caused Block's cancer?"

"Oh, no, this would not have been in his system long before it killed him."

"How does that fit in with your theory—and Jake's—that it worked on a delayed release basis?"

"Good girl, Jenn. That's just the question the professional detective asked. Jake says they also found traces of some sort of a buffer, an agent that protects the system from the harmful effects of the poison for a brief period, not longer than twenty-four hours. And once that buffer has been eaten away or is absorbed into the system, the dioxin is left to its devices. Almost instantaneous death at that one hundred per billion concentration. They're sending a sample from Adrienne's body down there too."

"It'll show the same, won't it?"

"Likely."

"What do you make of their starvation diets? Were they setting themselves up for this? Is it still possibly a double suicide?"

"It's possible, but I can't figure the delayed effect part of it. If you're going to kill yourself, particularly in a double death pact, why not do it quickly and together? Who wants to inject himself and then wonder when it's going to happen?"

"Maybe he did it, and she knew how he did it, so she followed suit."

"Maybe," Duffy said. "But it isn't a normal double suicide modus operandi."

"It's not a normal *murder* modus operandi, Cap."

"True enough. That's another reason I doubt the suicide idea, even though I thought of it first. Where does a guy get access to dioxin? Jake says the only place he knows of is at one of the disease control centers, and you'd have to be a physician or a scientist to even study it. You'd have to be a criminal to remove it from the laboratory."

"Where do they get dioxin, Cap?"

"Researchers bring samples of contaminated floodwater in for analysis. When dioxin is found, people are evacuated from their homes, the substance becomes quarantined in the lab, and the local or state Department of Health moves in to treat the area."

Duffy agreed that Block's notebooks were the key to the success of the rest of the investigation, particularly when he got a glimpse of how detailed they were. "If Sisk is innocent, as I fear, we're probably looking for someone we haven't considered yet," he said.

"That's going to be the point of my first couple of columns about this case," Jennifer told him.

"Futility?"

"You bet. Dead ends. Long hours. Frustration. It's like running in a maze. You see an opening, you charge through, you hit a wall, you go back, you start over. You enjoy this?"

"I enjoy knowing that a break will come that will make everything make sense. When it starts to fall into place, it'll all happen at once, and we'll be saying, 'Ah ha! That's why this and that's why that.'"

"I hope so."

"We have to stay optimistic, Jennifer. If you don't believe a break is coming, it's hard to stay in the game."

"Tell me one thing. Is this a typical investigation?"

"I'll say this: It's not a typical way to die, but it's a very typical investigation. It's like a crossword puzzle. If this word is right, these will be right; but if that word is wrong, we start from scratch. We're starting from scratch, in effect, now, but at least we've got a lot of the underbrush cleared away. We can start to get to the heart of the matter. We can say, who really did this if it wasn't all the people who could have or should have?"

"I think you just mixed a few metaphors there," Jennifer said, "but I see what you mean."

"Tell me what a metaphor is, and I'll try to unmix them for you."

"Forget it, Cap. That's my job. Listen, you're not sure about Sisk yet. How will you determine whether or not she's telling the truth?"

"About all I can do is assign some people to check out her background with a fine-tooth comb to see if there's a link to dioxin or someone with access to dioxin there anywhere. See, the poison that killed Block—and most likely Eden too—is the smoking pistol. Whoever's got the dioxin source has the means. None of the people we've investigated so far had more than motive and opportunity, and that's not enough. When the means is as bizarre as it is in this case, if we can find someone with the means, we may not have to work so hard to establish the motive and opportunity."

"Interesting," Jennifer said.

"Exhausting."

"I hear you."

Duffy paged carefully through the first Block notebook, which covered almost the first two weeks of January. "I can't make heads or tails of it," he admitted. "I can make out the dates and times, but little else. Can you read it, Jennifer?"

"I can read it, but it doesn't mean much to me either. See, here in mid-February of the fourth notebook I recognize his notes from a Police Department press conference we both attended."

"What's it say?" Duffy said. "Anything interesting?"

"Nah. It was just that thing about the police pension fund and benefit committee."

"Not interesting, all right. I had hoped these notebooks would reveal something good."

"You want me to just read through them aloud? You can make notes of anything you think is worth checking on."

"I guess."

For sounding so unenthusiastic about the exercise, Duffy took a ton of notes. Every time Jennifer read off a set of initials or tried to guess the meaning of an abbreviation, he jotted it down. Often he looked over her shoulder to help her make out a particularly scribbly entry. Their break came early that evening when she read a note entered 9:00 A.M., Monday, February 28.

It appeared like this:

> Recd. perm. fr. PT on exp. Can use A if kp hm pstd.
> Phd. BC off. for appt. Thu. 10.3 a. K. Av.

Jennifer interpreted it this way, laboriously, for Cap:

"Received permission for, or maybe from—and I assume PT is someone's initials, yeah, the, uh, managing editor at the *Trib* is Phil Thornton. That a safe assumption then?"

"If you're sure that's his name—yeah, let's run with it."

OK, then he received permission from Thornton on e-x-p. Hm. E-x-p."

"Explanation?" Duffy said.

"I don't think so. It's something he needs the boss's permission for."

"Experience?"

"Maybe. Permission for experience doing what? Something undercover maybe? Maybe it's an exposé on something or someone."

"E-x-p short for exposé?"

"Yeah!" Jennifer said. "I just said that, didn't I? OK, he received permission from Thornton for an exposé, but on what? Can use A if he keeps him posted. I don't know who A is, maybe someone else on the staff, but he can use A, I'm guessing, if he keeps Thornton posted. Why would he have to keep Thornton posted if he used someone else on staff? Maybe it's someone not on staff. Adrienne!"

"You're assuming a lot," Duffy said, "but keep going. He can use Adrienne in the exposé?"

"I think so. Then he phoned BC office. BC is obviously someone's initials. And got an appointment for Thursday at ten-thirty in the morning. K Avenue—oh boy, that could be anything."

Duffy furrowed his brow. "If I had the manpower, I'd call every place of business with the initials BC on every street in Chicago starting with a K and find out which one of 'em had an appointment with Block on—what would it be? Thursday, March third at ten-thirty in the morning."

"But Cap, you're assuming too much. We don't know if BC is a person's name or a company name. We don't know if the Thursday was the immediately following one. We don't know if Block used his own name in making the appointment, but I would highly doubt it. All BC would have to do, whoever that is, is see Bobby's name in the paper as a police reporter, and if the exposé is anything serious, Block is a dead man."

"I agree I don't have enough yet to start the search, Jennifer, but do you realize what you just said? You said if BC, the company or the person, found out who Block was, he'd be a dead man. And he is a dead man. You keep studying the notes—my advice would be to jump to the following Thursday—while I call, what was the editor's name?"

"Phil Thornton."

"Yeah, Thornton, to see if he knew any of the details."

Jennifer found the entry for Thursday, March 3 and read:

> Init. int. unevent., BC not in. Set for
> diag. tsts., EKG, etc., Mon. No break. Mon. ur. samp.

At the bottom of the page, she read "Ken. Ave." and was eager to tell Duffy. He returned with bad news from Thornton.

"He really wants to help all he can, but he said he simply agreed in principle to Block's exposé—he makes it a practice not to involve himself, even to the point of not knowing the target. He just wants to know in advance in case legal questions arise. He was very curious to know where we got Block's notebooks. I told him we uncovered a lot of stuff in the course of the investigation."

Jennifer made a face at him.

"You didn't want me to tell him you stole them from Young who had stolen them from Block's desk, did you?" Duffy asked.

"No, but I didn't want to be responsible for your lying to him either."

"Did I lie to him?"

"By omission you did."

"Same way you did when you didn't tell me you were seeing Young in the park?" Duffy said. Jennifer winced. "You could have gotten yourself killed. He was a murder suspect, you know."

"I know. I almost killed *him*, Cap."

She showed him the entry she had been studying. "If this is the address down here, that narrows it down some, it?" she said.

"Some. Kenmore? Kendale? Kendall? Kenwood? Should be able to find a BC on one of the Ken-something streets."

"But his use of BC this time makes it look more like a person, doesn't it? And if he has to bring a urine sample and have diagnostic tests the following Monday, is he meeting with a doctor? Is BC a doctor? It wouldn't be the same doctor who's treating his cancer if it's tied in with this exposé."

"If it *is* an exposé, Jennifer. We're still guessing."

"C'mon, Cap, we're onto something and you know it. Where's the optimism?"

"I left it in bed last night."

"Let's look at Monday the seventh of March."

> Gluc. tst. Foul. Boring wtng. Fml. Orntl. Dr. elus. abt. educ., dbt.
> MD. BC not in. Off. grl. says seldm. Inj. appt. supp. Prt. lks. lk.
> commrcl. stf.

"Now I'll admit you may be onto something, Jennifer. Translate that mess for me."

She studied it for several minutes. "I think he's saying he had a glucose test he didn't like, probably where they make you drink that concentrated Coke-type stuff. He waited a long time, like you do with those crazy tests, and he was bored. The next part I don't know. Is he saying there's a female doctor who's elusive about her education? He's doubting her M.D. degree?"

"What's 'Orntl.'?"

"I couldn't tell you, Cap. Ornithologist?"

"Ha!" he said. "Now I've got one on the brilliant columnist! He's going to a bird doctor?"

Jennifer smiled. "Chalk one up for Broderick Crawford. Twenty-one-fifty to headquarters."

"Headquarters by," he said. "Only a true 'Highway Patrol' devotee could appreciate *that.*"

"You're talking to one," she said, extending her hand.

He shook it. "The originals?"

"Of course not," she said. "You've got me by ten years. Reruns only."

"I'm sure," he said, turning back to the notebooks. "I can see we're going to need Jake's input on this."

THIRTEEN

Dr. Jacob Steinmetz arrived with a large brown paper bag filled with Chinese food carryout specialties. Trying to suppress a grin, he growled about having to work on a Saturday night, but it was apparent to Jennifer that he secretly enjoyed playing detective.

"Jennifer thinks she's onto something here, Jake," Duffy said, "and it's obvious to us we're heading in a medical direction."

Jennifer flipped back to the Monday, March 7, entry as they sampled Jake's gifts. "I love Oriental food," she said.

"Oriental!" Cap said. "Maybe that's what 'Orntl.' stands for!"

"Lemme see that," Jake said. "Wow, you guys are reaching. It could mean Oriental, I guess, but what does that tell you?"

Duffy took over. "That he had a foul, boring glucose test and that there was a female, Oriental doctor who was elusive when he asked about her education, so he doubted her medical degree."

Jake almost doubled over in laughter. "It sounds like a Peter Sellers movie! What else is there?"

Duffy was not amused. "If you see any other possibilities, Jake, we're open. We've been staring at this scribbling long enough."

With his mouth full, Jake waved an apology and bent over the notebook. Jennifer continued, "BC not in. I'm guessing now that that's the doctor he wants to see. Office girl says seldom?"

"That would fit," Jake agreed with a twinkle. "If he's the main doctor, he would seldom be in, right?"

"But what kind of a doctor is he?" Duffy said. "He gives glucose tests, EKGs, and all that."

"I don't know, Cap. There can be a lot of reasons for both those tests. What else can you make out here?"

"I haven't been able to make anything out of the next few lines," Jennifer admitted. "He's making some kind of a point here. What do you think?"

The three of them sat on the edges of their chairs and hunched over the little notebook, staring at the entry:

Inj. appt. supp. Prt. lks.
lk. commrcl. stf.

Jake tried, "Injection appointment support. That makes no sense, and I don't know what p-r-t is."

"The capital P means a new sentence," Jennifer said, "so the first three words stand alone. I don't know what p-r-t is either, but the rest of that last line is 'looks like commercial,' um, maybe 'staff' or 'stuff'."

Steinmetz suddenly stood and bent from the waist, raising his glasses to his forehead and pushing his face a few inches from the page, blocking Duffy's and Jennifer's view. "May I?" he said, picking up the notebook and carrying it near an overhead light.

"By all means," Duffy said, "What is it, Jake? What've you got?"

"If p-r-t means 'protein,' he's saying it looks like the commercial stuff, which is just what the lab thought of the stuff they found in his kitchen cupboards! BC could stand for bariatric clinic where they give these glucose tests and EKGs before starting people on these liquid protein diets!"

"Are they legit?" Jennifer asked. "Why would he expose them?"

"If they're prescribing stuff that they then supply, and it's commercial protein powder, then they're breaking the law. And of course, if the doctor's staffing his office with nonmedical personnel, they're likely counseling, diagnosing, and administering tests that only an M.D. is licensed to do."

Jake turned back to the page, then sat heavily as if it had all just hit him like a ton of bricks. "If i-n-j means injection, then a-p-p-t s-u-p-p could mean appetite suppressant, of which we found traces in both bodies! It *is* a bariatric clinic!"

"But why would he say BC is not in, if he was referring to a bariatric clinic?" Jennifer asked.

"Yeah," Duffy said, "and do you know of any bariatric clinics on a street like Kenmore, or Kendale, or Kendall, or Kenwood, or something like that?"

Steinmetz squinted in thought. "The only doctor I can think of on a K Street is Duke Creighton on Kendall. He's been known to follow the trends, put people on severe diets, that type of thing. Used to be quite the playboy too, owns a yacht and all the rest, but he's getting up there now. Must be close to retirement."

"Duke his real name?" Duffy asked, pulling a fat phone book off the top of a file cabinet.

"Seems maybe not," Jake said, "but I don't think I know his real name."

"Duffy leafed through the phone book, stopped in the Bs, ran his finger down the page and peered intently at the entry for Creighton on Kendall. He straightened up and twirled the book around on the table so it was right side up for Jennifer and Dr. Steinmetz.

They bent close to read: "Brewster (Duke) Creighton, general practice, specializing in nutrition and bariatrics."

"OK," Jake said, "let's just slow down a minute. Block may have been doing some kind of a series on Creighton, and it may have been an exposé. He may also have simply been on a doctor-supervised, liquid protein diet."

"Jake, it's the first solid lead we've got. Let me ask you something. Is there a traditional location for appetite suppressant shots?"

"Not really. It's fairly common to administer them to the patient just below the hip, while the patient is standing. But Cap, Duke Creighton is a fine physician. Always has been. Was some sort of a Chicago sports hero years ago, an Olympian or some such thing, maybe on a rowing team."

"So we shouldn't check him out because he rowed a boat for the U.S. of A., Jake?"

"I'm not saying that. I just think you have to move cautiously when you start accusing a renowned physician of running a clinic worthy of an exposé."

"That's not all I'd accuse him of, Jake," Duffy said. "I think he figured out who Block was and added a little something to Bobby's last appetite suppressant."

Jake looked stony, but he didn't argue.

"It'll all be in here if it's true," Jennifer said, patting the stack of notebooks.

The three spent until 11:00 P.M. piecing together startling information from the scribbled cryptic notes of a dead man.

On March 14 Bobby had involved Adrienne in the scam under the name Betty Miller. The entry for March 17 revealed he was using the name Daniel Edmonds.

March 23 revealed a note that indicated that the office girl, a Kirsten Moon, had offered to aid him in getting more than he was entitled to from Blue Cross/Blue Shield for his treatments. "You pay $50, I put down that you paid $75, and they pay you 80 percent of that, or $60."

Block's notes indicated that he asked if she wanted a cut. "I wouldn't know what to do with more money," she had replied.

"It still doesn't prove anything about the murders," Jake said miserably, late in the evening. But his futile defense of an old acquaintance, one he admitted he had not seen for more than five years, was hollow and nearly unheard.

Block's research into the records of one of the leading home-based mail-order business in the country revealed that Dr. Brewster Creighton was its leading seller of protein powder and had won innumerable trips and other prizes.

"I can't believe Duke would do that," Jake lamented. "It's against the law to prescribe the stuff, and no doubt it's against the buying service rules too."

Jennifer interpreted a March 30 entry this way:

> My own doctor says the weight loss is OK and the protein and vitamins are not harmful, though the big C is acting up again. I'll look trim in the coffin.

"You gotta admit that's ironic," Duffy said, shaking his head.

"Big C mean colon or cancer?" Jennifer wondered.

"Either one," Jake said. "What's the difference?"

The April 1 notes showed Block's confidence that his cover was still intact.

> I never want my picture in the paper like my former boss. Her undercover days are over.

April 8, Block noted that he had told Phil Thornton that he would be ready with the first installment of the big exposé by the last week of April for the Sunday, May 1 *Tribune*.

I asked if he wanted to know what it was all about. He said no, but if it was big enough he could try to get it in the *Tribune Magazine*. I said no, because once it broke, it would have to run everyday for at least a week. He asked if my weight loss had anything to do with it. I lied and said no. He'll find out soon enough.

April 19, Block wrote that he was looking forward to the appetite suppressant shot the next day.

They start to wear off now after about five days. It's all I can do to hang on until Wednesday afternoons. Cheated only twice. No noticeable difference in weight loss pattern. Medical records show no listing for Filipino female 'doctor' who handles most of the work. Still have never seen BC. On his boat somewhere KM says.

Several records indicated a discrepancy in charges and mode of payment, depending on which of the staff waited on Block and/or Adrienne. Her weight loss was slower and less dramatic, but she cheated more.

The next entry, under the same date, made Jennifer teary.

Wrote to Jenn. Fence-mending long overdue. Guess I'll just tell her straight out. No excuse, but a reason. Hope she agrees to see me. Wouldn't blame her if not.

She only hoped he had gotten her message to phone back.

"I've got enough to get a warrant right now," Duffy said.

"You may be able to get a coroner on a Saturday night," Jake said. "But I'd like to see you rouse a judge. Anyway, you don't know where to begin to look for Creighton."

"I don't want Creighton yet. I just want access to his office tomorrow. Nobody will be there on a Sunday. If I can get clearance for you, Jake, will you join me? I'm gonna need help deciphering medical notes and records."

"I guess so," Steinmetz said. "But this is going down hard."

"I can imagine," Duffy said. "How long have you known Creighton?"

"A couple of decades at least. I met him when we were both on an emergency public safety board for the Fox Lake River flood project."

Jennifer and Duffy stared at him. He looked from one to the other before realizing what he had said. Creighton was the type of doctor who would have access to disease germ samples and poisons. Jake buried his head in his hands.

"OK if I go now?" he asked finally.

"Sure, Jake. And thanks a lot. Can I call you tomorrow if I get the warrant?"

Jake nodded.

"And you won't tell a soul what we uncovered here tonight until we make an arrest, huh?"

He nodded again and pulled on his coat as he shuffled wearily out the door.

"I'm sorry to be calling so late, Mrs. Cole. This is Detective Cap Duffy of the Chicago

Police Department calling for the Judge. . . . Thank you, ma'am.

"Judge, I'm terribly sorry to wake you, and you know I wouldn't if it weren't important. . . . Yes sir, we met once in the late sixties during an Illinois Bureau of Investigation drug bust in the western suburbs when you were with the State's attorney's office, and we met again during the Tylenol murder investigations . . . in Mr. Fahner's office, yes sir.

"Well, it's this double poisoning murder of the newspaperman, Block, and his fiancée, Adrienne Eden. . . . Yes, sir, if I can get a warrant to search a doctor's office tomorrow, I feel confident we'll be able to make an arrest. . . . A messenger? No, sir, if you did that, I'd come myself to pick it up tonight. . . . Thank you, sir. I appreciate that. Here's the doctor's name and address."

The judge also recognized Creighton's name and asked several questions about the investigation before issuing a warrant that Duffy himself drove over to pick up.

When Duffy returned at about midnight, Jennifer had more information for him. "Look at this entry for April 15. It looks like he's saying, 'Told Mac about BC. Probably shouldn't have, but he'll keep it. As appetite suppressant wore off early last week too. She had another yesterday morning.' So, Cap, Bobby has his next shot the following Wednesday afternoon and dies Thursday morning. She has hers that same Thursday morning, a week after this entry, and dies the next afternoon.

"You realize what that means, Cap? She had her injection and had that poison in her system by the time she showed up at his apartment just after noon on the day he died."

Cap still had his hat on, and now he pushed it back on his head and folded his arms. "What we have to determine tomorrow is how Creighton got onto Block and Eden and who gave the lethal injections. If one of these office girls did it, which is unlikely, whether Creighton himself actually prepared the shots, or whether he even administered them. Anything on that in Block's notebook?"

"No. The twelfth book ends April sixteenth. He died on the twenty-first."

"Well, there should be a lot of corroboration in the doctor's office, unless he was smarter or more careful than we thought. I'm gonna grab some shut-eye and then visit that office first thing in the morning. You?"

"I'm afraid I can't join you tomorrow, Cap."

"*What*? We're getting to the best part, lady!"

"I know, but I go to church on Sundays, and I try to work as little as possible."

He smiled at her. "Where do you go to church?"

"These days up in Waukegan at Jim's church."

"How about a deal?"

"A deal?"

"Yeah. My wife and I will join you for church, then you two join Jake and me at the doctor's office."

"Jim would love that."

"Yeah. My wife doesn't like that snooping around sort of stuff, so I'd drop her off at home maybe after dinner and before we head to Creighton's office."

"You're not worried about losing time on this?"

"Nah. The only other people who know about it are Jake and the judge, and they won't be telling anyone. I'll be hard pressed to get any help rounding up Creighton on a

Sunday anyway. My plan is to get everything we need at his office and try to collar him Monday. We got a deal?"

"Sure, Cap. Are you sure you want to?"

"If your church is like the one I went to when I was nine, where they still believe, how did you say it—?"

"That there's a God who loves you and a Jesus who saved you from your sins?"

"Yeah. Then I'd like to check it out. It'll be a little late notice for Maryann, but she's always game."

FOURTEEN

Cap and Maryann Duffy were so impressed with Jim's church that they asked if they could come back the following week.

"You could even come tonight," Jim said at lunch.

"That would be even better," Maryann said, surprising everyone, including herself. "I mean, it's just that everyone seemed so happy and at ease and—well, enthusiastic."

"We are," Jennifer said.

"What impressed me," Cap said, "was how obvious it was that everyone just *believes*. I mean, they talk about it, sing about it, pray about it, smile about it."

"Not *it*," Jim said, smiling.

"Yeah," Cap said, slightly embarrassed. "I know." He pointed up.

"I was almost going to join you on your little escapade this afternoon," Maryann said, "just so maybe we could talk a little more about it. But if we're going tonight, I won't have to."

"I don't know how you can pass it up," Jennifer said.

"Believe me, it's easy," she said. "I know it's important, and I'm proud that Harold is good at it. But it always gives me the willies to be poking around in other people's things."

"But we have a warrant, Hon," Cap said.

"I know, and if that makes you comfortable, enjoy yourselves. I'll pass."

"But you *will* come tonight?" Jennifer asked.

"I wouldn't miss it," she said. "I confess it was not at all what I expected. I was really afraid at first and almost didn't come. But Harold told me about the good times he'd had in church as a child, so I thought it was worth a try. It left me with a million questions, I'll tell you that."

"Well," Jim said, "we don't have all the answers, but you can try us, and we can at least point you to someone who could be more helpful."

Dr. Jacob Steinmetz was waiting in his car across the street from Brewster Creighton's office when Cap Duffy pulled up with Jim and Jennifer.

Cap stopped next to Jake's car, and it was immediately obvious that the coroner was in a bad mood. "Let's park a couple of blocks down and not appear so obvious," Cap suggested. "I've tipped off the burglar alarm company and the local precinct station in case we can't get past the wiring, but Jim has the tools we need."

"Duke is in town," Jake said.

"How do you know that?" Cap asked.

"I couldn't help myself, Cap. I drove past his place. His mobile home is parked at the side, and the boat's in the garage. I saw him in the yard this morning."

It was all Duffy could do to keep from exploding. "Did he see you, Jake? If you blew this thing for us, he could have already been in there destroying all the evidence and—"

"I didn't say anything to him, Cap. He didn't see me. But I almost wish I had tipped him off."

"What if he's guilty?" Cap asked.

"That's the only thing that kept me from it. That, and the fact that you made me promise last night. I'm a man of my word, Cap. But breaking into a doctor's office goes against everything I've ever believed in."

"So does murder, doesn't it, Doctor?"

Jake stared at him. Cap pointed down the street, and Jake followed him. When the cars were situated, Jake joined the other three in Cap's car. "Jim will go first," Cap said, "and try to get in without tripping the alarm. Once he's in, we follow nonchalantly, as if the office is open and we're expected."

"You don't see any value at all in allowing Duke to come down here and let you in so you don't have to break into his files and everything?" Jake tried.

"Doc, I gotta tell ya, that's a little naive. He'll call a lawyer to get a temporary restraining order on the warrant, and that will give him all the time he needs to destroy anything that would prove his guilt."

"Or innocence," Jake said.

"If there's nothing in the office that implicates him, then maybe he *is* innocent. We're not gonna plant anything, Jake. I'm going in there with you and one of the straightest cops I've ever worked with. Jim is Officer Friendly, for pete's sake, and Jennifer would never let me get away with anything underhanded, which I wouldn't try anyway. You can be of great help to me today, Jake, if you're not just in there trying to defend your buddy."

"He's not my buddy," Jake said, "but he's a brother in the profession."

"He also took the Hippocratic oath, right?" Cap said.

Jake nodded.

"And if he violated that, you want to see him answer for it just as much as I do, maybe more."

Cap took Jake's lack of response as consent and nodded to Jim, who left the car and walked briskly a block and a half to the Creighton Medical Building. Jim tried the front door, then moved around to the back where he slipped a thin strip of metal between the door and its frame, slicing the wire to the burglar alarm. That took care of the remote feed to the police station, but opening the door would trip the local siren on the building.

Jim used a bent wire pick to trip the lock almost as quickly as a key would have done the job, then placed one hand on the glass next to the door and the other hand on the handle. He spotted the wire to the siren inside the building. He yanked open the door and heard the scream of the horn as he raced through the shallow lobby and swiped at the nearly hidden wire with his metal strip. The siren ceased.

Jim returned and relocked the back door, then made his way through to the front where he unlocked the door and pushed it open a few inches to signal the others to join him. When they were in, Jim locked the front door and moved cautiously toward Creighton's private office. He dropped to the floor and peered through the crack under the bottom of the closed door.

He motioned to Cap to join him in the front lobby again. "There's a unit next to Creighton's desk that could be any medical device, but if it is, it's the only one in that office."

"What are you saying? What do you think it is?"

"A sound-activated alarm."

"Have no fear," Duffy said with a grin, and he produced from his pocket a high frequency tone generator.

"You think of everything, don't you?" Jim asked.

"I'm an old thirty-nine," Cap said. "There's a reason for that. Would you like to do the honors?"

"Sure, what do I do?"

"Just aim it at the machine and give it one shot with this button. You won't hear a thing, but if we were outside, dogs would come running."

Purcell edged back to the door and carefully laid the corner of the palm-sized device in the crack under the door. He pushed the button. "How do I know if it worked?" he whispered.

Like this," Cap said, and he rapped loudly on the door. "Gimme your pick." And he popped the lock. The device had indeed been a sound detector, and if it had been on, it was now off.

"Did I do that?" Purcell asked.

"We'll never know," Cap said. "But who cares? We now own this place."

After a quick tour to get the lay of the land, Duffy pulled everyone back into Creighton's private office. "It's possible that people in the neighborhood are already suspicious. If they call the cops, a squad will come and then tell them that we're authorized to be here. If they call Creighton, we could have trouble when he shows up. If anyone notices him arrive, let me know so I can get some back up. Since he's unaware of this, he could shoot us and not suffer for it.

"Jennifer, I want you to dig through the files in the reception area. See what you can find on Bobby and Adrienne's aliases, Daniel Edmonds and Betty Miller. Jake, check the medicine storage cabinets. You know what you're looking for."

"Dioxin," he said.

Duffy nodded. "I'll go through the doctor's office, and Jim will float around, opening anything you want opened, damaging as few locks as possible. Jake?"

"Yeah."

"If you find anything significant, don't touch it, hear?"

Jake nodded.

"Work quickly, because if someone *does* tip off Creighton, he'd be here how fast, Jake?"

"Oh, forty minutes I guess."

"All right, we meet back here in twenty-five minutes with whatever you've got."

Jake found six vials of unidentified substances that were clearly labeled as dangerous poisons. Yet they were in the same cabinet as the appetite suppressant. He wondered whether the poisonings could have been a mistake and if other victims might turn up. Yet the poisons would have to be evaluated to see if they contained dioxin.

Jennifer found a raft of information on patients Edmonds and Miller from appointment times to payment receipts, from prescriptions to diagnostic test results. She found one report that seemingly indicated a cancer-related blood problem, along with a note that the information was classified and not to be discussed with the patient. Attached to this report was a handwritten note from Dr. Creighton stating that this "problem shall in no way affect or be affected by the protein diet program."

But she also found strange financial documents. The K. M., who must have been Kirsten Moon, had indeed falsified many records to Blue Cross/Blue Shield, initiating overpayments to patients from that company.

The plum of Jennifer's search was a small stack of notes concerning Edmonds and Miller that began early in March. The first several were copies of notes to Dr. Creighton that Mr. Edmonds was continually requesting an appointment with him. The doctor's replies recommended stalling as long as possible, promising that perhaps he would see Edmonds in May, if his schedule cleared.

Suddenly, on April 18 there was a note from another girl in the office to Miss Moon, informing her that the doctor had called from his Wisconsin cabin on the weekend to find out when certain patients were scheduled for appointments. The note added, "Kirstie, please call Dr. C. at his cabin and tell him when the following six are scheduled." Among the list were both Edmonds and Miller.

A general note went to the staff the afternoon of April 18, informing them that the doctor would be in Wednesday afternoon and Thursday morning and could then be reached at his home until Sunday afternoon at three when he would return to Wisconsin.

Duffy had all but struck out until he searched the cabinets lining the walls of Creighton's office. He had been through correspondence files, a petty cash fund, prescription pads, and equipment chests. But in one corner of a locked door of a locked cabinet was a small cash box, also locked. When Jim popped it open for him, Duffy knew he'd hit pay dirt.

In the box he found just over $11,000 in cash and a small ledger book with a rubber band around it, noting various payments and deposits. Creighton had apparently kept a stash of $20,000 in the box. But a payment was noted for Thursday evening, April 21, for $8,950 "to retire E.M. auto loan."

Duffy made a fast phone call to an associate and asked him to check telephone and bank records on two people, one of whom was Dr. Brewster Creighton. When Jennifer told Cap what she'd found, Duffy asked his boss to stake out the streets around the Creighton residence to see if he indeed planned to leave at 3:00 P.M. It was two-thirty.

When everyone had gathered in Creighton's office, Duffy summarized. "We can place Creighton himself here at the time of Block's and Eden's last injections. Whether he administered them or not, we don't know. He could have prepared them anyway, then this Kirsten Moon or someone else could have given the shots without being aware of the contents of the syringes.

"We'll have to examine the vials," Jake reminded him.

"Of course. The key is, what made Creighton call from Wisconsin last weekend and decide to come in when Block and Eden were scheduled for appointments? Obviously, someone tipped him off, but who was it and how did they get his number in Wisconsin?"

"Would it had to have been either Young, McDevitt, or Sisk?" Jennifer asked.

"Likely," Duffy said. "Sisk probably knew nothing about it. What motive would she have had for exposing the scam? Young may have had the notebooks before Block died, but I can't figure his motive either. He told you, Jennifer, that he hadn't read them, but for some reason he thought they might be important. Does that add up?"

"Really it does," Jennifer said. "As a newspaperman, he would know that there would be detailed information in there, even if he didn't read it."

"When was that entry in Block's journal that said he had told someone about BC?"

Jennifer pulled out the notebooks. "Friday, April fifteenth. Says he told Mac. What are you thinking, Cap? McDevitt?"

"Could be. Say McDevitt calls here to rat on Block because he can't stand sharing Josie with him. He wants to sell the doctor some information that would save his practice from a ruinous exposé. The doctor isn't in, and to protect him, the staff probably says they can't give out his number but that they will call the doctor and give him a message. McDevitt makes the message provocative enough that Creighton indeed calls him back. Within a day or two, Creighton makes arrangements to be back in his office for the two appointments, and once the deeds are done, he settles with McDevitt."

"But what do you make of the cash journal entry, Cap?" Purcell asked.

"A good way to launder the money," Duffy said. "It goes from Creighton to McDevitt in cash, McDevitt deposits it in his account, then writes a check for that amount to pay off his car loan. He's that much richer because he now has the money he would have spent over the next three or four years in high car payments, but he's not all of a sudden flashing bills around. I've got someone checking on his bank statement right now. They're also working on the phone calls between here and Creighton's Wisconsin cabin during the last week."

The phone rang, and everyone looked to Duffy. "All right," he said, "it could be my man, or it could be that someone has tipped off Creighton. Jennifer, you answer it, and if it's Creighton, make him think it's his answering service."

She picked up the phone. "Doctor's office."

"Dr. Duffy, please."

She smiled and handed Duffy the phone. "Yeah, Frank. . . . Oh, no! No mistake? Thanks, and stay close. We may need you. I may have to bluff him pretty good, but we'll want to make the arrest today."

Duffy hung up without another word and began scrambling to put the office back in shape. "My guys are tailing Creighton. He and his wife have left the house in their mobile home, but it appears they're headed this way. Jake, you and Jennifer and I will make it look like we haven't been here while Jim finds us a place inside here to wait for him."

FIFTEEN

It seemed to take longer to put the office back the way it was than it had to put it in disarray. And things were slowed when Jim returned by Duffy's deciding to let him reorganize Creighton's office while Cap was on the phone to his contacts, pushing for information before Creighton showed up.

Jim had located a second floor hallway that overlooked the back lobby and much of the reception area where at least three of them could watch Dr. Creighton as he entered. Duffy, because of his size, would fit in a cabinet at one end of Creighton's office, and, blocked by a file cabinet, he could leave the door open far enough to view most of the room.

Meanwhile, with Duffy on the phone, Jim straightening Creighton's office, Jennifer tidying up the reception area, and Jake on the lookout after having relocked the medicine cabinets, they awaited Brewster Creighton.

"I see a couple of cars near yours!" Jake said. Duffy quickly ended his call and jogged to the front door. He peered down the street through the tinted glass lobby and pulled a walkie-talkie from his belt.

"One-nineteen to one-sixteen."

"One-sixteen," came the static filled response.

"Bill, you don't want three unmarked squads that close together and that close to this building, do you?"

"Ten-four, Cap. Repositioning. Any guess where the mark will pull in?"

"Ten-four, sixteen. Vehicle size should force him into north parking lot entrance. He's likely to enter the building from the back. What do we know about his current ten-twenty?"

"Stand by."

In less than a minute, Duffy's associate came back on with Creighton's approximate location and said, "E.T.A. fifteen-hundred-fifteen."

"What's he saying?" Jake asked.

"Estimated time of arrival is three-fifteen," Cap said. "Everybody ready?"

"What'd you get on the phone and bank stuff, Cap?" Jim asked.

"Plenty."

Dr. Steinmetz, Jim, and Jennifer stationed themselves on the second floor, overlooking the back door, the main hallway, and the reception area, while Duffy climbed into the cabinet in Creighton's office.

"Nineteen to sixteen."

"Go ahead, Cap."

"Let me know when you spot the vehicle. I'll go off the air but will click you twice if I need you."

"How do we get in, sixteen?"

"Stand by," Duffy said, then hollered, "Jim?"

"Yeah!"

"You'd better unlock the front door—in case we need help."

"What if he comes to the front door? If it's unlocked it'll tip him off."

"He may already know we're in here, Jim. That may be why he's coming. Well, pick a door to leave unlocked so I can tell my backups."

"I'll unlock the back, Cap."

Duffy told his backup.

At seventeen minutes after three, Duffy's walkie-talkie crackled the message. "Nineteen to sixteen, vehicle sighted. Entering north lot. Parking at edge of lot in back. Driver leaving vehicle. Heading toward back door."

"I'm going off the air, sixteen!" Cap said, "And we're switching your unlocked door." Then he yelled, "Jim! Lock the back door fast and unlock the front. Hide where you can. This is it!"

Jim could see Brewster Creighton across the back parking lot about thirty feet from the back door, walking slowly, head down. Jim put one foot on the railing and leaped to the first floor, bending low as he hit to cushion the impact. He flew into the lobby and turned the knob on the back door, stealing a glance at Creighton before running back through the hallway. The doctor did not appear to have seen him.

Jim slid into the front lobby and unlocked the door, but as he turned to dash back upstairs, he heard Creighton inserting his key into the burglar alarm shutoff, then into the back door. Jim plastered himself against the wall in the lobby and held his breath.

Creighton moved purposefully through the main hallway carrying a black leather duffel bag. The broad, only slightly hefty, grey-haired doctor wore white buck shoes, rust-colored trousers, a white turtleneck sweater, and a pale yellow sports coat. He opened examining room doors on either side of the hall, quickly scanned them, and shut the doors again. Occasionally he would drop something in his bag.

When he got to the reception area, he pulled two of his medical degree certificates from the wall, then rummaged in the bottom of the desk drawer and replaced them with old photographs. At the end of the hall, he took down a photo of himself and the rest of the 1940 United States Olympic rowing team and replaced it with a photocopy of his undergraduate diploma.

He also retrieved a couple of photographs of his wife and family, one of his parents, and a gold inlaid letter opener. From a hallway closet he took his golf clubs and shoes and a camel hair sports coat. He then made a quick trip to his motor home, chatted briefly with his wife as he dropped off the stuff, and returned to the building.

He surveyed the rest of the first floor one more time, picking up a few keepsakes here and there and dropping them into his coat pockets. From one of the medicine cabinets he removed the six vials Jake Steinmetz had identified as poisonous. Just outside his office he inserted a special key into a mechanism above his door to turn off the sound-activated alarm, then unlocked his door. Inside he moved quickly to a cabinet at the other end of the office from where Duffy hid.

Dr. Creighton slid open a door and pulled an expensive leather briefcase from the shelf and placed it carefully on his desk. He opened it and emptied nearly $80 from his petty cash fund into it, replacing the box in his desk drawer. He pulled two folders from his file cabinet—stepping within three feet of the motionless Detective Cap Duffy—paused only briefly to leaf through them, and deposited them in his briefcase as well.

Creighton looked around the room once more and retrieved a couple of personal knickknacks and keepsakes, packing them neatly in his case. He then unlocked the cabinet in the corner, unlocked the smaller door, unlocked the cash box, and left it open.

Creighton went to the phone, dialed a number he read from a tiny slip of paper, let it ring once, then hung up. He closed his briefcase, spun the combination locks, unplugged the sound alarm, and sat on the edge of the desk, looking at his watch.

Within seconds the phone rang once and fell silent. As if on cue, Creighton slid the briefcase off the desk, left his office without relocking the door, left the building without resetting the central alarm, and locked the back door. He strode to his vehicle and pulled away.

"He's gone!" Jim shouted from the front lobby.

"He get anything significant?" Duffy asked, turning on his radio and announcing that he was back on the air.

"He took the poison," Jake called as they met in the hallway.

Duffy called his backup. "Nineteen to sixteen. Bill, he set this place up for someone. Don't let him get too far. He's got evidence we need, and we can't let him dump it. Let him get out of sight of here and take him."

"Is he armed, nineteen?"

"I doubt it, but be careful." He turned to the others. "Let's clear out so we can stake this place out. Someone is coming, probably after dark. Anyway, I need time to figure out why Creighton takes eighty bucks and leaves more than $11,000 unlocked."

By early evening Maryann Duffy had been called to cancel her evening plans with her husband and Jim and Jennifer. Jake Steinmetz had received permission to go home. Jim had been stationed with one of the three back-up cars situated within view of the front of the building.

Jennifer was in the backseat of Duffy's squad car, now positioned on an east-west street a half block behind the medical building, with a clear view of the parking lot and back door. Duffy sat behind the wheel, alternately watching and reading a report hastily scribbled by one of his men, telling of the telephone bank activity of Brewster Creighton. Several of Creighton's phone calls from Wisconsin and his office had been to a pay phone on the Northwestern campus.

Duffy had also been filled in on the preliminary questioning of Dr. Brewster Creighton, who had refused to answer any questions until his lawyer arrived. The vials had been sent to the lab, and the results, showing concentrated dioxin content, came back at about the time Creighton's lawyer arrived.

Creighton apparently refused to tell even his lawyer what he had done in his office, other than pick up a few items. The lawyer had demanded that charges be filed or his client released, but the Homicide Division was stalling as long as possible, using Sunday as an excuse not to have all the documents and personnel they needed and knowing they'd have an easier time if they had Creighton's accomplice.

At approximately 11:30 P.M., after Jennifer had exhausted her "what-if" questions and was beginning to wonder if they weren't on a wild goose chase—which, Duffy told her, was not only entirely possible, but probable, given the odds in such situations—Duffy was informed by radio that an old car had been parked about three and half blocks from his location and that the driver was now walking in that direction.

Duffy and Jennifer peered out and soon saw a figure approaching from the north, occasionally illuminating a piece of paper in its hand with a penlight. Reaching the north edge of the parking lot to the medical building, the figure stayed in the shadows near a row of hedges and then angled directly toward the back door.

Duffy left his car with Jennifer right behind him and sidled up to the hedge row to watch the figure unlock the back door, apparently with a key. As the figure edged down the hallway, again illuminating the paper with a light, Duffy crept through the back door and deftly stayed about thirty feet behind, Jennifer still on his heels, her heart racing.

The figure located Creighton's office door and pushed it open, using the light constantly now. Duffy and Jennifer slipped off their shoes and stole down the carpeted hallway, stopping a few feet from the office.

From inside, they could hear the opening of the cabinet, the inner door, the box. Money was being stuffed in pockets. Duffy sneaked to the other side of the door where he could see in through the crack.

The figure reached inside a short coat and withdrew two thin pint bottles, which looked like whiskey containers. These were splashed around the floor from the cabinet, past the desk, and to the door, where the figure now stood not four feet from where Duffy crouched, his hand on the snub-nosed .38 in his shoulder holster.

As the odor of gasoline wafted into the hallway, the dark figure pocketed the penlight and produced a disposable cigarette lighter. Backing up and reaching for the door behind it, the intruder carefully held it open, still gazing into the office, lighter poised.

Duffy moved up from behind and stuck the barrel of his pistol into the back of the man's neck, just above the spine, reaching around to the chin with his left hand. "Drop it or you're a dead man, Ed," he said, as McDevitt jumped, then struggled. The tall collegian whimpered and pulled against the force of Duffy's strangle hold, and somehow ignited the lighter and flipped it into the room.

The force of the blast drove both men into the hallway, and Duffy's gun bounced near McDevitt. Ed grabbed it and handed it to the detective, swearing and screaming. "Kill me, you liar! You said I'd be a dead man! Shoot me! Shoot me!"

Duffy holstered his weapon as flames from the office licked at the hallway. McDevitt lay in a heap on the floor, sobbing. "I had to make Bobby pay!" he said. "I had to make him pay!"

"You're *all* going to pay," Duffy said, grabbing the big man by his collar and his belt and using his own lithe strength and balance to drag McDevitt toward the back. Jennifer held the door open as Duffy yanked McDevitt to his feet and sent him stumbling past the bushes and safely out of range of the roaring fire.

Backup cars slid into the lot, and Cap's aide from the Chicago Avenue station jumped out and ran toward the back door, shouting for Duffy.

"Over here, Bill!" Cap called. "We're all OK."

As Ed McDevitt was handcuffed and led to a squad car, Cap squeezed Jennifer's shoulder. She was shaking. He winked at her. "You and Jim up to a little coffee at my place later tonight? We owe it to Maryann, don't we?"

Jennifer could hardly speak. "Ask him," she said, as Jim came charging around the corner of the burning building. He threw his arms around her and held her tight, not thinking, or at least not caring, that it was the first time he had held her in front of anyone.

Relief lit his face as it sank in that Jennifer was safe.

Gateway

ONE

Jennifer Grey and her fiancé, Jim Purcell, sat silently in the west parlor of the Norman Funeral Home on Chicago's Near North Side.

None but the macabre enjoy funeral homes. But those who have lost close loved ones develop a particular aversion to them. It can resurface and drag them back to wrenching memories at the mere smell of a sickeningly sweet floral shop years later.

Jennifer herself had been widowed young. So quickly, so painfully, that it had taken her months to regain a semblance of normalcy in her life. She had not been married a year when her husband was killed on the highway.

But she had dealt with that. Time, so the cliché goes, was a healer. So were close parents; understanding friends; a good church. And when she carefully ventured out into the real world again, Jennifer found she could function alone.

The loss made her reluctant to untie her emotions, hesitant to respond to her cautious new admirer. For a while she was able to hide, even from herself, her deepest feelings for Jim. Only sharing their own crisis and learning to depend upon each other had brought her to where she could no longer pretend she didn't care for him.

And now, after a long courtship, they would be married in a few months. She had said yes to Jim, resulting in the second to the last change in her life since her first husband's death. Until now, most of the changes had been for the better.

She had moved from the women's page of the *Chicago Day* to the newsroom under legendary City Editor Leo Stanton. She and Jim had survived an ordeal in his career on the police force that, while it seemed to Jennifer almost as grieving as losing a mate, was really the beginning of their love relationship. She had been promoted to columnist with her own location on the front page.

Jim had only recently been promoted to sergeant and would soon be a plainclothes detective. Today he sat stiffly in his dress blues, wearing his funeral face, the one worn by all who were only loosely associated with the deceased.

Even Leo had been promoted. He had become managing editor just two months before. That meant a huge office on the sixth floor, a secretary, more business suits, less action, more headaches. He pretended not to like it, to be hemmed in, restricted from the fun of the daily grind, the hands-on editing.

But in truth Leo loved it. He deserved it. He had more policy input on the entire paper. Jennifer missed the measured casualness of dress that had characterized his reign of mock terror in the city room.

Leo had always been one for soft leather loafers or wing tips, gray woolen slacks, pastel button-down shirts, navy or camel blazers, always draped neatly over a chair by mid-morning.

He liked to loosen his tie and roll up his sleeves, but there was still something formal about that informality. Worst, he had always felt the need to temper the whole Ivy League look with a soggy, unlit cigar lodged in his right cheek.

He never smoked and frequently reminded everyone of that. Somehow, during the several weeks since he'd been promoted, he'd given up the cigar. Everyone guessed that Publisher Max Cooper had made it a prerequisite.

Jennifer nodded red-eyed at her many colleagues as they somberly stepped into the chapel. Mr. Cooper and his stately, white-haired wife sat near the front, behind the family. How strange not to hear his loud voice, his bellowing laughter. He had a reputation for bluster behind closed doors, but with the rank and file, he always seemed to feel required to joke and laugh and tell inane stories.

Jennifer turned to glance at Jim. His uniform made him look so young. The hat in his lap had left its telltale impression on his whitish-blond hair. His pale blue eyes noticed her looking up at him, and he pressed his lips together to acknowledge her.

The parlor was nearly full, though there was a line back to the lobby where many were still signing the guest book. Jennifer leaned to one side and peered up to the front row where the family sat, still stunned at their loss of just three days.

Leo sat in the middle of a nine-chair row, his left arm around his married daughter who sat next to her husband and their two young children. They had flown in the morning before from California. Leo's right arm was around his bachelor son from Maryland, who sat next to his mother's best friend—June Roloff—and her husband, Kent, assistant managing editor at the *Day*.

Someone had coached the grandchildren, who only occasionally looked at each other to whisper. Jennifer watched Leo for several minutes and wondered if he had even blinked. She didn't see him move.

He just stared straight ahead, not tightening his embrace on either his son or daughter, not looking at them, not speaking to them. It didn't appear he was crying. He simply sat with his arms around his family, like a statue.

Directly in front of him and about ten feet beyond lay the body of Samantha, his handsome, red-haired wife of thirty-seven years.

One of Jennifer's hands hid her eyes as she lowered her head and cried for Leo. Jim held her other hand in both of his. She had not known what to say to Leo from the moment she had heard of Samantha's death. She knew what not to say, and from her too-fresh memories of just a few years before, she decided her silent presence was the best she had to offer.

Had it been over a month ago that she and Jim had visited the Stantons' home? Jennifer had been amazed at the beauty and charm of their old West Town neighborhood place, a narrow, three-story Georgian brick they had lived in since their marriage.

Jennifer had met Leo's wife at office functions, of course, but she had never been to their home until Samantha called one morning and asked if she and Jim wanted to celebrate their engagement over dinner.

Jennifer laughed at herself for being surprised that Leo would even share such news with his wife. He didn't seem the type, but then, certainly, it was the type of thing a man would talk about with his wife.

Samantha had been in her usual bubbly form the morning she phoned. Her unusually low voice and rumbling chortle were in fine fettle as she joked about planning such an evening without Leo's knowledge.

"You wouldn't really, would you?" Jennifer had asked, alarmed, making Samantha guffaw all the more.

"'Course not, Honey. But it'd be fun, wouldn't it, to see the look on that ol' bulldog's face when company shows up for dinner? Ha! The biggest surprise for him would be something decent to eat, know what I mean?"

Jennifer liked the woman immediately.

Their home was quaint and lovely, as one might expect when the wife is a world traveler and the man runs in fast company. Samantha was co-owner of a travel agency and taught a night school college course in oil painting.

At first Jim and Leo seemed a bit ill at ease with each other that night. Neither was a big sports fan, but each felt obligated to talk about the Bears and the Blackhawks, under the assumption that the other wanted to.

When the ice was finally broken and they admitted that their real love was literature, they headed to Leo's study to discuss the editor's library. As they moseyed down the hall toward the book-lined cherrywood paneled den, Jennifer heard Leo tease, "So how does a literate, non-jock wind up a cop, anyway?"

"He scream and holler at you a little now and then?" Samantha asked Jennifer after dinner.

"I was going to ask you the same thing," Jennifer said, laughing.

"No, he doesn't," Samantha had said, suddenly serious.

"I didn't think so."

"Then why were you going to ask?"

"Because he screams and hollers a lot at the office. Yet here he seems so peaceful. And I like the way he's not afraid to hold your hand or put his arm around you in front of people. It's almost out of character for him."

"I know what you mean, Jennifer. After all these years, too. I love it."

"You're lucky."

"Don't I know it," Samantha said. And with a twinkle she added, "And so is he."

"Don't you two ever fight?"

"Nope. I do, but he doesn't. I'm the one with the Irish temper."

"And he isn't?" Jennifer couldn't hide her incredulity.

Samantha smiled and tucked her feet up under her on the sofa. "That's what so many of his employees say," she said. "You should have seen him with our kids."

"Tough?"

"The opposite. A pussycat."

Jennifer shook her head slowly.

"All his employees do that," Samantha said. "Nobody believes me."

"Because you're putting us on, or because he's so consistently on our cases at the office?"

"Well, I'm not putting you on," she said. "I think jumping all over his employees is just his way of drawing the best out of people. He drew the best from you, didn't he? You were on the society page or the women's page or something, weren't you? Now you're better known than he is."

"Which is a little embarrassing for me," Jennifer admitted.

"And which suits him just fine," Samantha said.

The following week in the office, Jennifer had chatted with Leo about Samantha. "You don't talk about her that much," she said.

"Sam? Nah, I guess not. Think about her all the time, though."

"I wouldn't have believed that until I saw how you treated her the other night."

"We get along."

"You do better than get along. You enjoy each other."

"Yeah, and after all these years."

"That's what she said, Leo. Has it always been that good?"

"Mostly. Never any big problems. We disagree on politics, you know."

"Really? She's not a conservative?"

"Anything but. Kids are the same. Drives me nuts. We don't talk about it much."

"You have a super marriage," Jennifer said.

"You sound surprised."

"No, it's just that good marriages are so rare these days."

"I know they are, but that's not why you're surprised. You think the only good marriages belong to you religious types."

"Leo, you know religion has nothing to do with—"

"Yeah, yeah, all right. Born againers, then. Christians, evangelicals, whatever. You think they're the only ones with good anything. Good relationships. Good morals. Good marriages."

"Not necessarily. They have bad relationships too."

"Yeah, but they're the only ones with good marriages, am I right?"

"Apparently not," Jennifer said.

"And you gotta admit that surprises you."

"OK, maybe. But I'll tell you one thing: if your marriage is as good as it appears, I'll bet you're living under God's principles whether you know it or not."

"How would we know? We're basically humanists. She more than I."

"Let me guess. I'll bet you're faithful to her and always have been."

Leo reddened. "It's only fair. We promised each other that, and I know she's upheld her end of the bargain. That's why I do."

"That's the only reason?"

He fidgeted. "You know, I don't have to tell you—"

"I know, Leo, and I'm sorry. That was too forward."

"That's OK, as long as you realize it. Another reason I'm faithful to her is because I love her, and I always have."

"That's a biblical principle that works for you."

"We aren't faithful because we think God wants us to be. We hardly believe in God. She doesn't at all."

"But you do?"

"Sometimes. He fits my politics."

"And I'll bet you don't go to sleep angry with each other."

Leo looked at her, surprised. "That's true," he said slowly. "How would you have guessed that?"

"Another biblical principle that makes for good marriages."

"It's not because it's a biblical principle," he said, growing louder. "It's just that neither of us likes any tension hanging in the air, so we compete to see who can get the thing straightened out first. It works for us."

"God doesn't require pure motives for His principles to work. They work no matter who uses them."

"Lucky for us," Leo said with an inflection that signaled the end of the conversation. Jennifer had felt more freedom in that discussion with him than ever before. She was glad she and Jim had visited their home. Maybe that had made it easier.

Four Fridays later, Jennifer had noticed Leo outside her glassed-in office visiting the newsroom. As a reporter said something that made him laugh, he was paged to the telephone.

Leo's face lost its color and he hurried to a phone. Jennifer stood and moved to her door. Just as Leo slammed down the phone and jogged to the elevator, his face taut, she stepped out and grabbed Neil Scotto, the scurrying young reporter, on his way out.

"No time, Jenn," he said. "Got a possible death in West Town."

She held his arm firmly. "Is that what you told Leo?"

"Yeah!" he said, pulling away. "I said it couldn't be him 'cause he was here. He said somethin' about nothing would surprise him in that neighborhood anymore. Jenn, I gotta go."

"Where's your car, Neil?"

"In back," he called over his shoulder.

"Pick me up out front," she said. "I'm coming with you."

He looked annoyed, but she knew he'd pull around and wait for her. She gathered up her bag and threw her coat over her shoulder. On her way out through the lobby she paused just long enough to ask the receptionist, "Who was that calling for Mr. Stanton?"

"A neighbor. Some kind of emergency."

Two

Jennifer had waited at the curb on Michigan Avenue for less than a minute when Neil screeched up and popped open the passenger door from the inside.

"Where you been?" Jennifer kidded him as the skinny, goateed reporter wheeled back into the traffic.

"Funny," he said. "I know we have to cater to you hotshot privileged columnist types, but what makes you want to ride along on a police call? Miss the old beat?"

"Sometimes. What's the call?"

"Lady saw her next door neighbor's car in the garage later than usual. She wasn't worried. Figured she'd taken the day off. Wanted some company, gave her a call, no answer. Went over. Door was open, woman on her bed upstairs. Couldn't wake her."

"Dead?"

"Who knows?"

"That's Leo's neighborhood, you know."

"Yeah, that's why I said somethin' to him. He laughed."

"He's not laughing now. He got paged. The look on his face could have made me believe in premonitions, Neil. And after he took the call, he went past without even acknowledging me."

"Doesn't have to mean anything, Jennifer. Not everyone bows before your altar on their way out of the city room."

She ignored his crack. "The receptionist said his call was from a neighbor. I don't like it."

Neil fell silent. "I don't either," he said finally. "We'll know soon enough."

Jennifer was amazed at how different the neighborhood looked in the daytime. The lawns seemed brighter, the alleys grimier, the houses smaller and closer together. Her mind raced as they neared Leo's home.

She began to speak, but Neil shushed her with a gesture. He was listening intently to the squawking from his police radio scanner when Jennifer heard the familiar address.

"Neil, that's Leo's house," she said quickly. "Is that where we're going?"

He nodded ominously, the humor gone. "That's where we're going."

Police had already cordoned off the house, and Neil had to park half a block away. Dozens of neighbors crowded the scene, pushing at the edges of the area.

A paramedic vehicle had backed into the Stanton driveway. Neil was still trying to talk his way past the police lines when Jennifer found Steve Jeski, an old cop she knew from her police beat days, and was escorted in the side door.

"So what's the deal, Steve?" she asked. "I understand she didn't answer the door."

"She's dead, Jenn," the veteran said. "Suicide."

Jennifer wondered if she'd heard him right. "Surely not," she said. "I knew this woman, Steve. No way."

He motioned for her to follow. "You ain't got a camera, right?"

She nodded.

He led her in through the kitchen, down the hall, and up one flight of stairs. Other officers leaned against the wall in the hall, giving Officer Jeski dirty looks as he and Jennifer picked their way through to the bedroom.

"Whadya need, Steve?" the officer in charge, a Lieutenant Theodore Crichton, asked as they approached the door.

"Just a peek," he said, nodding at Jennifer.

Crichton recognized her. "No pictures," he said. They both nodded. Steve stepped back so Jennifer could peer in.

"Steve, she doesn't even look dead," she said, without turning around. "Are you sure?"

"She's dead all right, ma'am," a paramedic said. "Excuse me."

He and his partner edged past her, wheeling a litter into the room. Samantha Stanton lay on her side on her bed. The bed had been made, and she was fully dressed and made up, including jewelry, as if for work.

It appeared she had perhaps stretched out to relax a moment. Her face was nestled in one hand and she looked peaceful.

Jennifer took a quick peek back over her shoulder at the officers huddling in the hall and leaned into the room. "What was the cause of death?" she whispered.

"Self-inflicted poison," a paramedic said.

"How do you know that?" she asked, insistently.

"They told us," one said, pointing a thumb into the hall.

"*They* told *you?*" she asked. "Aren't *you* supposed to tell *them?*"

The medic picked up Mrs. Stanton's purse and tossed it to Jennifer, who had the presence of mind to jump out of the way and let it fall to the floor. "You shouldn't be touching anything in this room that you don't have to!" she scolded, nearly shouting. "You may not know it, but this is a crime scene."

"This is a suicide," he said.

"Suicide is a crime too. Don't touch anything more! Didn't you even try to revive her?"

"Sure we did! Hey, who do you think you are anyway?"

"Shut up," his partner said. "She's a reporter."

"Then get out," the first said.

"I want to know how you could have tried to revive her in the position she's in."

The police photographer entered. "Everybody out," he barked. Jennifer glared at the paramedics as she moved into the hall. "She back into the position you found her?" the photographer asked.

They nodded.

Jennifer stuck her head back in. "You're shooting a re-created scene?"

"Who's askin'?"

"Jennifer Grey, *Chicago Day,*" she said.

"Talk to public relations downtown," he said. "I don't have to talk to you. In fact, I'm not s'posed to."

"I just want to know if you're shooting the body the way it was found."

"Yeah, sure."

"How do you know?"

"'Cause the paramedics got no reason to lie."

"But they tried to revive her?"

"'Course."

"Not in that position they didn't."

"Right again, Brenda Starr. You want a nice eight by ten glossy of this dame, or what?"

"So the paramedics worked on her and then put her back in the position they think they found her?"

"Somethin' wrong with that? Should they have waited till I got here for a few snapshots before they tried revivin' her, or what?"

"Leave 'im alone, Miss Grey," Lieutenant Crichton said, touching her shoulder. "He's just doing what he's told."

"Your crime scene is being destroyed," she said. "One of the paramedics grabbed her purse with his bare hand."

"We've already looked in her purse," the lieutenant said. "That's how we know it was suicide."

"Your own men and the medics have contaminated the crime scene!"

"Nobody's contaminated nothin'," he said, pointing at the floor where the contents of Mrs. Stanton's purse had spilled.

Jennifer stared in disbelief at five booklets on suicide that had slid from Samantha's purse. She quickly scribbled their titles and publishers into her notebook as she heard commotion outside. Several officers bounded down the stairs to quell the disturbance. She moved to a window from which she could see Leo fighting to get into the house.

"Let me tell you something, Lieutenant," she said, surprised at her own bravado. "This woman's husband is Managing Editor of the *Day,* and he'll find a way in here soon enough. There'd better be no more messing up of this scene than there's already been, or a lot of people here are going to be in big trouble."

Crichton screwed his face into a dirty look but stuffed the suicide booklets back into the purse himself. "Jeski!" he hollered, putting the purse back next to the bed where it had been discovered. "Get down there and tell them to let the husband in!"

He shooed the photographer and the paramedics from the room and pulled the door shut. When Leo reached the top of the stairs, huffing and puffing, he saw Jennifer and the lieutenant and slowed to a stop.

Jennifer burst into tears at the sight of him, and the desperately angry look on his face melted into disbelief. "Jenn?" he said pitifully, asking the question without saying the words.

She nodded.

"I want to see her."

"You won't touch anything, sir?" the lieutenant asked.

He shook his head, and Crichton slowly opened the door. Leo knelt by the bed and impulsively felt Samantha's wrist for a heartbeat. He buried his face in her neck, and his sobs turned into a mournful, muffled wail that sliced through Jennifer like a winter wind.

She was tempted to make a deal with Lieutenant Crichton. The negotiation actually entered her mind, but she couldn't bring herself to broach the subject with him. It went against everything she believed in, and yet, in this case, she could have almost justified it.

She wanted to agree not to write about all the obvious errors in judgment and the sloppy evidence-gathering techniques during the last few minutes if he would agree to withhold from the other newspapers the discovery of the suicide booklets until the true cause of death had been determined.

But too many people already knew about the literature. Hiding it would be impossible—and unethical. Not writing about the shoddy police work would be wrong as well.

Her motive had been to protect Leo from embarrassment, she knew. Good motive, bad solution. She felt ashamed. The death *was* apparently a suicide. But how in the world would they ever know, the way the scene had been violated?

That night in Leo's home, she and Jim and Max Cooper and Assistant Managing Editor Ken Roloff sat with the stunned widower and gently urged him to make funeral plans. He had spent much of the day on the phone to relatives, but he couldn't bring himself to talk about the cause of death.

"I don't know what we can do about it in the *Day*, Leo," Roloff whined, tugging at his over-the-calf stockings and twitching his narrow shoulders, as was his custom. He pushed his wire-rimmed glasses closer to his eyes with one finger and, in the same motion, dragged his hand back through his thinning hair.

He was wearing the threadbare gray plaid suit he wore nearly every other day, an ensemble that didn't seem befitting of a man who had enjoyed the same responsible and profitable position for more than a decade.

Max Cooper, ever in character, stood and pushed his pointy tongue out the edge of his mouth and swore. His white, bushy eyebrows set off the red face and jaunty, thick little body that always seemed ready for action. "Of course you know what we can do about it, K.P.! It gets listed as a death of undetermined causes."

Leo shook his head. "That won't solve anything," he said weakly, as if drained of life himself. "Everybody knows that means suicide. Anyway, who's going to get the *Trib* or the *Times* to·call it unknown causes?"

He buried his head in his hands and cried anew. By mid-evening the funeral arrangements had been set. "Just family and close friends," Leo repeated often. "No press outside the *Day*."

"That doesn't sound like you," Roloff said, slapping Leo on the back.

"It does too," he said flatly. "I was never one for covering funerals, not even of mobsters. You know that. You tried to get me to cover enough of 'em. Made me cover a few."

"Can't make you do anything now, can I?" Roloff said, smiling sympathetically.

Cooper swore again. "You're unbelievable, Kent, you know that? You think it makes

Leo feel good to be reminded that he's your boss now? That really makes everything all right, doesn't it? You ever stop to think that maybe your lack of tact is the reason you've been stuck in the same job for years?"

Roloff was embarrassed. "I, I didn't mean anything, Mr. Cooper. I—"

"I know!" Cooper thundered. "You never—"

"Hey," Leo said, smiling and reaching out with both hands to the squabblers. "Can you guys fight somewhere else?"

"I'm sorry, Leo," Roloff said. Cooper stomped off.

"I want this thing covered in the *Day* the same way it'll be covered in the other two papers," Leo said.

Cooper came back in an arguing mood. "It's my paper," he said. "If I wanna protect my editor and his family, I can, can't I?"

"You can, Max, and I appreciate it," Leo said. "I really do. I don't believe Sam would have taken her own life any more than any of you do, I hope. In fact, I know better than any of you that she couldn't have. But if this happened to the wife of the editor of one of our competitors, I know we would cover it straight. We'd call it an apparent suicide, because that's what it is."

"You believe that?" Jennifer asked.

"I believe it's apparent," Leo said. "I just know that what's apparent is not what is true. But there's only one way to cover it. The truth will come out eventually. My family and I will survive."

Jennifer wasn't so sure. She pulled Mr. Cooper aside and told him she wanted to write the story in her column. He scowled and shook his head. "I don't think so," he said. "I don't think Leo'd go for it."

"I think he might," she countered.

"Then *I* won't go for it," he said. "Clear?"

"Why?"

"I don't need to tell you why, young lady, but I will. Your coverage will impugn the police department, which may have to be done anyway. But it will carry the bias of a personal friend and employee who doesn't believe what happened here any more than the grieving husband does. You're stunned. We're all stunned. Let the reporter— what's-his-name—handle it."

"Neil."

"Yeah, Scotto. It's the only way, Mrs. Grey. You're usually able to stay away from sentiment, but how could you here? It's not worth a column, outside of the fact that you work for the man and you knew them both. Am I right?"

Jennifer nodded, disappointed. "Would you give me a short leave of absence?"

"For what?"

"To check this thing out. The coroner ruled it a suicide because of the books the police found and the poison he found in her system. The autopsy will find nothing else, and that'll be the end of it. You can't let Leo investigate it. He's not up to it, and he'll make himself miserable."

"He's already asked for some time off himself. I hope it's so he can rest at his Wisconsin place."

"Maybe if you told him I was going to check it out, he'd be able to rest. Otherwise he won't. When the shock wears off, if it ever does, he's going to want to get to the bottom of this. No matter what."

"And what if you find that it *was* suicide, Mrs. Grey? We never know the private torment many people carry in their minds."

"Then I'd have to think that would at least satisfy Leo. He'd want to know the truth, either way."

THREE

The Saturday morning papers, all three major dailies, carried the stark story of the apparent suicide of the wife of a prominent editor.

The *Day* also carried a note that columnist Jennifer Grey would be on assignment for approximately two weeks.

In truth, she had been granted a leave of absence for not longer than three weeks.

Jennifer and Jim had invited Leo to church on Sunday, the day before the funeral, and he had almost accepted. "Good strategy," he had said wryly. "Catch me at a vulnerable time." But his family had flown in, and he would be at the funeral home all day.

Family, close friends, and no press except the *Day* turned out to be about three hundred people. The Monday morning funeral became more of an ordeal than Leo expected. He had to be supported as he walked from the car to the grave site.

His older child, Mark, arranged to be away from his own business for a week and was set to go through his mother's things with Leo and then spend a few days at the Wisconsin cottage with him. Jennifer was glad Leo could get away and have company, but she wanted to talk to him first, if he was up to it.

Tuesday evening, when only Leo and Mark were in the house and Jim was on duty, she visited. Mark, a tall, brooding, darkly handsome man in his late twenties, sat in on the conversation but said nothing to Jennifer. He'd been away from home for many years, but it was apparent he knew his father.

Whenever Leo seemed to be losing control, when his breath came in short spurts and his lips quivered, Mark would change the subject or bring him something to drink. More than once, Jennifer got the impression that Mark felt she was intruding, that everything was happening too quickly, that his father needed time to himself to deal with his grief and put it behind him.

But Leo persuaded her otherwise. "I need you to do this for me, Jenn," he said, his voice breaking. "I appreciate it more than you know. I wish I could help with strategy, but I can't think. You know what I mean."

"Of course, Leo. You want to know where I'm going to start?"

He nodded.

"I've gotten copies of the literature that your wife had in her purse."

"That was *planted* in her purse you mean," he said quickly. "That's the farthest thing from what Sam would have chosen to read, isn't it, Mark? Show her what your mother liked to read."

Mark produced books on art and literature and, of course, geography and travel. Jennifer nodded and smiled.

"Still I feel it's important to know what those booklets are all about, don't you, Leo?"

He nodded again. "I'd like to see 'em myself."

Jennifer had them in her handbag, but she hesitated. Mark spoke up. "No, you wouldn't, Dad," he said firmly. "Maybe someday. Not now."

"Why not?"

"Trust me, Dad. Not now, all right?"

Leo smiled and clapped a hand on his son's thigh. "All right, big guy. All right."

Jennifer was relieved. She hadn't had a chance to read through them herself, but she knew they were nothing for a grieving man to see.

"I couldn't sleep in our bed," Leo said suddenly, quietly.

"I can imagine," Jennifer said, fighting tears herself.

"No, you can't, but thanks for saying so."

"Leo," she said, hoping the sound of her voice would remind him that she certainly *could* imagine, that she too had lost a spouse, that she could remember all too well the haunting emptiness of a bed that threatened to swallow her if she dared sleep in it alone. Even in his grief she couldn't permit him to pretend that he was the only one who had suffered this kind of grief, especially not in front of a fellow sufferer.

He looked up at her sadly. "Jennifer, forgive me," he said. "I know you know. I remembered when you didn't try to say all the things everyone else tried to say."

Mark glared down at her. She stood. "I'd better go, Leo," she said. "I'll see you again whenever you say."

"No!" he said, desperate and suddenly lucid. "I want to know what you're going to do and how you're going to do it. I can't think clearly right now, but maybe if I know what you're up to, I'll think of something that'll help. Samantha didn't kill herself, Jennifer. You know that. And even if you don't, *I* do. If anybody can find the truth, you can."

He was crying again. "Leo," she said, softly, "you're not ready for this, are you? Let's talk again tomorrow, OK? I'll see you in the afternoon after I've talked to the coroner and the police and the woman next door."

He nodded, his head in his hands.

Mark helped her with her coat and walked her to the front door. "Thanks for being sensitive," he said. "You're very special to him."

Jennifer was surprised. If anything, she had expected a lecture from the stern-faced son. In the light from the porch she could see that he was smiling a grateful smile at her. And he opened the door, gently guiding her through it with a hand on her arm.

He let his hand slide down into her gloved fingers, which he squeezed briefly while thanking her. "We'll see you tomorrow," he said.

Jennifer lay in bed till two in the morning reading the short booklets. They were as scary and bizarre as anything she had ever read, not because they were horrifying or macabre. Rather because they were so reasoned, so deftly crafted, so persuasive.

The first made the clear point that the only prospect worse than an unacceptable life was a failed effort to terminate it. The book was the text for a euthanasia society that had nearly ten thousand members, all dedicated to the lofty ideal that they would rather take their own lives in relative peace and gentleness than to suffer a horrible end while enduring the ravages of disease.

The justification was on the basis of the reluctance of the dying to become burdens on their families or to suffer unduly themselves when the results would be the same regardless. They were going to die, so they wanted a hand in it.

Of course, the philosophy centered on the assumption that death was the total end of life. That's why the booklets, as genteel and slick as they were, stuck in Jennifer's craw. Because she believed that God was the author of life and that it was His to give or to take, euthanasia, regardless of the wrappings, was unacceptable.

Another booklet extolled the virtues of peaceful death, making it sound not only soothing, but desirable. Jennifer wondered what that might mean to those who weren't pain-wracked by disease or so old that they would rather be gone. She disagreed with suicide in any case, but making it so easy might tempt people who had even shallower reasons to consider it.

Everything she read pointed to suicide as an escape. There was no compulsion to face life head-on or to seek God or to serve others. One booklet referred to "assisted suicide" as the "compassionate crime."

Assisted suicide, Jennifer thought. *I wonder what my homicide detective friends would call that?*

Another booklet presented the case for dual suicides and called self-inflicted death "self-deliverance." Jennifer shuddered. The language and the logic was not unlike what she had read in sales pitches for retirement villages in Florida.

One of the guides justified itself by hoping that it would aid in cutting down the incidences of botched suicide attempts. While making the case that suicide should be a last resort—at least a moderate approach compared to the others—it went on to prescribe specific doses of drug combinations that would result in deaths so peaceful that the body looks dead, but not disgusting.

Jennifer couldn't help but think of how Mrs. Stanton had looked on Friday morning. She would ask Jake Steinmetz, the Cook County Coroner, about the drugs found in the body.

Early the next morning, Jennifer visited the University of Chicago Law School library where she learned that in England it is a crime to aid a would-be suicide. In the U.S., she discovered, suicide, and even attempted suicide, are ironically punishable crimes and that assisting a suicide is also illegal.

She asked a law student, "If it's illegal to aid a suicidal person in his effort, why can this material be printed and sold?"

"You ought to know that, if you're who I think you are," he said. "The First Amendment guarantees that you can write and publish anything you want. And so can the euthanasiasts. Don't threaten their freedom unless you're willing to have yours threatened as well. There are plenty of books available on how to lie, cheat, steal, and even murder."

Jake Steinmetz was, as always, pleased to find a few moments for his favorite newspaper reporter. They had worked together many times in the past. He was shocked when she guessed the precise dosage of drugs found in Mrs. Stanton's system.

"Jennifer, I'm afraid I'm going to have to remind you that I am a friend of the court."

"What do you mean by that?"

"Just that I'm sure that your boss has not been entirely ruled out as a suspect, and if you somehow know the dosage—well, that can't look terribly good for him. I would only be doing my duty to report it."

"Jake, my boss would love nothing more than to think that this case was shifting in suspicion from a suicide to a homicide. Please tell me you'll do that, put him under suspicion, get them to admit that this could have been a murder."

Steinmetz smiled his knowing smile. "You set me up," he said. "All I was fishing for was how you knew the dosage. The cops aren't at liberty to release that yet."

"I read it in a book, OK?"

"How did you know about the books?"

"I work hard, Jake. Just like you do. I do my homework. I have sources. Anyway, I was there."

"I won't pursue that, Jennifer."

"Thanks."

"I'm satisfied it was a suicide."

"Apparently for the same reason I'm convinced it wasn't," she said.

"How's that?"

"Because the dosage matches the prescription in the book."

"That's right."

"Why not prove it?"

"We already know it, Jennifer. It's proven."

"I mean prove the drugs were purchased by Mrs. Stanton. That should be easy enough. Wouldn't a pharmacist recall selling her lethal dosages?"

"No pharmacist in his right mind would fill a prescription like that."

"Then where would she get it, assuming she got it?"

"Probably from two different druggists. The ingredients are not alarming in themselves. Only when mixed do they result in the deep, peaceful sleep."

"That results in death."

"Precisely."

"That should be easy enough to check too," Jennifer said. "How many pharmacists are there in the area?"

"Hundreds. Be my guest."

"I just might."

"You probably will. That's what I admire about you, Jennifer. Naturally, if anything turns up, I'll be eager to hear about it."

"Naturally. But you want me to do the legwork."

"Right again. As I said, I'm—"

"Satisfied. Yeah, I know. At least tell me how she ingested the dosage."

"With water."

"You're sure? It wasn't mixed with her food or dropped in her orange juice?"

"You're impugning your boss again, Jennifer."

"I am not! Please quit saying that. If there's one thing I'm certain of, it's that Leo had nothing to do with his wife's death. I have to think someone poisoned her. If so, how would they have done it?"

"The autopsy showed a light breakfast and residue of an extremely fast dissolving mixture of the lethal chemicals, possibly in tablet form, but more likely mixed in water."

"You're guessing."

"Yes, I'm guessing she mixed it in water."

"Why? To fit your suicide theory? Where are the prescription bottles? The spoon? The water glass? Would there not be residue on her water glass?"

"There was none. That's why I said possibly in tablet form."

"You said it was more likely mixed in water. Why would she have been careful to clean the glass? Would she have had time?"

"Barely. She would have grown heavily drowsy almost immediately."

"She took it in tablet form, Jake."

"So?"

"One tablet she made up herself? No one would sell her that small a quantity of each ingredient, so where is the rest?"

"I don't know, Jennifer. This is your fairy tale, not mine."

"Did you check any medicine bottles in her purse?"

"Of course, but this is totally off-the-record, Jennifer. No one has this. You can't print it yet."

She raised her eyebrows. "Deal," she said.

"There was a bottle of plain, white aspirin tablets, the large type you take one at a time."

"And?"

"Microscopic residue of the poisonous mixture on one of the tablets. Not enough to hurt a flea."

Jennifer leaned forward in her chair. "Jake! That means the death tablet could have been in that bottle, doesn't it?"

"What if it was?"

"Then it could have been planted!"

He shrugged and raised his hands in protest. "Could have, could have," he repeated, as if she were dreaming.

"There was no suicide note, Jake. How often does that occur?"

"I don't concern myself with suicide notes."

"You never let a note help you determine a suicide?"

"Well, sure, I mean, sometimes it's obvious, and the note confirms it, and—"

"The woman was dressed for work, Jake. She had eaten a light breakfast. Don't you sometimes have to wonder why someone kills herself without a hint of the normal suicide pattern or even a reason?"

"Sometimes."

"This time, Jake."

"Happy hunting, Jennifer."

FOUR

"Are we off-the-record, Miss Grey?" Lieutenant Crichton asked, leaning back in his chair with his hands behind his head. She nodded. "I've got to tell you I was on pins and needles all weekend waiting for your story to take us apart."

"It could have."

"Of course it could have. I'm fully aware of that. You were right. Why didn't you print what you saw?"

"I'm not on the story. Too close to it. Leo Stanton is my boss, and I knew his wife. The guy who's covering it, Neil Scotto, didn't see what I saw."

"I'm glad, because we almost blew it."

"Almost?" she said.

"You don't still think this was other than a suicide, do you?"

"I do."

He shook his head slowly. "Well, I feel some obligation to you for not making us look bad. We did a lot of things wrong, I'll admit that. But not publicly. I'm still convinced it was a suicide. But if there's any way I can help you, let me know."

"Did you check it out, Lieutenant, or are you basing everything on what you found in her purse?"

"We checked her out some. You know, her interests and politics point to this sort of, ah, liberal, um, mercy-killing type of thing."

"Euthanasia?"

"Right. She could have easily been into that."

"But was she? Do you have any evidence that she belonged to any such group or was on any mailing list?"

He shook his head. "That would require a lot of man hours, and the coroner is satisfied that it was suicide."

"But how about drugstores? Wouldn't it pay to find out where she got the ingredients?"

"We don't think so. I'm sorry. We just don't."

"Yet you're willing to help me?"

"Sure, what can I offer?"

"Put Cap Duffy on this case."

"Duffy? The homicide detective? I can't do that."

"Why not?"

"First of all, I'm not in homicide. I can't go assigning their people. Second, if I *were* in homicide, I wouldn't put a homicide guy on a suicide."

"Then what do you mean when you say you owe me, you're obligated to me, you want to help me? How can you do anything for me if you can't help me prove this wasn't a suicide?"

"You're gonna have to prove that on your own."

"So you're not really willing to help me. You just appreciate that I didn't blow the whistle on your sloppy work at the scene of the crime."

"At the scene of the death. When I offered to help you, I was thinking in terms of any driving or parking violations that you'd like me to investigate for you. Perhaps something I could check into more carefully than the arresting officer did."

"Wonderful. You want to fix a ticket for me."

"Oh, my—no, ma'am. I would never do something like that. However, I *do* have the power to interrupt the judicial process on certain violations if my investigation turns up mitigating circumstances, if you know what I mean."

"I know what you mean. Fortunately, I don't speed, and the *Day* pays my parking tickets."

"That *is* fortunate."

"Yeah, for you too."

"Me?"

"You just offered to fix a ticket. I could get you in big trouble."

"I would never do anything of the sort. Maybe you have friends or relatives or acquaintances who might like to take their kids to the circus, but who can't afford it."

Jennifer stood. "Tell me you're kidding. You want to thank me for not writing the truth, which was hardly as a favor to you. And you want to show your appreciation by compounding the problem? No, sir! It's a wonder any crime gets solved in this city."

Crichton smiled condescendingly. "If I weren't still afraid you might point your poison pen at us, I'd warn you that a remark like that could result in your hoping you never *do* get a ticket in my precinct."

Jennifer left without another word, more determined than ever to find out the truth on her own. She might seek Jim's counsel, but she couldn't involve him in the investigation.

Just after lunch she pulled into the driveway next to Leo's house. It appeared his car was gone. She hoped Mark had taken him out to lunch.

Mrs. Wilma Fritzee, Leo's neighbor to the south, was a lonely, talkative, sixty-five-year-old widow of nearly a decade who carried her age well. She fussed over Jennifer, bringing her tea and cookies and leading a tour of the house.

"I know what it's like for Leo," she said. "The suddenness of it and everything. Edgar was older than I was, you know. Ten years. Retired from the foundry not three months. Died on our way to Florida for the big vacation we'd saved years for."

"I'm sorry. I lost my first husband too."

"Oh, my. And so young. But you're married again?"

"No, I shouldn't have said first husband. My only husband. I'm engaged."

"How wonderful! I was almost engaged again myself, but I'm afraid my new man thought I had more money than I did. When he checked into that, he lost interest."

"I'll bet you're glad of that."

"Oh, in the long run I am. Who wants a man who marries for money? I always thought it was women who did that, but you know, I'd never do that. There are days, though, when I could go crazy without someone to talk to, and I wonder if the loneliness is worth it."

"Worth the principle you mean?"

But Wilma Fritzee was lost in thought. Her eyes glazed over. "Samantha was good to me," she said. "I can hardly believe she's gone. I would listen for her car leaving just before eight-thirty every morning, and I don't mind telling you I was always just a little disappointed when she left. She owns that company, you know, and she could pretty much come and go as she pleased."

"And sometimes she didn't go to work?" Jennifer asked.

"Sometimes. Not very often. Usually she was out of there like clockwork. Leo—Mr. Stanton—he always left pretty early in that little car of his. 'Course he *never* misses work unless he's on his deathbed—oh, excuse me, I didn't mean to say it that way, but you know what I mean. Of course, you work for the man, so you know exactly what I mean."

Jennifer nodded.

"But every once in a while, after Mrs. Stanton—Sam I always called her, it was all right with her—after she'd been on one of those one- or two-week trips to who knows where, she might be home a day or two the next week."

"Resting up from the trip?"

"Well, I guess so, but you know, it was never the first day or two after she got back because I guess she had to go into the office and get back on track or something. But after the trip and then after she'd been in the office a day or two, it would be like she wanted to wind down or take a break or something. That's when I would listen and hope I wouldn't hear that car of hers leaving the driveway."

"And if it didn't?"

"I'd get right on the phone to her."

"Weren't you afraid of disturbing her so early?"

"Oh, I'd look for the paper first. Leo, he leaves the morning paper for her because I imagine he gets one free at the office. If the paper was still out there, I'd leave her alone. But if it was gone, I'd know she's up. Know what? She usually was too."

"Was what?"

"Up early, even on the days she took off. That's the kind of a woman she was. I loved her. Always have. Did anyway. It would make me so sad to think she really, you know, did it herself. I can't believe there could have been that much going on inside her head without me knowing about it."

"You were that close?"

"We're the only two houses on this block that still have the same people in 'em for thirty years. We've been here since long before Leo and Sam moved in, honest. I remember when they moved in. Didn't even have kids then. Remember the kids bein' born, babysittin' 'em. Never had an argument all these years, though I used to get after those kids when they were little. But Sam didn't mind. She told me to holler at 'em if they were into somethin' they shouldn't be. What was your question?"

"I was just wondering if you were really close enough to know whether she was having some real difficulty, either physically or mentally."

"I don't know. Maybe not. I know she just has tolerated me for the last several years since Ed's been gone. Not that we did much together as couples. Just a few cookouts each year, and Leo and Ed might sit out in the yard with a beer and watch a ball game on the portable."

"Why do you think she was just tolerating you?"

"Well, because I was always the one to call her. She'd never call me first. And I don't blame her. Heaven knows I never gave her the chance. If her car was in and her paper gone by eight-thirty, ol' Wilma was on the horn. Never gave her much chance to even read the paper, I don't s'pose."

"Did she ever make you feel like you were intruding?"

Mrs. Fritzee stood and moved toward the large picture window in her living room and leaned over the couch to peer out past the shared driveway into the front yard of the Stanton home. She took a deep breath and let out a rattling sigh. Her voice was thick with emotion when she spoke again.

"No," she said, straightening but not turning around. "She never once made me feel anything less than a million bucks. Her and Leo both. Treated Edgar the same way. We talked about that nearly every day of our married lives, I'll tell you that. Here was a foundry worker and a housewife. I never worked. Ed wouldn't have it. We suffered for it, but I wouldn't trade—"

Her voice trailed off as she remembered her other loss. But when she was ready, she picked up right where she had left off. "Here was Leo, always a big shot with the news- papers. You know, before they started this new one you work for, there was five of 'em there for a while. Seems there was more than that years ago, maybe seven.

"But Leo was always right in the middle of one of 'em, bein' the number one guy in some section or another. Always movin' up. And Sam, she was makin' money from day one in that travel agency as soon as her kids was in high school; it had to been before Edgar died when she bought into the company. She's the only owner who works there, you know."

"I didn't know that."

"Oh, yeah. I think there's four other owners, something like that. But she owns half of it and runs it. I guess. I don't really know. That's sorta how it is. How it was, I mean. I don't know what happens now. Do you?"

Jennifer shook her head. Mrs. Fritzee seemed almost embarrassed, as if she suddenly realized that she was standing nearly in another room, forcing herself to talk loud enough for Jennifer to hear.

She shuffled back over and sat heavily, covered her mouth with an open palm, and let it slide down her chin. "I was tellin' you what Ed and I used to say about them, wasn't I?"

Jennifer nodded.

"It was just that they always seemed to do good. Leo I'm sure was makin' OK money, and Sam did at least that good. They always had everything they needed and wanted, and they dressed well, traveled a lot, that type of thing.

"Edgar was a good worker, but there was never any money for him at the foundry. In forty-five years he worked up to quality control inspector and was shop union steward. We saved for that Florida trip for years and years, and the farthest we ever got away from here before that was a train ride to my sister's in New Mexico. We knew who we were and who we weren't, and we were happy, you understand."

"I sure do."

"You have children, young lady?"

"No, ma'am."

"That's good. I mean, that's good that they wasn't left without a father, you know what I mean? Only grief we ever had was our two boys. Neither one of 'em have amounted to much, but at least Edgar never really knew that. Both of 'em have kids their wives won't let 'em see. Pitiful."

Jennifer silently agreed. Here was a lonely old woman with no-account sons who just lost the only apparent listener she had left in the world.

The old woman sighed again and seemed on the verge of tears. "I keep gettin' off the track," she said. "The thing that Ed and I used to always say about Sam and Leo was that they treated us like friends."

"Oh, I'm sure you *were* their friends, Mrs. Fritzee."

"I know, but not really. I mean, we never went anywhere with them. We couldn't really talk about their lives. But Leo knew how to get Ed talkin' about the foundry, and Sam always told me about where she'd been as if next time I went anywhere, that's where it would be. I'm not kidding. She'd say stuff like, 'You gotta watch it in the market there and make sure you get your best deal. Don't let 'em smooth talk you, Wilma,' she'd say. And I'd laugh, 'cause there was no way I was goin' to wherever she was talkin' about, but it was fun to pretend.

"There's enough snooty people in this neighborhood who got nothin' to be snooty about. And here was a couple who had every right to act above us all—because they was—and yet they was good as gold."

She dabbed at her eyes with the end of her apron and stood again. "Do you know," she said, almost unable to speak, "if either of us was ever in the yard when Leo or Sam had some big shot over, they would introduce us."

"That's Leo," Jennifer agreed.

"Both of 'em!" Mrs. Fritzee corrected. "Sam too."

Jennifer nodded. And the old woman wept.

FIVE

By the time Jennifer was able to pull away from Mrs. Fritzee, Leo's car was back in his garage.

"Dad has had a rough morning," Mark said, as Leo seemed to nap on the couch. Jennifer could tell Leo was wide awake, but he lay there on his side in casual clothes and stocking feet with his eyes closed.

Jennifer was struck by how much he looked like his wife in her last repose, but of course she couldn't comment on it.

"How rough?" she whispered.

"He just wanted to go to a park they used to visit. We strolled around awhile and then sat at their favorite picnic table. It wasn't easy for him. I hope it accomplished whatever he wanted it to. Strange though, I never went to that park before."

"Why is that strange?"

"I just meant that it was apparently a place they had discovered after my sister and I had left home."

"Wrong," Leo mumbled, eyes still closed. Mark and Jennifer jumped. Mark smiled. "Wrong?"

"Wrong. It was where we went alone, even when you two were around."

"Hm. I feel left out."

"That was the point."

Mark laughed, apparently encouraged that his father's sense of humor was returning.

Leo sighed heavily and turned over, facing the back of the couch. "Shall we leave, Dad?" Mark asked.

Leo shook his head.

"Maybe talk in another room?" Mark suggested.

Leo shook his head again. "I like you right where you are." Soon he was breathing deeply, as if asleep.

"If he is, it's the first sound sleep he's gotten since Friday night," Mark said.

Jennifer grimaced in sympathy, but Leo stirred, and she wondered if he could sleep soundly even now.

"I need to talk to my fiancé and make several other calls anyway," she said. "Perhaps I should come back later."

"Oh, please stay," Mark said. "I enjoy your company." His direct gaze made her uncomfortable, and she couldn't return it, though she was flattered. "If Dad's not awake in an hour, I'll get him up with the smell of coffee and tuna fish, one of his favorite light meals. He hasn't eaten much."

"You don't think you should let him sleep?"

"Oh, sure, if the smell of coffee doesn't wake him, I won't push it."

"I needed to ask him about your mother's morning habits," she whispered, "and after talking to your neighbor, about the other partners in the travel agency too."

"Well, I wouldn't know anything about the agency. I never took much of an interest in that, though I was proud of Mom for jumping into it. It made me want to start my own business. Which I did."

"And which is?"

"Small sub-contracting firm. Plumbing and electrical. I know nothing of either one." He smiled.

"I'll bet," she said.

"Really! Well, just enough to keep my people honest. But my thing is business. I'd electrocute myself or drown if I started messing with the actual work."

Jennifer almost laughed, but she saw the same look come to Mark's face that came to Mrs. Fritzee's when she realized she had joked about death when everyone's grief was so fresh. She changed the subject quickly.

"You don't recall anything about your mother's morning habits."

"Not really. I suppose they're different now than they were when I was in high school. That was just before she started working. She was always a crack-of-dawn type. Up with Dad, breakfast for everybody but herself, then shooing us all out the door. Good mood in the morning. More than I can say for me or Dad."

"She didn't eat breakfast?"

"Oh, yeah, but it was sort of her reward when she had everybody out the door. She'd settle in at the dining room table with her newspaper and her toast and tea. And some kinda jam."

"Marmalade," Leo said.

With that, Mark stood and motioned for Jennifer to follow him to the kitchen. Leo grunted in protest when he realized they were leaving, but he stayed where he was and said nothing.

For half an hour or so, Mark and Jennifer sat across from each other at the kitchen table, chatting about everything except the Stantons. She told him about her husband, her home, her family, her job, and her fiancé.

Mark didn't appear to want to discuss Jim. Yes, he had met him at the funeral, but "of course you realize I wasn't thinking rationally. I'm still not. I noticed *you* though; I do recall that."

Jennifer didn't know what to say. "So, your father likes tuna sandwiches? I don't think I ever knew that."

"Only the way we make 'em here at home," Mark said, rising and expertly preparing a pot of coffee. He noticed Jennifer's surprise. "From years of living alone," he said. And she looked away.

He popped a can of tuna into the electric opener as if he'd done it every day of his life, picked the meat from the can with a fork and got every morsel, and mixed it in a plastic bowl with plenty of mayonnaise. Then he added diced onion, sweet and dill pickle, and celery.

"You like olives?" he asked, suddenly looking up.

She smiled and shook her head. "Not in tuna," she said.

"Shoot," he said. "I was looking for a reason for us to make a run to the store."

"You shouldn't leave Leo right now anyway, should you?" she asked, wishing she'd been bolder and just told him to back off. She was, after all, engaged, not available, off limits, not interested. Well, at least three out of four.

"I s'pose not," he said, rummaging around for a platter for the sandwiches and a bowl for chips. "You want Coke, milk, tea?"

"Coffee is fine," she said.

He placed everything in the middle of the kitchen table, and as if on cue, his father padded in from the living room. Noticing the table, Leo couldn't suppress a sad smile. "Always said you'd make somebody a fine wife someday."

Mark shook his head in mock frustration. "Sit down, you old coot."

Mark was pouring the coffee when his father surprised him. "I want Jennifer to say grace," he said, more as an announcement than as a request. "You mind, Mark?"

His son was taken aback, but he just shrugged.

"Jennifer, would you?" Leo asked.

"Sure," she said, panicking. Wasn't it Leo who had advised her to quit praying over her meals at the office and with her colleagues? She had never prayed aloud, of course, but she had always felt she should just bow her head.

She had told Leo she didn't feel she was making a show of it, and he told her it made everyone uncomfortable. She asked a few friends, who agreed with Leo and who added that it seemed a little holier-than-thou.

She had even talked it over with her parents, who thought she should continue it as a witness. "You never know who might be affected by that little gesture," her father said.

But she had decided to stop doing it. She wasn't doing it for a witness, and she certainly didn't want to make a show of it, which was hard to avoid because people noticed, no matter how subtle she was.

It had been months since their discussion, and she had felt a little guilty about bailing out. But she had gotten over that. She and Jim prayed together, of course, and even at meals. And she prayed during her own time alone.

But now Leo wanted her to pray, aloud and in front of his son—a self-proclaimed humanist, basically agnostic, almost atheist—and himself, a basically patriotic right-winger whose god was conservative politics and the free enterprise system.

She bowed her head and closed her eyes, her heart drumming. "Father God," she began, "thank You for Your love and for Your provision of food. Thank You for a family of people who care for each other. Be with them in their time of grief. In the name of Jesus Christ, Amen."

There was a moment of awkward silence before Leo reached for a sandwich. Though he didn't speak, it was obvious he was overcome with emotion. He fought tears and chewed slowly, as if not really hungry.

Mark ate quickly, nervously.

"Delicious," Jennifer said.

"Yeah, Mark. It's good," Leo said.

Mark nodded. He had quit staring into Jennifer's eyes, as he had done all afternoon. She decided that if her prayer had had no other effect than to put him off a little, that would be fine. And then, of course, she felt guilty for that.

Except for those brief compliments to the chef, they sat in silence. After a few minutes, less than half a sandwich, and one cup of coffee, Leo rose unsteadily and apologized.

He shuffled from the room with the fingers of his right hand pressed to his forehead. He peeked under his hand to see where to walk. Jennifer and Mark stood quickly and watched him amble back to the couch where he sat and cried, his head in his hands.

Suddenly, Jennifer wasn't hungry. Mark encouraged her to finish, but she couldn't. He wolfed another half sandwich and took his cup with him into the living room. Jennifer followed.

"Enough action for one day, Dad?" Mark said smiling. "Shall I kick her out or take her somewhere?"

Leo wiped his eyes and tried to force a smile. "I'd rather kick you out and let her stay," he said.

"This may not be the right thing to say, Leo," she said, "but it hurts me to see you hurt."

"I appreciate that," he managed. "I'm all right." He winked at Mark. "It's just that his mother made those sandwiches so much better than he can!"

"Ouch!" Mark said. "I thought they were particularly good."

"So did I," Jennifer said.

And the awkward silence returned. The sun was setting, and Mark stood to close the drapes. "Leave them open, if you don't mind," Leo said. He sat with his hands in his lap, his shoulders sagging, staring out into the twilight.

"You haven't seen me like this, have you, Jenn?" he said.

She shook her head, not able to speak.

"Big tough guy editor, never needs anything or anybody, right? That's me. I can hassle everybody, afraid of nobody. I'm champion of the old-fashioned cause. We do it right because that's the only way to do it. Credibility and trustworthiness and our reputation is all we have, right?"

Jennifer didn't know what he was driving at, but she nodded. It reminded her of his late-night harangues against sloppy journalism or management selling editorial out for the sake of an advertising dollar.

Leo would fight with anybody, even Max Cooper, over principle. And Leo usually won.

"But the only reason I could do that without fear," he was saying now, "is that I came home to the Rock of Gibraltar." His face contorted, and the tears flowed, but he made no move to hide them or wipe them away.

Jennifer impulsively sat next to him and put her arm around his shoulders. He sobbed.

She peeked at her watch. She would meet Jim in an hour, but she needed information from Leo first. She wanted to be clear on his wife's morning routine. She wanted to know of the other partners in the travel agency. And she wanted to know what drugstores the family frequented. But she didn't dare ask.

She tried another tack. "When are you heading for your cottage, Leo?"

He shrugged. "The sooner the better, I guess. Do you think I'm weak, Jennifer?"

"Leo, you're one of the strongest men I've ever known. You've meant more to me in my career than anyone. You're hurting and grieving, and you shouldn't fight that. Let it happen. If you weren't tender right now, after a long and good marriage to a wonderful woman, I'd worry about you."

He nodded. "I'm not going to sleep tonight. I just know it. And I need to. I'm exhausted."

"You must be," she said. "Do you ever use sleeping pills?"

"Never have," he said, "but right now I'd be willing to try."

"Where would you get them?" she asked.

"I'd want a prescription," he said. "None of these over-the-counter things."

"I can call your doctor, Dad," Mark said. "You still see Billings?"

Leo nodded.

"What pharmacy do you use, Leo?" Jennifer asked as Mark went to the phone.

He thought a moment. "Hargreaves on Western," he said. "Or the one next to the grocery store on Kedzie."

When Mark returned, he told his father that Dr. Billings had advised against sleeping pills. "He said he'd be glad to prescribe valium—"

"No way!" Leo said, almost shouting. "I've read enough about that to know I wouldn't touch it. Forget it. I'll just ride this out."

"He also said that in case you were still as belligerent about valium as you were the last time he saw you—which, he wanted me to remind you, was more than eighteen months ago—a change of scenery might be the best medicine."

"You tell him we were going up to the cottage tomorrow?"

"Yeah. He said make it tonight."

"Tonight?"

"Tonight. He said you'd probably sleep in the car on the way up there, which would be good, even if you didn't sleep well once you got there."

"If I'm sleepin' when we get there, leave me in the car. When do we leave?"

Leo had so brightened at the prospect of the trip that Jennifer knew she could ask him what she needed to. "Why doesn't Mark pack a bag for you while you chat with me," she suggested. "Just give me enough to keep me going on this until you get back."

Six

Leo painfully told Jennifer the mundane details of his wife's morning routine. For some reason he found it particularly difficult. Just thinking about her in her normal habits of life seemed almost too much for him.

Several times Jennifer offered to put it off till another time, but Leo wouldn't hear of it. "In the middle of this pain, I feel more strongly than ever the need to prove she didn't kill herself, Jennifer."

He told her his wife rose with him, made their breakfast, and just before her last cup of tea, she would finish dressing and making herself up for work. Then she would clear away the dishes, run upstairs for a final shot of mouth wash and some lipstick and peek in the mirror, and then head back downstairs to read her paper until it was time to leave.

The phone rang. It was Kent Roloff's wife. "Yeah, June, how ya doin'?" Leo asked. "Oh, I'm OK, thanks. It's not easy, June. . . . Yes, I know, it's hard on all of us. You were close, yes. . . . Twenty years? I wouldn't have guessed it was that long. . . . Well, I don't believe it either, but I'm working on that. . . . Yeah, Mark's running me up to the cottage for a few days. . . . Right, last summer. . . . Uh-huh, that was fun. Maybe we can do it again this year. You two and me anyway, I mean. . . . Oh, I'm sure Kent is taking care of everything for me. Tell him I appreciate it, if I don't get to talk with him. . . . Oh, he is? Well, all right. . . . Hi, Kent. . . . Yeah, I hope to see you next Monday. . . . No, I won't rush it. I'll let you know. Thanks for everything, buddy."

Leo hung up and rolled his eyes. "If the truth were known, I can hardly stomach the man," he said. "June's a doll, though. Always fun to be with. She and Sam were like sisters. This is as hard on June as it is on me."

"Surely not."

"Well, she thinks so. I don't think she has any idea. But they *were* close. June helped Sam in her travel class. She took the course and then served as sort of a volunteer aide. Did that for years. Could probably teach the course herself by now. And when Samantha won trips for two and I couldn't go, which was at least once a year and sometimes two, June was always her first and only choice. Their friendship was developed around the world."

"She never took Mrs. Fritzee?"

"You know, she asked her once. June couldn't go for some reason, and Sam bucked up her courage and asked Wilma."

"Why did that take courage?"

"You've talked to the woman. Sam was afraid she'd talk all the way to Bangkok and back. Probably would have, too."

"Why didn't she go?"

"Didn't have a dime for clothes or souvenirs or incidentals, and Sam didn't want to offend her by offering to give her cash too, though she would have been happy to pay for the companionship. Sam was really quite relieved when Wilma said no. She wound up taking one of the gals from the office."

"Do you feel up to telling me about her business, Leo?"

"Yeah. She owned half of it, and there are four other shares at twelve and a half percent each."

"Who owns them?"

"I hardly know. One's an investment banker who just sees it as a good investment. There's a retired couple in Texas who own a piece. And then there's a holding company of some kind—it's got initials in its name—that owns the two other shares."

"Is it worth checking into, Leo?"

"What—the ownership? Aw, I doubt it. They're mostly friendly. They have semi-annual meetings where the couple from Texas, the banker from downtown, and a local lawyer representing the holding company meet with Samantha. Guess I'll have to get involved in all that baloney now. She left me forty percent of the company."

"Only forty? That means you still have controlling stock by quite a significant margin. But if that holding company buys one of the other small shares out, you'd only have a small edge on them."

"Good grief, Jennifer, I could hardly care less. I'd be happy to sell it out to them myself."

"Do you mind telling me who your wife left her other ten percent of the company to?"

"Not at all—it was a wonderful gesture. Just a little nest egg for June Roloff."

"That was a nice thought, Leo. But do you see how it threatens your control of the company?"

"I suppose, but I'd always have June in my corner, so there's no way anyone can get more than fifty percent. In that sense, it's just like it's always been. I'll wind up splitting my shares between my kids someday anyway. Problem is—unless I sell, which I really shouldn't—I have to be chairman of that fool board. Major stockholder gets that dubious honor. It made sense when Sam was the owner. They pretty much liked having the chairman of the board running the company because she had more at stake than any of them. They had to know she'd run it for profit."

Jennifer had the uneasy feeling that she should check into the ownership a little more thoroughly. "I know you think it's a dead end, Leo, but is there a file or anything I can see that would give me a little more on the agency?"

"It might be at her office; it might be in her desk in the den upstairs. If the permission is mine to give, you have it. I'm not sure it's all legally mine yet until it goes through litigation, so you might have trouble getting into the files at her office. Check the den; be my guest."

Mark came down with two suitcases and carried them out to the car. "I'd really like to look through her papers, Leo, but I don't want to hold you up."

"Nonsense, you won't hold me up. Just lock up when you're through. The lights are on timers. You might let Mrs.Fritzee know so she doesn't call the cops." He embraced her briefly and gently and thanked her for listening and understanding.

"Just take care of yourself," she said. "I'm not goin' back to work until you do."

Mark winked at her, but she pretended not to notice. After calling Mrs. Fritzee, Jennifer phoned Jim to tell him she would be a little late. "But I still need to talk to you tonight," she said. "Nine o'clock too late?"

"Are you kidding? Anytime, anywhere, kid."

She laughed. "The Pancake House on Western."

"Pretty late breakfast," he said. "See you then."

Jennifer had always been fascinated by personal papers. She would rather nose around in someone's desk than in their closet or even in their safe.

It didn't take her long to determine that Samantha Stanton kept excellent records, and while most of the day-to-day business papers were apparently kept at the office, what Jennifer really needed was right there.

In a file labeled "Board," Jennifer found the minutes of the semi-annual meetings of the stockholders of the Gateway Travel Agency. Most were mundane financial reports and guest appearances by various staff members, reporting to the stock holders on different aspects of the company.

Jennifer traced the history of the company from the time Mrs. Stanton bought in and became the major stockholder. The technology and the relationships with airlines were the most dramatic differences, with Samantha campaigning for total computerization of the operation.

Most interesting, she found that the two most vocal members of the board were Kimberly Rand, the wife half of the Texas couple—Mr. and Mrs. T. J. Rand—and a lawyer named Conrad Dennison, who represented the holding company K.R.C. Limited.

The investment banker, Wilfred Griffin, seemed a positive man from the minutes, always the first to express appreciation ("I'm sure on behalf of the entire board—") for anything and everything presented.

Mr. Rand always backed up his wife, but rarely led any dissent. Dennison was the troublemaker, frequently asking tough, accusatory questions and debating the majority on almost every vote.

On three separate occasions, Dennison tendered cash offers for the stock of both the Rands and Griffin in the middle of a business meeting. On two other occasions, official complaints were noted in the minutes—once by the Rands and once by Samantha Stanton herself—citing the lack of proper procedure in tender offers he had made between meetings.

> Chairman: "Let the minutes show that the representative for K.R.C. Ltd. made an improper offer to purchase 60 percent of my stock or 30 percent of the company, tendering his offer by phone and without proper documentation."
>
> K.R.C.: "What's the purpose of putting that in the minutes? I have every right to make a bid for a total majority, and you have every

right to refuse it. It appears here as if I've broken some law."

Chairman: "If you need the reminder, our bylaws call for the knowledge of the entire body notified by mail before any such transaction is undertaken. And for the record, my stock is not for sale at any price."

K.R.C.: "We'll see. I just wonder how profitably this company could be run with proper majority control."

Griffin: "I feel very good about how the company is being run. We survived the recession with just one losing quarter, and we've been very profitable for many years."

K.R.C.: "Perhaps our ideas of profits differ, Mr. Griffin. This company is mostly a liability to my clients, almost a tax write-off. It could be twice as profitable."

Jennifer wanted to meet the Conrad Dennison character representing K.R.C. She also wondered who was behind K.R.C. If, by any chance, it was connected with anyone already owning one of the smaller shares, the purchase of the remaining small share would put half the stock in their hands. Then the *real* battle would begin.

The addresses and phone numbers were all there, so Jennifer took as many notes as she could and tried to keep it all straight in her head. Just as she was about to put everything back where she found it, she noticed a pile of unopened mail.

Much of it consisted of bills and junk mail addressed to Leo. But a few pieces were for Samantha. Apparently, Leo had dumped everything on her desk that wasn't obviously a sympathy card.

At the bottom of the stack was an unopened six by nine manila envelope from K.R.C. Ltd., addressed to Samantha over her agency title. Leo had said to be his guest. Did that permit her to open his mail? His wife's mail? Would she be violating the law—opening a dead woman's mail? The woman's heir had given her permission, sort of.

This was agency business. Leo would be inheriting majority stock. Did that give him total right to this envelope? And if so, had he given Jennifer the right to open it?

It was much too early to call Wisconsin and get Leo's permission. What about the *Day* lawyer who had represented Jennifer a couple of times? No, he would want to know who she was talking about, and he would advise against it.

He would advise against it, she knew, because it was wrong. Maybe Jim would know if there was any way she could justify it. She dialed. No answer at his apartment. She called his precinct station house. No, he had already left for the day.

Jennifer looked at her watch. It was almost time to leave if she was going to meet Jim at nine o'clock. She held the envelope up to the light. Nothing. Too thick. She studied the outside carefully.

It had been typed in legal typeface, and the name Dennison had been added, also typewritten, above the return address logo. K.R.C. Ltd. had an Evanston post office box, but the office address was on North Sheridan Road in Chicago.

Was it a firm in its own right, or was it simply represented by Conrad Dennison's law firm? How could she know? How could she find out?

Curiosity was killing her. The postmark was the previous week. It must have arrived

Friday or Saturday. No earlier, or Mrs. Stanton would have opened it.

What if it was a proper legal offer, a copy of which was mailed to all the other stockholders? Shouldn't Leo be made aware of it? But then, nothing could be transacted until Samantha's will was executed, right? Leo'd be protected.

But what if an offer was being made on another minority stockholder, and Leo wanted to match or beat the offer? If they didn't hear from Leo by a certain time, the deal would be consummated. Then what?

And what if Jennifer was right about K.R.C. representing someone else on the board? Leo could get back into his daily routine, show up at his first board meeting, and find he was majority stockholder with just forty shares to K.R.C.'s thirty-seven and one half.

All of a sudden the bidding for the remaining two shares—June Roloff's 10 percent and the unsold 12 1/2 percenter—would become fierce. Leo should be aware, shouldn't he? Wasn't it Jennifer's duty to her boss and friend?

She knew it was not.

Twenty minutes later Jennifer was pouring out the story to Jim in the parking lot of the Pancake House. He tried to slow her down and quiet her down as they entered and found a table, but she was going on and on about her dilemma.

He smiled, just listening to her. She sped through the information she had read in the minutes and dwelt on the curious envelope, the one she just didn't think she could resist. It drew her like a magnet.

"I worked like everything to talk myself out of opening it," she said.

He nodded. "Good."

"And then I tried everything to talk myself *into* opening it."

He stopped nodding. "You didn't."

She dug in her bag and produced the envelope. "I hoped it would have one of those gummy flaps that could be pulled apart and then resealed."

"But it didn't?"

"No."

"That's good, because that wouldn't have made it any more right or wrong to do."

"But, Jim, you should see what it says."

His eyes fell. "You didn't."

She held it up to his face. The envelope had been slit. "Just wait till you hear what it's all about."

SEVEN

"Just water, please," Jim told the waitress evenly. "I'm not eating."

"I am!" Jennifer said. "I'm famished. Give me the blueberry pancakes and the works."

"The works?"

"Whatever comes with it—everything. Hash browns, toast, milk, orange juice—whatever."

"Only syrup and whipped cream comes with it, ma'am."

"Fine."

Jim was stony. His eyes appeared hooded, and he sat with his chin in his hand, staring at her, expressionless, as she recounted what she'd found in the envelope. "I'm not sure I want to be party to this," he said at one point.

"You don't have to be," she said. "I know I'm in this alone. But Leo won't mind. Believe me—I know him."

"He may forgive you, Jenn. But it was still wrong to do it without asking first."

"I couldn't reach him! And I couldn't wait. I was right. It's important, and he needs to know about it."

Jim shrugged, and Jennifer sensed frustration building inside her. He was coming off a little pious in this, as if he and the rest of the police didn't go snooping when they felt like it. "You want to hear this or not?" she asked.

He didn't respond, which embarrassed her. So she began without looking at him. "You see, it's notification to all stockholders that K.R.C. Ltd. is making an official offer to buy out Mr. Griffin's twelve and a half percent. He's the investment banker with one of the small shares.

"The way it works in this kind of company is that the offer does not have to be matched or even accepted. But if it *is* accepted, or if there is an indication that it will be accepted, other stockholders may tender private bids of their own, without knowing the original bid."

She waited to see if Jim had any questions. He remained in the same posture, staring at her as if disappointed. He *was* disappointed. He had already made that clear.

"So," she concluded, "K.R.C. has notified the seller and the other stockholders of its intention. If the buyer doesn't hear anything by Friday of this week, the offer will be official. Now this Griffin has always been happy with his investment, but with the death of the principal stockholder, he may accept a good price. He's no dummy, and he has not been real active in the decisions of the company. He's just gone along with everything Mrs. Stanton wanted to do."

Jim would not participate in the discussion.

"Don't you think Griffin might want to get out," she pressed, "knowing that Mr. Stanton has no interest in running the business and also knowing that K.R.C. will undoubtedly take over the majority stock eventually?"

No response.

Jennifer ate, occasionally glancing up to see Jim staring at her, still unsmiling. She smiled at him. He looked away. She'd rather he told her off than put her off like this. She lost her appetite quickly.

"OK, all right," she said. "I think you've carried this judgment far enough. I was wrong. I admit it. I'm frankly glad I did it, though, because I think Leo will want to know. All right? Are you going to hate me forever because I didn't live up to your ideal of me?"

Jim just sat looking at her, letting the words echo in her mind so she could hear herself. She only felt worse.

"Do you realize," he said finally, "that you're sidetracked from your mission?"

She looked puzzled.

"Your job is to prove that your boss's wife didn't commit suicide. Based on what was found in her body, it was either suicide or murder. Couldn't have been an accident. How has this mail you've tampered with helped you determine her murderer?"

Jennifer sat back and sighed. She was still upset at Jim's condescending attitude, but she wished she had an answer for that one. All of a sudden she was running the travel agency instead of protecting Samantha Stanton's reputation.

"Jennifer, you have to tell Leo what you've done. You can't let it go long. These things have a way of catching up with us."

Now she was mad. "All right, Jim, I'll call Leo now! Is this thing so serious with you that it harms your view of me?"

"Why put it on me? It was wrong, and we both know it. You're entitled to mistakes; that doesn't shatter me. But I *do* wish you'd quit trying to justify it and would just deal with it!"

She stomped off to the pay phone, knowing Jim was right, wishing he wasn't, and mad at herself for going against her own conscience. She also wondered what Leo would say.

"He's sleeping, Jennifer," Mark said. "And guess where?"

"Not in the car."

"In the car. And I mean he's out like a light. The weather's nice, and the car's right next to my bedroom window, so I can keep an eye on him. I'm gonna let him sleep. I'm glad you called though. Dad got all worked up when he remembered that some letter was still on the desk from one of the company stockholders."

"That's what I was calling about."

"Good. He called the lawyer at the newspaper and the guy agreed to represent Dad in the agency, help him hire someone to take it over, and all that. He said to just leave that envelope unopened, because if it's any kind of official business, it'll be null and void or something like that as soon as the lawyer points out that it arrived during the week of my mother's death. OK?"

"That's the problem, Mark. I opened it."

"You opened it? Why would you open it?"

"I thought it might be something important. And it was."

There was silence on the other end for several seconds. "Oh, boy," Mark said finally. "Dad's not going to like that. Neither will his lawyer."

"I was trying to help."

"By opening his mail? I'm not sure how that helps, Jennifer."

"Me either," she muttered.

"Pardon me?"

"Listen, Mark, since what's done is done, you'd better get the message to the lawyer so he can do something about it."

"What's done is done? That's your view of it?"

Jennifer sighed and rolled her eyes. *Not from this guy too!*

"I'm sorry. I shouldn't have. I tried to reach you, but it was too early."

"We tried to reach you just before nine," he said.

"I was gone already. Are you going to chastise me for it, or are you going to tell the lawyer?"

"I'll tell him," he said. "But I think I'll let you tell Dad. You owe me that, at least."

"I *owe* you?"

"*I* didn't open his mail."

Jennifer reminded herself that Mark was grieving. Maybe if nothing else came of this, his interest in her would wane. That would almost make it worth it. Problem was, she feared the same was happening to Jim. Maybe he'd back off if he knew she knew he was right. And if he knew his prediction was right. It had indeed caught up with her.

She trudged back to the table and told Jim. He reached across the table and took her hand. "I was a little rough on you, and I shouldn't have been."

"Of course you should have," she said. "*I'm* even disappointed in me. I could have helped more by leaving it alone. They would have beaten it by not opening it. Now they have to go on the offensive. And like you said, it's totally off the subject of her death."

"Totally?"

Jennifer shot him a double take. "What are you saying?"

"Think, Jenn. You didn't get into that desk to look for some partner buying another partner out, did you? Didn't you have a reason you wanted to know more about that business? Wasn't it related to your original purpose here?"

"Yes, I was looking for a murderer."

"Of course. That might sound a little silly now, but you can't leave any stone unturned. It was a hunch, and you played it. What did you expect to find?"

"Some irregularity, some enemy, some reason someone might benefit from Samantha Stanton's death."

"And did you find it?"

"I'm not sure."

"But you've got plenty to go on, lots to check out before you pull out from under this rock, am I right?"

"You're right. When do you become a detective, Sweetheart?"

"Not soon enough."

"Tonight, I think. Thanks. Now aren't you hungry?"

"As a matter of fact, I am. You got time to watch me eat?"

"Depends. What are you ordering?"

"Just what you did."

"Want what's left of mine?"

"Oh, sure. Cold pancakes are one of my favorites."

The next morning she called Jim before heading out to talk to the two pharmacists on her list. "I saw you angry with me last night."

"For the first time?" he asked.

"You tell me. Have there been other times?"

"I dunno."

"You do too! I can tell from your voice! When?"

"I don't remember."

"You do—"

"No, I really don't. I just know it hasn't been the first time, that's all. Maybe a long time ago. Last night I just decided to let you know it, that's all."

"That one of your philosophies? If it's important enough, you'll tell me, and if it isn't, you'll let it slide?"

"I guess."

"Is that good?" she asked.

"I think so."

"So do I. Any more thoughts before I go out and play detective today, Sergeant Purcell?"

"Uh, what are you expecting from the pharmacists today, Jenn? They're a pretty tight-lipped bunch unless you have a warrant or something."

"I know. But apparently there was nothing wrong with the two isolated ingredients she might have gotten at different times."

"Still, they're prescription drugs, so there would have to be a record."

"Of course, my theory is that there will be no record whatever of her purchasing the ingredients."

"I thought of another obstacle you should be aware of. Maybe you already know."

"Go ahead. I need whatever I can get."

"It's just that Mrs. Stanton's philosophy and politics are not in your favor. The minister, or whatever he was, did a good job avoiding the suicide angle at the funeral, but the fact is, she might have been comfortable discussing just those ways to die. Not that she would have. Nothing in her history or personality indicates that she would have chosen it for herself, but can't you see her arguing for euthanasia under the right circumstances?"

"I guess, but unless she had some terminal illness, which the coroner didn't find—either that, or Jake's not saying—she certainly wouldn't have been preoccupied with it from the perspective of her own life."

"I agree. Just something to think about."

"Anything else?" she said.

"Yeah, matter of fact. Just before we left last night, you recounted Mrs. Stanton's morning regimen. Did you come to any conclusions based on that?"

Jennifer thought a moment. "Well, yeah," she said. "I guess I just thought they were kind of obvious."

"Don't ever assume that."

"Well, I thought they all pointed to the fact that she was on her way to work, not on her way to commit suicide."

"I agree," he said, "but tell me why."

"Dressed. Made up. Had her tea. Did the dishes. Brought the paper in. Had brushed her teeth, rinsed with mouth wash, and put lipstick on."

"You know that for sure?"

"I know about the lipstick from Jake Steinmetz. I'm guessing on the teeth brushing or mouth wash."

"Jake could tell you that. Better find out."

"Important?"

"Sure. Any change at all in her morning routine could blow your theory. Anything at all that even hints that her mind was elsewhere. So far, everything rings true. She was in a pattern, a habit, nothing changed. That's not how suicides work. They might get gussied up or do a few habitual things, but not everything. What would be the point? And what would it say about her state of mind?"

"Jim, I'm saying the woman was doing what she always did. She was on her way to work."

"Why did she take a pill, Jennifer? If someone forced her, they had to have been there. And if they were there, someone would have seen them. And they would have had to have known her habits, her schedule, when she did what. Any evidence of that?"

Jennifer thought. "No. I'll ask around, but up to now, no. Nothing like that. You know my theory on that?"

"Hm."

"That pill was in her aspirin bottle, and it was a time bomb. Someone planted it— who knows how long ago—and waited for her to get to it."

"Would Leo remember if she had a headache the night before? Or that morning?"

"I'll check. Why?"

"Maybe it wasn't even a bottle she always carried with her. Maybe it was a common bottle they had in the cabinet in the bathroom. If she had a headache, she might have grabbed a tablet and tossed the bottle in her purse for the work day."

"Could be. And if so, what are you thinking?"

"You sure they didn't plant it in the bottle when the bottle was in the cabinet?"

"Jim! It sounds like you're still thinking it could have been Leo!"

"Not at all. What I'm suggesting is that the intended *victim* could have been Leo."

EIGHT

Jennifer knew she'd hit some sort of pay dirt the minute she walked into the Hargreaves Drugstore on Western Avenue a few blocks from Leo's house. It was as if she was expected.

As soon as she mentioned wanting to ask some questions, she saw movement in the back, and by the time she mentioned her name, her newspaper, and the name Stanton, someone was gone out the door, and the ledger book was pulled off the counter.

Angry and full of adrenalin, Jennifer spotted a service entrance and dashed outside just in time to see an older man getting into a late model Oldsmobile, a raincoat over his white smock.

She ran up to the car door before he could shut it and leaned in, daring him to slam it on her. "You must be Mr. Hargreaves," she said sweetly.

"That's right," he said, shoulders slumping, hands in his lap.

"Apparently you know what I want to talk to you about."

He nodded miserably. "Do you know this could ruin a family business that's been in this neighborhood more'n fifty years?"

"What could?"

"What you want to talk to me about."

"What do I want to talk to you about?"

"You tell me."

"Let's quit playing games, Mr. Hargreaves. You've as much as admitted that your pharmacy made available drugs that killed someone. Why not just tell me about it?"

"For the paper? I don't have to talk, you know."

"Off-the-record. For my peace of mind. And the husband's peace of mind. For your peace of mind too, I imagine."

That struck a chord with the old man. "Take a ride with me," he said. She ran around and jumped in the other side.

He drove about six blocks to a muddy public park where baby-sitters watched day care center kids playing on the swings and bars. He turned off the engine and swung his right knee up onto the seat beside him.

Jennifer guessed him at about retirement age. He was dark complexioned and had long, wavy, salt-and-pepper hair. His accent had a faint British clip to it. He sounded weary.

"I ran errands for my father in the twenties in that store," he said.

She nodded.

"I'd hate to see anything happen to it. If you'll tell me again you're not going to print this in the paper, maybe I *can* tell you something that will help everybody concerned."

She nodded again.

"Well," he said with a sigh, "we have rules. We're pretty strict. Have to be. State agencies are tougher on us all the time with all the dope problems and everything. The people who work for me are either family or they're carefully trained. I mean, the family is trained too, you understand, but they're making a career of it. Everyone has to take all the classes, pass all the tests, get all the apprentice licenses and all that."

"I see."

"What I'm getting at is this. Yes, sometimes we make an exception, do somebody a favor. But there are a lot of prerequisites, if you know what I mean."

"Tell me."

"For instance, I might fill a prescription two or even three times past what the physician has indicated on the slip. But, nobody else in the shop can do it. They have to call me. And first, I have to know the customer."

"And the doctor?"

"That goes without saying. I would never, ever fill a prescription from a doctor who didn't have references, a local address, all that, at least with your dangerous drugs."

"OK."

"So, I'm at home, all right? I get a call early one evening from one of my nephews. A good kid. A little young, but a lot of promise. Goes by the book. I like him. He'll make it. He asks me if he can give Mrs. Stanton a few grams of something. It was nothing, but it was a puzzle because she had called it in first. Said she had had to get it somewhere else last time for some reason—which puzzled me because she trades with us all the time, and we're usually open.

"But anyway, she's told my nephew that she needed a little more and that she would read it to him from off the prescription slip. He'd asked her if there was a filling limit. She'd said no. Now normally, he could have filled that because she would then bring the slip in, and he would match it with the dosage and everything would be kosher.

"But the reason he calls me is that she's done all this, but when she gets there, she's forgotten the slip. She says she'll bring it in sometime, and he knows I'll have his hide if he doesn't check with me."

"So what did you do?"

"Without a second thought, I thanked him, praised him for calling me, told him 'no problem, it's always smart to call.'"

"And?"

"And I tell him to give her the prescription and don't make a big deal about bringing the prescription in. We don't want to treat her like we don't trust her, a longtime customer like that."

"When did you realize you'd given her something that would prove lethal?"

"Not till I heard about her suicide. I'm tellin' you, I cried. I was scared. I still am. I'm kickin' myself. Not that I could have stopped her. A woman wants to kill herself, she's going to do it with or without my help, you understand. But if I'd been firm, not made exceptions for an old customer and a respected doctor, who knows? Maybe I could have slowed her down, made her think twice. You know."

"Did you check with her doctor?"

"Billings? I was afraid to. What if he says, 'No, I never prescribed that'—which he probably didn't, because by itself it's virtually worthless. Then he would find out I filled a bogus prescription, and there goes my credibility with him, let alone everyone else."

"Aren't you curious to know where she got the other ingredient?"

"Sure. I assumed it would be from the drugstore up here on Kedzie, being so close, but again, I wasn't about to call and ask."

"Did Mrs. Stanton pay by check or put it on her bill?"

"Neither. She paid cash. That was a little unusual, come to think of it, because she has an active account with us. Her husband usually picks up the medicine though. But it *was* a small amount, so I didn't think anything of it."

Jennifer was crushed, and it showed.

"I'm sorry," he said. "I feel terrible about it too."

"It's not that Mr. Hargreaves. I appreciate your telling me, and I understand why you'd be scared. It's just that up to this moment, I didn't believe Mrs. Stanton committed suicide."

He nodded slightly, understanding. "And now you have to tell her husband?"

"Eventually."

"I wish there was a way you could tell him that we did it in good faith, if you have to tell him."

"I believe you did it in good faith. There's no doubt it was her, was there, sir?"

"Not really, no. It's kind of embarrassing, but I always thought Mrs. Stanton was a pretty nice looking woman. Didn't you? Did you know her?"

"Yes. Yes I did, and yes she was."

"Well, I asked my nephew when he had her standin' right there in the store, I says, 'Is she a good-lookin' redhead?' and he kinda whispered into the phone, 'That's her, Unc.'"

Jennifer used an entirely different strategy at the Allen Drugs chain store adjacent to the big grocery on Kedzie. Knowing it was a huge place that used a lot of employees, she just marched up to the counter and asked to see the head pharmacist.

"He's off until tomorrow, ma'am."

"Then I'd like to talk to someone who has the authority to let me look through your prescription records for the last two months. I'm from the *Day,* and I'm exercising my right based on the Freedom of Information Act."

The young man looked concerned but huddled with an associate pharmacist for a few seconds. The associate approached. "How may I help you?" he asked.

"Exactly the way he told you," she said firmly.

"May I see some identification?" he asked.

Jennifer pointed to the front page of the *Day,* which was in a stand near the counter. He looked at the picture of her on the front page, along with the note that she was on assignment. He smiled. "You're prettier in person," he said.

She didn't respond, which seemed to upset him. "I still need to see some identification," he said coldly. She showed him her press card and driver's license. He studied them briefly and pushed them back to her, and as she replaced them in her wallet, he slid the big book around toward her so she could see it.

He said, "You know that the Freedom of Information Act doesn't give you the right to print any of those actual names without permission."

"Journalism one-oh-one," she said, and immediately felt that had been too cold. She added a wink and a smile. He blushed and walked away.

Within seconds, Jennifer located the notation for the small amount of the ingredient needed to make a lethal dose. The date matched the one from Hargreaves, and the doctor was listed as Billings. "An appropriate name for a doctor," Leo had once deadpanned, but now it didn't seem so funny.

Next to the listing, however, was a notation. *No prescription. Verified with phys. by phone. Pd. cash.*

Dr. Floyd Billings was a stocky, pleasant, soft-spoken man who agreed to meet with Jennifer at the end of his office hours, about six-thirty. He loosened his smock and sat across the desk from her in a small examining room.

"I was as shocked as anyone when Mrs. Stanton took her own life," he said. "I knew she had not told her husband of her problem, but I assume she left him a note."

"There was no note, doctor. That's why we've been convinced it was not a suicide. What was her problem?"

"Oh, I'm afraid I would not be at liberty to say, even though she's dead. That is very privileged information. She made me pledge not to tell her husband, a pledge I would now break. But you understand that I couldn't tell you."

"But you would tell Leo?"

"I would."

"I understand. Could you at least tell me if her problem was terminal?"

"I really shouldn't discuss it. I'm sorry."

"Dr. Billings, do you recall receiving a phone call—it would have been two months ago to the day yesterday—from Allen Drugs?"

"Well, I get so many—"

"Mrs. Stanton was there without a prescription, but they called you to verify that it was all right to give her the medicine."

He furrowed his brow. "I *do* recall something like that. Yes! I remember."

"Do you recall what the medicine was?"

"I didn't ask."

"Excuse me?"

"I didn't ask. I had my girl look up her charts real quick and tell me if we had prescribed anything out of the ordinary lately. She said no, so I told the druggist to refill whatever she was asking for."

"Would you like to see what she asked for?"

He nodded and leaned forward to take the small slip of paper from Jennifer. Reading it, he winced and paled. He carefully laid the paper on the desk in front of him and ran his fingers over his face.

"She was a patient of mine for decades," he said, his voice weak. "I mean it. At least three decades. She must have had a breakdown of some sort. She must have."

"You've said you were shocked when you heard of her death, and you can't believe she would do something like this after you had known her for so long, so I'm guessing that whatever physical problem she might have had was not terminal. Otherwise this might have all made some sense to you. Am I right?"

"I'd rather not discuss it. Are you going to report me for this lack of discretion? In retrospect, of course, I can see what a terrible mistake I made. Those precautions we're supposed to use are to protect us from drug addicts, not our own patients."

"I don't think anything would be served by my telling anyone. When you tell Mr. Stanton about his wife's problem, you might want to tell him these details."

"Perhaps you're right. I don't look forward to that."

"You'll have some time," she said.

Jennifer didn't look forward to talking to Leo again herself.

NINE

The next morning, Jennifer phoned Leo's Wisconsin cottage. As expected, Mark answered.

"Is Leo mad?" Jennifer asked.

"Well, I don't think he cares to speak to you, if that's what you mean."

"Are you serious?"

Mark didn't respond, and Jennifer was worried.

"Mark, I need to know if your mother was ill, either in the night before she died or that morning. Was there a headache or any other sort of ailment? Can you find out from your father and let me know? I want to know why she took an aspirin."

Mark was still silent.

"Mark?" she said tentatively.

"Hm."

"Are you there?"

"I miss you," he said, flatly.

She pursed her lips. She was thinking, *Oh, for pete's sake, grow up. You're acting like a child! I'm engaged, I'm busy, and I don't have time for fun and games right now.* But she didn't respond. She decided she could play the game the same way he did. She figured there was nothing quite as frustrating as being ignored by phone.

She pretended Mark hadn't said anything. "Can you find out for me?" she repeated.

"I know how you feel about me," he said, desperately.

That's a laugh, she thought, pitying him.

"And you'll either call me or have your father call me, OK?"

"Bye-bye," Mark said endearingly.

Jennifer nearly gagged. This was all she needed in the middle of a frustrating and disappointing investigation. She was trying to muster the courage she would need to tell Leo the bad news—that his wife had indeed apparently stretched the truth to the breaking point to get the combination of contraband drugs that killed her.

Jennifer spent the rest of the morning studying her notes, wondering where to turn and what to look for that might make the evidence look less certain. She and Jim would be going to prayer meeting at their church that night. She had already requested prayer for her boss, whose wife had died. But how could she ask for prayer that it was other than a suicide?

She finally decided to console herself by making an appointment to talk with someone who would likely agree with her—someone who would feel too that, in spite of all the evidence, Samantha Stanton could not have taken her own life. She called Mrs. Stanton's best friend.

June Roloff invited her to lunch. "As long as you don't put yourself out," Jennifer said.

"Nonsense," she said in a pleasantly low voice.

"I could just as easily pick you up and take you out somewhere," Jennifer suggested.

"Really, it'll be no problem," Mrs. Roloff said.

Jennifer had met the striking fifty-year-old brunette before, but she had not realized what a swank neighborhood the Roloffs lived in, or even that they had domestic help. Their exquisite lunch of light crepes and fresh fruit was served as they sat on a wrought iron and glass sun deck.

Jennifer wanted to blurt out the question: Where in their world did the Roloffs get the money for a place like that? But she just tried to take it in stride. It was apparent that Mrs. Roloff was still grieving. Her eyes filled with tears whenever she reminisced about Samantha.

"I'm being asked to teach her class and even to lead some of her travel tours now," she said. "I just don't know if I can, or if I should."

"Why not?" Jennifer asked. "It would be for her, wouldn't it?"

"I suppose, maybe. Yes, it might. But it would be so painful, so difficult. I'm not another Samantha, and I don't want to pretend to be."

The woman spent much of the afternoon talking about her many adventures with Samantha. "We traveled quite a bit together, you know."

Jennifer nodded.

"She left a little piece of Gateway to me," June said. "I was so touched, I cried and cried. It was so sweet of her."

"When did you find out?" Jennifer asked. "I was under the impression that the will had not been executed yet."

"Oh, it hasn't, but Samantha told me she was going to do that about six months ago. She even showed me a copy of the will."

"You must have been very moved."

"It was unlike any feeling in the world. That agency had become her life, outside of Leo, of course. She couldn't have left me anything more personal unless she had left me her family."

And she clouded over again.

"Mrs. Roloff, I know you're upset, but I want to confide in you, and I have to admit, the news is not good. May I?"

"I guess."

"I've been researching this death under the assumption that Samantha Stanton would be the last person in the world to commit suicide. I admit I was biased. I was looking for the evidence I wanted to find. Much of it is puzzling, but the majority is troubling."

"In what way?"

"In that it is becoming apparent that Mrs. Stanton may have indeed taken her own life."

"And that surprises you?" Mrs. Roloff asked.

"Your response surprises me," Jennifer said.

"Why?"

"Well, I, because I just assumed, I mean—I didn't think you thought it was suicide."

"Why not?"

"Because you knew her. Leo lived with her, and he's convinced it wasn't suicide."

"If it wasn't suicide, what was it?" Mrs. Roloff said. "An accident?"

"I was thinking more in terms—"

"Because if it wasn't an accident or suicide, it was murder, and one thing I'm certain of, Sam didn't have any enemies—at least not any who would have murdered her."

"Who were her enemies?"

"I wouldn't even know that. I know she had some run-ins with certain stockholders in her company, but nothing serious. She always speculated that one of the representatives of one of the owners was in cahoots with some old couple on the board, but I never got any of the specifics, and it certainly didn't sound like she had developed any serious conflicts."

"Then you think it was an accident, Mrs. Roloff?"

June Roloff stood and stared out through the glass at her withering garden. "You mistake grief and loss for naiveté," she said. "You forget that we were like sisters."

Jennifer was shocked. "Are you telling me you think she committed suicide?"

"I try not to think about it," she said.

"But were you close enough to know what Dr. Billings knew?"

"Of course. I always thought she should have told Leo. It wasn't going to kill her. The sugar in her blood would eventually affect her eyesight. It already had, of course. But she was a lot of years from hardening of the arteries. She had a lot of good years left. Maybe as many as twenty."

"Why do you think she didn't tell Leo?"

"I think she thought it would make her less of a woman. She was within a year of having to give herself insulin injections. I don't think she was quite ready for that."

"I still don't see her killing herself."

"It's hard for me too," Mrs. Roloff said. "Though not totally surprising."

"Why haven't you told Leo?"

"I didn't know if he really didn't believe it, or if he simply wasn't accepting it. He will eventually. He needs his illusions right now."

"Then I'm wild-goose chasing."

"Jennifer, there is nothing that would please me more than for you to discover that I'm wrong. It horrifies me to think that she's gone, and to add the nightmare that she is gone by her own hand when Leo and I and so many loved her so deeply. I just don't want to accept that either. But it happened, and I'm trying to cope. Keep searching until you're satisfied."

"But you're implying that I am not going to like what I find."

"You haven't so far."

"For the most part, no."

"For the most part?"

"Well, there was shoddy police work that could have messed things up. There was the fact that Samantha wasn't despondent, that Leo or anyone knew of anyway." Jennifer's listener betrayed a sad, knowing smile. "And she was all ready for work when she died. Why?"

"Probably because she didn't want anyone to notice," June said. "She wasn't the type to do anything for show. She wouldn't have faked an attempt just to get Leo's attention. She did it so it would be discovered after it was done. That's my guess."

"That must be very difficult for you to even think about."

"Right."

"Is there more?" Jennifer asked.

"More?"

"More reason to believe it was suicide and not an accident or murder."

"Well, a person doesn't accidentally kill herself with a dose like that one. That rules out accidents, unless it was intended for Leo, and everyone knows that's ludicrous."

Jennifer nodded. "But couldn't it still have been murder?"

"That's almost as painful to consider as suicide."

"But we have to consider it, Mrs. Roloff. Because if it was murder and everyone thinks it's suicide, that means there's a murderer around somewhere. Someone who knew an awful lot about Samantha Stanton's habits."

"Don't go implicating Leo now," Mrs. Roloff said.

"I wouldn't think of it," Jennifer said. "Never."

They sat in silence for several minutes.

"Anything else that will help me?" Jennifer asked finally.

"Nothing you'll be happy about," she said.

"I'll be happy for anything that will bring an end to this assignment I once so eagerly wanted."

"Even if it ends the way you don't want it to?"

"I'm afraid so now. I just have to know, one way or the other."

"You'll need to keep this confidential."

"Of course."

"From everyone."

"Everyone?"

"Absolutely."

"Let me think about that for a moment." Jennifer had the feeling that Samantha's best friend in the world could shed some light on the truth, that she might say something that would be difficult to take, but that there was something to the cliché that the truth hurts. "All right," she said, "I'll keep your confidence."

"How do you think Samantha got those euthanasia booklets?"

Jennifer blinked. "I've been hoping to prove that they were planted by a murderer."

"In a way, I wish you were right. Like I said, knowing she was murdered is not any more pleasant than knowing she killed herself, but somehow I feel so guilty about her suicide."

Jennifer wanted to hear where June Roloff thought Samantha had gotten the suicide manuals, but she couldn't let that comment go. "*You* feel guilty about it?"

"Certainly. I was her best friend. Her confidante. I was committed to her. I had responsibilities and obligations to her." She began to cry. "And she did to me too!"

"Such as?"

"She had a commitment, a responsibility to stay alive. I resent that she's gone! I need her! I loved her and cared about her and gave of myself for her. And she did to me too, until this. Leaving without so much as a note or a good-bye—I can hardly bear it."

"But she left you that most personal gift."

"That was a gesture that came long before she died. It was sweet and thoughtful, but I didn't want it this way."

"But why should you feel guilty?"

"Because I was inadequate. I wasn't what she needed. I wasn't enough! She had such deep needs and causes, and I was not up to the challenge. Because she couldn't find answers anywhere—not even in me—she left us all."

Mrs. Roloff hid her eyes with her hand, but Jennifer had to ask. "Do you know where she got the booklets?"

The older woman nodded, her tear-streaked face finally showing its age. "She dragged me out to one secret meeting of the SMS. You know, Sam and I agreed a lot philosophically, but we parted there."

"The SMS?"

"Simplified Method Society."

"Method of what?"

"Self-euthanasia. Assisted-euthanasia. Call it whatever you like. They advocate suicide as a humane method of death for the terminally ill, or really for anyone who chose it and didn't want it to be painful or messy."

"You actually went with her?"

"She bugged me for ages to go. Asked me to think about it. To consider it. She hit me with dozens of hypothetical situations. What if this and what if that? Some of them were hard to argue with. I suppose there would be situations where I would rather be put out of my misery, even by a friend or relative than to suffer on for years."

"Where does a group like that meet?"

"In local hotels or restaurants. When you come in, they ask if you know what they meet to talk about and to promote. If you say no, they tell you you're not welcome. If you say yes, they ask you to state it briefly. If you're right, you may come in."

"What's the purpose of all that?"

"To make sure no one gets in the wrong room, is then shocked and tells someone who won't understand what it's all about."

"And they distribute this literature?"

"Free. But not to me. No, ma'am. I even used a phony name when I attended. I got the impression most people did. Not Sam though. Nobody could make Sam pretend she was someone else. So there was ol' Samantha Stanton, visiting the euthanasia meeting with her frumpy friend Claudia Brown."

"Frumpy?"

"I even disguised myself, Jennifer! New name and new look. It was creepy, and I never went back." She began to become emotional again. "You see why I can't be terribly surprised at her death—at least her method?"

TEN

"I agree it looks bleak," Jim said after prayer meeting that night as he and Jennifer strolled a Lake Michigan beach. Strolled might not be the word for it. She huddled against him and hid her face and neck from the chilling wind—happy to be with him, but regretting the choice of the beach.

Finally they sought shelter behind a gigantic tree trunk about sixty feet from the water's edge and settled in the sand with their backs against the wood. Out of the wind and nestled against Jim's chest, Jennifer felt relaxed and secure in the silence.

She had told him the story of her day while they rode to and from the church. "These people seem so empty," she said. "Leo and his son and even Samantha. Mrs. Fritzee. Mrs. Roloff. It's depressing."

"Seems it would give you a chance to talk to them about God," he said.

"You'd think so, and I know this sounds like an excuse, but I start listening to them and empathizing with them, and I get emotional and can't bring myself to tell them of the most important things. I'm overwhelmed with how they're looking in the wrong place for their peace and their answers, but so much so that it's as if I'm incapacitated."

He nodded in sympathy. "What are you thinking now about Samantha's death?"

She shook her head. "I don't know anymore. I just don't know."

"That's a good sign," he said. "Good or bad, depending upon how you look at it."

"What do you mean?"

"I mean it's apparent you haven't made up your mind yet, even though you have evidence heavily weighted one way. That's healthy skepticism in my book; it might be delusion to some people. That's why it's good or bad, depending—"

"My guess is I'm deluding myself, Jim." He didn't respond. It was *her* theory, not his. She continued. "The only reason I think it could still be murder is that her morning routine didn't change one iota and because I knew the woman."

"You *thought* you knew the woman," he said.

She nodded. "Leo thought he knew the woman too."

"I would agree with Leo."

"But Jim, Leo says she didn't commit suicide."

"I'd say he knows better than anyone."

"You agree with him?"

"That's what I said."

"I do too."

"I know you do, Jenn."

"How did you know?"

"Besides the fact that it's written all over you?"

"Uh-huh."

"Because you're staring at two drugstores, a doctor, a best friend, a coroner, the cops, and the evidence, and they all say it was suicide. Yet you're undecided. To me, that's not undecided. To me, you're coming down on the side of murder."

"But why am I, Jim? Am I that smart—or that stupid?"

"I'd like to think your intuition is good. It could be blind loyalty to your boss."

"Which he could also be guilty of Jim: blind loyalty to his wife."

"Right. But I am sure of this, the truth will surface. It always does."

"Always?"

"As long as people keep looking for it."

"How long will I have to look?"

"That's entirely up to you."

"And up to my bosses," she said. Jim chuckled. "I'm not sure I know where to turn next."

"That's a detective's greatest position," he said. "When you don't know where to turn next, turn everywhere. Get general. Stop being so specific. Think of all the places and people you've heard about so far, what you've learned, what questions have been raised. Anything you're thinking or wondering about?"

"Yeah," she said. "I'd like to meet some of the people behind Gateway Travel. I'd like to check in again with the coroner to find out about toothpaste or mouth wash in Mrs. Stanton's body. I want to hear back from Casanova about whether his father remembers if his mother had a headache sometime just before her death."

"Go for all of 'em, Jenn, but don't leave out an important one."

"I'm listening."

"Hadn't you better attend an SMS meeting?"

"In disguise, of course."

"Of course."

Coroner Jacob Steinmetz, M.D., stared at Jennifer from over the tops of his half-glasses the next morning in his office. "I said nothing about sugar content in the blood," he said, "and I dare say her personal physician didn't either."

Jennifer just returned his gaze.

"We noted something about the eye muscle and tissue," he said. "That's all, if your sugar guess is based on the transcript of the autopsy. You can't necessarily assume diabetes based on glaucoma."

"Any evidence she was a marijuana user?"

"That would be extremely difficult to determine by autopsy unless she had inhaled the smoke shortly before death. We didn't find any such trace. Why?"

"Isn't it common for glaucoma sufferers to even be *prescribed* marijuana?"

"Not common. Bandied about in sensational journals, I suppose. But no, not common in this country. Don't impugn a fine doctor like Billings. He's a good man."

"Tell me about the residue on her teeth or gums."

"Standard. Food particles. Tooth paste. Mouth wash."

"Alcohol?"

"Only from the mouth wash."

"How do you know that?"

"From the amount. C'mom, Jennifer, you're fishing. Let's get on with this so I can get back to work, huh? I wish *you* would too. I like you better when you're interviewing me for a story, not as an amateur detective."

"That hurt," she said, seriously. He didn't respond. She quickly recovered and plunged ahead. "I want to know," she said, "if you could tell whether Mrs. Stanton had a headache within twelve hours of her death or whether the poison would have obliterated such evidence."

"No, the poison would not have duplicated the blood vessel trauma created by a headache. However, death sometimes releases the pressure on the brain, and the headache symptoms go away."

"Was that the case in her death?"

"Why are you curious about a headache, Jennifer?"

"Well, I don't know, but apparently my hunch was right, because you're already evading the question."

"I won't evade it if you'll tell me where you're going with this."

"You've got a deal. You first."

"The woman was suffering from a severe headache, just short of a migraine, possibly up to six hours before her death. There's evidence she took some aspirin in the middle of the night."

"I don't recall that from our first conversation, Jake."

"We didn't have a deal then, Jennifer."

"Must I always make a deal to get straight answers?"

"Always," he said, smiling. "Now what're you making of all this?"

"The woman was murdered, Jake. Someone slipped a bogus pill into her aspirin bottle. If she wanted to kill herself, why not in the middle of the night while her head was throbbing?"

"Maybe she didn't want her husband to wake up next to her corpse."

"And maybe I'm right," she said.

"So you're saying someone slipped the pill into her bottle, possibly a long time before her death. Because they couldn't know when she was going to have a headache."

"I guess."

"Unless they poisoned her just a little the day before to make her feel the need of an aspirin." He was teasing her, and she resented it. "And how were they to know that she wouldn't share the bottle with her husband and wind up killing him unintentionally? Really, Jennifer, you're barking up the wrong—"

"The woman was dressed for work, Jake, and she completed her morning regimen right through to the tooth brushing and the mouth wash."

"And if the murderer planted the suicide pill, how did he know when to plant the euthanasia booklets so it would look like a suicide?"

Jennifer didn't know what to say. A murderer would have had no way of knowing when Mrs. Stanton would take the fatal pill, so how *could* the books have been planted?

Jennifer stood. "I'm going to prove Samantha Stanton didn't kill herself, Jake. But it won't be out of any malice toward you. Can we still be friends, no matter how it turns out?"

He smiled weakly. "Sure. Just promise me you won't have the body exhumed. I hate disinterred bodies. Messy all the way around. Families don't like it. Nobody does."

"I promise to avoid that if possible," she said, knowing Leo would probably oppose it too. That is, unless he felt it was absolutely necessary to clear his wife's name.

Mr. T. J. Rand—even by telephone from Texas—was not at all what Jennifer expected. She thought he'd be a big-talking loudmouth with a twangy drawl. The drawl was there all right, but with no twang, no volume, and no bragging.

"I don't rightly know why Mr. Dennison is makin' a bid now for Mr. Griffin's share. But I cain't hardly blame the man for sellin', now that the principal owner has died and we'll be lookin' frantically for a new working manager, understand?"

"Will you be selling too?"

"Oh my, no!" came the shrill voice of Kimberly Rand, whom Jennifer had not known was even on the line. "Things may never be better! We're still happy with our investment, and frankly, I can get excited about Mr. Dennison's clients taking a little more control in the company."

Jennifer decided to go on the offensive. "There are those who suspect that Mr. Dennison actually represents some other stockholder and that the purchase will then represent an even larger portion of the company."

"I have to get off now, T. J.," Kimberly said. "I got no more time for speculation with someone I don't even know. You get off the phone soon too, you hear?"

"Yes, dear. Well, Miz Grey, I never really thought o' that. But if the company that Mr. Dennison represents is actually a front for one of the other smaller stockholders, it could only be us. If it was Griffin, he'd be buyin' himself out. Dennison's K.R.C. Limited owns two small shares, so that leaves only us to be the sneaky partner. Is that what you're implyin'?"

"Yes, sir."

"Well, I resent that. First of all, you shoulda just come out an' said it. Second of all, I don't know how you get K.R.C. out of T. J. Rand. Good day, Miz Grey."

Jennifer's appointment with the seller, Wilfred Griffin, was for the mid-afternoon. She found him in his suburban Niles office, which also housed several similar firms. Griffin was one member of a five-principal company that invested mainly in municipal bonds.

"But this deal," he said brightly, with a big smile she assumed was normal, "is strictly independent, strictly personal. I'm rather proud of it. On my own, even when I was a junior member of this firm and didn't have my name on the stationery, I tried to get them to invest in Gateway Travel. It was voted down twice out of hand, and then I was allowed to pitch for it officially, I mean with the whole dog and pony show, you know what I mean?" He didn't wait for a response.

"I mean I had Mrs. Stanton in here, and I had flip charts and slides and earning curves and flowcharts and graphs. I'm tellin' ya, if I'd have been an investor, I'd have jumped at it."

"But they didn't?"

"No, they didn't. But did I rub it in when I invested on my own and made a nice piece of change? No, ma'am. Not my style. I didn't even brag about it. But I *did* make it clear I had taken a chance on my own, just so I could kinda live and die by that one risk—

'course, I was convinced it was safe and in fact had great potential—"

"I gathered that."

"Huh? Ha! Yeah! I guess you would. Any-hoo, I never bragged about quarterly or annual earnings unless someone asked. But when they asked, as they always did—independent of each other and always claiming that if it had been solely up to them, they would have voted for it—I was ready with a little printout to show just how successful and profitable it had been for me. They're all a bunch of liars, of course, because the vote was unanimous against it every time. I mean *every* time. But I don't mind. Those are the kinds of lies I tell too. None of us are actually dishonest; in fact, our firm is honest to a fault. Never cheated a client. Never will. But fudge a little on your own reputation, well—you know what I mean. That's why I was always ready with the printout, because no one would have believed me otherwise.

"Why, would you believe that each and every one of them at one time or another has asked how they can buy into the company *and* whether they can buy *me* out! Would you believe that?"

"Every *one* of them?"

"Every one."

"No, I wouldn't believe that."

"Well, you catch on fast, sweetie, 'cause you're right. Only three of the four have asked to buy me out, but they've all asked the other questions. Believe me?"

"Never again," she said laughing. "I'll never trust another investment banker as long as I live."

He laughed too. "Now, what can I do for you? You're probably wonderin' why in the world this idiot is selling out. I'll tell you straight. I got an offer I couldn't refuse. I got an offer twice what the stock is worth. It's such a good offer that I'm not even worried—and I know the buyer isn't worried in the least—that the other owners will even come close to it. 'Course they won't know what it is, so they'll be at a disadvantage. But I'll bet no one comes within fifty percent of it when they try to *beat* it."

"So, strictly a money deal."

"Exactly."

ELEVEN

Jennifer's hope that there was something to chew on in the relationship between Wilfred ("Call me Freddie") Griffin and Samantha Stanton was short-lived.

"I just admired the woman, that's all. Met her husband once. Whale of a nice guy, and talented newspaperman, I understand. But this woman ran that agency like a pro from the day she bought in and became the manager. She'd been there before, you know, but after she came up through the ranks to assistant manager, she had to scrape up some money somewhere and buy in to become manager."

"Was there a problem with the previous manager?" Jennifer asked.

"None, except that the board disliked him. I wasn't there then; this is all hearsay. 'Course, K.R.C. never liked anything or anybody in management, so when I came I tried to balance 'em out a little. Never worked."

"They were right in that case, though, and when Mrs. Stanton bought in and took over, profits went up right away. Wasn't long, though, before Conrad Dennison became the representative for the holding company, and he was pickier than the last guy."

"Do you happen to know where Mrs. Stanton got her money?"

Griffin smiled. "Sure. She told us plenty of times. It was one-third inheritance, one-third saved up, and one-third borrowed, long since paid off. Remarkable woman."

"Truly. Do you think there was trouble between Mrs. Stanton and the previous manager?"

"Nah. Just the usual frustrations of workin' for somebody who doesn't do as good a job as you could do. We all deal with that, don't we? Ha!"

"But there's no lingering problem that you know of?"

"Oh, no. I don't even remember the guy's name, but he became a ticket counter man at one of the big airlines at O'Hare. Died about three years ago. Heart attack, I think. I got his name in the file if you want it."

Jennifer shook her head. "Do you think Mrs. Stanton had any enemies on the board?"

Griffin's smile faded and he squinted at her. "You mean *real* enemies? Like murderin' enemies? No. None. We had our squabbles, but no, not at all. Not even Dennison, and he was her biggest critic."

"We'll see," Jennifer said. "Now, Mr. Griffin, I've looked over several sets of minutes of your meetings over the past few years, and I have to ask you why you finally relented and will sell to Dennison. I know the money was good, but aren't you worried about the character of the company?"

"Not really. I know what you're thinking, and I know I've been less than cordial in disagreeing with Mr. Dennison a lot in the meetings, but my share won't give K.R.C.

Limited enough power to do anything. Unless he thinks he can buy out the Stanton heir, he's not really helped himself except financially. And despite how much he paid me, if they can find the right manager, he'll have his money inside a decade."

"A decade? Isn't that a long wait?"

"Not for that kind of dough. 'Course, K.R.C. couldn't have known that Mrs. Stanton was going to die, but I'm not going to let him out of the offer. He may try to pull some legal shenanigan now, but I've got him by the short hairs. I was going to turn him down, you know, even at the price he settled at."

"You were?"

"'Course I was!"

"What changed your mind?"

"What else? Mrs. Stanton's death."

"You wouldn't have sold even for a big price with her running the show?"

"Nope. Said that many times. I think Mr. Dennison has bought himself a pig in a poke now, but that's his problem."

"Do you think Mrs. Stanton committed suicide?"

"Well, yeah! 'Course! I didn't know that was even a question. I didn't really know the woman enough to know what was troubling her. She certainly couldn't have had money problems unless she was way overextended. But we'd have known if the agency wasn't in tip-top shape, and it always was. I don't know why she killed herself."

"You can't consider the possibility that it was not a suicide?"

"Hm, I don't know. I guess not after seein' the news and readin' the paper. Nah. It was a suicide all right. You got any evidence says it wasn't?"

"Not enough," she said.

He smiled at her. "Pity. I liked her. Didn't know her well, but admired her. Seemed a good woman, and she sure was a good agency manager. I owe her a lot. In fact, I owe her double, triple maybe. Gettin' out when she got out is gonna make me richer than the agency ever did in the past, and that wasn't half bad. Gotta admit I had perfect timing this time."

"Getting out when she got out?"

"I didn't mean any disrespect by that. Just a manner of speaking. I really was shocked and sad when I heard she was gone, and gone that way. Depressed me for a while. But I was sure glad I hadn't turned down K.R.C.'s offer. I was about to, but when I heard the news, I sat on it."

Jennifer felt a little sleazy leaving Griffin's office. He had, at first, seemed so bright and optimistic. He fit the image she had built of him from reading the minutes of the meetings.

But in the end he was the same as most of the other financial wizards she knew: out for himself, caring only about the bottom line, the buck. It was disappointing.

She had an evening appointment with Conrad Dennison in his North Sheridan Road office, but a message on her phone answering machine made her call to change that to the next morning.

"Jennifer, this is Jim," the recording said, "and there's an SMS meeting tonight. Check your newspaper's personal column."

With Leo coming back around noon the next day, she wanted to have all her facts straight. It would be bad enough facing him with bad news (and after having opened his mail), but she certainly wanted to have enough information so that she knew for sure whether Samantha Stanton had taken her own life or was murdered.

She didn't need a suspect—just a clue.

Tossing her raincoat over the edge of the couch, she grabbed a piece of chicken from the refrigerator and laid out the newspaper on the table with her other hand.

Jim was right. In among all the love notes and prayers for the now departed, she found a simple message. "SMS tonight. Surf and Turf Inn. Estes Avenue. 7 P.M. Word to the wise."

She didn't want to go alone. She didn't want to be recognized. Of course, she would not use her real name. But Jim couldn't go with her; he was on duty.

Jennifer rummaged around in her closets and trunks for—what was it June Roloff had said?—something frumpy. The clothes and jewelry were easy. Jennifer looked frumpy all right. A bandana in her hair set the tone. But what finished the look was when she found the pink eyeglass frames she had worn in high school, just before she had switched to contact lenses.

She wore her contacts to drive to Estes Avenue off Sheridan, then removed them and put on her old glasses before leaving her car several blocks from the Surf and Turf. A quick glance in the mirror made her chuckle at the dowdy, middle-aged matron who peeked back.

As Jennifer walked down the rain-swept street, she caught glimpses of herself in the reflections of puddles, but her humor couldn't override her fear.

What if someone recognized her?

What if they asked for identification?

What if she saw someone she knew?

What if they didn't let her out?

What if she forgot what to say when they asked her if she knew what the meeting was about?

But she didn't. "Euthanasia," she said.

"Ten dollars," the woman responded.

"Oh, my," Jennifer said. "I didn't expect that."

"It gets you on our mailing list, honey. And we have expenses. Sign the book up front on the right when you get in the room."

No one seemed to notice when she entered, though forty or so people sat in stacking chairs in a dark-paneled room. She went and stood in line, about sixth, to sign the book. She prayed no one would stand behind her so she'd have time to peek back in the registry to see if she could find Samantha's name—or June Roloff's "Claudia Brown."

But someone came in when Jennifer was second in line. "Go ahead," she said. "I just want to tie my shoe." He passed, and she bent down to tie the old oxford she hadn't worn for years. When she stood, no one was behind her, so she leafed through a few pages before signing, "Louise Purcell."

She didn't see any names she recognized, but she did see a lot of names she assumed were phonies. She had to hand *that,* at least, to Mrs. Stanton. There was no hiding for her. That's why the escape of suicide seemed so incongruous.

From the looks of the garb and the demeanor, she was guessing she was with a fairly sophisticated intellectual crowd. A spokesman began by passing the notebook around and reminding everybody to add their address so they could be on the mailing list.

As soon she as heard that, Jennifer headed for the back row where she would have time to scan the book without suspicion.

While she waited for the book to make its rounds, a black-bearded man, who appeared to be in his late thirties and who wore an Indian chain and necklace, made an announcement:

"For those of you who have been worried about our being found out and hassled and turned away from meeting rooms and such, you'll be happy to know that our lawyers, of whom there are four here tonight—raise your hands; oh, five!—are making real progress with the American Civil Liberties Union in allowing us to meet in the open and say and do what we want."

There was a certain amount of clapping and subdued cheering. The rest of the surprisingly short meeting consisted of various updates on the chapters in other cities, recent developments in court cases, the sharing of anecdotes about terminally ill patients who suffered unmercifully for years, and more stories of people who were aided in their efforts to die peacefully.

More cheering greeted every such story, and then a list was read of people who belong to the SMS worldwide who had died peacefully, either self-induced or aided, in the last month. There were oohs and aahs when the reader announced that there was a possibility that someone who had attended one of "this very chapter's meetings may have died of her own choosing very recently. It was definitely done to specification and of her own volition."

By then Jennifer was casually looking through the book and unaware of anyone noticing. Sure enough, from the beginning of the book, Samantha Stanton's name appeared on nearly every list. The night they met in Alsip, south on the tollway, a Claudia Brown had signed, but there was no Samantha Stanton.

Jennifer couldn't figure that out and assumed she had missed Samantha's name. She was searching the list one more time when someone nudged her and asked for the book.

On the way home, she detoured farther north on Sheridan Road to check out the address she'd been given for K.R.C. Limited. Her suspicion had been correct. The initials K.R.C. did not appear on the directory in the lobby. The building housed law firms.

Discovering who was represented by Conrad Dennison would be tougher than she thought. She searched the board for his name. It was there alone in suite 4404.

She scanned the board for other names in that same suite. There were three or four listed singly, as Dennison was, and there was another listing of the name of the firm itself, "Cocharan, Thomas, Rand, and Kahill."

Rand, she thought. *Coincidental? Has to be.* The next morning she asked.

Conrad Dennison got a big belly laugh out of that question. He had come out to the waiting room himself to invite her into his beautifully appointed office, pretty nice for someone who wasn't yet a partner.

"*Yet* is right," he said, sitting at his desk in green suit slacks, white button-down shirt, striped tie, and vest. He also wore alligator cowboy boots. He was in his early forties and had wavy, longish hair that gave him a slightly outdated look. "If you think *this* office is nice, you should see the partners' offices."

He made a clicking sound with his mouth to indicate, she supposed, that they were top dog. "But I'll be there soon enough," he said. "Just a matter of time. They take care of me, and I've been doing the job for them for years."

She nodded.

"So you thought Rand was ol' T. J. Rand, did you?" he said, laughing again. "Nope, not even close, and am I glad of that! This Rand is one of the Boston Rands," he added, raising his eyebrows as if certain Jennifer would immediately recognize that name. She didn't.

"Tell me about K.R.C.," she said.

He stared evenly at her, not moving. He smiled. "What do you want to know? I thought this had to do with the travel agency."

"Doesn't K.R.C. have anything to do with the travel agency?"

"Well, just in the sense that they own a quarter of it, that's all. I handle that for them."

"Who are they?"

"A holding company. They have several interests."

"Who are they?"

"Business people. A small concern with a lot of irons in a lot of fires. They do well for themselves."

"Who are they?"

"They're private, anonymous people who, if they wanted nosy reporters to know who they were, would have used their names in their logo. Since they didn't, and since I am paid handsomely to represent them in the strictest confidence, you can quit hoping I'll suddenly spew forth the name just because you keep asking."

She stared him down. "Just one name?" she said.

"Name, names—what's the difference?"

"The difference is whether it's one person or more than one person. It'll make it easier for me to get the name from public records if I know a little more about this out-of-state group."

"You're really being childish for a big city reporter, you know that? You think that by saying they're out-of-state, you're going to get me to think that you really believe that so I'll confirm that they're local. It could be one name and more than one person, you know. Or vice versa."

"Not vice versa," she said sweetly. "That would be stupid. One person and several people's names? Silly."

"Perhaps," he said, reddening. "Do yourself a favor and give up on the name, OK?"

"What do you suppose the odds are that Wilfred Griffin will accept your generous offer?"

Dennison flushed again and clenched his fists. "How do you know about that?"

"I'm a big city reporter," she said.

He softened and smiled, but his fists were still balled. "I'm not at liberty to speak to that either," he said.

"Uncanny sense of timing on that offer," she pressed. "Would you have made it if you'd known?"

"Known what?"

"About Mrs. Stanton."

"I didn't make the offer. I represented it."

"Will you withdraw it now that she's out of the picture?"

"That's none of your business."

TWELVE

Jennifer was desperate, but Dennison didn't know it. And that was all she had to go on. "I've made it my business," she said. "I have to know who's behind K.R.C., and if you don't tell me, I'll find out somewhere else."

"What's the big deal?"

"The big deal is that Mrs. Stanton, the majority owner, was murdered, and now here you are making a big play for more of the company for who knows who?"

"Whoa! First, she wasn't murdered! Second, I've always made pitches for more of the company, which a look at any of our records will prove. And third, you'll note that this latest pitch was tendered *before* she committed suicide. You think it drove her to suicide?"

"Not a chance," Jennifer said. "She was never intimidated by you or the company you represented. And while she was alive, there was no way you could have dreamt of getting more than half the company. Even if you bought out both the other minority partners—which would be foolish because K.R.C. is undoubtedly in collusion with one of them—you would still have only fifty percent."

He sat smiling smugly at her. "Well, if I'm in collusion with another partner, it'd have to be the Rands, wouldn't it?"

She nodded.

"I like the old girl—not so much her ol' man—but she's fun, and we think alike. Unfortunately, she's too shrewd to sell. Maybe if the business flags a little during the transition of managers, the Rands will reconsider."

"There's nothing to the initials relating to the woman's name, is there?" Jennifer tried, feeling foolish.

But Dennison was visibly shaken. "What are you saying?" he managed, eyes narrowing.

"I'm saying I think it's an interesting coincidence that the woman you so enjoy has the initials K. R. Could K.R.C. be the Kimberly Rand Company?"

"You're joking."

"You're stalling."

"No! Of course not! How could she have me representing her business without her husband's knowledge? Well, let me just say you're not going to get any information out of me, but I'll give you my solemn promise and guarantee, K.R.C. Limited has no more to do with the Rands, either of them, than it does with our own firm."

"And why should I believe you?"

"Maybe you shouldn't. You decide. You're not going to find out one way or the other anyway. But let me save you some time and trouble in your little mission; forget the Rands. I'm serious."

"You only make me want to focus right on them," she said.

He shrugged and raised his hands in surrender. "Suit yourself," he said.

On her way out she paused at the directory board again and stared at the names of the law firm. Cocharan, Thomas, Rand, and Kahill.

Kahill. Rand. Cocharan. Could it be? What would be in it for them without the association with another stockholder? Dennison had said that K.R.C. had no more to do with the Rands than it did with his own firm. Maybe there was more truth to that than he intended. But would he have simply handed her that big of a clue?

She needed to talk to someone, and Leo and his son would not be back until about one o'clock. She called Jim, hoping she wasn't waking him. He usually rose by ten or eleven after working the night shift. That would all change when he became a detective. Which would be just before their wedding. *Good timing,* she thought.

"Did I wake you?"

"No, Jenn. I've been up."

"Hungry?"

"Yeah."

"Let's kill two birds with one stone. I need help."

They met at a popular luncheon spot where they found it nearly impossible to talk. They ate quickly and then sat in his car.

"You're right on the button," Jim said. "The problem is, Dennison's offer—on behalf of K.R.C.—*was* made before Samantha's death. But regardless, unless he was aware that the majority stock would fall from fifty to forty upon the execution of Samantha Stanton's will, the purchase doesn't make sense."

"Unless he's just advising K.R.C. that the company will be run better now," Jennifer suggested.

"But he couldn't have known of her death at the time of the offer."

"Or could he?" Jennifer asked.

"Maybe as the representative of K.R.C., Conrad Dennison didn't know," Jim said, warming to her idea. "But K.R.C. knew, whoever they are."

"Can we say that K.R.C. Limited is a suspect—at least one of their people—because they knew of the death in advance and assumed that it would make the sale more attractive?"

"It's a long shot," Jim said, "and the problem is that it points only to greed as a motive."

"What's wrong with that? It's a solid enough motive, isn't it?"

"It's a little galling," he said.

"Granted. But now how do we establish means and opportunity if we don't know who K.R.C. is?"

"We don't. But let's try something."

Jennifer knew not to ask what Jim was up to when he was in that mood with that look on his face. He liked surprises, and he also liked play-by-play announcing them as he went along.

About halfway downtown, he announced that they were going to speak with his soon-to-be superior, Detective Lieutenant Grady Luplo. "He'll know if we have enough to get a warrant to search for the name in private records."

"I implied to Dennison that I would find it in public records," Jennifer said. "But it would also be like looking for a needle in a haystack."

"Were you bluffing, or did you really think you could find it?"

"I don't bluff, you know that."

"Well, you weren't going to find it in public records, and Dennison probably knew that. Don't suppose he gave you much in exchange for that threat."

"Matter of fact, he didn't."

Grady Luplo was an interesting looking character who seemed to enjoy wearing his plainclothes suit, but wearing it less than tidily. The jacket was unbuttoned, and he stood with his hands jammed into the front pockets of his trousers.

"Wow," he said, after a half hour of listening to Jennifer's story and Jim's question. "I don't think so, Jim. No, you haven't nearly enough. There's an awful lot of speculation there, grasping for straws, you know what I mean. I mean, with her buying the drugs herself? I could call my buddy in the D.A.'s office, and he could look up the information for me without a warrant. It wouldn't be totally legal, but—"

"Then we don't want to do it," Jennifer said earnestly.

"Now, wait a minute," Jim said. "I want to get this straight. Is it actually a crime for us just to *know* this information?"

"No," Luplo said. "It's a crime to use it."

"Is it illegal for you or your friend to dig it out?"

"No. But it can't be used without cause. It'll be thrown out of court. You'll lose your case."

"But the problem is, Lieutenant, that we could use the information to expose a murderer."

"Yeah, you probably could. But if it ever came out that you got the information illegally, you've shot your case on a technicality."

"What would make it legal?"

"The D.A. You want me to call him? I'll call him."

Luplo spoke for several minutes with a contact in the District Attorney's office whom he called Larry. Larry dug out the information for him by computer and read the name to Luplo over the phone. "Thanks, Larry," he said. "I'll probably have to talk to a judge before I can do anything with this, but I'll let you know."

He hung up and turned back to the young couple. "They gave me the name," he said. "I know what it stands for, but I really shouldn't tell you if you're going to pursue this."

"What if we used the name to flush out the killer and got him to admit it himself?" Jim asked.

"Good question. But if it *ever* came out that you got the information without due cause or a warrant, the case would be jeopardized."

"Did you say name, singular?" Jennifer asked.

Luplo smiled. "I did say that, didn't I?"

"Can you tell me if it's a man or a woman's name?"

"I can tell you that I don't recognize the name. You might, but I don't. It's not a usual name, and I have this feeling that I might have seen or heard it somewhere before, but it doesn't send off any rockets with me."

"Ooh, this is frustrating!" Jennifer said. "That name could be the name of the murderer, someone who had enough knowledge of the business and of Samantha Stanton's life that he or she could have pulled this off. But for what purpose? For what gain?"

"The D.A.'s office agrees we don't have enough, ma'am," Lieutenant Luplo said. "I can ask a judge directly, but they don't like going through us. They prefer their own kind."

"Isn't there a judge in Chicago who was a cop once?" Jim asked.

"Yeah! There is. I'll try him if you want, but you know Saturday is a court holiday. He won't like being bothered at home."

"How long will it take?" Jennifer asked.

"I'd prefer waiting until early afternoon," he said.

"We'd better go, Jim. I've got to meet Leo."

"Yeah. And lover boy Markie."

"Oh, please."

Leo was almost chipper compared to how he had been before he'd gone to Wisconsin. He still had his teary moments, but mostly he was characterized by an attitude that signaled he was ready to get back into the fight.

Jennifer pulled him off to the side to apologize for opening his mail. "Ah!" he said. "It's all right. I was surprised, yeah, and the lawyer was ready to have you fired."

"Really?"

"Yeah! But you know what? I told him to cool his jets. I told him I'd have done the same thing myself. We nosy journalists are all the same. Proves your qualifications."

"It was still wrong, and I'm sorry," she said.

"Granted," he said. "In truth, you owed me that apology, and I accept it." He gave her a little hug. "And I owe you an apology too, or I should say Mark does. You won't get one from him, so it'll have to come from me."

"What are you talking about, Leo?"

"About the way he talked to you on the phone the other night. If he'd been younger, I'd have tanned his hide. He was humiliated to know I overheard him, but I gave him what for anyway. You won't have any more trouble from him."

"Oh, it was all right, Leo. I'm flattered that he was—"

"Nonsense. He knew all along that you were both a widow and engaged. It was foolish and inappropriate, and I told him that. And I apologize."

"I admit I got a little tired of it," she said. "Apology accepted."

By the time she and Jim had filled Leo in on the progress of her investigation, Mark had called a cab and was waiting for his ride to the airport. He was sullen and hadn't looked Jennifer in the eye.

When the cab arrived, Leo stood and embraced his son, both crying. It was difficult for Leo to let go, but the cabbie was honking.

As Mark left, Jennifer thought she saw a look of apology on his face when he finally looked at her. So she smiled her forgiveness, hoping she was guessing right and praying he wouldn't misinterpret the smile.

"Timing," Leo said, as he settled back into his chair. "That's the key to all this stuff. I want to know what you found and when you found it. I'm tellin' you, Jennifer, you're going to get your break when you put it together in sequence and relate it to other events. You'd be surprised how the whys and the whens of what people do are related."

Jennifer looked at Jim, wondering if Leo knew what he was saying. "Well, boss," she said, "when I'm finished telling you what all I've found, you may lose the equilibrium you gained with your rest."

"Not good, huh?"

"Not all good, no. Some very confusing and troubling."

He looked woefully at her. "Some of it point to, ah, suicide?"

She nodded. He shook his head slowly. "If it makes any difference to you, Leo, Jim and I are still convinced it was murder."

"Against heavy odds?" he asked.

He held his head in his hands as he heard what she had found at the drugstores. He covered his mouth with his hand when he heard of the diabetes and the glaucoma. He wept when he heard of the meetings she attended.

"It just doesn't sound like her," he said. "Maybe hiding the illness from me. She was always considerate. But this other stuff. It's almost as if someone put her up to it. But nobody could ever put Sam up to anything she didn't want to do."

He sat rocking back and forth, hands on his head. "What in the world have you found to overcome all this evidence?"

She told him of her investigation into the travel agency business. He didn't brighten, but he seemed to listen intently. He agreed there might be something to the name, "and my curiosity is killing me," he said. "When are they going to get back to you on that?"

"Anytime," Jim said. "We hope soon, but if they don't think she's turned up enough evidence, they won't give it to us at all."

"Are you kidding?" Leo said, "Those cops are just like we are. They like a good fight. If they think there's anything in that name, they'll let it out. Either that or they'll go after it themselves."

Realizing a cop was in the room, he winked at Jim. And the phone rang.

THIRTEEN

It was Lieutenant Grady Luplo, calling for Jim. He wanted Jim and Jennifer to come back downtown to talk to the judge.

Leo wanted to be in on everything. "I'm tired of hibernating," he said. "Gotta get back in the game. Besides, I can sense you're onto something. This may not be fun, but I want to see it happen—whatever it is."

On the way downtown, Leo wanted to know how Jennifer figured the murderer planted the booklets. "I was afraid you'd ask," she said. "That's the biggest stumper right now, along with the drugstore purchases. It's apparent the pill was made up several days before Samantha died, based on when the ingredients were purchased."

"But how do you explain her buying the ingredients, unless she was despondent over Dr. Billings's diagnosis?"

"I'm not sure of that either," Jennifer said. "Maybe she was forced to buy them, or maybe it wasn't really her. You see, Leo? There's a lot to overcome. I hope the judge doesn't ask the same questions."

"You can bet he will, unless he's in a bad mood. Did they say which judge it was?"

"Ottomeyer," Jim said.

"Crazy old coot," Leo said. "Funny, engaging guy, but coasting. He won't ask a thing, but he'll listen a lot. Be careful not to tell him more than you want to."

Suddenly, Leo was tired. He leaned his head against the window of the back door and tried to sleep. "I can't get past the booklets, the drugstores, and the meetings," he said. "I want to believe what you believe, Jenn, but a gut feeling is all I have."

"And timing," Jim said. "You said it yourself, Leo."

Leo nodded.

Jennifer rifled through her notebook, comparing dates and times and places. "Leo!" she shouted, making everyone jump. "Samantha was out of the country when the drugstore purchases were made! Why didn't I see that before?"

Stanton shuddered. "I can hardly believe it," he said. "Even though it's staring me in the face. It *was* murder." He shivered again. "What a feeling," he said, staring out the window. "To think someone would do that to my wife." He added quietly, "Timing."

Jennifer kept reading, flipping pages back and forth and making new notes. Leo grew sullen. "I have to know who," he said, "legally or otherwise. If the judge won't give the police a warrant, I'll get your lieutenant friend to tell me anyway."

"Leo—" Jennifer said.

He held up a hand to silence her, as if to tell her not to even waste her breath.

Leo was right about the judge. He was full of jokes and wisecracks, but he did listen to Jennifer's story of the investigation.

"You'd make a good policewoman, anybody ever tell you that?" the old man cackled.

"My fiancé has told me many times."

"This guy here? You a cop?"

"Yes, sir."

"Good. A detective?"

"Soon," Luplo said.

"Hire the woman instead," the judge said, laughing. He slapped his palms onto his knees and rose unsteadily. "All right," he said, "down to business."

He motioned for Luplo to follow him out into the hall, and as they left, Jennifer heard him begin: "Grady, I'm gonna get a warrant delivered to the D.A.'s office. Now you take over the thing from here and—"

When Luplo returned, he grinned slyly. "Jim," he said, "you can come along on official business. Mr. Stanton and Mrs. Grey, if you're up to it, I need you as decoys."

"Decoys?"

"Yes, ma'am. We may need you to role play to flush out the quarry."

They mapped strategy in the car, and it was four in the afternoon when they arrived at the offices of the *Day*. On the way through the lobby, Jennifer tugged at Leo's sleeve. "The drugs were purchased the day after your promotion was announced," she said.

"Timing," he whispered. "I'm nervous."

"Me too," she said.

When they entered Leo's spacious office next to a conference room on the sixth floor, Luplo was introduced to the secretary, who explained how the intercom worked.

"Let's try it," he said. "Leo, you and Jennifer go into your office and talk in normal tones." After a few seconds, "Ah, that's good. Now, is there a way we can signal that office from out here?"

The secretary showed him a button that emitted a beep so innocuous that the occupants of the office would have to listen for it and know it was coming. "Perfect," he said. "Make the call, Jennifer."

"Mr. Roloff? Jennifer Grey. Fine, thank you, and you? Good. Listen, I'm doing a piece on Mrs. Stanton for the Sunday paper, and I was wondering if you knew whether your wife would be available for a few follow-up questions."

"Follow-up questions?"

"You knew I interviewed her the other day?"

"Ah, no. No, I didn't. But, uh, she's coming to pick me up. We're going out tonight. She should be here any minute. When would you need to talk to her?"

"Right away, if possible, sir."

"Well, we are going out."

"So early? If I could just have, say thirty minutes, I could wrap this up and not have to come in tomorrow. Could you have her call me when she arrives? I'd appreciate it."

There was a pause. "I suppose. You won't be long?"

"Not at all. In fact, Mr. Stanton's secretary has given me permission to use his office, so we'll have complete privacy."

"Oh."

"So she can reach me here. I just want the best friend angle, you understand."

"Sure. I heard Leo had gone to Wisconsin. How's he doing?"

"Under the circumstances, I'd say as well as could be expected."

"Uh-huh. Well, good. Good man. Need him back here. Hey, here's June now!"

"Thanks, Mr. Roloff. I'll be waiting in Mr. Stanton's office."

Leo and Jim and Grady Luplo stepped into a conference room and waited for the secretary's signal that Mrs. Roloff was in with Jennifer. Then they stepped back into the outer office and had the secretary phone Kent Roloff again.

"Mr. Roloff, Mr. Stanton would like to see you in his office, please."

"Leo's back?"

"Yes, sir."

"I didn't know. I mean, when did he get back? Is he all right?"

"He returned this afternoon, and he seems to be doing fine. May I tell him you'll be right up, sir?"

"Absolutely. Is my wife up there?"

"Yes, sir."

Roloff arrived buttoning his coat and straightening his tie. "Leo, man, how are ya?" he said, shaking Leo's hand. "I mean, *Mr. Stanton,* right? Gotta give the boss his due, don't I?"

Leo nodded and smiled weakly. "Kent, this is Lieutenant Grady Luplo, Chicago PD. And you know Jim."

"Nice to meet you—yeah, hi, Jim." Jim nodded. Roloff was still trying to put it all together. "You guys ride home from work together or something?"

"They're here on business, Kent," Leo said. "Let's have a seat right here, huh?"

"What's it all about, Leo? And where's June?"

Leo nodded to his secretary who pressed the button, privately signaling Jennifer that everyone was in place and simultaneously opening the intercom so the four men in the outer office could hear the conversation.

"So I'll start teaching the class on Tuesday nights, and I'm still debating whether to accept an offer to take over the travel agency."

"Who made that offer?" Jennifer asked.

"Well, someone from their board, I guess. I suppose Leo would know him. I'd do it if he thought I should, I guess, but it's hard, you know, like I told you, with all the memories and everything."

"Would you wear a red wig if you ran the agency?" Jennifer asked.

"Pardon me?"

"Would you try to look like Samantha? I mean, it sounds like you're trying to keep her alive by living her life for her."

"I'm not sure what you're driving at," June said, suddenly emotional, "but it's not easy losing your best friend."

"I don't imagine it's easy losing your wife to murder either." Jennifer said.

"You still think it's murder?"

"We know."

"We?"

"We. A serious mistake was made when the murderer bought the ingredients for the fatal dosage, posing as Mrs. Stanton, when Mrs. Stanton was out of the country."

"Really?"

"Really. There was interesting timing there, Mrs. Roloff. It was right around the time of her husband's promotion. Remember when Leo was promoted?"

She nodded.

"Promoted right past your husband?"

"We didn't view it that way. Kent has been at this same level for many years and enjoys it. He's been passed over before. I mean, not passed over. We don't see it as being passed over."

"Anyway, he has enough outside business interests, does he not?"

"Outside? Oh, I suppose. I don't get too much involved in that."

"You don't? The Kent Roloff Company Limited owns a quarter of the stock of the Gateway Travel Agency. And if everything goes as planned, K.R.C. will purchase another twelve and a half percent from Mr. Griffin. When Mrs. Stanton's will is executed, you stand to pick up another ten percent, giving you majority control."

Silence. In the outer office Kent Roloff leaped to his feet and had to be restrained from bursting through the door. He started to yell, but Jim Purcell wrapped his hand around Kent's mouth.

"One thing I can't figure, Mrs. Roloff," Jennifer said. "How you planted the booklets with such excellent timing. I've already figured out that it was you who went to all those SMS meetings, signing Samantha's name each time. And the one time you badgered her into going, *she* signed the phony Claudia Brown name, and you must have signed something else. I mean, you couldn't get away with signing her name right in front of her, could you?"

Mrs. Roloff licked her lips, but her eyes never wavered. "You figured that out all by yourself, did you?"

Jennifer nodded.

"You get a gold star. You'll never prove anything."

"When handwriting analysis is done, you'll be finished," Jennifer said. "And when the young boy in the drugstore gets a look at you with a red wig. No, you were just a little too eager to have it all at once, you know that?

"You were so jealous, so envious of Samantha that even your friendship couldn't stop you. She always had the spotlight, because she was real. She never had your money, but she had grace you could never muster.

"She saw herself and everyone else as common people. She taught the class. She led the tours. She managed the agency. You were second fiddle. She had the talented and respected husband.

"And when he was promoted over your husband, that was the last straw. You took your knowledge of her illness and put it together with your knowledge of her habits, her shopping, her druggists, her doctor, and even her purse.

"When did you take the opportunity to plant the pill in the bottle, June? Was it when she had to leave the room for a minute and was trusting you to watch it, the way we do with the one person we know we can trust?

"Did you wait on pins and needles, and for how long, before she finally got enough headaches and got around to the fatal pill? Did you ever wonder if you should grab the bottle and change your mind?"

Mrs. Roloff shook her head. She had worked up tears the first time around. None were necessary now.

"C'mon," Jennifer said. "Tell me about the booklets. How did you plant them at just the right time?"

June Roloff sighed heavily. "That was just luck," she said softly. "I gave them to her about a week before and asked her to hold them for me because I knew Kent wouldn't want them in the house. He wouldn't even want to know I had them. She said Leo wouldn't either, but I said Kent had even been known to go through my purse. She said Leo had never once gotten near her purse, even when she asked him to bring her something from it. So she kept them for me in her purse. Twice she told me she was bringing them back, and I asked her to just wait another week."

"She waited long enough, didn't she?" Jennifer said.

Mrs. Roloff nodded. "Kent had nothing to do with this, you know."

Jennifer flinched. "Are you serious?"

"Yes. He didn't know I was getting ten percent of the company. He knew I owned a quarter through the private corporation, and we kept that from the Stantons over the years. But everything else was on my own. He knew nothing of it."

Jennifer shook her head in disbelief.

"Oh, it's true," Mrs. Roloff said in a monotone, staring straight ahead. "And you almost assessed it correctly too."

"Almost?"

"Almost."

"Where was I off?"

"The reasons."

"Not jealousy?"

"Oh, I suppose. But it was Leo I wanted, not Samantha's life. Not her beauty. Not her visibility. Not her job or her teaching or her travels. I wanted him."

"Did he ever know that?"

"Never. I never had the nerve to make a pass at him. Too much character there. In him, not me."

"How was this going to get Leo for you?"

"Oh, I was only halfway there when you stepped in."

"You mean—?"

"Uh-huh. Only half the job was done."

"Your husband—?"

She nodded. "—would have been next."

When Jennifer reached the outer office, she fell into Jim's arms. June Roloff walked past two weeping men, both slumped in chairs. And into the custody of Lieutenant Grady Luplo, Chicago PD.

THE CALLING

ONE

Her high heels echoed eerily in the frigid parking lot beneath her apartment building. Jennifer Grey could see her breath as she dug for the keys to her Camaro.

Strangely, it was even colder in the car. She started the engine and tugged the hood of her down-filled coat up around her head while she let the car idle a bit.

It wasn't like Jim to call her out in the middle of the night, especially a night like this. Late January. Chicago. Two degrees below zero. Wind chill factor: thirty-five below. Temperature on the windshield of a sleek car doing fifty miles an hour down Lake Shore Drive? Nearly incalculable.

Jim had sounded so earnest, so excited, so urgent. "Don't ask any questions, Jenn," he said. "I need you to meet me at Rasto's as soon as you can. Don't tell anyone you're coming."

"The motel?"

"Yes!"

"The one down there, uh—"

"South on the Drive, yes! Hurry, Jennifer."

"Jim, what time is it?"

"I don't know. C'mon! You know I wouldn't ask you if it wasn't important."

"Jim, I can't meet you at a motel in the middle of the night. It would look terrible."

"I'm not alone, sweetheart," he said. "Room fifty-eight, all the way around the back. Park in front and walk."

"Who's there with you?"

"Jennifer, please!" And he hung up.

At least he hadn't sounded in trouble. If he had, she wouldn't have taken the time to comb out her long brown hair and apply her makeup. The invitations had gone out two weeks before, and the wedding was less than a month away, but there was no way Jim Purcell was going to see her at less than her best until he had to.

As she pulled out onto the street and headed toward Lake Shore Drive, Jennifer glanced at her watch. Two-thirty. Jim was still on duty, she remembered. This would be unique. Not since she had been a *Chicago Day* rookie police reporter and he a Chicago Police Department precinct deskman had she seen him while he was on duty.

Now she was a front-page columnist, and he was about to be named a detective sergeant. *Whatever he wants, it must be important,* she decided. Anyway, she wanted to see him, anytime, all the time, anywhere.

Thinking of Jim almost made her quit wondering what he was up to. Tall, whitish blond hair, pale blue eyes, trim, soft-spoken, serious, devout, considerate. She had to admit he reminded her—except in looks—of her first husband. But she rarely mentioned that to Jim.

She would be glad when Jim was a plainclothes detective, and not just because he would be through with those crazy eleven to seven hours. It was simply that despite all the years and the living alone and the counsel of her father, Jennifer couldn't shake the memories that were stirred by the sight of a young policeman in uniform.

It had been a very young state trooper who had come to her door with the news that her husband of less than a year had been killed in a car accident. She had done well, considering. She was fortunate to have close friends, a good church, a tight family.

But she had never quite gotten over the impact of the police uniforms. She had forced herself to put it out of her mind while on the police beat, but even then, the younger men—the ones who kept their uniforms and shoes and leather belts and holsters spotless—they were the ones who transported her back to the painful memories.

But now she felt privileged. After having decided that she could never fall in love again, it had happened.

She was helplessly, hopelessly, totally in love. It had happened so gradually, so methodically, so certainly, and in such an unlikely way that when she and Jim realized it, they knew it was right.

It wasn't as if they hadn't had problems. Their relationship had been tested from the beginning when Jim was implicated in a scandal and charged in an Internal Affairs Division shakeup.

He was cleared, of course, but the ordeal only drew Jim and Jennifer closer together. Recently, though, another problem had arisen. Just a few weeks before the wedding, Jim decided that God had called him and Jennifer into missionary work.

She wanted to pass it off as immaturity on Jim's part. But that was inconsistent with his character. Maybe *she* was the immature one. Maybe she wasn't spiritual enough to be open to what God might be telling them.

She would never forget the Thursday night Jim told her. They had been attending their church's missionary conference, a week of famous speakers who were there to get the congregation fired up about missions.

Jennifer had always been interested in missions. Some of her childhood friends were missionaries. She sent them money every month. She also contributed to her denomination's missions program. She had even visited missionaries both times she'd traveled outside the United States.

She had never felt called to serve, but she wasn't closed to that either. At least, maybe not until now. And she didn't know why. When she had been at her most tender point in her relationship with God, she had told Him that she would do whatever He wanted.

At that point, He had brought Scott Grey into her life. Her job then, she felt, was to follow his lead.

Scott was a quiet man, always looking for ways to serve God through his church. He was so old-fashioned that he didn't want Jennifer to work, not that he would have stood in her way if she'd wanted to. In a way she did want to, but she knew she would have to get used to being at home when they started a family, so she didn't look for a job.

She was soon bored and threw herself into more church activities than even Scott could keep up with. They had begun talking seriously about starting a family when he was killed.

Even with the heater on full blast, Jennifer was cold. Maybe it was the wind chill. More likely, it was the memories. She saw the billboard—the only one Rasto's had ever rented—that told her the dingy little motel was still eleven miles south. The only other drivers on the road at that time of the morning were cops, cabbies, drunks, or truckers; but no trucks were allowed on the Drive. Jennifer assumed there weren't too many young women rendezvousing with their young men either.

She could hardly get over how differently she was approaching marriage the second time around. She and Jim had talked very little about starting a family. She didn't know what she would have thought if he had resented her working or just didn't want her to for some reason.

Admittedly, her work had left less time for church work, but she was still as active as possible. She would give up her job for a family too, but now that she was in her thirties, it was something they'd have to discuss.

She had never dreamed of becoming a daily columnist, but it had certainly given her a platform from which to speak out about ethics and social problems from a Christian perspective. In many ways, she felt her job was almost a ministry.

Jim hadn't even suggested she give it up for homemaking. They agreed that if they had a family, she wouldn't work until the youngest was in school.

But now, with Jim's seeming call to missionary work, Jennifer's future was less secure and more indefinite than it had been since Scott had died. She had always assumed that God called people to His service individually.

Sure, if He calls a man, his wife will go along. But what happens when the man is called and the woman isn't his wife yet? And she doesn't sense the same call? In fact, it makes her nervous. Makes her second-guess herself. Makes her question whether she would really follow her love anywhere, at any price. And what a price!

Was she reluctant to consider giving up her job just because it paid more than twice what Jim's paid? Or would she miss seeing her face on the front page of the *Chicago Day* five times a week?

Jennifer should have realized something was different about Jim when they left the church during the missionary conference eight days before. Usually, Jim was eager to get out of the pew and start circulating. He liked to greet people, to ask about them, and—he admitted—to be asked about the upcoming wedding.

Then in the car, he would usually try to engage Jennifer in a discussion of how the meeting, particularly the message, applied to their lives, their jobs, their futures.

But that Thursday night Jim was strangely quiet at the end of the service. When she gathered up her things, she realized he hadn't even stood yet.

She turned to him and smiled, as if to ask if he were ready to leave. Jim looked at her, wide-eyed, as if trying to communicate something—something he apparently thought she should be able to read on his face.

But she couldn't. He almost appeared overcome, but rather than concerning her, it embarrassed her. And that troubled Jennifer. She knew she shouldn't care what other people thought, especially if Jim had something on his mind.

But all she could think of was that people who knew them, the friends who would be coming to their wedding, might think there was something wrong between them.

Jennifer stood and moved toward the aisle, feeling terribly self-conscious when Jim remained seated, staring at her. She glanced back and let her smile fade to a puzzled look and then almost a scowl. It was as if she were willing him to stand and come with her. Finally, he did.

"What's the matter, Jim?" she whispered as he joined her.

"In the car," he said huskily.

It was unlike him to be coy with her. He wasn't a game player, and he had never been brusque. But as they wormed their way out of the crowded church, Jim just stared straight ahead, merely nodding to anyone who greeted him.

Jennifer tried to cover for him by becoming more gregarious than normal. But Jim's gentle pressure on her arm urged her out to the car.

"Did I do something to upset you?" she asked as he opened the door for her.

He shook his head, but he didn't speak. Jennifer decided that when the time was right, he would tell her what was wrong. She wasn't going to push him. But by the time he stopped at her apartment, she feared she had made the wrong decision. He had said nothing for almost an hour.

Rather than seeing her to her door, as was his usual custom, Jim led her to the end of the hall where a small couch sat by the windows in a sitting room near the stairwell. He unbuttoned his coat and sat on the edge of the couch, elbows on his knees and hands clasped.

"I really got blitzed tonight," he said finally, so soft she almost couldn't hear.

"He really got to you, huh?" Jennifer said, referring to the speaker.

"It wasn't him so much as the Lord speaking to me," Jim said.

Jennifer was taken aback. Jim was a very spiritual guy, a Sunday school teacher and a deacon. But it was rare that he ever said such things. "About missions?" she asked.

He nodded. "About being a missionary."

She froze. Was he serious? "About your being a missionary?" she asked, wishing he'd simply been inspired to give more money, or whatever.

He shook his head. "Us. Both of us."

She nodded slightly and looked away.

"Better pray about it, Jennifer," he said.

"You took my very words," she said.

"You know what this would mean for our careers."

She didn't even move. When he said no more, she put a hand on his shoulder. "Let's talk about it when you've had more time to think about it."

Jim answered, "I'll never waver from this, Jennifer. It's of God."

Again, his vocabulary jangled in her ears. In a way, she had always wished he felt more comfortable talking about the Lord, but this was weird. She didn't like it. It didn't make sense. It was all coming too fast.

"I'll talk to you tomorrow," she said.

He looked quickly at her, as if surprised that she was unwilling to discuss it right then. "Too tired right now?" he asked. She nodded and stood. He followed her to her door. "I won't be tired for a week," he said.

She feared he was speaking the truth.

For the next several days their conversations were the same. Jim felt God was trying to tell him something. That he was supposed to give up his job, his career, his life-style, and go to Bible school. He was to prepare for missionary work.

They had hardly ever argued about anything, and Jennifer certainly didn't want to start with something as crucial as this. She remained guarded, almost aloof. She knew it was frustrating for him, but she couldn't even nod in agreement without his assuming that she was buying the whole package.

He never said it in so many words, but she got the impression that he thought she should share the vision, quit her job, and follow him to wherever God would lead.

When she asked a probing question or two, implying that maybe he should back away a bit and get counsel from trusted friends about such a decision, she sensed it almost angered him. In a way, she hoped he would hit a boiling point. She wanted it all out, but she knew if she angrily confronted him about it, it would appear she was not open to God's leading.

And she was. She thought.

A week and a day after the Thursday night meeting, Jennifer pulled off Lake Shore Drive and into the parking lot of a seedy motel where she was to meet her fiancé. And who knew who else? Or for what reason?

TWO

Not even Rasto's was hopping at that time of the morning. Jennifer wheeled to the end of the first two-story wing of rooms and parked in the shadows.

The long drive had made the car toasty, and she had been able to take off her gloves, lower her hood, and unbutton her coat. But as soon as she stepped out into the air, she turned her back to the icy wind and hunched her shoulders, ducking to bring the hood back up while she quickly buttoned her coat and fumbled for her gloves.

As she walked across the parking lot and past two more buildings, she wished she had worn quieter heels and had brought a smaller handbag. She stopped and looked behind her every twenty or so steps, and her handbag slid off her shoulder or banged her hip each time.

She heard nothing but the wind with her hood up. But that crazy, irrational fear that comes with hurrying through a dimly lit parking lot in the middle of the night and in the dead of winter made her heart crash against her ribs.

Jennifer had been to Rasto's only once, and then only for a clandestine meeting in the parking lot for a story she had written while on the police beat. The contact person turned out to be a phony, and the story never ran in the paper, but Jennifer never forgot the almost unbelievable tackiness of the place.

Many times she had pointed out the motel to Jim as they flew by on the Drive. It almost became an inside joke with them. If she neglected to notice it, he'd remind her, "That was the place that you met the guy who didn't pan out and—"

"Yeah, yeah," she'd say, mimicking how he reacted when she pointed it out to him.

Jennifer determined where room 58 would be by a process of elimination. Only every second or third sign telling which rooms were where had survived the vandals and the years, so when she reached the back of the last row of rooms, she edged away from the crumbly walkway and out into the parking lot to squint up at the second floor.

There were no lights in the parking lot back there, and only a few lights were working outside the rooms. She saw room 51 at one end and 60 at the other, but no other numbers were visible. The only room with a light shining from the inside of closed drapes was the third from the right end, the one she assumed had to be 58.

She edged back closer to the building and felt her way to the outside stairwell. The wrought iron steps seemed to almost give way as she gingerly, and not too quietly, trotted up to the cement platform leading to the rooms.

She would rather have taken the steps more slowly and carefully to ensure against tripping, but she decided the risk was worth it to get on a flat surface again. The stairwell was pitch dark, and she imagined hands darting toward her legs as she moved up the steps.

She slowed and tried to catch her breath as she walked toward the room with the light. Just as she leaned close to see if she could make out the number, the light went out, and she heard the door jerked open just far enough to pull against the chain.

She gasped.

"Jenn?" Jim whispered.

"Yes," she mouthed, but no sound came.

"Yes," she tried again, squeaking it out.

The light came on, the chain came off, and Jim, in his stocking feet and street clothes, reached out to pull her in. "Anybody out there?" he asked, still whispering.

"I hope not," she said, moving toward him and expecting a warming embrace. He edged past her and flipped the light off again, sticking his head out the door to watch and listen. She hadn't noticed anyone in the room, but a second after Jim darkened the room, she noticed a light go off under the door to the bathroom.

Jim pulled back in and shut the door, and in the darkness she heard him set the lock in the knob and reattach the chain before he turned the light back on. As he fussed with the drape to be sure it fully covered the window, she finally got a good look at him. His hair was mussed, his collar unbuttoned, his tie loose.

He placed both a cheap, rickety chair and a heavy table up against the door, a thick green ashtray sliding around as he moved the table. Then he looked Jennifer full in the face with that same smile of wonder and excitement she had noticed in the church a week before and came to her. She withdrew her clenched, gloved hands from deep in her pockets and held him.

The room was cold, and the heater was laboring. "Ooh, you're freezing," he said, pressed against her coat. But he didn't pull away for a few seconds. "Sit down," he said finally.

She looked around and noticed that the room's only chair was the one Jim had pressed into service as a door stop. She sat on the edge of one of the two double beds set a couple of feet away from each other.

She lowered her hood and shook out her hair, and her hands found their way back into her pockets and she sat with her knees and ankles pressed together for warmth. Jim deftly crawled atop the other bed and sat Indian style facing her.

"Still cold?" he asked.

She nodded, smiling only slightly. She wasn't going to beg, but her reporter's curiosity was about to get the better of her. She wished he'd get on with it.

Jim took a deep breath and looked at the ceiling, then back at her. "There's someone I'd like you to meet."

"I gathered that," she said.

"But first I have to tell you about them."

"Them?"

"Them. There are two. A boy and a girl."

"Kids or a couple?"

"Both."

"Both? You mean four?"

"No, two kids. A couple. They're about twenty-one, I guess."

She wanted to ask who they were, where they were, where he'd met them, and why they were holed up here. Not to mention why he wasn't in uniform on a work night. But she got the impression he wanted her to ask all that, one question at a time, and she wasn't in the mood for the game.

"You won't believe it," he said, pausing. She assumed he was trying to get her to keep pumping him. He couldn't. "They're from Russia. The Soviet Union."

"What are they doing here?" she asked, unable to stifle the question.

"They escaped! They're seeking political asylum."

"What are you doing with them?"

"Hiding them. We have reason to believe the KGB is after them, and the last thing they want to do is be dragged back."

"Start from the beginning, Jim. I don't get this."

"Fred and I were on patrol when we got a call to ten-nineteen the station and ten-twenty-five the captain."

"It's been too long, Jim. Refresh me."

"Return to the station and meet with the captain."

"For what?"

"That's what we wanted to know. I mean, we've got a watch commander, the sergeant. His boss, a lieutenant, certainly doesn't work the graveyard shift. And they want us to come in and see a captain at midnight?"

Jennifer took her gloves off and entwined her fingers, leaning forward toward Jim.

"So we get there, and there's Captain Bram with the lieutenant and our watch commander. We figure maybe we're in trouble for something, you know?"

"*Norman* Bram?"

"The one and only."

"How long's he been a captain? Seems only yesterday he was still a sergeant."

"Well, he was made lieutenant just after you became a columnist, and he was made captain during the new commissioner's shakeup."

"Must be nice. He couldn't have been a lieutenant for even a year."

"Nine months to the day. Anyway, he's all serious and everything—they all are—and he invites us into this training room."

"Not his office?"

"Nope. That big schoolroom-like place where they train cadets."

Jennifer nodded.

"Bram motions for us to pull chairs up around the table at the front of the room, and he sits on the table. By now we're really scared, and I can tell Fred's thinkin' the same thing I am—that we messed up somehow, and royally. I couldn't think of anything we'd done wrong, but I was sure my promotion was down the tubes.

"Bram tells us they've gotten a call from federal agents in Detroit. Seems this young Russian couple—they're not married, but they will be soon—had escaped the Soviet Union through Canada somehow and made it all the way to Detroit. They turned themselves in and were protected by federal agents for a couple of days before it was determined that no one was following them. Then they were freed."

The room was warming, and so was Jennifer. She shed her coat and kicked off her shoes.

"They took a bus to Chicago late last night, and a couple of hours after they'd left Detroit, the feds were tipped that three Soviet diplomats—ones they had been carefully watching for a year—had been seen in the bus station that night."

"The agents think these guys are spies?"

"They thought they might be. But now they suspect they're KGB. Well, they didn't have time to fly to Chicago to protect the kids, so they got hold of the federal office in Chicago, who asked us to protect them for a while."

"While *they* do what?"

"The feds?"

"Uh-huh."

"Handle the KGB, I guess. So Fred and I were told to change into our street clothes and take our own car—we took Fred's—and meet these two as they got off the bus in Chicago. That was easy enough, but they were scared to death when we approached them. We had trouble convincing them we were really American policemen and not KGB until we told them the names of the agents who had protected them in Detroit."

"So, why didn't you take them to the police station?"

"They'd be too easy to find. We were supposed to find a remote, unpopular, and not auspicious place to hole up for a while."

"You sure found it."

"It was the first place I thought of, Jennifer. You know, this is the place you—"

"Yeah, yeah. Where's Fred?"

"Home. He's gonna relieve me in the morning. But there's no way I'm going to sleep, and I knew you'd want to meet them."

"I do, but I suppose everything has to be off-the-record and that if I write anything at all about them, you're in big trouble."

"Nope. Just the opposite."

Jennifer stood. "You're kidding."

"I'm not."

She paced. "We've both been warned, you by your bosses and me by mine. You can't give me scoops."

"This is an exception."

"Why?"

"'Cause Bram says so. Why do you think they just happened to choose Fred and me for this assignment, of all the guys on the street tonight?"

"They chose you for me?"

"You got it."

"Bram has that authority?"

"Right from the top."

"The commissioner?"

Jim nodded, still in a cross-legged position, smiling up at Jennifer. "Apparently, the feds say the best thing we can do for these kids—now that the USSR is on to them—is to make them visible, not to the KGB, but to the public."

"In other words, get some good quotes from them so there would be a real outcry if the KGB tried to say they were coerced or kidnapped or brainwashed?"

"I guess."

"Too good to be true."

"Jennifer, I hope you care as much about them as about the columns they might be worth."

"You know I do."

"No, I don't."

She smiled. "I don't either. But I can be won over. Get them out here. They must be boiling in that bathroom."

"You kiddin'? That's the coldest room in the place."

"Sergei!" Jim called. "Natalya! Come on out!"

Indeed, a cold blast of air greeted Jennifer when the young couple emerged. They both wore short, dark ski-type jackets, jeans, and leather boots. Sergei Baranov was a tall, rangy, bony boy with fair skin and dark hair. His cold, black eyes belied the expectant expression on his face. He seemed genuinely pleased to shake hands with Jennifer.

Natalya Danilin hung back, almost hiding behind her boyfriend. But Jennifer gently tugged the tiny girl toward her when Natalya offered her hand, and they embraced awkwardly.

The girl's eyes were a transluscent hazel, and while her hair was almost a nondescript brown, her long nose, pearly teeth, and full lips made her stunningly pretty, especially when she smiled.

"We would love to talk to you at length," Sergei said, his voice low, his accent thick, but his English perfect. "It means security for us. But we are so tired. We have not slept well. I don't believe we are up to it yet."

Jennifer was glad she hadn't reached for her notebook when Jim first told her she could interview them. "I understand," she assured them. Natalya looked relieved. She sighed.

"As long as I can talk to you before four o'clock tomorrow afternoon," Jennifer said. "We can get something in the weekend papers. And the Sunday editions have the most readers."

"Big paper?" Sergei asked.

"Biggest in Chicago."

"Bigger than the *Tribune?*" he asked, surprising her.

"As of last fall, yes," she said. "The *Chicago Day*."

"New," he said. "News of it has not reached our country."

"It will soon enough," Jennifer said.

THREE

Patrolman Fred Bishop, a thick, balding, forty-five-year-old double divorcé who aspired to little beyond his current job, tapped on the window at ten-thirty that morning. Jim leaped to his feet, his snub-nosed revolver seeming to jump from an ankle holster into his hand.

He peeked through the curtain and unlocked the door. Bishop backed through the door, laden with steaming styrofoam boxes. "Hungry, comrades?" he asked. Jim winced at his crudeness, shushed him, and pointed to the beds. Sergei and Natalya, still in their clothes, lay sleeping in each. Jennifer had been napping on the floor between the beds.

"The smell of the food will wake them soon enough," Jennifer said, greeting Bishop, who pretended to be surprised to see her, yet had known to bring her breakfast. He usually liked to flirt with her, in front of Jim or not, and she was just as accustomed to ignoring him. She hoped Jim would stay around until she was finished interviewing the Russians, but she knew he needed to get home for some rest before standing guard again that night.

The squeaking of the boxes made Natalya sit up, and for a moment she look scared and puzzled. "How 'bout a scrambled egg, Olga?" Bishop asked, displaying a fork full.

She squinted at him and mouthed, "Olga?"

Jennifer scowled at Fred and motioned for Natalya to join them. The tiny girl scooted to the end of the bed, stretched, and let her legs dangle. Jennifer handed her a fast-food breakfast and a small cup of coffee.

Natalya said something in Russian, then realized that no one awake could understand. "Hungry," she said, smiling at Jennifer. Fred laughed loud, and her smile faded. Already it was apparent she didn't know what to make of him.

Sergei rolled onto his back, and Jim stood with another box. But Natalya, her mouth full, waved at Jim and shook her head. "Not awake," she said. Sergei snored.

"He'll be hungry," Jim whispered. "And this won't stay hot long."

"Hot, cold," she said. "Never mind to Sergei. He not sleep well for many nights. He must feel safe here."

"He'd better!" Bishop said. "He's got Chicago's finest lookin' out for the Russian goons!"

Jennifer put a finger to her lips, and Natalya wondered aloud, "Goons?"

"He means the KGB," Jim said. "It's just an expression."

"Goons," she repeated softly. Gobbling her food, she was quickly finished and drank the rest of her steaming coffee in a few gulps. "I take shower?" she asked, rummaging through her backpack for a change of clothes.

Jim nodded, and she headed toward the bathroom.

"You need any help, you let Fred know, hear?" Bishop said, grinning and winking at her. Natalya looked puzzled again, and Jim and Jennifer quickly chastised him.

"What's the matter with you?" Jennifer asked.

"Yeah," Jim added. "This is hardly the time or place or person for that."

"Hey, I was only kiddin', all right?"

"Your humor doesn't translate well," Jennifer said. "How's she supposed to know what you meant?"

"She knew well enough; I think she likes me."

Jennifer rolled her eyes and shook her head. When Jim announced that he was leaving to get some sleep and that he would be back for a seven to three shift, she tried to tell him with her eyes that she wished he would stay. But he simply stood, bent to kiss her, and pulled on his coat as he left.

"Should we bolt the door?" Jennifer asked, but knowing as soon as she said it that she had opened herself to one of Bishop's lines.

"Not unless you're afraid of me," he said, grinning.

"If there's anybody I'm not afraid of, Fred, it's you."

He shook his head and turned back to his food. He started to open the one remaining box.

"If that Russky's gonna sleep through chow, I'm havin' his."

"No, you're not, Fred," Jennifer said. "The boy's going to be starving when he wakes up. Just leave it for him." She stared at him until he put the box back down, but like a child who didn't get his own way, he left it open to get cold. Jennifer stood and bolted the door, then closed the breakfast box and put it next to her handbag.

A few minutes later Natalya emerged from the steaming shower, dressed as she had been before but with clean clothes. Her head was wrapped in a towel, and she was vigorously trying to dry her long hair. "Cold in there!" she announced, shutting the door behind her.

"I should have brought my hair dryer," Jennifer said. "You can never go out in this weather if your hair is even damp."

Natalya looked genuinely shocked. "What surprises you?" Jennifer asked.

"You think this weather is bad?"

"You said the bathroom was cold," Jennifer said. "You must know it's terrible outside."

"This would be mild in Leningrad. You really have hair dryer?"

"Sure. I'll bring it for you next time I come."

"Then I can go out in your terrible weather with my dry hair?"

Jennifer smiled, but Fred Bishop broke in. "You're goin' nowhere, Olga. Least not till we get clearance from the feds."

"Natalya," Natalya said timidly, pointing to herself.

"Whatever," he said.

"Not everyone in America can pronounce three-syllable words," Jennifer told her. "And if you didn't know any better, you might think that because a famous gymnast was named Olga, all Russian girls are."

"Olga Korbut!" Natalya whispered loudly. "You know Olga!"

"Do you?" Jennifer asked.

"Everybody in homeland knows Olga. Not in person, of course, but yes. You know her?" she added, looking at Fred, who still appeared to be smarting from Jennifer's shot.

"Just from TV," he said. "She was big stuff in Munich in seventy-two, right?"

"Olympics," Natalya said. "I remember well because I was nine then. She became big hero."

"You were nine then?" Bishop said, swearing. "I was still married to my second wife then, but it doesn't seem that long ago."

"Long time," Natalya said. "Olga old married lady now. Almost thirty."

"You're kiddin'!"

"I'm what?"

"You're joking," he said. "It's an expression."

"Expression," Natalya said. "Like goons?"

"Whatever. Olga's really that old, huh?"

She nodded. "I teach you say *Natalya*, OK?"

"Nah."

"That's good start! *Na, tal—*"

"Nah! No!"

"Come on! *Tal—*"

"Natalia, OK?" he blurted.

"No, not four, um—"

"Syllables," Jennifer helped.

"Right. Just three. *Na, tal, ya.* You try."

"I don't wanna say yer dumb name. I'll call ya Natalie or Olga, whichever you want. Just quit teaching me."

"Natalie? OK. But not Olga."

"Awright! Hey, when's yer ol' man gonna get up?"

"Old man?"

"Well, he's not yer husband. What is he? Yer lover?"

"Sergei? He'll get up when he's rested."

"Then I'm gonna eat his breakfast."

"Then what will he eat?"

Jennifer and Natalya both looked at Bishop, wondering if he had an answer. He didn't. He just waved disgustedly and turned his back on her, then went to peek out the window. The bright morning sun shone directly into Sergei's eyes, and he stirred.

Slowly he sat up. "Officer Bishop," he said thickly. "Good morning to you."

"Good morning to you too, Stosh."

Before Sergei could react, Jennifer was yelling at Bishop. "Honestly, Fred, can't you call a person by his name once in your life? You've even got your bigotry mixed up! Stosh is a derogatory nickname for a *Pole*, not a Russian. Is Sergei too hard for you? Two simple syllables—*Sir* and *Gee*. Try it."

"Get off my back, Jennifer, huh?"

"Actually, it's more like *Sare Chee*," Sergei corrected her, a twinkle in his eye. It was obvious he was aware of the tension between Jennifer and Fred, and he enjoyed it. Jennifer liked him already. He wolfed down his breakfast and headed for the shower.

"What are you going to be doing while I'm interviewing these two?" Jennifer asked Fred.

He continued staring out the window. "Watchin' TV, I guess," he said. *"Wide World o' Sports* is on, I think."

"That's going to make it difficult for me to concentrate, Fred. Do you have to?"

"What else am I gonna do, listen in? That would bother you too, wouldn't it?"

"Well, yes."

"Then what am I supposed to do, take a walk? I get myself kidnapped, you wind up dead, and Stosh and Natalie'll be doin' hard labor in Siberia by next week!"

"I thought maybe you'd ignore us and read or something."

"Hey, this is *my* gig, not yours. This interview is a favor to you. What I'm doin' is my job whether I like it or not. It's like guarding the enemy."

"Fred! These kids *left* Russia and are seeking asylum here."

"They could be spies."

"Silliness. Spies don't make noise by defecting."

"Hey, Jennifer, why are you on my case today? I always thought we had fun together. What's eatin' you?"

"I've just found you crude and a little prejudiced today, that's all," she said.

"Your man, he's never curt with me. He's always the perfect gentleman."

Jennifer flushed. "Well, I know. And I'm sorry. I should be as nice to you as Jim is. But you're not always the perfect gentleman with me, are you?"

"I try to be. But, hey, you're a good lookin', uh, lady, and any guy likes to have fun with the ladies, right?"

"Well, I'm flattered that you find me attractive, but there are more appropriate ways of expressing it."

"Yeah, well, if I knew more about what was appropriate, I'd still be married, wouldn't I?"

"Perhaps. But I'm sorry, Fred, if I've been nasty to you. I just don't want you giving these kids a hard time, even out of ignorance, OK?"

"So now I'm ignorant."

"That's not what I meant."

"It's what you said."

"I'm sorry."

"That's all right. And speakin' of married, you're next, huh?"

Natalya, who had been pretending not to listen for several minutes, looked at Jennifer.

"Yes, it won't be long," Jennifer told Fred.

"Us too," Natalya said. "Sergei and I want to marry as soon as possible."

"Don't rush into anything," Fred said.

"We are not rushing. We have been promised to each other five years."

"Wow," Fred said. "Maybe you oughta rush into it, huh? Bet you're not a virgin like Jennifer here though, right?"

Jennifer's jaw dropped, and Natalya turned away from Fred, picking up a local restaurant directory and pretending to thumb through it. "You see what I mean, Fred?" Jennifer said. "How can you talk that way to her?"

"Hey, what's wrong with the truth? Isn't that true about you?"

"Fred, my father wouldn't even ask that."

"Why, 'cause he knows better or he's just a classier guy than me?"

"Both."

"See, you're bein' mean to me again. Here I am, all fascinated by this beautiful woman who's still, how to say it, *pure*. And you want to climb on my case."

"For your information, I happen to be a widow. I saved myself for marriage and was faithful to my husband, as I plan to be with Jim."

"Yeah, but in the meantime you've stayed straight—that's what I can't understand."

"That's true, but it's also none of your business. How do you know what I've been or haven't been?"

"Because Jim talks about you all the time."

"He certainly doesn't talk about *that*!"

"Just once, when I was asking him about himself and how a guy his age could still be, you know, inexperienced. He said that it went along with what you two believe. Sounds pretty boring."

Jennifer hated herself for saying it even before it came out: "But then, divorce is boring too, isn't it?"

"Ouch."

"I shouldn't have said that, Fred. I'm sorry. That was cold."

"But a nice shot. I deserved it. I just always figured maybe you *were* a fun-loving type, and who knew what kind of a chance I might have, you know?"

Jennifer shrugged, not wanting to appear to condone his behavior now or previously.

Natalya turned to face him. "And that is why you asked me that question?" she asked, eyes flashing. He winked at her. Jennifer shook her head disgustedly. And Natalya said, "Sergei would kill you."

"With what?" Fred asked, turning away from her. Under his breath he muttered, "A hammer and sickle?"

"You're hopeless," Jennifer whispered, and Sergei appeared, drying his short hair.

"You two up to answering a few questions?" Jennifer asked him.

Sergei smiled and in his charming bass voice asked, "Is that your way of asking if we are ready for two hours of questioning?"

Jennifer nodded. Fred Bishop looked annoyed. Sergei and Natalya sat next to each other on one bed, and Jennifer sat facing them on the other. As she pulled her notepad and pen from her handbag, Bishop dragged his chair over in front of the television, turned it away from the others, found his sports show, and put his feet up.

Jennifer was grateful that the sound was low enough not to distract them. Her new friends stared briefly at each other and held hands, then looked at Jennifer without smiling. They were eager to get started.

"Does the name *Chulkov* mean anything to you?" she began.

"Does it mean anything to us?" Sergei repeated. "They were our models. Our idols."

"And they were from Leningrad," Natalya added. "Tchaikovsky Street."

"You knew them?" Jennifer asked.

"Never met them," Sergei said. "But we knew people who did. We know their whole story. They are why we escaped. How did you know?"

"Just guessing," Jennifer said. "I read about them and wondered, that's all."

"You want their story the way we heard it?" Sergei asked.

"Precisely."

"OK," he said. "And then you'll want ours."

"Right again."

FOUR

"Perhaps you should tell us what you know already," Sergei suggested.

"All I know is what I read from the wire services," Jennifer said. "I tried to reach the Chulkovs by phone in England, but I never got to them. A piece was published out of London, and as I recall, they were a young married couple."

"Yes," Natalya said. "Oleg and Irina."

"And he was a sailor with the Russian navy," Jennifer said.

"Fourth officer on the Soviet cargo ship *Mekhanik Evgrafou,*" Sergei said. "You'll find we know everything about them. *Everything.*"

Jennifer smiled at the young couple. "All I remember is that he stowed her away on his ship, and they escaped to England."

"Oh, it was much more exciting and romantic than that," Natalya said. "They did it for love. The love of each other."

"And is that true with you as well?"

"Yes and no," Sergei said, and Natalya nodded. "We would have done this had we been just friends or brother and sister. We had wanted to leave Russia long before we met. Just like the Chulkovs."

"He actually stowed her away in his own room on board ship, am I right?"

"Yes, yes," Sergei said. "They did not even tell their families good-bye. They were so tired of the special treatment that was reserved for only those who were active in the party and the four and five hours of standing in line for food. The state makes use of you, Miss Grey. Everyone loves the motherland so much and hates the oppression. Everyone wants to flee, and everyone wants to stay. We will miss so much."

"OK. Start at the beginning of Oleg and Irina's story."

Sergei began, "Oleg's mother had been to Britain when he was ten. She was there on a course; she was a teacher. They told her not to return to Russia praising Britain, but she couldn't help herself. She didn't get in trouble for it, but she certainly made her son hunger to see the world. That's why he joined the merchant navy. He saw so much of the world that he knew he must escape. When he fell in love with Irina, he knew he had to find a way to take her with him."

"And he did this how?"

"He only had one place to hide her. Under the bed in his small cabin. There was little more than a foot of space under the bed, and it was taken up by two huge drawers for storage. He smuggled a power saw on board and cut the drawers to half their width, leaving room for Irina when they appeared to push all the way back in."

"How she could stand that for so many days and nights is a mystery to me," Natalya said. "I would not have been able to take it for one hour. People visited his cabin, a maid made up his bed every day, and Irina had to stay there when the ship was in a storm. She could only get out for a short time every few hours."

"It is an amazing story," Sergei said. "When they finally got to England, Oleg told the sailor guarding the gangplank that he could go to bed early because Oleg was not sleepy and would cover for him. As soon as the man was gone, Oleg got Irina, and they jumped to the pier and ran through the rain to the authorities."

Sergei and Natalya were beaming, Natalya on the verge of tears. "We heard and told their story so many times, and we read copies of it that were smuggled in from the West," Natalya said with her thick accent. "No one admits, even to each other, that they envy Oleg and Irina, but many do. And many will try to do as they did."

"How will they do it?"

"The way we did it," Sergei said. "With some variations, of course."

"I'm dying to know," Jennifer said, realizing she had never used that in an interview before.

Natalya looked at Sergei, and he laughed. "Our friends will be shocked."

"Why?"

"They think we hate each other," Natalya said.

"They do?"

"We have pretended to hate each other since we first fell in love."

"I don't understand."

"We met in school. Sergei had moved in from Kiev. All the girls were crazy for him from the beginning."

"But my heart went only to Natalya. Probably because she didn't pursue me."

"All the others went after him, and he ran the other way. I waited for my chance. At last it came."

"When we finally had the chance to talk, someone interrupted, and we ended up arguing. I thought all was lost and that she would never speak to me again. But she started passing me notes."

"How old were you at this time?"

"I was fourteen. He had just turned fifteen. One day we went into the city together, just us two. We went to the park and talked and walked and talked some more. No one saw us. The next day we met again, and we knew something was happening between us. We laughed about how we argued the first time and how everyone thought we hated each other, and yet we were starting to care for each other."

"I had started to care long before," Sergei said. "But now it was mutual. When we got serious, we finally admitted to each other our dreams of defecting. We told no one at school that we were seeing each other, and we never let anyone see us together alone."

"During our first year in love, we came up with the plan," Natalya said. "We had been playing this game, pretending we did not care, just so our friends would not tease us and ask questions. Then we decided to use it to make people believe we were enemies."

"For what purpose?"

"To aid in our escape. So we could leave together with no one suspecting."

"I don't understand."

Sergei explained, "The reason that Oleg and Irina Chulkov had to devise such a plan was because they were in love and then they were married. The state watched them carefully. Oleg could not be at sea when his wife was visiting the West on business. So she had to go with him in that very dangerous manner."

"We could not do that," Natalya said. "My Sergei is not a sailor, and I am afraid of closed-in places."

"Claustrophobic."

"Yes. And so all the while—and I mean for *many* years—Sergei and I played an act in front of everyone, including our families. They all thought we despised each other. And the whole time we were madly in love and had promised ourselves to each other forever."

"I guess I still don't understand how that helped you."

"We had been studying English since our first years in school. When we studied advanced English in later years, no one was suspicious of our being in the same class. We each even convinced everyone that if the other turned up in the same Intourist training program, we would quit. When it happened, Sergei's friends told him to ignore me and not worry. 'So you hate her,' they said. 'So what? Just forget it. She can't hurt you.' Meanwhile, my friends were saying the same things. I told them, 'Do you realize that I might have to travel to another country with that monster? I would not be able to stand that!' And they said, 'Just ignore him.'"

"So you were both studying to be guides for tourists from English-speaking countries?"

"Right."

"And you hoped someone you met would help you defect?"

"No. Too risky," Sergei answered. "Our plan was to travel to other countries on get-acquainted tours and establish that we really couldn't tolerate each other. It worked quite well. The instructors counseled both of us to be sure that we didn't let our animosity show through to the tourists or to our hosts in Britain and Canada. In Britain, Natalya purposely got herself in trouble by not returning to the group on time. I had been so convincing in expressing my dislike for her that I was assigned to find her and drag her back. We almost escaped then, but another girl stayed with Natalya, and we wouldn't have succeeded. Anyway, we wanted to get to America, and we didn't know how we would get there from England. It was a perfect rehearsal for Canada though."

"So you had a trip planned to Canada."

"Yes, about a year later. We were both tour guides in Russia, and we saw each other in public occasionally when we had training or short tours. Without overdoing it, we clearly established that we would just as soon not be associated with each other. Privately, we were engaged, of course."

"And you trusted no one with your secret? No one at all?"

"No," Sergei said, but Jennifer sensed he was holding back.

"We can tell you," Natalya said finally, "but you must not write it."

"Fair enough."

"We each had one very close friend who knew. But they did not know each other, and as far as we know they never told anyone else. We trusted them, and they were just as afraid as we were of what might happen if the authorities had known about us."

"Will they be escaping too, or trying to?"

Both shook their heads. "They have their reasons," Sergei said. "But they will not be coming."

Natalya added, "Now because people know they are our friends, they will likely be questioned about our disappearance."

"And they're probably saying that they always thought you hated each other," Jennifer supplied.

"Probably. But they will not be believed, and they will be watched for a long time."

"So how did you finally make it out?"

"The Canadian trip," Sergei said, "was to be the end of our playacting. We became so good at being terrible to each other in public that it became difficult to remain in love in private."

"But we manage," Natalya said.

"Before we left for Canada," Sergei said, "we heard a heavy speech of patriotism. We were reminded that we had been chosen for the Intourist training because we had been good students, industrious citizens, lovers of the motherland. We were reminded also of the basic tenets of communism and the evils of capitalism. That was when I knew we could wait no longer. We had planned for a long time to escape in Canada, but we had always held out the possibility that something could go wrong and we would abandon our plans. I remember telling Natalya after that meeting that we would go for it all, no turning back, no matter what. We agreed it was worth the risk."

Natalya nodded.

"What so upset you about that last speech?" Jennifer asked. Natalya started to speak, but couldn't articulate it and yielded to Sergei again.

"Basically, we were told why things that might look attractive in the West were not all they appeared to be. And we were told that we were indeed the most free people on the face of the earth. No one could have believed it, but we all sat there obediently."

"How could they pretend that you were free?"

"I don't know. I think it's because they truly believe that the current dictatorship is still temporary."

"Temporary?"

"Yes, that was Lenin's idea in 1917. The dictatorship was to be a temporary government to rule over the landlords and the overthrown capitalists. This was supposed to make the proletariat and the peasant equal and evolve into a classless society. It has never happened. It never will happen. Lenin actually intended for the state as we know it to become unnecessary and wither away."

"Then how would the republic be governed?"

"If it all worked according to plan, there would be no people governing *people,* just people governing things and systems."

"Why didn't it work?" Jennifer asked, looking toward Natalya.

"Don't ask me—he is the history expert."

Sergei smiled. "After Lenin died, there was what looked like very successful economic planning. The five-year plan made for a healthy economy. And then the border nations seemed hostile, even though they might say the hostility was coming from our side. So the power of the Soviet state, it seemed to the leaders, had to be increased. There is a pretense of representative government, but all is done for the sake of the state as a whole. Everyone can vote except those who have been declared insane. And if you do not wholly support the party—"

"—you are insane," Natalya finished.

"Right," Sergei said. "Even though the constitution of 1977 says that citizens have the right to profess or not to profess any religion, atheism is a party tenet. Religious instruction is against the law, so what is the future of religion in Russia?"

"Do you care about that?" Jennifer asked.

"Do we care? Of course, we care! I am not an atheist. Natalya is not an atheist."

"Forgive me, but I thought you would be."

"I understand, but you might be surprised how few true atheists are in the Soviet Union. Some of the party leaders may really believe they are atheists, but most citizens, like Natalya and me, we are agnostics. Thinking people in the Soviet Union do not agree that there is no God just because the party says so. I know many scientists and scholars who refuse to subscribe to atheism."

"Do you know of any Christians in the Soviet Union?"

"Many! Most are Russian Orthodox, but they cause no trouble. The ones we admire are the radicals, the underground Christians, the ones who meet in homes and in the forests, who risk their freedom and their lives, worshiping and teaching their children. How free is a man who cannot teach his children what he believes most deeply? We had to get out. How free were we that we had to flee through deception?"

"Tell me, Sergei," Jennifer said, "what really happened to people who got out of line?"

"People who resisted the government, you mean? Who acted independently, as if they really had the freedoms the constitution promises?"

Jennifer nodded.

"KGB."

"KGB what?"

"KGB is the answer to opposition. The secret police of the committee of state security. They are big, widespread, and have tremendous power."

Natalya pulled her feet up under her and clasped her hands in front of her knees. "Do you know that I had been in love with Sergei for a year before I was entirely sure he was not KGB?"

"You're serious?"

"Absolutely."

"I feared the same of her," Sergei said. He poked her. "And you shouldn't be so sure now, my love."

Natalya laughed a hollow laugh. "Many in Russia do not trust their own families. Anyone can be KGB."

"What can they do to you?"

"The most common punishment for betraying the motherland is hard labor at one of the camps in Siberia. Camps that Russian history will tell you were closed in the nineteen fifties."

"And that's what you risked by defecting?"

"Fifteen years hard labor is lenient," Sergei said.

"How severe can it be?"

"For people like us, in positions of trust and authority, we would have been eligible for death."

"So that was really what you risked."

"Of course. And we would do it again."

"And *how* did you do it?"

Natalya and Sergei looked at each other and then at the dozing Officer Bishop. Jennifer leaned over and turned the TV sound off.

FIVE

"This may make us sound crazy," Natalya began quietly in a delicate, thickly accented voice. "But trying to escape and dying for it would have been better than to go on living in the Soviet Union."

Sergei put an arm around her shoulder. "We had to believe that with all our hearts before we left for Canada, because once we got on that plane, we had no alternative plan."

The young couple told Jennifer how they had all but scripted their lines and actions but, of course, weren't foolish enough to put anything in writing. The plan was that Natalya would act impetuous again in the airport, make everyone wait by being late from shopping, and act frivolous. She pushed it to the point where she was lectured by the group leader.

Once in the air, Sergei went to the leader and recommended that Natalya be returned to the Soviet Union immediately upon their landing in Montreal. "The leader told me he had dealt forthrightly with her and that her discipline was not my concern unless I wanted the responsibility. Which, of course, was *just* what we wanted."

"Why?"

"Child psychology," Natalya said carefully, smiling.

Sergei explained. "Soviet administrators are insecure. They do not like being told what to do by subordinates. They will often do the opposite of what they think you want. We believe it is because they must obey the party and their many superiors, so they protect the little authority they *have* been charged with."

"So how did it help you that the group leader was upset with Natalya, but not upset enough to make her return to the Soviet Union?"

"Well, she was one of the best tour guides, and he knew it. She had never misbehaved while leading a tour in Russia. She was only disruptive when the whole group was together. The leader scolded her for not being serious and responsible enough. She was also warned that she would never get to go on another trip like this one. We thought that was funny, because we knew she would either wind up in America or Siberia anyway."

"Why run the risk that the leader might take you up on your suggestion and send her back?"

"Ah, it was really no risk," Sergei said. "I didn't present it as a request. I presented it as a *demand*. I insisted that she be sent back. That got me in trouble, and I wound up getting lectured too."

"And that was part of your plan?"

"Yes," Natalya said. "Remember child psychology. What do you think our leader planned to do?"

"Tell me."

"He decided to fix us both by making some switches. He put me in Sergei's group so Sergei would be responsible for me and for six others. He knew we hated each other. He wanted to make me behave, and he wanted to get back at Sergei for telling him what to do. He also knew that Sergei would be particularly strict with me, and that would keep me in line."

"Pretty crafty."

Sergei smiled. "We thought so. We had been working on the plan for two years. I can't tell you the number of times we rehearsed our lines, our little speeches to the group leader. He was a very nervous, very stern fellow. He had people to report to, and he had a very sensitive job. Our task in Montreal was to see how Canadian guides handled the many tourists in so many languages. The city itself has two languages you know, French and English. Well, of course, you know. Excuse me."

Jennifer smiled at him. "So you landed in Montreal."

"Yes, and Natalya was wonderful! She pouted, she argued, she giggled, she took other girls running here and there."

"And you?"

"I was cross with her, warning her, threatening her, staying close and keeping an eye on her. I also reported her to the group leader. I was so earnest that he almost took charge of her himself. That was the scariest part, until we actually made our break."

"What would you have done if he had taken charge of her?"

They looked at each other and shrugged. "It simply couldn't happen, that's all. He had too much on his mind. He was frustrated, and we were convincing, but he just looked me deep in the eyes and pointed at me and said, 'You, Baranov, will answer for Danilin. You will see that she behaves in Canada and that she is delivered safely back to the Soviet Union with us. We will deal with her there, and with you, sir, if you do not succeed. We will not be embarrassed. She is *your* problem.'"

"He played right into your hands."

"Right. We spent several days in Montreal, visiting the site where Russian athletes had performed at the 1976 Olympic Games. We toured the city and studied how the guides handled us and the English and French speaking tourists."

"It must have been fun."

"It was horrible," Natalya said. "We could not help but feel pride in the history of our athletes, and the Canadians had obviously been cautioned not to criticize us or our country or government. They were wonderful to us, and it was difficult for both Sergei and me to maintain our hatred for Soviet life, which we needed to carry out our plan."

"You mean you were actually getting a new view of your home country?"

"Yes!" Sergei said. "But we had to keep reminding ourselves that we knew the truth. Each of us feared the other was wavering, and it was difficult not to become emotional at hearing our national anthem every night at various events."

"But we could not talk together," Natalya said. "We could have given great encouragement to each other, but we could not be seen together unless we argued."

"Then you escaped from where? Montreal?"

"No, no," Sergei said. "We wanted to wait until the last day when the group would be heading home and could not wait around to see if we were located. The trip was two weeks. We spent most of the first week in Montreal, then traveled by bus to Ottawa and on to Toronto."

"So Toronto was your spot."

"Right. And as we drew closer and closer, we became more and more nervous. It was very draining. We did not sleep well. We were irritable. I was trying to act irritated with Natalya, yet I was truly irritated with everyone else. I heard them talking among themselves about how Canada was not really that impressive, and how the people didn't seem happy, and how they were really much happier and freer and more productive in Russia. They were lying to themselves! I wanted to stand and shout at them and show them how wrong they were. I wanted to remind them of the oppression, the sadness, the frustration. I know that with a few well-placed questions I could have started many of them thinking about doing what we were planning, but it was not worth the risk. I had never done it before, and I would not start now. Who knew how many KGB might be among our group?"

Sergei had become emotional and stopped to collect himself. Natalya stroked his arm. "People who lead uprisings," she said, "who stir up the passions of others, who urge them to look honestly about themselves and decide if they are really free in Russia— those people are gone. Reassigned. Transferred. Moved."

"Siberia," Sergei said. "Many people joke about it, even in Russia. But it is not funny."

"I was careful as we got into Ottawa," Natalya said. "I did not want anyone thinking that I was unhappy with the Soviet Union. I just wanted the reputation of being flighty and of not liking this beast, Sergei Baranov. If I grew moody and sullen and disrespectful of all authority, I would have been watched even more closely."

"So when the guides got into discussions comparing Canada and the USSR, Natalya argued passionately for Russia. It was very difficult for me, because I wondered if she was trying to tell me that she had changed her mind."

"It was difficult for me too," Natalya said. "Because I was being so deceitful. I wanted to be a behavior problem so they would keep Sergei watching me. But I did not want to be thought of as a traitor, or we would have never had the chance to escape."

They waited, they told Jennifer, until the last day the group was to be in Canada. The group was to fly out of Toronto early in the evening. Each small group was free from before lunch until they had to be back on the bus at five-thirty for the ride to the airport.

"I split my group into four pairs," Sergei said, "just to show them I trusted them. They loved it. They were excited and kept asking, 'Really? Can we really split up and meet back together later?' I told them they could, but that each pair had to stay together. I also told them where I'd be, because that was part of Natalya's and my plan."

"The first thing I did," Natalya said, "was to find out what my partner, Raisa, wanted most to see and do. First, she was hungry. Then she wanted to see the Royal Ontario Museum. That was the best news I'd heard all day. We picked up some brochures that told us how to get to the museum, and we decided to walk. I noticed on the map that there was a shopping mall before the restaurant and also a movie theatre several blocks before the museum. It couldn't have been better."

Natalya told Jennifer that she first talked excitedly to Raisa about their afternoon and how they should find a cute restaurant and take their time eating, then stroll to the museum and spend the rest of the afternoon there.

"Raisa was very excited, and I hated to spoil her fun, but she was simply a pawn in our plan."

"What did you do?"

"Well, I kept talking about food and how we might like some more of the Western cuisine we had enjoyed in Canada so far. I could tell she was really getting hungry, and we located a little place on our map that we decided would be perfect. But I walked very slowly and window shopped for about one hour.

"When we finally got to the shopping mall, a couple of blocks from the restaurant and about half a kilometer from the museum, I begged Raisa to let me walk through the mall. She started getting irritated with me, but I insisted, and she finally followed me through the mall, urging me along. 'I'm hungry, Natalya,' she kept saying. She would have made me hungry, too, if I hadn't been so nervous.

"Finally, Raisa pleaded with me to come eat with her. I told her to go on ahead. She said she did not want to go alone, so I said, 'Well, just a few more minutes then.' Twenty minutes later she was almost in tears and threatened to tell Sergei about me. I told her to go ahead. She waited another ten minutes or so, then told me she was going to tell him. She left. But I did not believe her. I knew she would give me one chance more. I just kept browsing through clothing, and sure enough, she returned. 'Are you coming, Natalya?' she asked timidly. I was cruel to her. I said, 'No, little Raisa. I thought you were going to get me in trouble with Baranov, so I decided to just stay here and wait for him to come and yell at me.'

"'Come on, Natalya!' she said. And I said, 'No! You go on. I'm happy to stay here shopping.' When she left that time, I knew she was gone for good. So I quickly spent almost two hundred dollars that I changed into Canadian money at the hotel. I bought clothes and backpacks for Sergei and me, and on the way out of the mall, I bought sausages and bread."

"So, did Raisa get to you, Sergei?"

"Oh, yes! I had told everyone where I'd be with Alexsandr. He was quite a lover of trains so we were spending a lot of time at the station. Actually I was expecting Raisa much sooner, and as Alexsandr and I sat in the depot restaurant, I was afraid he would notice that I was preoccupied or looking over his shoulder or something.

"But when Raisa finally arrived, I looked genuinely surprised and upset over how she described Natalya's behavior. 'She just wants to shop, shop, shop!' Raisa complained. I suggested that she ask her to compromise and please hurry to lunch and then to the museum. I didn't want to be too quick to offer to trade partners. Raisa assured me that she had tried everything and that Natalya was just being impossible. Inside, I was cheering for her great job and hoping she was getting everything arranged.

"'Can't you go talk to her, Sergei?' Raisa asked. 'It's your responsibility, and I can't get through to her.' I asked her where Natalya was, and she showed me on the map. Just to be certain they would suspect nothing, I said, 'Alex, old friend, do this for me, will you? Run and tell this spoiled girl that she has to go with Raisa, and that I said so.'

"I was so relieved when he said, 'Forget it, Sergei! She's *your* problem!' I said, 'Well, then, would you mind switching partners? I'll go find Natalya and make her behave, and you let Raisa finish my lunch here and then take her to the museum.' He said he'd already seen enough trains for one day, and he readily agreed."

"Which we knew he would," Natalya said, smiling. "It was the plan all along. We could see they had eyes for each other, but they had not declared themselves yet. It was the whole reason for the original pairings."

"Yes," Sergei said, "and to make sure they didn't follow too soon and find us heading another direction, I ordered another sandwich for Raisa. But as I was leaving the restaurant I went back to Alexsandr and said, 'Are you sure you won't do this for me, Alex? I'll owe you one.' He waved me away, and I stalked out with an angry look. 'I'll see you on the bus at five-thirty,' I said. By the time I was out the door and looked back, they were already smiling and talking."

Natalya turned to lie on her stomach and rest on her elbows, facing Jennifer. "By now I was done with my shopping and running toward our meeting place, the bus station. I was lugging two full backpacks, but I was so excited I hardly noticed. I bought two tickets to Windsor and then ran into the washroom where I changed into my Western-style clothes. I sat on a bench pretending to read an American novel with my backpacks next to me, hoping I looked like a Canadian."

"And she did," Sergei said. "I almost ran right past her. I knew she would be there, but the look was so total, the boots, the jeans, the blouse, the jacket. She had even worked with her hair, tied it back or something. But she couldn't hide her tininess or her beauty. I recognized her soon. She tossed me my backpack, and I went and changed. We looked like twins." He laughed. "Except for our height, of course, and the colors of our backpacks."

"That's when we changed our plan slightly," Natalya said. "We were going to change nothing, but we decided that if someone got suspicious and we were reported missing, they would look in bus and train stations and taxi companies and ask if a couple of our description had been seen. We decided to travel separately. On the same bus, I mean, but not together."

"We worried," Sergei said, "that someone would think we looked a lot alike because of our clothes, but Natalya had done such a good job of buying what was popular that we just looked like everyone else. She'd had to memorize my sizes, of course, because if she'd ever been found with them written down, it might have given us away."

"So, you took the bus from Toronto to Windsor, but you didn't sit together?"

"No, and it was difficult," Sergei said. "We almost felt free, but we didn't want to defect in Canada while our group was still there. The KGB has a way of talking authorities into forcing you to at least talk with them. Then they forge a confession and drag you back to your group, announcing that you had your fun and now you're changing your mind."

"So we listened carefully to the conversations around us," Natalya said. "And we tried very hard to sound Canadian, or American, if we were ever asked any questions."

"Did you know the difference between Canadian and American accents?"

"Not really, because we didn't know if the people talking were one or the other," Natalya said. "The only thing Sergei wanted us to learn to say as clearly as possible and without giving away our accents, was 'Canada. Yes. Pleasure. A few days.'"

"That was all?"

"I hoped so," Sergei said. "If they asked us anything else at the border, I didn't know what I'd do. I was afraid that by the time we got there, our bus in Toronto would have been waiting for us for about an hour, and the authorities would already be looking for us. When we got off the bus in Windsor we didn't see anything suspicious, so we took a cab to the border and walked together to one of the crossing stations, trying as hard as we knew how to look like Canadians."

Six

"The cab was easier," Sergei said, "because the driver didn't care who we were or where we were from or how we talked. All he cared about was where we were going and how much he could charge us for getting there."

"Sergei asked him to let us off a few blocks from the border station so it wouldn't look suspicious—I mean our taking a cab to the border and then walking across."

"So," Sergei continued, "we walked up to a station, feeling very self-conscious because we were the only ones in that line who were not in a car. But there were other lines that had people standing in them, so we knew it was all right. We picked the longest line so the guard would be in a hurry to move people through.

"When it was our turn, the guard asked, 'Traveling together?' I said, 'Yes,' and Natalya nodded. 'Born in Canada?' I said, 'Yes,' again, and Natalya nodded. He looked directly at her. 'You too, honey?' he asked. She said, 'Yes,' just as plain as could be. 'How long in the U.S.?' he asked. 'A few days,' I said, trying to emphasize my uncertainty over the time to take his mind off any accent that might slip through. He looked away from us and was writing on a clipboard. 'Business or pleasure?' he continued, sounding bored. 'Pleasure,' I said. The best thing we did, I think, and Natalya was so good at this, was to pretend that we did this all the time. We acted as bored as he did, and we didn't look nervous or worried. 'Have a good time,' he said. I just nodded and smiled, and we walked across."

"Then we went straight to the American authorities," Natalya said. "Sergei told them, very proudly and in his best English—though no longer worrying about his accent—that we were Russian defectors from an Intourist delegation in Toronto and that we wanted political asylum."

"I also told them that we wanted to tell our story before the KGB came looking for us and trying to get us back. We wanted to ensure against any false confessions or crazy stories about our being undesirables or criminals."

"And how did the authorities treat you?"

Sergei smiled at Natalya. "Like dignitaries," she said. "They called in a lot of other people who greeted us like old, welcome friends. They fed us, interviewed us, assured us that we would be protected, and carefully searched our bags. They did ask a lot of questions about our status with the Soviet Union, any friends who might be following us, everywhere we had been, and what we had done since we had been in Canada, and lots of other things."

"They were simply trying to be sure that we were not bad people," Sergei said. "They were impressed with how much money we had; but we had been saving for many, many years. They were very curious about what we planned to do. We said we wanted to be married as soon as possible, and they said that we would at least have to have blood tests first and that there might be a little more processing and checking before we could settle somewhere. I had always wanted to come to Chicago, so we decided we'd come here. They told us we should stay there in Detroit for two or three days while they established that we were not being hunted down and while they saw that we were officially listed as defectors with the proper documents and testimony."

"I'll never forget the day that they told us we were free to go and encouraged us to take a bus to Chicago," Natalya said. "They told us of safe, inexpensive places to stay."

"Sort of," Sergei said, laughing. "Places like this one. Not cheap. Not fancy, but not cheap."

"We sat next to each other on the bus from Detroit to Chicago, and we finally felt free. Scared, but free."

"What were you scared of? You must have thought the KGB had given up on you and that you were fairly safe."

"You never feel safe from the KGB, no matter how long you are away. Anything can happen. But we were most scared of our freedom."

"You'll have to explain that," Jennifer said, scribbling furiously and flipping pages to find blank ones. Officer Bishop's hands dangled at his sides, and his head had rolled to one side.

"With no restrictions," Sergei said, "we almost didn't know what to do. The authorities in Detroit had started the paper work on naturalization so we can someday become citizens. We had temporary work permits so we could get work and be paid. But we realized that when we got into Chicago and found a cheap apartment, all we knew to do then was to try to get married and find work. No one would tell us where to go or not go. No one would tell us what we could do or not do. Few requirements. Just freedom. True freedom. To do what you want, when you want, how you want. We had lost the security of oppression. That sounds crazy, doesn't it?"

"No. I see what you mean. But didn't it also excite you?"

"In a way, yes," Sergei said. "But in another way, it will take a lot of getting used to. It was all we talked about on the bus from Detroit, and that was a long ride. We decided not to circulate each time the bus stopped. Others were getting snacks or buying souvenirs, but we either stayed on the bus or strolled near it. We still didn't want to take any chances. We decided that we wouldn't feel totally free until we were safely in Chicago."

"It was such a strange feeling," Natalya said. "To be on a bus and going to a big city, and the only people who knew were the authorities in Detroit, and with them it was OK. They had advised us where to stay and what to do, but they hadn't commanded us. There were a few things we were required to do, yes, like getting the proper permits and starting our citizenship process, but you see, after that we could do what we wanted. Literally, do what we wanted." She looked above Jennifer's head, as if into a limitless horizon.

"You see why it makes such an impact on us?" Sergei asked. Jennifer nodded. "It's almost as if we have so many things to choose from we don't know where to begin. We decided that when we got to Chicago, we would stay in a hotel for one night and eat there. We understand that at some of the big hotels, like on Michigan Avenue—is that right—?" Jennifer nodded again. "Yes, that the restaurants at the hotels are as fancy as any. We wanted a big American meal and a fancy hotel room. They might even serve the meal in the room, no?"

Jennifer smiled. "Yes," she said, "and in the morning you would have a bill you wouldn't believe."

"How much, in American dollars?"

"Depends on what you had to eat and how nice your room was."

"Say a regular room and a big dinner for two."

"Well over one hundred dollars; maybe two hundred."

"Oh, no!" Natalya said. "We would have been in for a surprise! We have only six hundred American dollars left."

"And you'd better guard that six hundred with your lives because you'll need most of it for a deposit on your apartment. And then you'll have to find work as quickly as possible so you'll have money to live on."

"Sergei can teach history, and I can teach Americans to speak Russian."

"Do you both have degrees?"

"Not actually degrees, but we were both honor students at university and can probably pass whatever test is necessary to teach here."

"Perhaps. And I'm guessing that some colleges here would love to have the real thing teaching their students, degrees or not. You may have to finish your education to get far here though."

"The real thing?"

"I just meant native Russians, who not only speak the language and know the history, but who have also lived there all their lives. And you're both so fluent, really."

"Sergei is better at speaking English than I," Natalya said. "But I will catch up when I've been here long enough."

"You shouldn't have any trouble here. Nothing will be as frightening for you as what you have already come through."

Sergei stood and walked to the window, leaning back against the wall next to it. "That's the problem," he said quietly so as not to awaken Fred Bishop. "We haven't come through it yet. You can't imagine how scared we were when we stood to get off the bus in Chicago and saw your Jim and Officer Bishop standing at the door."

"Did you know they were policemen? They were in plain clothes, weren't they?"

"Yes, but when two serious-looking men are standing one on either side of the door and carefully peering into the face of every passenger, it can mean only one thing."

"Sergei was worried," Natalya said, "but I couldn't see the men over the crowd in the bus. I kept telling him that we were not in the Soviet Union anymore and that unless the men looked like Russian KGB, we had nothing to worry about."

"But when they spotted me," Sergei said, "I could see it in their eyes, and I knew they were talking to each other without looking at each other, which is always a sign. They were saying something like, 'That's him. Where is she? There she is.' I wanted to run out through the back, but there was no exit. And there were too many people behind us. Then I thought about pushing the people in front of us into the two men and trying to just break away through the crowd and see if we could escape."

"In fact," Natalya said, "Sergei was quite upset with himself. Here he had kept his head through the toughest part of our plan, and now he was giving himself away by looking all around and appearing scared."

"Oh, I definitely confirmed our identity in their minds, because I looked at them as if I knew they were looking for us. There was no turning back now, and I was terribly frustrated. If I could have thought ahead a little better, I would have tried to fake my best English and act upset that anyone was trying to detain us. But I had lost my composure, and unless I wanted to create a terrible scene, I knew we'd been caught."

"Did you know they were Americans?"

"Oh, yes. I don't think I ever thought they were Russian. I don't know why. I can tell the difference, I guess. I just didn't think about it. When we stepped off the bus, Officer Bishop identified himself as the Chicago Police and said, 'You're coming with us.' I asked, 'What've we done?' and noticed that Jim—of course, I didn't know his name yet—was giving his partner a dirty look. He said to us, 'If you are Sergei Baranov and Natalya Danilin, we'd like you to come with us for your own protection.'"

"Did that put you at ease?"

"Not entirely, but I certainly could tell that Officer Purcell meant us no harm. I couldn't understand the other one's attitude. It was as if we were being arrested. We were glad that Officer Purcell took over as soon as we got past the crowd and into a little office in the bus station.

"Jim told us who he was and showed us his badge. He told us that federal officials in Detroit had reason to believe we were being followed by KGB, and he and his partner had been assigned to protect us until we had a chance to decide whether we wanted to talk to Soviet authorities."

"Sergei immediately told them that we had decided that a long time ago," Natalya said, "and that he could be sure that we wanted no contact whatever with KGB. He asked how we could be protected from them, and Officer Purcell explained the plan."

"Which is?"

"We would be brought here and protected until federal authorities had time to negotiate with any Soviet officials. We knew what the KGB would do. They would represent themselves as diplomats and try to strong-arm the U.S. into letting them talk with us. They'll make all kinds of threats and try to make it appear as if we have been kidnapped or brainwashed or held against our wills. Our not wanting to talk to them would only make it appear that they were right, but we absolutely refuse to do it anyway."

"Are you afraid of them?"

"Absolutely! It would not be beyond the scope of the KGB to drug us while we are talking with them. They could harm us, take us back, make up stories about us. More than likely, they would come from a private meeting with us with a signed confession and also a written request that we not be subjected to any more harassment from U.S. authorities. They would insist that no one from the U.S. be allowed to talk with us again and make it appear, and convincingly so, that we had requested that ourselves. Then we would be lost. Siberia, or worse."

"Would U.S. authorities stand for that?"

"What recourse would they have? They'd have to embarrass their Soviet contacts and call them liars. By that time, we would be threatened with harm to our families if we did speak to U.S. officials. No, Miss Grey, once we fall into the hands of KGB, or however they represent themselves here, we're as good as back in Russia."

Jennifer took a deep breath and looked at the two young defectors. "Everything we've said here has been on-the-record, except for what you specifically asked me not to print, am I right?"

"Right," Natalya said. "The truth is our best defense. Sergei has been saying that for years."

"Wait," Sergei said, looking deeply troubled. "If it is not too late, and if you are indeed allowing us the freedom to request this, I wish that you would not write what I said about the KGB threatening our families."

"It's pretty powerful stuff, Sergei."

"I know," he said. "And true too. And I know that truth can only help us. But I would hate to give the KGB any ideas. If the word came out of Russia that our families were suffering for our freedom, I don't know if I could live with it."

"There is already much pain involved with our families," Natalya said, and her voice quavered. "We may never have contact with them again, even indirectly."

"They can't write to you? You can't get your address to them somehow? Won't they try to write to you through the international news agencies?"

"No, no!" Sergei said, waving. "They could if they wished, but all mail going in or out from them or to them will now be subject to investigation. But more important, they will have disowned us. In their minds, we will no longer exist. Everyone in Russia is subject to the oppression, but leaving is unforgivable. They will never want to think about us again."

"In their minds, perhaps," Jennifer said. "But do you really believe you will leave their hearts?"

Sergei and Natalya looked at the floor, and then at each other. Natalya began to weep. "I love them," she said.

Sergei stood straighter and turned his back to Jennifer and Natalya, pretending to look out the window through the side of the curtain. Soon his head dropped and he rubbed his eyes with his hand.

"If by any chance anything you write would find its way into Russia," he said with difficulty, "it would maybe be good for us to tell how we feel about our parents, whether they accept or believe it or not. The most difficult thing about leaving was knowing that we were losing them forever. They had nothing to do with our escape, and they had no knowledge of it. Whatever they hear from whatever source, they should believe only what we say to you. My parents hardly know Natalya's parents, and they might each try to blame the child of the other. But we share whatever blame there is to share. Our love and our need for freedom—true freedom—forced us to follow our consciences. You may write that."

SEVEN

This time, Jennifer's and Natalya's embrace was not awkward. Jennifer got the impression that Natalya understood her intentions and accepted her support, her best wishes, her welcome to a new homeland.

Sergei, in what Jennifer thought was a rather transparent attempt to avoid an embarrassing situation, approached Jennifer and offered her his hand, which she gripped warmly. "Will we get to see what you're going to put in the paper before it appears?" he asked.

"No," she said quickly. "That's a policy of the paper and of the reporters too. You'll have to trust me."

"How do we know we can?"

"You don't. You tell me tomorrow, after you've seen it, whether I'm trustworthy or not. And if I am, I'd like to ask you not to contact any other reporters until you come out of hiding."

"You want an exclusive," Sergei said, smiling.

"You're well read," Jennifer said.

"What if other reporters contact us?"

"They won't. I won't give away where you are. I'd have the Chicago Police Department, not to mention untold federal agencies, down on my neck. They want this publicity for you; it makes their jobs easier. Giving away your hideout would only make it more difficult."

"We want the publicity too," Sergei said. "That's why we are forced to trust you, even though it goes against everything I have learned in life."

"But you learned your suspicion in the Soviet Union," Jennifer said.

Sergei nodded. Natalya spoke. "Also, Sergei, you have always been a good judge of character. That's why you didn't care so much for him—"she pointed at Bishop—"from the beginning, but you like Mr. Purcell. And his girlfriend is the same. Can't you tell?"

"Of course, I can," Sergei said. "But Miss Grey also understands my fears. Don't you?"

"I do," she said. "And I'm eager to prove my trustworthiness to you. I'll find out from Jim if I can deliver the paper to you tomorrow myself. By then, they'll probably have come up with a rotation of officers to stay with you, one every eight hours.

"But now," Jennifer said, "I have to get to the office. I normally write my Sunday column before noon on Saturday, even though my deadline is four P.M. My boss will probably be looking for me when he finds out I'm not in yet."

As she zipped up her coat and unlatched the chain lock, Bishop stirred. When she opened the door and the sub-zero wind blew in, he stood quickly, his hand on the revolver at his hip. "Oh, you leavin', Jenn?" he asked. "I musta dozed off there a minute."

Jennifer was right. Leo Stanton, her boss, was on the phone when she arrived, calling his various contacts among her colleagues, asking if they had seen her. "Oh, here she is now," he said. "Sorry to bother you."

Leo stood. He was dressed the way he might be during the week, except today there was no tie or jacket. But the woolen slacks, the Oxford broadcloth shirt, the cardigan, the ever-present unlit cigar, the half-glasses pushed up to his forehead—they were all there. He cursed under his breath. "Where you been, girl?" he asked. "You know I always call Saturday mornings to see what you've cooked up for Sunday."

"I know, Leo, and I'm sorry. But this one is worth it."

"It'd better be. I'm only in here because you weren't. You know I hate to come in on Saturdays."

"I would have called you in anyway," she said, producing her dog-eared notebook. "You won't believe I got this from the cops."

"I'd believe anything. Just tell me you didn't get it from Jim."

She looked up at him with one eye shut. "Well, I did, but it's all right. Trust me."

"*Trust* you? You're not on the police beat anymore, Jennifer. We're talkin' front-page feature column stuff. It's not often the police blotter has the grist for that. You realize you're competing with probably the most famous local columnist in the country in this town."

"No, Leo, really? You mean there's another columnist in this town? How would I know that? I never read the papers!"

"All right, I'm sorry. Get on with it. What've you got, and how am I gonna keep city hall off my back if it's obvious you got this from Jim?"

"It was the brass's idea, Leo. Now sit down, and let me give it to you."

He pointed to a chair and then came around and sat on the corner of his desk facing her. He let his head fall back, and he rubbed his eyes with the tips of his fingers. The pressure loosened the grip of his glasses on his forehead, and when he took his hands away and looked down at her, his glasses slid down and settled on the end of his nose. He stared at her over the top.

Within minutes, Jennifer had him pacing his office. "Dynamite," he said over and over. "It's great! How much space will you need?"

"I can go as long or as short as you want, Leo, but there's a lot here. It's going to take me more than an hour to bang it out if I start right now while it's still fresh in my mind."

He called the production room to check on the first two pages of the Sunday edition. He was assured that a hole had been left for Jennifer Grey's column.

"I don't care about that," he said. "I need room for about twice her normal column on page one and about half of page two for a sidebar and the continuation of the column. Yes, the column will be that long. Send me up a proof of what one and two look like right now, and I'll tell you what can be moved or killed."

Leo turned to Jennifer. "Better get started."

She dumped her things on a side chair in her office and turned on her video display terminal. She began her column:

A young Russian couple defecting from the Soviet Union have chosen
Chicago as their new home. But if the KGB has its way, they could
be living—or dying—in Siberia by the end of next week.

While Jennifer was working, Leo assigned a reporter to write a sidebar for page two,
to run alongside the continuation of Jennifer's page one column. The sidebar would tell
of some of the more celebrated defections from the USSR, including Oleg and Irina
Chulkov and several dancers and athletes.

Little more than an hour later, Leo was thrilled with Jennifer's column. "We'll follow
it up every day next week with more quotes from them, the progress of negotiations
with the Soviets, the whole bit. You have access to them?"

"Sure."

"I can't think of better columns for next week," he said. "Can you?"

Jennifer got no answer on the phone at Jim's, so she decided to go to her own place
and get some rest, hoping to call him at Rasto's during his shift. But when she got
home, her own phone was ringing. It was Jim.

"I was hoping to get to the mortgage company today before I have to go back on
duty," he said.

"The mortgage company? Aren't we all set with the house? I thought everything was
signed and all we have to do is close next month."

"But, Jennifer, if we're not going to even be in the Chicago area, we need to bail out
of this house deal as soon as we can."

Jennifer was silent. It wasn't that they hadn't discussed it. She knew his feelings, his
leanings, his convictions. But she hadn't conceded that it was all going to happen just
the way he said. She had never agreed to quit her job or help put him through Bible
school, seminary, or missionary training.

"Do I have any input on this at all?" she asked finally, weakly.

"Sure, yes, of course you do, Jennifer. But you know how it's probably going to go if
the Lord wants us to do this. Don't you think we should put the brakes on for this deal
and if things change, we can look for another home?"

"Jim, we can't talk about this over the phone. I felt God led us to that house. He was
in that too, you know. You said so yourself. It was a good deal, a good location, the right
timing. Were we wrong about His leading us there?"

"Maybe it was a test, Jenn. He wanted to get us excited about that and then see if we
were willing to give it up for Him."

That didn't sound like the God of order that Jennifer worshiped. Hers wasn't a God of
games and tests. But when Jim was excited about something, convinced about something, wrapped up in something, there was no talking him out of it.

"Jim, I really am not prepared to take this step just now. I think we have time to wait
on the house deal, and if God confirms that this is what He wants for us, He'll provide
the time to get out of the arrangement. Don't you agree?"

"Jenn, what more does He have to do to show us this is what He wants for us?"

She paused, seething. She didn't want to fly off the handle, but she feared the day was
going to come when she would have to either blow up at Jim or push him to blow up at
her. "He has to tell *me*," she said.

"Jennifer! He's telling you through *me!* That's how God works with husbands and wives."

"We're *not* husband and wife, Jim!" she said, knowing how it sounded and wishing she hadn't had to say it. Finally, she had elicited nothing from him but silence. It was the best part of the conversation from her perspective.

"Apparently, we *do* need to talk face-to-face," he said. "And soon."

"That would be good, Jim."

"Oh, Jennifer, don't you see how this assignment of protecting Sergei and Natalya is just further affirmation that God wants me in missionary work? It's as if He brought someone from overseas into my life just to show me the need and the potential and how I could serve Him so much better if I am willing to go wherever He sends me."

"I can see how you might feel that way, especially after hearing the sermons we heard at church last week."

"But you think I'm putting two and two together and getting five."

"I just don't want to discuss it by phone, Jim. This may be the most important thing we ever talk about."

"*May* be? What could be more important?"

"Nothing, I know. And you'll wait on the mortgage thing?"

"I can't do anything without you on that anyway."

"I appreciate that, Jim."

Immediately after Jennifer hung up, she dialed her parents' home in Rockford, Illinois. "Dad, I was wondering if you and Mom might be able to visit me tonight."

"Something wrong?"

"Oh, not really. I just need someone to talk to."

"Well, your mother can't come. She's on some ladies' retreat until late Sunday afternoon. I guess I could make it, unless you thought you could come this way."

"I wish I could, Dad, but I'm on a story that requires I stay around here if at all possible. Does the *Morning Star* still carry my column?"

"Are you kidding? They always identify you as 'Rockford's own Jennifer Knight Grey.'"

"Well, by tomorrow morning you'll know about the big story if you stay there and wait for the *Star.* But if you come in time for dinner tonight, I'll give you a sneak preview."

"I can't pass that up. But Jenny, listen—no cooking for me tonight. You couldn't make me happier than to let me take you out, just the two of us, hear?"

"Are you sure?"

"Never surer. Please let me do this. After next month I may never get to do it again. I'll always have that husband of yours along. And you know I think he's the greatest, but—"

"He's not my husband yet, Dad."

"You know what I meant."

"Yeah, I know. When can I expect you?"

"Well, I'll have to get gussied up a bit here, but I'll leave within the hour. Then give me another hour and a half."

"Sounds good. You may have to wake me with the doorbell or call when you get here. I've been up since about two this morning."

"Good grief, Jenn. Are you sure you're up to this?"

"Up to it? I *need* it, Dad. See you soon."

Jennifer showered and laid out her clothes for the evening, then slept soundly for a little more than an hour. She was awakened by the phone. She was groggy, and she couldn't believe her father could be there already.

"Hello?"

"Jenn, it's Jim. We may have a problem at Rasto's. I just wanted you to know. I called to see how Fred was doing and to tell him I was going to be there a little before seven, but I'm getting no answer."

"Uh, maybe he took them out for dinner," Jennifer suggested, still trying to clear her head.

"No, he knows better than that. Something's happened. We're sending a car over there."

"Did you talk to the people at the desk?"

"At Rasto's?"

"Yeah."

"Well, we kinda didn't want them to know we had three or four people in the room. When we checked in, we just told 'em there would be two of us."

"They could at least tell you if anyone was there when they cleaned up the room."

"That's just it. To make sure not even the maids knew how many people were there, we hung the do-not-disturb sign on the doorknob and called the office to tell them not to bother with cleaning the room today."

"Somebody could at least tell you if Fred's car is still there."

"We'll know soon enough. I'm going over there too."

"You know, Jim," Jennifer said, finally sitting up and thinking more clearly, "Fred was sleeping most of the morning and into the early afternoon, from the time I started interviewing Sergei and Natalya to the time I left."

"He was sleeping when you left?"

"He woke up just as I was going out the door. And he had been inappropriate with both Natalya and me earlier."

"You're kidding!"

"That surprises you?"

"Well, you're just talking about what he says, aren't you, Jennifer? I mean he was just the same old Fred, right? He didn't try anything, did he?"

"No, but I wouldn't put it past him. He's really quite crude."

"You sound like his first wife."

"Thanks."

"No, you know. I mean, she always said that about him."

"Didn't the second one too?"

"Sure. Still does. He knows his shortcomings, but I don't think he means any of it. He's harmless."

"I hope so."

"I'm sure of it," Jim said. "I just hope he's safe."

Jennifer wasn't sure she cared about Fred Bishop's welfare. She knew she should. But she was really worried about her new young friends, and she hoped Fred's irresponsibility had not cost them their freedom. Or their lives.

EIGHT

Jennifer felt so whipped, so dead tired, that she wished she could just lie back down, roll over, and tune out again. But she knew she had to call Leo. Of course, he wasn't still at the *Day* offices.

"Leo, I'm so sorry to have to call you at home."

"Hey, no problem, as long as you're not gonna tell me that the young aliens are phonies or criminals or something."

"None of the above. But they *are* missing."

"No."

"Yup. At least Jim can't get an answer at their hotel room. He's on his way there now. He'll probably be calling me with whatever they find."

"I know this sounds morbid, Jennifer, but it's almost more difficult for us if they find nothing."

"For the paper you mean."

"Yeah. I mean if they find KGB or foul play or whatever, at least we'll know what's going on. But what if someone has simply messed up, the cop maybe?"

"Entirely likely, but I'm worried."

"I can imagine. But if they just don't know where the cop or the other two have gone, we can hardly mention it in the later editions tomorrow."

"Too late to insert something in the column now to say that they're already missing?"

"Oh, yeah, way too late. They're rolling with the first edition right now, Jenn. I mean if we knew for sure they were dead or kidnapped or something, then we might justify stopping the run, but nothing short of that."

"Well, I'm sorry to disappoint you, Leo."

"Jennifer, you know I'm just being realistic. We just don't have enough here yet to hold the run, do you think?"

"I suppose not, but to me that's good news."

"Well, of course it is. You stay on top of it now, you hear? Because as soon as we know anything definite, we'll want to adjust for the later editions for tomorrow. You have a schedule of the press times?"

"Yeah, around here somewhere."

"I just can't see putting something in—not even in the second run—that says that they might be missing. We just don't know that. I agree it's scary and there's no reason they're not getting an answer at the motel room, but it doesn't tell us anything. It could be a phone problem. It could be they've decided not to answer. They could be out to dinner, anything."

"They're not supposed to be out to dinner."

"I know, but that's what I mean about the cop maybe messing up. If we go to press with your great column *and* this dramatic business that they've only been in town a few hours and they're missing already, and later we have to say, 'Oh, they were just at dinner with a cop who blew it,' we're gonna be the laughingstock."

"I know. I'll stay on it, Leo, but I need some sleep. I've been up since two, you know."

"Get what you can while you can," he said. "You'll want to stay as fresh as possible for this one. Let me know as soon as you have something solid."

A few minutes later, when Jennifer realized that she was indeed falling asleep again, she felt guilty. She had a foreboding sense of danger about what might have happened to Sergei and Natalya, yet she was going to be able to sleep in spite of it. That, she knew, was real fatigue.

When Jennifer awoke an hour and a half later to the ringing of her doorbell, she threw on her robe and padded out to look through the peephole. "Come in, Dad," she said, opening the door.

The big, white-haired man embraced her and held the back of her head in his massive hand. "I'll be right with you," she said. "I've got to make a couple of calls first."

"You usually do," he said, smiling, unbuttoning his trench coat and his suit coat and vest before settling down on the couch. "That's why I made the reservations for a half hour from now, even though we're just ten minutes away."

"Where're we goin'?" she called out from the bedroom.

"Ritz Carlton sound all right?" he asked.

"The Ritz? Are you serious?"

"'Course! Nothin' but the best for my girl."

"You didn't have to do that!"

"But you never would've forgiven me if I hadn't."

Jennifer got no answer at Jim's. Nor at Rasto's room 58. Neither Jim nor Fred Bishop could be located by their precinct dispatcher. "Is Captain Bram in?" she asked.

"Matter of fact, he is, Mrs. Grey. How'd you know that?"

"Just lucky, I guess."

"Yes, Jennifer, this is Captain Bram. It's been a long time."

"Yes, it has, Norman. Good to talk to you again. Congratulations on your promotion. I appreciated your thinking of me on this defection case. Of course, you know why I'm calling."

"I do, and I'm afraid we know nothing. Jim and a couple of other men from here should be at Rasto's now, but we're getting no answer by phone or radio. I'll have Jim call you as soon as I hear anything, all right?"

"That would be fine. Could you tell him that if I'm not at home, I'll be at the Ritz Carlton. In the restaurant."

"Oh. A date, huh? Ha! Have a good time."

"It's with my father, Norm."

"I figured as much. I'll have him call you, Jennifer. And I'm looking forward to your column tomorrow."

"Thanks. I'm looking forward to finding Sergei and Natalya."

"Me too."

George Knight didn't act like an out-of-towner. He'd had a successful business for many years before retirement, and he had traveled all over the country. He had been successful. "Not successful enough to retire to some sunny clime," he always said, "after putting a son and two daughters through college. But successful enough."

He wasn't awed by the Ritz. He slipped the maitre d' a few dollars for a very secluded table with a lovely view. "She may be getting a phone call," he told the man. "Will she be able to take it at the table?"

"Certainly, Mr. Knight."

"Her name is Jennifer Grey."

"Yes, sir. I know."

"Oh, ho," he whispered as they sat down. "He *knows!* Did you set that up? Sort of like having yourself paged at the airport!"

She laughed.

They studied the menu for a few minutes. "Say," Mr. Knight said, "since this was your idea and you're planning on seeking a little counsel from your old man tonight, how 'bout lettin' me play the chauvinist, just this once."

She gave him a puzzled look.

"You know, Jenny, I know how far we've come in society and all that, but you wouldn't think it demeaning if I ordered for both of us, would you? I mean, I won't presume to tell you what to eat; I want you to order anything you want. But let me tell the waiter for you, the way I was taught to do it."

"Sure, Dad, if you want to. It doesn't bother me. I want the oysters Rockefeller. And by the way, who taught you to do this?"

"My father."

"Really? I never would have thought Grandpa was learned in the ways of the world."

"Oh, yeah. Just before I went off to college, he and Ma took some of their savings and we dressed up, the four of us, and went to a fancy restaurant in Madison. The Exeter. Doesn't even exist anymore. Looked it up a few years ago. Parking lot."

"The four of you? Aunt Lucille too, you mean?"

"Yup. Lucy would've been in high school at the time, probably a sophomore. Yeah, a sophomore. Anyway, my pa said we were gonna pretend this was a double date, like I might have to endure in college—that was the way he put it. And he coached me for several nights at the dinner table before the big night."

"How'd it go?"

"Frustrating. Lucy was thrilled with it. Neither of us were allowed to date until we went off to college, so this was the closest she'd come to a night out with a guy. I was wanting to cut up and be silly, and that made Pa mad. Lucy was takin' the thing so seriously that she kept trying to tell me what to do and when and how to do it."

"Like what?"

"Letting her out of the car, opening the door, helping her with her coat, pulling out her chair. I'll never forget her sayin', 'George, if you even pretend to pull that chair out from under me, I'll scream! And I laughed and laughed. But you know, it was kind of fun, and I did learn what I was supposed to do. It was only a few months later that I took a beautiful young blonde from Beloit out to dinner. Gal named Lillian."

Jennifer smiled at the mention of her mother's name. "Dad, since you're being chauvinistic tonight by your own admission, can I ask you how you treated Mom early in your marriage?"

After Mr. Knight had ordered and while they were having their appetizers, he tried to reconstruct the first year of the marriage, nearly forty years before.

He admitted, "There was a lot to get used to. For both of us. I guess I was the strong, silent type, or at least I wanted to be. And she wanted me to be too. In many ways, I think she found some security in letting me handle the things a man was supposed to handle. We've changed a lot over the years, but I recall that I made the big financial decisions, and she handled the checkbook. I decided who we would or would not have over to the house, but she served as hostess when they came. I think I saw the inequities in all of that long before the women's movement raised the issues. But I can't take the credit for having noticed it right off or all by myself."

"You mean Mom pointed some of those things out to you?"

"Oh, yes. See, one thing she wanted me to lead in that I ran from was the spiritual aspect. She had always seemed more devout than I was. I mean, I was a churchgoing man, and I was a believer. Even read my Bible and prayed a lot. I prayed before every meal, but that was the extent of my spiritual leadership in the home, 'cept I drove to church, of course."

Jennifer smiled. "How did that change? I always remember you as the spiritual leader."

"Yeah, well, by the time your memory would have kicked into gear, your Mom and me had it out about a lot of things."

"A fight?"

"Naw. Never. You know better than that. I worship the ground she walks on. I could no more have a fight with your mother than stay mad at you when you were a stubborn high schooler with the temper of a sailor."

"So how did you have it out?"

"She just told me that there were some things she had to know, some things we had to get straight, for her own peace of mind. Boy, I wish she was here tonight to tell you what led up to that. She's got a good memory, you know."

"I know."

"Well, all I remember about it is that I was real hurt. I was hurt deeply because I could see what I'd done to her. I hadn't meant it, and she knew that, and she said that, very clearly. That helped, but not much. It was such an effort for her to say anything critical of anybody at all, especially her own husband. And I hated myself for whatever it was I had done or not done that had driven her to the point where she had to do that. It was as painful for her as for me, I think, and that's what hurt."

"Hard to talk about, huh?"

"You bet. I don't believe I had ever cried in front of anybody since I was about fourteen and learned that my cousin had drowned over in the Rock River. I was the tough guy, you know. But I hated to see a woman cry. Still do. But no one can get to me with tears the way your mom can. Not that she'd ever use crying just to make a point. Never. She's not so quick to cry herself.

"But when she was carefully and lovingly trying to tell me what she needed more of from me—and what she needed less of—well, that made her cry. And it made me cry too. We haven't cried together more than four, five times in forty years, but we cried that afternoon. Hot, Sunday afternoon. We cried when she miscarried between Drew and you. We cried when you left home for good. We cried when we heard about Scott. And when Tracy made high school homecoming queen, we cried for happiness and pride."

"So did I," Jennifer said. "Dad, I need to know what Mom talked to you about that day. I have to sort out how Jim and I are going to relate to each other. I want to be a good wife. I want to be a biblical wife. I want to be submissive and let him lead in a spiritual sense, but I have to know what that means. Where it starts and ends. What I have to say about anything."

Her father fell silent and studied her before responding. "Times have changed so much," he said. "What was appropriate forty years ago may be the opposite of what you'd want or expect today. While your mom needed me to take more of a leadership role in what I thought were women's things—like church and devotions and stuff—you may want to play a bigger role in that yourself."

"But the Bible doesn't change, Dad. Who did I learn that from?"

"I never got the impression you learned it, Jenny, but I confess I hammered you with it constantly."

"I learned it. And you know something? You're still the only person in the world I let call me Jenny."

"Honest?"

"Absolutely. Anybody calls me that but you, I correct them."

"Even Jim?"

"It's never happened, but I would. 'Course he calls me Jenn the way no one else can say it."

"Is the reason you correct everyone because you really don't like the name Jenny and you wish I wouldn't call you that either? You're just afraid to hurt my feelings, right?"

"Wrong. I'll never be anybody else's Jenny, that's all."

"I love you, Jenny."

"Thanks, Dad. I'm glad. Because I have a serious problem, and I need your help."

Nine

As the dessert dishes were removed, Jennifer finished her story—the whole thing, Fred Bishop and all. Her father dragged a linen napkin across his mouth and let it drop to the table before him. He entwined his fingers under his chin and studied his daughter without speaking.

On his face she read deep concern. His brow was knitted, his eyes narrow, his jaw set. As was his manner, he thought a long time before he spoke, and he started with memories that took him back to long before the last few weeks.

"When you were a little girl, I worried about you. I wanted to see a happy face every time I looked at you. You had a smile that would melt ice, but you were independent. You were a thinker. You were a doer. You had justice in your head, and things had to make sense to you.

"You had to have reasons for things. You were never simply happy for no good reason. If you were smiling and bubbly and up, it was because you had seen or heard or done or realized something. If you were happy, I could ask you why, and I would get an answer.

"You felt things deeply, as deeply as an adult by the time you were nine or ten years old. You and your sister were every bit as beautiful as each other. Only she was a people person, eager to make other people happy whether she was happy or not. That made her more popular, more noticed. But I told you the night she was named homecoming queen that you could have won it hands down three years before if it had been your goal. I meant it, and you knew I was right.

"But your priorities were somewhere else. I loved the simplicity of your faith. You questioned the things you didn't understand, and you questioned my explanations for things you didn't think I understood either. And when I admitted I didn't have all the answers, it was no surprise to you, but you were content to trust God and accept by faith that He knew better than we did and that He was trustworthy."

He paused and waited for the smile of recognition that would tell him Jennifer saw the connection between his memories and her encounter with the too-soon grown up Russian boy. "Sergei had to trust you because he had no choice," her father said. "I wish I could see the look on his face when he reads your column tomorrow. Remember it for me, will you, and share it with me someday?"

She nodded, unable to speak.

"Ah, Jenny," he said, picking up his napkin again and twisting it in his hands. "I'm out-of-date. I'm a broken-down old businessman who raised a son and two daughters the best he knew how. I'm tired, but I'm happy, and I'm proud my kids turned out the way they did. Who but Drew could endure the woman he married?"

"Dad!"

"I know. I'm sorry. But she's so obvious it's not even a judgment call. You know I love Francene. Two, three days max, is all I can take at one stretch, but she's a good mother and a good wife. But I was talkin' about Drew. I was trying to make a point about him."

"I know. But Francene thinks the world of you, Dad. It would crush her to know you think she's a nag."

"Did I say that? See, I said nothing about her whiny nagging, and yet you knew what I meant."

Jennifer laughed. "You're terrible."

"You think I'm terrible? Wait till you hear what I think of Tracy's airhead boyfriend."

"Dad!"

"Is that the right use of the term? She uses it herself."

"Not for him, she doesn't," Jennifer said, shocked at her father's uncharacteristic bluntness. "I don't remember the last time I heard you badmouth anyone."

He smiled a knowing smile at her. "Gotcha," he said.

"I don't understand."

"Yes, you do. Or at least you *will,* soon enough. I set you up. I stepped out of character. I let you hear how it sounded when I not only talked behind backs, but hit close to home. You'd have been surprised, but a little less shocked, if I had talked about someone else. I could have agreed with you about Fred Bishop. But I don't know the man. I suppose you have the right to complain to me about someone I don't know and whose reputation can't be hurt by your telling the truth about him. But when I start talking about people you know and love, that shocks you. That hurts. How would you have felt if I had said that Fred Bishop sounded like a real louse?"

"I probably wouldn't have given it a second thought, but I still don't know what you're driving at."

He reached across and gripped her wrist gently. "That's all right. You're tired, and have a lot on your mind. What I'm getting at is this: You're not prepared for me to speak the truth even about your brother's tiresome wife or your sister's spacey boyfriend."

He stopped to let it sink in.

"And so," she said, getting the point, "you're not about to speak against my off-the-deep-end fiancé, even if you agree with me."

"Right on the button."

"You're no help."

"In a way I am. You don't hear me defending him, do you?"

"Then you agree with me? He's being unreasonable?"

"No comment."

"Oh, Dad!"

"Not on your life. I'll listen all you want, but my opinion is you're going to marry this guy, and I don't want to go on record saying anything against him."

"So if you can't say something nice about someone, you won't say anything at all. So why should I marry him?"

"Are you wavering?"

Jennifer's eyes filled with tears, so suddenly that even she was shocked. "I'm tired," she said.

"I know," he said, gently stroking the back of her hand. "Maybe you shouldn't think about this tonight."

"That's the problem, Dad. I *have* to think about it constantly. It isn't like I have a choice. And I'm worried about Sergei and Natalya too. What's happened to them and to Jim? Why hasn't he called?"

"Then, while you're spending the last of your energy worrying and wondering, answer my question."

"Am I wavering on whether to marry Jim? Yes!"

Mr. Knight looked at her with compassion. "I'm sorry to hear that," he said. "May I speak in his favor?"

"Of course."

"He's a fine young man. Honest, sincere, spiritual, in love."

"I want him also to be sensitive and caring."

"If he's not, it's temporary."

"How can you know, Dad?"

"It's out of character for him to be insensitive to you, is it not?"

"Well, yes. But how do I get him to snap out of it? Especially when he thinks he *is* being sensitive. He sees himself as my spiritual guardian, with authority over me."

"And you don't like it."

"No, I don't. But is that just because I'm stubborn and independent? Is that why you brought all that up?"

"That wasn't all I brought up. I also talked about how thrilled I was that you were a thinker and that you thought for yourself. Even if your husband is to have spiritual headship over you, that doesn't mean you leave your brain at the altar. If Jim thinks he can run a marriage and a family and a household without an intelligent, contributing wife, he's going to come to a sad realization."

"Dad, I don't *know* that God hasn't called Jim to be a missionary."

"Of course, you don't. Do you know that God *hasn't* called you?"

"I don't feel a call, but I don't know that you're supposed to feel anything when God calls you."

"Then how does one know? One must feel or sense something. God must impress it upon one's heart some way, Jenny."

"That's just it. Jim thinks God is using *him* to call me. The soon-to-be-husband has been called, thus the soon-to-be-wife is along for the ride."

"But you feel fortunate that it happened before you were married because you feel free to decide for yourself."

"I guess."

"And if Jim insists on this and doesn't give it up, the marriage is off unless you feel God tells you otherwise."

She nodded, but didn't speak.

"And what if it had happened a week or a month or a year after you were married? What would be different?"

"That's what I'm afraid of, Dad. Will I magically change overnight when I'm Mrs.

James Purcell? Will I not worry whether I feel the calling, as long as Jim is in tune with God?"

George Knight was not in the habit of answering rhetorical questions. He pressed his lips together and displayed both palms to her.

"Dad, this is what has me so torn up. I feel that because this happened now, I was saved by the bell. It's as if I grabbed the last twig before I fell off a cliff. I'm sitting here wearing this diamond, and yet I feel it means nothing. I'm safe, I'm free, I'm not married. If I were married, I'd be trapped, in trouble, no option."

"You'd have an option."

"Divorce is not an option, Dad."

"Of course, it isn't. But you have the same option your mother had. You could sit down with Jim and tell him, as painful as it would be, that there are some things that have to change for the sake of your love, your sanity, your life, your future, your marriage."

"Mom said that to you?"

He nodded. "Is your marriage worth that, or are you just so relieved to have not tied the knot that you're going to throw it away because of a temporary lapse in Jim?"

"You agree it's *his* problem?"

"Jennifer, I'm not going to get into that. I'm just speaking from your perspective. You think he's wrong in this."

"I think he's wrong for me. I can't speak for him."

"Yet he's trying to speak for you."

"That's it! That's what I can't handle."

"You've prayed about it, thought it through, sought the Lord on it? You don't feel God is calling you to follow Jim in this?"

"I don't."

"And thus you feel that's a sign you shouldn't marry the man?"

"What else can I think? He's not reasonable, even if he is right. The way he presents it makes me want to run the other way, and he's not hearing me, not even listening."

"That sense of commitment and purpose is something you've always admired in him."

"I know, but it's never been directed *against* me before. And that's how I feel, that we're suddenly adversaries."

"You are."

"I know. But am I fighting Jim, or am I fighting God?"

"Do you feel you're fighting God?"

"No, but if I were married, I'd feel I was."

Her father rubbed his ruddy face with both hands, and Jennifer felt bad for keeping him from getting back home. "Jenn, I agree with you that when you're married, you're going to have to work in harmony with Jim, but I really wish you'd see the spiritual headship issue as a last-ditch defense against stalemates. When you're at loggerheads, and you're married, trust God to lead you through Jim. Otherwise, campaign for your opinion. Not for your rights or your position, but for your judgment. You deserve input, and you'll deserve it as much or more then as you do now."

"Dad, my feeling right now is that if I had a heart-to-heart talk with Jim and he was in the same frame of mind he's been in for more than a week, I'd have to tell him that the wedding is off. If God called me to follow Jim or join Jim in missionary work, I believe I'd go. Jim will tell me that God is calling me through him, and I would say I was sorry but I didn't think so, and that would be the end of the relationship. I just know it."

"Then so be it."

"You mean that?"

"What's the alternative? You give in because you want to marry him, leaving the core of your being at the door, and you give up not just the things you like and want, but the things you feel God has entrusted you with."

"My job, my town, my friends, my church, my responsibilities."

"Right."

"But isn't that what I'm supposed to be willing to give up when I marry?"

"I won't even attempt a guess."

"Dad, I need help, not therapy."

"And I need therapy," he said. He could always make her smile.

"Just tell me you don't think I should get married in my present state of mind."

"I think that's obvious and safe to say."

"So one of us has to change viewpoints."

He cocked his head. "I'd hate to see you make a mistake, Jenn, the way you're think-ing. More important, you have to realize this issue could come up again when you're married, and you'll have just as much right and duty to get Jim's attention then as now. Maybe more so. You'll owe it to him."

"Is that it, Dad? Is it a matter of getting his attention?"

"Sure sounds like it."

"Will telling him the wedding is off get his attention?"

"Would that be the only reason you'd say it?"

"No. You know I'd mean it."

"I think you know the answer."

The waiter brought a cordless telephone. "For you, Miss Grey," he said. "And for you," he added, handing the check to her father.

"Jim?" Jennifer said.

"No, Jennifer, this is Leo. Listen, Bram didn't think it was worth bothering you with, but the story is this: Jim and an associate found no one in the room at Rasto's but followed a suspicious car into Indiana, outside the range of their dispatchers. That's why they were unaccounted for until just a little while ago. They finally pulled the car over and discovered three Soviet diplomats who denied having been in the parking lot at Rasto's when the officers arrived. Jim and his partner, guy name of, uh, Carling East-man—you know him?"

"Sure. Jim's watch commander, a sergeant."

"Yeah, anyway, he and Jim know they followed this car from Rasto's and, of course, suspect these boys are KGB. But now they're in the middle of a hassle, with the diplo-mats claiming they've been harassed. They're all back in Chicago now and are scheduled for a meeting on Monday in the federal court building with some real mucky-mucks."

"So, where do they think Sergei and Natalya and Bishop are, if not with the three Russians?"

"That's just it. Bishop shows up at a South Side precinct station with a story about the young couple telling him they didn't want his help anymore and making off with the keys to his car. Crazy thing is, he still has his weapon. Why he couldn't overpower a couple of young people is beyond me."

"He was probably sleeping. Sounds phony to me."

"Well, me too, Jennifer, but I don't know what to make of it, and we kind of have to go with his story, whether we imply we believe it or not."

"Believe me, we'll imply that he was irresponsible and sloppy in his technique, at least. Any lead on where the defectors are?"

"Your fiancé thinks he and Eastman were led on a wild goose chase to throw them off the trail. He thinks other Russians, maybe KGB, have already spirited them away. The three diplomats, though, have indicated to somebody at the fed headquarters that they're going to accuse the police of kidnapping the two. Should be interesting."

"What do you want me to do, Leo?"

"Get some sleep. Then enjoy your Sunday. I'll knock out a few update graphs to carry us through the late edition. If you get onto anything late tomorrow, I can take a last-minute column by midnight and make the Monday first edition."

"I should hope we'll have something by then. If nothing else, the story of the scheduled diplomatic negotiation."

"I hope we know where the kids are by then," he said.

"I'll be spending time with Jim tomorrow; I'll get what I can."

"He's a little nervous about your date tonight, Jenn. Bram told him you were out with your father, but Jim said he would have known about that."

The waiter hovered as if to suggest that Jennifer was taking too much time on the phone. "Do you need this?" she asked him, covering the mouthpiece.

"When it's convenient, ma'am," he said, meaning, "Yes, as soon as possible."

"I *am* with my father, Leo," she whispered into the phone. "It was a spur-of-the-moment thing. Don't worry about it; I'll straighten it out with Jim when he picks me up for church tomorrow."

TEN

"Hoo, boy," George Knight said, settling heavily onto Jennifer's living room couch. "I ate too much. Always do in places that charge like that."

"I did too, Dad, and I'm exhausted. More important, don't let me keep you from getting home before midnight."

"It's already too late for that."

"I mean, I appreciate your coming and spending all this time and—"

"Then let me give you one more reaction, Jenny. Then I'll be outta here so we can both get some shut-eye. You know better 'n anybody that I'm no psychologist—but Jim is under a lot of pressure. He's got a lot of changes coming. He's going to change ranks, change life-style, be responsible for two people. My business partner used to tell me not to count on anything of any substance from an employee who's within two months of marriage. They tend to go stir crazy."

"So he's crazy?"

"Only temporarily."

"But what if he doesn't snap out of it?"

"That's your problem," he said, not unkindly.

"How well I know."

Her father stood and reached for his coat. "All I'm saying," he said, "is that you have to attribute some of this, at least, to the fact that he's nervous—maybe without even knowing it—about getting married. He's probably questioning his own ability to take care of you, to lead you the way he knows he should, and he's probably scared to death that you aren't sure he's up to it either."

"But I was sure of it until this."

"Then he may be testing you. He may be forcing you to decide if you really trust him."

"You mean like God with Abraham and Isaac?"

"Yes, except I don't think Jim is doing this on purpose."

"So what should I do?"

"If you agree with that assessment, it gives you an option besides having it out with him or telling him the wedding is off. You can tell him that you're so convinced that he's trustworthy and that he loves you as much as he says he does, and that you're so sure he loves God and will continue to seek His will in this, that you'll cast your future with him, trusting him, by God's grace, to do what's best for you as well as for himself."

Jennifer sat down. "That would have sounded so good and so right two weeks ago, but I sure wouldn't be able to say that now, at least not until after a good night's sleep and a lot of prayer."

"But isn't it what you really want to do when you get married, to cast yourself and your future with your husband?"

"Sure, but you have to really feel it, believe it, and mean it."

Jennifer slept long and soundly and was up an hour before Jim was to pick her up for church. While rested, she was nervous. She opened the door as soon as she heard his knock, and for some reason, she sensed it was the old Jim who stood there smiling at her.

She had hoped to start the day off by establishing a bit of cool distance between them. She was going to be cordial and pleasant, but not affectionate or warm. But Jim seemed so much like his old self that she couldn't help responding to his kiss of greeting.

His eyes were alive; he was attentive to her. He seemed to listen and to hear. "I have good news for you," he said. "But it'll have to wait for after church."

During the ride north he reached over the back of the seat to pull the Sunday *Day* from under his Bible.

"I didn't even have time to peek at mine," she said, quickly scanning her column and the sidebar on pages one and two. She liked how it had come out. It was a first edition, so there was no mention of Sergei and Natalya's disappearance.

All during Sunday school and the worship service, Jennifer prayed that her hunch was right: that Jim had seen the error of his thinking and that he was at least going to discuss such major decisions with her. Somehow, she hoped, he had snapped out of the emotionalism that had driven him for the past several days.

He was vocal during Sunday school and outgoing after church, greeting people and interacting with them in his usual manner. He beamed when people complimented Jennifer on the exclusive story they had seen that morning.

At lunch she told him she could wait no longer. "What's the news?"

"Well," he said with a twinkle. "All is not as it appears."

"Deep," she teased. "Shall I write it down?"

Jim suddenly grew serious. "There are things I can tell you and things I'm going to tell you even though I shouldn't. Everything has to be off-the-record until we've discussed it; then we can decide what you can use and what you can't."

"You mean the good news you were saving for me is not *personal* news?"

"In a way it is. On the whole, no, it's not."

Jennifer was curious because he was obviously sitting on something hot. Yet she held out hope that his seeming reversion to the old personality might mean that things between them would improve too.

"OK," she said simply.

"I have been in contact with Sergei and Natalya."

"Since when?"

"Since early this morning."

"Where are they?"

"We have them in custody. They're safe and hidden. I might be able to take you there, but we have to talk first. Very, very few people know we have them. The Russians are going to be accusing us of having kidnapped them, and if it gets out that we *do* have them, it would be hard to explain."

"Start over, Jim, please. How did you get in touch with them, and what's their story about leaving Rasto's?"

Jim looked over her shoulder and out the window of the small restaurant. Jennifer felt the chill from the window on her back and pulled her coat collar up to drape it around her shoulders. "This is *really* off-the-record," he said.

"Jim, you're talking to your fiancée, not Dan Rather."

"Jenn, I know. But I have my instructions, and we were the ones who put you onto this story. Now we have to keep control of it."

Jennifer wanted to scream. What he said went against everything she had ever learned or had ever been taught about journalism. Sure, the cops had given her this story. But there could be no strings attached. That's why the later editions of that day's paper would carry hints that regardless of what happened, Fred Bishop was not without implication for some of his incompetencies.

"Meaning?" she said evenly.

"It's just that in exchange for our having given you the scoop, we need assurances that some of the other things you come across may be less appropriate for publication."

Jennifer set her fork down and stared at him. She was sure she reddened. "You sound like some bureaucratic windbag." His eyes narrowed. "I'm sorry, Jim. I hate to talk to you like that, but I hate worse your talking to me like I'm some business associate. Speak English, and remember who you're talking to."

Jim appeared shocked. Jennifer knew she was using the frustration that had built up over their personal problems to load her artillery for this battle, but she felt it was worth it. When Jim spoke again, it was obvious she had gotten to him.

"Well, uh, Sweetheart, you know I've been told to say that."

"Well, then say so. You only guessed that you were chosen for this assignment with Sergei and Natalya because of me, and now it's very clear that that was the case. So don't pretend to be one of the engineers of it. All of a sudden it's we/they, and it makes me nervous. For one thing, I never agreed to any strings attached to the exclusive interview. Maybe you ought not to tell me where you have the two hidden if the extent of your generosity was one Sunday column."

"That's just it, Jenn. We want you to keep writing about it; I mean *they* want you to keep writing about it. But you can see that some of the information necessarily has to be, ah, colored, or uh, slanted—what am I trying to say?—*manipulated* to help us in our negotiations."

Jennifer pushed the uneaten half of her meal away and sat back with her arms folded. Jim looked sheepish, as if he wished he'd remembered not to use "we" for the police brass when he meant "they."

"Since we're still off-the-record, I have a few questions for *you*," she said, using her most professional and unfriendly tone. "Did you know where the two defectors were when you spotted the Russians in the parking lot at Rasto's and chased them into Indiana?"

"We didn't chase them; we followed them."

"Then why didn't you pull them over where you had jurisdiction, not to mention radio contact?"

"When you're working under the auspices of the United States government, you have jurisdiction anywhere inside the continental United States—Hawaii, Alaska, the District of Columbia, and any U.S. territories."

"You sound like a bureaucrat again, Jim."

"I'm sorry. So do you."

"Are you going to answer my question?"

"I must have missed it."

"Did you know where Sergei Baranov and Natalya Danilin were when you were chasing—excuse me—*following* the Russians through one of the United States' many territories?"

"No."

"How did you know the car you were, ah, following, had KGB agents in it?"

"We didn't. We still don't. They could be diplomats without being KGB."

"And I'm the Easter bunny."

"Sarcasm doesn't become you, Jennifer. It was a rented car. It contained three middle-aged males in dark suits. When we pulled in at Rasto's and ran up to the room, the car pulled away to another location in the lot. That's when we decided to approach it and question the occupants."

"And they said, 'Follow us'?"

"Hardly."

"They pulled away."

"Yes, but not fast."

"So you were following, not chasing."

"OK! At times they appeared to be trying to lose us on the Dan Ryan and the Skyway. So following might have been described as chasing at that point."

"Didn't the fact that they were apparently unaware that Sergei and Natalya were gone lead you to believe they had not abducted them?"

"We didn't know what their involvement might have been. We thought maybe they had taken them, or that some of their associates might have and that they were assigned to see who came to check it out."

"Oh, come on, Jim. I'm not even a cop, and I know that if Russian agents were sent to stake out the site of a kidnapping where a policeman was still there, they're going to be so careful and so secluded that they wouldn't be recognized by the first car that appeared. They had to be staking out the place without knowing that Sergei and Natalya had already left. They were probably hoping to follow the Chicago PD if they tried to move the two somewhere."

"Maybe."

"Did you know where Sergei and Natalya were when you talked to Leo last night?"

"While you were having dinner with your dad—thanks for telling me—no. I didn't know where they were then."

"But you did promise him you would let him, or me, know when you did find them."

"I probably did."

"And does he know?"

"No. but you're about to find out, if you're still with us."

Jennifer shook her head slowly, not taking her eyes off Jim's. "You still don't get it, do you? I'm *not* with you. I must have independence. I must retain some credibility. Why do you think the paper has the policies it has, and why do you think I have never been allowed to get leads and tips from you before? It's not a you-scratch-my-back-I'll-scratch-yours arrangement, Jim, and I deeply resent it if you or Bram or Eastman or anyone thinks it is."

Jim shrugged. "I don't like to fight with you, Jennifer. I'm not trying to be difficult. The fact is, we know where the two kids are. We're protecting them. We don't want the Russians to know we have them again. You see why?"

"I can guess. I'm just glad to know the disappearance wasn't staged and that the newspaper wasn't used to publicize that for the sake of negotiations."

"It wasn't. And I know now how you're going to feel about this, but what I've been driving at is that we would like to go into tomorrow morning's negotiations under the guise that we have not only not 'kidnapped' Baranov and Danilin, but also that we have reason to believe the Russians have them already. It would scramble their brains and give us the edge in the negotiation."

"I can confidently speak for Max Cooper and Leo Stanton and the *Day,* Jim, you know I can. And I'm telling you, we would not be used for such a purpose, as patriotic as we are and as interested in justice and fair play as we are."

"That's it?"

"That's it."

"You aren't curious to know where they are, how and why they left, and what Bishop's story is?"

"I'm *dying* to know, but if I can't use it, or if I'm asked to publish something else, I won't. Oh, I wish I had never gotten into this mess. If I had known before I went out in the middle of the night, I'd have never gone to Rasto's."

"You know I couldn't tell you over the phone."

"Of course, Jim, but you could have told me before I interviewed them that the police brass was expecting me to play the shill."

"I didn't know that at the time myself," he said. "And I'm not so sure of it now."

"What would you call asking me to slant the story for the sake of the negotiations? Journalism?"

He didn't reply.

"Jim, off-the-record, as a friend, as my fiancé, no obligations, tell me the rest of the story. I will not write it your way, but I won't write it at all either, if you insist."

"I'm still your fiancé? The way you were looking at me, I wondered how long that would last."

"We need to talk about that, but first, tell me where Sergei and Natalya went, how and why."

"We need to talk about our engagement, but first you want the story? That makes it kind of hard to concentrate, Jenn."

"I know. I'm sorry. I shouldn't have said that way. Forget that for now."

"But we will talk about it?"

"Of course."

"All right. According to Sergei, Bishop got fresh with Natalya."

"Oh, no."

"Yeah. I guess he didn't really try anything, but he was much more suggestive verbally than he had been even when you were there, and Sergei threatened him. They almost came to blows."

"Bishop admits this?"

"No."

"You know it's true, though, don't you Jim?"

"I believe it's true, yes."

"That's a relief. What's Bishop's story?"

"He says Sergei drugged him by putting something in a drink and that when he woke up several hours later, he discovered they had taken his keys and his car."

"Where was Sergei supposed to get a drug or a drink?"

"Well, *nobody* believes that story, and when we found American whiskey in the room, we knew Bishop had run out for it himself. Sergei's story is that he was so upset with Bishop that Bishop was apologetic and wanted to make it up to him. Sergei said he missed good Russian vodka and that they should share a drink. Of course, Bishop is in big trouble for leaving them, but he admits now that he ran out for some booze and that Sergei, or Natalya, must have put something in it.

"Sergei says that he and Natalya just sipped the booze and pretended not to like it, meanwhile, continuing to fill Bishop's glass until he had drunk several glasses. Then they were just silent and let him talk, and nod, and doze off again. Apparently he collapsed in his chair, and when they took his keys, he didn't even stir. We think Bishop even slept through our phone calls."

"How did Sergei and Natalya think they were going to get away with a policeman's private car, Jim? As soon as he came to, he would have phoned in the information."

"They knew that. That's why they drove north on the Drive for as far as they thought they could, then got onto Sheridan and took it even farther up. They dumped the car and used cash to check into a hotel in Highwood."

"That's where they are now?"

He nodded.

"How did you find them?"

"We didn't. We were notified that the car had been located and started a search, but Sergei called a message in to me downtown."

"A message?"

"Yes. It said, 'Tell Miss Grey: Trustworthy.'"

ELEVEN

"Mean anything to you, Jennifer?"

"Yes!" she said. "But how did *you* know what it meant or who it was from?"

"I didn't until I heard it on the tape. All those calls are taped, so I hurried downtown. When I heard the accent, I knew it was Sergei. By then the call had been traced to Highwood, and we headed back up north."

"I didn't think they could trace a call that fast."

"With the new equipment, calls to the police department are automatically traced, in case the phone goes dead before someone tells his address in an emergency."

"So when you located Sergei, he told you what he meant by 'trustworthy'?"

"Yeah. I was proud of you, Jennifer. I still am."

"Would you be if I kowtowed to your bosses?"

Jim ignored the question. "And Sergei told us his version of how they got away from Fred. Of course, Sergei's in trouble for that."

"And Fred isn't for what he did?"

"Sure. In fact, he'll be suspended for a good long time and maybe reassigned after that. But we don't think it ought to be publicized."

"Making a pass at a young woman defector, leaving her and her fiancé unprotected long enough to buy liquor, drinking on the job, and sleeping on the job?" Jennifer said. "Sounds like a guy who ought to be protected. Coddled maybe."

"C'mon, Jenn. Nobody's going to try to cover for Fred. It's just that you wouldn't have known if I hadn't told you, and—"

"I've been onto Fred from the day we met, Jim! And earlier yesterday he slept through my entire interview with them!"

"—anyway, we want to trade Sergei and Natalya's silence for not pressing charges on what they're guilty of."

"Which is?"

"Grand theft auto."

"Oh, for pete's sake."

"How can you deny they stole Fred's car?"

"They didn't intend to steal any car."

"Intent is irrelevant. They took it without permission."

"Put yourself in their places, Jim. Their only hope is their protection in Chicago, and it turns out to be a scoundrel like Fred Bishop. Sergei probably would rather have killed Fred."

"So they're innocent because they could have done worse, Jenn?"

"They're forgiveable because they're scared-to-death aliens who don't know where to turn."

"Well, everything I've told you so far is off-the-record, so don't print the stuff about Fred and you won't have to print the stuff about their stealing the car."

Jennifer had to fight a smile.

"What's funny?" Jim asked.

"Their stealing the car is the best part of the story so far," she said.

"Do we have a deal?" he asked.

"I wouldn't call it a deal. I would say you told me a lot of things off-the-record, and unless I get your permission, I can't print them. How is that a deal?"

"You mean what do you get out of it?"

She nodded.

"You get to see them again."

"And I get to write up another interview?"

"Right."

"And what do I say about their disappearance and relocation?"

"Could you see your way clear to imply that it was part of a master police plan to remain elusive?"

Jennifer excused herself for a few minutes. When she came back, she said, "Jim, this morning when you showed up I thought you were yourself again. When I hear you talk like this, you sound like someone else. Is this the way you're going to act when you become a sergeant?"

"A company man you mean?"

"Yeah, I guess that *is* what I mean."

"I don't want to cop out, Jennifer—excuse the pun—but I am only telling you what I've been instructed to tell you."

"Can you see how I feel I'm being used?"

"I guess."

"And do you agree with the logic of your superiors?"

Jim thought a moment. "Let's say I can see your point too. But journalistic standards are not laws. They're rules, and they make a lot of sense, but sometimes it seems it would be better to ignore those standards for a higher good. You wouldn't print something that would endanger lives or the security of the country, would you?"

"No, but does that pertain here? What you're talking about is protecting the reputation of a man who should not be protected."

"I admire your convictions, Jennifer, I really do. But even if you convinced me and I totally agreed with you, I can't change what I was asked to communicate. That's the deal. If you want to see Sergei and Natalya for more interviews, we have to keep the stuff about Fred Bishop off-the-record."

"Is that Sergei and Natalya's wish too?"

"They're willing to abide by it so they don't suffer for stealing the car."

"You'd actually press charges on that?"

"Bishop might."

"But only if they pressed charges against him for his failure, right?"

"Probably."

"What if they tell me the Bishop story *and* why they took the car, but still don't press to get him in trouble?"

"Still no good. No deal. You can't use it."

"Then I don't want to interview them again."

"You're not curious about where they are and how they are?"

"Of course, but I'm being used, and there are too many strings."

"Will you be printing that fact?"

"That the police department is trying to manipulate the story?"

"Yes."

"No. I won't. I'll give you that much."

"Thanks."

Jennifer didn't respond.

The tension between them was thick as Jim drove in silence to the home where they had chosen to begin their married lives. It was barren, and the heat had been turned way down. Jennifer wondered why he had brought her there.

Jim pointed to a short stepladder in the living room, then brought a wood crate from the kitchen. They sat awkwardly facing each other. Jennifer was still upset over the lunch argument and had decided not to speak unless Jim spoke first.

"Can we disagree and still love each other?" he asked suddenly.

"About journalism and public relations, of course," she said. "I can't expect a non-journalist to be sympathetic with journalistic standards."

"And I can't expect a non-cop to understand how important it is to us to protect our reputation and our people."

"Fred Bishop is one of your people, Jim? Do you put yourself in his—"

"Jenn, we've been over that. Can we leave that subject?"

"Yes, I'm sorry. But if I thought you saw yourself as some sort of a brother to Fred Bishop, I'd hate it."

"You know better than that."

She did, but she decided not to say so.

"I suppose you're wondering why I've called this meeting," he joked. She forced a smile. "I just thought this was as good a place as any to discuss our future."

Jennifer knew she looked distant, but she didn't care. He continued. "I feel God has used this encounter with the Russians to confirm my calling to missionary work. I need and want your support."

Still she didn't respond.

"Do I have it?" he asked.

Jennifer felt herself becoming emotional, but she fought back the tears. "How could I not support you if God has called you?" she asked.

"I sense you're not totally behind me, though, Jenn."

"I'm not."

"Why?"

"Because it carries too many implications. If I'm going to be your wife, I must share the call."

"I feel that way, yes."

"Jim, I don't feel the call, and please don't tell me that my call is coming through you. I have obligations."

"But weren't you going to sacrifice some of your obligations to get married, just like I would?"

"You never asked me to give up my work. I'm under contract. You know the *Day* has made a substantial financial commitment to me and my column."

"I know you're almost in six figures, but I can't believe you wouldn't give that up for your faith."

"Jim! How can you say that? I'm thrilled and overwhelmed by how much the *Day* thinks I'm worth, but I can live without the money."

"Then why did you mention the financial commitment?"

"Because they've signed me to a long-term contract. It runs almost four more years. They've advertised my column, built their front page around it, won awards because of it. And Jim, you *know* God has used it. They have never restricted one thing I've wanted to write, and they've syndicated the column all over the country. I can reach more people in one day than I could reach in a year of public speaking."

"But if God called you away from that to a ministry that wasn't in the limelight—?"

"I'd go in a minute. But He hasn't yet."

"Have you examined whether you just don't want God to call you out of such a public role?"

"Yes! I believe I'm open to Him, Jim. I really do. But your questions make me wonder if you're jealous of my visibility."

Jim stood and shook his head. "No," he said. "I've searched myself for that. Really, Jennifer. In fact, if anything, I take too much pride in your accomplishments and notoriety."

"Then give me the benefit of the doubt. I can believe you're not jealous; believe I'm not hanging onto the job for my ego or my budget."

He walked to the drapeless window and stared out into the snow. "I've been thinking about this house," he said. "And maybe you're right. Maybe we should go ahead and buy it, and I can leave the police department and study at one of the local Christian colleges or seminaries."

Jennifer stood and moved to stand behind Jim, but she didn't touch him. "So I can keep working and support us?" she suggested.

He turned to face her. "Is that too much to ask?"

"Not at all," she said. "It will give me time to get used to the idea of missionary work. And it will allow me to fulfill my commitment to the *Day*."

"But what if you don't feel the call when the time comes to go?"

"I'll decide what I'm going to do before I marry you, Jim. Once we're married, I go where you go. But I still want to be involved in the decisions that affect us. I won't question how God calls a person, but I confess I wonder about the quickness of your decision. I don't like what it has done to you."

"What has it done to me? I've felt like I was walking on air ever since."

"You have been. You've been unreachable. I haven't felt like I could communicate with you until today, and then we were arguing about something else."

"I'm sorry about that."

"Don't be. In a way, I loved it. We were disagreeing, but we were communicating. I went several days without feeling we were making any real contact at all."

Jim put his hands on her shoulders and rested his forehead on hers. "That's scary," he said.

"Yes, it certainly is," she said. "I was prepared to give you your ring back today and call the wedding off."

He winced and closed his eyes. "And now?"

"I love you. I know that. But I cannot be shut out of your life or just dragged along for the ride."

"Do you think I should go to school and prepare for missionary work?"

Jennifer didn't respond quickly. When she did, she said, "Jim, I just can't argue with you about God's call on your life. If He called you, He called you. Who am I to say that He didn't, or wouldn't? God's ways are not our ways, though He does honor us when we honor our commitments.

"God's calling you from a successful law enforcement career may just be the test you think it is. But you're a good policeman, highly thought of, about to be promoted. That carries with it a certain implied commitment too, doesn't it? Your employers are counting on you in their future. I think God wants you to consider that carefully."

Jim took the crate back to the kitchen and walked Jennifer out to the car. As they headed to her apartment, he said, "For strictly personal reasons, I wish you'd come with me to see Sergei and Natalya."

"I can't, Jim. I am so fond of them that I'm afraid if I meet with them again, I'll be tempted to give in on my convictions and write the story your people want, rather than the one that should be told."

"But, Jennifer, I got a chance to really talk to them this morning."

"What do you mean?"

"Well, they asked about us. About why we were different. They've met several officials since they arrived, some they liked and some they didn't. But Sergei said he sensed something different about you and me, mostly you, I'm sorry to admit."

"So you got a chance to tell them about our faith?"

"Yes. For almost an hour."

"Almost an hour? I had no idea you had that much time with them."

"Yeah. He called downtown very early. Apparently, that hotel gets the morning paper just after midnight. I'm not sure when he got it, but as soon as he read it, he called in his message. They'd like to see you, Jennifer. And I think you might be able to add to what I said this morning."

"No wonder you seemed so high when you picked me up today. Maybe you *are* cut out for missionary work."

"Will you come see them then?"

"Not just yet."

TWELVE

Leo reacted even more strongly than Jennifer had when she told him what the police wanted from her. Through the phone she could hear him slam a fist on his desk. "Come on in, Jennifer. I want to talk about this in person."

When she arrived, he was still fuming. "Imagine the nerve of those guys! I don't know how long I've been in this business, and we still can't seem to get through to city officials that we aren't a PR sheet."

"So I made the right decision?" Jennifer asked.

"Of course. I just hope they don't go after someone from the *Trib* or *Times* now."

"Oh, I never thought of that. How can we ensure against it?"

"We can't, unless you want to be guilty of the same things the cops are guilty of. Tell them that we're gonna run with everything you heard this morning unless they keep it away from our competitors. Wouldn't that be a wonderful way to show our consistency?"

"And trustworthiness."

"Yeah. All I'm sayin' is that we have weapons we could use too. We just choose not to because we play by the same rules we expect others to play by."

They sat staring at the floor, enjoying each other's company and their common misery. Jennifer felt good to be with her boss, who understood and agreed—at least on this.

"What I want you to do," Leo said, "is keyboard everything you know at this point, as if you were going to use it."

"You mean write it up in column form?"

"If that would help. I just want to be sure we have everything at this point, whether we are free to use it or not."

"You think something will break and we *will* be able to use it?"

"You never know. It's good to be prepared."

When Jennifer finished several hours later, she had composed four columns. "There's a lot in each one that cannot be used," she told Leo. "It's a pity."

"It sure is," he said, calling them up on his video screen and scanning them quickly. "They're beautiful. I feel like calling the Chicago PD or the feds or whoever and threatening to use them."

"Too bad that's not how we work, Leo."

"I'm glad it's not. At least we have the information for posterity. Any ideas for tomorrow's column?"

"I'm not supposed to have a column in Monday's paper."

"I know, but we're gonna look silly if we don't follow up on the hottest story of the year."

"The year isn't very old, Leo."

"You never were any good at taking compliments. You know what I mean. We can't be silent on this one. We'll look terrible."

"You want me to write a follow-up story with everything I have that's *not* off-the-record?"

"How much is that?"

"Precious little."

"You used a lot the first time, and what's left, other than what you learned today, would be fluff, right?"

"Right."

"I'd almost rather be silent than not bring the reader up-to-date."

"Me too, Leo."

He sat teething on his unlit cigar and staring past Jennifer. "Jenn," he said quietly, as if something had just come to him, "I wonder what the federal authorities think about this. I wonder if they even know about it."

"They must know most of it," she said, "because they entrusted Baranov and Danilin to the Chicago PD, and I'm guessing they've kept in close touch."

"I'm gonna call them."

Leo dialed and let it ring for a long time. "Somebody's gotta be there even on a Sunday," he told Jennifer. "Maybe no receptionist, but surely someone working on this case and preparing for tomorrow's—

"Oh, hello, yeah, who've I got? . . . Ah, Leo Stanton from the *Day.* Just wondering if Chick Alm is around today? . . . Yeah, I'll wait." Leo motioned to Jennifer to listen in on the other phone.

"Hey, Leo," Agent Alm said, "'S been a long time. What's shakin'?"

"Oh, I'm just looking for some more background information on this Russian defector thing."

"Yeah, you and every other paper in town. I just got off the phone with the *Tribune*, and the *Sun-Times* called earlier."

"They base their questions on our piece, Chick?"

"A little. But mostly on what they got from this Bishop."

"The cop?"

"Yeah! They're askin' if we're gonna deport these kids for rollin' him and stealing his car. He told 'em if he hadn't fallen on his weapon when he was hit, they'd have taken that too."

"What *are* you going to do, Chick?"

"We don't know yet, Leo. We were really hoping nothing like this would go down before the meeting with the Soviets tomorrow. They'll probably make out like Baranov and Danilin are criminals in the Soviet Union and that they want 'em back so they can prosecute. That's gonna make your story in today's paper look sick."

"Chick, I have to ask you. Were you aware of this before Bishop told you?"

"Ah, funny you should ask. We off-the-record?"

"I'd rather not be, but if we have to be."

"Off-the-record, no. The cops told us there was a mix-up. The officer who was supposed to take over for Bishop was late or went to the wrong place or something, and they got their signals crossed. Then they decided to move the couple. That was all we knew. But you know, the guy from the *Times* told me this morning that one of the cops on this case is the boyfriend or husband or something of your columnist, the one who wrote the story. He says she got a break, so he wants one. I couldn't give him anything, and you can't print what I said either, Leo. We're keeping it under wraps until this meeting tomorrow."

"Chick, when the other two papers print this stuff about the Russians overpowering Fred Bishop, your cover is blown. The Russians will know you have Baranov and Danilin in custody again. Chick, I think you've been lied to by the Chicago PD, and I know the other papers have been lied to by Bishop. The police can't be too thrilled when all that comes out, because it's going to make it difficult for them to reprimand Bishop when he comes off looking like a victim."

There was silence on the other end for several seconds. Then, "I see what you mean, Leo. I'll talk to our police contacts and get back to you. But do me a favor and don't print any of this."

"I've got until late tonight," Leo said. "And it won't break my heart if the competition comes out with the wrong story. But we have to print something, Chick. If I don't hear from you, I'm going to assume the restrictions are off and we can go with everything we've got. Fair enough?"

"I'm sorry, Leo, I can't let you do that."

"Why not?"

"Because I might get tied up and be unable to get back to you. Then what? You print something that may be true but damaging to our diplomacy and we've all got trouble. Promise me you'll wait until you hear from me."

Leo hung up. "Why'd you do that, Leo?" Jennifer said. "He's going to think you're going to press without his permission."

"That guarantees he'll call me. You'd better get to Bram and get the same kind of guarantee."

"Norman, I must see you," Jennifer said when she reached Bram at his home.

"Jennifer, do yourself a favor and interview the kids on *our* terms, huh?"

"I can't do that, Norm, and you know it."

"You don't appreciate the tip that got you the big exclusive this morning?"

"I *do*, but I didn't know it had a price. It made you guys look pretty good for being so wonderful to Chicago's guests, but I could have included Bishop's first bit of inappropriate talk to both Natalya Danilin and to me, and I could have included the fact that he slept a couple of hours while I was interviewing Natalya and Sergei. That wasn't off-the-record. I could still use it."

"Let *us* handle the discipline, Jennifer. What he did later was worse, we admit, and he's going to suffer for it."

"*You're* going to suffer for it."

"How do you mean?"

"He's gone to the other papers, and they've gone to the feds, with an invented story. It looks bad for the defectors and should gain a lot of sympathy for Bishop. How are you going to suspend him or reassign him or whatever it is you have planned if the public thinks the poor man was mugged by Russian criminals?"

"Let's get together, Jennifer. I'm supposed to meet Federal Agent Chick Alm at my office in an hour, and this must be what he wants to discuss. Can you be there before that? I'd like to have all the ammo I can."

Not long later, after Jennifer had laid out everything she knew from the first call from Jim at two in the morning until now, Bram asked Alm if Jennifer could sit in on their meeting. "Only if she can shed some light on the problem, Norm. I'm telling you, we're going to have to have it out about why our office didn't get the straight dope on what happened."

"Believe me, she can help," Bram said. "You can trust her."

Bram had to take a lot of heat from Alm about not only the lack of communication between the federal and the local agencies, but also the misinformation that was apparently fostered. After they heard Jennifer's rundown of what had happened, they sat staring at each other.

Finally, Alm spoke. "Norm, we've got to let the *Day* print the whole story. And you've got to can Fred Bishop."

"He's as good as gone," Bram said. "And there's another wrinkle, Chick. You remember you told me the Soviets wanted Baranov and Danilin at the discussion tomorrow, no strings attached? Well, Sergei and Natalya have a condition."

"I can't wait to hear it," Alm said.

"They'll come if they can be accompanied at all times by Jennifer Grey."

With the freedom to print anything and everything she thought was relevant, including the bungling of information between the police and federal agents, Jennifer had to fight to watch the speed limit as she wheeled north.

Two uniformed police officers outside the hotel room door made it obvious that security was tight. They had apparently been tipped that Jennifer was coming and was welcome, because one opened the door and the other waved her in.

Sergei and Natalya were huddled in a corner with Jim, but three other plainclothesmen were also in the room, one on the phone and two chatting by the window. Natalya squealed and jumped to her feet when she saw Jennifer. They embraced, and so, this time, did Jennifer and Sergei. And of course, Jim and Jennifer. "Somebody win a gold medal?" one of the cops quipped.

"Is there another room where we can talk?" Jennifer asked Jim. He led her to a smaller suite where she briefed him on what had happened.

"I'm happy for you," he said. "So you were right all along. And I was wrong."

"You were doing what you were told," she said.

"That's no excuse. I've got a lot to learn."

"So do I, Sweetheart," she said.

They returned to Sergei and Natalya, and the couples sat directly across from each other in love seats. "Thanks for inviting me to the meeting tomorrow," Jennifer said.

"It wasn't exactly an invitation," Sergei said. "It was a condition."

"I know, but I'm grateful. It means a lot to me."

"Your article was wonderful," Natalya said.

"Thank you."

"Really," Sergei said. "I know my message got us caught again. But I wanted to tell you that you had for sure proved that you were trustworthy. If I had read the article before it was printed, I would have changed not a word."

"He means it," Natalya said. "I know because he has been saying that all day."

Jennifer filled them in on all that had happened from her perspective since the last time she saw them. They were shocked to hear of Bishop's account of their crisis.

"I want to interview you for several columns this week, but most of them are written already. They just have to be updated with quotes from you, and I need to add the information about Officer Bishop going to the other papers with his story."

"Will the other papers tell it the way he told it?" Sergei asked.

"In a way, I hope so," Jennifer said. "I know that sounds a little cruel, but if they print that without substantiating it, it's their own fault. We would certainly never run a story like that without making sure of it first."

"But your article will make them look bad, won't it?" Natalya asked. "Or do people here like to believe lies over the truth?"

"When lies are all they read, it's all they can believe," Jennifer said. "But when both the truth and a lie are printed, the truth looks and reads and sounds like truth. People will know the difference. Especially when Officer Bishop is fired. They wouldn't fire him if they thought he was telling the truth, would they?"

Sergei and Natalya shook their heads. "We want to tell you whatever else you need to know, because we know we can trust you," Sergei said. "But there is one thing that worries us. These men who call themselves Soviet diplomats, they are KGB for sure. You must promise that you will not let us out of your presence tomorrow. They will want to meet with us privately for a few minutes, I am sure of it. And no one can imagine how much they can accomplish in those few minutes. I heard of a Russian defector to England who was taken into a back room for less than five minutes, and when the 'diplomats' returned, they had taken a self-developing photograph of him and attached it to a phony arrest record from Russia. They also had a written confession signed by him, along with his request not to be interviewed by the British again. Do we have your word that you will stay with us all the time?"

"Every second," Jennifer said.

THIRTEEN

Late Sunday evening, when Jennifer had finished getting the information she needed for her columns and started feeling the pressure to get downtown to the office, a message came for her.

"Ma'am," one of the policemen said, "we've been asked to tell you to call your boss."

"Shall I wait down here, Jennifer?" Leo wanted to know.

"Nah, I don't think so. It's going to be dynamite stuff."

"So Chick Alm told me. I'm proud of you. You're gonna let me read about it in the morning, huh?"

"It's basically the stuff you saw earlier today anyway, Leo. They've just corroborated everything and clarified a few things. It'll be better, but not wholly different."

"And are we scooping the competition?"

"As far as I know."

"All right, I have arranged it so you can just key your copy directly in to composition, as long as they have it by midnight. Watch your length and your formatting, and I'll give you a call after I've read the paper at home in the morning."

"Leo, do me a favor, huh?"

"Anything."

"Call me closer to noon."

"You've got it."

Jennifer intended to get brief good-byes out of the way and get downtown in plenty of time, but it was apparent that something was on Sergei's mind.

His serious look accompanied myriad questions designed to keep her there. "Well, better run," she said.

"Ah, one more thing," he said, looking around and leaning in closer to Jennifer, Natalya, and Jim. "I have many questions regarding what Jim talked to us about today."

Jennifer couldn't help looking at her watch. She hated herself for not hiding it better, but it *was* nine o'clock. Sergei hesitated. "You have no more time?"

She decided that if she left by nine-thirty, she would be OK since she wasn't creating a column from scratch. "It's all right," she said, also leaning toward him.

"This was something new to us," Sergei said. "We are aware of Christians in the Soviet Union, but we have never known what they *really* believe. Schools in Russia are not afraid to teach what religions believe, because they are so convinced that they are all stupid and baseless, and they ridicule them."

"So you did learn something of religion there?"

"Oh, yes. But, of course, we also had courses in dialectical materialism and atheism."

"Actual courses?"

"Oh, yes."

Natalya explained, "Neither Sergei nor I are still atheists, though we were when we were children. It's sort of a special thing with teenagers in Russia to secretly believe in God or to at least allow for the possibility that there is a God."

"It's a form of rebellion," Sergei said. "I suppose young people in this country go against what they are taught just to get a reaction."

Jim and Jennifer nodded. Natalya continued. "We learned that Christianity was a set of beliefs like all other religions. Hindus have their beliefs, Moslems theirs, Buddhists theirs, and Christians theirs. Christianity was begun in the first century when Jesus was born, and a group of radical Jews believed He was the Son of God. When He was put to death, they made some sort of a martyr of Him, and they believed He came back to life and went to heaven, and that He's coming back someday."

"That's pretty good," Jennifer said.

"Yes, but we thought Christians in Russia—the Russian Orthodox and the Baptists—were sects, like other religions. We thought they studied their Bibles and said prayers and did good works, like everyone else."

"They probably do," Jennifer said.

"But if they know this faith the way Jim told us today," Sergei said, "it is much more than that, is it not?"

"*We* think so," Jennifer said. "What do you think about it?"

Neither spoke for a moment. "We aren't sure what to think," Sergei said finally. "I find it intriguing and different, just because it is so personal, but the personal quality of it repels me as well."

"Why?"

"Because it is so far removed from anything we've ever heard that we wonder if we can adjust our thinking to allow for this approach. Is it fairly common in America?"

"What aspect are you referring to, Sergei?"

"This, this *personal* approach. Jim talked about knowing God, knowing Jesus Christ. And there is the exclusivity."

"The exclusivity?" Jennifer asked.

"Yes, where Jesus is supposed to have said that He was the only way to God. We have been taught that all religions believe that they are the way to God, but that only some small cults are the ones who believe they are the only true religion. Now you say this is true of Christianity and the Man who founded it. Yet Christianity is no small group or sect. It is a major world religion, and the dominant religion in America. Do most Americans feel that their religion is the only way to God?"

Jim caught Jennifer's eye, then spoke. There are many who believe as we do that the Bible is God's Word and that where it quotes Jesus as saying He is the only way to God, it is a true account of what He said. We don't understand it all, but we believe it. You know what I mean?"

"I think so. Would you know if the Russian Orthodox and the Baptists also believe that each individual Christian can know God and commune with Christ?"

"I'm afraid I don't know," Jim said. "But I'm sure that many Christians in Russia enjoy that relationship with God."

"That is shocking," Natalya said.

"Why shocking?" Jennifer asked.

Natalya appeared unable to express herself. Sergei offered, "It is just so different from what we have heard or known." Natalya nodded.

"Does it appeal to you?" Jennifer asked.

Sergei shook his head. Natalya said, "No. It is too different—puzzling. And we wonder why it is not known better. It would seem that this would in many ways be a more attractive religion than the sets of beliefs and creeds."

"Oh, we find it so," Jennifer said.

"It makes you different," Sergei said.

"It's supposed to," Jennifer said. "It doesn't always, because we often get in the way of God working in our lives. But we are supposed to be known by how we love one another and other people."

"I think that is what we see," Natalya said.

Jennifer asked, "Why does it not appeal to you then, if you think it would be more attractive than other religions you've heard about?"

"Well," Sergei began, "it seems it would be more attractive to religious people. I can see why you would like this religion better than another, but we are not religious people. We allow for the possibility that God exists, but it is such a jarring thing to think that He wants to be friends with people."

Sergei paused, then added, "It's very interesting. A new lesson for us. We like to study and learn."

"Can you think about the fact that God might love you and care about you personally?" Jennifer asked. "I mean, if He made you, would He not want to communicate with you?"

Sergei smiled at her. "Like your husband-to-be, you are going to be a proselyter, no?"

"I don't know," she said. "Maybe."

"Jim tells me that he may go to other countries to tell people about his religion."

Jennifer looked at Jim and smiled.

"Tell me," Sergei said, "how many people in the United States believe as you do?"

"Many," Jim said.

"How many?"

"Hundreds of thousands, maybe more."

"How many do not?"

"Many, many more," Jim admitted.

"You are a persuasive speaker," Sergei said. "Do you tell those who do not agree with you or those who do not know?"

"Do I tell them?"

"About what you believe. I should think that people in America who are not atheists, even those who are, you would want to tell them about this. If you will be going to other countries to tell it, you must tell it here too."

"I do."

"Ah," Sergei said, nodding. "And there are no more to tell here?"

"Well, it's not that. I don't really tell it as much as I should."

"Why are you going far away to do this then?"

"I feel it's what God wants me to do."

Sergei smiled and looked at Natalya. "I would think you should tell everybody here before you go somewhere else."

"Perhaps," Jim said.

"You meet many people in trouble here," Sergei said. "Why would you want to go somewhere else?"

"I don't know," Jim said. "Maybe I should just tell everyone, wherever I am."

"Maybe," Sergei said. "I don't know. I am not a believer and maybe never can be. But your beliefs make you different, and you are in many ways as devout as a communist."

Jennifer wondered if this young man with the thick accent had hit on something and expressed it better than she had been able to in a week's worth of trying.

The next morning Jennifer's column hit the city, and Fred Bishop, like a bomb. It exploded in the faces of the competition who had published pieces critical of the agencies involved and sympathetic to Fred Bishop. As predicted, the truth rang true, and a general outcry went up.

When Jennifer showed up at the federal building, Sergei and Natalya had already had an encounter with the diplomats in the lobby. They requested a brief meeting with just them, insisting that they had urgent messages for the pair from their families. Natalya's eyes filled with tears, but Sergei quickly turned her aside and whispered in her ear. Jim and his associates expressed Sergei and Natalya's request against the brief meeting, but when it appeared to Sergei that the Americans were wavering, he began struggling and shouting, "This is not part of the agreement! Miss Grey is not here!"

The Americans hustled Sergei and Natalya away, and now the Russians waited in a meeting room while Jennifer and Jim and several federal agents waited with the young defectors in a sitting room.

Jim whispered to Jennifer. "Sergei really got to me last night."

"Really?"

"Yeah. I don't doubt God was speaking to me at the missions conference last week, but I'm wondering if I didn't overreact to my failures in sharing my faith by thinking that I had to become a full-time missionary."

In a way Jennifer was happy to hear him say that, but she wished she had the courage to tell him that he should let her know when he decided for sure. She thought it might have an impact on when they should get married. If he was that undecided and easily swayed, she wondered if he was ready for the big step. And she was afraid *she* wasn't.

But she remembered her father's counsel and knew that some of Jim's uncharacteristic immaturity was due to the impending marriage. She was confident God would give her the assurance that the wedding was the right step sometime during the next few weeks before the big day.

If He didn't, she would have to tell Jim that it would be postponed. The thought of it made her smile. No way was that going to happen.

A federal marshal stepped into the room. "Mr. Baranov, Miss Danilin, Mrs. Grey?" They rose and approached him. "Follow me, please."

Sergei and Natalya were apprehensive, nervous. They expected to face the Russian diplomats when they entered the big meeting room, as did Jennifer.

But no one was there. Jennifer and the kids sat next to each other on one side of a huge mahogany table and watched the marshal leave, assuming he would escort the three Russians back into the room. Sergei whispered something to Natalya. He turned to Jennifer, still whispering. "Don't be surprised at anything. They will try everything to get us alone. If you are called out for a message, do not go, or I will go with you."

Jennifer smiled and patted his arm to assure him she would not leave them. "I wrote all that in my column today," she whispered, "your predictions of what they might try. They will look silly if they try any of that."

The marshal came back. "Mr. Baranov, Miss Danilin, you are free to go," he said, smiling.

"Wait!" Sergei shouted, standing. "It's a trick!"

"It's no trick," the marshal said. "I saw them leave myself. They drove away." He pulled a piece of paper from his pocket. "Their message is this: 'The Union of Soviet Socialist Republics has no more interest in Baranov and Danilin, betrayers of the motherland. We are satisfied they have not been detained against their will, and they are refused reentry in the U.S.S.R.'"

Sergei was still squinting in disbelief. "I do not understand," he said.

"I might have had something to do with it," the marshal said, leaning over the table, both hands resting in front of Sergei. "Sit down, please, Mr. Baranov." When Sergei was seated, the marshal told him what had happened.

"I searched their briefcases before they entered this room," he said. "Standard procedure. They're used to it. Interesting thing was, one of them had a Polaroid camera. And I had just read your column, Mrs. Grey. The one about the fact that they might try to take Sergei and Natalya into another room and photograph them.

"I asked them if they had seen the morning paper, and they said, 'Only the *Times*.' I felt it was only fair that they see the *Day*. Wouldn't you agree?"

Jennifer nodded, smiling. Sergei embraced Natalya.

"Next thing I knew," the marshal said, "they were handwriting a message. Then they were gone. Welcome to America, kids. You're free!"

VEILED THREAT

ONE

Jennifer Grey didn't expect to be writing her nationally syndicated *Chicago Day* front-page column on her wedding day. Nor for three weeks after that in Hawaii where she and Jim Purcell expected to start their married life.

But then she didn't expect to still be single at the end of her wedding day either.

Things had gone smoothly once she and Jim had finally set a date—Sunday, August 19, 3:00 P.M. Jennifer had had to carefully explain to her mother, Lillian Knight, why the wedding really had to be in Chicago rather than Rockford. Her father, George, had been understanding and was an ally in the brief skirmish.

"All of our friends are here, Mom," Jennifer explained. "Jim's attendants are all from the church or the police department, and mine are from the church or the paper. Anyway, I promised only a few people from the national media that they could come, and Rockford is just not an easy place to get to."

Jennifer had heeded the advice of her boss, Leo Stanton, to resist the temptation to write about her wedding before it happened. "We'll just run your picture with a note that you're on your honeymoon," he said. "Then you won't get all the crazies and the groupies."

About four hundred friends and relatives had indicated that they would attend. Jennifer wished the church was air-conditioned. The forecast was for clear skies and ninety-nine degrees with humidity not far below that. When she awoke from a fitful sleep, partly due to the jitters and partly to the heat and humidity which invaded with the dawn, she knew the forecast had been too timid. By church-time, it was eighty degrees, and the wind was dead.

By noon it would be one hundred, and under a cloudless sky, no relief was in sight. Jennifer was glad she had insisted her parents stay in a hotel in Chicago the night before the wedding. "That way you'll be fresh, cool, and have a place to change without a long drive to look forward to." And The Consulate was a classy place. She picked it out herself.

Just before Jennifer left her apartment for church that morning, she got a call from Candy Atkins, her matron of honor. "Game plan still intact?" Candy asked.

Jennifer assured her it was. "I just wish Jim's parents were alive to share this day with him," she added.

Jennifer was taking her wedding dress and luggage, everything, to church with her. After church, someone would run out and grab something for the women to eat so they could spend the early part of the afternoon getting ready and supervising the florist.

At church Jennifer got tired of answering whether she was "ready for the big day today" and also of explaining that Jim had decided to attend another church that morning.

He was still hung up on some of the old traditions—like the groom not seeing the bride before the ceremony on the day of the wedding, but this was the first time for him. Jennifer had been widowed after only a short marriage to Scott Grey. She didn't want to think about Scott so much that morning during church, but she knew it was inevitable. The old emotions came storming back—the deep love she had felt for him, the excitement of their courtship, the wedding, the gifts, the friends, the honeymoon, the new home, the new church, the new social circle.

And the stark, black day in the winter when her phone rang and a state trooper asked kindly if he could come and visit her briefly. The premonition. She knew. She took the news of the accident almost in stride, yet found herself still grieving months later, almost as if in a trance.

Her new job at the *Day* helped, but it was being moved to the police beat and meeting the young, tall, blond policeman Jim Purcell that really healed her hurts, her memories. Theirs had been a difficult courtship, with Jennifer not knowing her true feelings toward him until he was in trouble, suspected of being a dope-dealing dirty cop with all the cards stacked against him.

After he was cleared and they found themselves deeply in love, moving headlong toward marriage, Jim suddenly felt the call to foreign missions. It was almost the end of them. Not that Jennifer wasn't just as devout a Christian. But she had discovered a side of Jim she had not suspected. An impetuous, emotionally oriented, impulsive side that scared her.

But they had survived that too. Jim realized that his conviction, the work of God in his life related to telling others about his faith, began with the people around him. He didn't have to travel halfway around the world to be a missionary, and if he wasn't ready to begin with his own circle of friends and acquaintances, he would never succeed anywhere else either, no matter how far away.

He had begun a Bible study at work for other Christian policemen and several who were not. Three had become Christians over the past six months. Just as important, Jim was growing.

When Jennifer found her mind had shifted from Scott to Jim, she was grateful, but even that thought brought her back to Scott. She knew she would have to deal with that somehow. Jim had been so understanding when she had wanted to talk about her late husband. And while he hadn't said so, she knew that after the wedding, Jim would probably be much more comfortable if she just dropped the subject. Jim was to be the primary focus of her attention, as she would be of his. But it would take work and discipline. And prayer.

She prayed right then that God would help her put Scott in the past once and for all. She thanked Him for the brief months she had spent with him and for the wonder he had brought to her life, but she asked that God would fill her mind and heart with the deep feelings for Jim that attracted her to him in the first place.

Suddenly, she was nervous. The church was stifling with the windows and curtains open, but no breeze. Her watch read almost twelve, and she knew the humidity was in the nineties and the temperature probably higher than that.

Her father and mother tried in vain to talk her into going to lunch with them before coming back to get ready. "There's a nice restaurant at our hotel," her father said.

"I know," she said. "That's one of the reasons I chose it for you. You go and enjoy a leisurely lunch. By the time you're done and freshen up, it'll be time to come back here."

Jennifer was amazed at how long it took the church to empty after the morning service. It was almost one o'clock by the time the pastor, Reverend Howell Cass, had shaken the last hand, listened to the last suggestion, smiled the second to last smile, and called his wife to tell her he was almost on his way home. She had imperceptibly slipped from his side a half hour before to get dinner on the table at the parsonage.

When Jennifer and Candy ducked into a back room for a final check of the fit of the bridal gown, Pastor Cass started from the back pew and worked his way slowly to the front, straightening the hymnals, replacing the pencils, replenishing the information cards, and picking up scraps of paper and works of art by four-year-old illustrators.

A few minutes later, with Jennifer in her gown and stocking feet, working on her veil, he knocked gently. "Excuse me," he said, as Candy opened the door. "Oh, my, Jennifer, you look radiant. Just beautiful." And he offered the last smile necessary before the ceremony that afternoon. "Need anything?"

"Just a sedative," she joked. "No, we're fine."

"A couple of carloads just pulled up," he said. "One full of your friends, I think. The other's the florist's van. I'll point them your way. And my office is unlocked in case you need to use the phone."

"What a sweet man to have for a pastor," Candy said when he had gone.

Jennifer nodded absently, something in the back of her mind telling her that Candy was right, that she did have a wonderful pastor and that she was fortunate. But her mind was elsewhere. She heard the giggling of her attendants as they bantered with the pastor, and she felt the stifling heat and discomfort from the exertion of having put her wedding dress on too early.

"I'm not going to sit around in this thing," she said.

Candy nodded. "I should say not. You ought to sit by the fan in your slip for a few minutes and cool off." She helped Jennifer out of her dress. And Candy was right; the fan felt good until her body was no longer fooled by the slight difference in temperature caused by the air blowing on her perspiring skin. Then she was hot again. And her friends were filing into the room, giving her quick hugs, oohing and aahing over the dress as Candy held it up to show them. And the phone was ringing in the pastor's office.

"I've got to try my dress on right now," one of the girls said. "I think I've gained five pounds since I finished it." She stepped out of her shorts and top. "Should someone answer that phone?"

"Nah. The pastor'll get it."

"Is he still here?"

"I don't think so."

"Yes, he is. Oh, somebody got it."

There was a knock at the door. "Jennifer," came the voice of the pastor. "Jim's on the phone. Didn't sound like him, but you know what wedding days do to grooms."

"Could you tell him I'll be a minute, or can I call him somewhere?"

"I told him you might be a minute and that I was leaving. I really must go."

"Thanks!" She turned to the other girls. "Any men out there in the hall?"

"Yeah. The florist and a custodian."

"Oh, great!"

"Here, wear my shorts and top to run to the phone."

Jennifer jumped into the slightly baggy substitutes and hurried to the pastor's office. "Hi, darling," she said, the phone to her ear.

"Excuse me, ma'am, but this is Jim McGraw at The Consulate. Your mother asked that I phone you to tell you that your father has become ill."

Jennifer held her breath. "Ill?" she managed. "What do you mean, ill?"

"He's apparently had a heart attack, ma'am."

"Where have they taken him?"

"Well, he's still here, Miss Grey. I think you might want to come quickly."

"Is he alive?"

Jennifer panicked at the pause she detected from the other end. "I believe he is, ma'am. But I would suggest you hurry."

Jennifer hung up, fighting tears. *I should have gone with them to lunch the way they wanted,* she thought. *It's too much, a wedding, this weather, the trip. But he's always been so healthy.*

Jennifer ran down the hall, hoping to pour out to Candy her need to get to the hotel. But the room was empty. The girls had moved into a restroom down the hall, so she just scribbled on a blackboard, *Candy, Dad may have had a heart attack. Will call you. Jenn.* She grabbed her purse, stepped into someone else's casual canvas slip-ons, and ran to the car. She could call Candy and the pastor from the hotel, and someone could get a message to Jim. He would understand that there couldn't be a wedding today. If only he could be with her now.

She didn't even have time to feel silly. She had pulled up her slip and stuffed it into the baggy shorts and wore nylons with someone else's shoes. She dug for her keys as she slid behind the wheel, and the vinyl seat burned her legs.

The wheel was hot to the touch, as was the ignition. She rolled her window down and started the car, cranking up the air conditioner at the same time. Normally she would have sat in the steaming car until it cooled down some, but now gravel and dust spit from under the rear wheels as she pulled the black sports car around the side of the church.

She braked quickly at the street, reminding herself that she was a good half hour from the hotel, even at top speed. She turned left, barely noticing the florist's van parked in front until she was about forty feet from it and accelerating. A dark-complexioned young man with curly black hair and a walrus moustache stepped out from behind it, skipped across the street into her path, and raised his arms.

All Jennifer could do was hit the brakes and jerk the wheel to the right, sending her into a broadside skid that just missed the man and left her perpendicular to the street on the grassy shoulder. In the microsecond since she'd just missed him, Jennifer thought about honking and yelling, and even about the irony of running a man down on the day of her wedding, which would be postponed by her father's heart attack. Emotionally, she was ready to burst.

She looked left and turned the wheel, but before she could gun the engine again, the young man shouted, "I heard about your father! Are you going to see him?"

The incongruity of it didn't hit her at first. Who could have told him? How could he have known? Who was he anyway? "Yes!" she shouted, as he slowed to walk in front of the car. She was dumbfounded. She just sat and watched as he came around to the passenger's side and opened the door. He wore a loose-fitting smock that made her assume he was with the florists and also made her find room in her boggled mind to wonder if he was very hot because of it.

"I'm going with you," he said, smiling and shutting the car door.

Jennifer put her foot on the brake. "You are not!" she said. "Now get out and let me—"

He reached over with his left hand and placed a long, smooth finger on her lips. With his right hand he reached down into the left side of his smock and produced an ugly, stubby weapon Jennifer recognized immediately. A *Uzi*, the same piece carried by the Secret Service men who guard the President, pound for pound, one of the most powerful weapons on earth.

As if reading her mind, the young man cradled the *Uzi* over his left forearm, aimed at her rib cage, out of sight of anyone driving by. "It will chew you up and spit you out and leave your body in neat little rows next to what's left of your car door," he said. "You wanna start drivin'?"

"Where?"

"Pershing, south of the Stevenson."

"Pershing is north of the Stevenson."

"Not east of Pulaski, it's not," he said.

"What's this all about?"

"No questions."

"You picked the wrong person then, pal. All I do is ask questions. Start with my father."

"Your father is fine."

"Are you sure?"

"You know better than we do. We only saw him at The Consulate to make sure everything would work. We got no problem with your father."

"You've got a problem with me?"

"Not if you cooperate."

"How come I feel like I'm in a B-movie?"

"You're gonna feel like you're in a casket if you don't step on it."

"C'mon, who are you, and what's so important that you need to scare the life out of me and kidnap me on my wedding day?"

"We need you, that's all. Or I should say, we need your audience. I'm Benito Diaz, and you're under arrest by the Guest Workers Party of the Estados Unidos Mexicanos."

Jennifer shook her head and pressed her lips together. "That's just Spanish for United Mexican States," she said. "Mexico. What's your problem?"

"You got a smart mouth, lady," Diaz said. "Shut up till we get where we're goin'. Then you can ask whatever you want." He turned in the seat and rapped on Jennifer's luggage with his free hand. "Honeymoon stuff, huh?"

She nodded.

"Good. You're gonna need clothes. We're gonna be spending a lotta time together."

TWO

Ricardo DiPietro and his family had been handling the floral arrangements at Chicago city and suburban weddings for decades. "And we've never lost anything off the truck before," he told Edwin Hines, the church custodian.

"What'd you lose?" Hines asked, his lined face showing deep concern. "I'm sure it wasn't any of our people."

"Oh, sure!" DiPietro said. "It's *never* church people!"

"I'm sure we'll be happy to replace whatever it is you lost," Hines said.

"Oh, it's just my son Richie's smock, that's all. But I saw him lay it across the bumper myself, and I don't like the idea of somebody messin' with my truck."

"I'm sorry."

"You got anyone who can keep an eye on it for me, or do I hafta lock it up?"

"You'd better lock it up."

"Then I'm gonna park it back here and unload a lot of the big stuff. Is there a room back here we can use?"

"I think the girls are dressing back here, but I'll ask."

Ed Hines knocked, then opened the door carefully when no one answered and he heard no activity. "The bridal gown is in here," he told the florist, "so at least the bride will be coming back to dress here."

"No, she won't," Candy said, approaching from behind the men and slipping into the room. "We found a better spot downstairs. Anyway, I have to do a little work on that dress." She gathered it up carefully. "Is Jennifer still on the phone? Could you point her our way?"

"Sure," Mr. Hines said. "Do you know if the men will be wanting to dress in here?"

"Don't think so. They're in another room downstairs."

She hurried out.

"Then I don't see why you can't use this room," Hines told DiPietro. He turned the blackboard toward the wall. "Let me just get this out of the way, and you can slide all those chairs into one corner if you want to."

"Thanks, man," the florist said. "I don't wanna be no trouble. I just don't wanna get robbed blind either. Richie!" he shouted out the door. "Bring the truck around back, and carry the candelabra in through here."

In the hall, Hines met Jim Purcell. He was wearing cutoff jeans and a sleeveless sweatshirt. Except for the tux in a plastic bag slung over his shoulder, he looked as if he was ready for a game of basketball. But he was also nervous.

"The bride isn't around here anywhere, is she?" he asked.

"On the phone in the pastor's office, I think," the janitor told him.

"Don't let me see her," Jim said, grinning sheepishly and heading for the stairs. Hines waited until Jim was out of sight before peeking into the pastor's office. It was empty. He shrugged and hoped bride and groom wouldn't run into each other before they wanted to.

Jennifer's fast-food lunch grew cold as the other girls wolfed theirs down and began to get dressed. In her long gown and bare feet, Candy skipped upstairs and poked her head into the dressing room turned florist headquarters. The busy DiPietro family hardly had time to look up.

"Anybody seen the bride?" Candy asked.

Several shook their heads. "I saw Mr. Hines with the groom near the pastor's office a little while ago," Mr. DiPietro said.

Candy nodded. *That must be where they are, then,* she decided. But as the parking lot filled with cars and the photographer came asking for the bride, Candy and the other girls grew nervous. Finally, she was selected to interrupt the couple in the pastor's office.

When she found it empty, she enlisted a few more people, and they went scurrying about the church in search of the missing bride. As a last resort, Candy rapped on the men's dressing room door. "Anybody know where Jim and—"

The door opened and there stood Jim in tux trousers, cumberbund, and loose bow tie. "I, uh, I was just looking for one of the girls," Candy said.

"No girls in here," Jim said. "Just us chickens. Who's missin'?"

"We'll find her," Candy said, hiding her concern. She found Ed Hines briefing Pastor Cass, who had just arrived, on the arrangements. "Excuse me, Ed," Candy said, "but did you tell Jennifer we had moved downstairs?"

"I'm sorry, Candy, but I haven't seen Jennifer since she took the phone call."

"Me either," the pastor said, smiling. "Don't imagine she's hiding somewhere, do you? A little case of cold feet?"

"Hardly," Candy said. "I know her better than that."

"I do too," the pastor said, quickly sobered to Candy's seriousness. "Well, listen, there aren't that many places to hide here. I'm sure she'll turn up. If we see her, we'll send her to you. You know, I recall a wedding where the bride and groom sneaked into the balcony and watched the preliminaries together, getting into their respective positions just in time for the processional."

"But Jim is accounted for," Candy said. "I didn't tell him that Jennifer wasn't."

"I'm sure there's some logical explanation," the pastor said. "It'll all seem quite silly an hour from now."

"I hope so," Candy said, a feeling of dread washing over her.

The three unsuccessful searchers got back together. "Is her car here?"

"She wouldn't have gone anywhere."

"Better check."

"What's she driving?"

"A black Firebird with the back loaded. You can't miss it."

A minute later the scout returned. "Only two Firebirds in the lot. Neither is black."

"I can't believe it," Candy said. "Why wouldn't she have said something? Could it be a prank?"

"Yeah, that's it! A joke. Someone talked her into running out for a Coke and is making her sweat getting back in time."

Candy looked doubtful. "That's not Jennifer," she concluded. "She'd never put up with it."

"Then what could it be, Can? She chickening out?"

"No way. That's not how she'd do it. She'd talk to Jim. Anyway, it's out of the question. There hasn't been one hint of that. Anyway, I just talked to Jim, and he was his usual self. If there had been some discussion about calling the whole thing off, he sure wasn't in on it and doesn't know anything about it."

"But didn't she take a call from him a little while ago?"

"That's what I thought, but I didn't want to ask Jim. There's no sense worrying him about this until we have to."

A woman knocked and opened the door a few inches. "Places," she called out in a singsong voice.

"Um, ma'am," Candy called after her. "Could you stall the organist for a few minutes? Jennifer needs a little more time."

"Oh! Well, I'll see what I can do. Do hurry though."

As soon as she was gone, all the attendants got in on the discussion with Candy.

"Then what? Something came up? She had to leave for some reason?"

"Obviously."

"But what could it have been? And why wouldn't she have told one of us or the pastor or at least left a note?"

"Maybe she did," Candy said. "It was while she was on the phone that we moved out of the upstairs room. Maybe there's a note in the pastor's office."

"Or in the first room we were in."

"Let's look."

On their way up the stairs they were met by the same woman. She was carrying Jennifer's wedding dress and was nearly in tears. "Here's the dress, but where's the bride?" she whined.

"Uh, we're not sure," Candy said. "We need a little more time."

"Oh, my. Oh, no!"

"Did you stall the organist?"

"Yes. He's going to play three more pieces. That might give you ten minutes. But where is she?"

"We don't know! Can you find the pastor for us?"

Without a word, the woman scurried away. The attendants, their hems gathered at their knees, continued up the stairs to the pastor's office. It was empty, and there was no note. As they hurried down the hall to the original dressing room, they passed the groomsmen.

"Thought you were supposed to come in from the foyer," one of them said. And Jim squinted solemnly, apparently wondering where Jennifer was and what was going on.

"We will," Candy said on the way by, as if the men should mind their own business.

She opened the door to the back room, and the rest of the girls followed her in to where the DiPietros were packing up.

"We'll be back to pick up the stuff from the sanctuary later," Mr. DiPietro said to Candy, as if she cared. "As soon as we put this room back the way we found it, we'll be outta here."

"Don't mind us," Candy said. "We're just looking for a note someone might have left us."

"Didn't see nothing like that," Mr. DiPietro said. His son backed out the rear exit with several empty boxes and rolls of crepe paper while his wife gathered up pin cushions and leftover bunting.

As Candy looked under books and papers for any sign of a note, another girl found Jennifer's Sunday clothes, as well as her going away clothes. "Jennifer either left in her slip or she's wearing my stuff, which she wore to the phone and which I don't see anywhere."

The pastor entered. "Still no bride?" he asked, no longer amused by the situation.

Candy shook her head. "And her car's gone. No one has seen her since she took the phone call. And no one saw her leave either."

"It's past time for the ceremony," Pastor Cass said. "I'm going to have to say something to the people."

"But there's nothing to say yet, is there?"

He shook his head, the look in his eyes making clear that his mind was working on something. But nothing was coming together for him. Mr. DiPietro enlisted his son's help in rearranging the chairs, then putting the blackboard back where they had found it.

The DiPietros ignored the writing on it, assuming it was Sunday school stuff. But as they left with an inane wish for good luck in finding the bride, the message Jennifer left for Candy stared the women and the pastor in the face.

Candy dropped into a chair and hid her face in her hands. "Why wouldn't she have at least told Jim?" someone asked.

"She probably expected me to," Candy said, her words muffled by her fingers. "And I'd better do it quick."

The woman with Jennifer's dress burst into the room. "The men were supposed to wait for you, Pastor," she said, "but the guests were getting restless. We let the men go out. You'd better catch up with them."

"I'm afraid Jim's going to have to find out about this along with everyone else," the pastor said. The girls followed him and peeked through a side door to the platform as he strode to the center.

The overhead fans were working overtime, accomplishing little more than moving the hot air around. People were fanning themselves with bulletins, wedding programs, even hymnals. But mostly they were murmuring among themselves about why the groomsmen had come out before the pastor and craning their necks to see where the bridesmaids might be.

"Wait a minute!" Candy whispered to the other girls. "Isn't that Mrs. Knight in the front row?"

The others crowded for a better look. "I don't know," one said. "It's been years."

"It *is* her!" another said.

"Ladies and gentlemen," the pastor began. "I'm sorry to report that the bride has been called away unexpectedly due to a sudden illness in the family." He held up a hand to silence the collective gasp. Lillian Knight lurched in her seat and turned around to seek out her husband, who was waiting in the foyer for Jennifer and the bridesmaids. He scanned the second and third rows behind his wife to be sure that his son and other daughter and their children were all accounted for.

Jim's eyes darted to his future mother-in-law, then to Mr. Knight, who shrugged.

"We don't know how serious the problem is at this moment," the pastor continued, "but apparently Mr. Knight, Jennifer Grey's father, has fallen ill. This will mean a postponement of the ceremony, and I would suggest that before we leave, we all bow and pray that—"

"Hold on a second!" Mr. Knight shouted, charging briskly up the aisle. "I'm right here, and I'm fine. What's going on?"

As the guests chattered and some even laughed—assuming the announcement was a cover for a bride who had changed her mind—Jim left his position and huddled with the pastor and Mr. and Mrs. Knight.

"What's the deal?" Jim asked. "Where is she?"

Reverend Cass told the three quickly of the note on the blackboard and of the fact that Jennifer had apparently left in her own car, leaving her wedding dress, Sunday clothes, and honeymoon outfit behind. "I want to see the note," Jim said, signaling Detective Sergeant Ellis Milton—one of his groomsmen—to join him. "Don't let anyone touch it."

"Take the men back," the pastor advised, "and Mr. and Mrs. Knight, if you'd just take your seats in the front row for a moment." Mrs. Knight complied. Mr. Knight did not. He followed the groomsmen to the back.

"I'm sorry about the confusion," the pastor announced. "It's clear we are not entirely sure what has happened, but the bride is not here, and until further notice, there will not be a wedding today."

THREE

If the ornery-looking *Uzi* hadn't convinced her, the dumping of her less-than-a-year-old car into Lake Michigan made Jennifer realize that she was in mortal danger.

What amazed her was the cool aplomb with which Benito Diaz, if that was indeed his real name, arranged for the dumping. He had directed her to drive to a secluded alcove at the beach, several miles south of where a thousand people were swimming and sunbathing.

"Pull up next to that van," he had said.

"You mean the green panel truck?"

"Call it whatever you want, Jennifer," he said, and she wished he hadn't used her first name. There was something distasteful about being on a first-name basis with a terrorist.

Terrorist. It was the first time she had allowed herself to mentally articulate it. But that's what he was. Even if he appeared in his early twenties at most, and even if the walrus moustache was the only hair he had seemed to be able to cultivate on his smooth, dark face. She wondered if a terrorist so young and with such delicate hands and slim, long fingers had the intestinal fortitude to use the ugly weapon he brandished. Or was he a complete phony, masquerading without even ammunition? Could the weapon be a fake? A Toys R Us special? She remembered the cold steel in her ribs in front of the church and knew she was kidding herself.

"Good," Diaz said. "Now pull around the other side of him, and park as close to him as you can."

Jennifer shot him a double take. The panel truck was situated out on a concrete pier and was parked parallel with the water, seemingly at the edge of the pier. As she pulled around the far side, she realized that there was just enough room for her car and maybe a foot or two to open her door.

"I should take a hard right and see who survives," Jennifer said, staring coldly at Diaz and edging as close to the side of the pier as she dared. She probably cleared it by four inches, but from the driver's side it seemed that half the car was over the water.

Apparently the effect wasn't much different from Diaz's perspective. "Hey!" he shouted, involuntarily leaning toward her, as if to keep the car from rolling into the drink.

"Scared?" she asked.

That had angered him. She was only dimly aware that the driver's side door on the other side of the panel truck had opened and shut, because the fire in Benito's black eyes burned into her own.

He raised the automatic weapon and pressed it against her right cheekbone, pushing her head back until it hit the window. He kept pushing until she winced in pain. "You're hurting me," she said softly.

He swore. "I'll kill you if you try to mess with me," he said. "You're worth nothing to me!"

She tried to nod, but the steel against her flesh paralyzed her from the neck up. Jennifer wanted to reach up and tear at the Mexican's eyes with her long fingernails, but he had finally gotten through to her. She believed him. He would kill her.

There was a soft knock on the window near her head, and Diaz slowly lessened the pressure on her face until she could turn to look. In the small area she had left between her car and the truck stood a taller, leaner, older, more Indian-looking man she assumed was also a Mexican.

"Roll the window down," Diaz said. "I want to introduce you to Luis Cardenas."

"What do you want me to do, shake his hand?" she said, tempering the sarcasm only slightly.

"Exactly."

But she didn't offer her hand. Cardenas, his weathered face eyeing her warily, put a hand through the window. Jennifer ignored it until she felt the *Uzi* on her cheek again. Then she raised her right hand to meet Cardenas's, but didn't squeeze when their hands met. Strangely, Cardenas didn't either.

"Pleased to meet you, señora," he said in an accent so thick it made Diaz sound like an Ivy Leaguer. She was amazed at the homework they had done. How could they know she was technically a married woman, being a widow, and that "señora" was indeed the correct address? Or had it been an insignificant lucky guess?

"Leave it in neutral and turn the engine off," Diaz instructed. "Then get out."

"You first," Jennifer said, wondering why she was motivated to be so smart with her captor.

"You have a wild one, Benito," Cardenas said, laughing. There was no way Diaz could get out on his own side without tumbling into the lake. He just stared at her. She shifted into neutral, turned off the ignition, and started to remove the keys.

"Leave them there," Diaz said. Jennifer stepped out and thought about slamming the door as he slid across the seat behind her. Cardenas awkwardly shuffled out of the way, and the three of them barely fit between the vehicles.

The shorter man tucked his weapon into his pants and leaned in the window to wrench the wheel hard, all the way to the right. Jennifer had not seen Cardenas's weapon yet and found herself looking for someplace to run. But there was nowhere to go. The pier was at least a quarter mile long, and even if they couldn't catch her on foot, there was plenty of time to run her down with the truck.

Cardenas opened the passenger-side door of the truck and motioned that Jennifer should climb in. "You can see from here," he said. When he shut the door and turned around, she saw a .45 automatic pistol wedged into the back of his pants.

The two men, whom she could now see were at least a foot apart in height, emptied the luggage from her car and piled it into the back of the truck. Then they pushed the Firebird from behind. The right front tire dropped off the side first, and the crunch of metal onto concrete sickened Jennifer.

Her car, the beautifully designed and fully appointed style she had been able to justify and afford only when her column became one of the most widely syndicated in the country, sat with its right front tire off the edge of a pier, the left rear off the pavement, and the undercarriage crumpled under its own weight against the cement.

The men counted aloud in unison in Spanish and heaved again at the back bumper, causing the left front tire to also drop off the edge. The left rear bumper creased the truck as the car turned toward the water, but now it was hung up, the front tires clear of the pier, the back tires only barely touching the ground, and the main weight of the car resting on the edge of the concrete.

Both men stood back and took deep breaths. *"Uno mas,"* Cardenas said, and he bent to the task again. They pushed and heaved and rocked, and the car lurched and scraped and inched until the weight of the engine was fully past the fulcrum of the pier, and the car's own momentum carried it clear of the pavement.

Jennifer could hardly believe the splash made by the short drop into the water. It couldn't have been two feet, but the water leaped at least twelve feet into the air, and a wave cascaded up over the pier, causing Cardenas and Diaz to dance back toward the truck.

They both entered from the driver's side, first the taller, older man, who disconcertingly sat directly behind Jennifer where she couldn't see him. He tossed the keys to Diaz, who fired up the engine and impetuously reached over and pinched Jennifer's cheek lightly. He winked at her and smiled as if he had just pulled off the greatest high school prank in history.

She turned away and stared out the window. "We could have just as easily left you in the car," he said. And she knew it was true. She breathed a silent prayer of thanks, wondering where this was all leading, when and where it would end, and how soon she would be reunited with Jim.

Within fifteen minutes, Benito Diaz pulled into a garage at the back of a dingy, two-story, redbrick building near the northeast corner of Pershing and Kedzie, in the shadow of the Stevenson Expressway.

Jennifer forced herself to drink in every sight and sound. She didn't know what these people wanted or what they expected, but she had the feeling she would need to employ every detail-oriented bone in her body if she had any hope of escaping.

A heavy metal overhead door rose and fell automatically as the truck passed through. As Jennifer's eyes slowly grew accustomed to the darkness inside, the threshold seemed to have worked magic on her captors' manners. They were suddenly deferential, almost to the point of being sickening. They treated her like a lady, opening the door of the truck for her, carrying her luggage, speaking softly, calling her Mrs. Grey.

She didn't know what to make of it, and while she was still determined to drink in every inch and every sound of her new surroundings, she was—she finally allowed herself to realize—weak with hunger.

And fear. She couldn't deny it. She wanted to be tough, once the initial shock wore off. She had been so relieved that her father was all right, that she had enjoyed a brief—and false—sense of well-being, the feeling that nothing could really go too terribly wrong.

But the cold steel in her ribs, the *Uzi* barrel in her face, her car in the lake, the entombing of the truck in the secluded, yet apparently well-equipped building, and the disconcerting turn to politeness by her captors gave her a sinking, almost helplessly hopeless feeling of dread.

Neither Cardenas nor Diaz had mentioned anything about anyone else being involved in her abduction, but Jennifer sensed such a feeling of anticipation in both men all along the way that their sudden personality change was the only further clue she needed. She was about to meet whomever else was behind this scheme, probably the mind that had conceived the plot.

She was eager to meet him or her and to find out, if possible, how the Guest Workers—or whatever it was they called themselves—knew so much about her and her parents' arrangements. She wondered who had placed the phony call purported to be from The Consulate Hotel. She wondered how Benito Diaz had gotten to her church. And she wondered if they would have any food.

Diaz and Cardenas pointed up a back staircase with a single light bulb burning at the top. When Jennifer reached a multi-locked door upstairs, she stopped. The two men stood on either side of her and moved close, as if they had a secret.

Diaz affected a heavy Spanish accent, easily as thick as Cardenas's, and it made Jennifer wonder if the latter's was phony too. "You are about to meet Adolpho Alvarez, our boss, and Maria Ruiz, his wife. We call him Double-A or A-A, but you will do well to call him Mr. Alvarez or Señor Alvarez."

What if I don't want to call him anything? Jennifer wondered. But she wasn't about to cause trouble now.

From inside the door she heard a female voice with a flat, Midwestern accent. "Benito?"

"Sí!"

"Luis?"

"Sí!"

"Mission accomplished?"

"Sí!"

Several locks began to pop open, and the door swung in. Jennifer was almost startled by the striking, smiling face of Maria Ruiz. It was so jarring and so unlike what she might have expected that she almost smiled back. It was the way Jennifer had been raised—to be polite, to smile when smiled at, to speak when spoken to. Jennifer wondered how such a delicately featured woman, apparently about her own age, could be involved in a terrorist organization.

"Welcome to the temporary headquarters of the Guest Workers Party of the United Mexican States," Maria said, extending her hand. Jennifer had to check herself to keep from reaching for it. Maria Ruiz never flinched. "Can you smell lunch?"

Jennifer nodded, wondering if perhaps she should have returned the handshake to be certain of getting some food. She was light-headed, having skipped breakfast. "My husband is the best Mexican cook I have ever seen," Maria said.

And Jennifer *could* smell it. She was able to pick out the fragrances of the slowly melting cheese, the flour and corn tortillas, the refried beans, the rice, even the guacamole. She envisioned tacos and enchiladas and burritos.

Still smiling, her even white teeth gleaming against the darkness of her face, Maria looked deep into Jennifer's eyes. "It is what we will all enjoy, if you cooperate. It is what four of us will enjoy if you do not."

Jennifer wanted to promise anything at that point, but she had established a smart mouth with Diaz and Cardenas, and already a cool distance from Maria. She feared she might be misguided, but she thought she should be consistent, in case that posture proved to be a strength. If it cost her a meal, however, she would have to rethink it.

Maria led her into what appeared to be a nicely furnished apartment. It was carpeted and decorated in a conventionally American way. In fact, aside from the aroma from the kitchen and the clothes of the three she had met so far, there would have been no hint of anything Mexican or Spanish about the place.

The strange thing about the large living room, with its television and couches and chairs, was that it had no windows. It was well-lighted and cozy, but somewhat claustrophobic. A huge wall air conditioner blasted icy air throughout the place with such power that Jennifer's hair danced in its wake.

Maria pointed to one end of a huge sofa, and Jennifer lowered herself carefully. She was tired, exhausted, having transferred her nervous excitement about the wedding to this fear for her life. "Adolpho will be right in," Maria said. "Please do not speak to him unless he speaks to you."

"I may not even then," Jennifer said, almost casually, surprising even herself. Diaz and Cardenas looked at each other and at Maria, and they all smiled knowingly. The men took Jennifer's luggage into another room, and she noted the loud knocking of the lanky Luis's cowboy boots on the hardwood hallway between the carpeted rooms.

When Benito and Luis returned, they detoured through the kitchen, and each carried in two large pitchers of beer. They set them on a coffee table in front of Jennifer and Maria. "You like?" Luis asked, smiling. Jennifer shook her head. "Somethin' else?" he asked, as if she had dropped in after church. Which, she realized, she had.

"Anything else," she said, hoping he knew she meant anything other than whisky or wine. He came back with a two-liter bottle of cola, which almost made her smile. It was so perfect and seemed so out of place.

From the kitchen Jennifer heard the low, rumbling voice of Adolpho Alvarez, who bellowed his wife's name with an accent. Maria jumped and hurried to the kitchen, returning a minute later with five large drinking glasses. She was pouring the beer for herself and the three men when Alvarez entered with a tray piled high with hot Mexican delights.

Jennifer almost studied the food before the man, but he was an imposing figure. Almost six feet tall, Adolpho was wide and stocky and muscly with long, black hair and a square jaw. She guessed him at least in his late thirties.

"The joke among my people," he said, "is that Americanos think our food is spicy. In truth, it is very bland—lots of bread, little salt. You season to taste." He smiled, displaying a silver eyetooth on the right, and produced several small saucers of hot sauce from the heaping tray.

Only Jennifer and Maria sat on the couch. Benito dragged a chair over to one end of the coffee table for Adolpho, then sat on the floor next to Luis, directly across from the women.

Without any amenities or any more talk—let alone any plates—the four dug into the treats. Adolpho sat on the edge of his chair and leaned forward. Gingerly picking up a steaming flauta, he cocked his head so as not to spill anything, laid one end across his tongue, and devoured half the flauta in one bite.

The others tore at beans and rice and guacamole with a fork each, their only utensils. Jennifer sat with her hands in her lap. Her mouth watered. Her heart raced.

FOUR

It was the first time anyone in the church, from the pastor to the organist to the groomsmen and bridesmaids and family and friends, had ever been involved in a wedding that didn't come off on schedule. Anyone, that is, except the florist.

Ricardo DiPietro shook his head and smiled as several hundred people filed out the back past his truck. Usually, he was long gone by the time the occasions broke up, and he, like most others, merely felt that the groom had been jilted, left standing at the altar.

"Happens all the time," he said to whomever would listen, not thinking that he attended several weddings a week and that the odds were better that he would have witnessed something similar. "I saw a guy leave a girl at the altar and come back later and talk the priest into marryin' him to one of the bridesmaids. Brought two witnesses. Just them and us in the big church with all the trimmings. Saw another one where a guy stood up when they asked if anybody had an objection. He said he did because the girl had told him the night before that she loved him but couldn't get out of the marriage. The minister handled it pretty well, I thought. Told the congregation he was going to give the girl one chance to publicly confirm or deny the story. She said it was true, and the pastor said he couldn't perform the wedding. Don't know if she married either one of the saps. I got paid for the flowers, that's all I know. Whether the wedding comes off is none of my concern. If the flowers are there, somebody pays. That's it."

Inside, there was a crowd on the platform that wouldn't have been bigger if the wedding had taken place as usual. The men and women in the wedding party were chattering, Mr. and Mrs. Knight were there, the pastor, the janitor, the woman with Jennifer's dress, all of them.

Jim pulled his best man, Detective Ellis Milton, to the side. The swarthy, thick investigator was sweating profusely. "Ellis, I need you, man," Jim said. "Can you handle this? I'm at a loss."

"I'll do whatever I can, Jimmy," the fast-talking Ellis said. "But we've gotta break up this crowd, find out who knows what, and get an order of events. Can you get me a notebook and something to write with?"

Relieved to have a chore, anything to do that would allow him to worry without having the responsibility for the investigation, Jim ran to the pastor. "I need paper and pen for Detective Milton, and I need to let everyone know that he's in charge. Whatever he says goes."

"Fair enough," Pastor Cass said, nodding to Ed Hines who came up with a notebook and a pen for Ellis Milton.

Ellis loosened his tie and took off his tux jacket, shedding also the cumberbund and slipping the suspender straps off his shoulders. The rest of the men immediately followed suit. "Could we all sit here in the first row or two?" he asked, exhibiting enough authority in his voice that everyone fell silent and complied.

"Now, I hate to be cold," Ellis began, "because I know you all care and are concerned. But if you did not see Jennifer between the end of the church service this morning and the time she disappeared, I need you to leave."

There were several groans from the groomsmen and the bridesmaids. "I know Jim and Jennifer will call you as soon as we get to the bottom of this, but you have to understand that if you have nothing substantial to contribute, you're going to be in the way. Do us all a favor and just go somewhere—out for dinner or home or wherever you want. I'm sorry, but I must insist."

Several stood to reluctantly step out. "What about me?" Mr. Knight asked. "Lil and I saw Jenn right after the service and tried to talk her into going to lunch with us." His voice nearly broke. "I wish she'd come with us."

"But she didn't, and that's the last you saw of her, and the first you knew she was missing was just now, right?"

The Knights nodded. Ellis had bad news for them. There was nothing they could do then and there. He searched his mind for a diplomatic way to get rid of them. "What I want to do," he said, "is to pick up the sequence from there, and I need only those persons who saw or talked to Jennifer after that. Mr. and Mrs. Knight, the most important thing you can do is go back to your hotel, in case Jennifer or whoever she's with tries to get in touch with you."

Mrs. Knight stood and began moving into the aisle. But her husband, the big, white-haired, independent father of the missing bride, remained seated and stared at the detective. Ellis just stared back, trying with all that was in him to look firm yet compassionate, urgent but not panicky, insistent but not insensitive. Finally, the father stood to leave. "We're at The Consulate," he said. "Don't hesitate to call."

"Thank you. Anybody talk to Jennifer earlier?"

"I did," Candy said. "I called her early this morning. Just to see how she was. I was curious, I admit it. Just wanted to see what a nervous bride sounded like. She wasn't nervous at all. Not harried—nothing. Same as ever. I had my own church to go to this morning, and when I got here, she was in the back, just waiting for help to get into her dress."

"It must not have been too long after that that I saw her," the pastor said. "As I recall, she was in her wedding dress, but was without shoes or veil. She said something funny, I think, but I don't remember exactly what it was."

"Something about needing a sedative," Candy said. "Wasn't that when you told her she had a phone call?"

"No, that wasn't until after the other girls got here."

"Oh, you're right," Candy said, "because Jenn borrowed someone else's clothes to run to the phone."

"That must have been at least a half hour after I saw her the first time," he said. "Maybe longer. In fact, I didn't see her the second time, I assume, because she was dressing or something. I was on my way out the door when I got the call from you, Jim."

Jim flinched. "From *me?* I didn't call here today, Howell, excuse me, Pastor Cass. Did the person say he was me?"

"Well, he said *Jim,* and I just assumed. He referred to Jennifer by Jenn, I think, and so, like I say, I assumed."

"But Pastor," Candy reminded him, "you said something to Jennifer through the door about it not sounding like Jim."

"That's right! I didn't think it sounded like him. But I still thought it was him because who else would be calling here, and who knows what a wedding day might do to a man's voice? Anyway, whoever it was didn't say much. Just, 'Hi, Pastor, this is Jim. Is Jenn there?' You can see how I assumed—"

"I sure can," Ellis said. "It's obvious already we're dealing with someone who's done some homework. What were the odds the pastor would answer the phone, as opposed to the custodian?"

"One in two," Edwin Hines said. "We would have been the only two men here at the time, and in fact, I don't think I was here that early."

"You were," Pastor Cass said. "You got here just as I was leaving."

Ellis Milton looked at Jim out of the corner of his eye. "The caller could have been someone who had already been in proximity of the church," he said. "Could have been calling from nearby."

"Or got a tip from someone nearby," Jim said. "Someone who told him the pastor was in or near his office."

Ellis nodded. "So Jennifer borrowed someone's clothes?"

"Mine," a bridesmaid said. "And they were a little too big for her."

"So she's wearing slightly baggy clothes. What did they look like?"

"Red long-sleeved top and khaki shorts."

"Would she have been barefoot?"

"When she left us she was," Candy said. "But my beige canvas slip-ons are missing from the back room now, so she may have put them on to go to her car."

"And if she took her own car," Jim said, "you can forget looking for her by her clothes. She planned on taking a lot of stuff with her. Several pieces of luggage."

There were several dejected nods. "Any chance she'd have left of her own accord?" Ellis asked.

"Ellis!" Jim scolded.

"I have to ask, Jim. She was here one minute and gone the next."

"Yeah, but we also know there was a bogus phone call, and she left a note. If she was going to run out on me, she wouldn't have had to invent anything."

Ellis leaned back against the piano and folded his arms across his chest. "So, our hypothesis at this point is that she was tricked by a caller into believing that her father had had a heart attack, and we have to assume it was supposedly at his hotel or en route, because it made her want to leave immediately, even without telling anyone. Pretty risky of the pranksters."

"How do you mean?" Jim asked.

"How did they know she would come out alone? Wouldn't it have been logical for him or her or them to assume that she would be surrounded by girl-friends at that moment? Wouldn't the natural thing be for her to tell the girls and have one or two of them go with her, maybe even drive her, maybe in one of their cars?"

No one said anything. "I can't make it make sense either," Jim offered finally. "There's just so much we don't know."

"Jim, do you feel up to helping out?"

"I have to do something."

"Then call downtown and have a detail assigned to The Consulate. See if they had a medical emergency this afternoon and whether they could have called the wrong contact person by mistake. I'm assuming that either Jennifer paid for her parents' room or at least made the reservation."

"Probably the latter," Jim said.

"See if anyone saw Jennifer around there today. And have them find out if there's a clerk there named Jim. I'm going to assign some people to canvass this neighborhood. Surely someone saw a Firebird leave here when there was little other church traffic around. Is it a Trans Am?" he called after Jim, who was heading for the phone.

"No!"

"Well, in a way that's a break," Ellis said, barely above a whisper. "A black Firebird that's *not* a Trans Am might be easier to locate." He looked back to the group. "OK," he said, "there's not much need to hold everybody here. Anything else I should know before I check out the pastor's office and the back room?"

"I was just curious," Candy said, "if Mr. Hines remembers when I asked him to point Jennifer our way when she got off the phone. We switched rooms, and if we hadn't, like you say, one or two of us probably would have gone with her. We wouldn't have had any reason not to believe the message. I mean, not until we saw her parents here, both healthy."

"All that tells me," Ellis said, "is that either the person was working *very* close to the church, or there was a contingency plan to take care of any extra riders."

"Meaning?"

"I wouldn't want to speculate. I couldn't even tell you if whoever lured Jennifer away abducted her or not. And if they did, whether it was in the parking lot or down the street or at The Consulate or on the expressway. Who knows?"

"I'd like to answer the question the young lady posed," Hines said as Jim came back. "I remember promising to send her to you, but the pastor's office was empty when I checked again. I believe I told you I hadn't seen her when you asked about it later."

"But you told me she was in there," Jim said. "Remember—when I brought my tux in from the car?"

Hines thought for a moment. "Yes, I did. When I told you, I thought she was in there, and you said not to let you see her. That was just before I checked and found out she wasn't there."

"Did you try to find her?" Candy asked. "To tell her where the new dressing area was?"

"No. No, I didn't, and I don't remember why now. I think I figured if she wasn't in the pastor's office, she must have been out of there quite some time and had likely already caught up with the rest of the girls."

"Uh-huh," Candy said. "That's why the florist told me he'd seen you with Jim near the pastor's office, and I assumed Jim was with her in there after that."

"But she was already gone," Ellis said. "That helps pinpoint the time. Jim, didn't you notice that Jennifer's car wasn't in the lot when you arrived?"

"Yes, but I knew she had to have parked around the side or the front, because it was her car we were making our getaway in. In fact, I was a little perturbed it wasn't right there handy so I could dump some stuff in it. But then I realized I didn't have the keys anyway, and I didn't want to see Jenn before the wedding."

Ellis Milton and Jim took a few minutes to debrief each other and to check out the pastor's office and the note Jennifer left on the blackboard in the original dressing room. Ellis called downtown and requested help canvassing the area. The response was not good.

"Wrong day to ask," he reported to Jim. "Lots of people off. Apparently, it's up to us."

"I gotta tell ya, it seems like a waste of time, El. Do we have to do it?"

"Oh, I think we definitely should, Jim. We have to have more than we've gotten so far. No doubt it was a phony call; at least, that's my guess. If it was just a mistake, the boys at The Consulate should be able to determine it quickly. But then Jennifer would have been back or called long before now. Let's ask for a couple of volunteers. There can't be that many homes around here, and we should do it now, while anything anyone might have seen would be fresh in their minds."

The phone rang. Ellis Milton picked it up. "Church office," he said, "Pastor Cass speaking."

"Pastor, this is Leo Stanton of the *Chicago Day*. Have the bride and groom left yet?"

"Is this for an article, sir?" Ellis asked.

"No, I'm Jennifer Grey's boss, and there's been some kind of a scam here. Could I speak to either Jennifer or Jim?"

"They're not available right now, Mr. Stanton," Ellis lied. "Can I help you in some way? What scam are you talking about?"

Jim's eyes lit up when he heard Stanton's name. He grabbed the phone. "Leo, this is Jim. What's up?"

"Well, well," Stanton said. "Are congratulations in order?"

"No, sir, I'm afraid not. Jennifer has been lured away or abducted somehow. Weren't you here?"

"No, that's what was so strange. I got a message to call my office just before I got to the church for the wedding. The reception on my car phone was fuzzy, so I called from a pay phone. The only person in the office on Sunday is the receptionist, who said there was an urgent, personal, confidential note waiting for me. When I arrived, the note was on my desk. It said that if I cared about my favorite columnist's health, I'd leave room for her column in tomorrow morning's paper. Jim, I didn't know what to make of it."

When Jim had filled in Ellis on the phone call and told him he didn't appreciate his deceiving Jennifer's boss, Ellis told him he was sure that a good, old-fashioned newspaperman like Leo Stanton had pulled a few similar tricks in his day and probably would get a kick out of knowing what had been pulled on him. "I'm going to ask him myself," Milton said. "Because if the only place we have someone actually contacting us in writing is at the *Chicago Day*, then that's where I'd like to set up shop."

Surprisingly, Ellis was right. In the midst of his confusion, turmoil, and fear over the life of his star columnist, Leo did remember a time when he was covering a tavern brawl where a man had been killed. The cops wouldn't let him in, so he went to a phone booth down the street, called the tavern, got the sergeant on the phone, and said, "This is Flanigan downtown at headquarters. What's goin' on over there?"

"And you got the whole story?" Ellis said, laughing.

"You bet!"

"Then we owed you one, didn't we?"

"I guess you did!"

Stanton agreed that Ellis could set up a command post at the *Day* after the neighborhood canvass. "Now all we need is to round up enough help to find out if anyone around here saw anything this afternoon," the detective told Jim.

Just before dismissing anyone who didn't want to help by asking basic questions door-to-door, Ellis asked if anyone had any more information about anything suspicious that might have happened at the church that day.

"There was one thing," Edwin Hines said. "The florist was convinced someone had been messing around near his truck. Said they stole his son's florist's smock. Don't know if that's significant or not."

FIVE

Double-A, Adolpho Alvarez, had largely ignored Jennifer during the first half of his repast. But when Maria attempted to pour Jennifer a cold drink, he flashed forward and batted the plastic, two-liter bottle against the wall. The cola fizzed and shot from the opening, splashing the carpet.

As if on cue, Luis Cardenas casually stood and went after a towel. He placed it over the puddle and set the bottle upright. He returned to his meal without finishing the cleanup.

Alvarez's eyes burned into Maria's face, but she acted as if nothing unusual had happened. Jennifer couldn't tell if Maria reacted calmly because such behavior was typical of Adolpho or because she knew that any resistance to his volatile temper would result in more violence.

"I'm thirsty," Jennifer had said, less calmly and evenly than she would have liked.

"She's thirsty," Alvarez said to Maria, ignoring Jennifer. "We haven't even talked yet. She's a guest in my house, and she asks for something to drink. She is a guest; she will be asked to cooperate, but we haven't even got that far, and she tells me she's thirsty. Tell her she will eat and drink from my table when *I* am ready, and I will not be ready until she agrees to cooperate."

"I have ears," Jennifer said. "You can talk to me."

She had clearly angered him now. Adolpho let his fork drop and, with his mouth full, he gripped the sides of the coffee table holding the food platter. Luis, Benito, and Maria leaned back, as if they knew what was coming.

The wide, hard man slid forward off the edge of his chair and squatted before the table. Still holding it only by the two sides of one end, he lifted it to his eyes. His biceps bulged, but there appeared to be no effort, no hesitation, no wavering. The table, heavy even if it hadn't been piled with food on a solid tray, was held flat, straight out.

Jennifer was impressed and pretended she wasn't.

"I could kill you with one bare hand," Adolpho said, slowly lowering the table. The others continued eating while he stared at Jennifer. "I don't need you," he added in his gravelly bass voice.

"Yes, you do," she said.

The other three looked up, startled. Jennifer had talked back to Adolpho after two outbursts and his show of strength. It was as if she was daring him to hurt her. "You need me for something," she said, "or you wouldn't have dared such a risky kidnapping."

He studied her and filled his mouth again. "When this is all over, you're gonna wind up gettin' yourself killed."

"Then why don't you let me eat anyway?"

Jennifer couldn't believe herself. For some reason, she was compelled to talk tough to this muscle-man. She had hope. Hope that she would see Jim again. Hope that she would be married. Hope that she would go back to work and see her friends and co-workers. Hope that she would be able to go back to her church and her fellow believers. But somehow, sitting quietly and hoping and praying didn't seem to be enough.

If she riled the man to the point where he hurt her, then maybe she would be quiet. But she was no good to him dead; at least she was fairly certain of that. She still didn't know what he wanted. But if he planned to use her for more than just ransom bait, she would have to be alive and well and fed to do him any good. So she said so.

"Let her eat," Adolpho said, and Jennifer jumped. They were only three words, and they carried good news. But they hadn't been so fast or so distracting to hide the fact that A-A had slipped out of character for a moment. Those words, so quick off his tongue and vibrating with his trademark bass tones, had been completely devoid of a Mexican/Spanish accent. And Jennifer had not been able to mask her surprise.

Adolpho immediately started in again with a tirade of threats about what would happen to her if she chose not to cooperate after she had eaten. His accent was back, full and authentic as from one who had learned Spanish many years before learning English.

Then Jennifer, as the other three had done, simply ate, ignoring him. How quickly, she thought, one learned how to deal with A-A. And she was amazed—despite the disappointment in her gut, the fear in her heart, and the confusion in her mind—how delicious the food tasted.

It bore the trademark of authenticity. Succulent, mellow though lightly bitter, the intermingled flavors of corn and meal and flour and beans and rice and guacamole and beef and chicken and cheese and lettuce and tomato satisfied her hunger with the first ravenous bites.

But she couldn't force from her being the knowledge that her life was in danger. She was confused, dying for information. Not knowing what was going on had always been one of her deepest frustrations and probably the guiding force behind her becoming a journalist. Not only did she hate to be left out, she didn't even like being the second one to hear any news. She had to know so she could be the one to tell. And right now, she knew nothing.

Just before Jennifer finished eating, Adolpho nodded to Benito and spoke softly to him. The younger man immediately put down his fork and went to another room. He emerged with a white business-sized envelope, which he was sliding into a 6" x 9" manila envelope. "Spell the name again for me, Maria, *por favor*," he said, pulling a black marker from a chest of drawers in the hall.

"S-T-A-N-T-O-N," she said, and he wrote in huge, block letters, adding, "URGENT."

Adolpho nodded to Diaz. "Come straight back," he said. "You'll need to take one of the eight-hour watches tonight."

Jennifer, who had casually been studying the room and whatever other parts of the apartment she could see, began to give up hope of an escape. If each of them were with her for eight-hour stretches, she wouldn't be getting far, even if she found a vulnerable window somewhere.

She didn't have to wonder which of the four would not be pulling guard duty, but she wished it were otherwise. She would have been willing to give up several hours of sleep—which she assumed would be fitful at best anyway—to talk with Adolpho Alvarez. Until now, he'd done most of the talking but hadn't said anything of substance.

Jennifer decided he was in his image-building mode. For all his braggadocio and showing off, she sensed a deep insecurity in the man. He felt the need to establish his power, his rank, his place, to beat his chest before not only Jennifer, but also his own underlings. In Jennifer's mind, Benito was quietly genuine. He was ruthless and violent without flaunting it. She almost feared him more. Because rather than trying to talk her out of her sarcasm, he'd just as soon blow her away.

Luis was much more quiet, fitting more Jennifer's stereotyped Mexican. She knew it was wrong to categorize any people, but with her limited contact with Mexicans and even Mexican-Americans—except at the office—she entertained the idea that the United States' immediate neighbors to the south were a quiet, easygoing type who took *siestas,* and then slowly got back to industrious labor.

Already she had met four in one day who, except for Luis, shattered the mold. Adolpho was as boorish as any obnoxious American she had ever known. And he was far from easygoing. Maria, though she was obviously American born and bred, was just as obviously a full-blooded Mexican. But because of more than her lack of Spanish accent and manner of speech, she was the least like what Jennifer pictured a Mexican to be.

When Jennifer and the remaining three had left nothing but scraps on the platter, Adolpho stood, looking down on Luis. For some reason, Luis took that as a cue and quickly began rearranging the room. He waited for Maria to remove the food tray, then slid the coffee table out of the way. Then he dragged Adolpho's chair over in front of the couch.

Jennifer had a knee-jerk reaction to help Maria with the cleanup and almost laughed aloud at herself. *Imagine,* she thought. *I'm kidnapped at gunpoint on my wedding day, see my new car destroyed, am brought who knows where for who knows what, and I still want to be a considerate guest!*

Instead, Jennifer sat where she had for the last hour or so and watched the silent theatre of Luis preparing the room for something and lazy Adolpho letting him do it, apparently to the do-nothing "Adonis's" specifications.

The air conditioner had quickly cooled Jennifer to the point that she was almost feeling a chill, but Luis was working up a sweat, rearranging the furniture. When Adolpho's chair was in place, he plopped down heavily, not because he was overweight—in fact, Jennifer thought he was in as solid good shape as anyone she had seen in a long time—but because of his big meal and maybe as a result of the fatigue showing in the redness around his eyes.

His chair was lined up with the center of the couch, and as Jennifer was sitting on the far end, to his left, she was able to avoid his squinting stare without having to turn too far away. "Excuse," Luis said, suddenly appearing in front of her. "You have my place."

She started to move, then stiffened. "Where would you like me?" she asked.

Luis motioned that she should move over to the middle of the couch, but that would have put her directly in front of Adolpho. She wasn't so sure she wanted to sit right next to Luis either. She slid down, past the middle to the other end.

Apparently, that was a breach of protocol. Both men looked shocked and angry and said in unison, "No, no!" and motioned her back to the middle. At first she didn't move, angered by the craziness of it all. But when Adolpho leaned forward and reached for her arm, she feinted back to avoid him and slid the other way toward Luis.

Fortunately, Luis seemed as uncomfortable with her right next to him as she did. She didn't want to think what it would be like to sit almost touching Adolpho. She hoped she wouldn't have to find out.

The two men seemed to be waiting for Maria who was cleaning up the kitchen. Jennifer was tempted to impatiently demand to know what it was all about, but she decided against it. Obviously, they were about to tell her what it was they wanted her to cooperate on, if she could only be patient. She figured she didn't have much choice anyway.

Maria returned with a smile as if she were a normal hostess glad to get back to her guest. If it hadn't been for Maria's earlier cold statement (behind as lovely a smile as she flashed now) that Jennifer would eat if she cooperated and wouldn't if she didn't, Jennifer might have wondered if Maria was in on this thing at all.

Maria sat next to Jennifer, who now had nowhere to look unless she wanted to encounter the high-eyebrowed look of Luis; the expectant, cheery smile of Maria; or the bleary-eyed stare of Adolpho. She looked down.

As if to heighten the tension and prolong the agony, Adolpho said something to Maria in Spanish. She jumped up again and hurried to the kitchen, returning quickly with a huge glass mug, easily containing a full quart of icy beer. If Maria was offended by Adolpho's constant demands, she hid it well. She served it as if she was more than happy to do so. Jennifer decided Maria would have made a wonderful in-flight attendant.

From the corner of her eye, Jennifer watched as Adolpho took several long swallows of the beer. He set the mug on the floor next to his chair and leaned back so his seat was still on the front edge of the chair but his shoulders rested against the back. That position tucked his square chin into his chest. Still he stared directly at Jennifer.

With her knees almost touching his and each of her shoulders touching her other two guardians, Jennifer had never felt so vulnerable in her life. She smelled the alcohol on three breaths, but she guessed that none of the three was new to drinking and that none of them was to the point of inebriation yet.

Suddenly, as if now he was finally ready to begin his discourse, Adolpho slowly hunched himself up to where he was leaning forward toward Jennifer again. "I want you to look at me," he said.

She didn't.

"When I talk to you," he said louder, almost slurring, "I want you to look at me!"

Peripherally, she could see that even Luis and Maria were looking at him. She decided not to push him. She looked up with contempt and locked her eyes on his, trying with all her might to communicate with her look that she found him disgusting, despicable, beneath value.

She thought she might have gotten through. Under his baleful stare she sensed a wavering, a flicker of inconsistency, maybe even fear. For sure, he hated her; she could tell that. And she knew it was her calling to love her enemy. He was certainly that. She would deal with the theology later. For now, she decided that communicating her true feelings to him through her eyes did not violate the broad truth that she should pray for him. She would pray for him later. Just now, she was praying for herself.

"I am the noble wolf," he said, but something was stuck in his throat. He said it as a pronouncement, but the obstruction in his voice made it sound like he had a bad connection. Jennifer almost laughed.

"You're the *what?*" she said derisively, pretending not to have completely heard him.

He cleared his throat, looking at her warily to decide whether she was mocking him or really wanting him to repeat it. He repeated it.

"I am the noble wolf."

He stared at her as if expecting some reaction. He should have been pleased with the first one. Jennifer had decided not to respond in any way. Let him wonder if she heard him this time. "And you," he said finally, clearly irritated by her lack of response, "will help the noble wolf and his Guest Workers Party."

Jennifer wanted to ask what she would be helping him accomplish, but she figured he would get to it.

"You will help us tell the United States about our plight. About our problems, the injustices, the needs of the Mexican people. You will help us tell your nation of the needy Mexican, the so-called illegal alien, and the charade your government called the Guest Worker program that allowed my people to come in and be taken advantage of. You will tell the story through your column that is sent around the country that if there are not changes in the way the United States treats Mexico and her people, violence will come to key people, the same way it will come to you."

Six

Candy Atkins, Pastor Howell Cass, custodian Edwin Hines, and Jim were the only volunteers for Detective Sergeant Ellis Milton's neighborhood canvassing detail. And after that, they would join Leo Stanton at the *Day*. Other police personnel would be assigned when they became available.

Having seen the florist's truck in the back parking lot, Ellis Milton erroneously assumed the petty theft of the smock happened there. He didn't know if it was related to Jennifer's disappearance, but if it was, he was guessing that Jennifer left by the back exit from the lot, rather than driving around the side of the church to the front.

"Pastor Cass and I will handle the street that runs behind the church at the far end of the parking lot," he told the four volunteers. "Then I'd like Jim and Candy to handle the houses across the street in front. Each of you start at either end, and when you meet in the middle, report what you've learned, if anything. Pastor, if either you or Candy come up with something interesting, tell your police partner, and we'll help you question the witness. Mr. Hines, if you'd stay here and wait for any phone calls, I'd appreciate it."

Ellis added to the canvassers, "I know time is important here, but I don't think we'll appear too authoritative or official in these getups. Let's change quickly and get to it."

After changing clothes, Jim and Candy talked briefly, then headed off on foot to either end of the block in front of the church. Jim found no one home at either of the first two houses, but the third had what appeared to be a family reunion going on in the backyard.

Jim flashed his badge and said, "Chicago PD," to the man at the outdoor grill.

"Hey, 'scuse me! We're not bein' too loud, are we? I mean, we got no music playin' or nothin' like that. You want me to tell 'em to keep the noise down—hey, I'll tell 'em. Someone squeal on us or somethin'? Probably the old bat next door. Always a busybody, but, you know, if we're guilty, we're guilty. Did you think it sounded too noisy when you came around the side here?"

Jim assured him no one had called in any complaints about noise. "We're just checking out a missing person's report from the church across the way there."

"Oh, well, we never went there. We go to church, I mean, but not there, you know. Well, we go sorta sometimes, not all the time, not every Sunday. Certainly not twice every Sunday the way these people do. And Wednesday. Anyway, that's not my church. Never been there. Been visited by the pastor though. Nice guy. Wants us to come. We probably won't. You know anybody who goes to church that much?"

"I go to that church."

"Do you? Hey, that's nice! You go three times a week?"

Jim nodded.

"Boy oh boy, imagine a church good enough to draw people that often. Pretty good, huh?"

"Pretty good. Listen—"

"Hey, what happened over there today? We thought the wedding went pretty quick. My brother Fritz here was goin' on about how somebody had to been jilted over there."

"You noticed the wedding went quickly, sir?"

"Oh, yeah, it seemed the last of the guests had just pulled in when we notice that they're all pullin' out. In fact, some of the latecomers were still gettin' there and the thing musta been already over! From the way the traffic came in, I woulda said there was a three o'clock wedding. But fifteen minutes later, it was a traffic jam. So, how you gonna find somebody missin' from that?"

"I don't know," Jim said. "Maybe I'm not. You hear or see anything strange or out of the ordinary around there today?"

"You mean, ah, when?"

"Before the wedding. Before most of the people arrived."

"Well, like what? I mean, we can't see much through the trees here, and we were all out here in the back."

"So nobody saw or heard anything unusual?"

"Don't think so. 'Cept Pudge, that's my son. Name's Paul, but we've always called him that. Tournament archer. You oughta see him shoot."

"He saw something?"

"Nope, heard something. The kid's a car buff, a whiz. He can hear a car that he can't see and can tell you what make, model, and year it is."

"He heard a car?"

"Heard screeching tires."

"And?"

"And what?"

"Did he see it?"

"No! He heard it! And he still knows what it was."

"Even the color?"

"Don't be silly."

"I could say the same to you, sir, to think anyone could know the year, make, and model of a car he can't see! The engines on several different makes and models are identical, made by the same suppliers even. How do you know he's right? Do you ever go check it out?"

"Never have to. We know he's right."

"Is he around?"

"Jes' a minute. Paul!"

A gangly, string-bean thirteen-year-old with taut muscles in his arms but nowhere else, jogged over to the two men. "Tell 'im, Pudge. Tell 'im how you can spot any car just by how it sounds."

"That's right, I can," the kid said, shaking hands. Jim was skeptical and didn't try to hide it.

"You heard a car screeching its tires between one-thirty and two o'clock over by the church?"

"Yes, sir, right out in front, just past those trees over there."

"Peeling rubber like it was taking off with a jackrabbit start, or slamming on the brakes?"

"Braking. Like it was going kinda fast, then hit the hooks, you know?"

Jim nodded.

"And then it drove off?"

"No, I heard a door open and shut, and then it drove off."

"So someone got out?"

"Or in."

"True enough. And you know what kinda car it was?"

"Nah."

"What?" his father demanded. "You always told us what kinda cars they are! What'sa matter?"

"Aw, Dad, all I can tell from the sound is the size of the engine and whether it's a four-barrel or not, that's all. And I can tell if it's automatic or stick, that kinda stuff. I always guess a kind of car 'cause I know you get a kick out of it. Half the time I'm right because there are only so many cars that have that kind of equipment."

His father shook his head, embarrassed and clearly irritated. "Well, don't be makin' up something for this guy, 'cause he's a cop. Give 'im the straight dope, and don't be givin' me tall stories anymore either. OK?"

Paul shrugged. "This was a big, four-barrel automatic. Could have been a Corvette or Camaro—though they don't make too many of the loaded Camaros like they used to."

"If it could have been a Camaro, it could have been a Firebird, right, Son?" Jim asked.

Paul nodded. "Sure. More likely. Probably a Trans Am."

"But it wouldn't have to be."

"No. I guess you *could* soup up a Firebird without havin' it be a Trans Am, but probably only a woman would do that, and no woman would have been driving like that today."

"If the driver was showing off, you mean?"

"Yeah, and that's what it sounded like."

"But if the driver really almost hit something or someone?"

"Then it could have been anybody."

"One more thing, Paul. What color did it sound like?"

"Hah!" Paul said, kicking the ground. "Cute."

When Jim went back around to the front of the house, Candy was coming up the sidewalk. "This is it?" she asked. "You've only been to three houses?"

"Yeah, sorry. How many did you hit?"

"Eight. I kept thinking I was going to run into you."

"This was the only place with anybody home. Didn't get much, except I think Jennifer must have come out of the lot the front way, hit the brakes, a door opened and shut, and took off again. How'd you make out?"

"About the same. My people were home, but only one would let me in. A couple said they noticed the wedding was pretty short. Three said they heard a near accident at about one-thirty or a little before. Only the little old lady in this brick house here next door invited me in. I think she saw Jennifer, Jim, and I thought you'd better handle the interview."

Jim walked toward the house. "What makes you think she saw her?" he asked.

"She's a widow. Four years. Gets her work done early in the morning, and I mean *early.* Like at sunup even in the summer. That gives her the rest of the day to watch out the window, she says. She's watching us now. She reads her paper on a little TV tray next to the window. Takes her phone calls there. Eats her meals there. Doesn't own a TV. Wouldn't know what to do with it. Sunday's her favorite day. Lots of people to watch twice a day, and even more today because of the wedding."

"I'm Jewish," the little, white-haired woman explained as she let Jim and Candy inside. "I go to synagogue on Saturday and have Sundays all to myself. I was getting myself a late lunch in the kitchen, or I would have seen where the little black car came from. It makes me so mad. I knew you were coming to ask me. I saw you come out of the church. I knew something was wrong because the wedding was so short, but I didn't know if the accident—or the almost accident, I should say—had anything to do with that or not. I feel so bad that I didn't see where that car came from."

"That's all right, Mrs.—"

"Freidrichsen," she said.

"Yes, that's all right," Jim said. "Could you just tell us what you did see?"

"Well, I watched all the people come to church this morning. They have some kind of religious training classes early, I believe, and many people come for that. But even more come later for the worship ceremony or pageant—I've never attended, of course—and though some of those who arrived early leave when the others get there, most don't, so the biggest total crowd is for the later meeting. Then I knew there was a wedding because I saw more than the usual number of cars stay behind at the end. And then I saw the florist's truck. Not enough cars arrived before one o'clock for it to be a one o'clock wedding, and no one has a wedding on the half hour, do they? So I watched the girls arrive and one or two of the men, carrying their fancy clothes. And I dashed to the kitchen some time after one-fifteen or so and made myself a tuna sandwich, which I love. Do you?"

Jim wanted to shrug, but he nodded, as did Candy, smiling.

"And as I sat back down by the window with my tea, I heard the roar of the engine in the black car, a little car, very fast."

"Tiny?" Candy prompted.

"No, not like a tiny foreign car. More like a teenager's fast car, only the driver was a woman. Not too young. Not too old. Long, brown hair."

"The car was going fast, but you could tell it was a woman driving?" Jim asked.

"Well, it was on my side of the street, and when she almost hit the florist, she stopped suddenly and sat there for a moment."

"She almost hit the florist?"

"Yes! What he was doing in the street, I don't know, because his truck was parked on the church side, and he certainly didn't need to get over here for anything. It was as if he jumped out in front of her on purpose!"

"How do you know it was the florist?"

"Well, florist's helper then."

"No, I'm not saying it wasn't the florist, ma'am, I was just asking—"

"I know it wasn't the florist because the truck had an Italian name on it, and this boy was not Italian."

"What was he?"

"Cuban maybe? Puerto Rican? South American? Something like that."

"Can you describe him?"

"Maybe twenty. Not too tall. Black hair, moustache."

"And you thought he worked with the florist because—"

"Because he had a florist's coat on, a green smock, the kind they wear."

"Uh-huh, and what happened?"

"Well, I heard the engine, so the black car was not going fast until it got near my house, I guess. Like it was going normally and then started going fast, you know?"

"Or as if it were coming out of the church parking lot from the rear?"

"I suppose, but I didn't see it in time. I'm sorry."

"That's all right. What else?"

"Well, just before she got up to the florist's truck, this young Latino man seemed to jump in front of her car, waving his arms. She slammed on the brakes and swerved onto my parkway there. You can see the tracks."

"And she missed him."

"Yes. She sat there for a moment and seemed to be putting the car in gear again or getting ready to go somehow, and the young man walked in front of the car with his hand up. He opened the door on this side and got in. They talked for a minute, and then she pulled away. That's all I know."

SEVEN

Adolpho Alvarez, the self-proclaimed noble wolf, was on a roll. Full of Mexican delights he had tastily prepared himself and loosened by a full quart of ice-cold beer (after having downed a few normal-sized ones during his late lunch), he sat before Luis Cardenas to his left, the abducted Jennifer Grey in the center, and his wife—if Jennifer could believe that—on his right.

And he was carrying on. Despite all the food and beer that made him groggy and short of breath, Double-A was not a fat man. Big, yes. Stocky. Not too tall. Muscle-bound, his sleeveless shirt displaying bulging biceps and a bulky, taut neck, he was engaged in a lengthy tirade about injustice.

Jennifer felt weak, despite having eaten heartily from her kidnappers' table. The air conditioner had long since cooled her past the point of comfort, yet it continued to labor and drone on. No one else seemed the least bit bothered by it, and she guessed that was because they had suffered so long in their native country without such a convenience.

"My country is made up of Spanish people," Alvarez was slurring, "Indians—about a third, and the rest a mixture. Mestizos. Luis here, he is Indian. Maria is Spanish, born in America of full-blooded Spanish Mexicans. Benito and me, we are Mestizo."

Jennifer wanted to ask where Adolpho had met Maria, but she was not in a reporting situation. The way the lecture was going, she figured he might get to that anyway. Sometimes, when Adolpho slipped into Spanish, Maria would quietly turn to Jennifer and translate.

"The most powerful organization in Mexico, before the noble wolf formed the Guest Workers Party, was the Partido Revolucionario Institucional."

"Institutional Revolutionary Party," Maria whispered. "Or the authentic party of the revolution."

"They have a rival in PAN," Adolpho said. "The Partido Acion Nacional."

"National Action Party," Maria said.

"Both *partidos* think that because Mexico has a so-called stable government—and I suppose it is more stable than anything else south of the United States—that it will soon become a major industrial power with all its oil reserves."

He paused for a reaction. Jennifer felt like screaming. Anything for a change. She was cramped, crowded, stifled. The three all had beer breath. "And you disagree, no doubt," she said.

That she said anything caused Adolpho to flinch, and he sneered as he fought to decide whether she had been disrespectful. He decided she had not, mostly because she had asked him a question he wanted to answer.

"Of course, I disagree," he said. "Mexico will never be prosperous until they make me at least governor of the federal district."

"I'm sorry," Jennifer said, wishing as she said it that she hadn't seemed subservient. "But I don't know enough about the inner workings of the government of your country to understand what that means."

She had irritated him. Adolpho was offended that she didn't know more about something so close to him. "The federal district!" he shouted. "I don't wanna be in charge of any of the thirty-one states. I want to be appointed governor of the federal district."

"And who makes that appointment?"

"The president."

"And he selected someone else?"

"Of course! He would not even speak to me, see me, return my calls, answer my letters. I had a petition from many hundreds of people who wanted to see me in some station of national authority."

"Did you have the credentials?"

"The credentials? I am the noble wolf! I am the one who saw through the crazy scheme our president and your president worked out at Camp David a few years ago. One hundred thousand guest workers were to be allowed to visit the United States for two years, and the number of visas for legal immigration to your country was supposed to be increased to forty thousand."

"And that didn't happen?" Jennifer asked.

"Yes! It happened! It was a success! So why has nothing come of it? Most of the guest workers, myself included, have been deported."

"Because the plan didn't work?"

"Because it *did* work! Americans are threatened by foreign workers who know how to work hard, who show that Americans are lazy and cannot keep up. The program worked all too well, and the American unions couldn't take it."

"You met Maria while you were here on the program?"

He nodded slowly. "I was not here the whole two years."

He had said it flatly, as if it was incidental. Jennifer picked up on it immediately. "Of course, you weren't," she said. "You were a troublemaker, a rabble-rouser, a malcontent. Am I right?"

At first he looked offended, then he smiled wryly as if he liked her spunk. "I was not thrown out, if that's what you think."

"Then where did you go?"

"Back to Mexico."

"For what?"

"To try to join the big labor union. The *Union Confederacion de Trabajadores de Mexico*. More than two million Mexicans belong to this union and still have to work forty-eight hours a week. Millions of Mexicans still can't read or write."

"And so you tried to improve things by working in the union?"

"I was not allowed in the union either. I had brought my American wife with me, and even though she is Mexican and looks Mexican, she did not sound Mexican, and we were found out. I had trouble finding any work at all, even though I am the noble wolf and had the best interests of my people at heart."

"But there isn't anything wrong with an American living in Mexico, is there?"

"Not officially, no. But when so many Mexicans are kept out of the U.S., they do not like Americans going down there either. I was not welcome among the very people I was trying to help."

"And so you—?"

"Came back here. I still had my visa, which had been canceled, but which I was able to duplicate."

"It must not have taken the authorities long to find out you were here illegally."

"Not long."

There was a knock at the door. One knock, then a pause, then another single knock. Maria ran to open it. "Benito?" she asked.

"Sí!"

Benito came in smiling. "Mission accomplished?" Maria asked, as she had when he and Luis had brought Jennifer up the stairs. He nodded.

"Anyone see you?" Adolpho asked.

"No. This was a perfect day for it because so few people were at the newspaper office. I waited until the receptionist was on the phone, then I left the envelope right in front of her where she could see it when she turned around."

"Do you think he got the envelope?" Adolpho said.

Benito nodded.

"And you weren't seen?"

He shook his head.

"Good job. Have a beer and sit down."

"Are you going to get to your point?" Jennifer asked.

"Sure," Adolpho said. "But first you're gonna hear how we kept your column open in tomorrow's paper."

"Impossible."

"No. We called Stanton on his car phone, Maria using her best English and yet faking a bad connection well enough to keep him from realizing it was a phony call. He was to head back to his office for an emergency. When he got there, no emergency, but a message from us."

"Which said?"

"Trust me," Adolpho said. "He will keep a spot open for you."

"So you needlessly scared him."

"Needlessly? You don't seem to realize how important your column is to us."

"This reminds me of those radio and TV station takeovers in the nineteen sixties."

"So we're behind the times? It seems to me we are on the forefront of revolutionary activity."

"What do you want from me?"

"It seems to me you could guess."

"I can't," Jennifer said. "And don't expect me to try."

"You will be writing your column for the next several days. Or weeks. As long as it takes for us to accomplish our goals."

"Which are?"

"Sympathy for our cause."

"You've been going on and on, and I still don't know what your cause is."

"That is because you are a true American. You could never see, never understand. That is why you must just listen and let me tell you what to write."

"You think anybody will believe that I wrote it?"

"Sure. You are going to phrase it in such a way as to give it, ah, credibility. It will be coming from you and not from me."

"And will you let me tell the truth? Will you let me tell that I have been kidnapped and forced to write?"

"Of course! Everyone should know that by now anyway. It will show the seriousness of our mission and our message."

"Which I still don't understand."

"You will when I tell you what to write."

"And where will I write?"

Adolpho beamed. "Come with me," he said. He stood and stretched and groaned loudly. Jennifer followed him down the hall to a big bedroom next to a bathroom. Her bags had been opened and ransacked, her clothes hung in the closet.

As she stepped into the room she realized that the other three captors had followed her. Now they and Adolpho stood with her, eager to see her reaction, as if she had just rented an apartment and they wanted to know how she liked it. She was expressionless. There was no window. Just a big bed, a big closet, and in the corner with a quaint lamp, a small, wood desk.

"Bring in the surprise," Adolpho said.

Luis moved to another room and returned, lugging a huge box that had not been opened. It was marked "fragile," and there were myriad instructions on how to store it, how to open it, how to remove the contents, and why to save the box. It took all three men to pull the heavy, gleaming typewriter from the box.

Had Jennifer not been used to video display terminals and state-of-the-art computer typesetting technology, she might have been impressed.

"Freshly bought, huh?" was all she could muster.

"Freshly stolen," Adolpho said with a grin. "In the name of the Guest Workers Party of the United Mexican States, we have appropriated the equipment. You will type your column on this, and we will deliver it to a different place each day. Then we will call your editor and tell him where to find it."

"You know, the other papers around the country who carry my column have been told that I will not be writing it for three weeks."

"They'll make room for this story, señora," Adolpho said. "We have done our homework. We know how rich and famous and important you are. When you are reported missing and still unmarried, it will be big news. And when the papers find out you are writing your column in exile, they will run it. Don't think they won't."

"You *have* been doing your homework, haven't you?"

"For this payoff, honey?" Benito said. "You better believe it. We been studyin' you and your boss and your boyfriend and your pastor and your church and everything for weeks. It'll be worth it."

"What he means," Adolpho said, glaring at Benito, "is that what we are seeking for our people is a big, important concession from your government, and so everything we do for the working man of Mexico is worth any sacrifice."

"Did you study enough to know when my deadlines are?"

"Your deadlines are when we say they are. They will hold the presses for you."

"But not forever. Especially if you have to deliver what I write."

"Then let's get started."

"Do you have paper?"

Adolpho swore. Maria told him they had some yellow legal pads. "That will have to do," he said. "Can you type on those?"

"I can type on anything," Jennifer said. "But the question is: Will I?"

Adolpho had had enough. He was troubled, frustrated, irritated at his insubordinate prisoner. He turned to face her, and the other three immediately left the room, sensing his anger and not wanting to be there if he erupted.

"Let me tell you something, lady," he said slowly through clenched teeth, leaning close to Jennifer so she could smell him and his breath. "Many writers would give anything for the opportunity you have. You were selected for a reason—because you are good, and your column is read by millions all over the world. You think we would have chosen just anyone? You should feel lucky. This will make you even bigger. What you write and the reaction you get could change history. You will be affecting U.S.-Mexican relations maybe for the rest of our lives. And you will be gaining for the poor Mexican working man a dignity and a life-style he deserves."

"Touching," Jennifer said.

Adolpho put both hands on Jennifer's shoulders, but hardly in a compassionate way. He was trembling with rage, and she was scared. "If you make light of me or my mission, or if you disobey me, I will kill you."

"And then what good will I be to you?"

"You will be, at least, an example to whomever follows you to my cause. But I will not kill you until you have served me."

"And if I refuse to serve you?"

"Then I will start with your man, Jim Purcell. I know where he lives. I know his phone number. I know his car. I know his schedule, his habits—everything. He would be easy. Almost as easy as your parents, George and Lillian Knight of Rockford. And your older brother. And your younger sister. And their families. You will do what I say, Mrs. Grey, because I know everything about you and them. I know how to get to you. You may not fear for your own life. I even know that because I have studied your religion. But you care for the lives of others, especially your loved ones. You wouldn't want to see them hurt or killed at the hands of the Guest Workers Party, would you?"

Jennifer shook her head, knowing that she would do almost anything he asked. She tried to pull back from his grip, but his fingers tightened. Maria entered with the paper, and Adolpho dropped his hands, backing away.

Maria plugged in the typewriter and turned it on. Jennifer fed the paper in and tapped a few keys to see what it looked like. It looked like nothing. Adolpho, leaning over her shoulder, swore again.

"There's no ribbon," Jennifer said. She looked at the box. "Ribbon and correcting tape not included," it read.

"Do you need it?"

"Correcting tape, no. Ribbon, absolutely."

"We gotta go get some. Luis!"

EIGHT

Jim and Candy jogged behind the church and into the parking lot where the pastor and Ellis Milton were strolling back. Ellis reported that no one on their tour had seen or heard anything suspicious, "except that the wedding or meeting or whatever it was supposed to be was certainly short."

Jim told him what Candy and he had discovered. "Let me get this down and draw some conclusions," the detective said. "Then let's get down to the *Day*, and we'd better take separate cars. I can't guarantee how long we'll be there or when any of you might want to get home and get some sleep."

While Ellis was making notes on the white-hot trunk of his car, Ed Hines emerged from the church with the news that the police investigators at The Consulate Hotel were satisfied that no one from there had suffered any sort of illness and also that there was no evidence that any calls had been placed from The Consulate to the church.

"That means that this man who jumped in front of Jennifer's car either placed the call that threw Leo Stanton off the track or tipped someone else off to make the call, and he probably called Jennifer at the church to flush her out. I can't imagine he's working alone, but on this part of it, he apparently was. We need to see if there's a phone booth close by, close enough for him to have placed the call and then still have gotten back to the church in time to intercept Jennifer."

Ellis instructed the others to drive on downtown to the *Day* offices and to let Leo Stanton know that he and Jim would be along. Ellis drove slowly down the street in front of the church. About two hundred feet from the front of the building was a gas station on the church's side of the street at the corner. Out in front was a phone booth.

"Help you?" the attendant asked.

"Yeah, maybe," Ellis said, showing his badge and identifying himself. "Looking for a male Latino, early-to mid-twenties, black hair, moustache, short and stocky but not too fat. Might have made a phone call here sometime after one o'clock this afternoon."

"Ah, I was workin' on a car between one and two. Lemme ask Rodney. Hey, Rod!" The attendant explained the question to the young pump man.

"Yeah, I saw him. Kinda strange. Looked like he was carryin' a piece too. Had it stuck in his belt and was tryin' to hide it with his black shirt. He was wearin' all black. Went to the phone, made a call, then watched up the street for about a minute and started jogging that way. Yeah, I remember him. He didn't say nothin' or do anything around here. Just made the call and ran up that way, that's all."

"How did you happened to notice him?"

"Well, I have this little old man who always pulls up to the self-service pumps and then gets someone to help him anyway. I was out there pumpin' his gas for him when this guy got off the bus, wandered up the street a ways, came back, made his phone call, then hurried up the street. I didn't see him again after that."

As both attendants got back to work, Ellis told Jim he was going to try something. "Put a watch on me," he said.

Jim looked at his watch and said, "Go."

Ellis stood at the bus stop and walked halfway down the street toward the church. "I can see the back and front at the same time," he said. "Can you?"

"Sure can," Jim said. "And took you less than a minute, moving casually."

"So, I go this way to determine that Jennifer's car is in the lot—that tells me she's in the church. I've already got my story concocted. If anyone else answers the phone, I tell them to tell her it's you. Makes sense. Unless you're already there, which I can also tell from just up the street. Then, when she comes to the phone, I tell her—what? That I'm from The Consulate and that her father has had a heart attack. No time for anything else, she has to come. Now, put a watch on me again. I'm going to jog up from the phone booth."

Ellis trotted from the phone booth to halfway down the street where he could watch the parking lot. "See?" he said, huffing as he moved toward the church. "From here I can see her come out to her car. I can dash up to the florist's truck and grab a smock— for who knows what reason? Maybe so that if she comes this way I can make her think I'm a florist. If she goes out the back, I can still run that way and head her off. But she goes this way, so I've got the smock, I jump in front of the car and make her stop to keep from hitting me. Gutsy. Then somehow I get in the car with her. If she's got any- one with her, I can do away with them or scare them or something."

"Probably do away with them if he's got a gun the way the gas station guy thought," Jim said. "Otherwise, they could identify him. Listen, would it do any good to see if the bus driver knows where he picked him up?"

"Might, but the odds are bad. He probably came a great distance with transfers, may- be part of the way by cab. It'd be awfully hard trying to trace him very far back."

"The only thing that doesn't add up so far," Jim said as they went inside the church, "is his risking the time to get the smock. Think that was planned or just a spur-of-the- moment thing?"

"Had to be spur-of-the-moment, because he couldn't have known for sure the florist would be here or exactly where he would park either."

"But would he really have had time?"

"I don't know. What'd you get on me from the phone call to where the florist's van was?"

"Less than thirty seconds."

"And what did Jennifer do in here? Let's run through it. She put the phone down here, then moved into the first dressing room and wrote the note after looking around for anyone close by. Maybe she was slipping on her shoes and grabbing her keys at the same time. Then she headed out the back to the car. How much time?"

"Almost a minute. He had plenty of time. Let's get downtown."

In the car, Jim asked, "What've we got? What do we know?"

"Precious little," Ellis said.

"That's what I was thinking."

"You worried?"

"Wouldn't you be? What kind of a question is that?"

"Well, we know for sure she was abducted. She didn't leave on her own. We know her father is all right, so a bogus message was used to lure her away. We know someone wants to use her column for some reason."

"Ransom?" Jim asked.

"Likely. Maybe something bigger. We'll learn more every time we hear from the abductors. The Latino appearance of the one may be a clue. But it may mean nothing. We can put our international terrorist specialists on it and see if any of the groups have been operating in or around Chicago or the Midwest. But he could just be a member of a bigger group."

"You don't think he could be working alone?"

"Unlikely. This thing is a little polished, even in its danger. I mean, kidnapping someone in broad daylight the way he did it is about as risky as I've heard in a long time. Usually, it's either your amateurs or your Mafia types that get away with that. It's either a spectacular success or a spectacular failure."

"I hope this is a failure," Jim said.

"So far it's a big success, and it's going to take all we've got to crack it. I hope you know that."

"I do. That's why I'm worried."

"You're a religious guy, Jim. Thought you weren't supposed to worry."

"I'm a human being."

"But isn't worry a lack of faith in God?"

"Oh, I don't think so. I have faith that God is doing His perfect will. But I worry that that perfect will might contain something I'm not ready for yet. Maybe I'm about to learn a tough lesson I didn't even know I needed."

"You mean like if God would let something happen to Jennifer, you would think He was trying to tell you something?"

"It's possible."

"And that's the kind of a God you believe in?"

"Hey, Ellis, this is a pretty tough time to make me try to defend God, you know what I mean?"

"Yeah, I guess. Sorry. It's just that you're a religious kind of a person, and yet something like this happens to you, just like anybody else."

"It's not as if God did it, though, Ellis. He may have allowed it, but I can't blame Him for it."

"But you'll pray it works out, and what if it doesn't?"

"Then I'll need God to give me the strength to bear it. Because I sure don't have that kind of strength in myself."

"But you're a religious—"

"How many times have you said that now, El? I'm not religious. If I were religious, maybe I would have some sort of strength in myself. A true believer knows he has no resources and trusts in a Person. That Person gives the strength that the believer would otherwise not have."

"And that Person is God?"

"Yes, in the form of His Son."

"Jesus Christ."

"Right."

"That simple."

"Not so simple, as you can see from the predicament I'm in now."

"Well, Jimbo, at least you're honest. I've seen religious types, I mean—sorry—uh, believers who pretend that nothing bothers them. They smile through the disappearance of a child or the murder of a spouse or the loss of their home."

"They may have peace from God."

"Yeah, but like you say, they're human beings. Doesn't God allow people to be weak, to grieve, to be honest, to face themselves and their losses?"

"I think He does."

"Well, so do I. And these people who put on this phony relig—er, 'churchy' facade as if nothing at all can get 'em down—they wind up on a funny farm somewhere, because eventually it all catches up with them. You know, the first time I encountered that, it was an old man whose wife of fifty-some years had been robbed and beaten to death right in front of him. Well, he was so calm and cool and collected that I was intrigued by whatever it was he had that I didn't have. He said he was a Christian. Well, who isn't a Christian, you know? But he had a different brand, a real church-goin', Bible-readin', life-livin' style that really got to me. He said he was frustrated and upset that he hadn't been able to help his dear wife, but that he knew she was with Jesus, which proved that the whole thing was meant to be."

"I can see how that would be confusing, Ellis. I really can. I'm afraid I wouldn't be that way. I'm afraid that in spite of my faith, I would be asking God a lot of questions. And I think my healing period would be lengthy. I don't even want to think about it."

"Like I say, Jim, at least you're honest. Realistic. Maybe that way, if anything bad happens to Jennifer, you won't wind up killin' yourself the way the old man did."

"He did, really?"

"Yup. He did. I always thought that if he had just let his faith in God be his comfort instead of his excuse, he might have been OK."

"I'll buy that. But you know, Ellis, the thing I always have to keep coming back to is that no matter what happens, there's a God out there who's personally interested in us. I mean, what kind of a God would He be if He wasn't? A God reserved just for churches smacks too much of institutionalized religion."

"Yeah," Ellis said. "The type that preys upon people and takes advantage of them."

"Sometimes it does, yes. But God Himself, the true God, doesn't. I believe that when someone honestly seeks God and asks Him to reveal Himself, He has to respond to that. I mean, if a person prayed, 'God, if You're out there, let me know,' God would have to somehow let him know."

Ellis was silent, staring straight ahead as he neared the *Chicago Day*. "I've been a Christian almost all my life, El," Jim continued, "and I have to say, that's the one thing that I've never gotten over. That God cares about people individually, you and me. The God who created the universe, if you can believe it, actually loves me. Loves you. Isn't that incredible?"

"Like you said, Jim. If you can believe it."

"I want to believe it, El."

"That's probably why you do."

"That's not the only reason. I asked God to reveal Himself to me."

"And did He?"

"Yes. It wasn't long after I asked Him to do that that I ran into people of faith, people who believed. I saw God in them. I was attracted to God through them."

Ellis Milton pulled into the parking lot behind the *Day* building. "If you're a praying man," he said in a conversation-ending tone, "you'd better start praying about this case. It's gonna be a tough one."

"Don't think I haven't started."

Pastor Cass and Ed Hines had already decided they would only be in the way and had left the newspaper office a few minutes before. "Nice couple of guys," Leo Stanton said, dragging a couple of extra chairs into his spacious office. Candy Atkins greeted Ellis and Jim, then resumed her posture with her head in her hands. She had been crying.

"You all right, Candy?" Jim asked.

"I'm not sure. This really has me spooked. I have this dread fear for Jennifer. And I feel helpless; there's nothing I can do for her."

"I feel the same way," Jim said, briefly resting his hand on her shoulder.

"Hey, let's not be so glum," Leo said, his tall, rangy, Ivy League look suffering only slightly from fatigue. "You know we're gonna hear from these guys, and they're gonna tell us what they want."

"And if it's not too unreasonable, we'll try to smoke 'em out," Ellis said. "That's all we *can* do."

"What's unreasonable?" Candy asked. "Seems to me if they ask for a million dollars, you still try something."

"Money is no problem," Ellis said. "You can always fake something with money. It's when they want to talk to the President or get a plane to somewhere or get some political prisoners released. That's when your hostage's life is in danger. They want to start proving they mean business. Remember the Arab-Israeli thing at the 1972 Olympics?"

Ellis filled in Leo and Candy on all the developments up to that point. Then Leo asked, "Now what?"

"Now we sit and wait," Ellis said. "The next move is theirs. We don't know where they are, who they are, how many there are, what they want—besides a column by Jennifer—or when they want it. I need to call downtown and get some telephone guys over here to try to trace any calls. Meanwhile, tell me what you've done, if anything."

"I put a note about Jennifer's disappearance out over the wire and gave strict instructions not to call here for details. I included the fact that she was abducted from her church on her wedding day and that we would send new information as it became available. I did notify the papers who carry her column that one would be forthcoming, but I made no promises when or what length, or whether it would be publishable. I didn't get any phone calls—which I appreciated—but our teletype machine lit up with requests from all kinds of papers, ones that never carried her column before, to be put onto the service immediately. They're also demanding to know if she's being forced by someone to write a column. Many are going to press within a couple of hours, and some are holding press runs already. They're onto the story, and I'm going to have to tell them the whole truth soon."

"Oh, do it right away," Ellis said. "The more people who print the abduction story, the more who will read it. I want the whole country to be looking for Jennifer. Also, their show of support could scare the kidnappers. Letters to the editor, offers of money to start a ransom fund. That'll make 'em nervous."

"I hope it doesn't make them do something rash," Jim said.

"Jim," Ellis responded, "they already have."

NINE

It had become quickly apparent to Jennifer that though Alvarez was the leader, Diaz the sergeant at arms, and Cardenas a follower, Maria Ruiz was the brains of the Guest Workers Party. Double-A had assigned Cardenas to "rip off some typewriter ribbons somewhere," but it was Adolpho's wife, Maria, who kept Luis from otherwise wasting his time.

When Alvarez was somewhere else, Maria tore the side of the typewriter box and slipped it to Luis. She told him in Spanish, "You must find only this kind, no other. Remember, nothing else will fit."

"Where should I look?"

"Not in a department store. It must be a specialty store or a stationery store. You might have to buy it to be safe. Otherwise, you will have to bring many kinds if you don't have time to read the serial numbers. Better to get help and ask for the right kind."

Cardenas found that humorous, but when he got out searching for the right ribbons, he soon realized he would indeed have to buy them rather than shoplift them. They were hidden away and complicated to figure out. And they were expensive. He embedded the name and location of the store in his memory so he could make up for the purchase some other time. He was a couple of hours getting back, and Adolpho was angry. He stomped around the apartment, breathing heavily.

"Let's get on with it," he said. Jennifer put the ribbon into the typewriter and asked Adolpho how he wanted to work.

"What do you mean, 'how do I want to work?'" he asked. "I'm gonna tell you what to write, that's what."

"And all these people are going to be in here watching me type, is that it?"

Luis and Benito sat on the bed; Maria was on the floor, her back to the wall.

"Yeah," A-A said. "You got a problem with that or what?"

"I guess not," Jennifer said, realizing that her wishes made little difference. "But I'll tell you this, unless you write like I do, this column is going to sound phonier than a Mexican leader who fakes his native accent."

Adolpho glared at her. He was silent for a moment, as if wondering how to save face in front of his people. "So," he said finally, "how do *you* propose that we work?"

"You let me interview you, and then you let me write the column my own way. If you expect anyone to believe you or think your cause has any credibility, you have to let me lend it. Otherwise, I'm just a kidnapped typist, banging out what you force me to bang out on your stolen typewriter."

"I'll think about it," Alvarez said. "What if you write what I don't like?"

"Then you change it if you must. I'll guarantee one thing: unless you force me to write something I disagree with, you won't like what I write. But you will get notoriety and attention. I have to hand it to you on that score; if my usual papers print me, you'll have quite an audience."

"OK," Alvarez decided. "You interview me."

Maria brought paper and a pen, and Jennifer began her questioning. "Tell me about yourself. Who are you? Where did you come from? And what do you want?"

"Adolpho Alvarez is the noble wolf. I was born in Monterey, Mexico, of poor parents, thirty-nine years ago. My father was a farmer and my mother a seamstress, and they both died at a very young age, younger than I am now. The work, the land, the poverty was too much for them. I worked in factories in the city when I was fourteen and began to learn the ways of management against labor. By the time I was twenty, I was a powerful union leader in my country. Though I never held an elected position, except in the local unions, many workers looked to me as their leader."

Alvarez quit talking as if satisfied with the portrait he had painted of himself. "How did you build yourself up, physically I mean?" Jennifer asked.

He beamed. "I was always a hard worker, and when the work began to develop the muscles, I decided to help the development along. I worked with weights, but we had to make them ourselves. We had no money for store-bought weights. We used pipes and buckets and cement, and we read books and magazines about how to build the muscles and the body. Good job, eh?"

Jennifer didn't respond. "Is that all you want to tell me?"

"I will tell you anything you ask."

"What do you want?"

"Justice for the people."

"What people?"

"*All* people."

"Even people like me?"

"Of course!"

"Was it 'just' to kidnap me?"

"On the day of your wedding, you mean?" he asked, eyes twinkling.

"At all, forget what day you did it on."

Alvarez walked over to the door and stretched to fill the frame with his arms. He pushed up and the wood creaked. He groaned loudly, as if tired. "Sometimes," he said carefully, seeming almost to stand straighter as he delivered the line, "a small injustice is worth the greater justice that might come from it."

Jennifer sat back and sighed after she had noted the quote. "That was almost poetic," she said. "The only potentially valid thing I've heard you say today."

He dropped his arms and stepped toward her menacingly. "Oh, quit trying to scare me," she said. "I'm getting a little weary of your posturing. You've got these people scared to death of you so they'll do anything you say. And I believe harm might come to my loved ones if I don't do what you say, so stop with the theatrics. You wouldn't hurt them yourself, because you're a coward. You'd send Benito with his weapon or Luis with his blind obedience. You might hurt me because you know I'm no match for you. If you want me to use my column, waste my space, use the readers and the editors who trust me to further your cause, you're going to have to get to it. What is it you want?"

"Justice!"

"You said that. What do you *mean?* Are you telling me that between the time you were twenty and a union leader in Mexico and the time you were chosen as a guest worker in the United States a few years ago that you were just plodding along as a common laborer? I don't believe it. You were probably serving time somewhere."

The two on the bed and the one on the floor jumped and shot Jennifer a double take. Alvarez came over to her and reached down with both hands to grab two of the chair legs. He stood quickly, pulling the chair from beneath her. Jennifer saw the room spin as she flew against the wall and slid to the floor, bruising her hip. "Where did you learn about me?" Alvarez shouted, and despite her fear and her aching hip, Jennifer smiled. It had just been a lucky guess.

When Alvarez boiled over at the sight of her smile and raised his fist, she held up a hand to wave him off. He turned to the others in the room and demanded to know who told her. No one responded. "I'll kill you, Benito!" he said. "Did you tell her? Luis? Maria?"

They all shook their heads and shook with fear. "They didn't tell me," Jennifer said. "It's just that there's a hole in your story, and prison is written all over you. Tell me, was it in one of the horrible holes in Mexico or in the not-much-better U.S. federal pens in Texas or Oklahoma?"

He didn't answer.

"Texas, huh?" she tried. He glared, and she knew she was right. "Then you were an illegal alien at one time. Or tried to be. And you still are, am I right? Tell me what you really want of me and my readership."

"Money for my people," he said weakly, and she nearly laughed.

Jennifer stood and retrieved her own chair. "Pretty good trick," she said, feeling desperately, almost suicidally brave for some silly reason and knowing that she would be in for a good cry of relief if she ever got out of this. "Can you do it with someone your own size sitting in the chair?"

Alvarez looked as if he might try it again. Jennifer braced herself and decided to be ready to roll with the fall. But he backed away, eyeing her. She picked up her pen and pad. "I've decided I'm not going to write a column for you," she said. "You write it, put my name on it, deliver it, and see who in the United States publishes it."

Adolpho sat on the end of the bed and stared at Jennifer. "You are something else," he said, with no trace of a Spanish accent. "I spent almost ten years in a federal penitentiary in Louisiana for arranging for Mexicans to stay in the United States after their visitation visas had expired."

"Why weren't you deported?"

"I was born in New York."

Jennifer nodded. "And you met your wife where?"

"She is not my wife. She is my sister."

"And the Guest Workers Party?"

"You're looking at it."

"And your cause?"

"Hah!" Adolpho grunted derisively. "Our cause is money!"

"This is all motivated by greed?"

"Tell me who isn't greedy, lady! Let me tell you something. When our scheme to bring you here succeeded, when Benito and Luis came through that front door with you, our ship came in too. You are loved, you have money, the people who employ you have money, the people who read you have money. We need it. We want it. And we will have it!"

The other three faces showed fear and anticipation, wonder at the prospect of actually receiving money from the prize in the chair. "How much do you figure I'm worth?" Jennifer asked, genuinely curious.

Adolpho Alvarez was quick with his answer. "A quarter of a million dollars for each," he said.

"Only a million total?" Jennifer asked, pretending to be offended. "I'm in so many papers every day, you'd think you could get a few thousand from each one. Is that what we're going to do? You're going to write a syndicated column-style ransom note to my family and friends and readers and employers, is that it?"

"You like it?" Adolpho asked. "I thought it was creative."

"I'll find out how much I'm worth, I guess. But tell me, how many papers do you think will cater to a terrorist?"

"What do you mean?"

"I mean, it's news that I'm missing, and the demands of my kidnappers are news. But would you devote a column to it if you were an editor or a publisher? I wouldn't. It would give too many crazies the same idea."

"You think I'm crazy?"

"Of course."

"You're going to wind up dead, you know that?"

"Because I tell the truth? The truth is what got me where I am today. Sitting here with four kidnappers. If I didn't tell the truth, you wouldn't have cared to kidnap me. I know one thing: I might be worth a million dollars to you alive. I'm worth nothing to you dead. Not one penny."

"That's why you have a smart mouth?"

"I guess. Don't think I'm not afraid of you or afraid for my family. But if you're going to do away with me anyway, I might as well get my last shots in, huh?"

"You would have done well as part of my team," Adolpho said.

"Don't count on it. I don't think you like people around you telling the truth too much. I do, however, have a suggestion of how best to handle this so-called writing assignment you've thrust on me."

"I'm listening."

"Let me do it straight. Let me tell the whole story, just as it's happened. Everything. The kidnapping, the lies, the fabricated cause, your story, the whole works. It'll all come down to the same thing. It may not be as noble a pursuit, but you can't deny that greed is your motivation. It'll be even more dramatic."

"What's in it for me?"

"It may work. Papers might run it. You might get your money—who knows?"

"What's in it for you?"

"I get to use all my creative energy telling the truth instead of making something up with a gun to my head. Or hands on my chair. And I get very few chances to tell my readers what makes me so foolishly brave sometimes. I can sure be forgiven for doing that here."

"What does make you so foolishly brave?" Adolpho asked.

"You'll have to read my column and find out."

"Will you use my real name?"

"I'd like to."

"I'd like you to. You see, we're going to succeed in this. And if it works out the way I hope, we will have no need to kill you. But one thing I want you to be very clear about. I have killed before. I. Me. I have killed with my bare hands. And I would do it again in a minute. If someone on the other end of this deal thinks I'm kidding or tries something cute, he'll find out. I'll deliver you to your public one piece at a time."

Jennifer's eyes showed that she had thought of another quick reply, but Maria quickly jumped in. "Mrs. Grey," she said, "I would humor A-A now. He is not kidding. He is serious. Your bravery has impressed him, but you will not humiliate him without paying a deep price."

"I want to be immortal," Adolpho said. "Don't you too, Benito and Luis? Maria?" They all nodded. "We will let her use our names, and we will take our money and escape, never to be found again. We will be the talk of the world until we die, and in our safe-deposit boxes in Argentina or Switzerland or wherever, we will reveal where we fled and how we lived on the greatest ransom payoff ever. No one will be able to duplicate it."

"Believe me," Jennifer said, "by tomorrow morning you will be one of the most famous men in America."

"And if that is true, and I have my money, you will be a free and happy and healthy woman. If there is a problem, you will die. You like truth. You live for truth. You write truth. You write that. That is truth."

TEN

The only calls that came through on Leo Stanton's phone at the *Day* during the next few hours were from George Knight, who had been informed by investigators at The Consulate that the command post had been shifted from the church to the newspaper office.

Finally, Jim was forced to promise him that he would keep him up-to-date at the first sign of any news. "Meanwhile, George," he said, "I have to tell you that no calls will be forwarded through to Mr. Stanton's phone unless they are from the kidnappers."

"Hoo, I hate that word," Mr. Knight said.

"Me too," Jim said.

"And I understand. Don't worry about us."

"I *do* worry about you," Jim said. "I worry about you and Jenn and Mrs. Knight."

"You can start calling us Mom and Dad pretty soon, you know."

"I should have been able to by now."

"You can if you'd like."

"I think I'd better wait."

"Suit yourself. But whatever you do, don't give up hope. We have the peace that passes all understanding."

"I'm glad to hear you say that. I'd appreciate it if you'd pray for me. I know Jennifer is uppermost in your mind, but this is very difficult for me."

"And for us, Jim. What say we pray for each other?"

Ellis was signaling Jim to free up the phone. And it wasn't long after he hung up that another call came through. Stanton put it on the speaker. The voice was muffled and staticky, as if there was an intentionally bad connection and the caller was using a kerchief over the mouthpiece as well.

"There's gonna be a heavy delay, man, because we didn't have everything we needed for your columnist. We'll be callin' you back when we know where you can pick up the column."

"Listen!" Stanton said, "I couldn't understand you! Is that all you want? A column? Is that all?"

"You got it, man." And the line went dead. One of Ellis's technicians leaned through the door and shook his head. "Too quick," he said. "These guys are no dummies."

"How long do we have to still be able to make the morning paper?" Jim asked.

"A couple of hours," Stanton said, "but the problem is that we have to see the thing before we decide to print it."

"What do you mean?" Ellis asked. "If they demand you print something and you don't, Jennifer's life could be in danger."

"I know that, sir, and I happen to be a very close friend of hers besides being her boss—so don't assume I don't have her best interests at heart. But there are considerations on any paper of this size and influence. We don't just publish anything and everything that someone tells us to, regardless of the situation. It might surprise you to know that I say yes or no on every column Jennifer writes, before it is sent to our syndicate and before it is printed in the *Day.*"

"Have you ever said no?"

"Yes, sir, I have."

"On what grounds?"

"It's irrelevant here."

"I'll be the judge of that."

"Trust me, Sergeant Milton. I'm telling you that the reason I might have stopped a column or two in the past has no bearing on why we might or might not print the one we'll receive tonight."

"And I'm telling you that everything Mrs. Grey has written, published or not, could have an impact on this case. Irrelevant or not, you can tell me."

Stanton shook his head in resignation and pushed his half glasses up onto his forehead. He sat back in his chair and shifted his ever-present unlit cigar from one side of his mouth to the other. "Jennifer, as you may know, has some rather strongly held beliefs. When she is able to work them naturally into a column of broad appeal and interest, I let them go. When they become part and parcel of the column, the whole reason for it, I suggest more subtlety. Since she's become a sort of national media star, it has been harder and harder to talk her out of using her privileged platform position, if you will, as a soapbox for her religious beliefs."

"How does she respond?"

"Graciously. It would be inconsistent with her stand to blow up and get angry and throw things like some prima donnas I work with."

"But, I mean, what does she do about the column in question?"

"Usually, she rewrites it and works the pitch in naturally as an organic part of the whole."

"But she never leaves it out?"

"In those instances, no. Of course, only infrequently does this come into play."

"I understand. But it sounds to me like she's not the type to roll over and play dead just because someone suggests she try something different."

Both Jim and Leo laughed at the suggestion. Candy Atkins couldn't take it.

"I don't understand how you can laugh at a time like this! Who knows what is happening to Jennifer right now? Isn't there anything, something that can be done?"

"I wish there was, Candy," Ellis said. "Believe me, I wish there was. The problem is that we have so little to go on from what we've learned so far. We don't know where she is, which direction she went, who has her, or why. All we know is that she *was* taken and that a column is supposed to arrive soon."

"I feel so helpless," Candy said.

"We all do," Jim said.

"I'm afraid for Jennifer, but I'm afraid she's *not* afraid."

"I know what you mean, Candy. Jennifer has this sort of 'take-life-as-it-comes' mentality that lets her shoot back rather than be intimidated."

"Don't say 'shoot back,'" Candy said.

Ellis Milton was the only smoker in the bunch, Stanton being a cigar chewer rather than a puffer. The detective went through half a pack over the next few hours, filling the ashtray on Leo's desk. Candy paced and gulped coffee, making herself even more frazzled.

"I know it's a horrible thing to say at a time like this," she said, "but I think I'm getting hungry."

"Best suggestion I've heard all day," Ellis said. "I'm starving too. Would it offend anyone if we sent out for something?"

"I'll send someone," Leo said.

They were all munching sandwiches, all but Jim, when the phone rang. "Lincoln at Foster," came the heavy Spanish dialect. "You got it?"

Ellis Milton was frantically waving to Leo, telling him to stall.

"No, I don't have it!" Stanton said. "What did you say?"

"One more time, and that's it, man—take it or leave it. Lincoln at Foster!" Click.

Jim headed for the door. "Jim," Ellis said, "I've got to call downtown, and it's time to inform the FBI. You know kidnapping is a federal offense, even if they haven't crossed state lines. Now that they've named a drop-off point, we've got to inform that level."

"Let's just get going!" Jim said. "There's been no ransom figure discussed, nothing we have to do."

"Yes, there has! So far the ransom is the publishing of a column."

"But there's been no deal! We don't get Jennifer if we publish the column."

"No, but we're wide open to their threat on her health if we don't!"

"Well, call whoever you have to call, and let's get moving."

"Jim, you asked me to handle this, so you have to let me. You have to report to me, or I'll have someone downtown take you off the case. You shouldn't be in on it anyway. You're too close."

"El, don't do this to me."

"I will."

"Please."

"Then you are subordinate to me, regardless whether you agree with everything or not. You can have me taken off it too, I know, but they won't replace me with you. They'll replace me with someone who'd never dream of keeping you involved till it's over."

"Fair enough. I agree. Let's move."

"Just a minute."

Milton called police headquarters and requested that the FBI be informed. "Get some brass with clout to tell 'em we're just informing them at this point. . . . We don't want help or supervision or anything until we ask. . . . I know, I know. . . . Just tell 'em that. Otherwise, I'll keep them in the dark too."

"I assume you want me to stay by the phone," Leo said.

"Exactly."

"I'm going," Candy said.

"Wrong," Ellis said.

"I can't just sit around here and—"

"Then go home! You're not going with us. I'm sorry. You've been a big help, and I don't mind your being in on things here, but this is a very dangerous mission. We don't know what we're getting into. We both have weapons, and we're prepared to use them. Do you and are you?"

She shook her head, almost in tears.

"Trust me, Candy. You'll help most by staying here."

Jim was the first through every door, first on the elevator, first off the elevator, first outside, first to the car, first in the car. Ellis hurried along behind him. He slid in behind the wheel. "Any bright ideas on the fastest way to get up there?"

"It's way up north, El. Probably the Kennedy to Lawrence and east."

"I think that's way out of the way, Jim. I think I'd get off at Western and go north. Sunday traffic won't be bad early in the evening."

"Whatever," Jim said, happy just to be moving.

It took Ellis a little less than twenty minutes to cruise up to Lincoln and Foster, and when he neared the corner, he told Jim he wasn't sure what he was looking for. "A manila envelope? A person? What?"

"Surely they wouldn't be stupid enough to send anyone. Then we'd be even. We'd have one of theirs; they'd have one of ours. Negotiations would be off."

"We won't be that lucky, but the turkey didn't tell us anything but the location. What does a newspaper column look like?"

"And who's this?" Jim said, nodding toward a black man walking along in the lengthening shadows from the hot sun.

"Just out for a stroll," Ellis said.

"I'm gonna watch him anyway," Jim said.

"Suit yourself."

Ellis was craning his neck to see if there was any obvious hiding or stashing place for an envelope or manuscript when the black man stepped into a phone booth and dug in his pocket. Before he could put a coin in, however, he picked up the phone and listened. He looked at the receiver and hung the phone up again. Then he placed his call, but said nothing and hung up.

Ellis was still looking behind them in the rearview mirror. Jim said, "El, pull over there by that guy." Milton popped a U-turn and rolled next to where the young black man would walk by. Jim rolled down his window but made no move as if to talk to the man.

As he walked by, he was shaking his head. Muttering to himself, he said, "Give me the girl's name, and I'll tell you where to look."

"What'd he say, Jim?" Ellis demanded.

Jim repeated it while reaching for the door handle. For once, Ellis was out of the car first, his gun in one hand, badge in the other. "Police!" he screamed. "Freeze!" Jim was out now and behind the man, both hands on his gun and in a low crouch, the weapon pointed at the man's face.

The black man froze all right. He almost fainted. "Hands in the air!" Milton shouted.

"Now over to the car and put 'em on the hood, feet back and spread 'em. C'mon, you've been through this before."

Jim searched the man. "What is it, brothers?" he asked. "I ain't carryin' nothin'! I'm clean!"

"You got a name, sir?" Milton asked.

"Yes, sir. You wanna see my ID?"

"Later. Just tell me your name."

"Am I under arrest?"

"Do I have to put you under arrest to get your name? I will!"

"Luschel Bradley."

"What did you say when you walked by our car a second ago, Luschel?"

"I don't remember sayin' anything. I mighta been talkin' to myself."

"You tellin' me," Jim said, "that you don't remember saying, *just a second ago,* something about a girl's name and where to look?"

"Oh, *that.*"

"Yeah! That!"

"The phone rang, man, just as I was gonna call my woman. I pick it up and a guy says that."

"Says what?"

"What I said. What'd I say? I don't remember."

"A guy says to tell him the girl's name and he'll tell you where to look?"

"Yeah."

"What'd he sound like?"

"Far away."

"Did he have an accent?"

"Yeah."

"Like?"

"Like maybe Puerto Rican."

"What'd you say to him?"

"I tol' him Gladys."

"Gladys!"

"Yeah, that's my woman. I figure maybe he's a Latin King or somethin' and he's got my woman. Scared me to death. 'Specially when I couldn't get her on the phone after that."

"What'd he say when you said 'Gladys'?"

"He said I was gonna regret that, and he hung up. I musta been runnin' that over in my mind when I walked by your car. Wrong thing to say, huh?"

"Sorry to detain you, Mr. Bradley. You're free to go."

"Man, this ain't my night," he said, wandering off. "Wonder where Gladys is."

The phone rang again. Milton ran and grabbed it. "What was that Gladys business?" came the telltale Mexican accent.

"That was an unfortunate coincidence. Now where's the column?"

"Give me the girl's name, and I'll tell you where to look."

"I mentioned the column and you still have to qualify me?"

"If you're tryin' to trace me, man, it ain't gonna work. I'm off of here now, but I'll call back in one minute. If the first thing I hear ain't the girl's name, she's dead."

Milton slammed his fist on the metal counter.

"What?" Jim wanted to know.

"I almost blew it, that's all," Ellis said. "He'll call back, and I'll play it his way. I just hate to cater to punks. I've been through all the training, know what to say and what not to say. But treating them with kid gloves while they're threatening someone, scaring 'em to death, and playing mind games with us, that goes against my grain."

"Play it straight, El—*please.*"

"I will, I will."

The phone rang.

"Jennifer!" Ellis said quickly.

"Greyhound Bus Station—downtown," the voice said.

"Where in the station, man? That's a big place!"

Click.

ELEVEN

The column had taken Jennifer more than two hours to write, and amazingly—she thought—Adolpho Alvarez had asked her to change only details that would have led the police to his door. He made her change the color and general description of the vehicle she was transferred to after her car was dumped in Lake Michigan, and he had her change the reference from Lake Michigan to the Chicago River.

Other than that, she had written the story exactly as it happened, from the bogus phone call to just missing running over Benito Diaz. She described the weapon he carried, the meeting with Luis, and the pushing of the car into the "river." She added a line at the end of that episode that slipped past her abductors, but which she hoped and prayed would not slip past her loved ones, her editor, her readers, and the police.

It was just one of those creative throwaway lines she used frequently to add spice to her writing. "My heart sank with my beautiful new car that Jim and I had already enjoyed so much. My only hope was that the alewives would appreciate it as much as we had."

Astute readers would catch the clue. Alewives were a Lake Michigan problem. They covered the beaches during the bad years for such fish. But Jennifer prayed that not only would Leo and Jim and whoever else was involved pick up on the obvious error, but that they would also comb the column for other clues. She realized that her only hope was to use her God-given ability to put words together. God had provided her best chance at escaping, and it lay within that brand spanking new typewriter Adolpho Alvarez was so proud of.

In describing her abductors, she wrote that Luis was "to me a cross between an Apache, a Sioux, and maybe a Cuban. He is a tall, lanky, hauntingly handsome man of slow pace and a certain dark grace. A follower. A doer. A thinker rather than a talker. Obedient. He'll do anything A-A tells him to do."

She described her ordeal thus far:

> I could as easily be writing an epic I'd call "My Experiences in the World War," and here I am only hours into my dilemma. I keep asking myself, *How did it happen? Why did it happen? What did I miss? Could I or should I have known that the first telephone call from the hotel was a bogus one?*
>
> There's something about the experience that is as embarrassing as it is frightening. It's that sort of hate yourself feeling that comes with a public goof like a run in your pantyhose or having your picture

taken with the hole showing in the bottom of your shoe. I've heard people say that when they've been robbed they feel as if they've been violated or their privacy has been invaded. I know the feeling now. And the questions. I keep asking myself the questions . . .

She told the whole story of the charade and how she was able to cut through the baloney and get Adolpho to admit that his was not a cause of justice or a torch for humankind, the working man, or anyone else except himself and his small band of members of the "Guest Workers Party of the United Mexican States."

In fact, I sit a bit stunned, amazed actually, yet knowing that the man has an ego that will let me write that he *has* such an ego without fear of reprisal. It isn't that he isn't a violent man or that he won't make good on his death threat if his demands are not met; it's just that he has a thirst for power and glory and immortality—worth gaining even through infamy—that is nearly as unquenchable as his greed. He reminds me a bit of Clyde Barrow of "Bonnie and Clyde" fame, who was so deeply touched by his girl friend's poems that chronicled their reign of terror. Even the lines memorializing those who were foolish enough to try to stop them and wound up dead in the process were precious to Clyde, because he had been immortalized on the front pages of papers all over the United States and Europe.

I am not without fear, that gut-wrenching, almost immobilizing terror that reminds you that you could be here today and gone tomorrow, and were it not for my deep belief that God is in control and that my future is secure with Him, I know I would be unable to function at all, even to maintain my composure, let alone to write.

For it is this God alone who is worthy of praise and power, and it is He alone who holds the keys to true immortality. Not the immortality that lets a Clyde Barrow live on in poetry and legend decades after his death, or a Julius Caesar for centuries after his, but rather the real thing, the actual, bona fide, eternal living immortality that allows a person to never really die.

Jennifer even wrote of her sarcasm and dark humor.

I dreaded and hated myself for it even as it was coming out of my mouth. But that too, I sensed, was born of a belief that I was where I was supposed to be and doing what I was supposed to be doing. When a man twice my size, in anger literally pulls my chair from under me and I see not only the ceiling and the walls whiz by but also my brief life and the face of my soon-to-be husband, yet still I am able to call my captor a coward and write the same for many hundreds of thousands of reading eyes, then I know that either I am the

most foolish woman ever to breathe or I have been gifted with a power outside myself.

Don't think that if you read of my death tomorrow, or the next
day, that my faith has been in vain. Neither blame God for all my
boldness, for no doubt much of it has been ill-timed and not so carefully conceived (an understatement, I realize, as I put it on paper).

While it is of some comfort to me to be in the familiar mode of
writing to you as I do several times a week, I am using equipment
that is unfamiliar to me. I am writing from a posture of pressure and
fear that I wouldn't wish on anyone. And lest anyone think there is
anything glamorous or positive about this experience, please know
that no matter how it seems, you would not want to trade places
with me, regardless of what may come of it.

I admit I have envied reporters who have voluntarily inserted
themselves into dangerous situations to help work out solutions. I
have also questioned their motives and assumed them glory-seekers.
But now that I have experienced that deep, mortal fear that battles
constantly against my faith, I know they could have had such surfacy
motives only the first time, never again.

For when a weapon is pressed against your cheek and you can feel
the cold steel and smell the acrid oil and imagine the sound and the
result of the explosion in the chamber that you would never hear,
you know that this is not cops and robbers in the backyard. This is
not a TV show or a movie. This is it. This is life and death in the cold,
stark reality of ugly weapons, selfish motives, and nothing-left-to-lose
characters who risk their precious anonymity, their freedom, their
futures for one big payoff, one booty of a million dollars in small,
unmarked bills to be split four ways.

The question, of course, is one which must be faced by the principals. Can they trust each other? Will a man who would mastermind a
kidnapping, concoct a story about fighting for the working man, use
the platform of a newspaper columnist, and terrorize her friends and
family and co-workers in the process, not make some attempt to skip
out with their share of the money?

Adolpho had enjoyed that paragraph. In his perverse way, he had taken delight in the
possibilities that he was worse than he appeared, that there was no honor among
thieves, at least not when this thief was tossed into the mix. But it was the next paragraph that caused him some grief and which changed his strategy. He would send two
pickup people rather than one.

Should Double-A, the noble wolf, be noble enough to trust whoever
he sends out to pick up the ransom? Or will he be able to send only
his own flesh and blood? And can he trust her? That, of course, is
when he will be most vulnerable. Will the pickup person return?

When he or she returns, will the split be equal? Will A-A then uphold his end of the bargain and deal with the payers?

Were it not I here in this situation, but rather some nameless, faceless columnist from some other daily newspaper, I might assert that the missionary agencies in South America have the best policy. They do not pay. They do not cater. They do not bend or bow. They lose missionaries too, but they believe—and probably rightly so—that they will lose those missionaries anyway. They do not trust the abductors. They could pay and still see their people killed. In fact, that is more likely.

That could happen here too. I hope it does not. Not because I don't believe that my afterlife is secure with God, but because I cannot bear to think of the grief it would cause my family and my fiancé. I enjoy my life, my love, my people, the place I work. I don't fear death, but I fear dying. I want to stay around until I'm 90 and then slip peacefully away in my sleep.

So, yes, it's selfish, this personal change of policy. I don't want my friends and family and newspaper maintaining lofty ideals and refusing to be moved to spend the money necessary to win my release. I promise to help in every way to find my abductors, but get me out of here first.

As I've said, I can't guarantee that they'll deal fairly, but since it's me, since it's someone I've grown close to over the years, since I have a personal, vested interest in the abducted, I'd rather not see a reaction that flies in the face of the captors and gives them no choice but to prove their mettle. There is something to be said for following the best police psychology of the day when dealing with short-fused, volatile people.

These words, I assure you to the best of my ability, I wrote on my own, without coercion. Only a few facts, protecting the location of my captivity, were adjusted. The following I write under instructions from the noble wolf, whom I would not describe that way, were I given the choice. (You see? He still allows me latitude even here.)

The payoff figure is 1 million dollars in small, unmarked bills. Forty-eight hours are allowed to raise it. A drop-off point will be phoned to the offices of the *Chicago Day* before dark on Tuesday night. If the pickup person either does not return to Adolpho Alvarez or there is any evidence that he or she has been followed, I will be killed. No question. No hesitation.

I'm back, on my own. I know my column is much longer than normal, that it will not fit on the front page of the *Day*, and that many of my regular papers will not carry it because they choose not to. It's not only because they thought I was to be off for the next three weeks, but rather because they do not cater to a criminal element.

But to those who carry it, I'm grateful. I had hoped that at least this would be a daily dialogue between my captors and the ransom payees, but perhaps this is best. Two days seems long enough to put off the inevitable. Something will happen; I hope no one is hurt. Most of all, I admit, I hope I am not hurt.

Should it turn out for the worst for me, either due to my paper or my family or the police being unwilling or unable to accede to the demands of the kidnappers, please know that I understand. Forgive the personal addresses in my column, which as a rule—as you know —I avoid wherever possible.

But Jim, I love you. Mom and Dad, I love you. Leo, I love you. My church friends, I love you. Most of all I love my Savior, Christ, and I know that to be with Him is far better. I believe that, though I won't really *know* it until I get there. Forgive the morbidity of these final few thoughts, and accept my greetings and expressions as sincerely and with as many heart feelings as they are offered.

Benito Diaz returned from the bus station downtown with the news of the misfire on the first phone call. "I couldn't believe it," he said. "Some dude tellin' me Jennifer's name was Gladys. I thought they were tryin' to do a number on me."

For only the second time since the beginning, Jennifer thought she saw some nervousness, some weakening in Adolpho. He paced more. He sat with his head in his hands. He seemed distracted. He looked at his watch. He kept asking Maria what was next.

"I don't know," she would tell him. "They get it at the bus station, they read it, they decide if they're gonna print it, they decide if they're gonna get the money and wait for our call."

"And we call 'em when the sun goes down Tuesday night," Alvarez said, "right? Is that right?"

She nodded.

"And should we have another column ready for Tuesday morning's paper? Something Jennifer would write tomorrow night?"

Luis and Benito looked at each other and then at Maria. It was clear to Jennifer that none of them were as comfortable with being immortalized in the papers as Adolpho was. They didn't look enthusiastic.

"How about you?" A-A asked Jennifer.

She shrugged. "I do what I'm told," she said.

"But do you want to?"

"I don't know what else I'd write. Unless I brought everybody up-to-date on my daily activities. What are we going to do tomorrow?"

She meant it as a joke, but Adolpho was tired and irritable. He didn't appreciate her sarcasm anymore. It didn't impress him the way it had earlier. "Sometimes," he said icily, "I hope they don't honor our demands and that it ends up in a big shoot-out and you go down with us in a blaze of gunfire."

Jennifer didn't respond. She could tell he meant it. He continued.

"And you *would* go down with us, because you would be the first person I would shoot. I would take Benito's *Uzi,* and I would turn you into hamburger and sling you out the door. And if the odds were against me, I would kill myself before I would let anyone else kill me."

"Your own people might kill you first," Jennifer said softly. Double-A heard her but pretended he didn't.

"Get some sleep," he advised. "There will be someone outside your door all night."

Jennifer went to bed exhausted, but too keyed up to sleep. She was miserable. She heard muffled conversations from the living room where Adolpho was working and re-working strategy, trying to determine if he or his sister should accompany one of the others for the all-important pickup.

Jennifer fought the stinging tears that welled up in her eyes. She knew she had to be strong, that wasting tears now would be useless unless the clues she planted in her column were successful. Would they bring rescuers to her, or would she have to take her chances with police strategy centered around the money drop?

All she could do was pray, and all she could think to pray was that by morning, someone would also be outside Adolpho's door.

TWELVE

Ellis Milton and Jim Purcell parked illegally downtown and raced into the Greyhound Bus Terminal, not knowing what or whom to look for. But they looked anyway. They ran up and down the corridors, in and out the doors, past the game rooms, past the cafeteria, past the waiting rooms and the benches and the vending machines.

They ran past the ticket counters, looking everywhere—up, down, sideways, in people's faces. All they got were blank stares, some half smiles. Jim and Ellis slowed and almost stopped several times when they saw someone who looked like Jennifer or who fit the description of the young Latino she had almost run down in the street in front of the church.

They looked in phone booths, and even in a few buses. "We're getting nowhere," Jim huffed and puffed at last.

"I know," the sweating and panting detective said. "We have to stop and think. Where *should* we look for something?"

They stood staring at each other, then at the ceilings and walls and people.

"Lost and found," Ellis said. "Make any sense?"

"Not much," Jim said. "But I'll try anything."

At the lost and found center, Ellis asked if there was anything there for a Jim Purcell.

"Like what?" the man asked.

"A manuscript, an envelope, a folder. Something like that?"

"Nope. Only envelope I got here is for a—ah—just a second—yeah, Grey—J. Grey."

"That's it!" Jim and Ellis shouted in unison.

"That's what?" the man asked. "You didn't say anything about a J. Grey."

"We've got no time to argue, pal," Ellis said, whipping out his badge as Jim did the same. "Just give me the envelope and tell me where to sign, and I'll take full responsibility."

"I'll have to see a driver's license."

"You'll see nothin' but a badge number. Now let's have it!"

In the car, Jim discarded the envelope and dusted the inside pages for fingerprints. They had all been wiped clean. "Crafty," he said. By the time he and Ellis got back to the *Day,* Jim had read the column aloud three times by the dim light inside the car. Every time he finished it, he slammed his palms on the dashboard.

"I don't see *anything* in here!" he said. "I mean it's an incredible story, but wouldn't she be trying to tip us off? Does our picking it up at the bus station mean they've taken her somewhere at least a bus ride away? What do you get from it?"

"Nothing yet. But you know her better than I do. Would she try to give you clues?"

"Of course! The only thing that doesn't make sense is that line about the fish in the Chicago River. I mean, there may be alewives there, but you never think of that. You associate them with Lake Michigan."

"Then she *is* giving you a clue!"

"Maybe, but what does it mean? So what if she was trying to say it was Lake Michigan and not the Chicago River. It doesn't help us."

"Maybe she's just telling you that every detail in the story is slightly inaccurate."

"But that doesn't help either."

"It helps her, Jim. Later she can show how she disassociated herself from the phony story."

"But that will be meaningless unless we can free her! Otherwise there won't be a 'later.'"

"Take it easy, guy. If there are clues there, we have people who can find them. Does she try to tell you anything by using the first letter of each sentence to form a word, anything like that?"

Jim studied the piece again. "Nah. Anyway, her abductors would have checked for that, wouldn't they?"

"I don't know. She doesn't exactly paint a picture of them as being too bright, does she?"

"Oh, no," Ellis said as he pulled into the *Day* lot and saw a dozen marked and unmarked squad cars from various agencies. "We've got all the help we need now."

"What's this all about?" Jim asked.

"Who knows? Somebody tipped 'em, and now they all want in on the act."

From the lobby Ellis phoned Leo. "I'm sorry," the editor said. "Once it got out over the wire and the radio and TV news guys got a hold of it, we were dead. It's been on the air for more than an hour, the whole thing, promising news of her column to come, all that. Did you get it?"

"Yeah, we got it, and we're gonna need help deciphering it. Can you start a copy machine smokin'?"

"Not until I've read it."

"I'm not asking you to decide on putting it in the paper; whether you do that or not, we need to see if she gave us any clues. Though if you decide against printing it, you'll have to have a pretty good reason."

Phones were ringing all over the place when they got to Stanton's office. He was taking no calls from reporters on other newspapers. "As for the other law enforcement agencies," he said, "Sergeant Milton, they're all yours."

And Ellis took over. He announced that the case was his from the beginning and that unless he heard from his own immediate superior or above, he was still in charge, and any and all activity had to be assigned by him or cleared through him.

"Do you have the column?" someone asked.

"Yes."

"What are you going to do with it?"

"The *Day* editor is perusing it now. Then he'll copy it for anyone who wants to help us determine if she has planted any clues for us."

"*If?* What do you mean *if?* If she didn't, she's got to be nuts."

"Or maybe she's being careful," Ellis said.

"There's such a thing as being *too* careful."

"Not with the group that has her, gentlemen."

"Well, we wouldn't know, would we?"

"Patience."

Jim and Ellis checked in on Leo, who was handing pages to Candy as he finished them. "This is great stuff," she said. "I mean, just the writing itself."

"It's *her* all right," Leo said.

"It is?" Ellis asked. "You're sure?"

"No doubt about it."

"No irregularities?"

"Plenty."

"You make anything of them?"

"Plenty."

"Really?"

Leo didn't answer. He quieted Milton with a wave of his hand as he finished the last few pages. "Let me speed read 'em again when you're through, Candy," he said. "Just to be sure."

"Can we copy them first and get others working on them?"

"In a minute," Leo said.

"We don't *have* a minute, sir. Can it be run in the paper?"

"Yes, in ours."

"In others?"

"It's up to each one. I'm guessing they'll run it with the full story of the disappearance. Most will only say that I believe the column is from her. We can't guarantee it."

"But you're sure?"

"I'd stake my life on it."

"Read fast, and tell me what you think," Milton said.

Candy confided that she had seen nothing in the column that gave her any hint where Jennifer might be. Leo handed the pages to Ellis. "Have Marge, outside, make as many copies as you want. But none—repeat, *none*—may leave this building."

"So, what did you find?"

Leo smiled faintly. "I'd rather withhold my guess until the others have a chance to corroborate it without any knowledge of what I'm thinking."

"All due respect, sir, but we don't have time for games."

"I'm not trying to play a game, Sergeant. I really need to know that I haven't planted ideas in people's minds that may not have been there otherwise."

When Ellis started handing out the copies to the various representatives of the local, state, and federal agencies, one commander said, "I need four copies. I brought along two cryptologists and a trivia buff."

"That's three."

"Include me too."

"What are your qualifications?"

"I read Jennifer Grey religiously."

It didn't take the cryptologists long to determine that no traditional or recently devised letter or word patterns had been used to transmit a message. One of them immediately noticed the mention of the alewives in the Chicago River, but when he mentioned it aloud, several others scolded him.

"We've all got that," they said. "But there has to be more."

Many of the cops and their aides were studying every word, looking each up in the dictionary and asking Stanton for access to reference books and maps. During the second hour of study, Stanton had the entire column transmitted over the news wires to hundreds of papers across the country who typeset it for morning editions. The *Day* itself would hit the streets at 4:30 A.M.

Finally, both a state police criminologist and a federal agent sat back and tossed their pencils down. "Giving up?" Ellis asked.

"Nope," one said, smiling. "We think we know where she is."

"So do we," came the response from a small cluster in another corner.

Candy and Leo emerged from his office. Jim stood. "Who wants to be first?"

"We think she's trying to tell us that the car is in Lake Michigan and she is at the Stevenson Expressway and Pershing."

"That's what I thought!" Leo said.

"Us too!" another group piped in.

"Where did you get that?" Jim said, shaking his head. But Ellis was dragging him to the door.

"Listen up, everyone!" the detective said. "If it's that clear to all of you, I have to buy it, even if I don't know how you did it. I also have to think there'll be a lot of amateur detectives reading the column who might beat us over there if we don't hurry."

By the time everyone was assigned locations at the stakeout and a vehicle with sophisticated communications capabilities was appropriated from downtown, it was near dawn. The *Day* had hit the streets, and a couple of national radio news networks had read the column on the air.

Ellis was right. As law enforcement officers began slowly converging on the only building at Pershing and the Stevenson, crowds had begun to gather. "There goes our hope of catching three of them asleep," Ellis moaned.

"I don't believe this," Jim said, pointing out a group of Mexicans who carried hand-painted signs reading "Mexicans Against Alvarez" and "Free Jennifer Grey."

"Where did they get the time to do that?" he asked. "Now all we need is for them to start chanting and blowing our cover."

Uniformed policemen cordoned off the area and kept the crowds back while Ellis and Jim planned surreptitious entry to the building. "It looks impregnable from here," Jim said.

"Worse," Ellis said. "We don't know who, if anyone, is in there."

"Don't bail out on all that expert help now," Jim said. "They couldn't have all come to the same conclusion by coincidence."

Just the same, Ellis assigned someone to see if a phone had been installed in the building. One had. The number was unlisted. Which meant it took the police a few minutes longer to get it. The billing went to AA, Inc., and the majority of the long distance calls in the last month had been placed to New York.

Ellis and three other plainclothes detectives from the Chicago PD approached the building from the angle of each of its corners. There were no windows. Just the garage door, securely locked, and a service door that had apparently been sealed shut.

"A clear violation of the fire code," Ellis radioed back to Jim in a command car.

Jim shrugged and looked at Ellis's watch commander, Lieutenant Steve Sykes, who had just arrived. Sykes deadpanned, "So what's he gonna do—bust 'em on a code violation or set the place on fire?"

When the four had all scrambled back to the safety of the car, Ellis reported: "I don't think we were seen or heard, but there's no way of getting in there by force without waking the dead. And I don't think they're gonna fall for any phony stuff in person."

"Then what?" Jim asked.

"Maybe they'll fall for something by phone."

"Like what?"

"Like this." Ellis dialed the unlisted number from the phone in the car. "You know Alvarez is not going to answer, so I've got a one in two chance of guessing right if a man answers. If it's a woman, it has to be Maria, right?"

Everyone nodded and held their breath. The phone rang three times, then a groggy voice whispered, "Hello?"

"Hey, Benito!" Ellis said urgently in a beautifully faked accent. "It's Chico from New York, man. I gotta talk to Double-A fast."

"This ain't Benito, Chico. This is Luis. Do I know you?"

"I don't think so, Luis, but I heard a lot about you from Adolpho. I know it's early, man, but can you get 'im?"

"Jes' a minute."

Ellis held up his free hand and crossed his fingers. Several minutes passed. Then came the voice of Adolpho Alvarez. "This is the noble wolf," he said, sounding still asleep. "Who is this?"

"This is Chicago Police Department Detective Sergeant Ellis Milton, Adolpho. I want you to listen carefully and be prepared to deal. Are you awake, sir?"

There was no response, but neither did Adolpho hang up. "I am going to assume you can hear me, sir," Ellis continued. "You are surrounded, with no possibility of escape. You have little time and no options. Can you hear me?"

The only sound from the other end was rapidly accelerating breathing. "Sir?" Ellis called. "Señor Alvarez?"

Suddenly, Adolpho was screaming, but not into the phone. "I don't believe this!" he shouted to his people. "Get her up! Get her out of bed! They're going to make me kill her! Get her up! Get her up!"

"Adolpho!" Ellis shouted. "Adolpho! Listen to me! There's no need to do anything rash. Let's talk! Let's deal!"

Finally, Adolpho acknowledged Milton. "No talkin'!" he yelled into the phone. "You said we can't escape and we got no options, man. Remember, *you're* the one who said it! We're gonna show you what kind of options we've got! You ever heard of a *Uzi?*"

"Yes, sir, but there's no reason to—"

"Shut up!" and he slammed down the phone. The command officers began organizing everyone into a huge circle around the building. They were back more than fifty feet and hiding behind cars. The crowd was pushed farther and farther back until everyone was outside the range of gunfire.

"Get some lights flashing!" Ellis hollered. "When he looks out to see if we're serious, I want it to look like Christmas."

Lights began flashing all around the building, and spotlights were trained on the garage door. "It's got to come up!" Ellis said. "It's the only way he can see us."

He was right. It came up about halfway, automatically, and was lowered quickly. When there was no activity from inside for almost four minutes, Ellis called the number again. Before he could say anything, Adolpho picked up the phone.

"I'm comin' out with the girl!" he said, "and my people will be behind me. I'm gonna have the weapon at her throat, and here's what I want. I want a helicopter and one unarmed pilot to take us to O'Hare and an empty jet with one unarmed pilot waiting for us. You got that?"

Ellis didn't respond. His watch commander pantomimed that he should at least pretend to accede to every request, and they would deal with it later.

"OK, all right," Ellis said. "It'll take a while. Just be cool."

"It'd better be fast. Anything goes wrong—*anything*—and she's a dead woman." And he hung up.

Ellis turned to Commander Sykes. "I'm sorry, sir, but I don't think that is the way to handle this guy. I know all the stuff about what to say and what not to say, but why cater to him? We can't deliver the 'copter and the jet, so why lead him on and pretend we can? Just to keep him from getting riled? He's riled already! How do you think he'll react when he finds out we've been lying to him?"

The commander pursed his lips. "You know department policy, Ellis, and—"

"I know we're gonna wind up with someone dead in there if you don't let me talk his language, Lieutenant."

"Meaning?"

"Trust me."

"It's all on your shoulders, Ellis, but I won't back you up."

"But you'll let me handle it?"

"I'll deny it later."

"But you won't stop me now?"

"You're on your own."

"That's all I wanted to hear," Ellis said as he dialed Adolpho again.

THIRTEEN

Adolpho answered, *"What!* If the chopper ain't comin', I don't wanna hear from you!"

"The chopper ain't comin', Adolpho, but you'd better listen to me."

"Talk!"

"You wanna deal?"

"You know what I want, man!"

"Yes, I do, Adolpho, and you're not going to get it. The deal will be my deal. It will be the only deal offered, and you can take it or leave it."

"Listen, man! I'm gonna—"

"No, you listen, and listen carefully, 'cause I'm only runnin' this down once. I call the shots here. I set the deals—not you. Now *we've* got lots of time. But you're limited by how much food you've got. We're gonna wait until you come out. I want you to surrender, to send Mrs. Grey out first, unharmed. Then I want you and your people to come out one at a time—six feet apart—you first, hands on your head. Leave your weapons inside. You got it?"

"Have I got it? That's *it?* That's no deal!"

"That's the only deal you're gonna get."

"What's in it for me, man?"

"This is what's in it for you, Adolpho. This is the deal, total and on the table, OK? If Mrs. Grey comes out unharmed, you come out unharmed and charged only with those crimes you have committed thus far. If you hurt her, we will hurt you. If you kill her, we will kill you. That's it. You decide."

And Ellis Milton turned off the phone, trembling. Commander Sykes sat in the backseat, palms cupping his temples, shaking his head.

The next twenty minutes crept by as the sun rose higher in the sky, and Jim Purcell sat in a pool of his own sweat, praying and hoping that Ellis had done the right thing.

The strategy went against everything they all knew about the psychology of dealing with an irrational, demented, violent terrorist. Jim shivered, imagining he heard a burst of automatic weapon fire inside the building. Had he imagined it? Was it real? If it was real, was it his beloved being made an instant martyr to a bad cause? Had Adolpho turned the weapon on himself? Or had one of his people murdered him?

Jim looked at his colleagues and sympathetic friends. And he realized that he had only imagined the sound. And then he imagined it again and again—until it was killing him, and he wished the bullets, real or imagined, were ripping through *him,* ending his nightmare. He didn't know how much longer he could bear the agony.

"Should you call him again, El?" he asked weakly. "What if he has a question, needs clarification? He doesn't know how to call you."

Ellis was pale. "He doesn't *need* to call me, Jim. I couldn't have been clearer. He's thinking. That's all I could have hoped for. The deal's the same now as it was twenty minutes ago, and it'll be the same twenty-four hours from now."

"I could never last," Jim whined. "What if he's killed everyone and himself?"

"That's what would have happened if we had stormed the place."

"Ellis, I can't help but think this is a reckless, dangerous move."

"No move I could have made would have been less dangerous, Jim. He has a no-win situation. I couldn't pretend to open a window of hope to him. I talked his language; he understood me. The rest is in his hands."

"That's what bothers me. The man least capable of making the right decision will determine what happens here."

"It was going to be that way no matter what. The terrorist always holds the trump card. But I set the parameters, Jim. The decision is his, but he's deciding between the options I gave him."

Jim felt as if he had to get out of the car, but he didn't know where he'd go. He wanted to pray, but he didn't know what he'd say. He wanted to take charge, but he didn't know what he'd do. He wanted to punch Ellis, but he knew in his heart of hearts that, right or wrong, Ellis had the same goal in mind that he had.

But it was *his* fiancée in there! It was his life, his love, his future. The helplessness and hopelessness of it all ate away at his bones and his brain.

At first, Jim had hoped and prayed and longed to see that door open and Jennifer come running out to him. But with every additional second, that hope seemed more and more remote until it was a foolish kid's dream, mocking him, making him feel the fool, the dunce, the joker. To think it would all turn out the way he wanted it, the way Ellis had laid it out!

Such trash! It would end in bloodshed. Jim prayed, *God, forgive these thoughts! It's hopeless. I can't stand it! How long will he wait? How long can I wait?*

"Ellis!" Jim said too loudly, making everyone jump. "What if he hurts or kills Jennifer and *he* comes out first, and you don't know what's happened to her until he's in custody?"

Ellis didn't respond.

"You can't take justice into your own hands then, can you, El?"

"I might have to, to keep my word."

"It would be the end of your badge," Sykes said.

"I wouldn't be able to live with myself if I let him get away with something like that anyway," Ellis said. "What's the difference how I end my career?"

"But, Ellis," Jim said, "I'm serious. What will you do?"

"If he comes out first, I'll drop him on the spot."

"But don't you owe it to him to warn him of that?"

"Jim! I owe him nothing! I told him the rules. If he breaks the rules, he'll suffer for it. If he comes out first, I can only assume that Jennifer is hurt."

"But maybe—"

"But nothing! Maybe nothing! She *must* come out first and reach us unharmed for him to be alive by the end of the day."

Weapons were trained on the garage door. Jim had to get out of the car. He pulled his gun from its holster and crouched behind the left rear fender. Ellis joined him with a bullhorn.

Without warning, the garage door opened, and hammers were pulled back on a hundred pistols. Ellis managed all the coolness and calmness he could in spite of the raspy loudness of the speaker as he said, "Easy, easy, easy—hold your fire, hold it, hold it, hold it."

And Jennifer emerged alone. She was dressed in her own clothes, and her hands were empty, her arms limp at her sides. She walked steadily toward a police car at right angles to where Jim and Ellis crouched. Jim wanted to shout, to run to her, to embrace her, to cry, to pray. He started to move, but Ellis's vice grip caught his arm. "We're not out of the woods yet."

Jennifer looked as if she wanted to run, to dive for cover, but she fought the urge. She could have been walking down the aisle, the way she forced herself to step slowly, carefully, methodically.

"Easy, Jennifer," Ellis intoned. "That's it."

When she reached the exposed side of the squad car, two uniformed policemen scampered out and pulled her between cars and to the ground where she burst into tears. They helped her crawl into the back seat and lie down. Shortly, the squad car pulled away.

When Jim turned back to the scene, the muscular Adolpho Alvarez was slowly walking across the same path, his hands on top of his head, no weapon visible. Not far behind came the lanky Luis Cardenas in the same posture, his face showing no emotion. Six feet in back of him was the petite Maria Ruiz, her eyes puffy and red, hands on her head, feet moving in double time to match the speed of the men.

It was her speed that made it less noticeable when Benito Diaz did not emerge at the proper interval. Ellis had been coaxing them along slowly with the bullhorn, soothing them, encouraging them, keeping his men calm at the same time.

Two officers stood to come around and meet Adolpho, but they froze when Ellis shouted through the bullhorn, "Wait for the other! Wait till he shows himself!"

And from inside the dark garage rang out the burp of six shots that tore through Adolpho Alvarez's spinal cord and heart and left him time only to wrench his hands from his head in an effort to break his fall.

But midway through his descent, the power source connecting his brain to his muscles had been severed, and he crashed face first onto the pavement. He appeared as if he would have twisted to get a look at his slayer, if he'd had the choice.

Policemen dived for cover, and Luis and Maria ran in opposite directions, their hands still in the air, pleading for the men not to shoot. Ellis was still on the bullhorn. "Wait, wait, wait—don't shoot, don't return fire, hold your fire."

The *Uzi* came clattering out of the garage into the dirt, Benito proudly following it, standing upright, head held high, empty hands atop his head. He walked straight to where Adolpho lay and screamed, "Coward!" at the corpse as he was taken into custody.

Jim slumped to the ground, his back to the bumper of the unmarked squad that contained Lieutenant Steve Sykes, the ashen-faced watch commander of Ellis Milton. And Jim wept.

EPILOGUE

The sleepy-eyed Jennifer was glad to see Jim at police headquarters. They held each other, long and silently, burying their faces in each other's necks. Later, when they were alone, they would praise God for His miraculous protection. Jennifer was eager to reset the wedding date for the next Sunday—after they'd both had some rest, and she was shocked to hear of Alvarez's death.

Still she was able to smile when Jim asked, "Is anyone going to tell me how Jennifer led us to her?"

"I would have thought you would be the first to catch it," she said. "John J. Pershing's memoirs were entitled *My Experiences in the World War*, and if there was any doubt, I said Luis looked like an Apache, a Sioux, and a Cuban. Which is ridiculous. No one could look like both an American Indian and a Cuban. But Pershing's first three tours of duty were in the Apache campaign, the Sioux campaign, and in Cuba."

"So that put you on Pershing Street," Jim said. "A big, long street."

"And the most famous picture of a hole in the sole of a shoe was taken of the foot of Adlai Stevenson."

"Thus," Jim said, "the Stevenson Expressway at Pershing."

"Right."

"Pretty obscure."

"Apparently, not to everyone—fortunately for me."

"And me," Jim said.